WRITTEN BY **Ezra Claytan Daniels**

ILLUSTRATED BY **Ben Passmore**

FANTAGRAPHICS BOOKS INC.
7563 Lake City Way NE
Seattle, Washington, 98115

Editor and Associate Publisher: Eric Reynolds
Book Design: Ezra Claytan Daniels and Keeli McCarthy
Production: Paul Baresh
Color Assistance: Luke Howard
Publisher: Gary Groth

ISBN 978-1-68396-206-9
Library of Congress Control Number 2018963543

First printing: June 2019
Printed in China

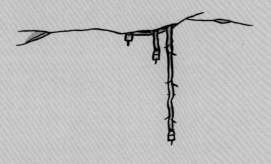

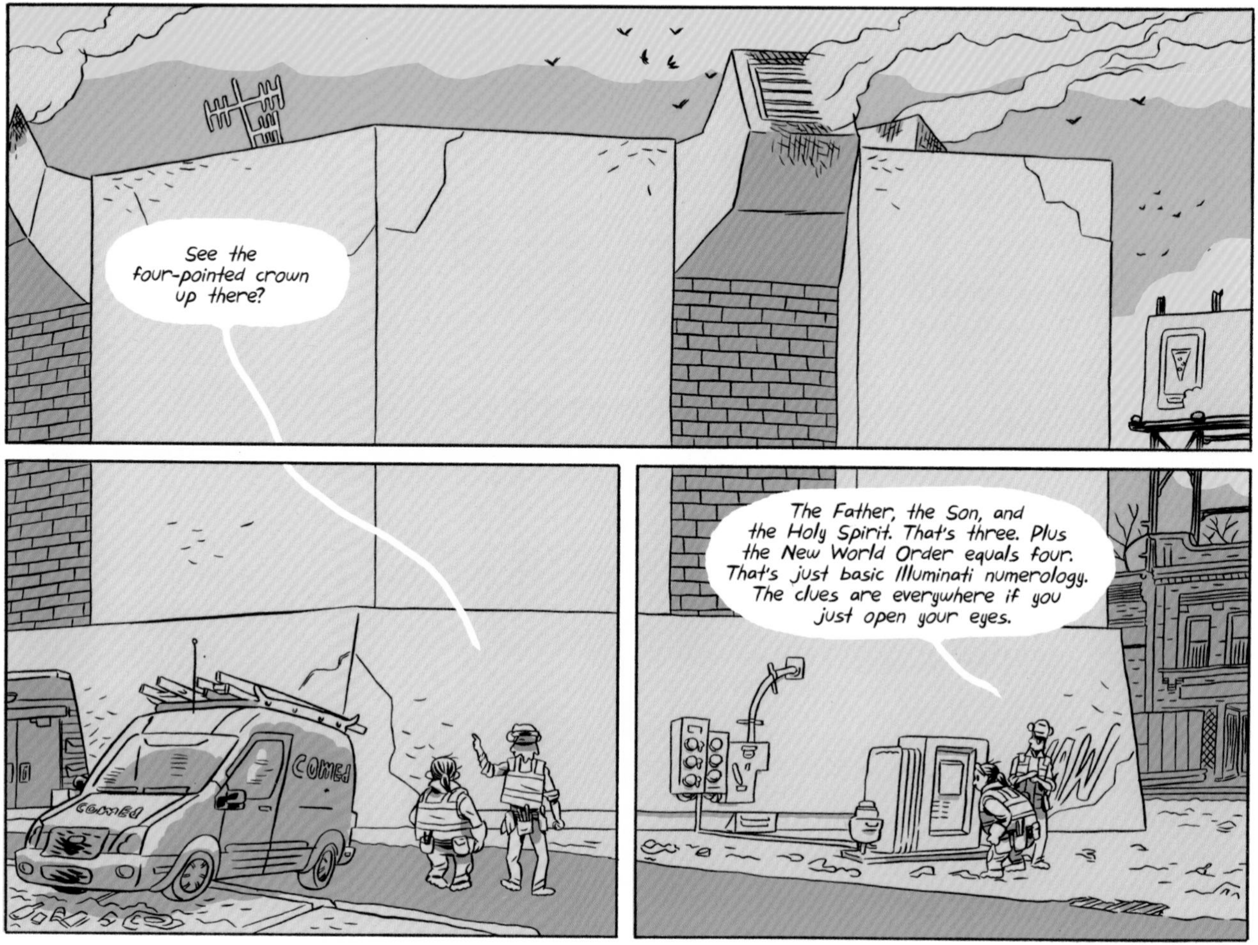
See the four-pointed crown up there?
The Father, the Son, and the Holy Spirit. That's three. Plus the New World Order equals four. That's just basic Illuminati numerology. The clues are everywhere if you just open your eyes.

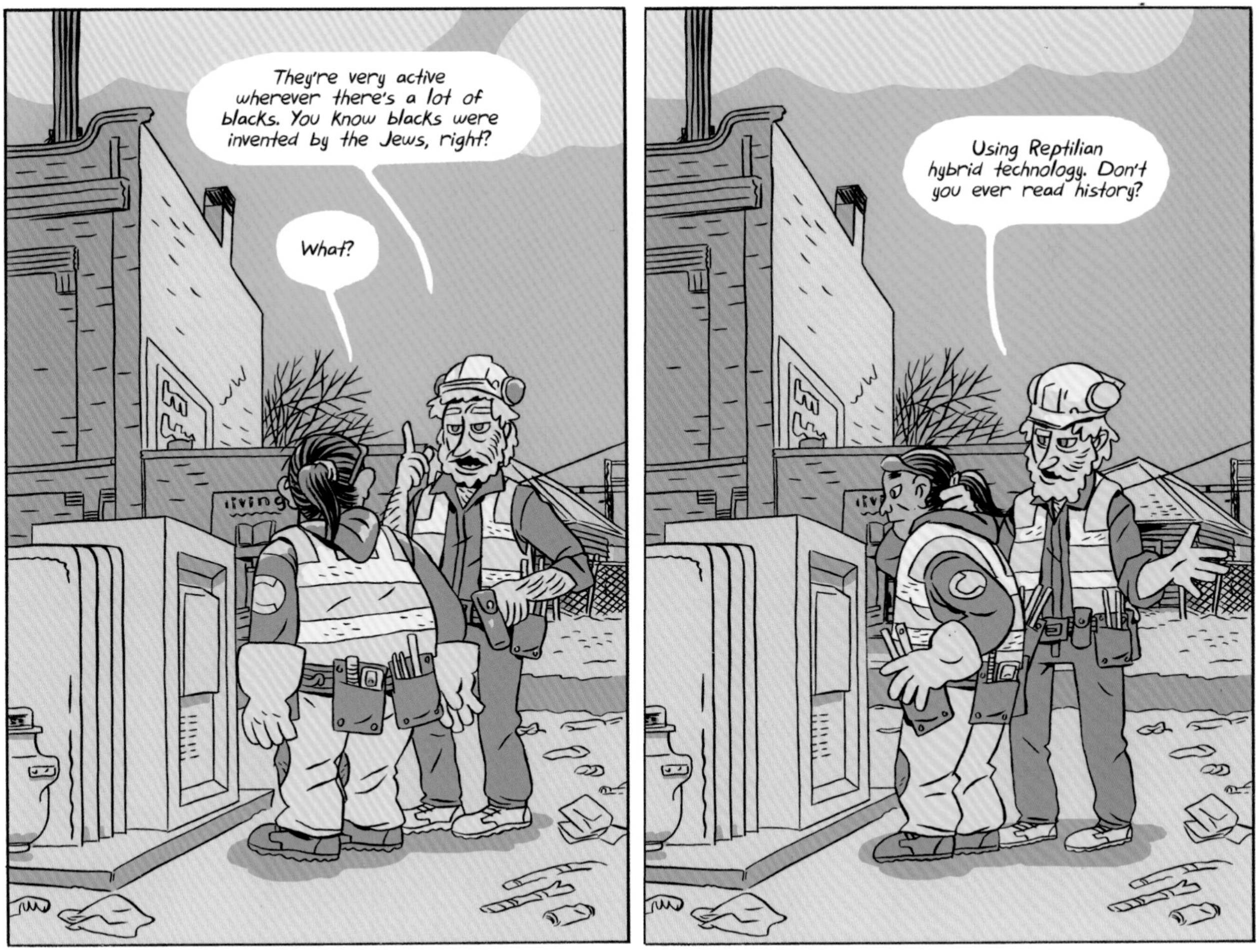
They're very active wherever there's a lot of blacks. You know blacks were invented by the Jews, right?
What?
Using Reptilian hybrid technology. Don't you ever read history?

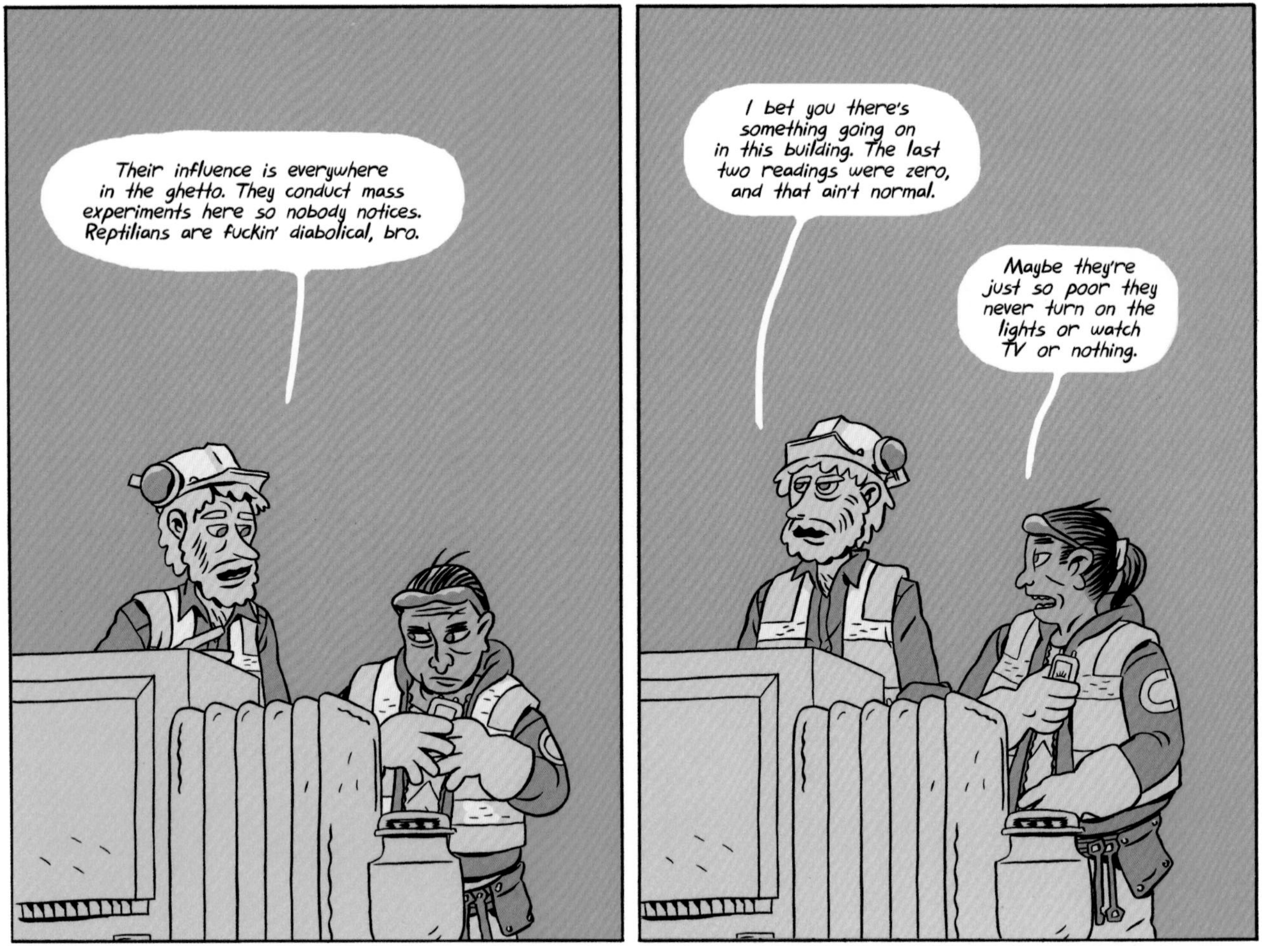
Their influence is everywhere in the ghetto. They conduct mass experiments here so nobody notices. Reptilians are fuckin' diabolical, bro.
I bet you there's something going on in this building. The last two readings were zero, and that ain't normal.
Maybe they're just so poor they never turn on the lights or watch TV or nothing.

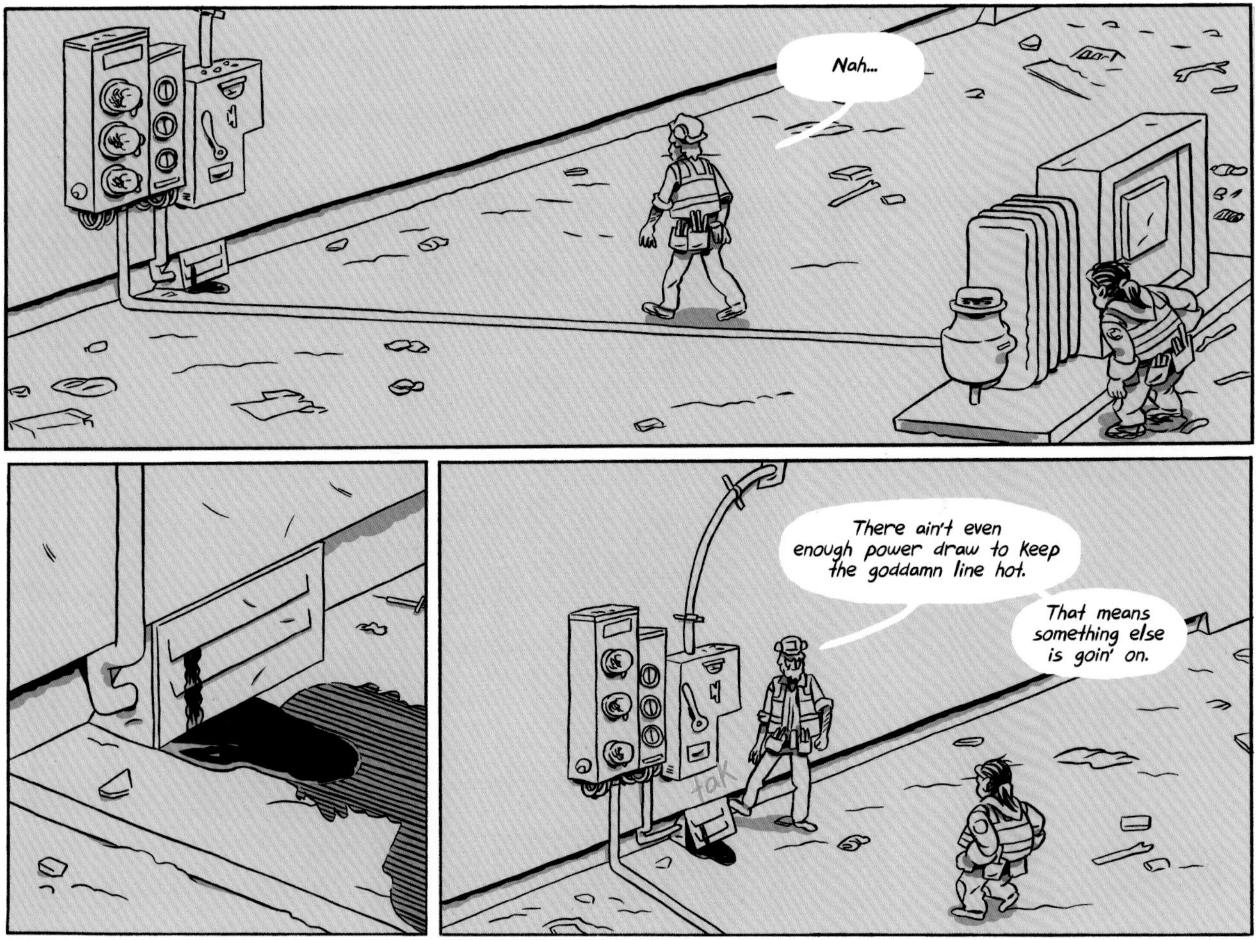
Nah...
There ain't even enough power draw to keep the goddamn line hot.
That means something else is goin' on.

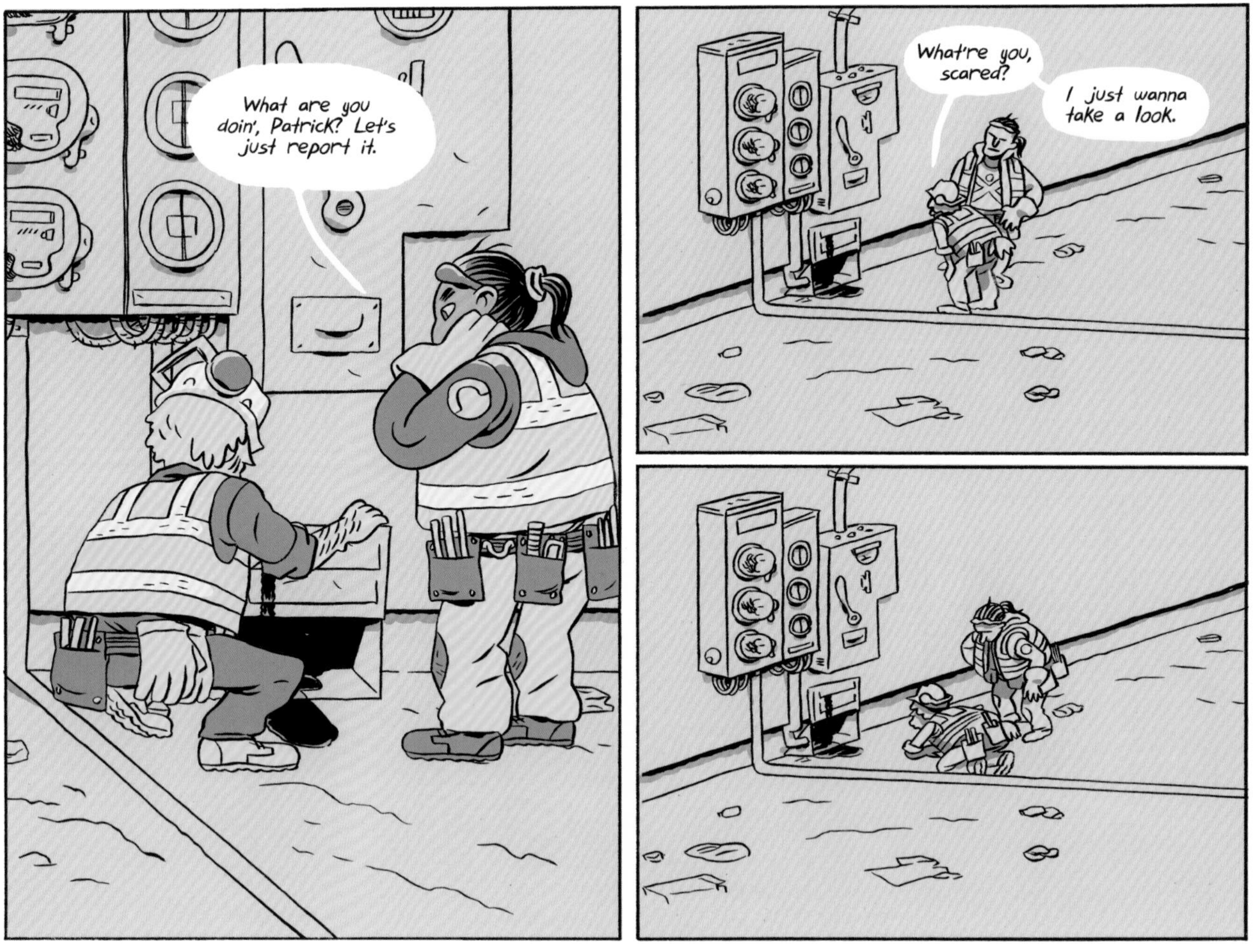
What are you doin', Patrick? Let's just report it.
What're you, scared?
I just wanna take a look.

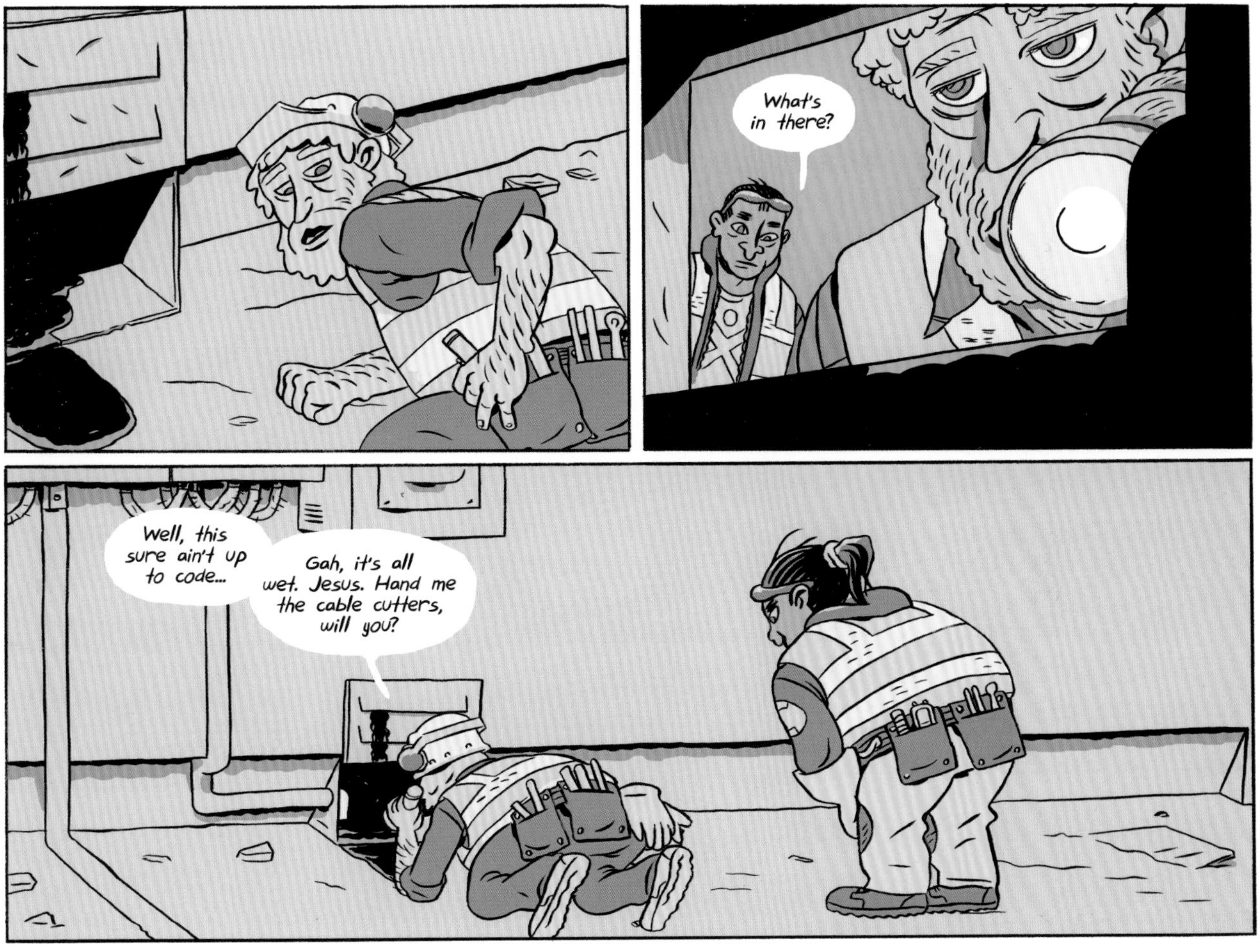
What's in there?
Well, this sure ain't up to code...
Gah, it's all wet. Jesus. Hand me the cable cutters, will you?

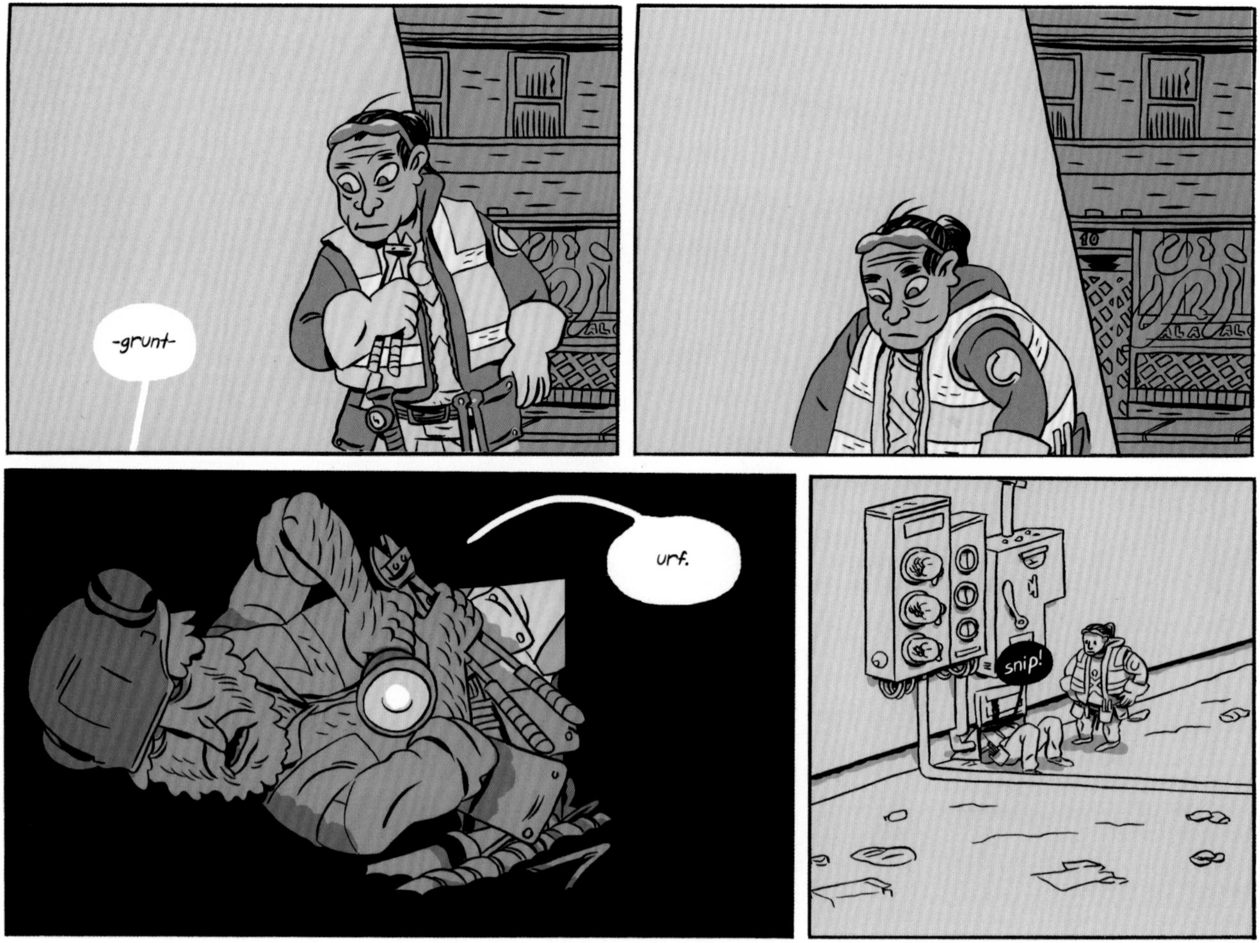
-grunt-
urf.
snip!

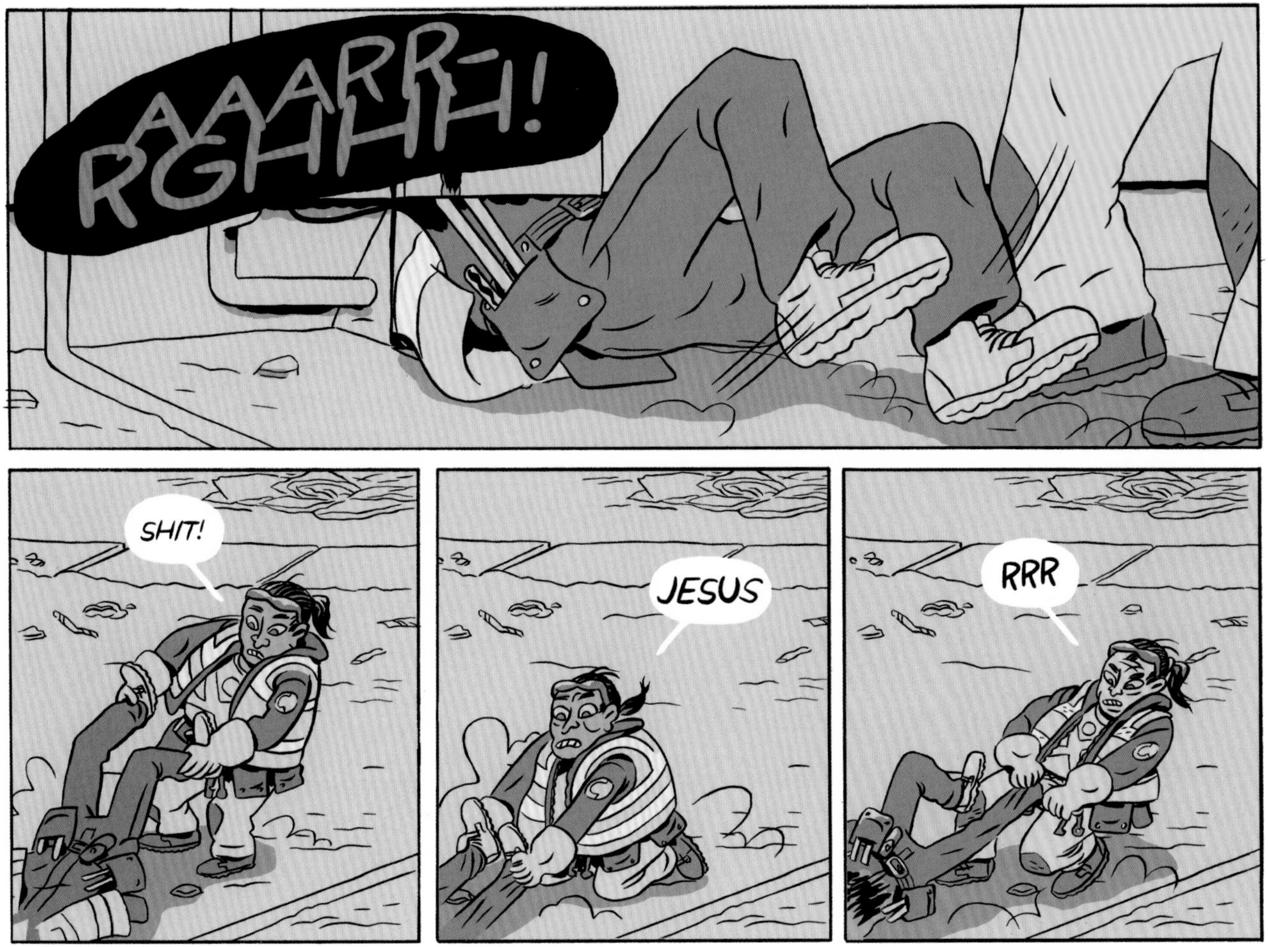
AAARR-RGHHH!
SHIT!
JESUS
RRR

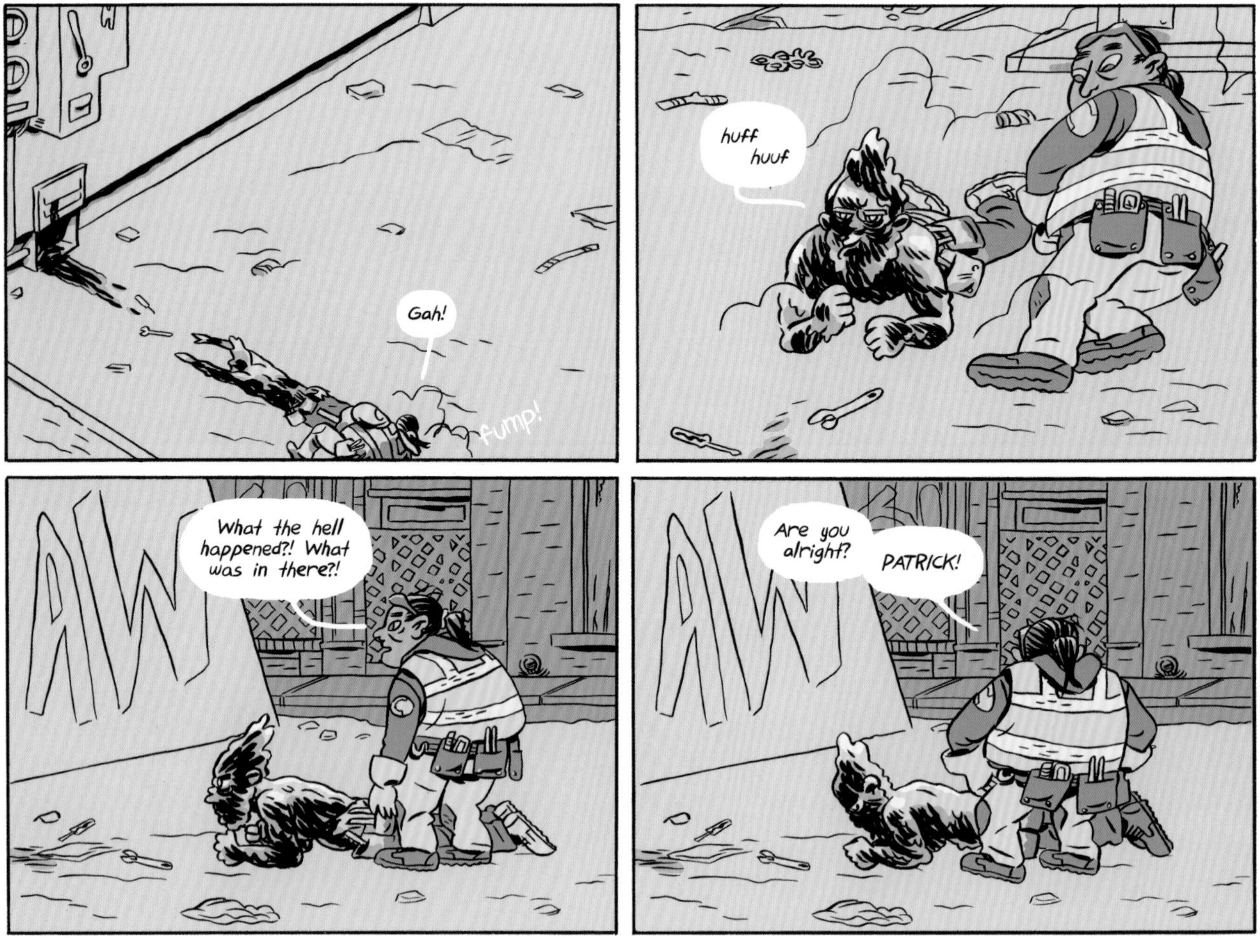
Gah!
fump!
huff
huuf
What the hell happened?! What was in there?!
AW
Are you alright?
PATRICK!
AW

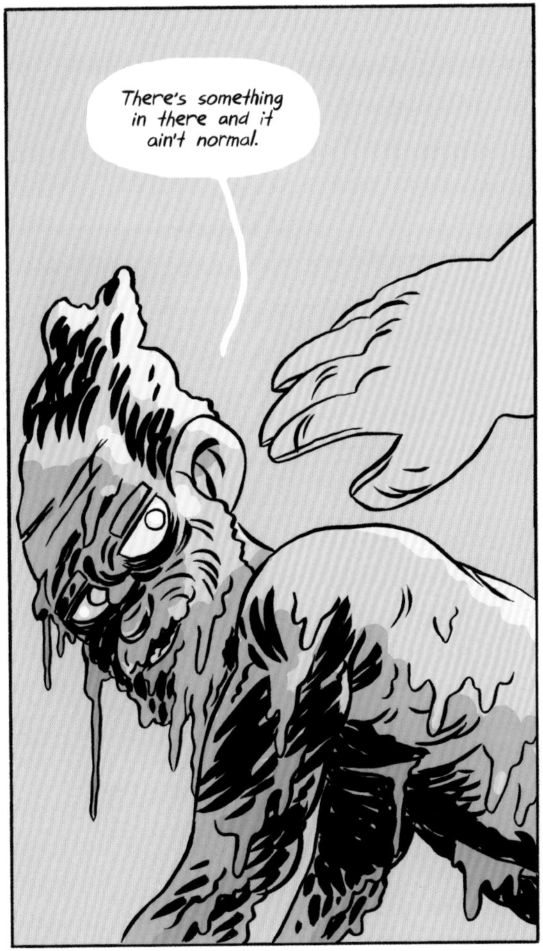
There's something in there and it ain't normal.

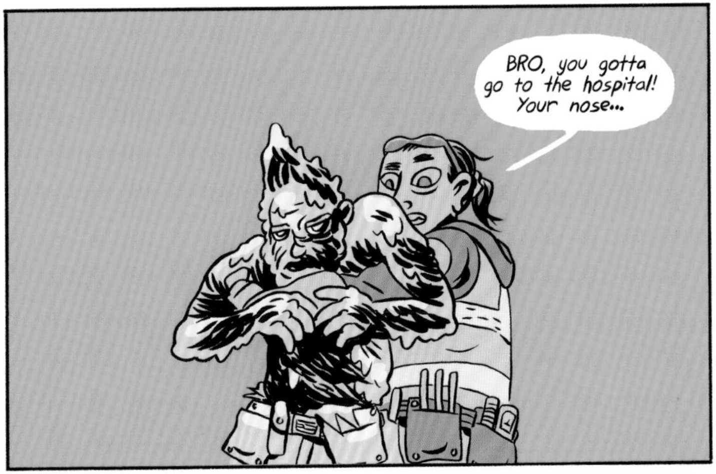
BRO, you gotta go to the hospital! Your nose...

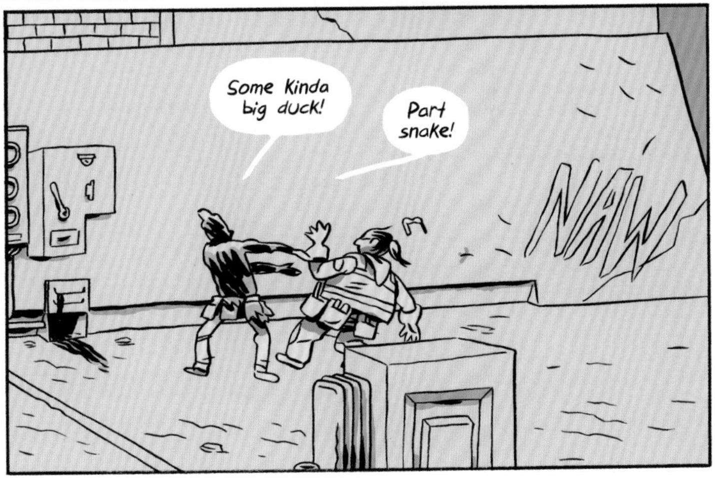
Some Kinda big duck!
Part snake!
NAW

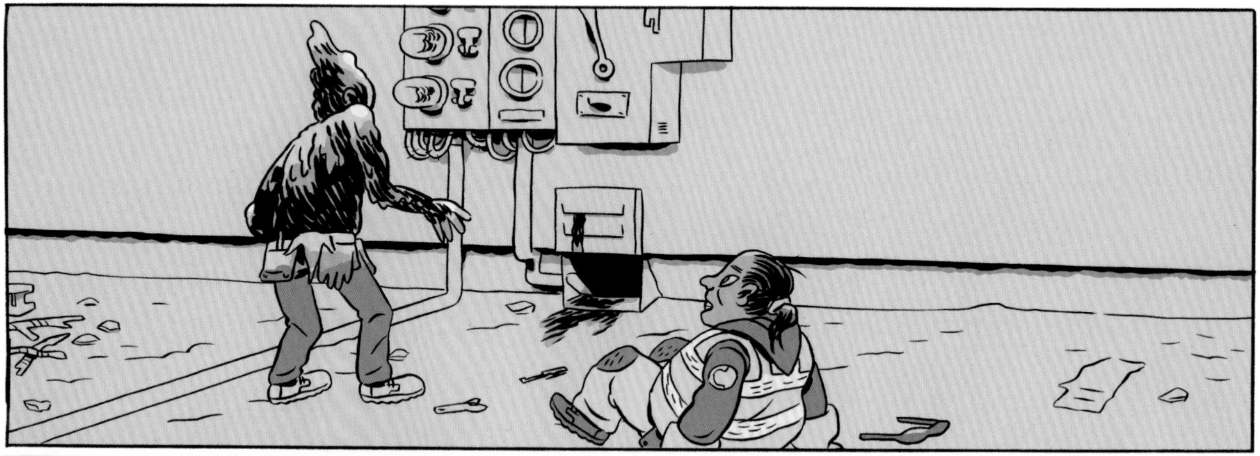

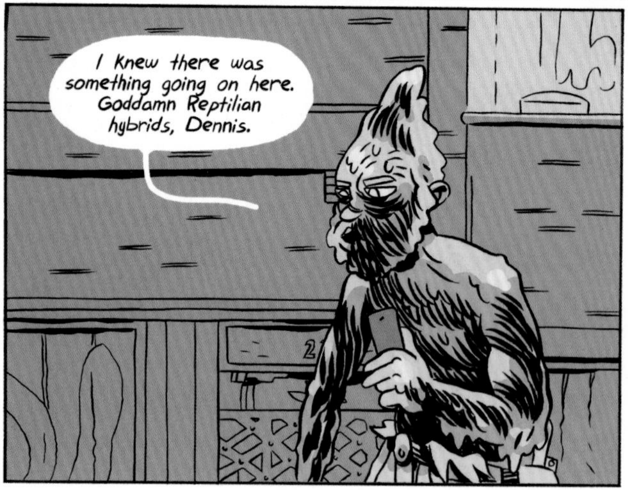
I knew there was something going on here. Goddamn Reptilian hybrids, Dennis.

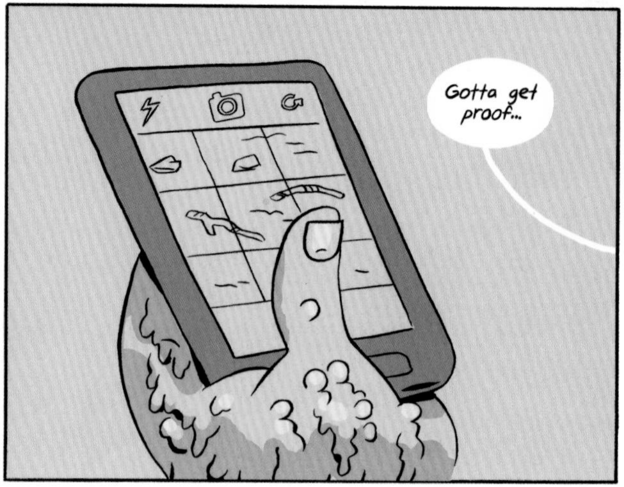
Gotta get proof...

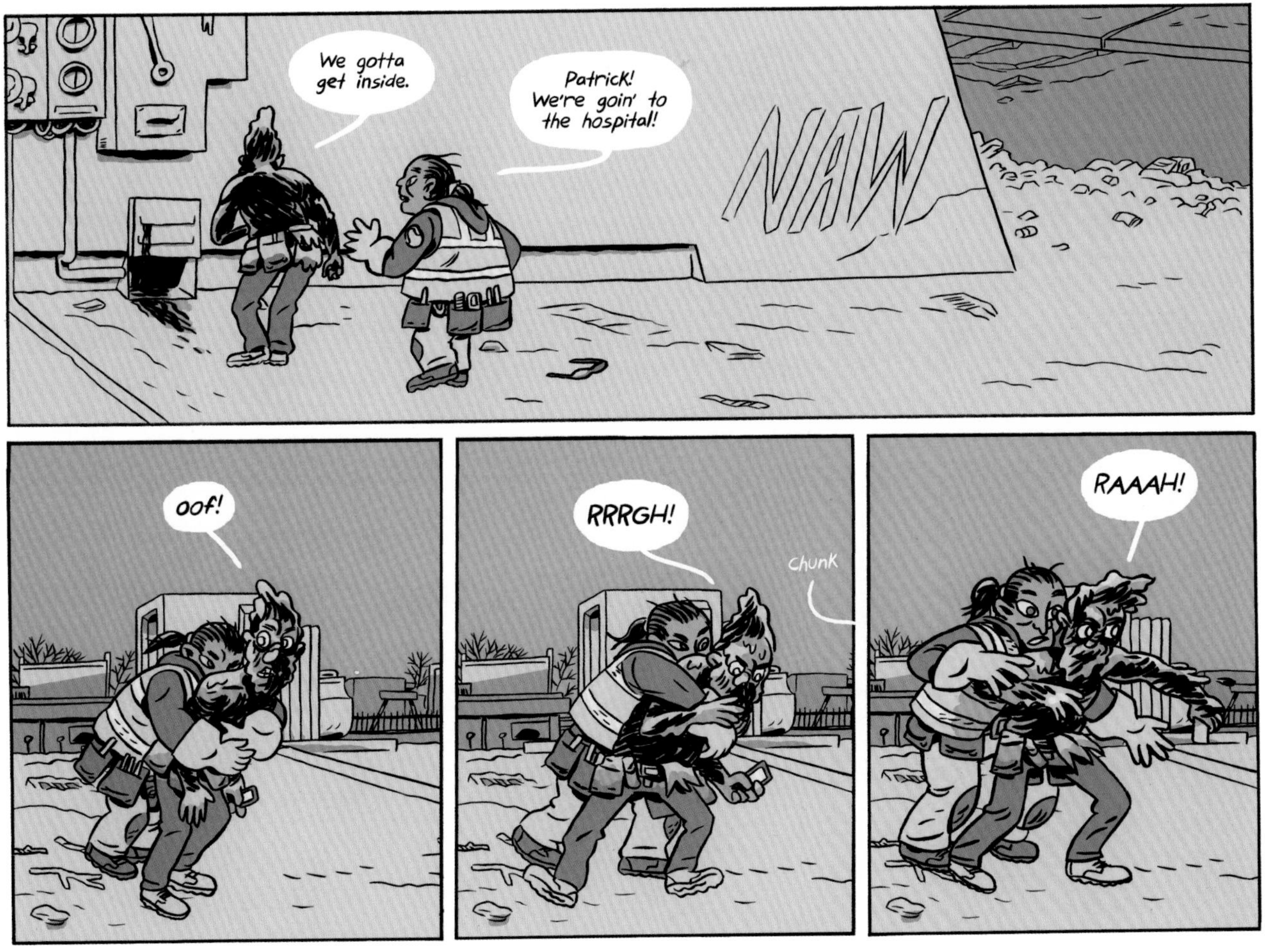
We gotta get inside.
Patrick! We're goin' to the hospital!
NAW
oof!
RRRGH!
chunk
RAAAH!

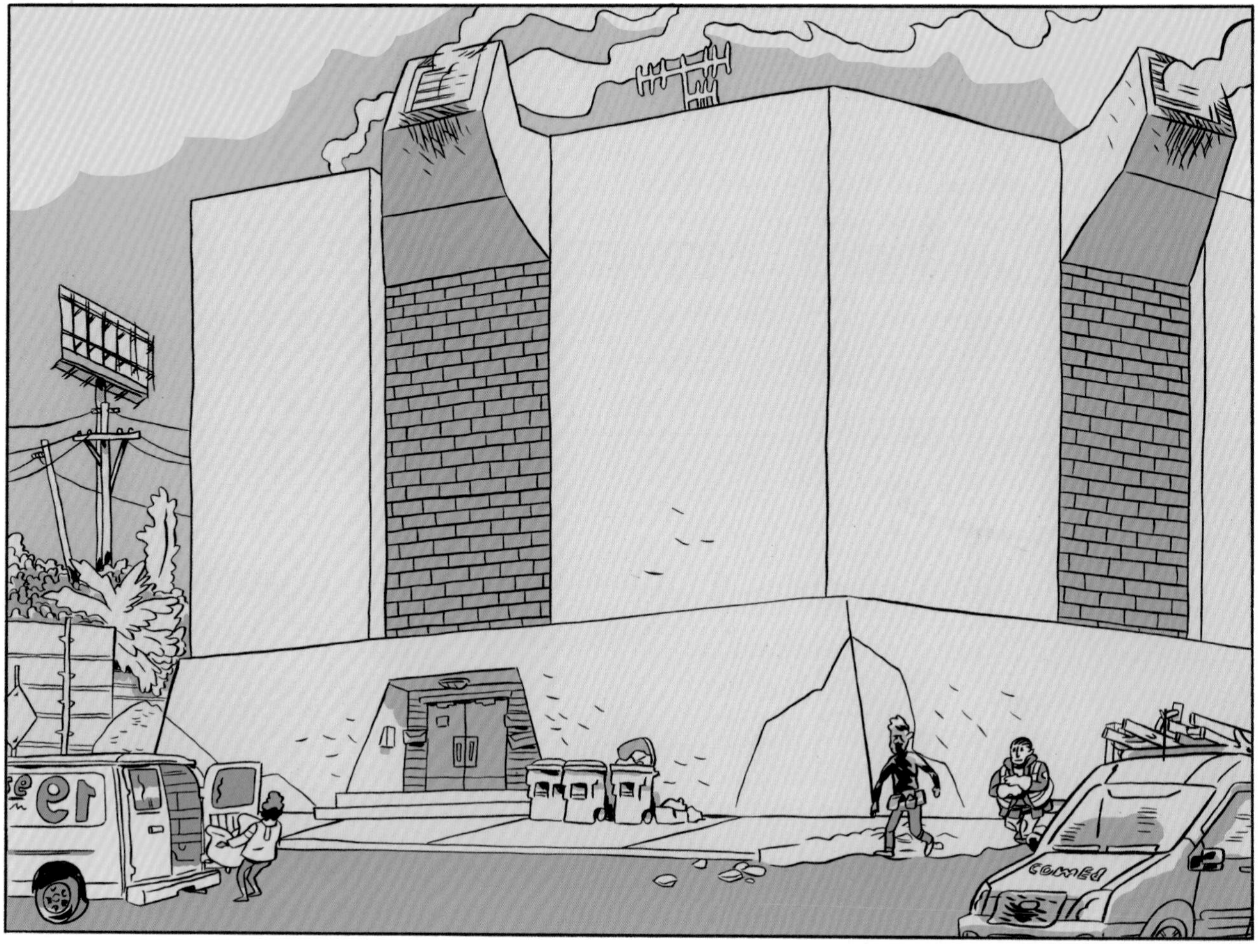

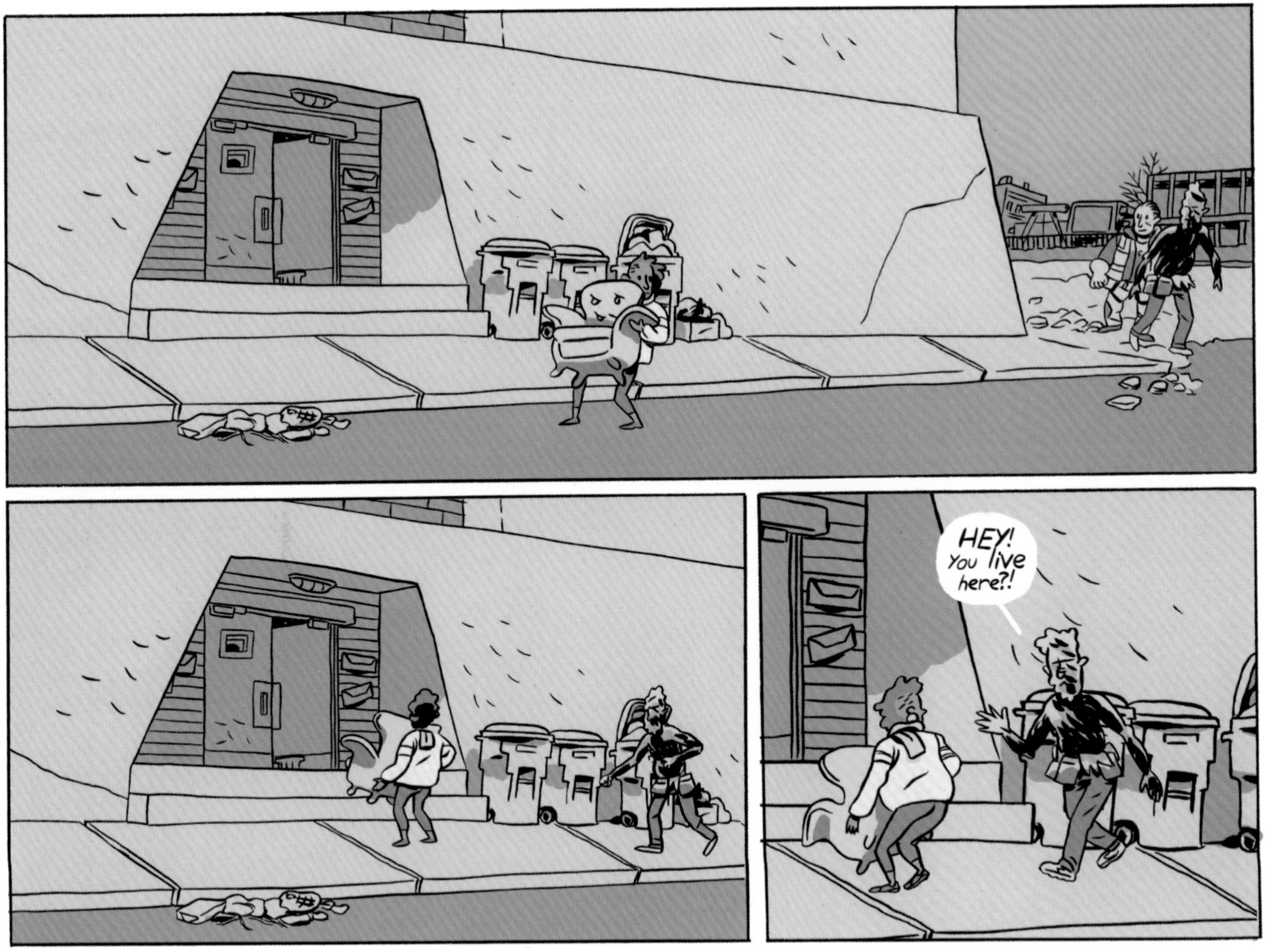
HEY! You live here?!

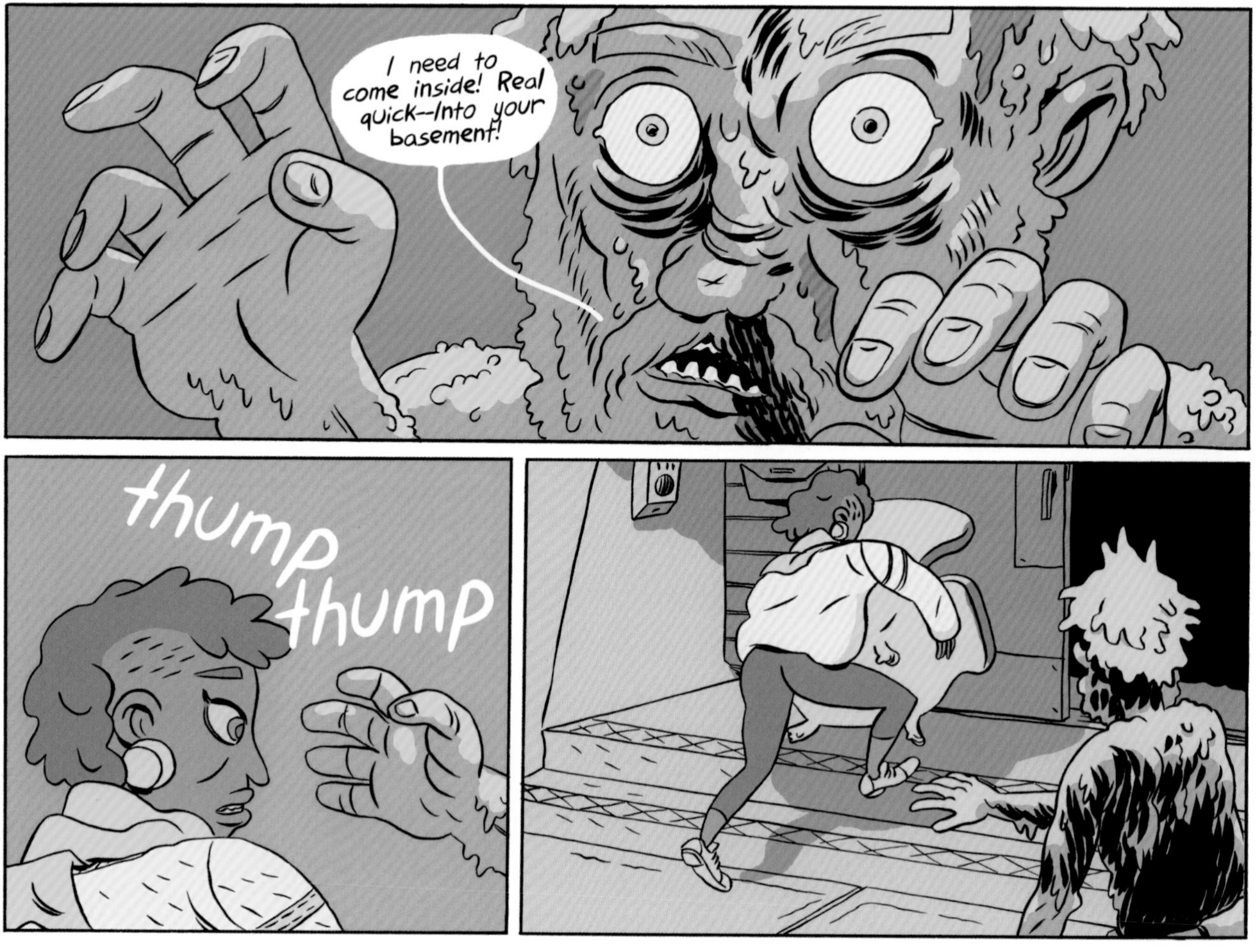
I need to come inside! Real quick--Into your basement!
thump thump

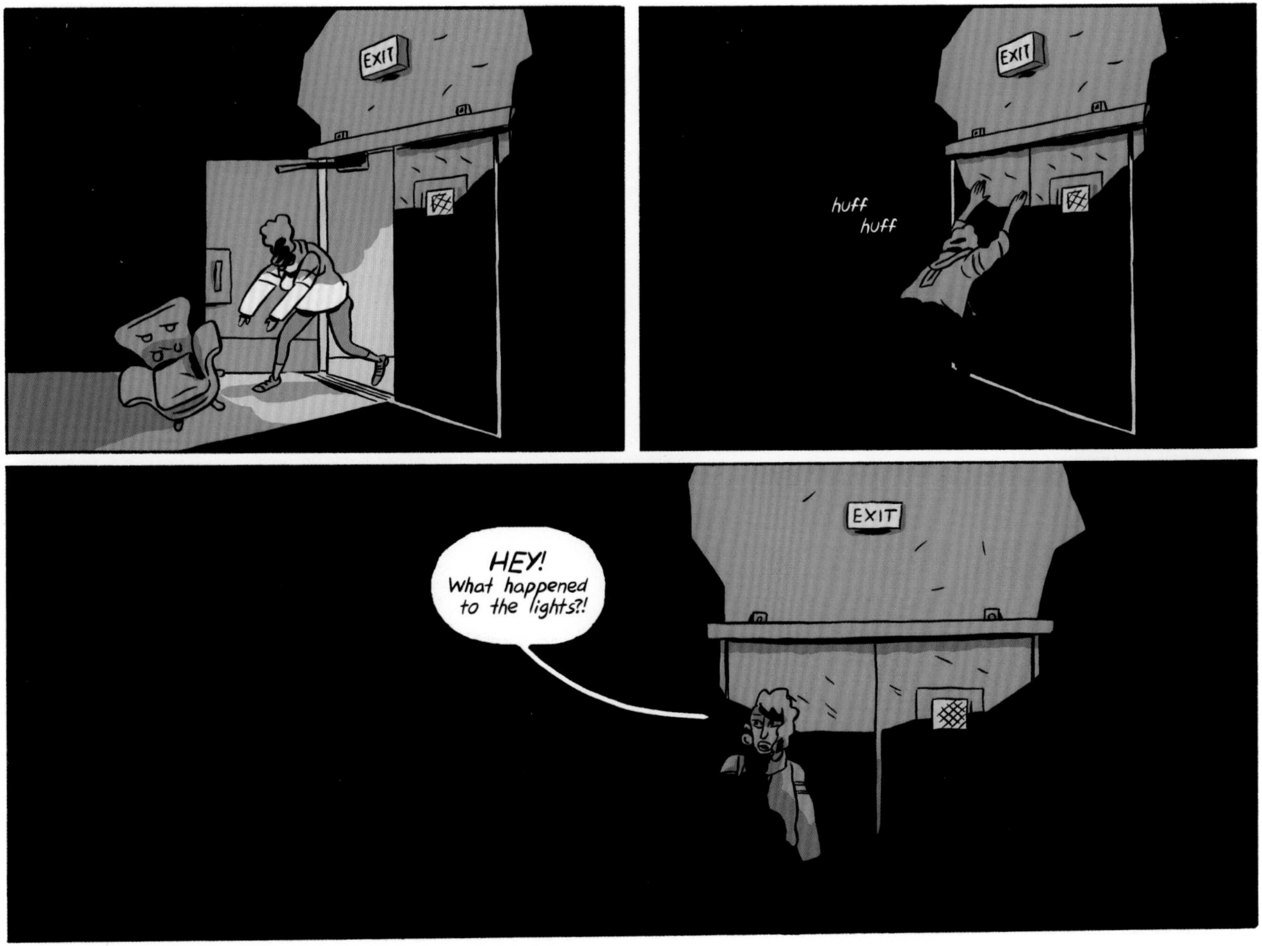
EXIT
EXIT
huff huff
EXIT
HEY! What happened to the lights?!

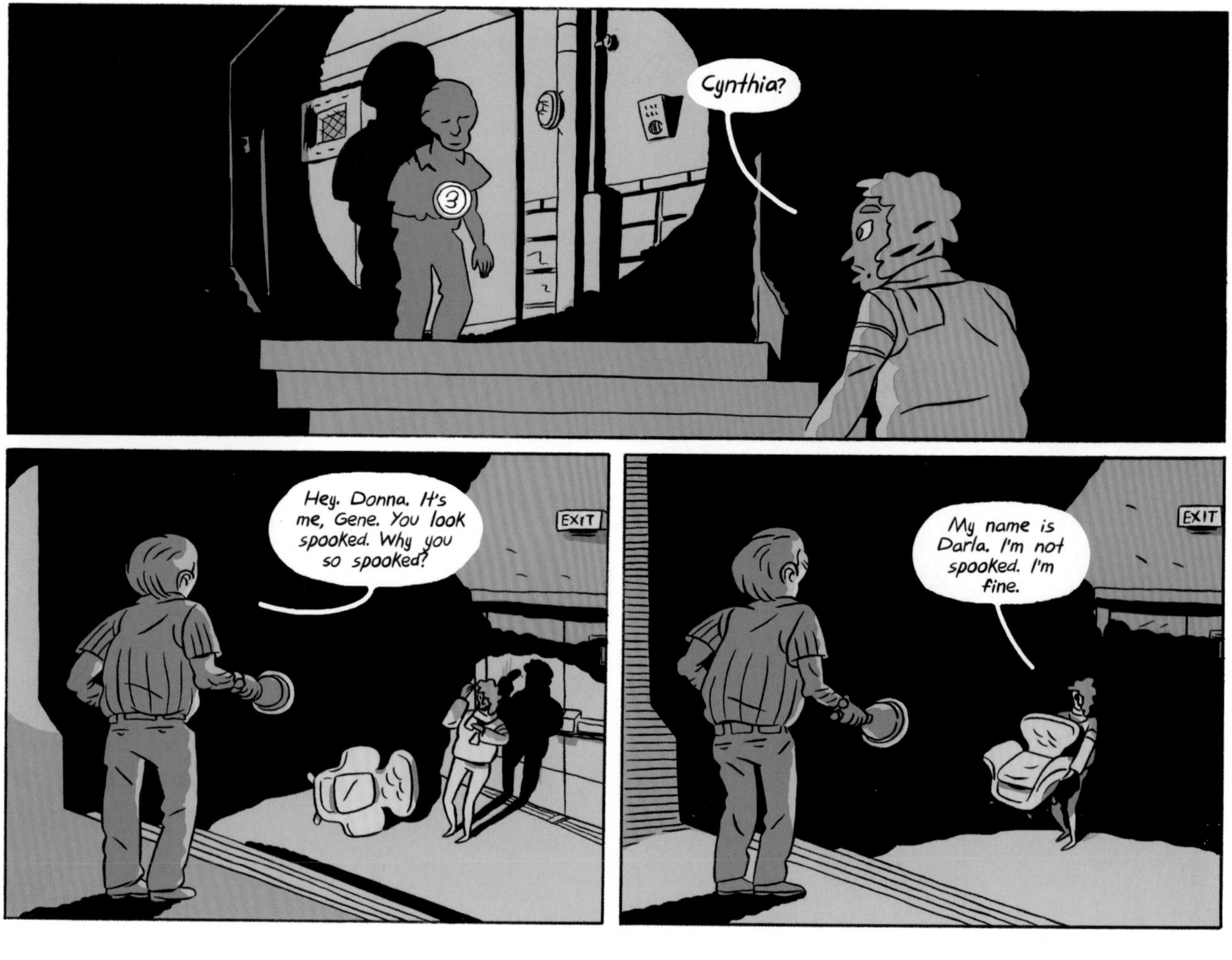
Cynthia?
Hey. Donna. It's me, Gene. You look spooked. Why you so spooked?
EXIT
EXIT
My name is Darla. I'm not spooked. I'm fine.

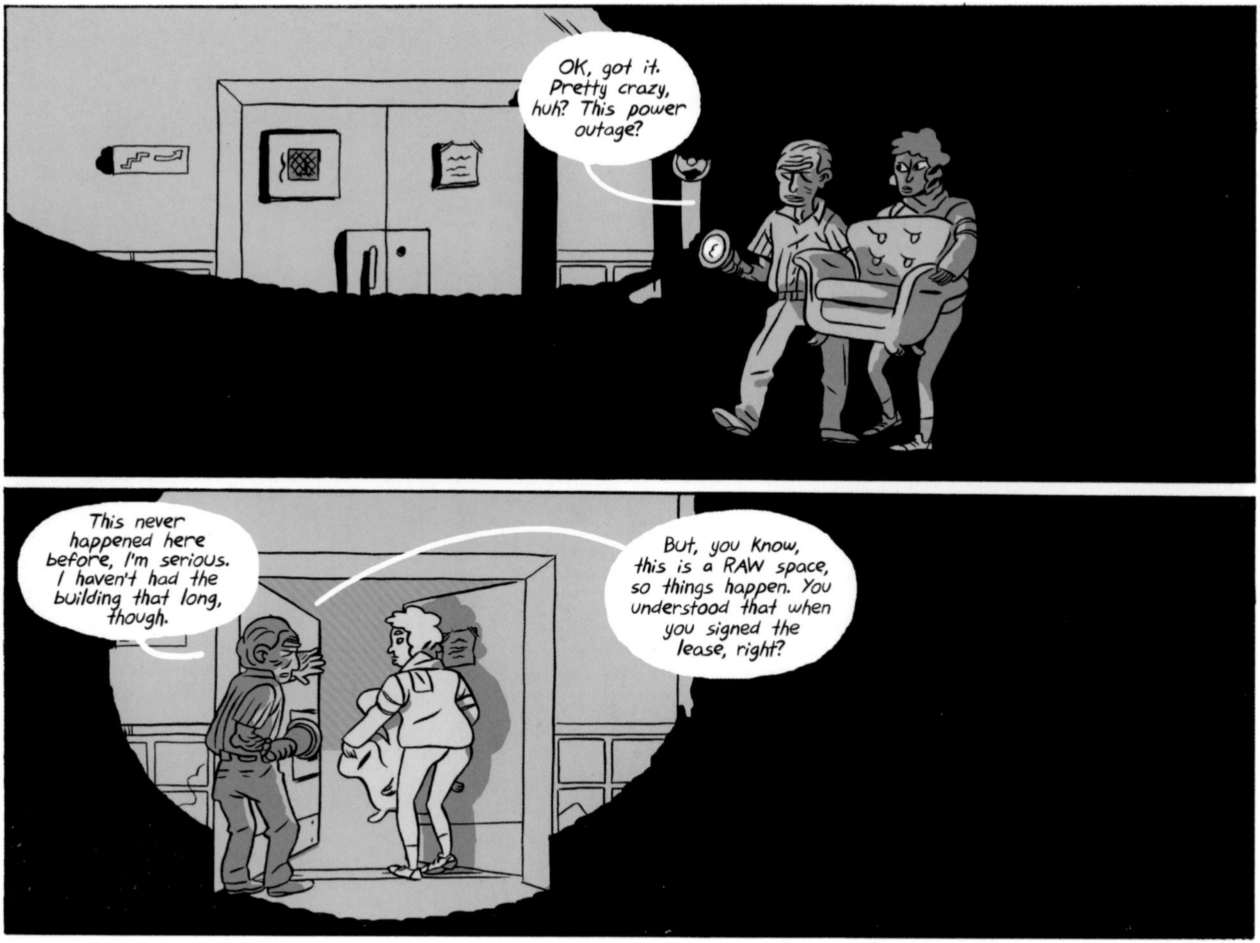
OK, got it. Pretty crazy, huh? This power outage?
This never happened here before, I'm serious. I haven't had the building that long, though.
But, you know, this is a RAW space, so things happen. You understood that when you signed the lease, right?

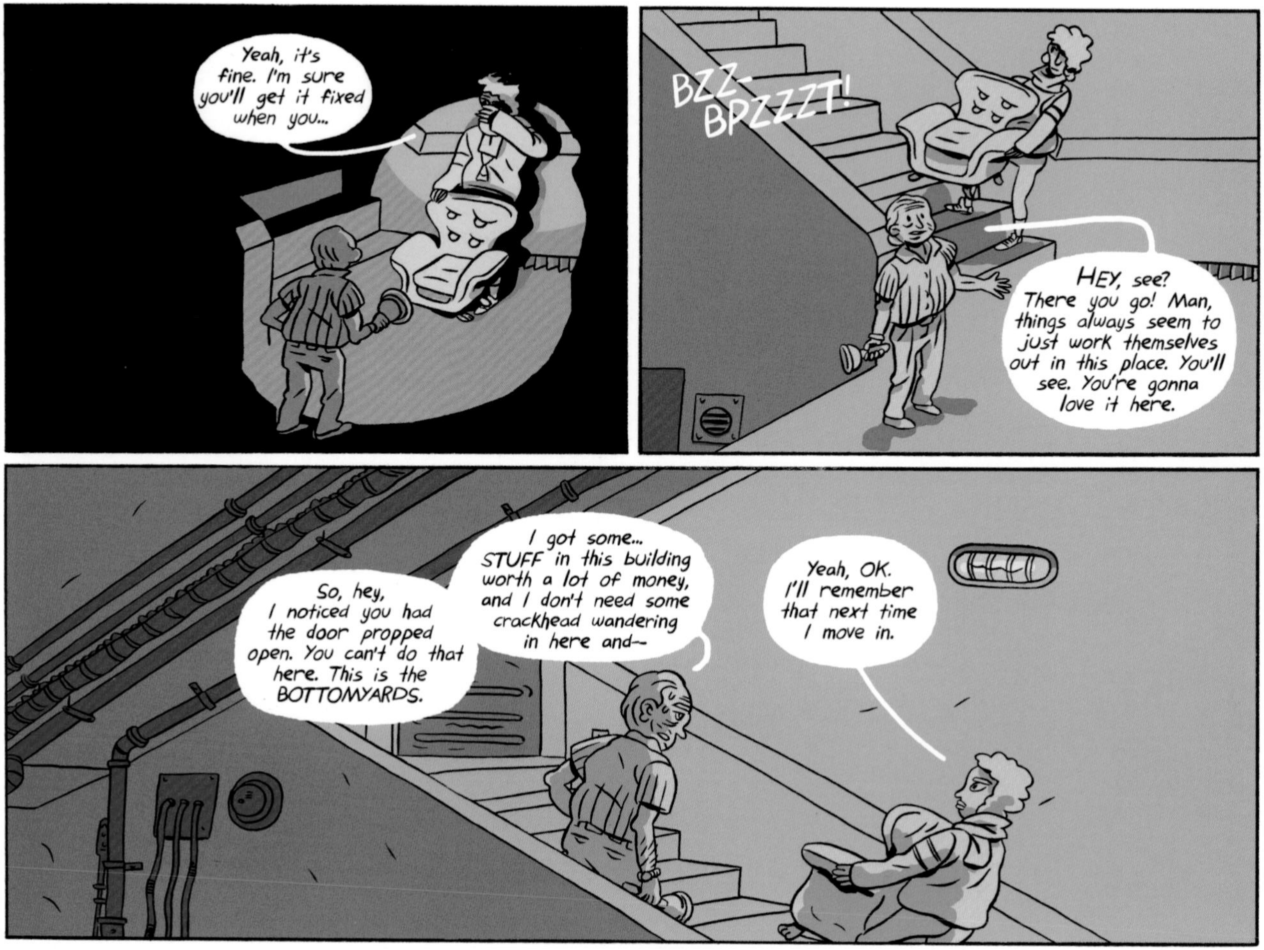
Yeah, it's fine. I'm sure you'll get it fixed when you...
BZZ-BPZZZZT!
HEY, see? There you go! Man, things always seem to just work themselves out in this place. You'll see. You're gonna love it here.
So, hey, I noticed you had the door propped open. You can't do that here. This is the BOTTOMYARDS.
I got some... STUFF in this building worth a lot of money, and I don't need some crackhead wandering in here and--
Yeah, OK. I'll remember that next time I move in.

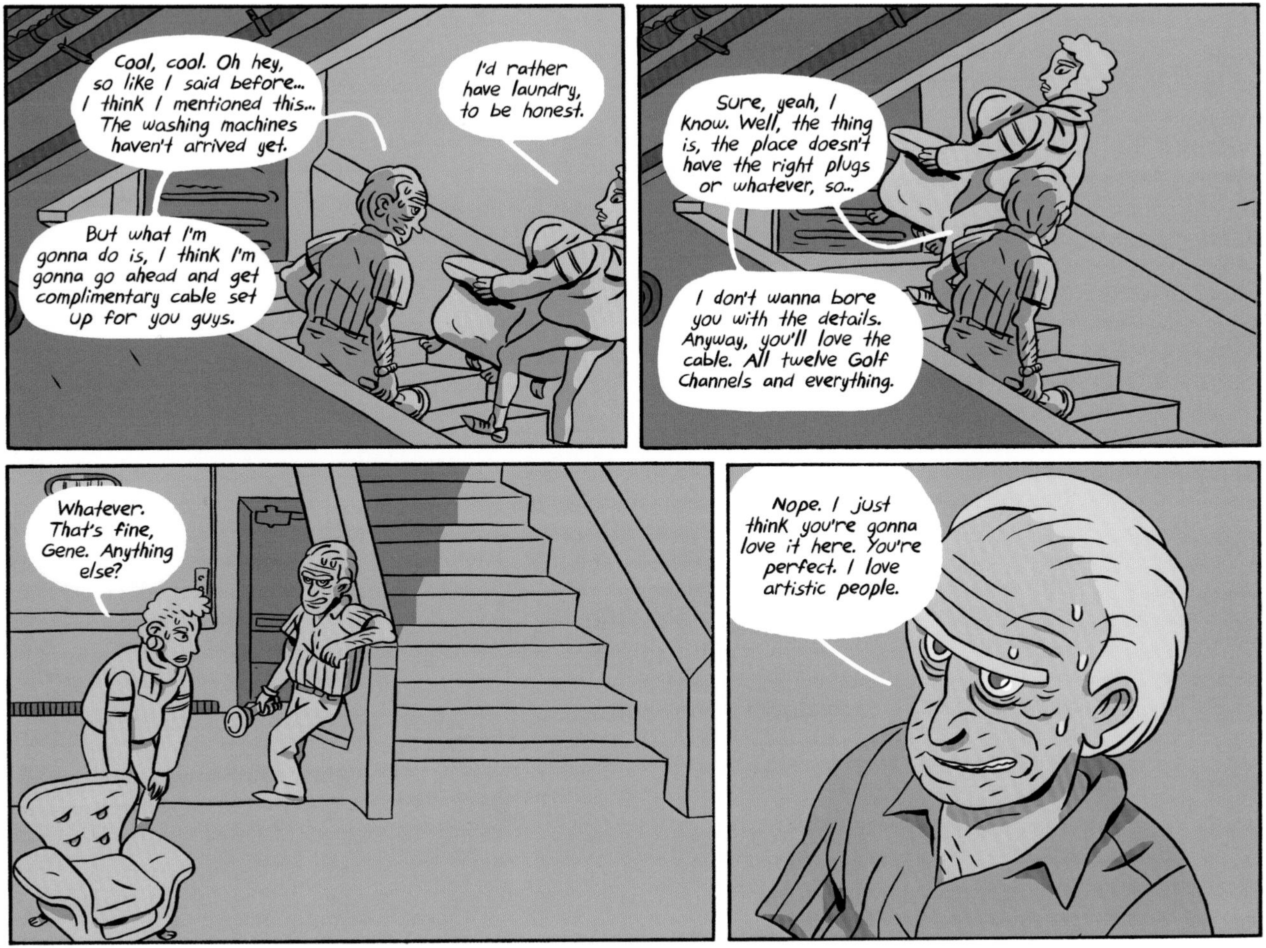
Cool, cool. Oh hey, so like I said before... I think I mentioned this... The washing machines haven't arrived yet.
But what I'm gonna do is, I think I'm gonna go ahead and get complimentary cable set up for you guys.
I'd rather have laundry, to be honest.
Sure, yeah, I know. Well, the thing is, the place doesn't have the right plugs or whatever, so...
I don't wanna bore you with the details. Anyway, you'll love the cable. All twelve Golf Channels and everything.
Whatever. That's fine, Gene. Anything else?
Nope. I just think you're gonna love it here. You're perfect. I love artistic people.

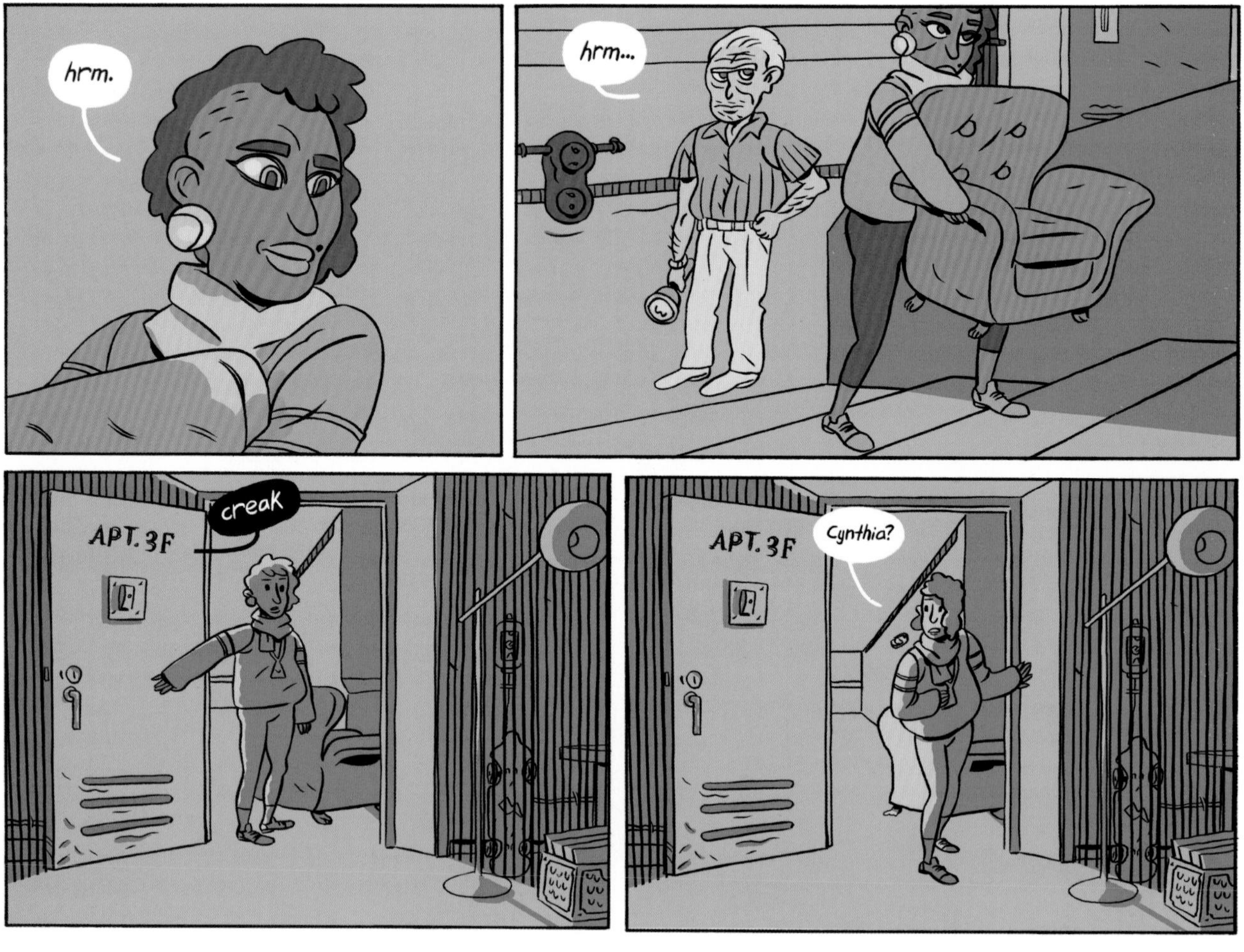
hrm.
hrm...
APT. 3F
creak
APT. 3F
Cynthia?

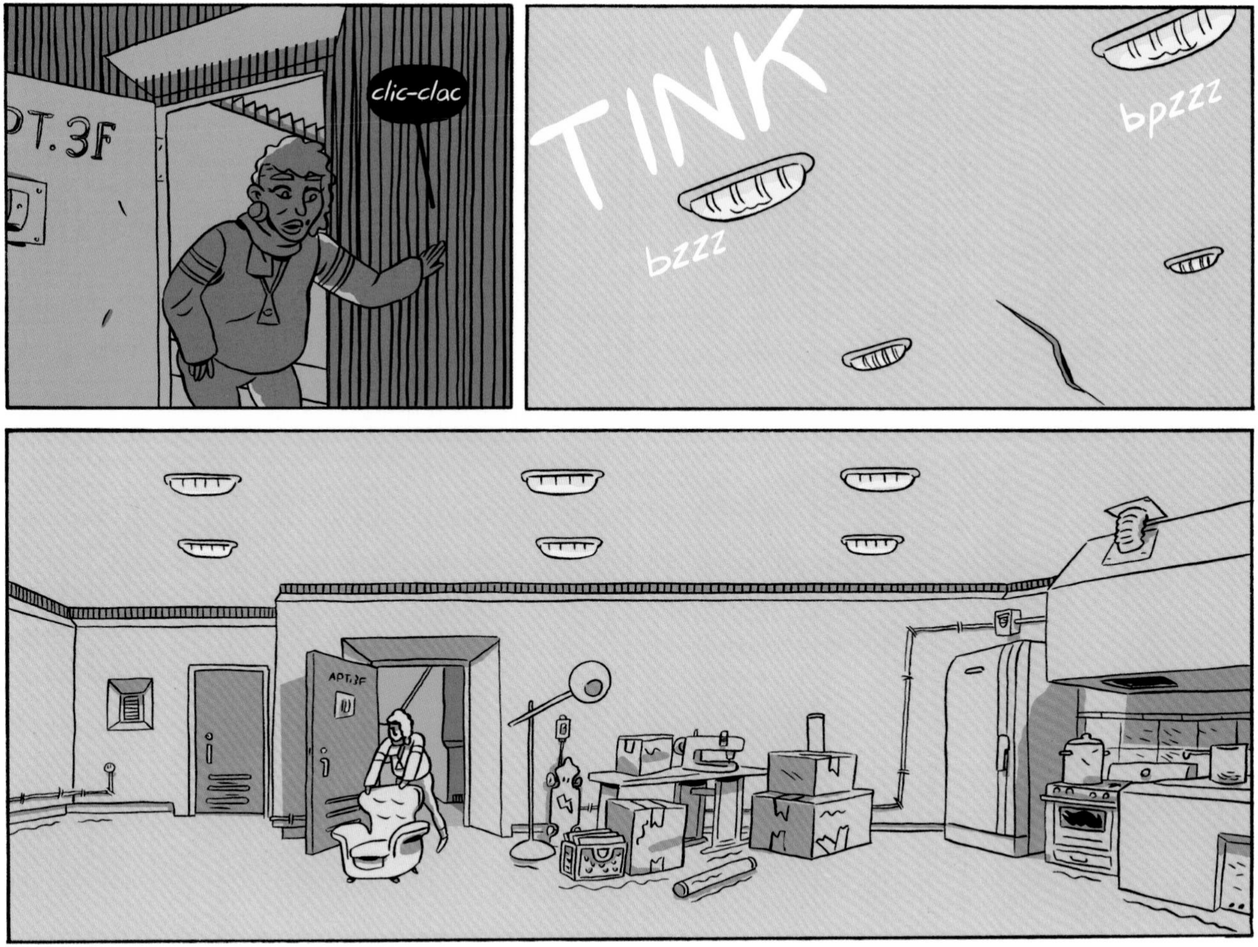
PT.3F
clic-clac
TINK
bzzz
bpzzz
APT. 3F

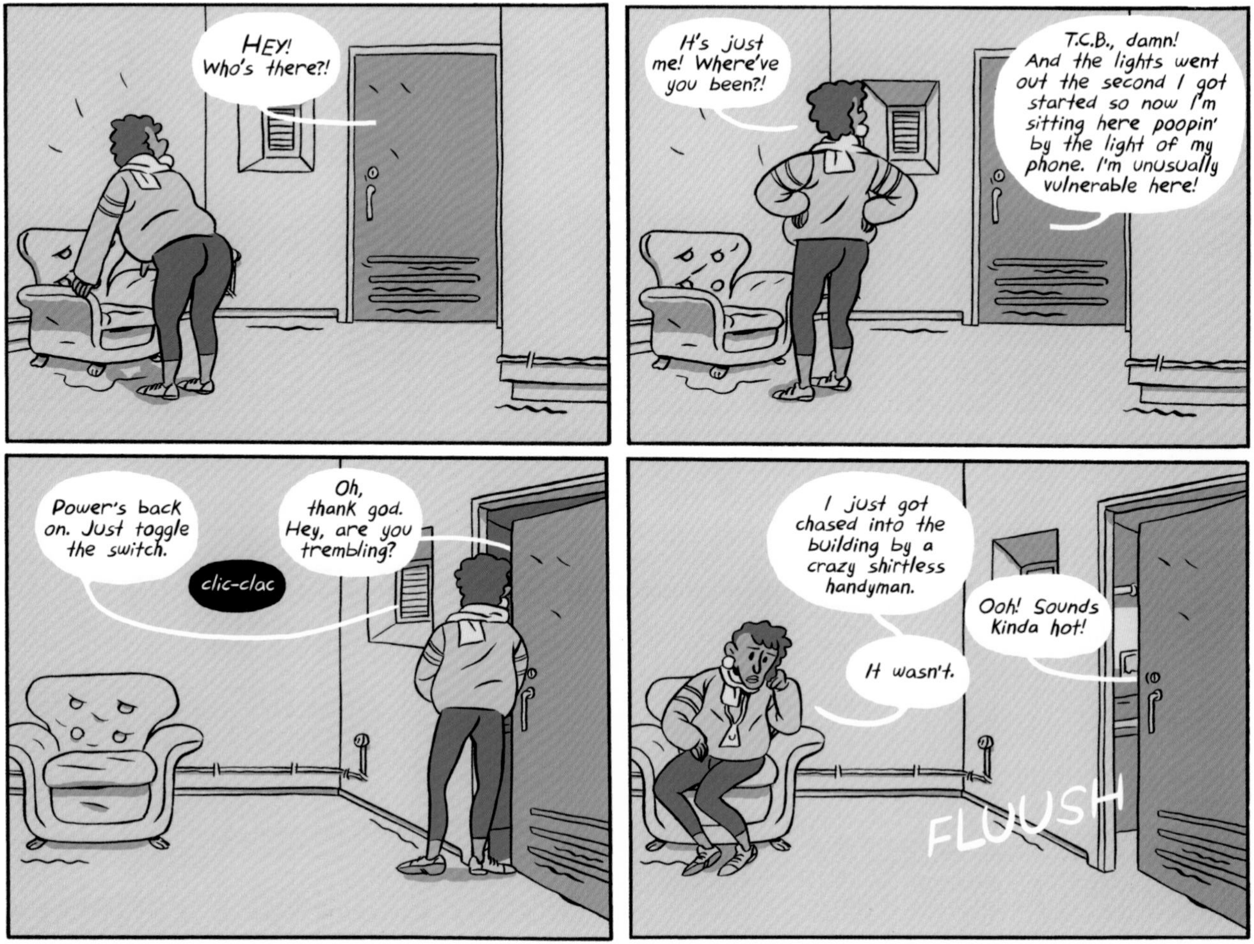
HEY! Who's there?!
It's just me! Where've you been?!
T.C.B., damn! And the lights went out the second I got started so now I'm sitting here poopin' by the light of my phone. I'm unusually vulnerable here!
Power's back on. Just toggle the switch.
clic-clac
Oh, thank god. Hey, are you trembling?
I just got chased into the building by a crazy shirtless handyman.
Ooh! Sounds kinda hot!
It wasn't.
FLUUSH

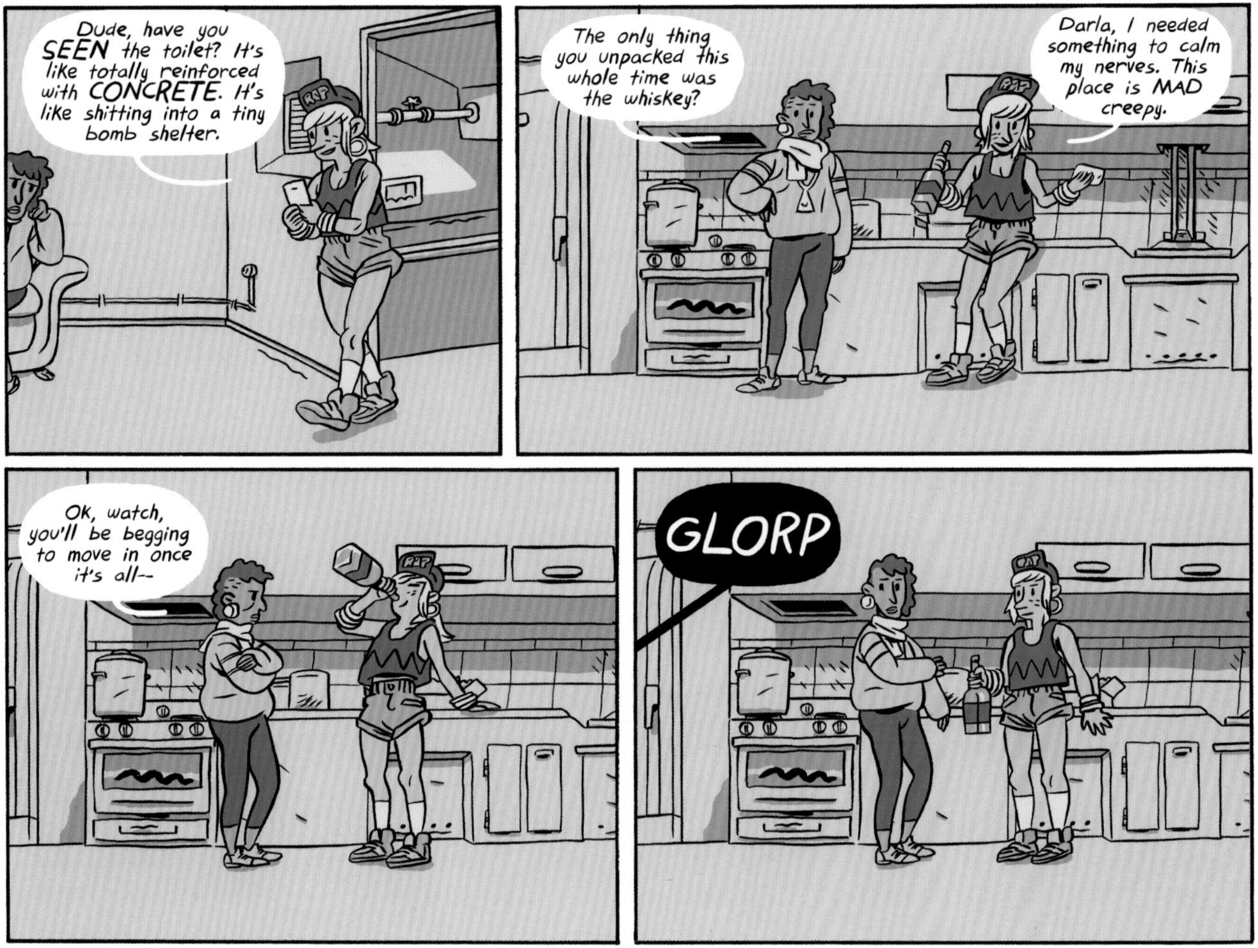
Dude, have you SEEN the toilet? It's like totally reinforced with CONCRETE. It's like shitting into a tiny bomb shelter.
The only thing you unpacked this whole time was the whiskey?
Darla, I needed something to calm my nerves. This place is MAD creepy.
Ok, watch, you'll be begging to move in once it's all--
GLORP

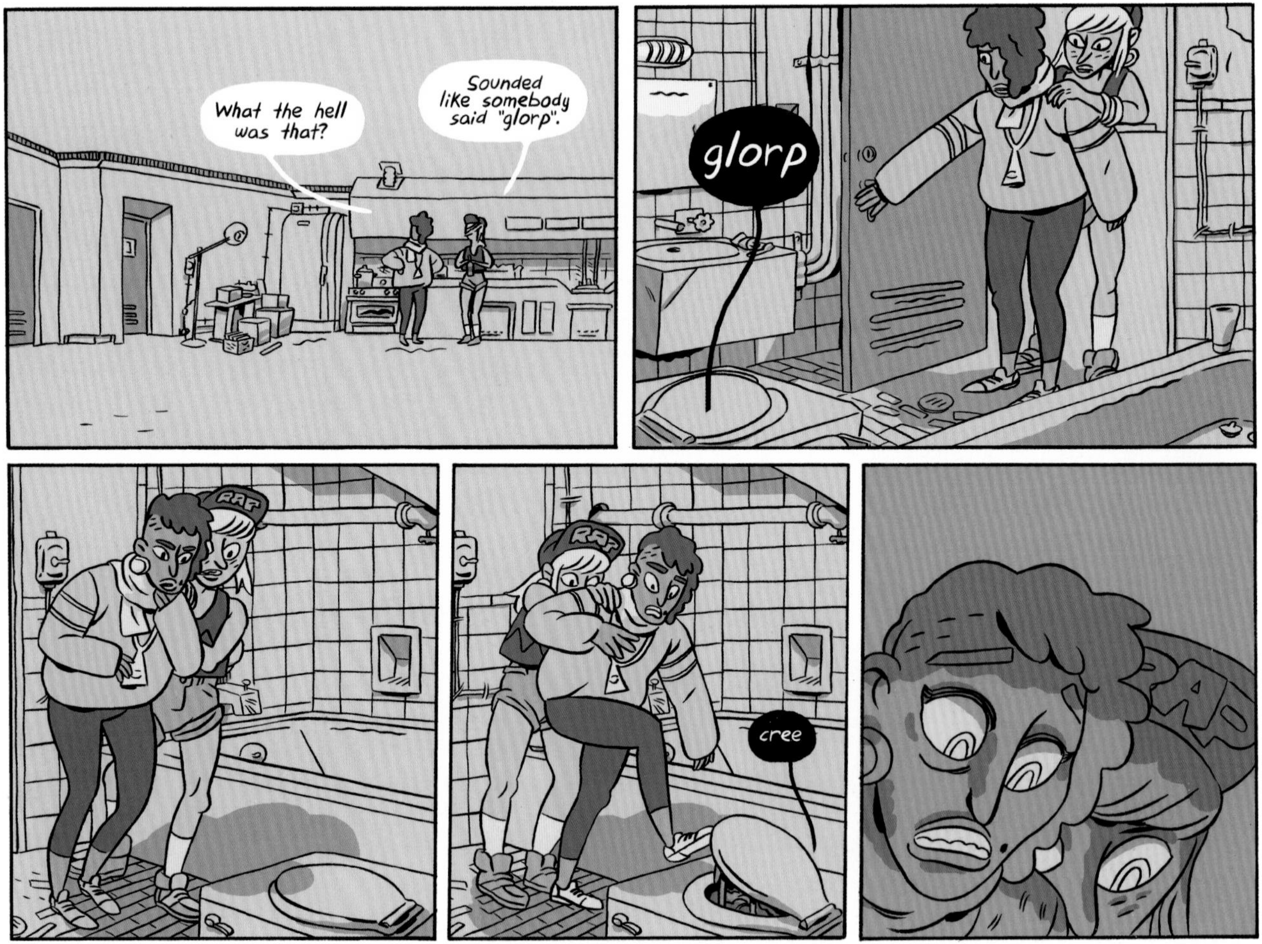
What the hell was that?
Sounded like somebody said "glorp".
glorp
cree

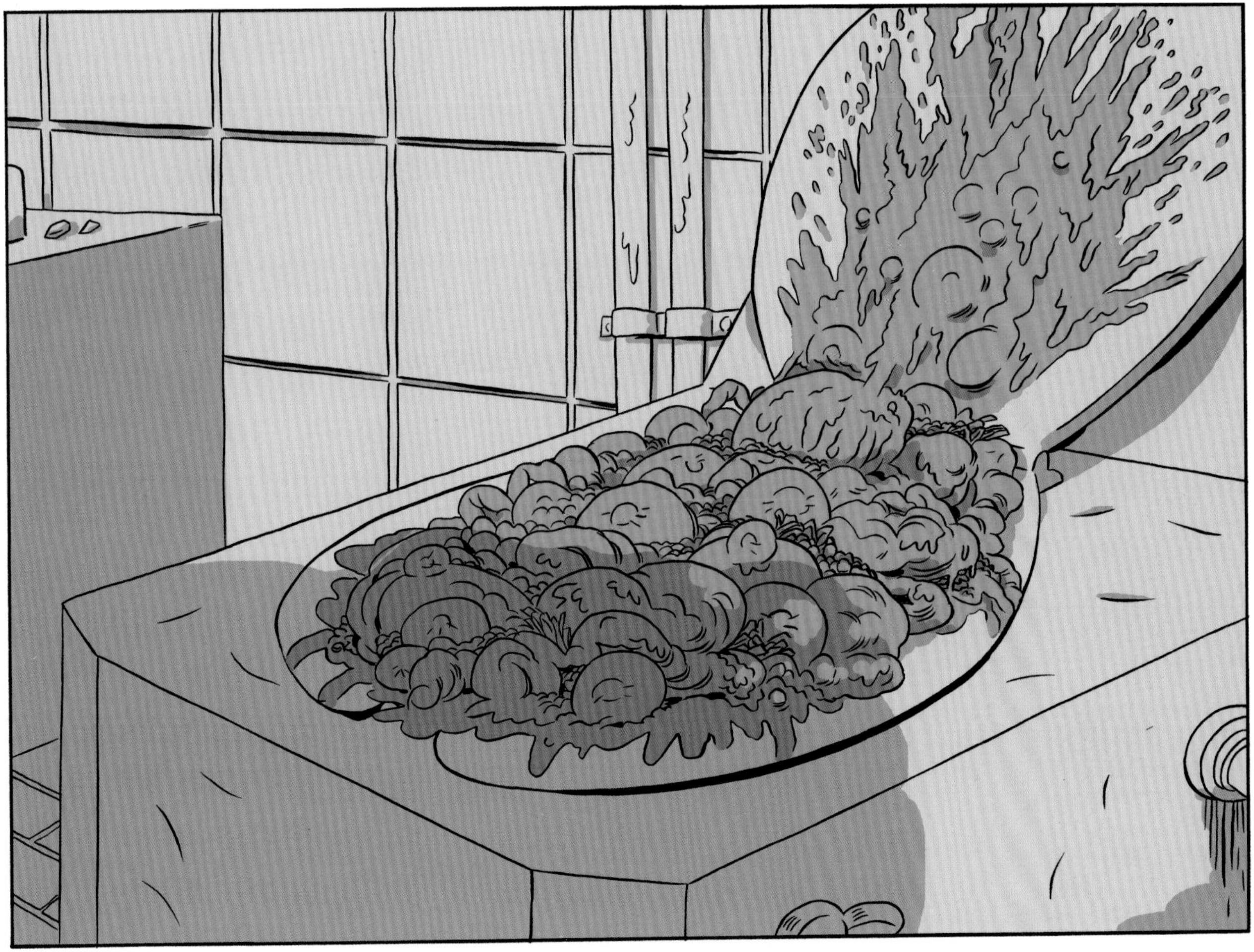

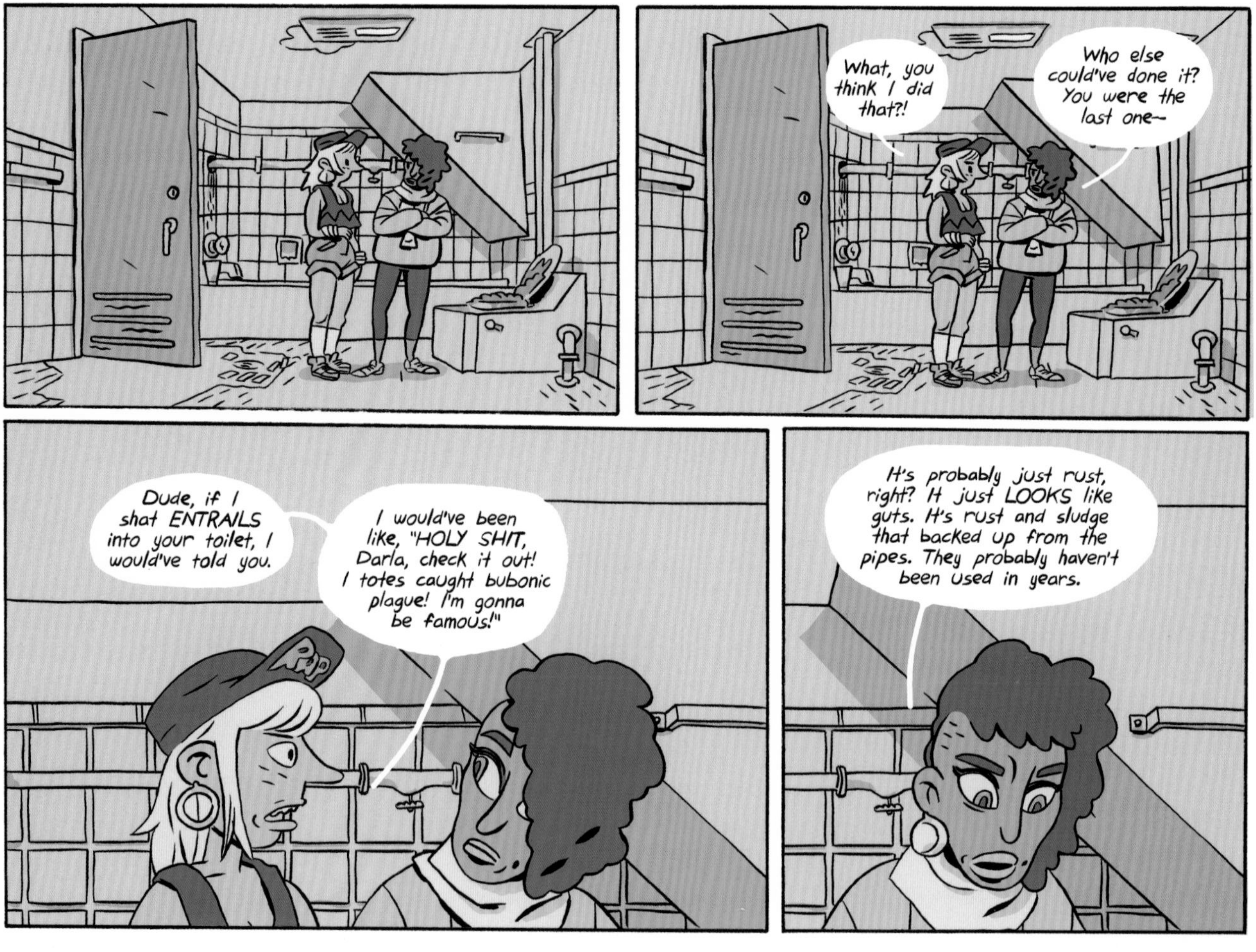
What, you think I did that?!
Who else could've done it? You were the last one—
Dude, if I shat ENTRAILS into your toilet, I would've told you.
I would've been like, "HOLY SHIT, Darla, check it out! I totes caught bubonic plague! I'm gonna be famous!"
It's probably just rust, right? It just LOOKS like guts. It's rust and sludge that backed up from the pipes. They probably haven't been used in years.

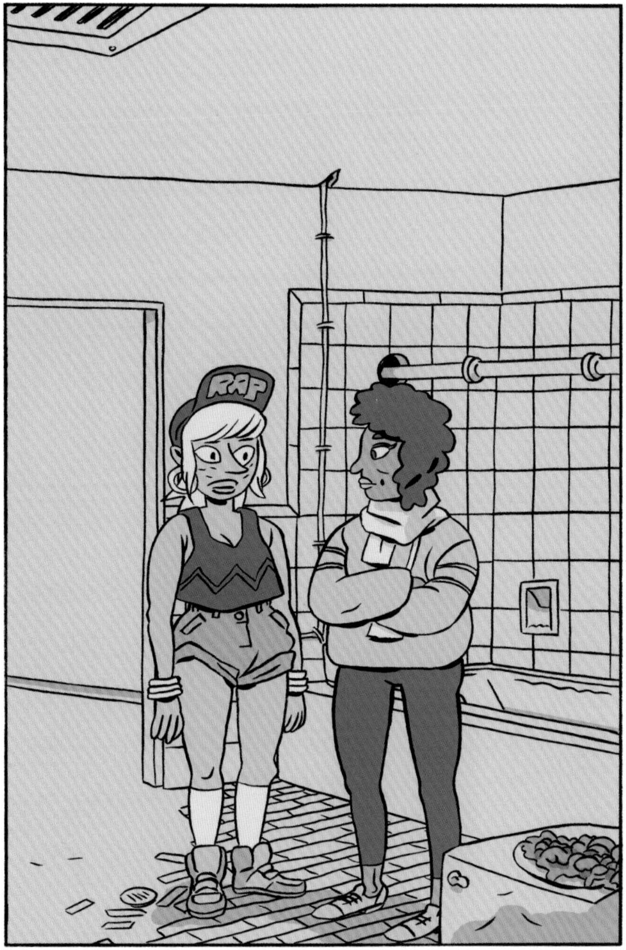

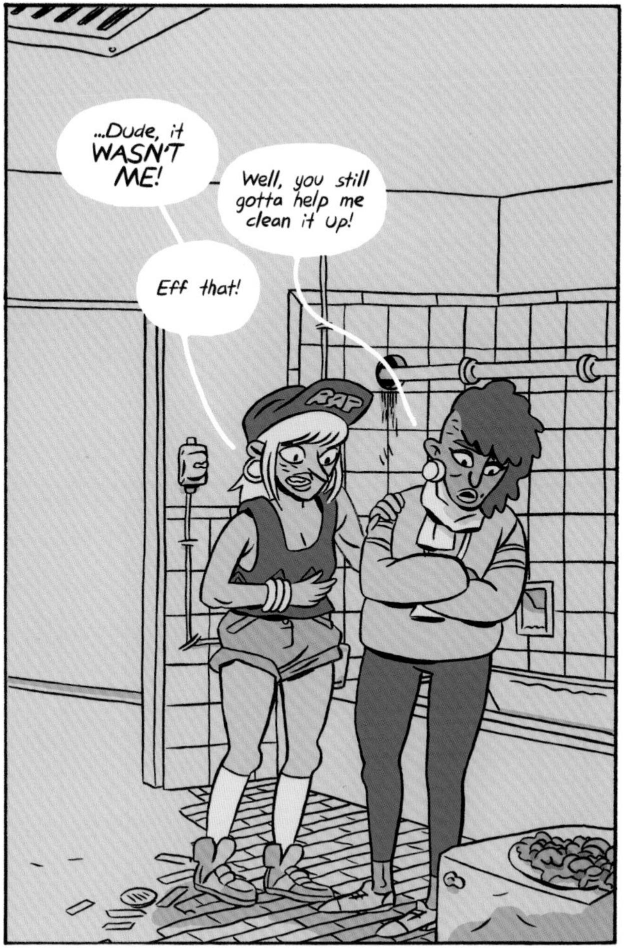
...Dude, it WASN'T ME!
Eff that!
Well, you still gotta help me clean it up!

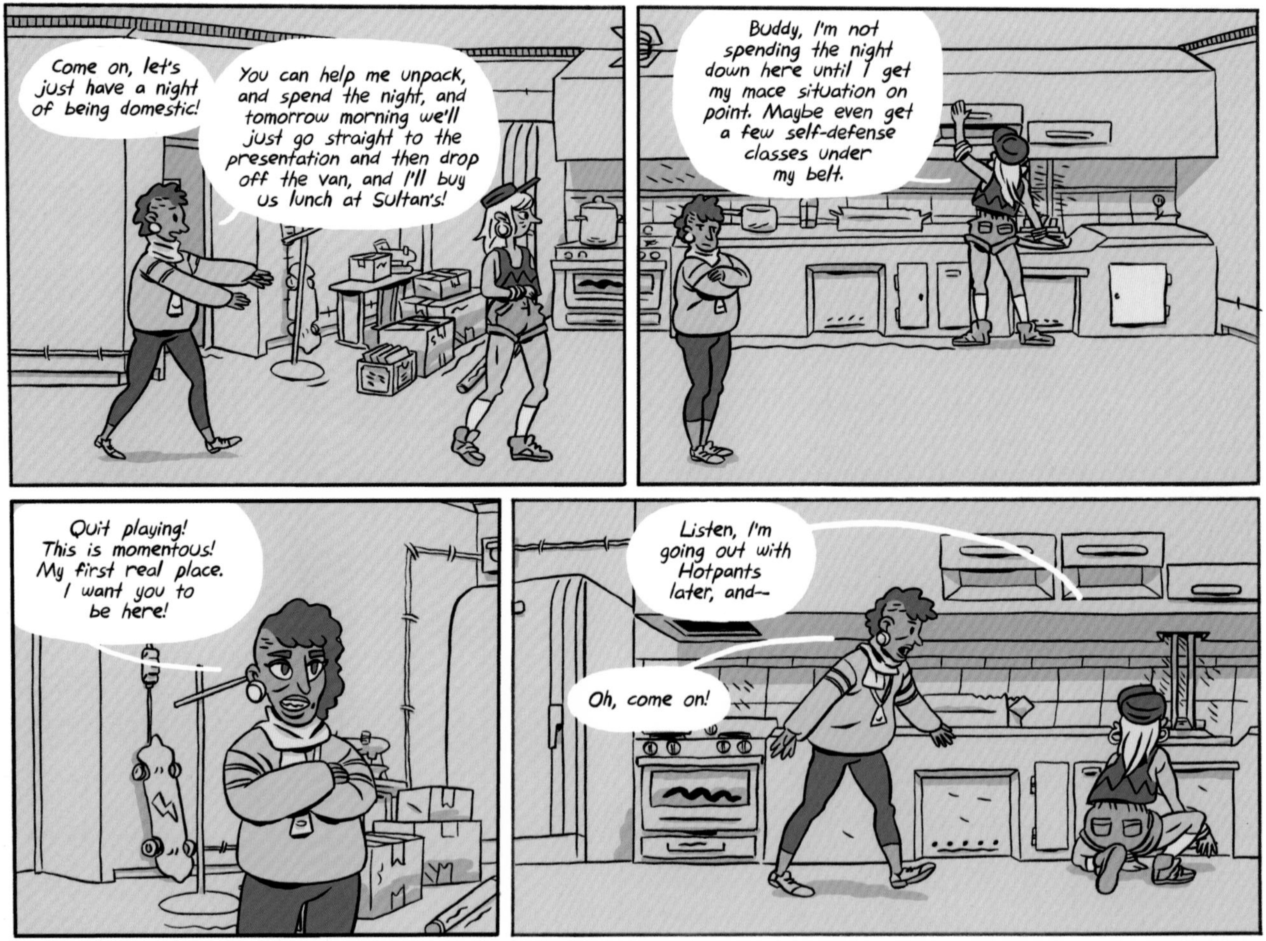
Come on, let's just have a night of being domestic!
You can help me unpack, and spend the night, and tomorrow morning we'll just go straight to the presentation and then drop off the van, and I'll buy us lunch at Sultan's!
Buddy, I'm not spending the night down here until I get my mace situation on point. Maybe even get a few self-defense classes under my belt.
Quit playing! This is momentous! My first real place. I want you to be here!
Listen, I'm going out with Hotpants later, and--
Oh, come on!

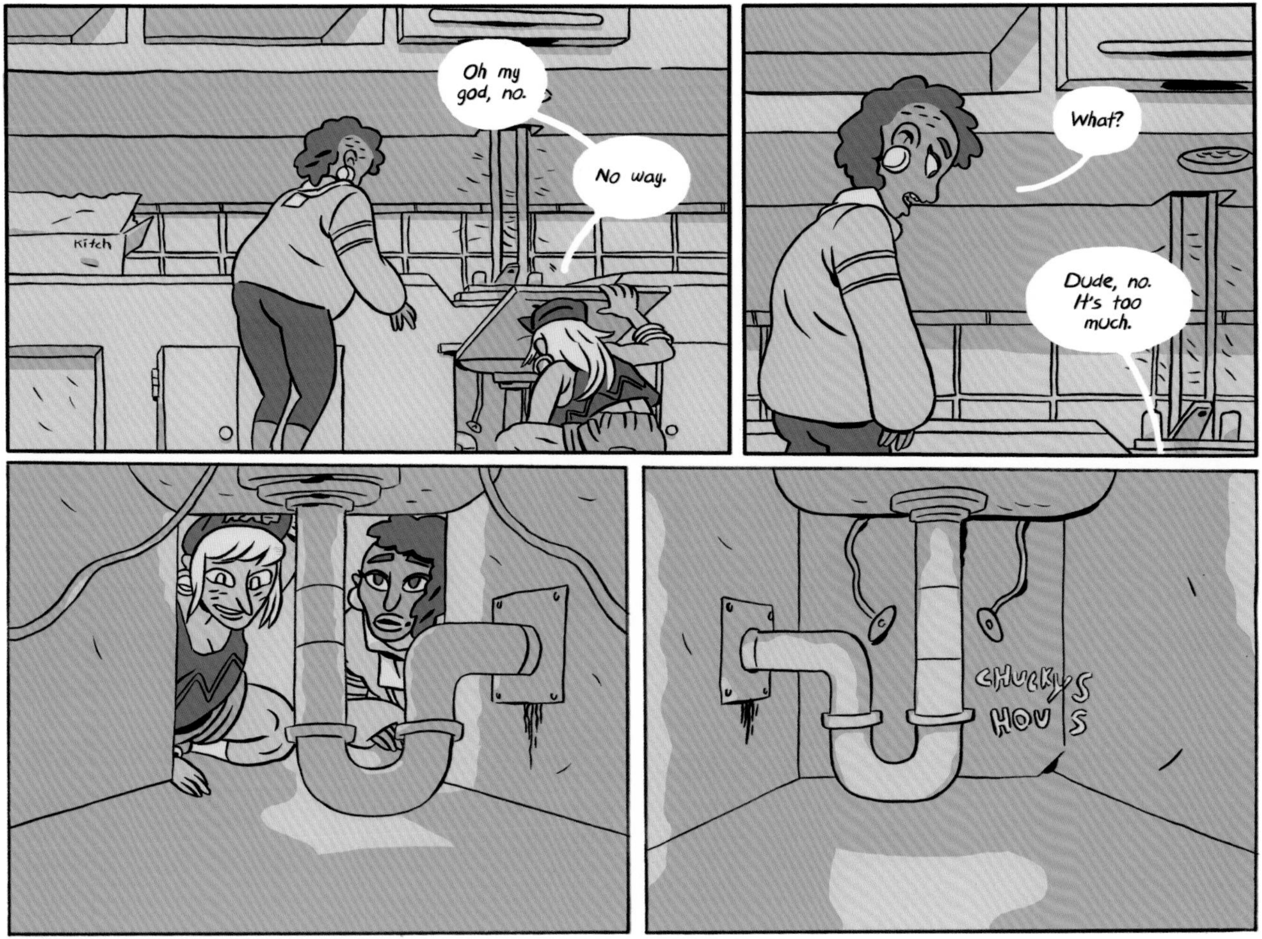

Kitch
Oh my god, no.
No way.
What?
Dude, no. It's too much.
CHUCKYS HOUS

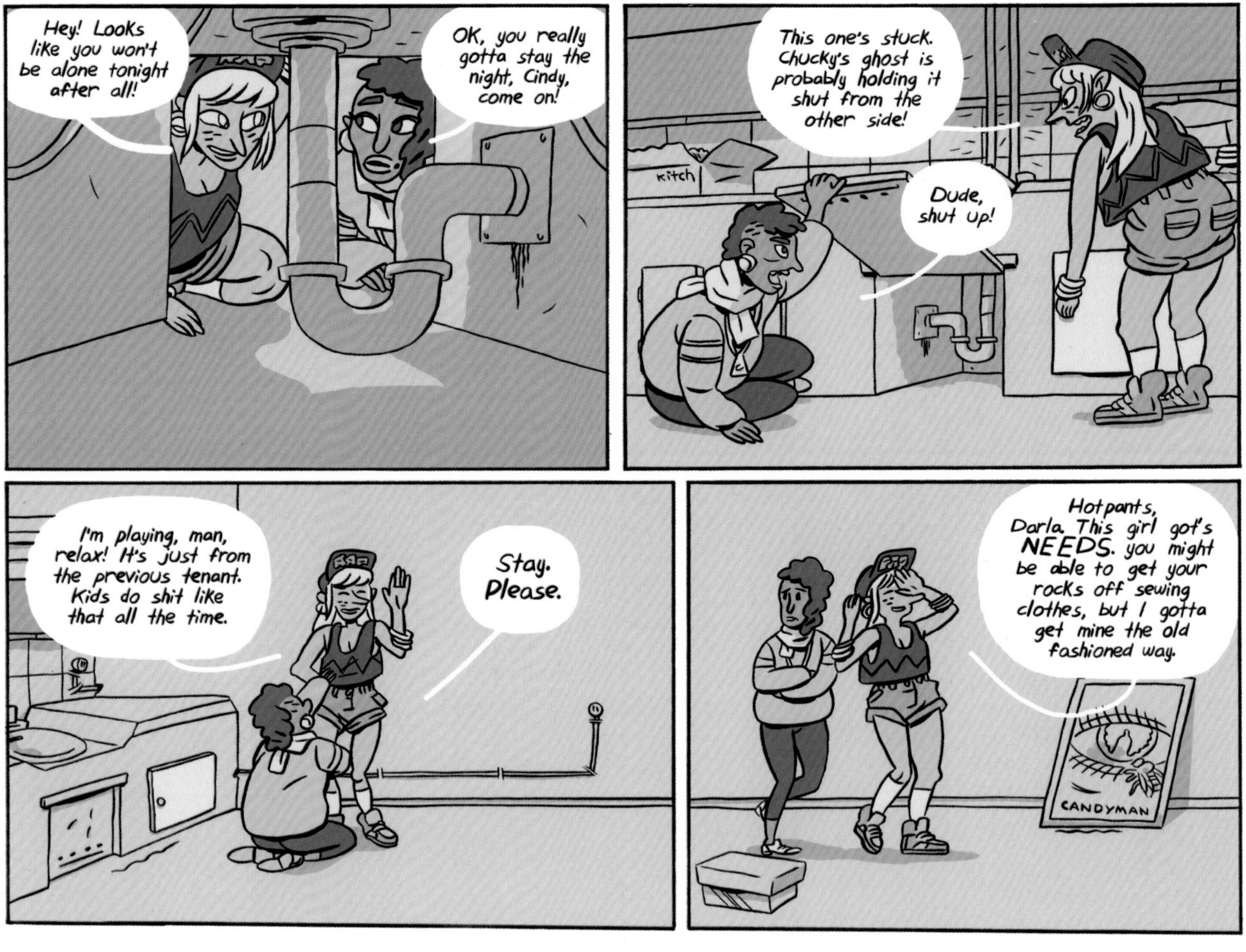
Hey! Looks like you won't be alone tonight after all!
OK, you really gotta stay the night, Cindy, come on!
This one's stuck. Chucky's ghost is probably holding it shut from the other side!
kitch
Dude, shut up!
I'm playing, man, relax! It's just from the previous tenant. Kids do shit like that all the time.
Stay. Please.
Hotpants, Darla. This girl got's NEEDS. you might be able to get your rocks off sewing clothes, but I gotta get mine the old fashioned way.
CANDYMAN

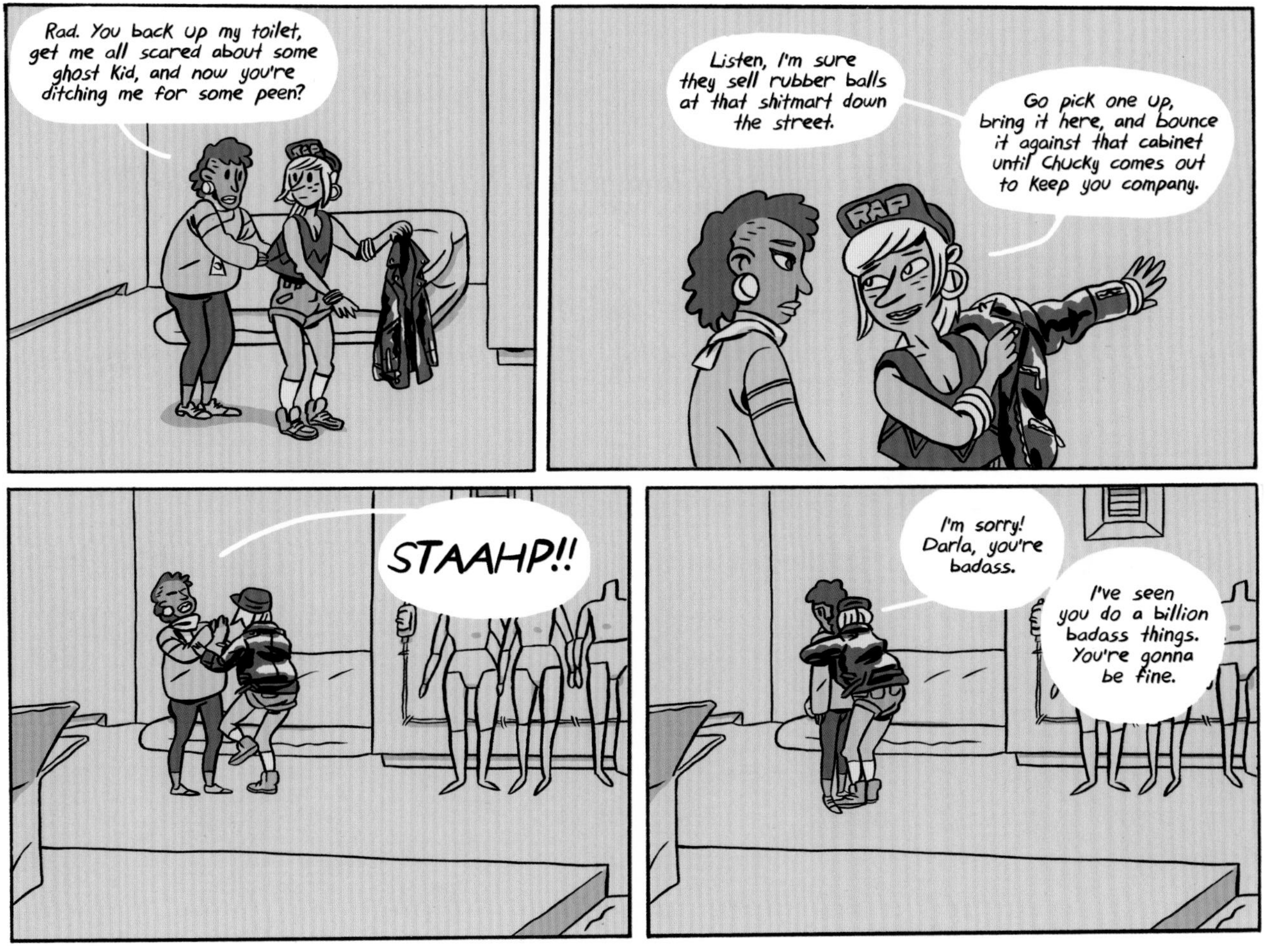
Rad. You back up my toilet, get me all scared about some ghost Kid, and now you're ditching me for some peen?
Listen, I'm sure they sell rubber balls at that shitmart down the street.
Go pick one up, bring it here, and bounce it against that cabinet until Chucky comes out to keep you company.
RAP
STAAHP!!
I'm sorry! Darla, you're badass.
I've seen you do a billion badass things. You're gonna be fine.

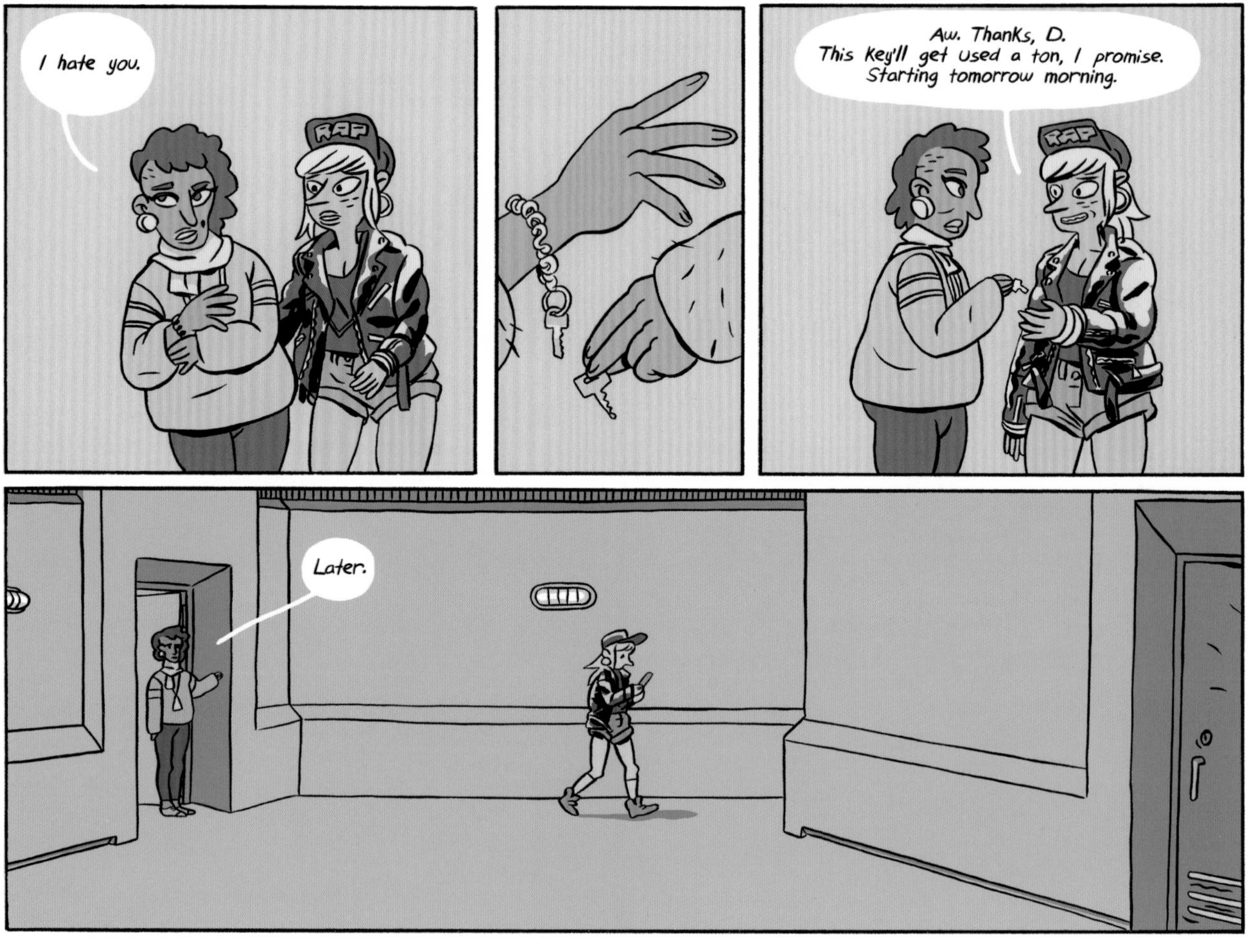
I hate you.
Aw. Thanks, D. This Key'll get used a ton, I promise. Starting tomorrow morning.
Later.

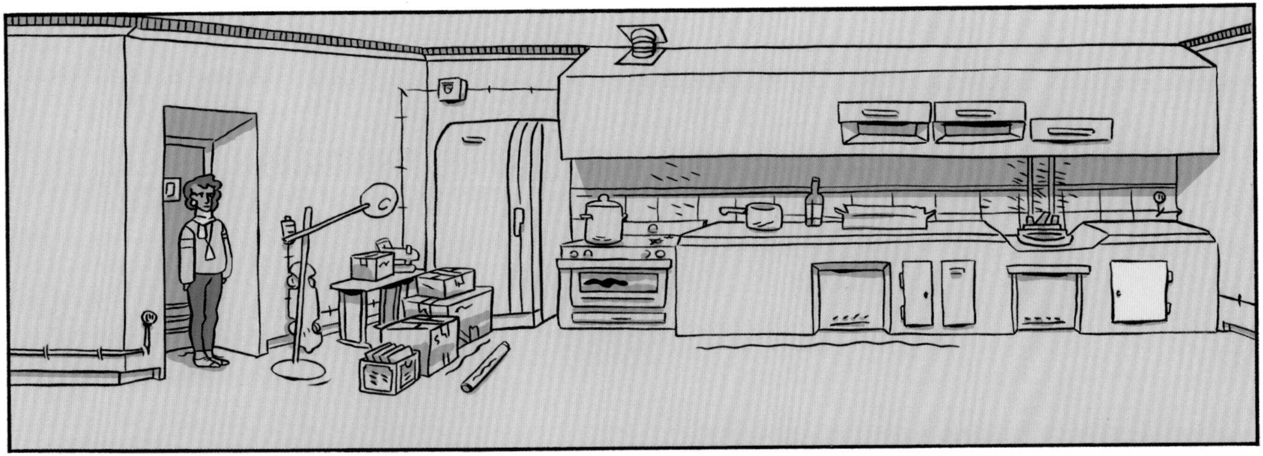

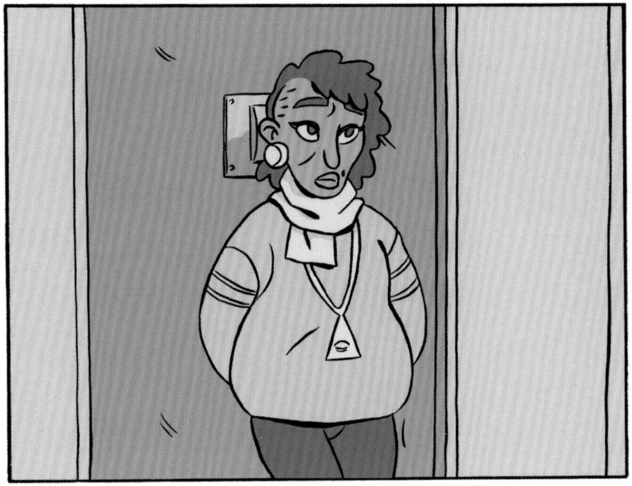

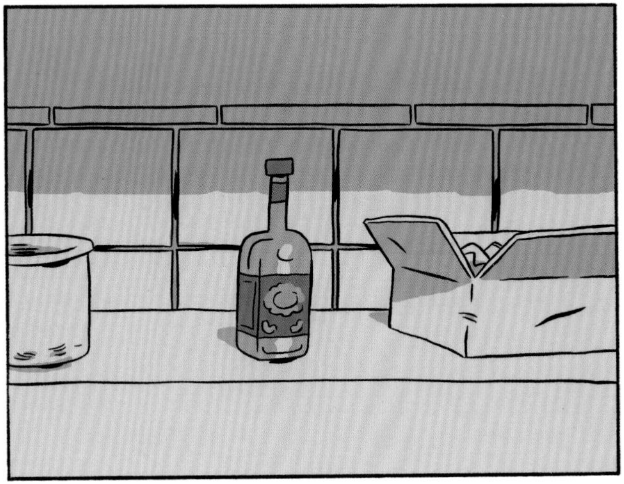

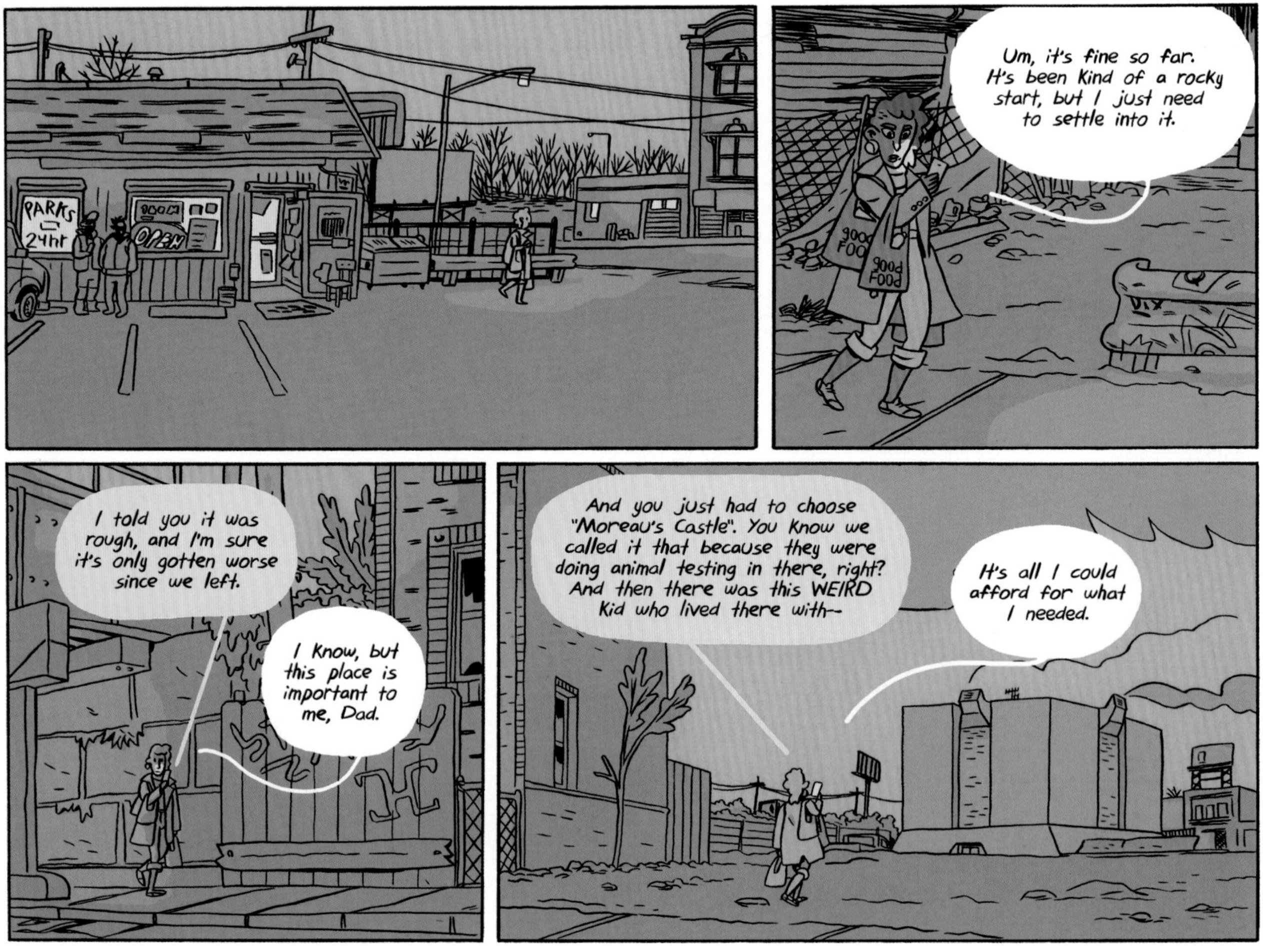
PARKS 24hr
OPEN
Um, it's fine so far. It's been kind of a rocky start, but I just need to settle into it.
good FOOD
good FOOD
I told you it was rough, and I'm sure it's only gotten worse since we left.
I know, but this place is important to me, Dad.
And you just had to choose "Moreau's Castle". You know we called it that because they were doing animal testing in there, right? And then there was this WEIRD kid who lived there with--
It's all I could afford for what I needed.

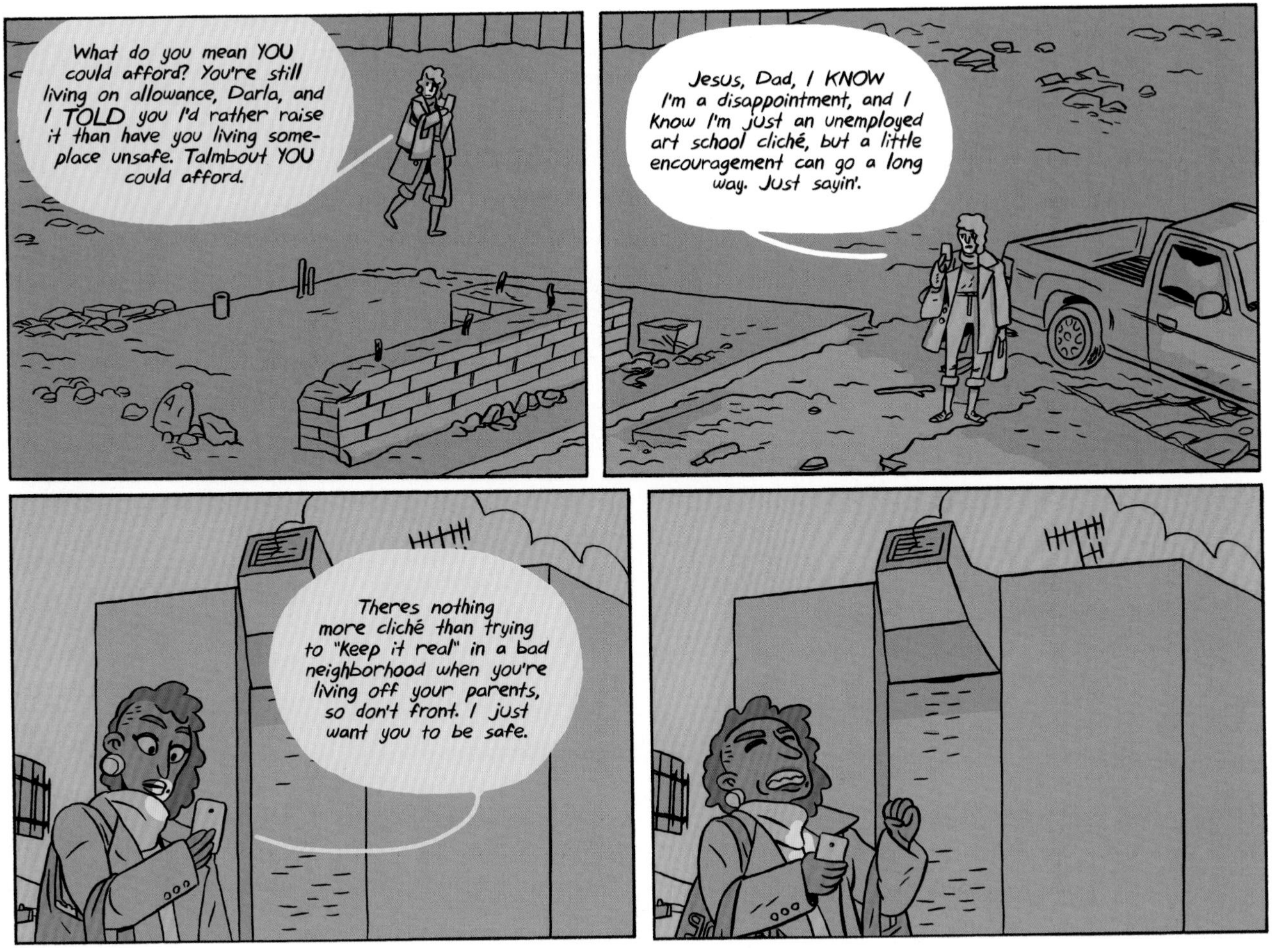
What do you mean YOU could afford? You're still living on allowance, Darla, and I TOLD you I'd rather raise it than have you living someplace unsafe. Talmbout YOU could afford.
Jesus, Dad, I KNOW I'm a disappointment, and I know I'm just an unemployed art school cliché, but a little encouragement can go a long way. Just sayin'.
Theres nothing more cliché than trying to "keep it real" in a bad neighborhood when you're living off your parents, so don't front. I just want you to be safe.

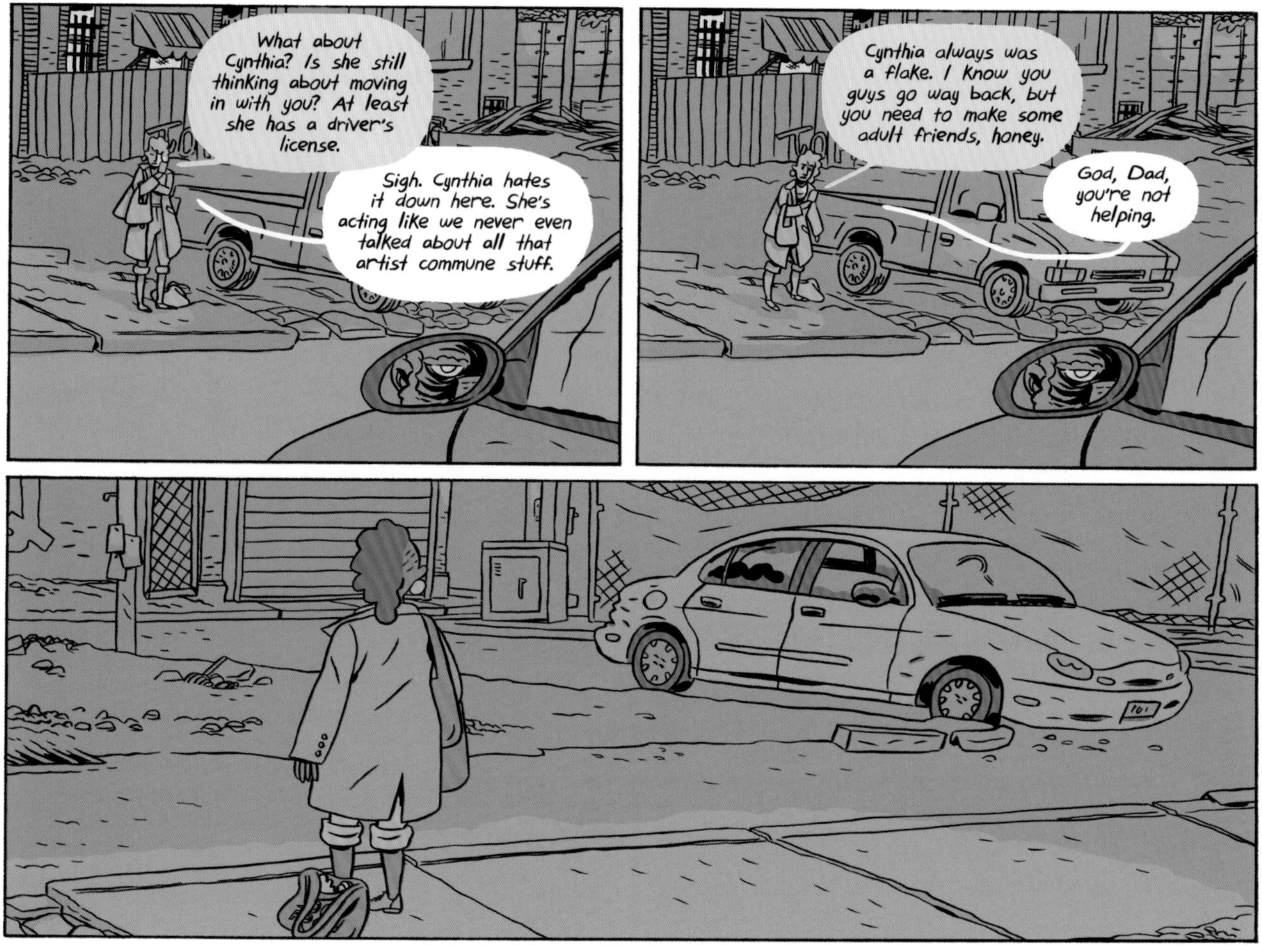

What about Cynthia? Is she still thinking about moving in with you? At least she has a driver's license.
Sigh. Cynthia hates it down here. She's acting like we never even talked about all that artist commune stuff.
Cynthia always was a flake. I know you guys go way back, but you need to make some adult friends, honey.
God, Dad, you're not helping.

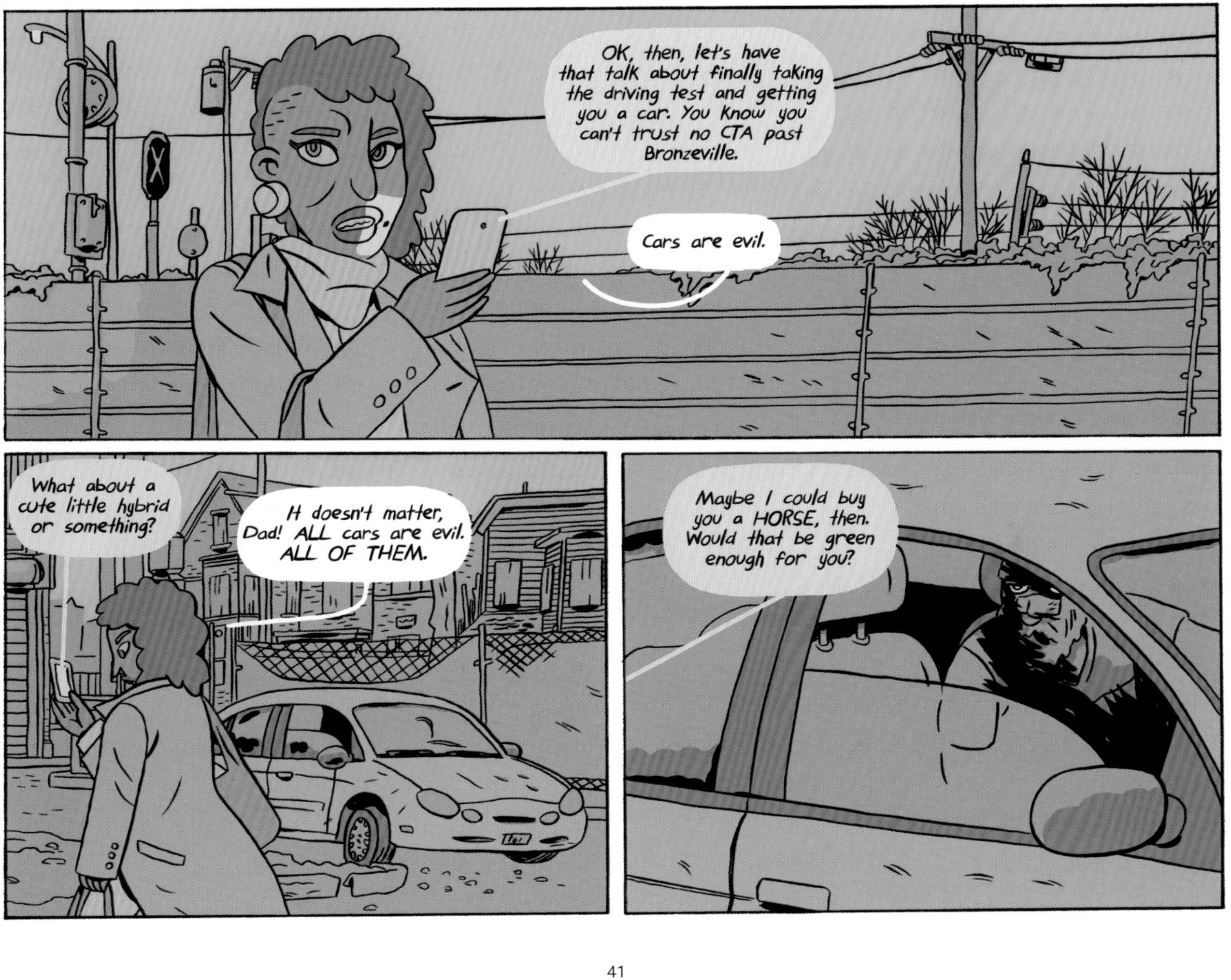
OK, then, let's have that talk about finally taking the driving test and getting you a car. You know you can't trust no CTA past Bronzeville.
Cars are evil.
What about a cute little hybrid or something?
It doesn't matter, Dad! ALL cars are evil. ALL OF THEM.
Maybe I could buy you a HORSE, then. Would that be green enough for you?

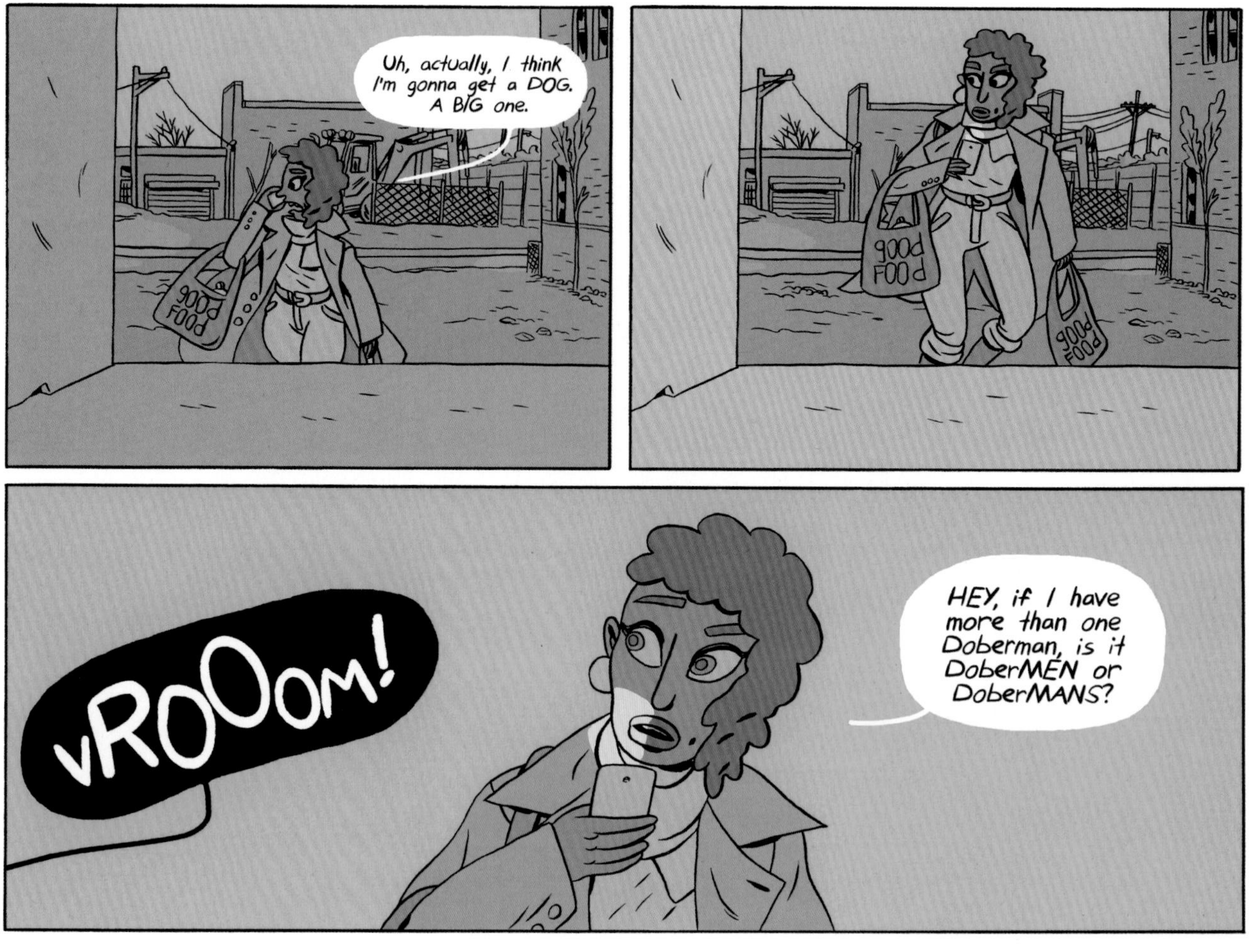
Uh, actually, I think I'm gonna get a DOG. A BIG one.
vROOom!
HEY, if I have more than one Doberman, is it DoberMEN or DoberMANS?

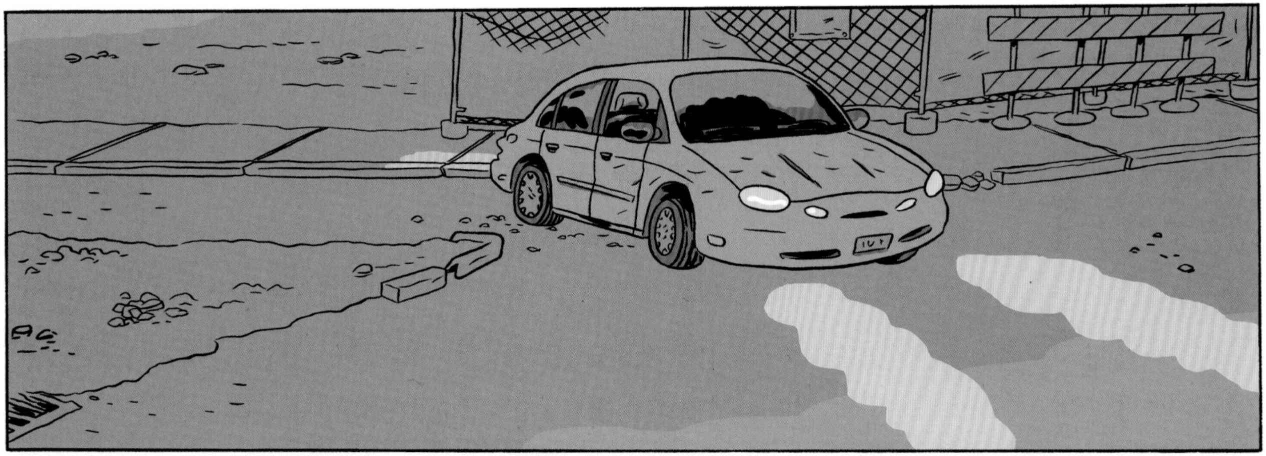

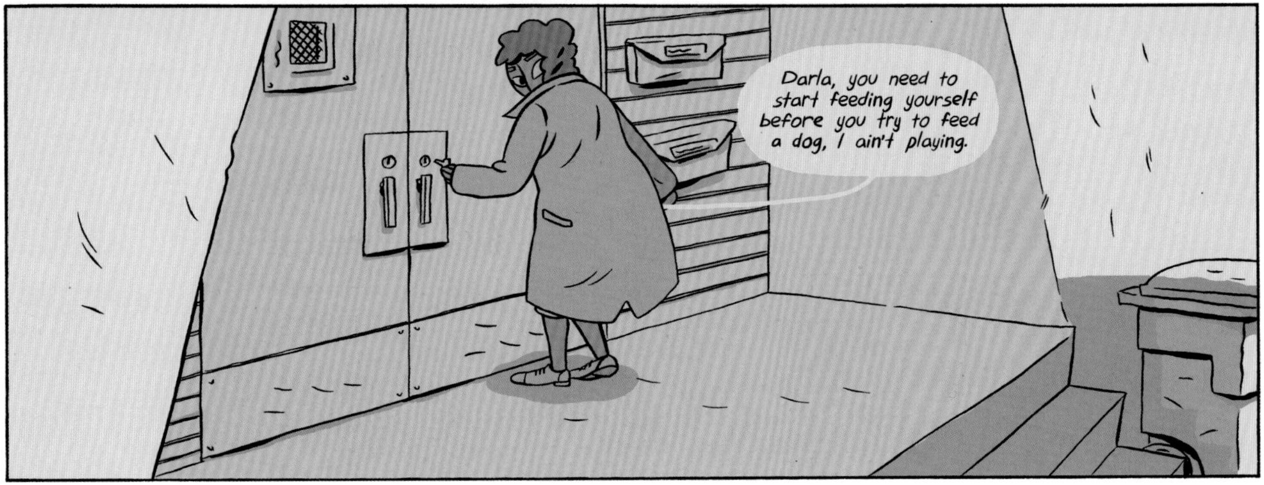
Darla, you need to start feeding yourself before you try to feed a dog, I ain't playing.

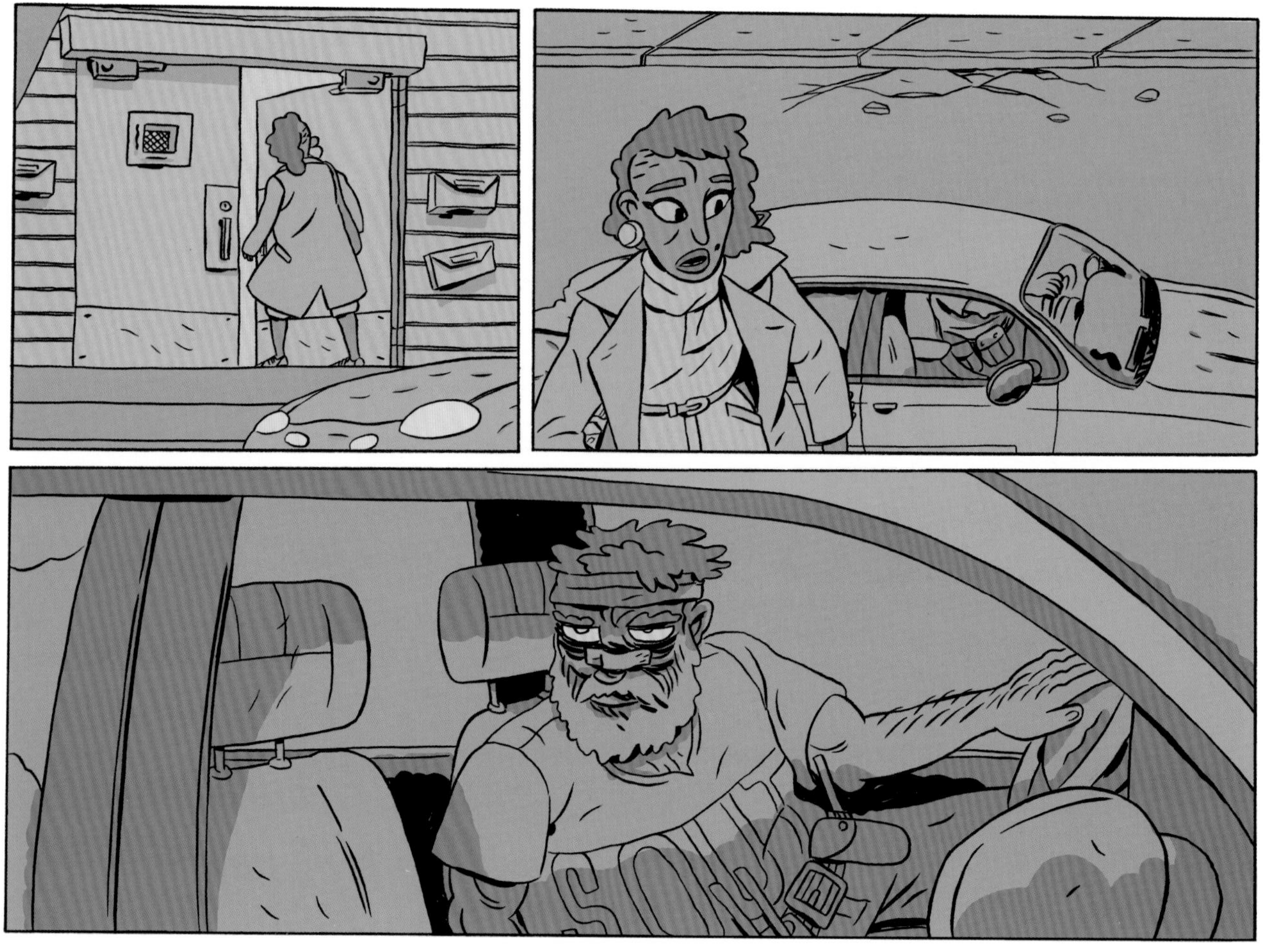

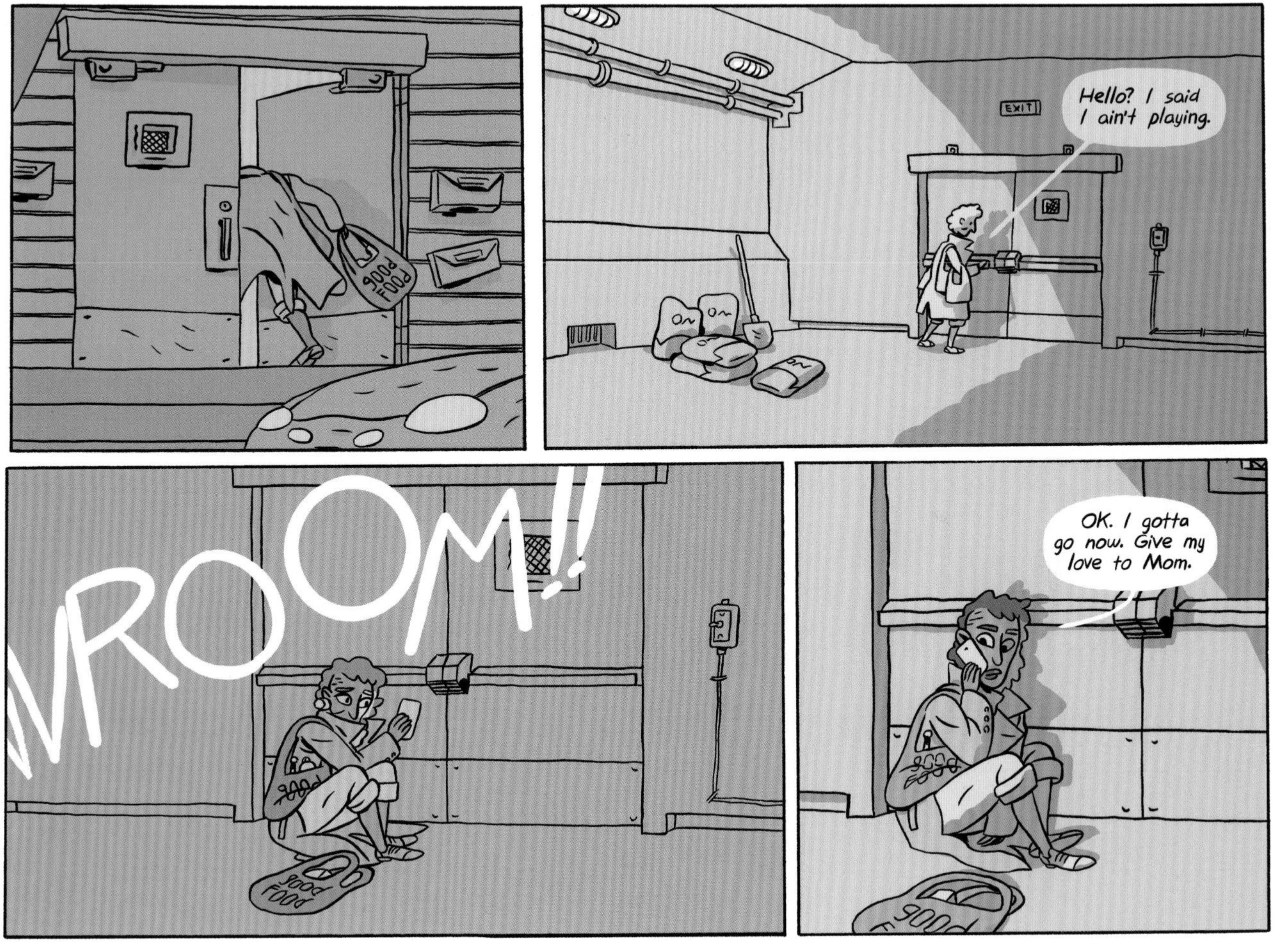
EXIT
Hello? I said I ain't playing.
VROOM!!
OK. I gotta go now. Give my love to Mom.

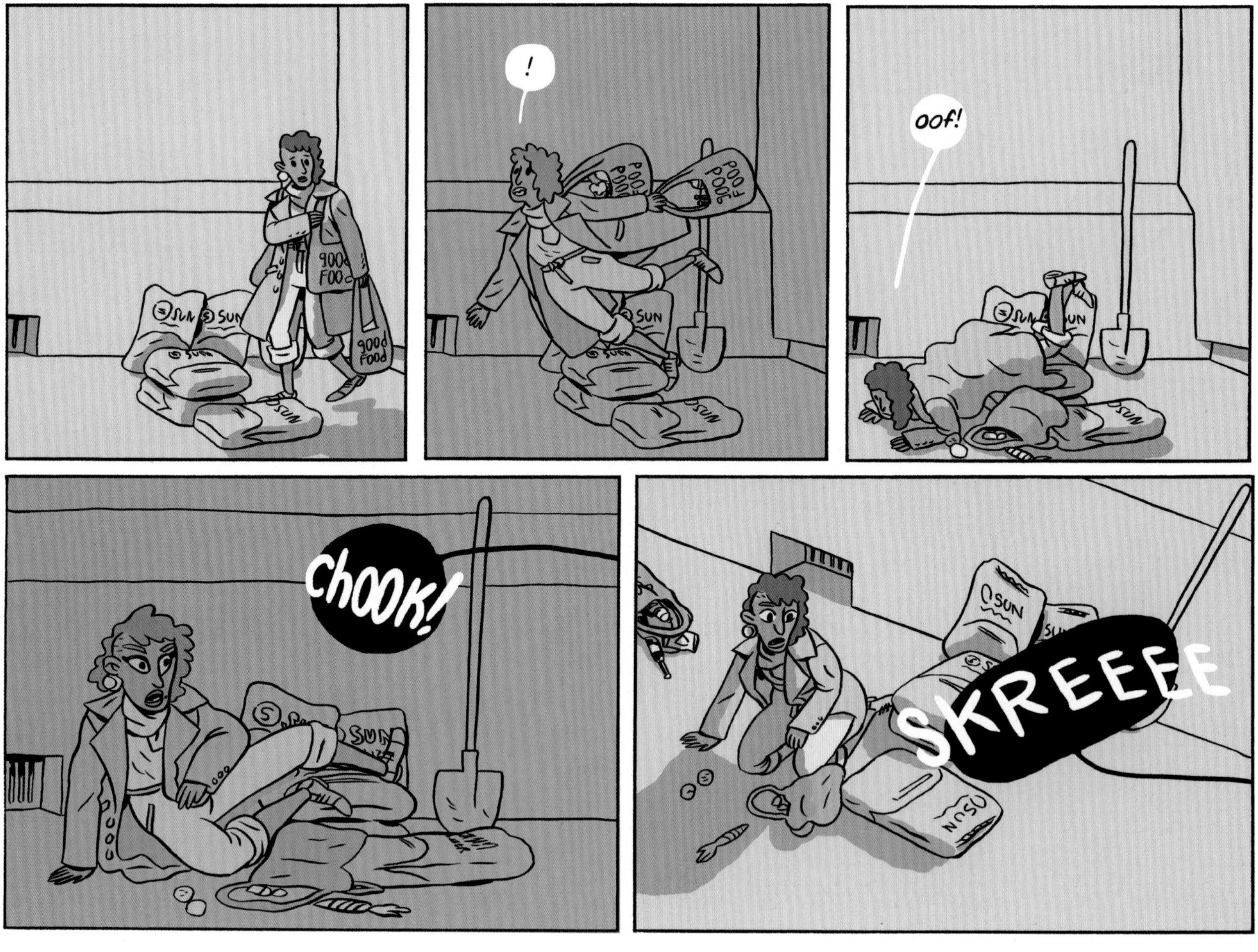
!
oof!
CHOOK!
SKREEEE

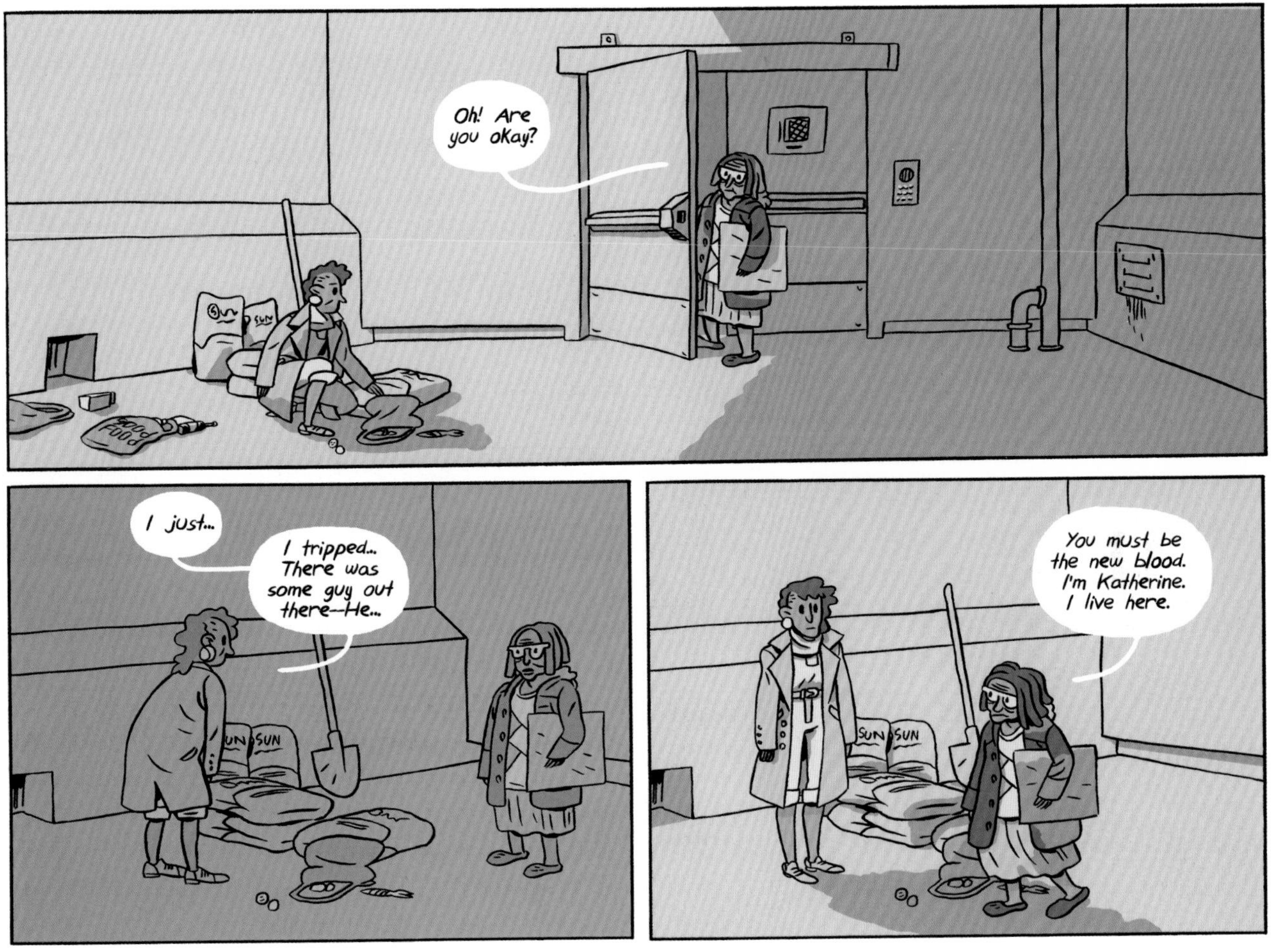
Oh! Are you okay?
SUN
SUN
FOOD
I just...
I tripped... There was some guy out there--He...
SUN
SUN
SUN
SUN
You must be the new blood. I'm Katherine. I live here.

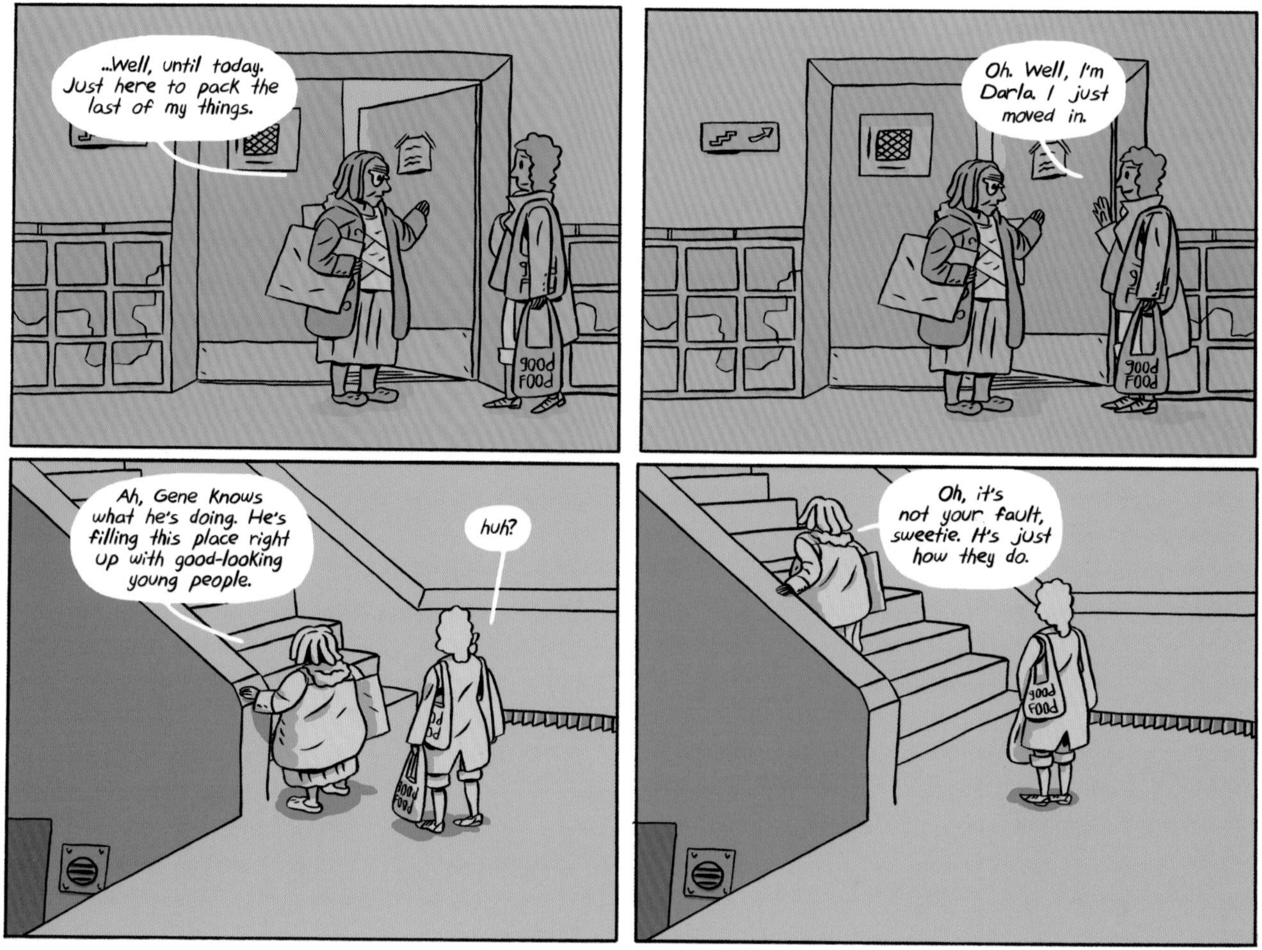
...Well, until today. Just here to pack the last of my things.
Oh. Well, I'm Darla. I just moved in.
Ah, Gene knows what he's doing. He's filling this place right up with good-looking young people.
huh?
Oh, it's not your fault, sweetie. It's just how they do.
good FOOD

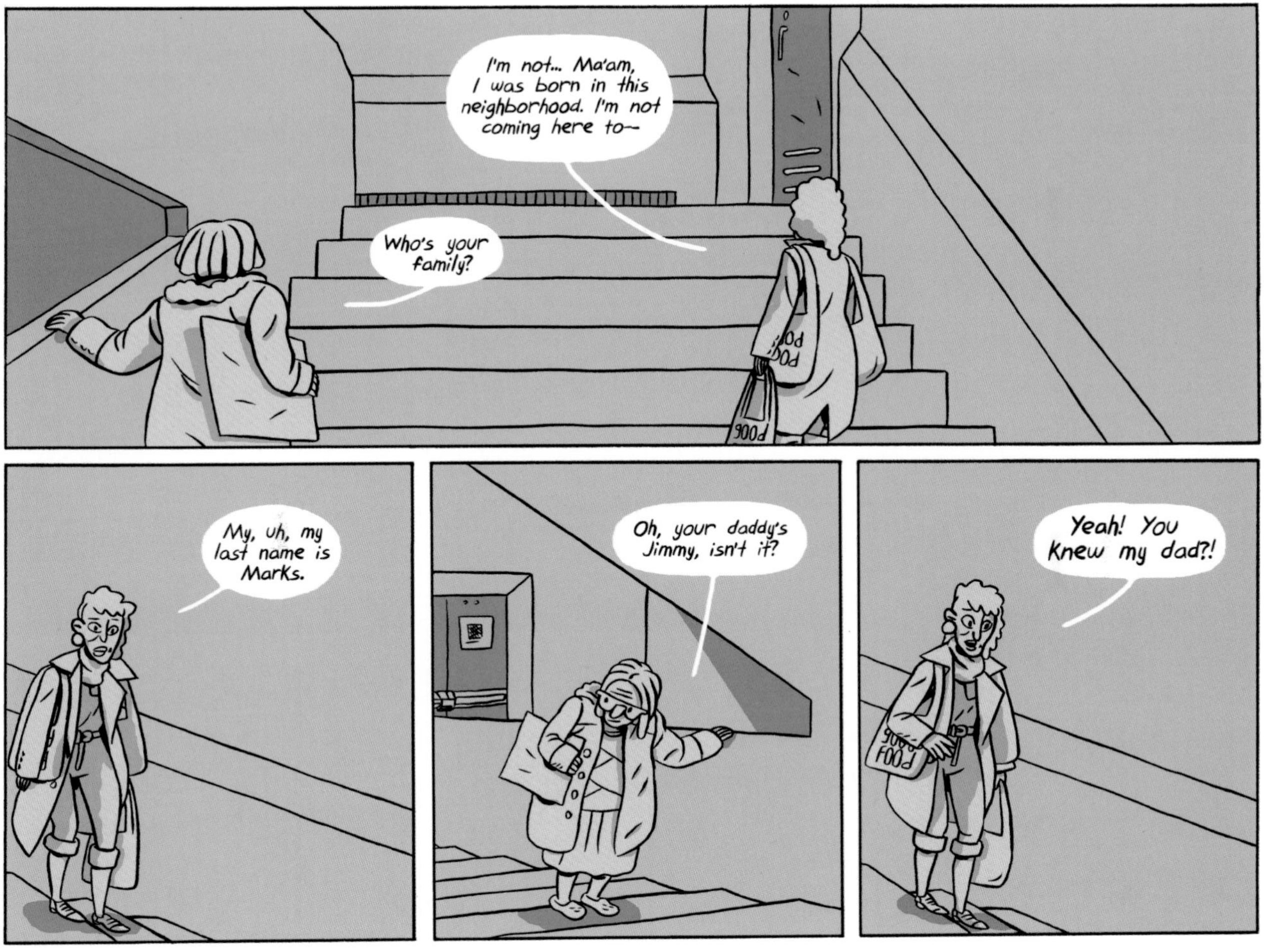
I'm not... Ma'am, I was born in this neighborhood. I'm not coming here to–
Who's your family?
FOOD
My, uh, my last name is Marks.
Oh, your daddy's Jimmy, isn't it?
Yeah! You Knew my dad?!
FOOD

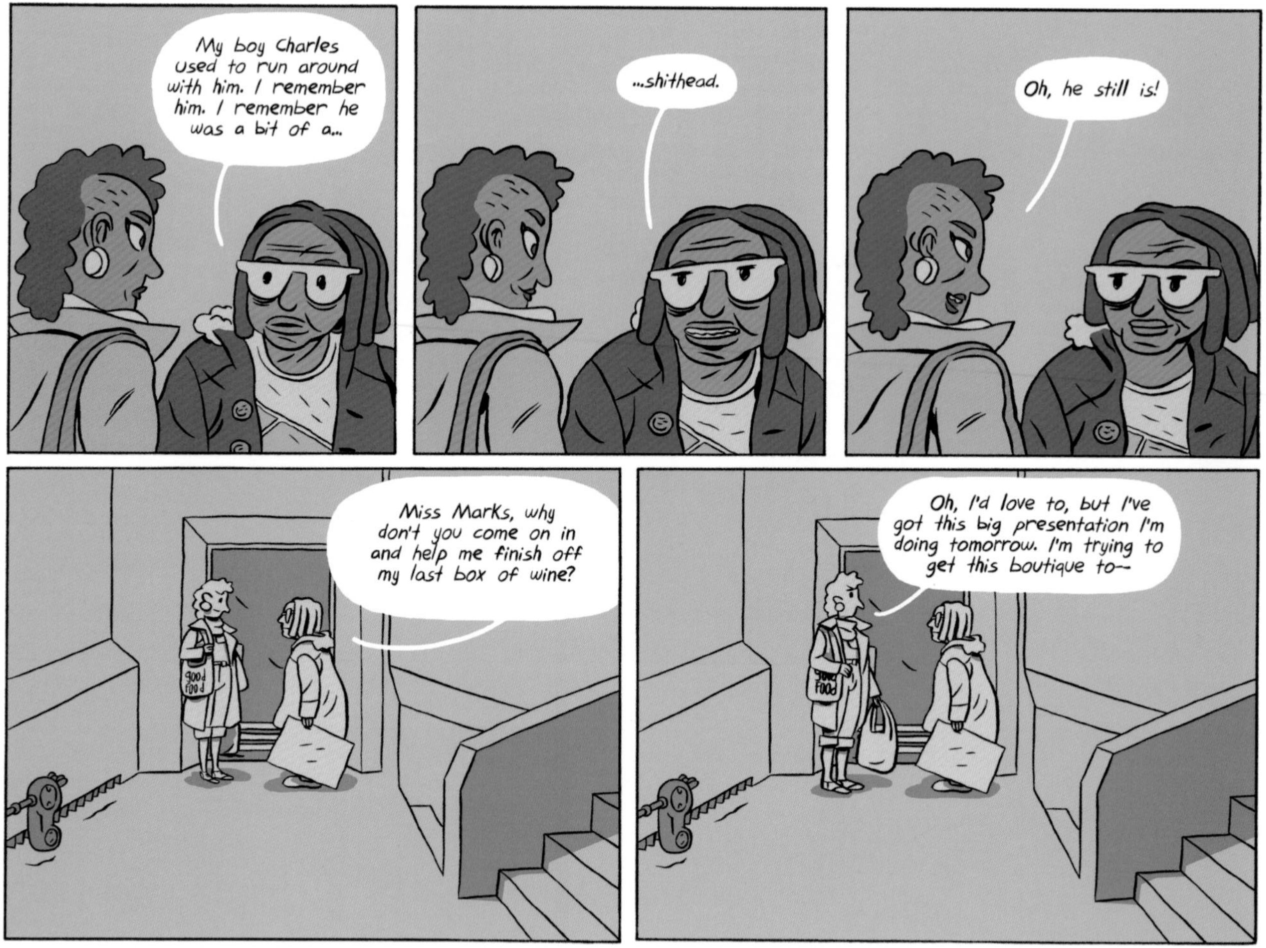
My boy Charles used to run around with him. I remember him. I remember he was a bit of a...
...shithead.
Oh, he still is!
Miss Marks, why don't you come on in and help me finish off my last box of wine?
Oh, I'd love to, but I've got this big presentation I'm doing tomorrow. I'm trying to get this boutique to--
good food

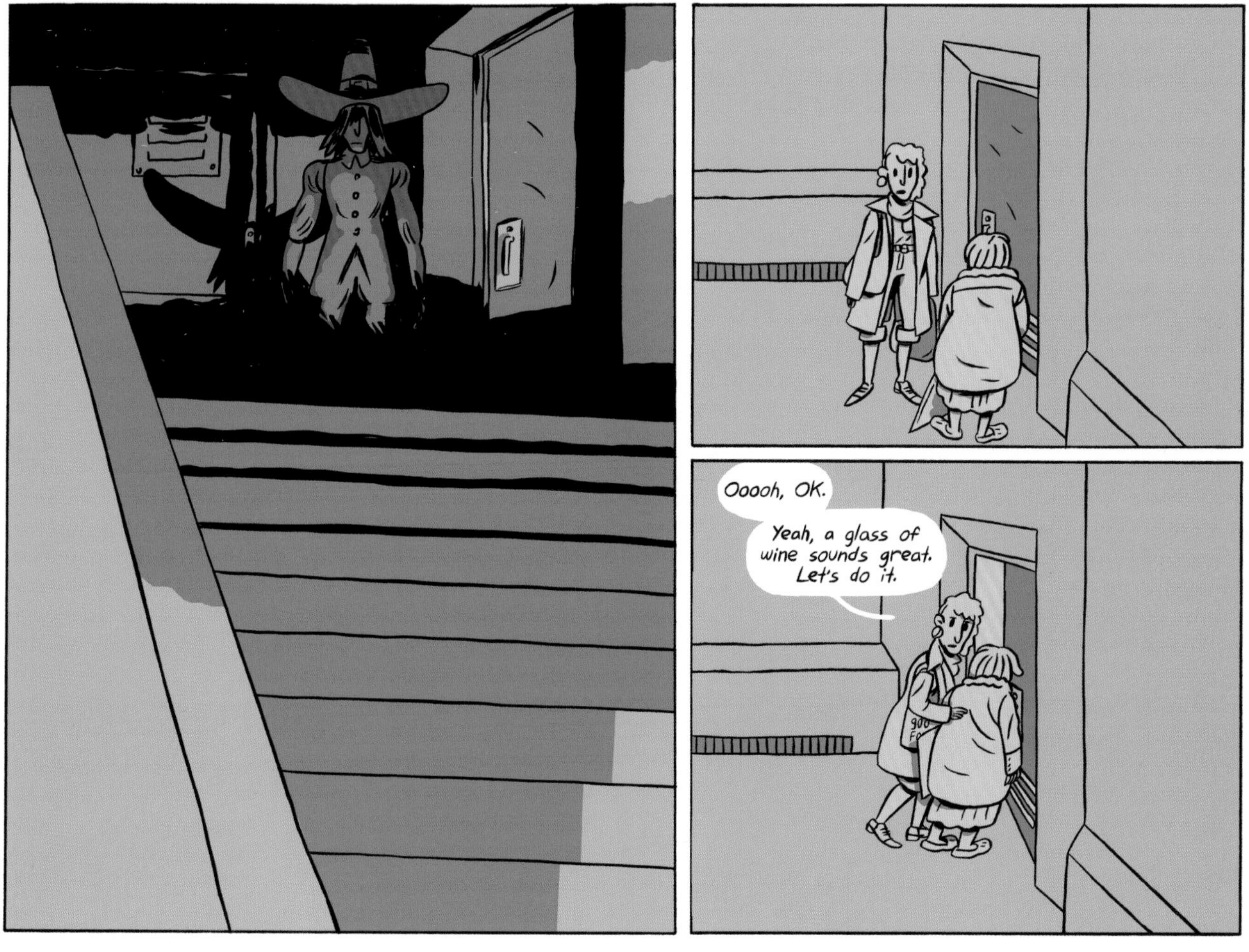
Ooooh, OK.
Yeah, a glass of wine sounds great. Let's do it.

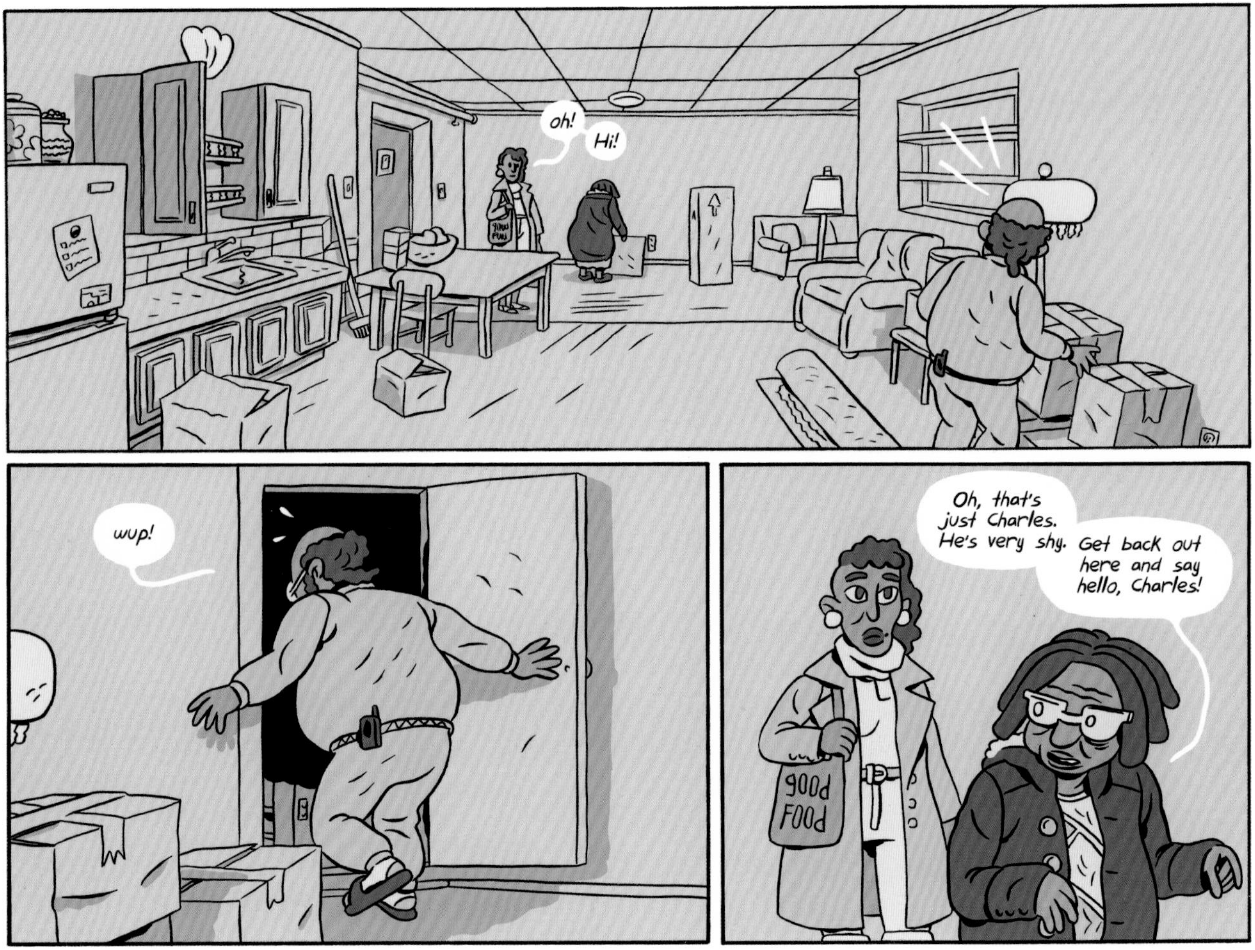
oh!
Hi!
wup!
Oh, that's just Charles. He's very shy.
Get back out here and say hello, Charles!
GOOD FOOD

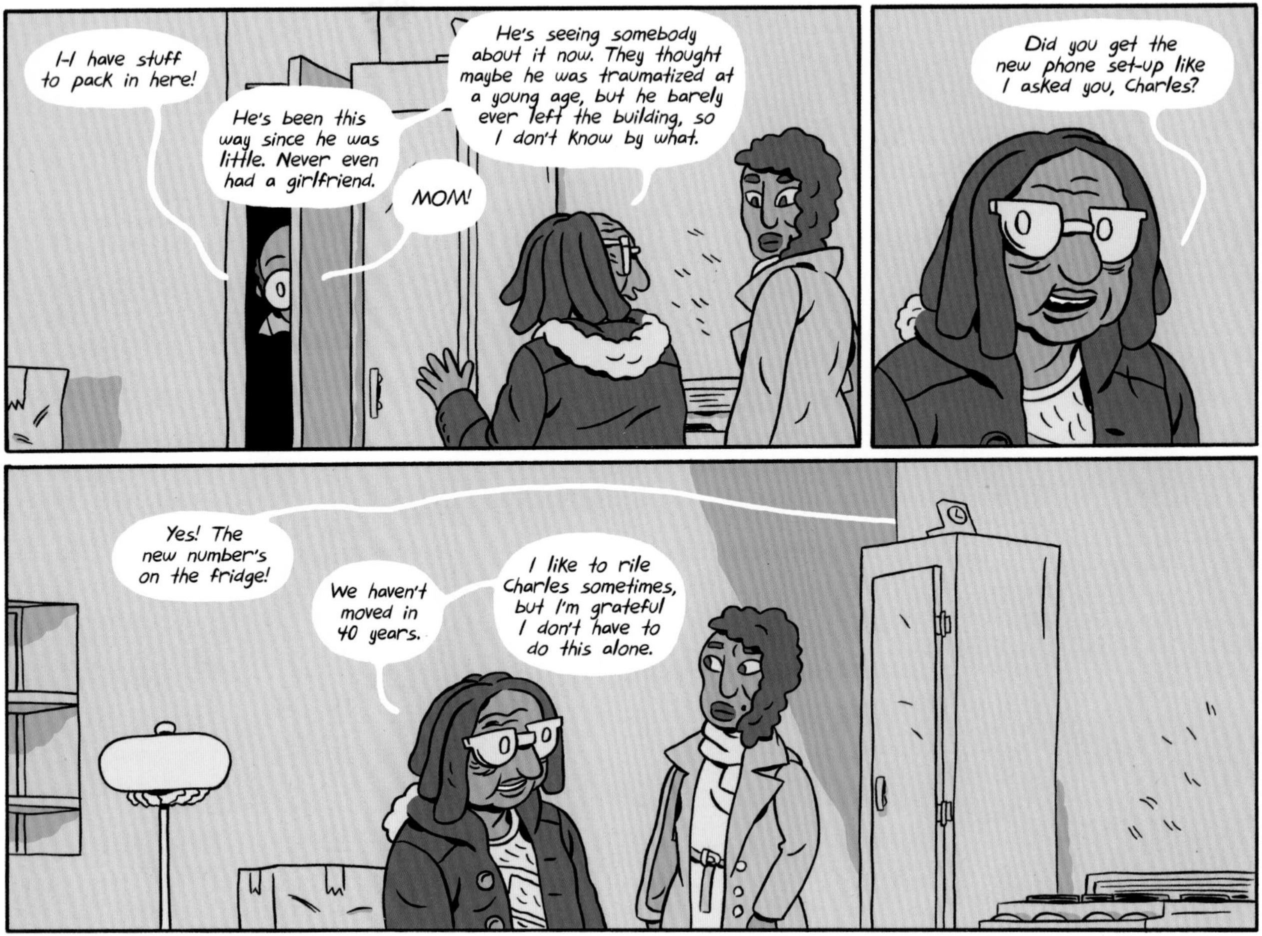
I-I have stuff to pack in here!
He's been this way since he was little. Never even had a girlfriend.
MOM!
He's seeing somebody about it now. They thought maybe he was traumatized at a young age, but he barely ever left the building, so I don't know by what.
Did you get the new phone set-up like I asked you, Charles?
Yes! The new number's on the fridge!
We haven't moved in 40 years.
I like to rile Charles sometimes, but I'm grateful I don't have to do this alone.

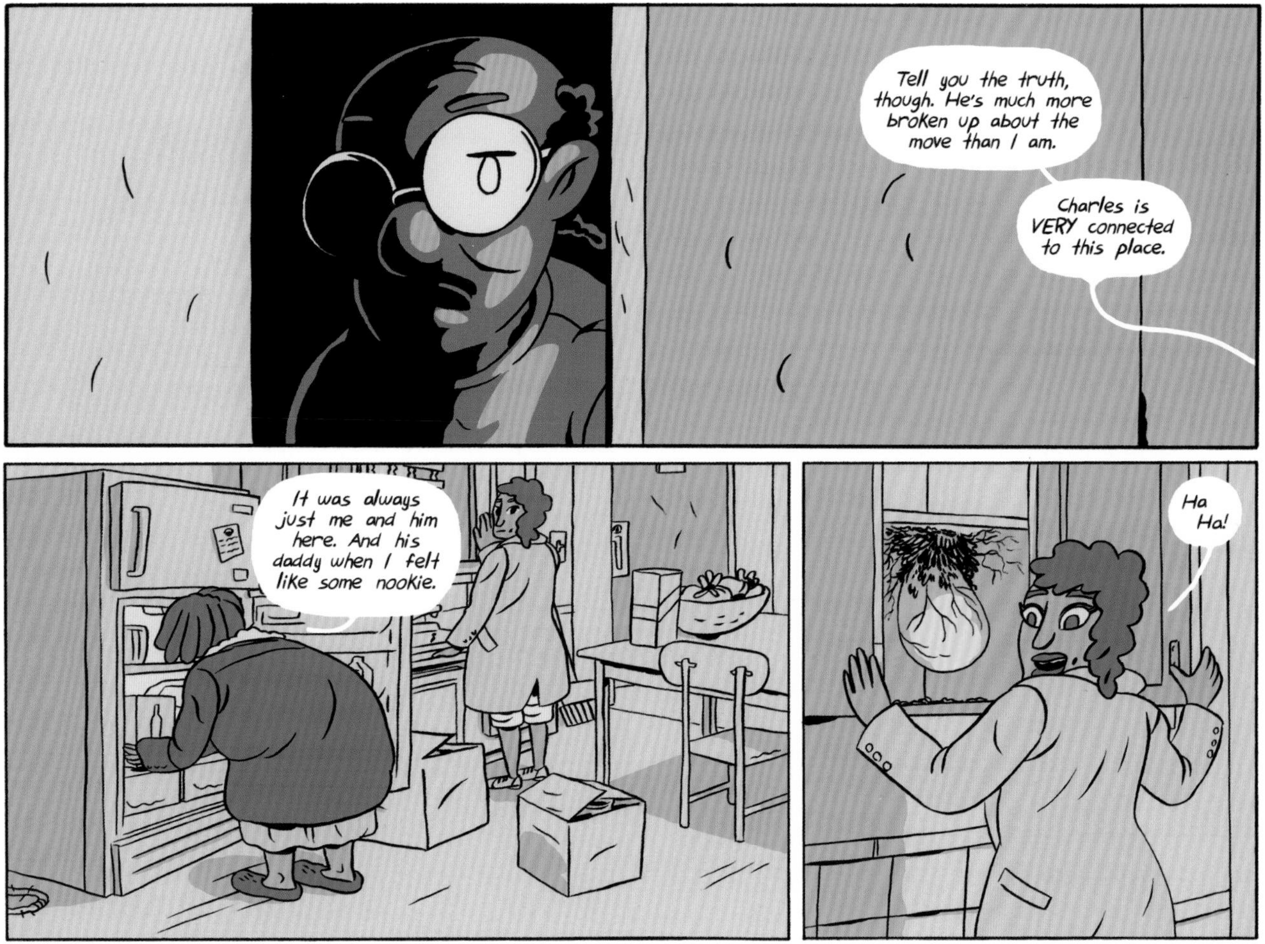
Tell you the truth, though. He's much more broken up about the move than I am.
Charles is VERY connected to this place.
It was always just me and him here. And his daddy when I felt like some nookie.
Ha Ha!

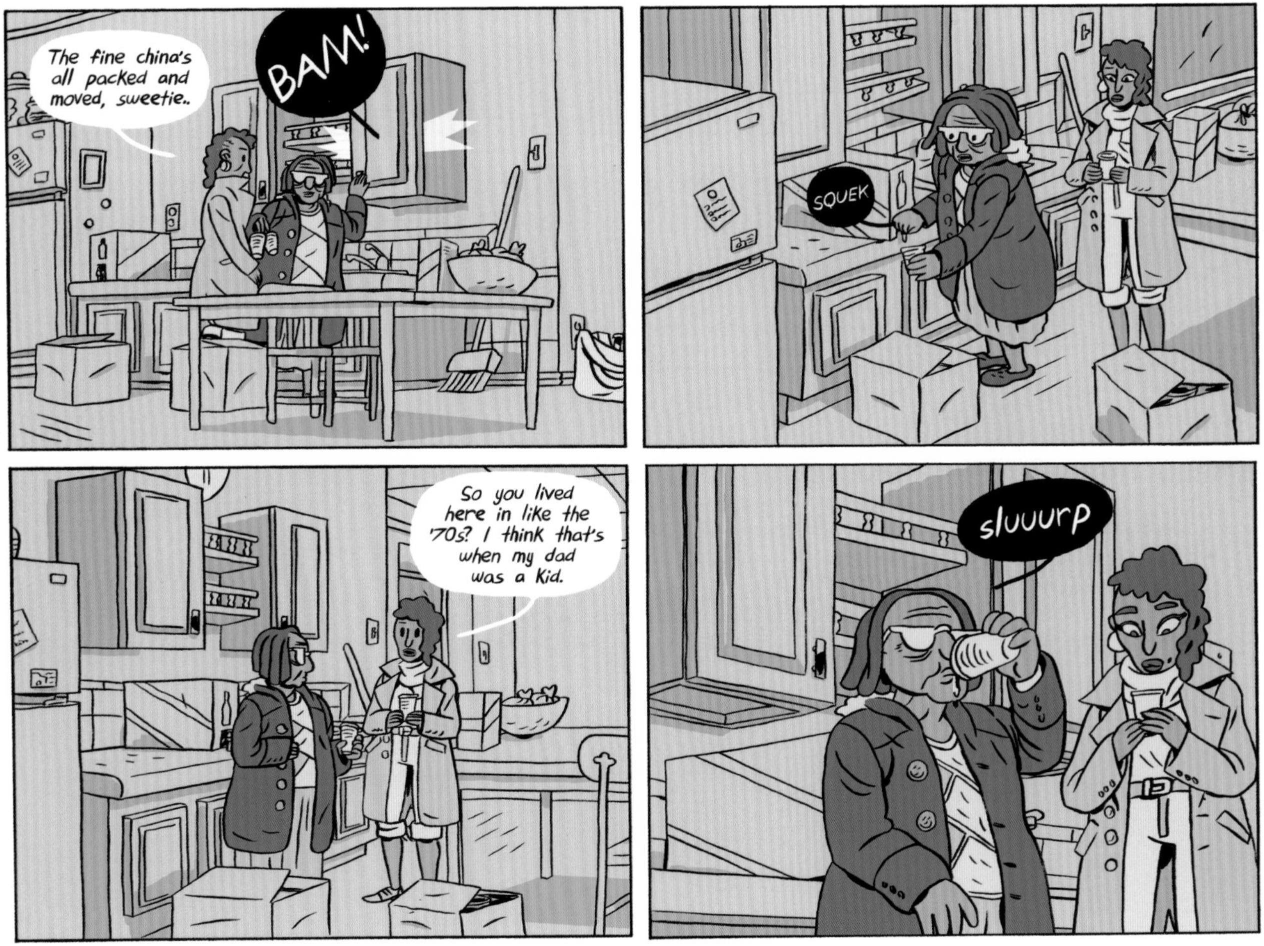
The fine china's all packed and moved, sweetie..
BAM!
SQUEK
So you lived here in like the '70s? I think that's when my dad was a kid.
sluuurp

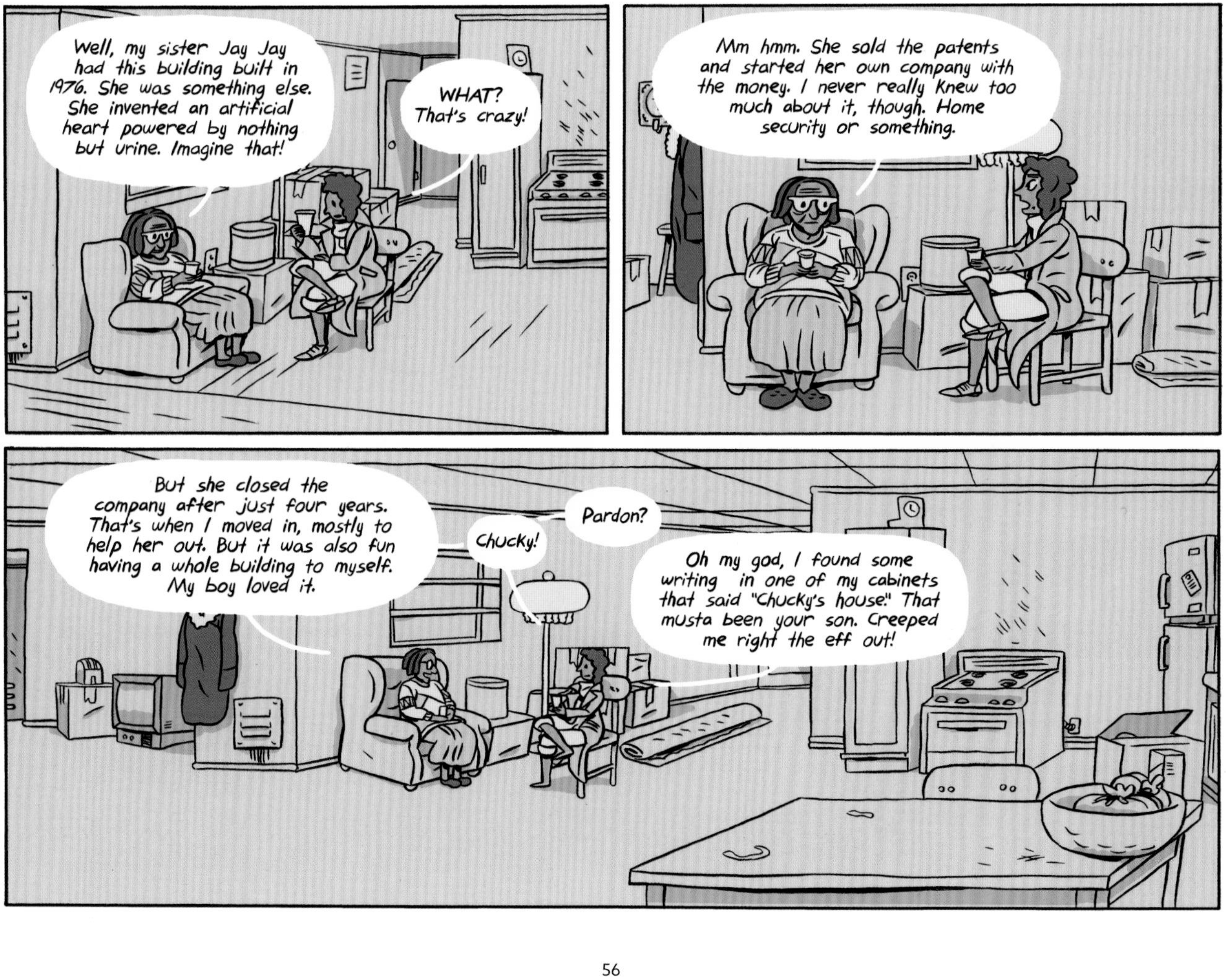

Well, my sister Jay Jay had this building built in 1976. She was something else. She invented an artificial heart powered by nothing but urine. Imagine that!
WHAT? That's crazy!
Mm hmm. She sold the patents and started her own company with the money. I never really knew too much about it, though. Home security or something.
But she closed the company after just four years. That's when I moved in, mostly to help her out. But it was also fun having a whole building to myself. My boy loved it.
Chucky!
Pardon?
Oh my god, I found some writing in one of my cabinets that said "Chucky's house." That musta been your son. Creeped me right the eff out!

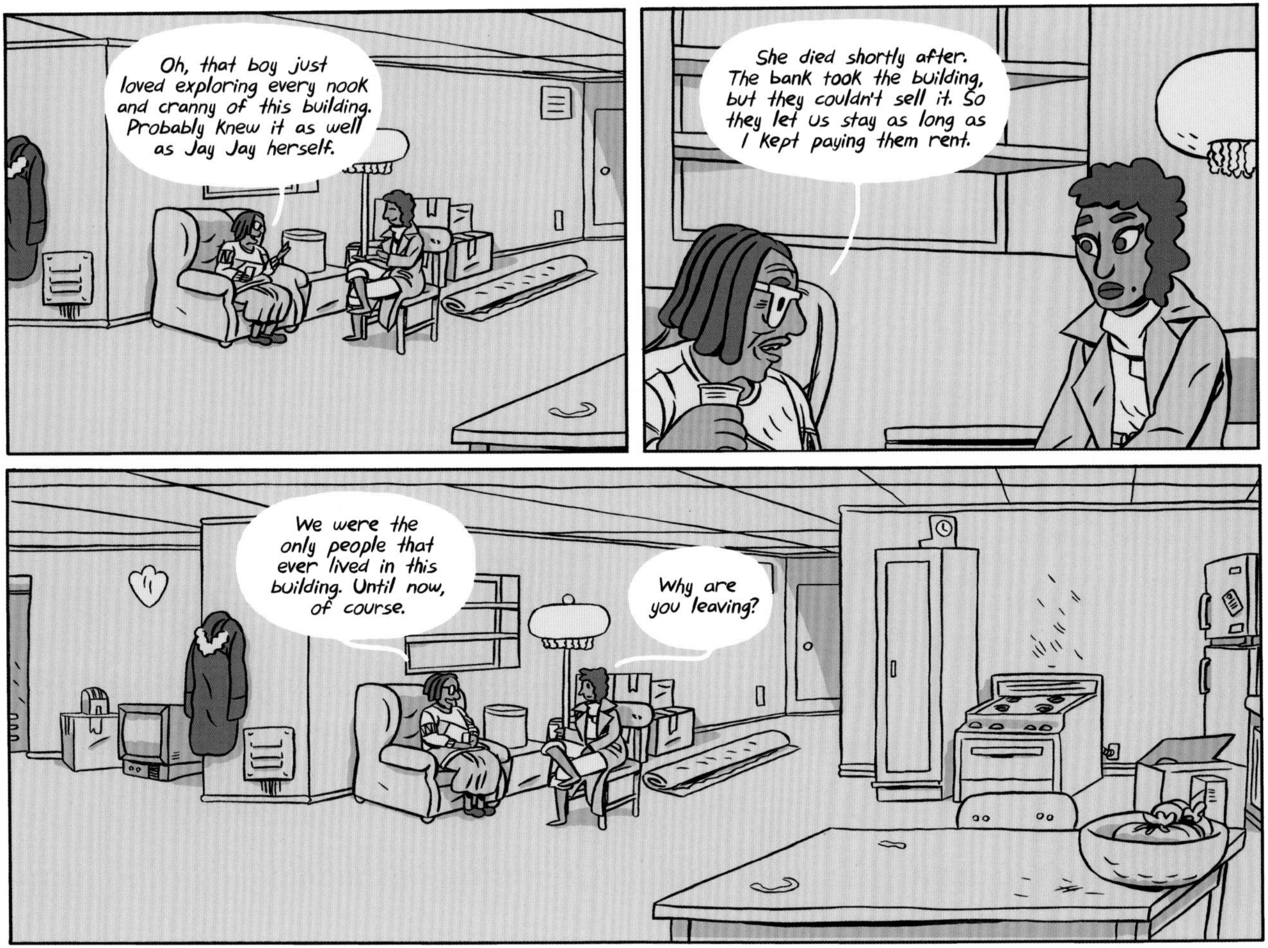

Oh, that boy just loved exploring every nook and cranny of this building. Probably knew it as well as Jay Jay herself.
She died shortly after. The bank took the building, but they couldn't sell it. So they let us stay as long as I kept paying them rent.
We were the only people that ever lived in this building. Until now, of course.
Why are you leaving?

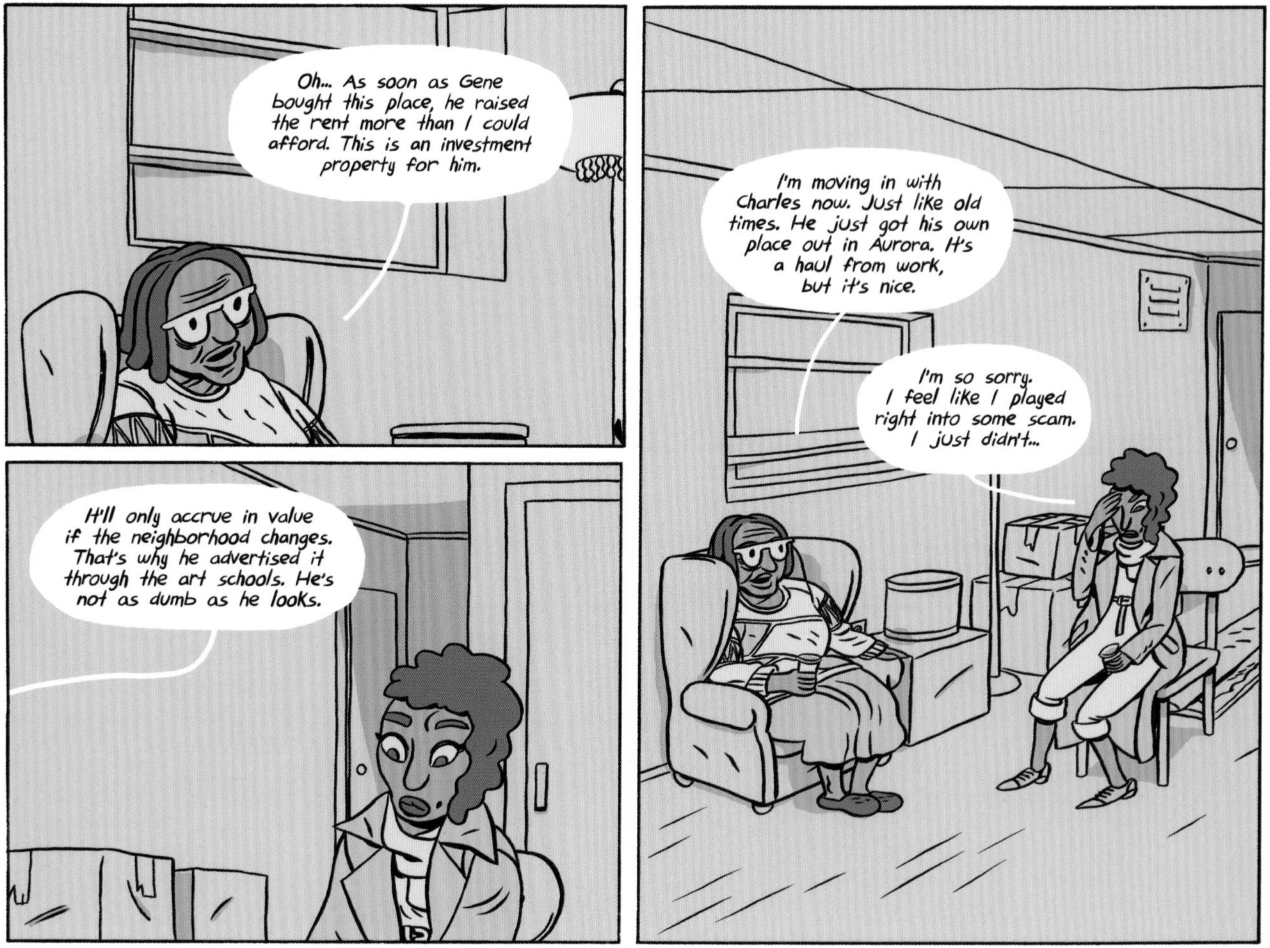

Oh... As soon as Gene bought this place, he raised the rent more than I could afford. This is an investment property for him.
It'll only accrue in value if the neighborhood changes. That's why he advertised it through the art schools. He's not as dumb as he looks.
I'm moving in with Charles now. Just like old times. He just got his own place out in Aurora. It's a haul from work, but it's nice.
I'm so sorry. I feel like I played right into some scam. I just didn't...

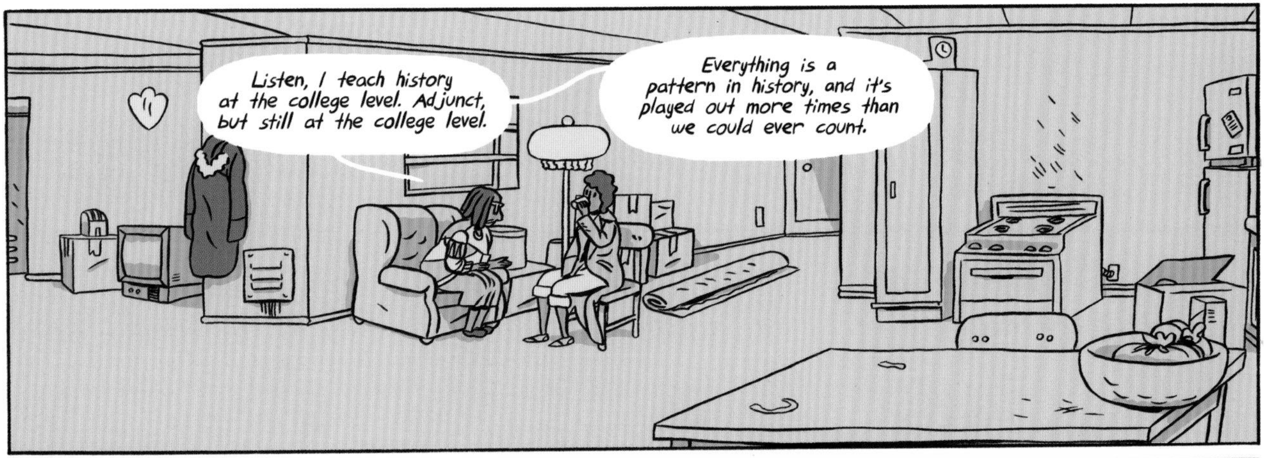
Listen, I teach history at the college level. Adjunct, but still at the college level.
Everything is a pattern in history, and it's played out more times than we could ever count.

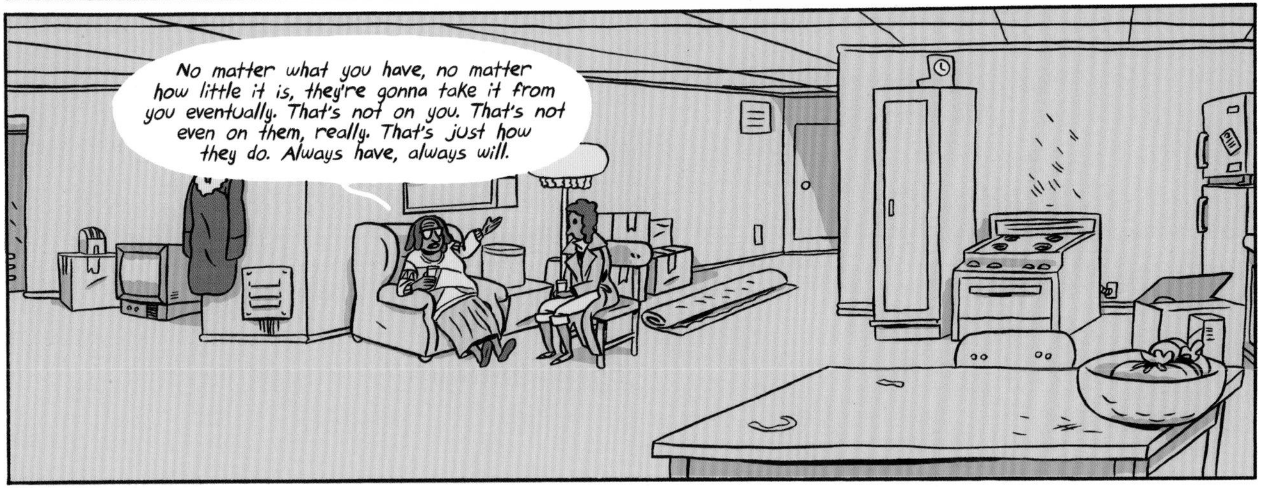
No matter what you have, no matter how little it is, they're gonna take it from you eventually. That's not on you. That's not even on them, really. That's just how they do. Always have, always will.

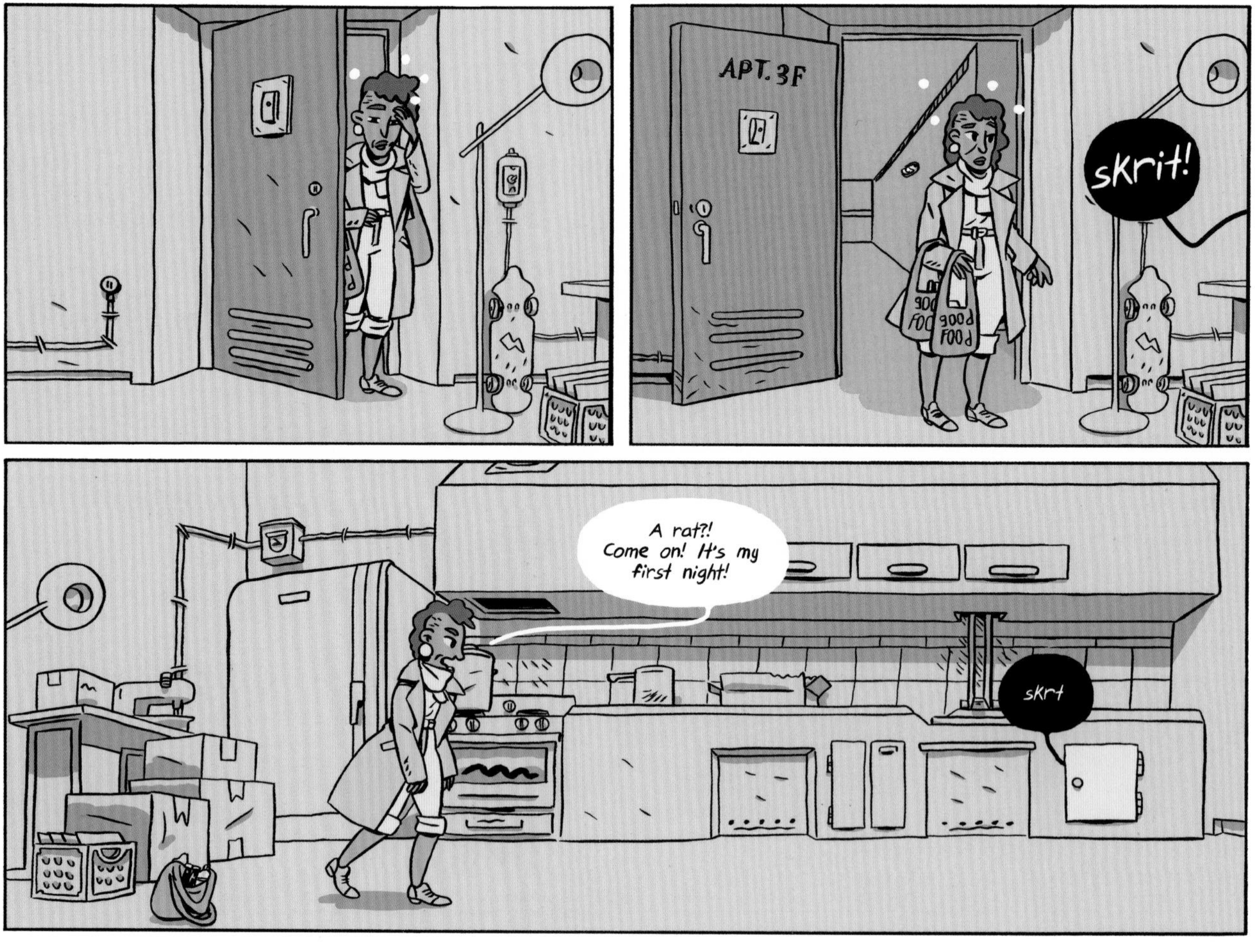
APT. 3F
skrit!
A rat?! Come on! It's my first night!
skrt

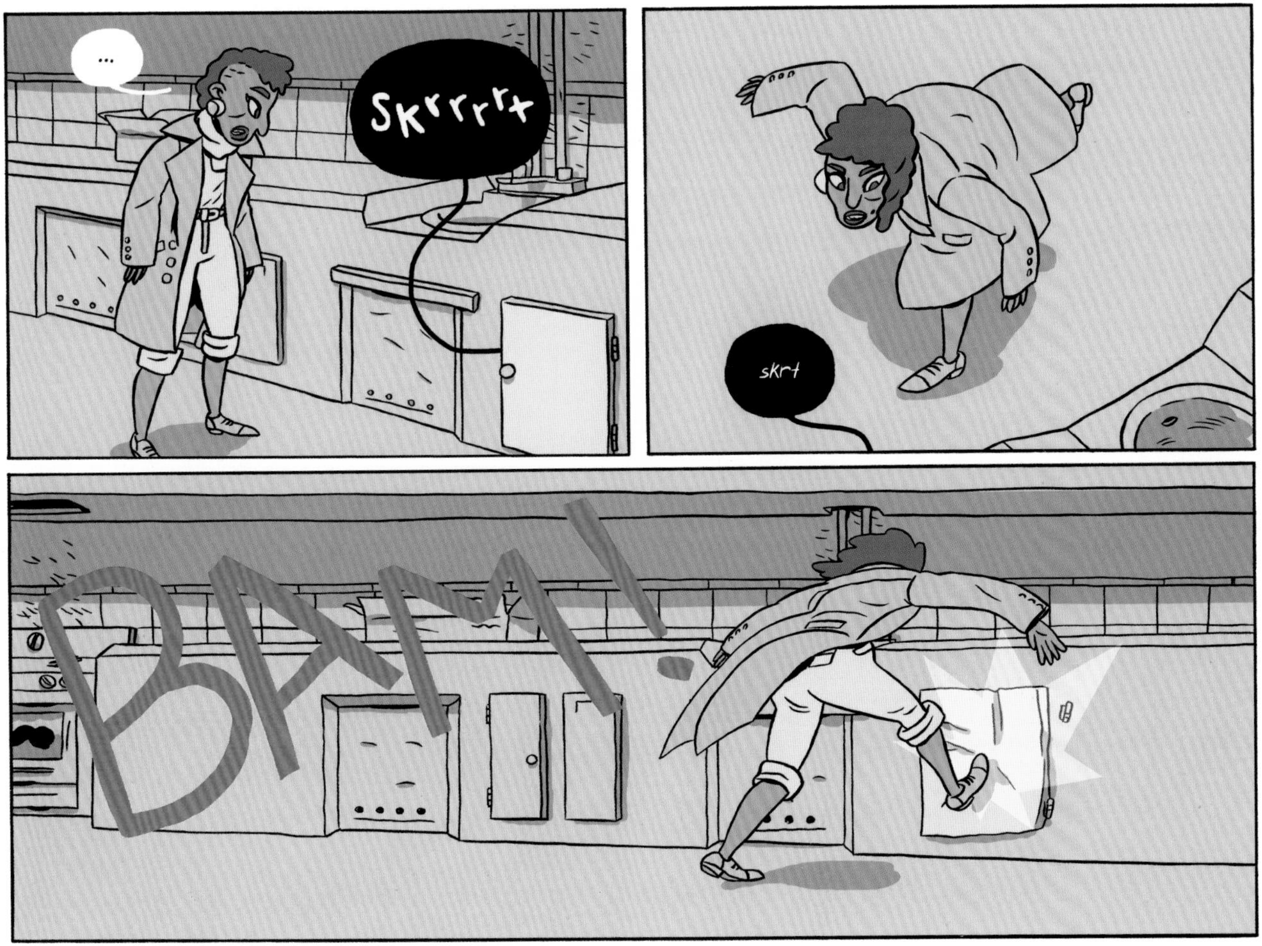
...
Skrrrrrt
skrt
BAM!

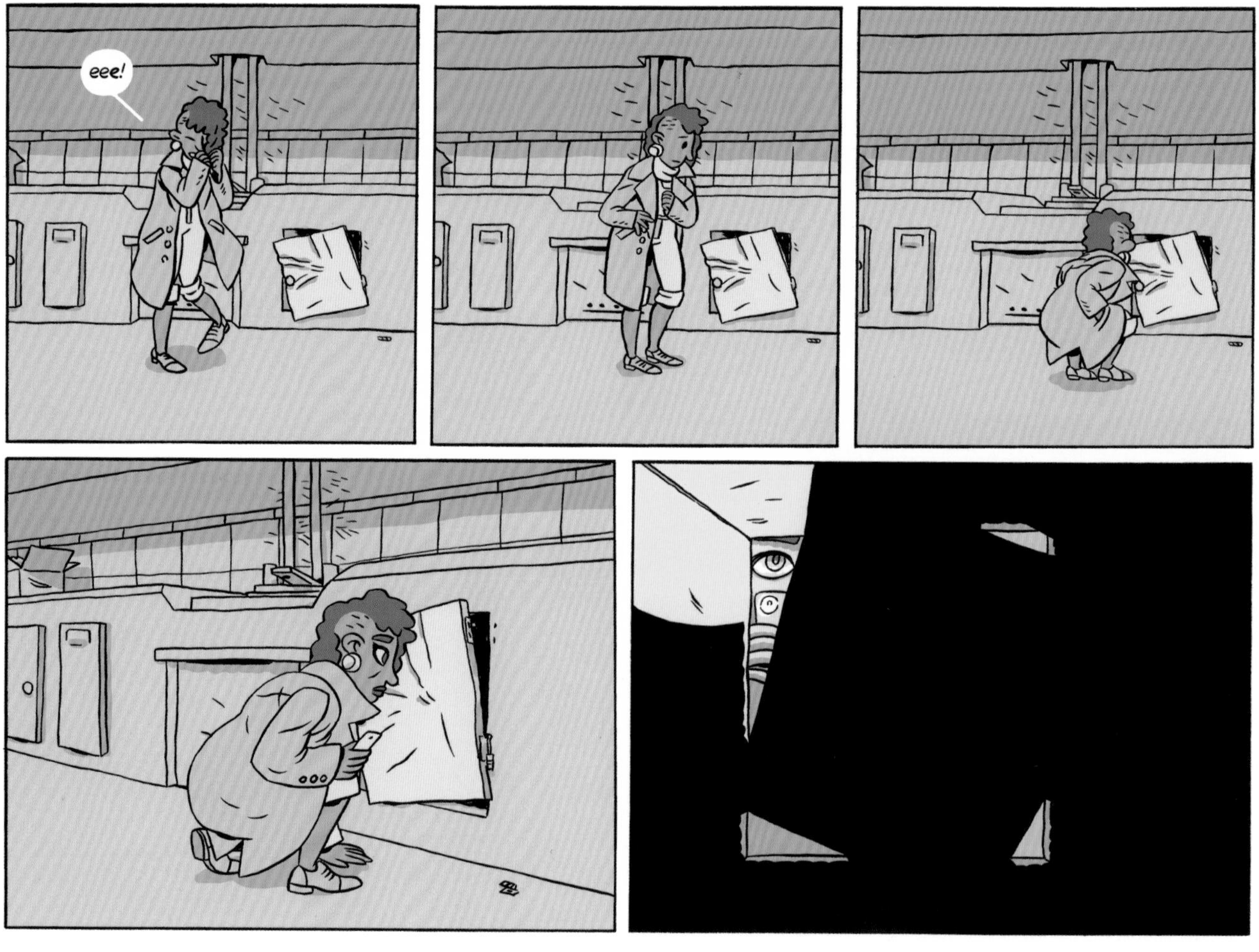
eee!

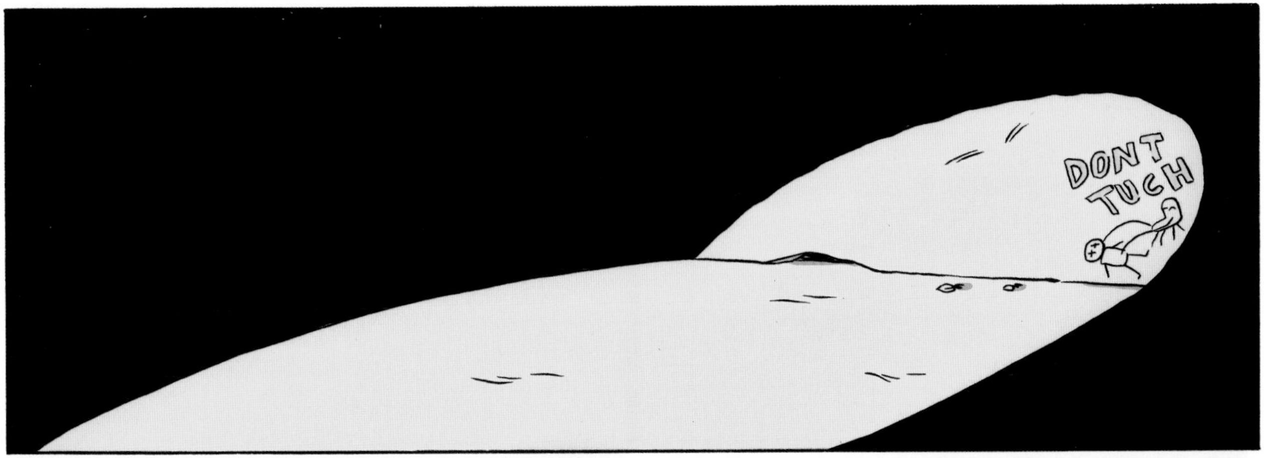
DONT
TUCH

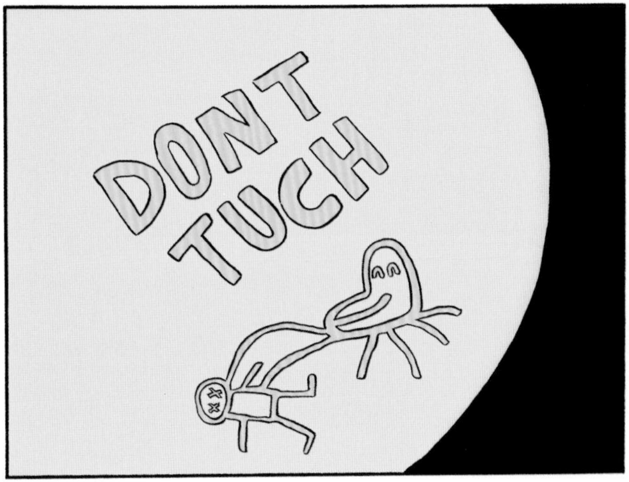
DONT
TUCH

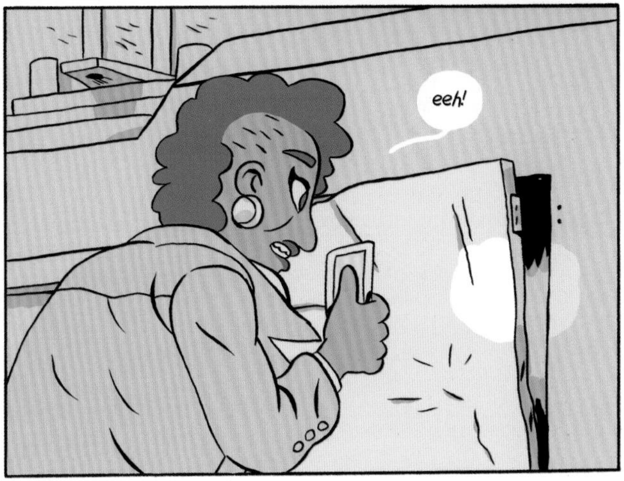
eeh!

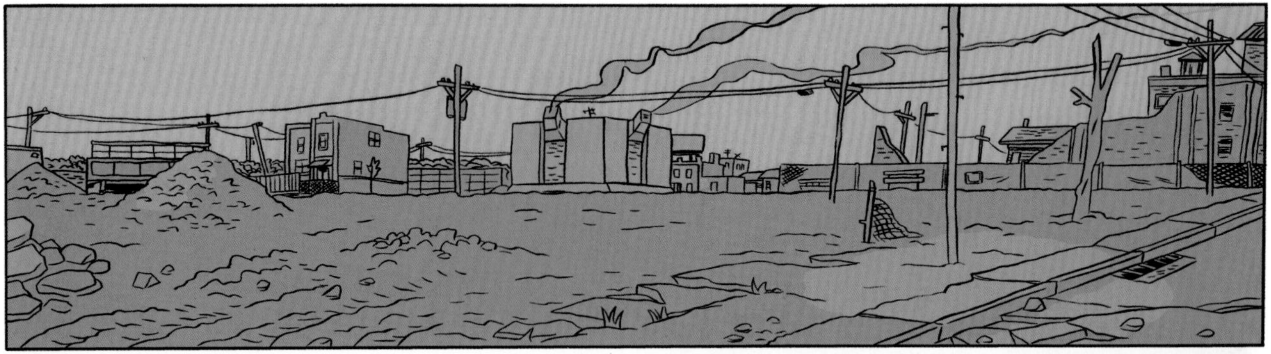

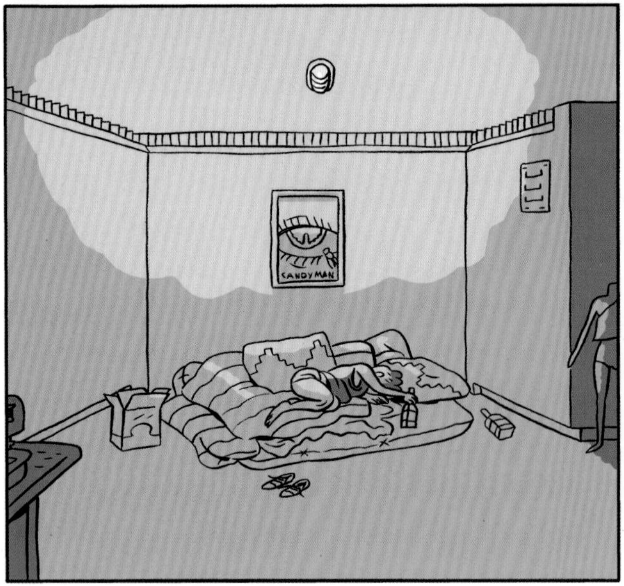
CANDYMAN

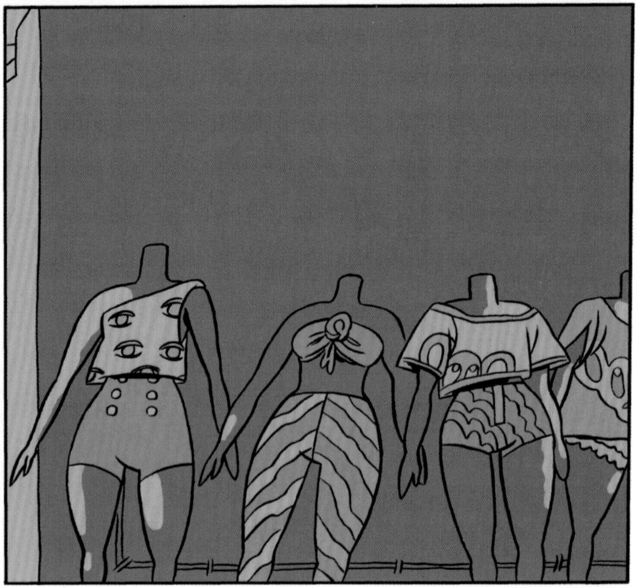

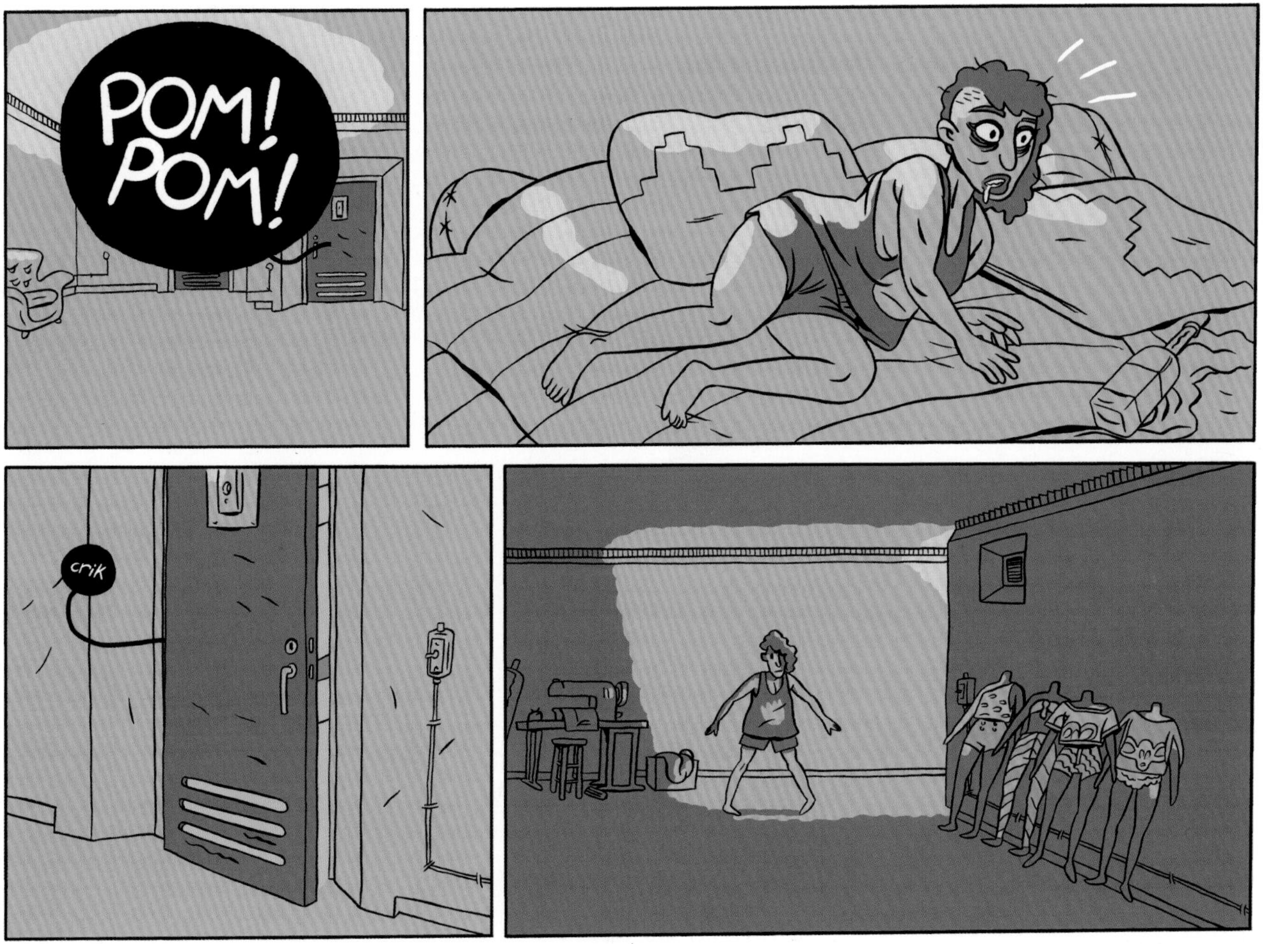
POM! POM!
crik

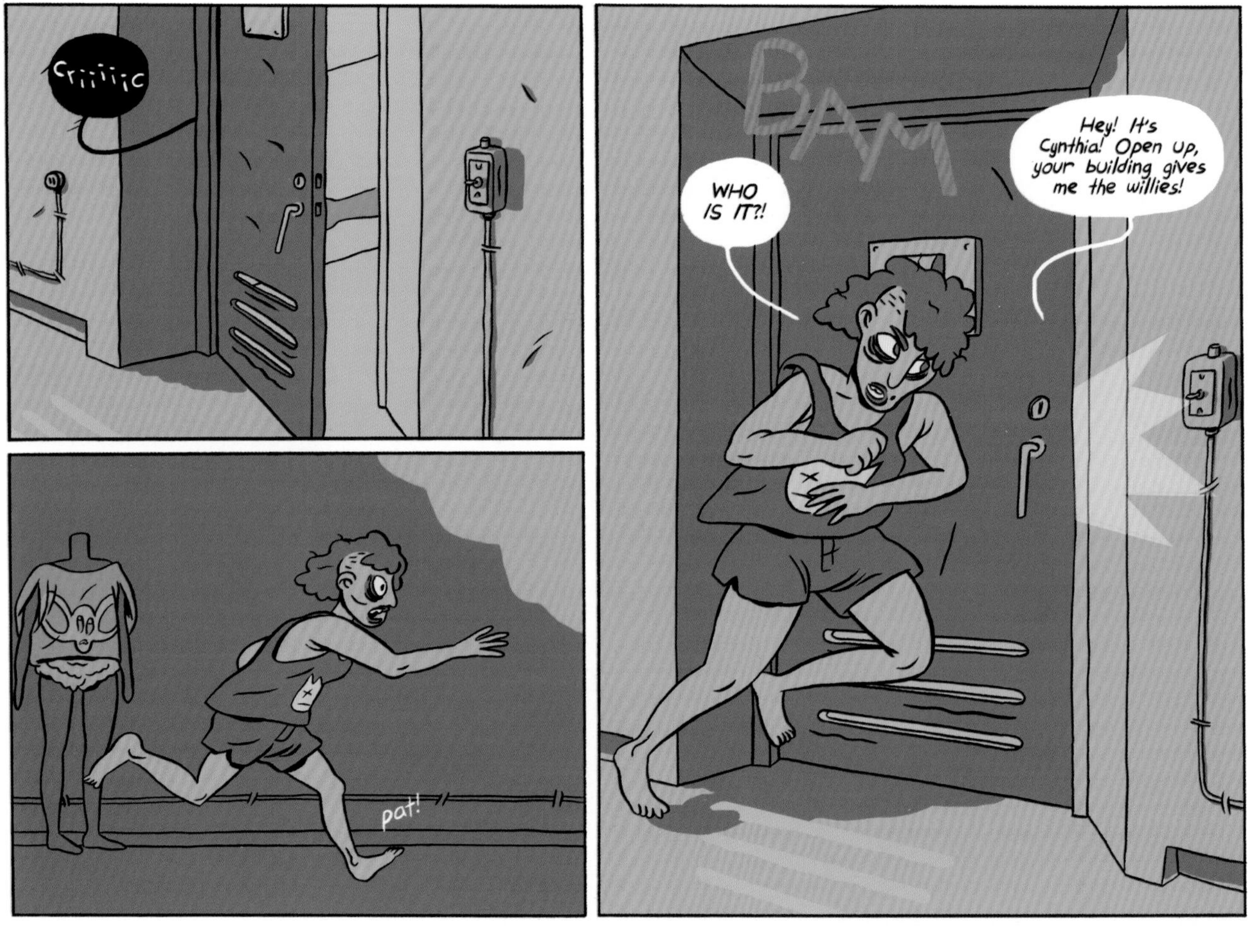
Criiiiic
pat!
BAM
WHO IS IT?!
Hey! It's Cynthia! Open up, your building gives me the willies!

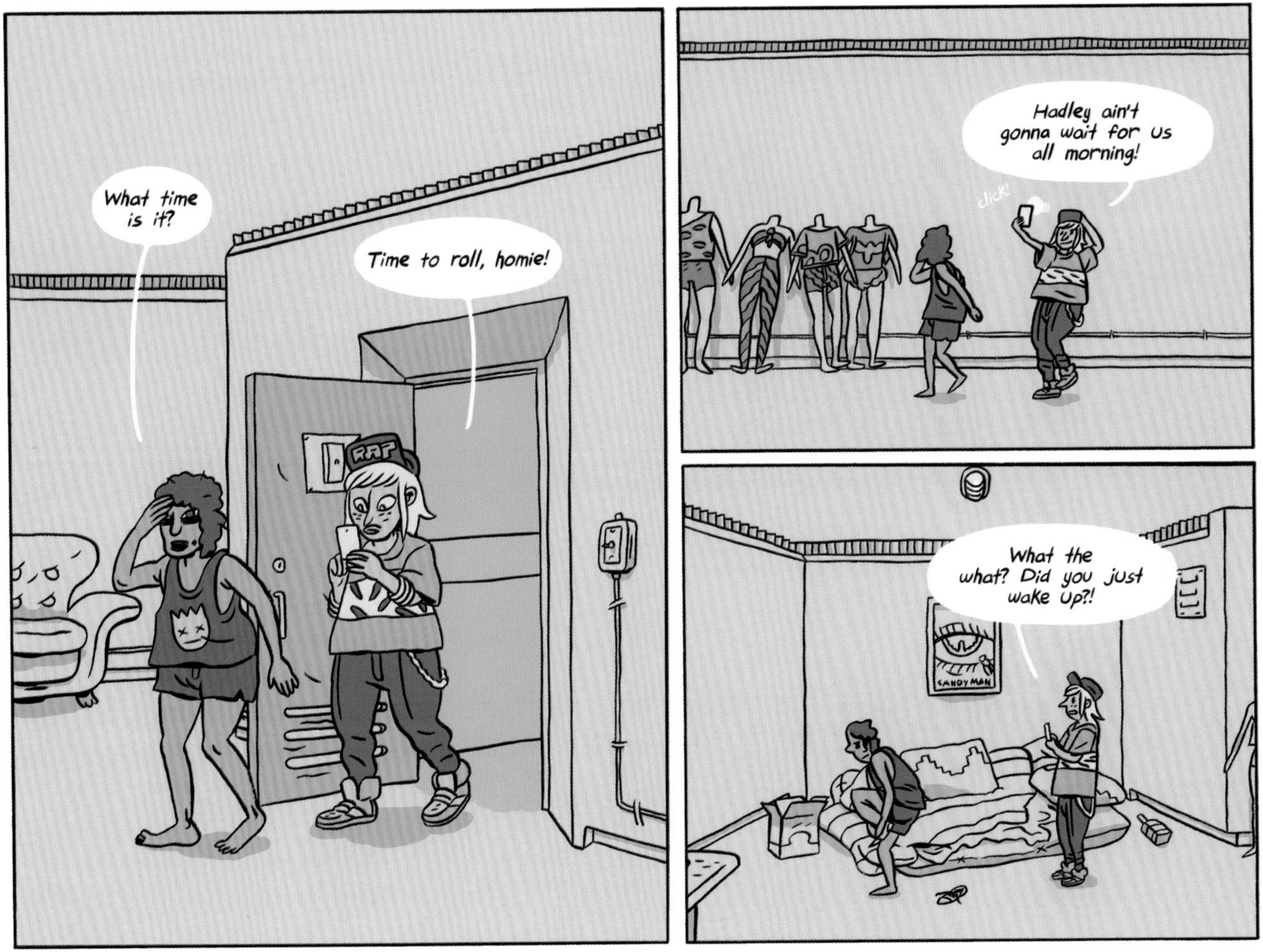
What time is it?
RAP
Time to roll, homie!
click!
Hadley ain't gonna wait for us all morning!
What the what? Did you just wake up?!
CANDYMAN

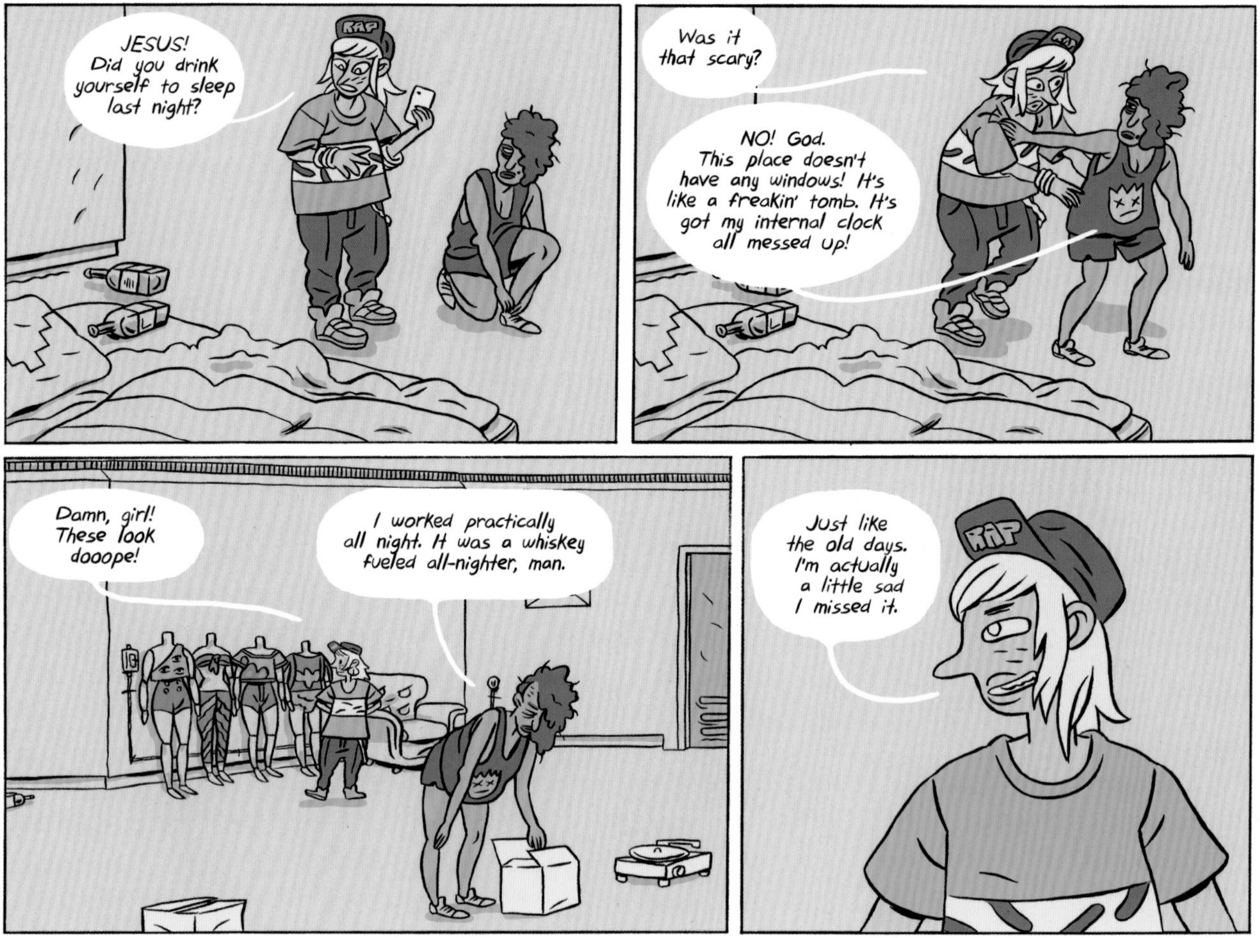
RAP
JESUS! Did you drink yourself to sleep last night?
Was it that scary?
NO! God. This place doesn't have any windows! It's like a freakin' tomb. It's got my internal clock all messed up!
Damn, girl! These look dooope!
I worked practically all night. It was a whiskey fueled all-nighter, man.
RAP
Just like the old days. I'm actually a little sad I missed it.

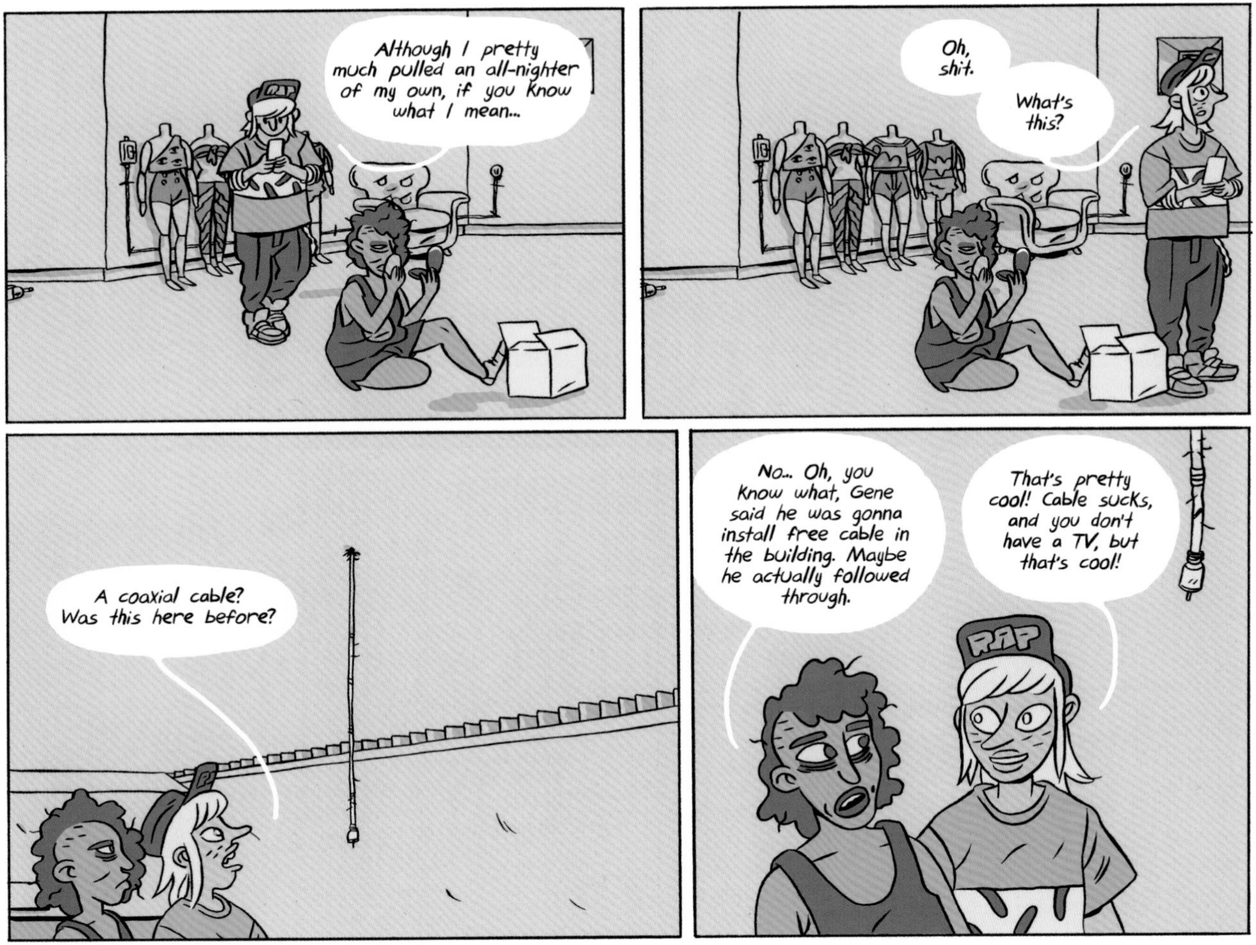
Although I pretty much pulled an all-nighter of my own, if you know what I mean...
RAP
Oh, shit.
What's this?
A coaxial cable? Was this here before?
No... Oh, you know what, Gene said he was gonna install free cable in the building. Maybe he actually followed through.
That's pretty cool! Cable sucks, and you don't have a TV, but that's cool!
RAP

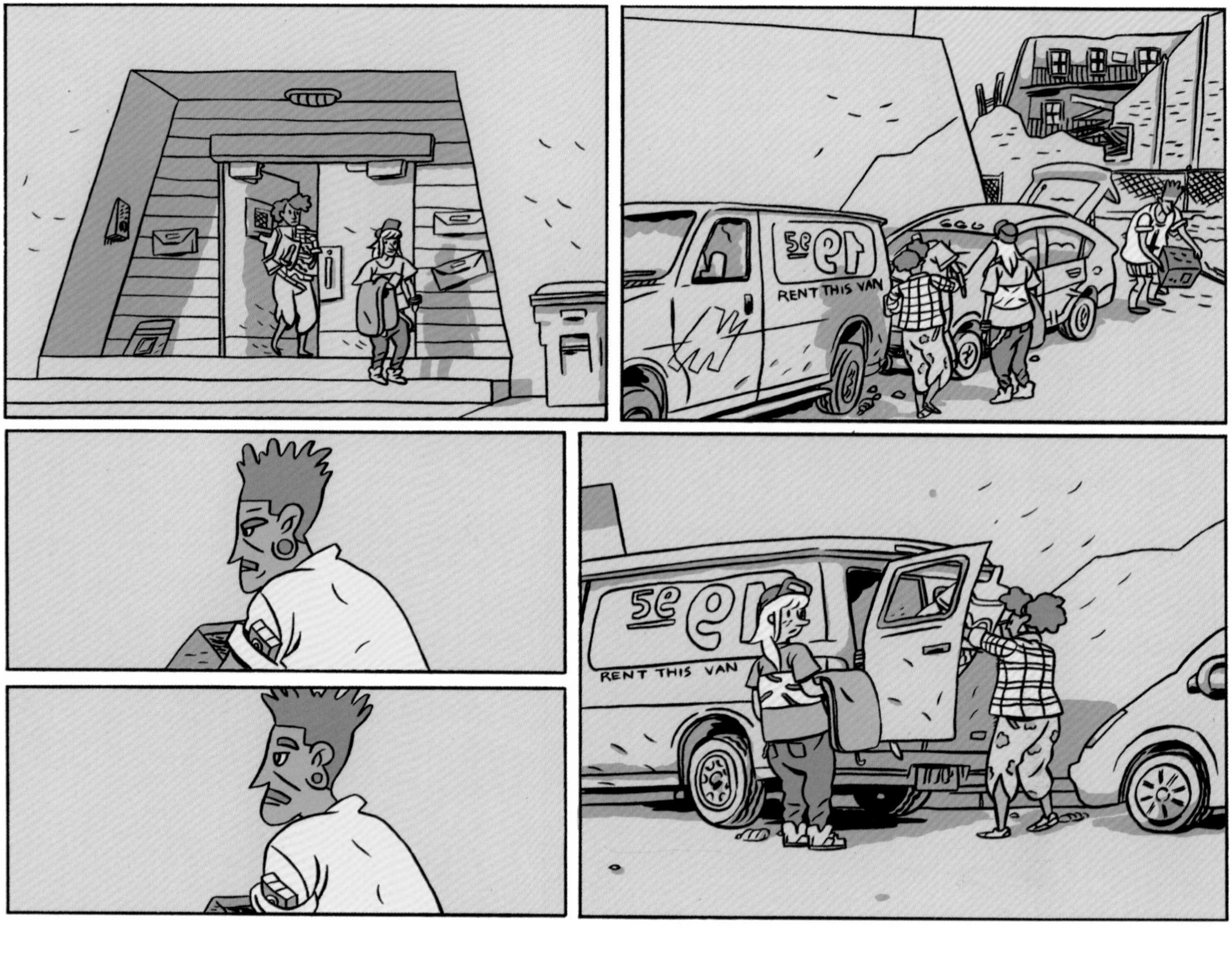
RENT THIS VAN
RENT THIS VAN

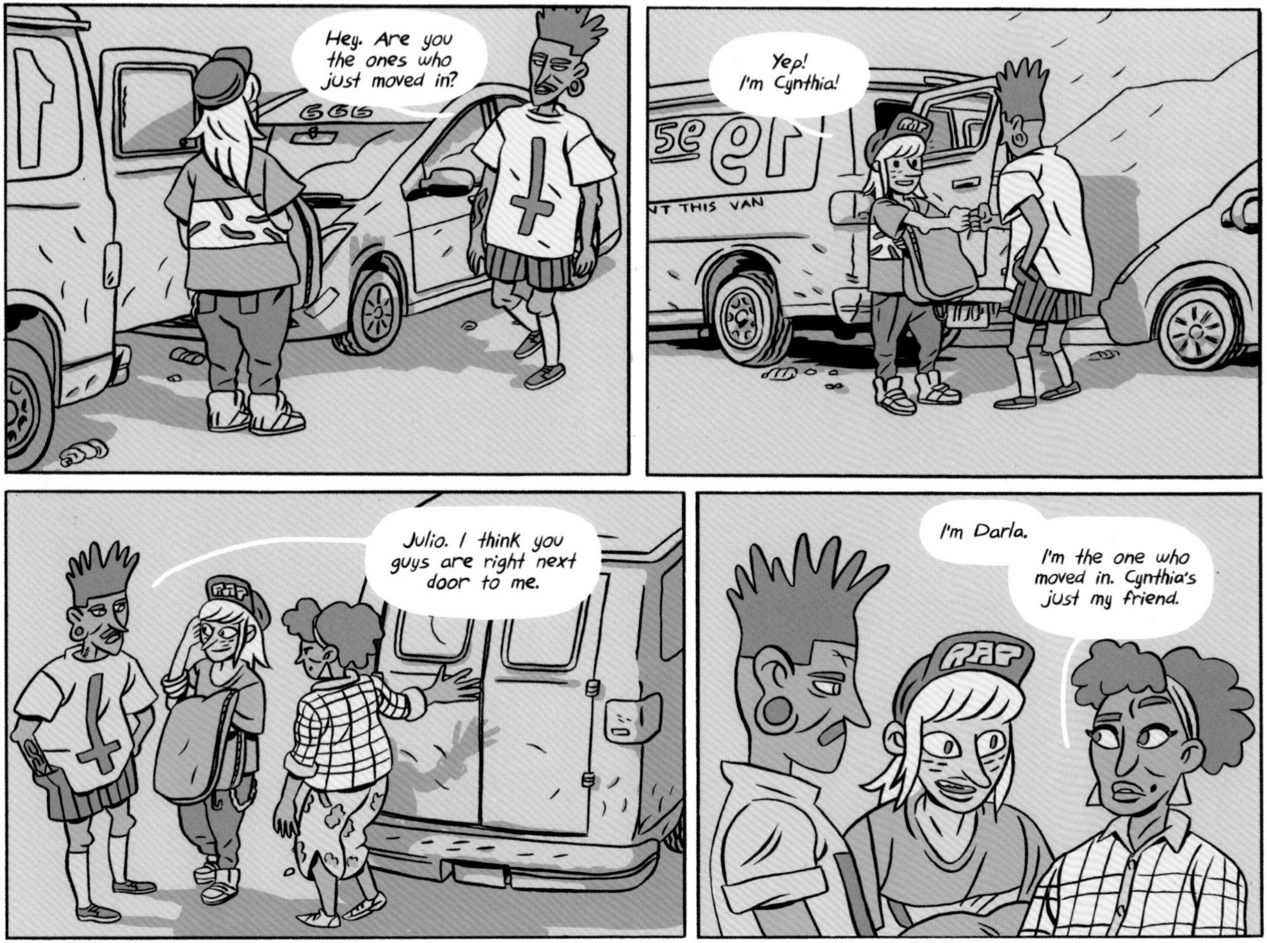
Hey. Are you the ones who just moved in?
Yep! I'm Cynthia!
Julio. I think you guys are right next door to me.
I'm Darla.
I'm the one who moved in. Cynthia's just my friend.

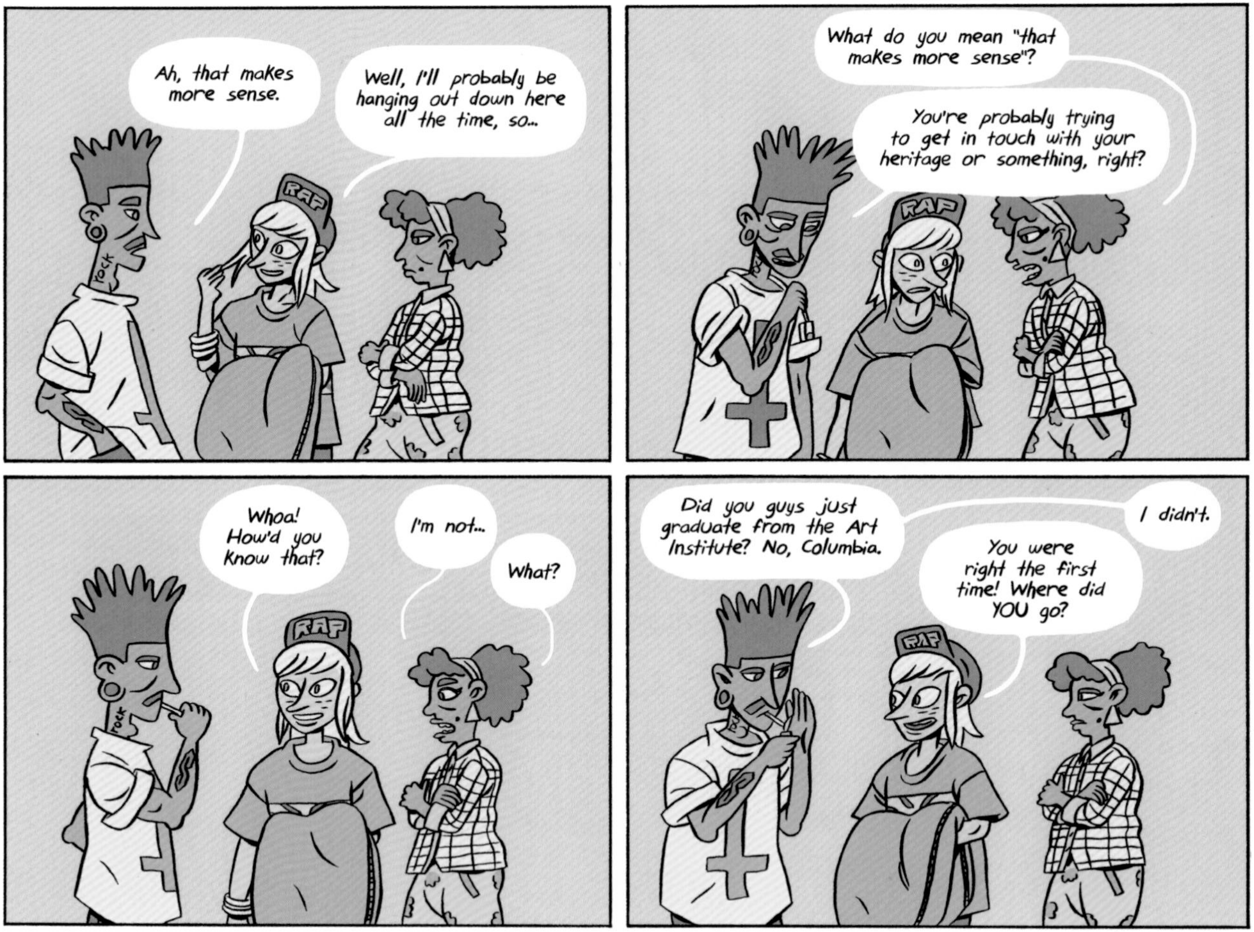
Ah, that makes more sense.
Well, I'll probably be hanging out down here all the time, so...
What do you mean "that makes more sense"?
You're probably trying to get in touch with your heritage or something, right?
Whoa! How'd you know that?
I'm not...
What?
Did you guys just graduate from the Art Institute? No, Columbia.
I didn't.
You were right the first time! Where did YOU go?

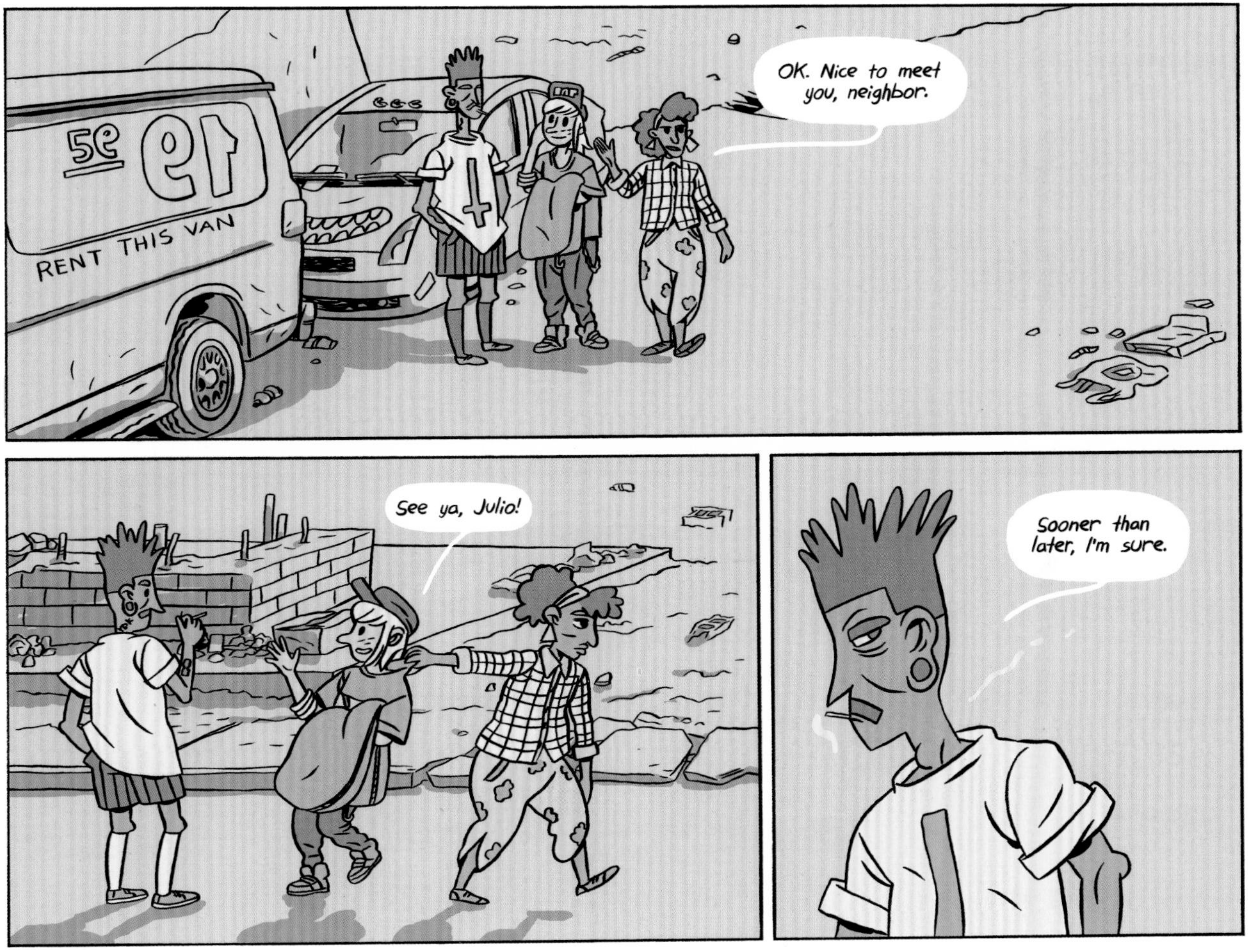
RENT THIS VAN
OK. Nice to meet you, neighbor.
See ya, Julio!
Sooner than later, I'm sure.

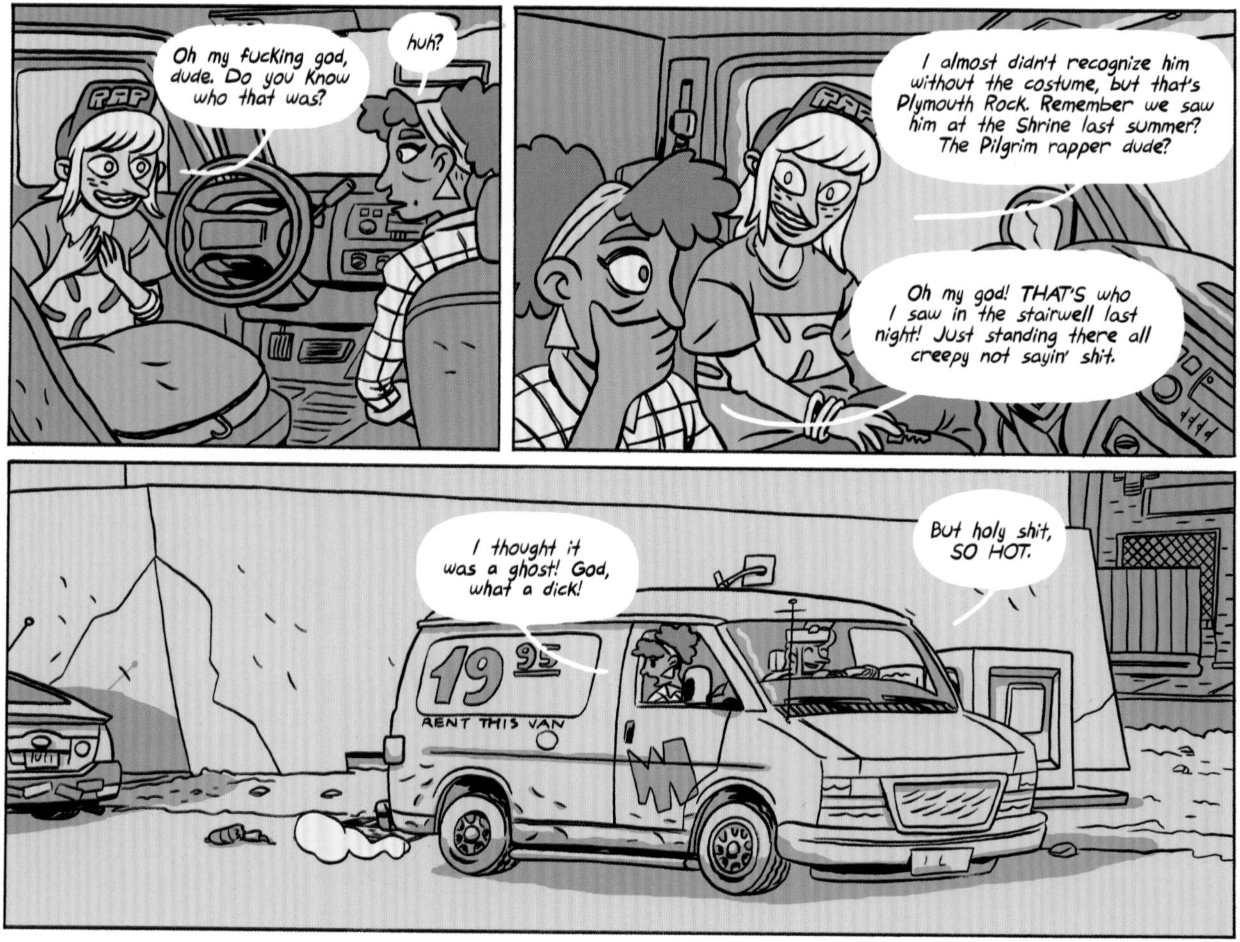
Oh my fucking god, dude. Do you know who that was?
huh?
I almost didn't recognize him without the costume, but that's Plymouth Rock. Remember we saw him at the Shrine last summer? The Pilgrim rapper dude?
Oh my god! THAT'S who I saw in the stairwell last night! Just standing there all creepy not sayin' shit.
RENT THIS VAN
I thought it was a ghost! God, what a dick!
But holy shit, SO HOT.

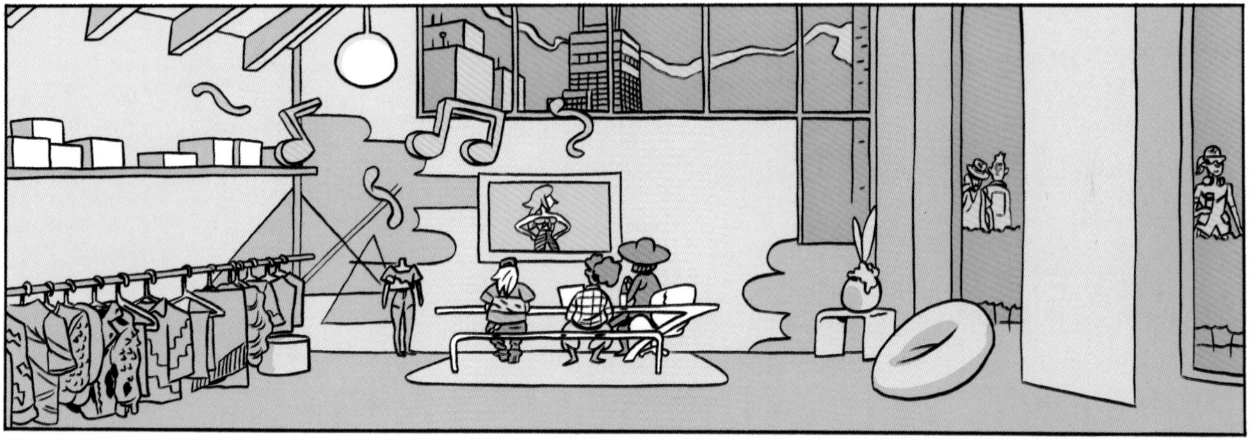

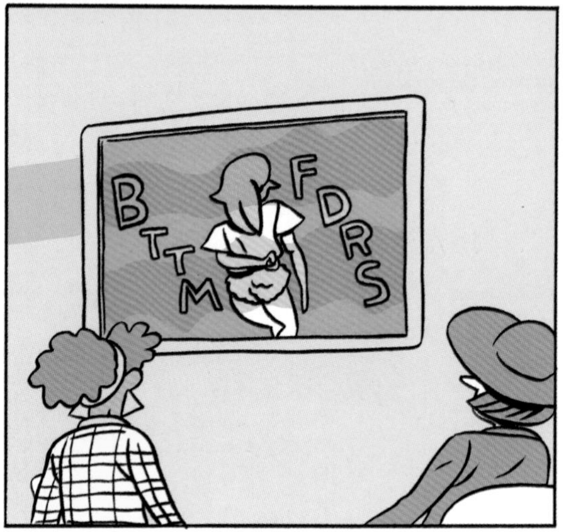
B
T
T
M
F
D
R
S

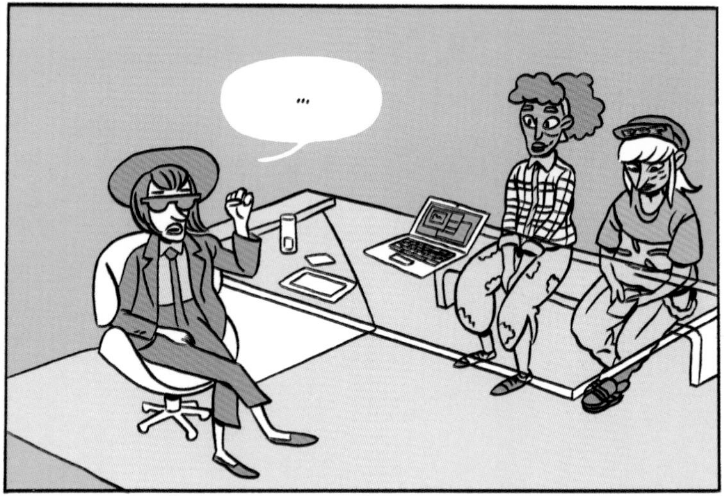
...

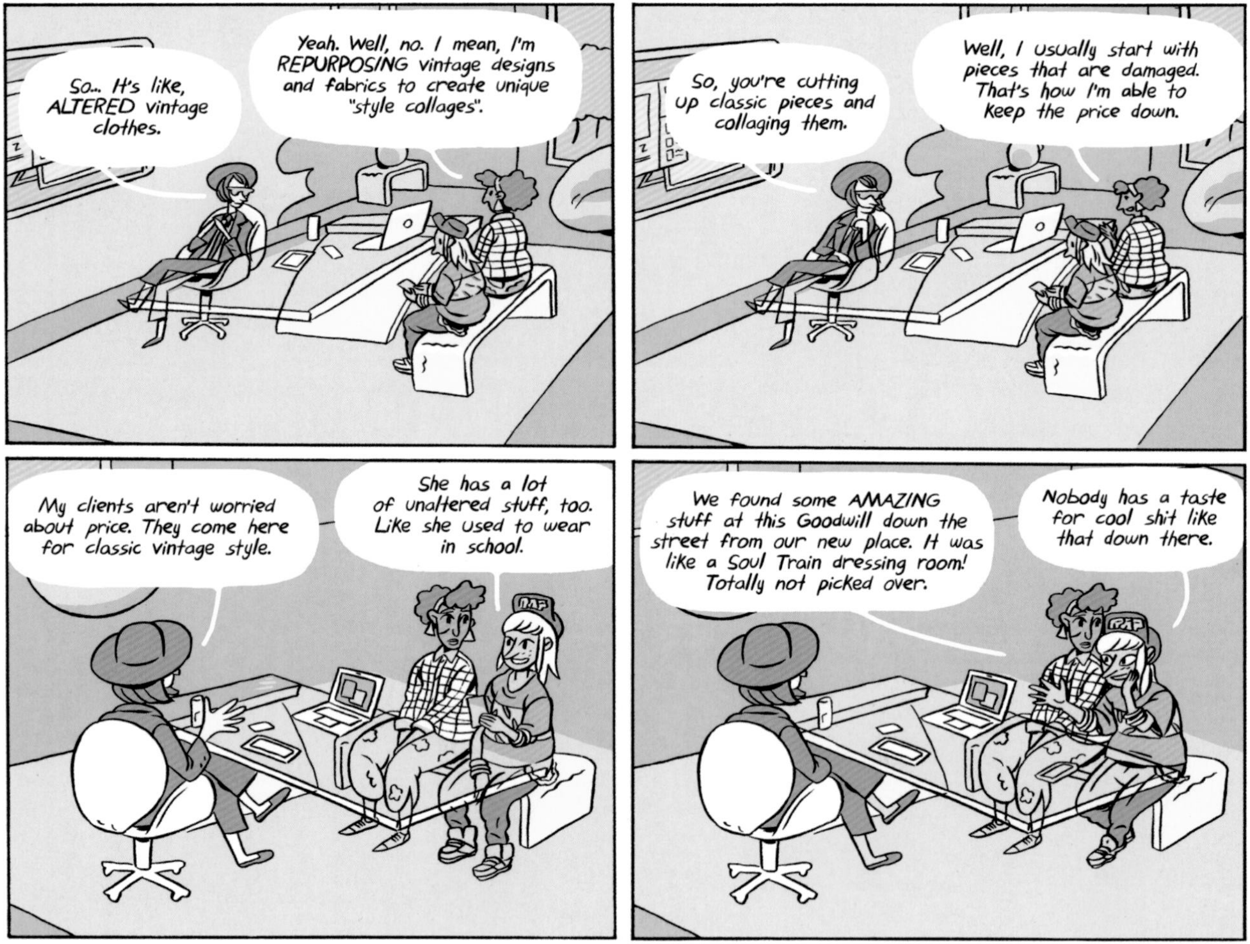
So... It's like, ALTERED vintage clothes.
Yeah. Well, no. I mean, I'm REPURPOSING vintage designs and fabrics to create unique "style collages".
So, you're cutting up classic pieces and collaging them.
Well, I usually start with pieces that are damaged. That's how I'm able to keep the price down.
My clients aren't worried about price. They come here for classic vintage style.
She has a lot of unaltered stuff, too. Like she used to wear in school.
We found some AMAZING stuff at this Goodwill down the street from our new place. It was like a Soul Train dressing room! Totally not picked over.
Nobody has a taste for cool shit like that down there.

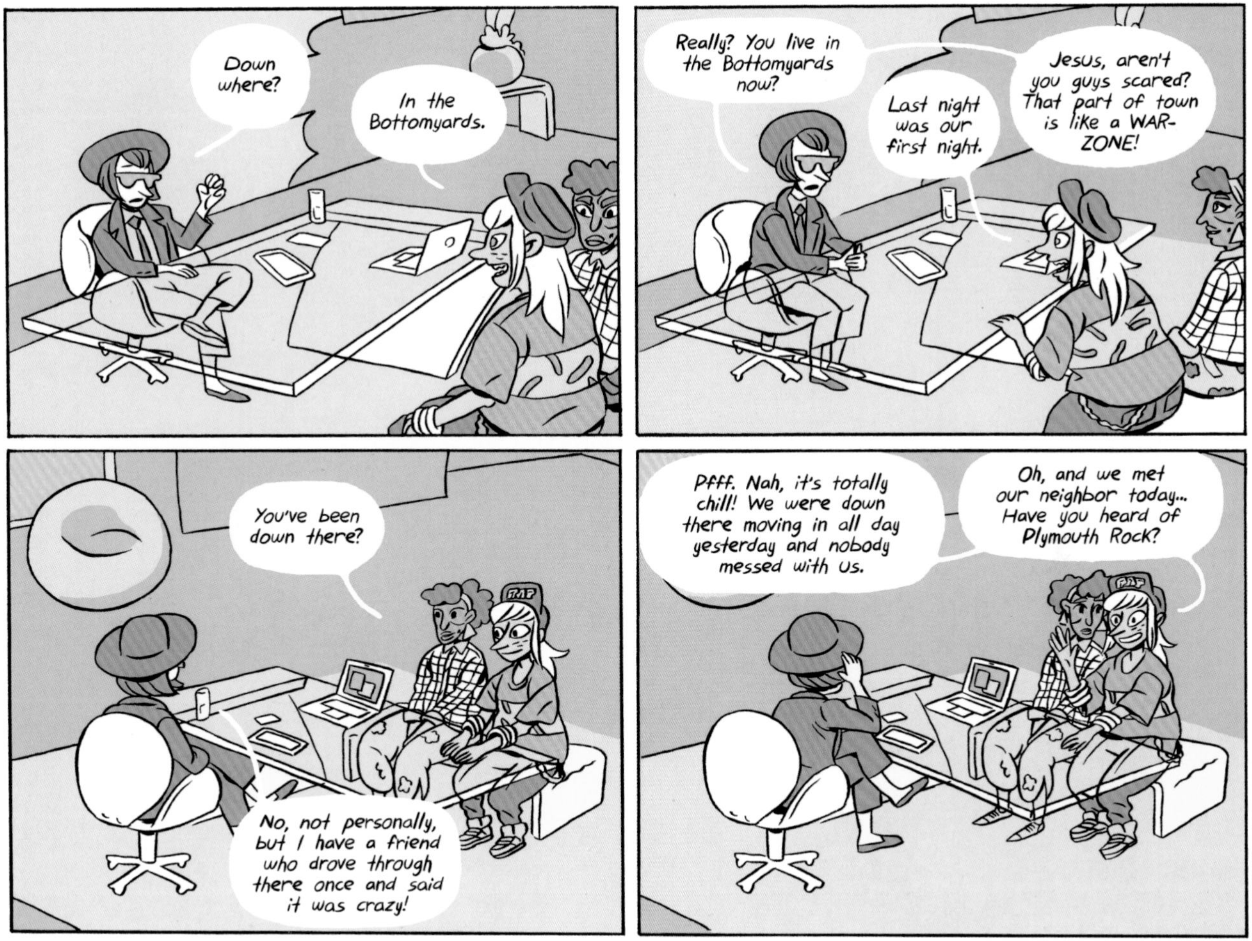
Down where?
In the Bottomyards.
Really? You live in the Bottomyards now?
Last night was our first night.
Jesus, aren't you guys scared? That part of town is like a WAR-ZONE!
You've been down there?
No, not personally, but I have a friend who drove through there once and said it was crazy!
Pfff. Nah, it's totally chill! We were down there moving in all day yesterday and nobody messed with us.
Oh, and we met our neighbor today... Have you heard of Plymouth Rock?

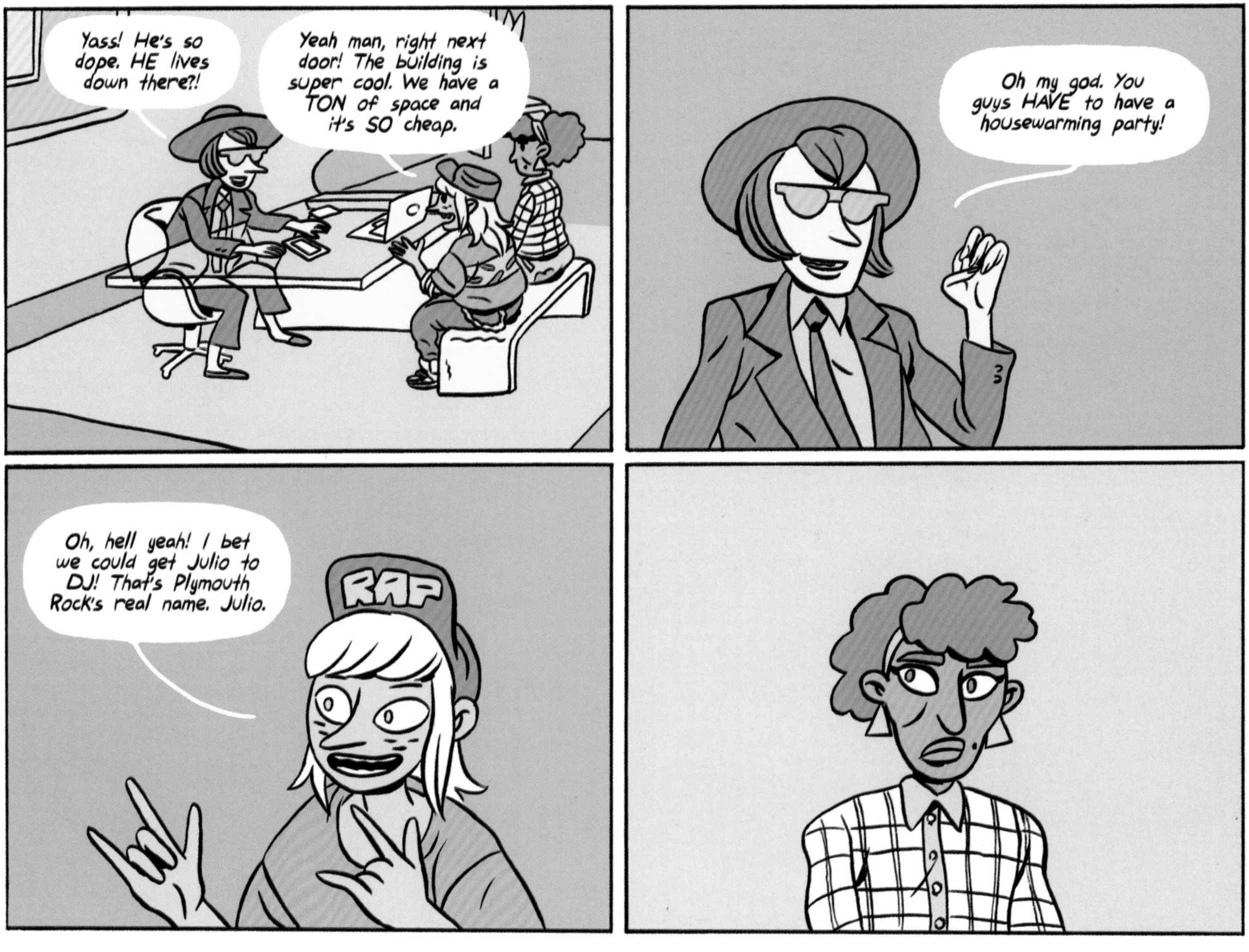
Yass! He's so dope. HE lives down there?!
Yeah man, right next door! The building is super cool. We have a TON of space and it's SO cheap.
Oh my god. You guys HAVE to have a housewarming party!
Oh, hell yeah! I bet we could get Julio to DJ! That's Plymouth Rock's real name. Julio.
RAP

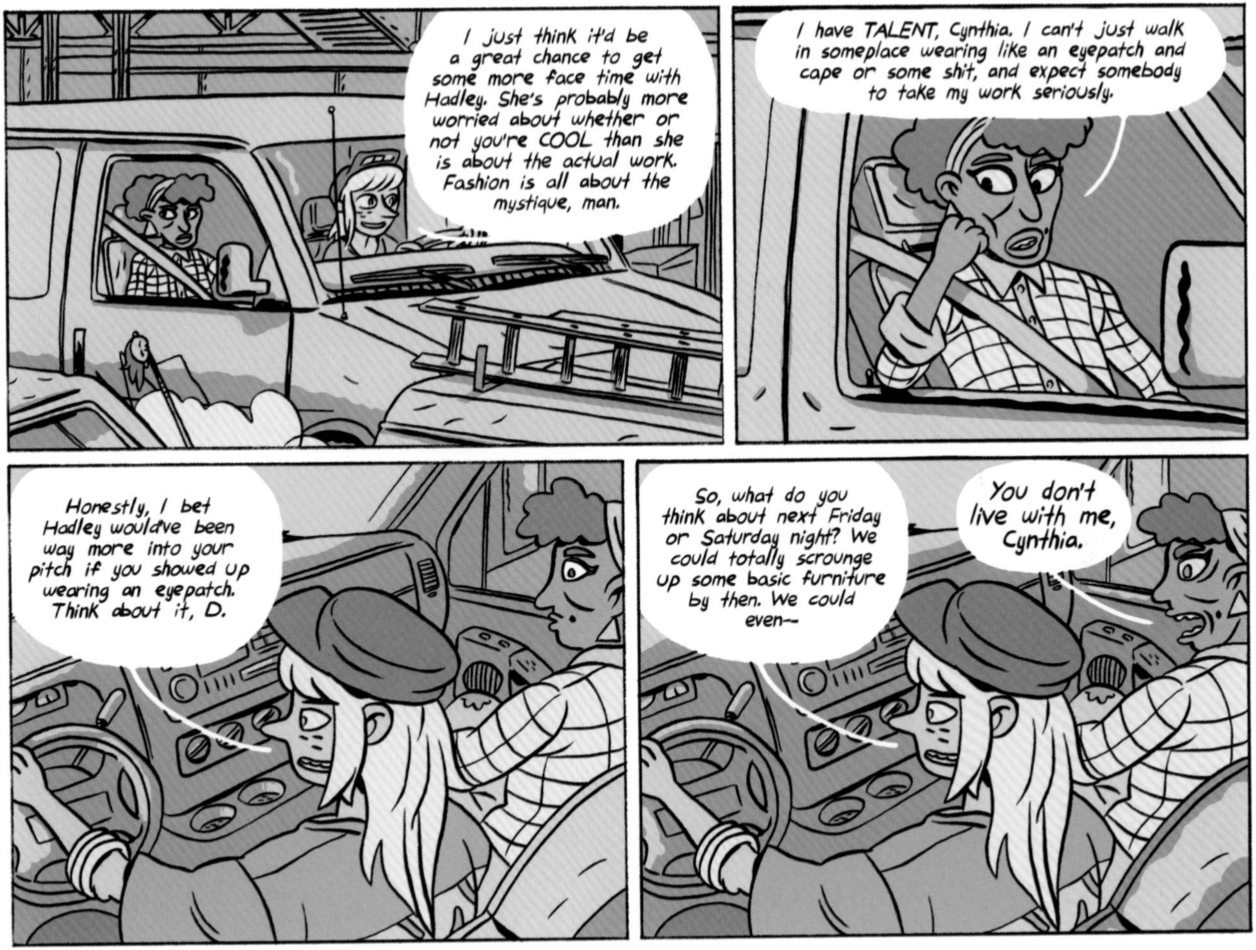
I just think it'd be a great chance to get some more face time with Hadley. She's probably more worried about whether or not you're COOL than she is about the actual work. Fashion is all about the mystique, man.
I have TALENT, Cynthia. I can't just walk in someplace wearing like an eyepatch and cape or some shit, and expect somebody to take my work seriously.
Honestly, I bet Hadley would've been way more into your pitch if you showed up wearing an eyepatch. Think about it, D.
So, what do you think about next Friday or Saturday night? We could totally scrounge up some basic furniture by then. We could even--
You don't live with me, Cynthia.

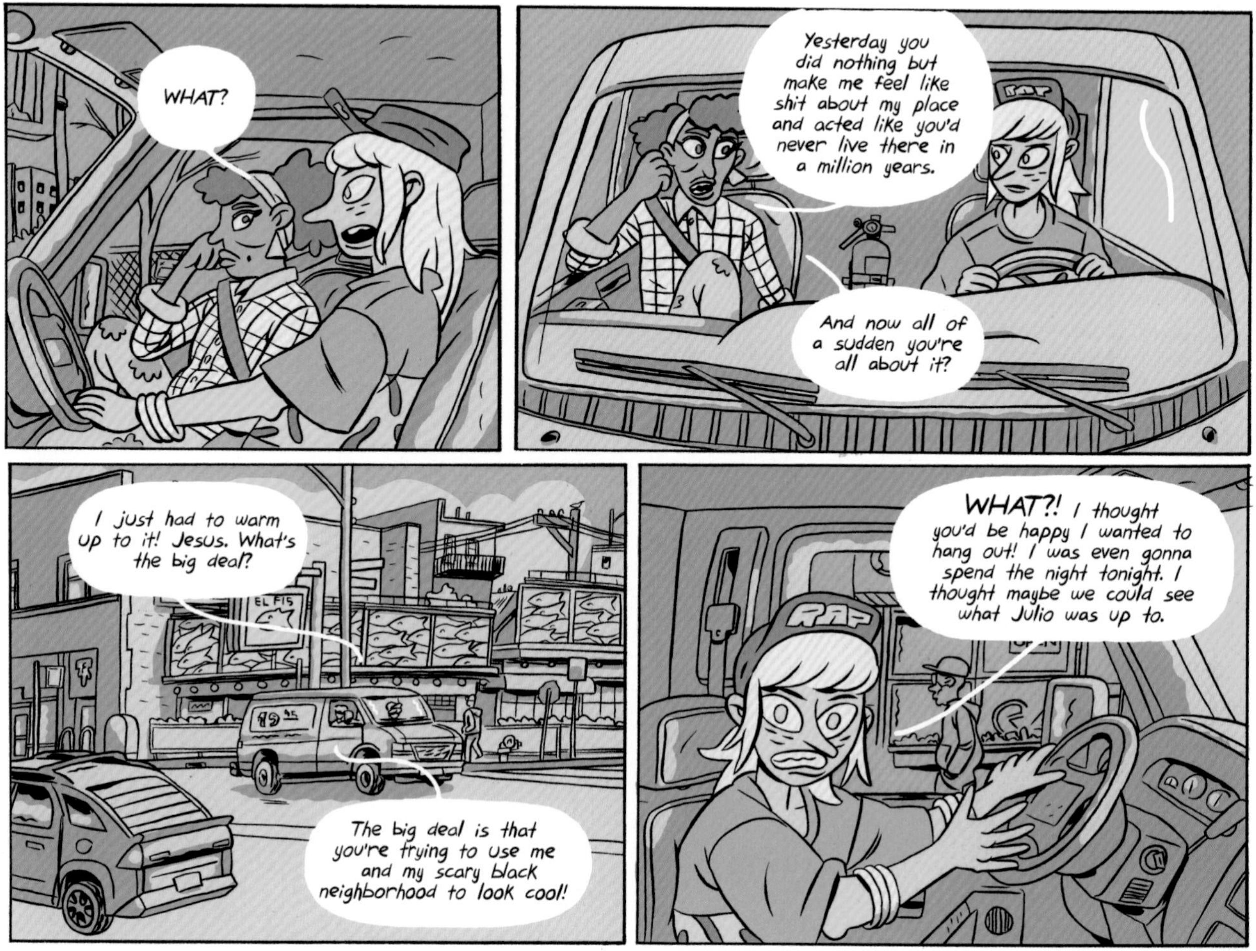
WHAT?
Yesterday you did nothing but make me feel like shit about my place and acted like you'd never live there in a million years.
And now all of a sudden you're all about it?
I just had to warm up to it! Jesus. What's the big deal?
EL FIS
The big deal is that you're trying to use me and my scary black neighborhood to look cool!
WHAT?! I thought you'd be happy I wanted to hang out! I was even gonna spend the night tonight. I thought maybe we could see what Julio was up to.
RAP

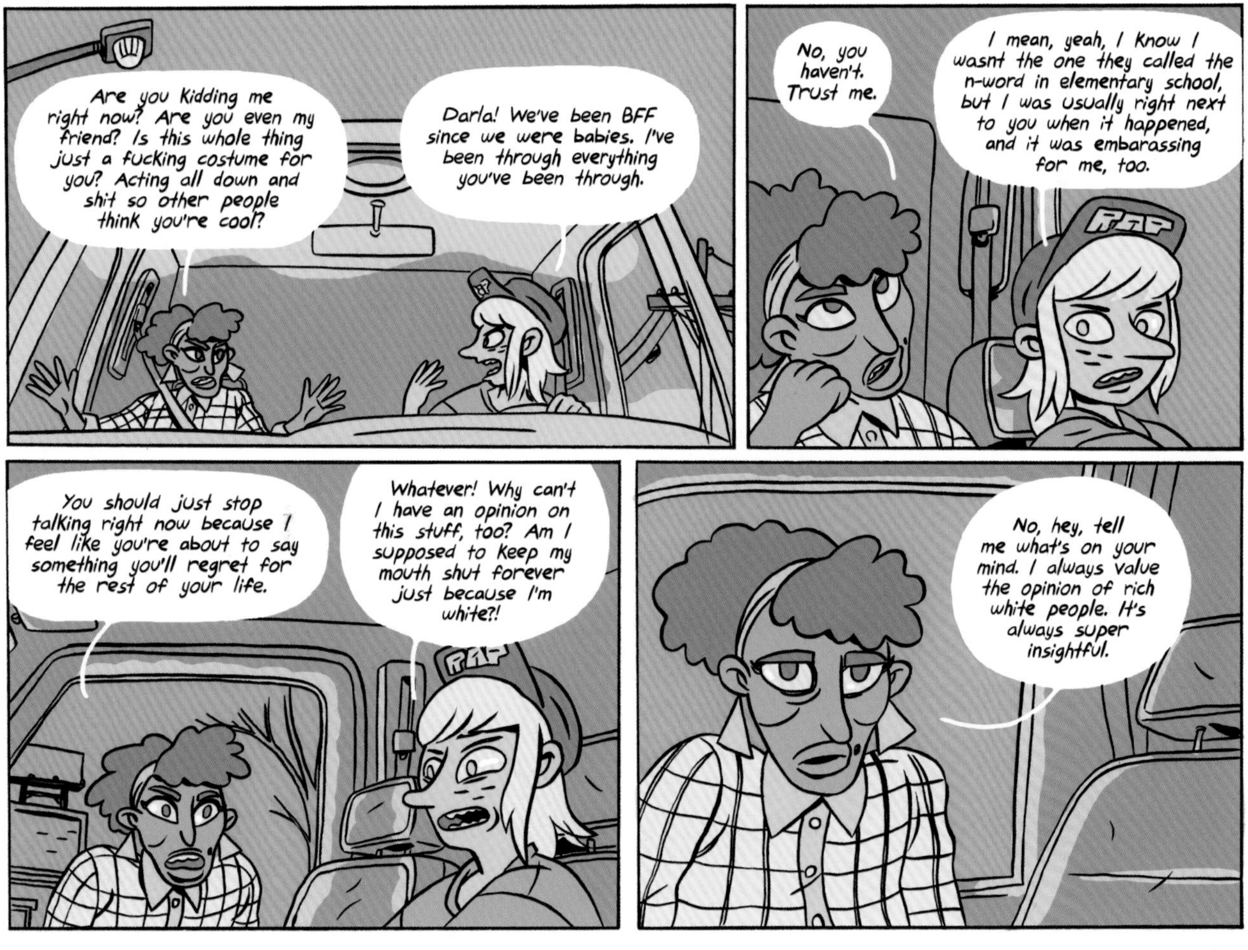
Are you kidding me right now? Are you even my friend? Is this whole thing just a fucking costume for you? Acting all down and shit so other people think you're cool?
Darla! We've been BFF since we were babies. I've been through everything you've been through.
No, you haven't. Trust me.
I mean, yeah, I know I wasnt the one they called the n-word in elementary school, but I was usually right next to you when it happened, and it was embarassing for me, too.
You should just stop talking right now because I feel like you're about to say something you'll regret for the rest of your life.
Whatever! Why can't I have an opinion on this stuff, too? Am I supposed to keep my mouth shut forever just because I'm white?!
No, hey, tell me what's on your mind. I always value the opinion of rich white people. It's always super insightful.

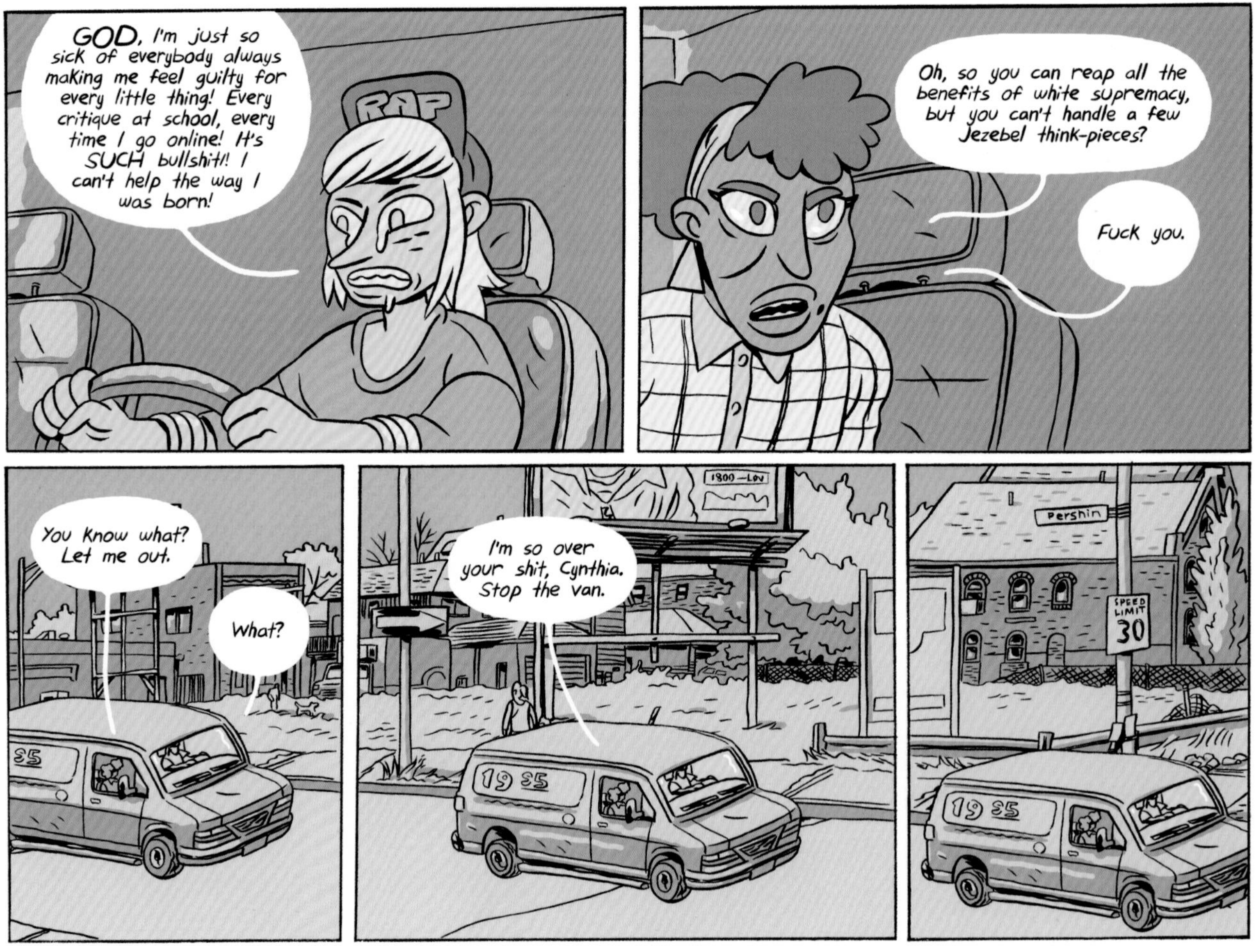
RAP
GOD, I'm just so sick of everybody always making me feel guilty for every little thing! Every critique at school, every time I go online! It's SUCH bullshit!! I can't help the way I was born!
Oh, so you can reap all the benefits of white supremacy, but you can't handle a few Jezebel think-pieces?
Fuck you.
You know what? Let me out.
What?
1800—LOV
I'm so over your shit, Cynthia. Stop the van.
1995
Pershin
SPEED LIMIT 30

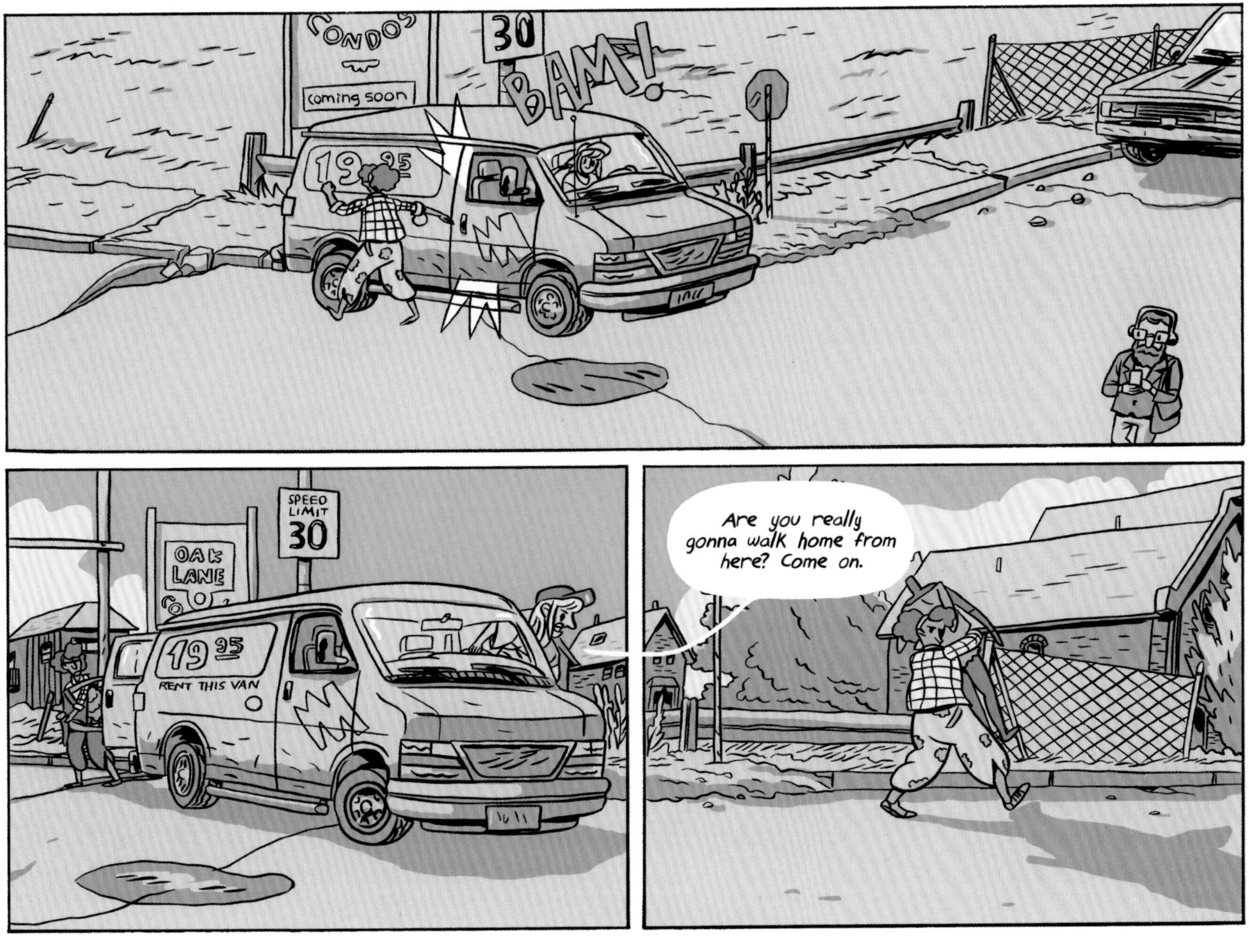
CONDOS
coming soon
30
BAM!
19 95
SPEED LIMIT 30
OAK LANE
19 95
RENT THIS VAN
Are you really gonna walk home from here? Come on.

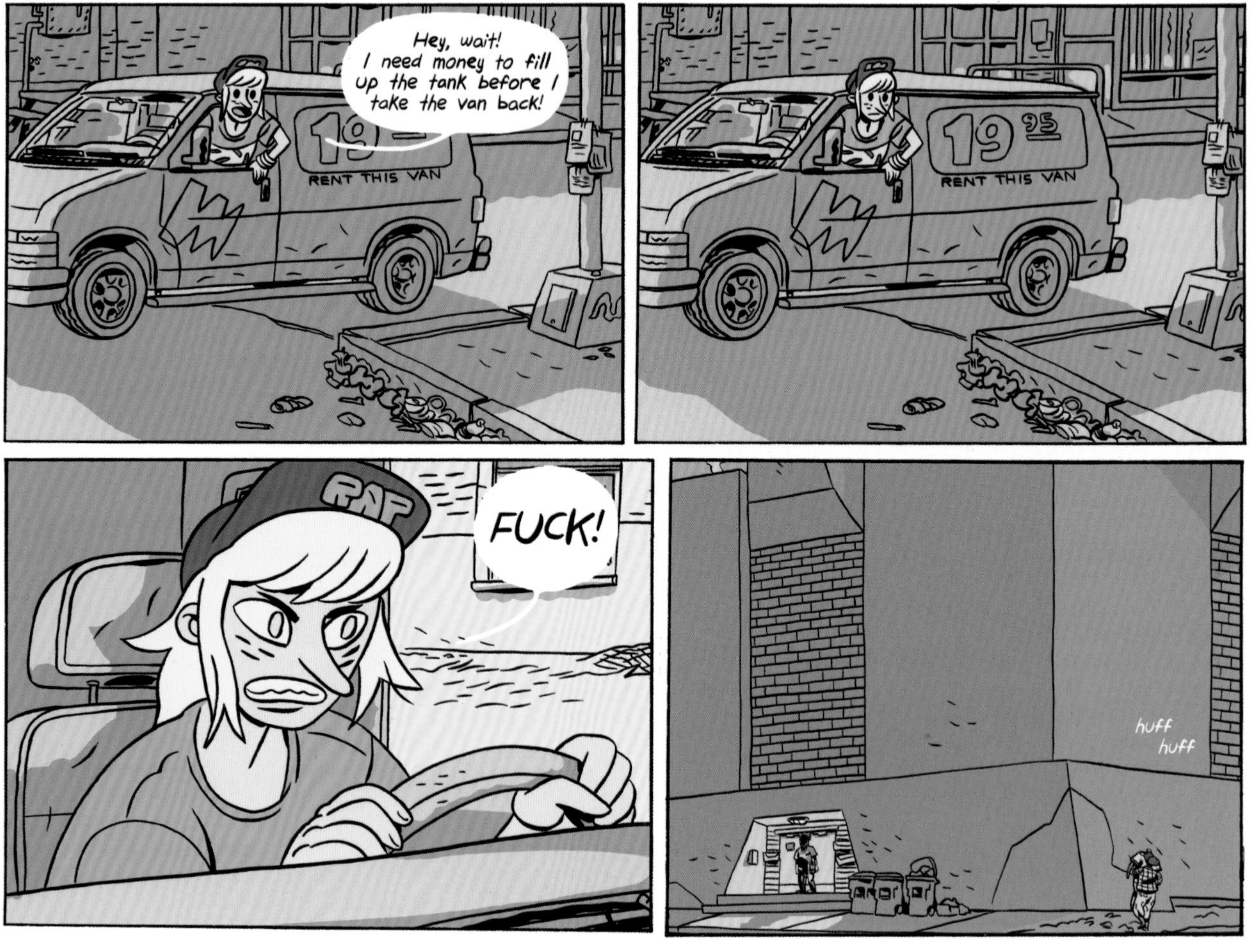
Hey, wait! I need money to fill up the tank before I take the van back!
19
RENT THIS VAN
19 95
RENT THIS VAN
FUCK!
huff huff

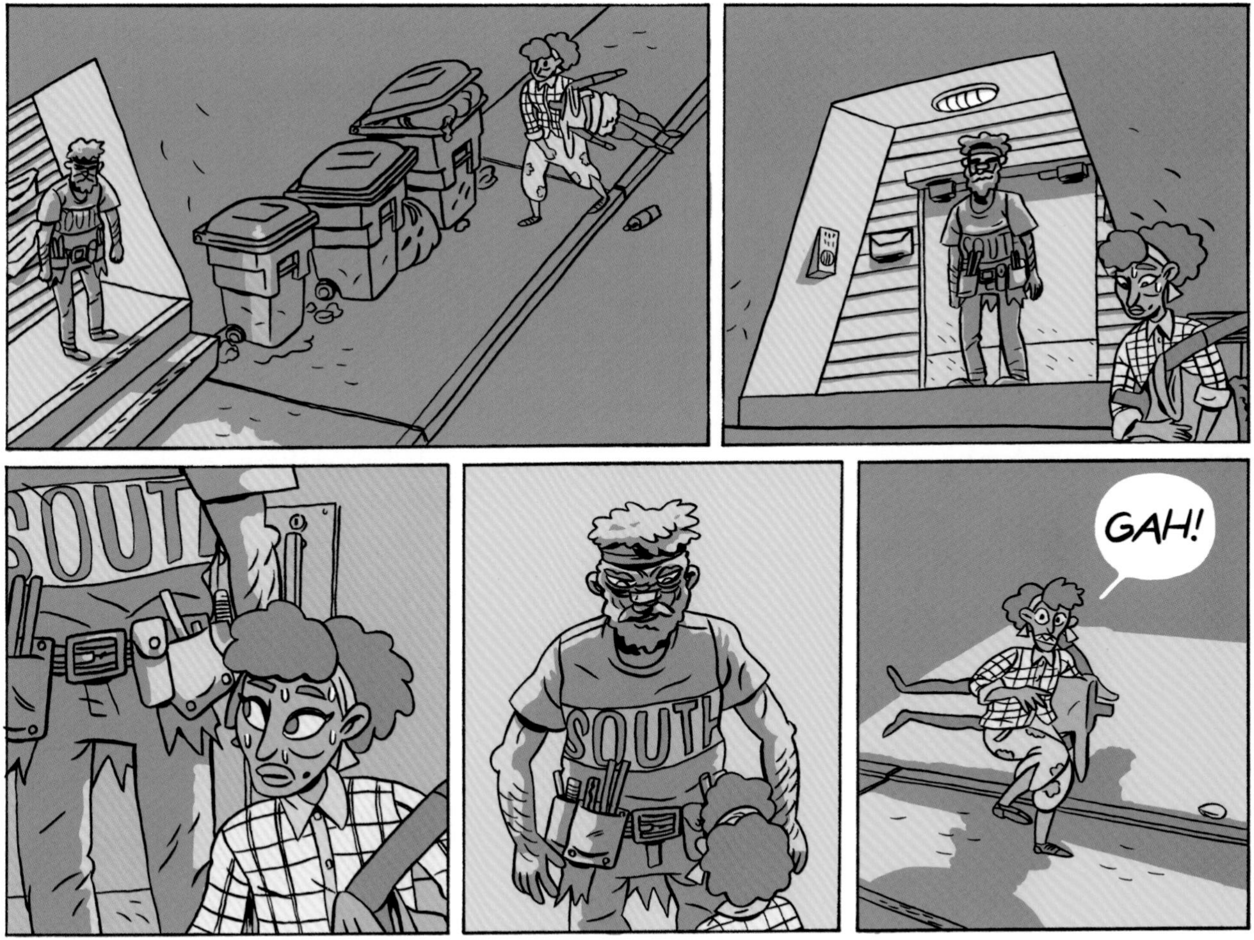
SOUTH
GAH!

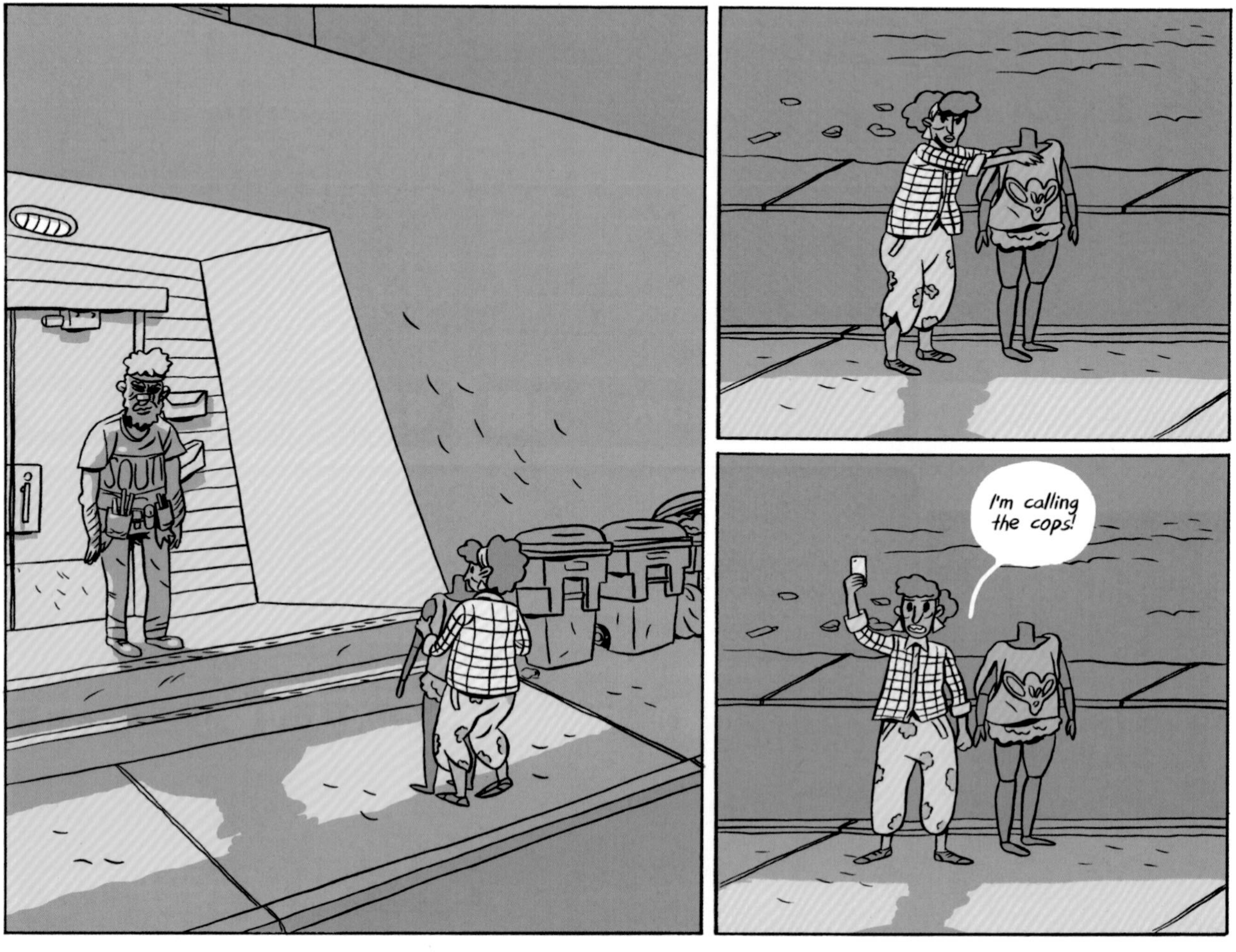
SOUTH
I'm calling the cops!

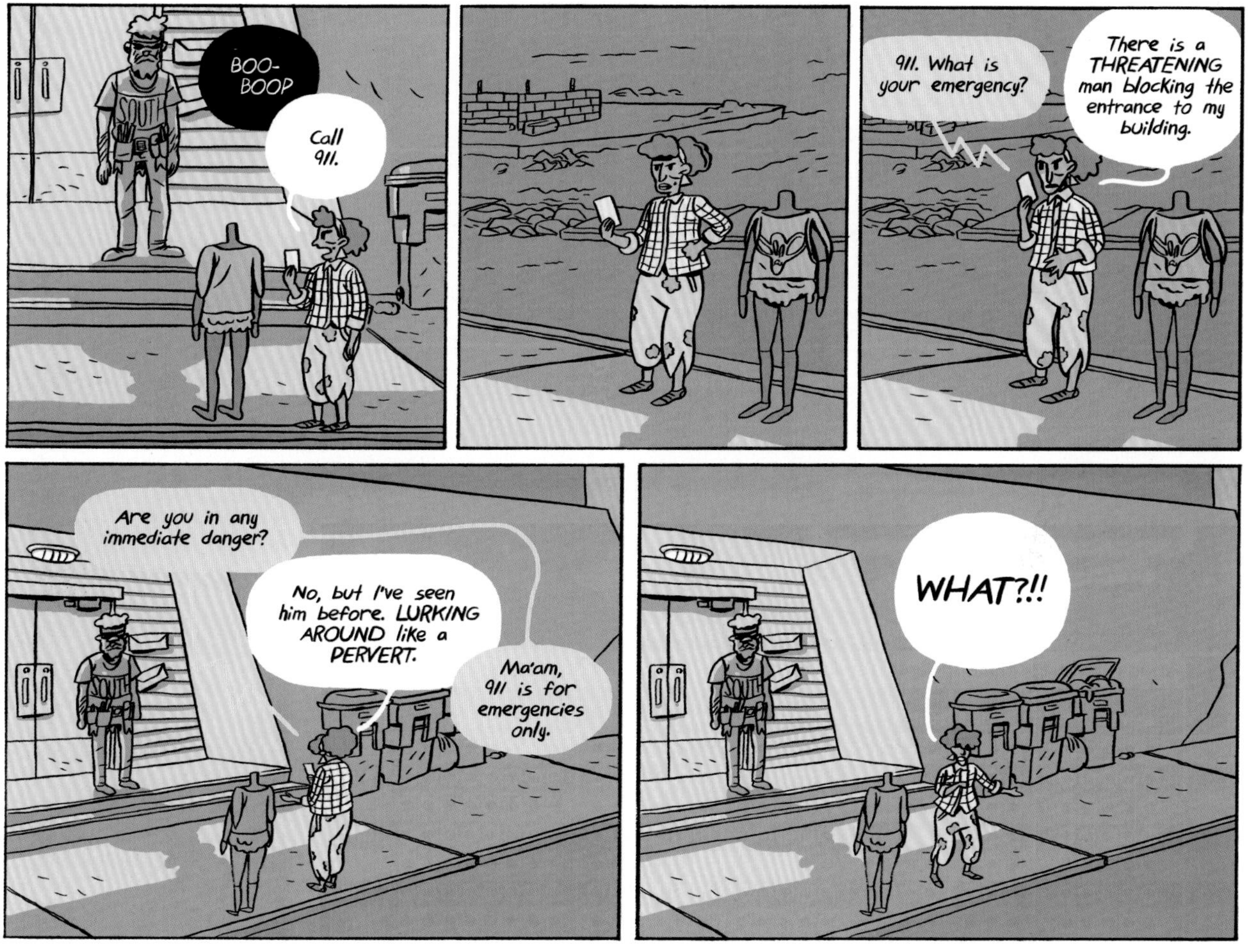
BOO-
BOOP
Call 911.
911. What is your emergency?
There is a THREATENING man blocking the entrance to my building.
Are you in any immediate danger?
No, but I've seen him before. LURKING AROUND like a PERVERT.
Ma'am, 911 is for emergencies only.
WHAT?!!

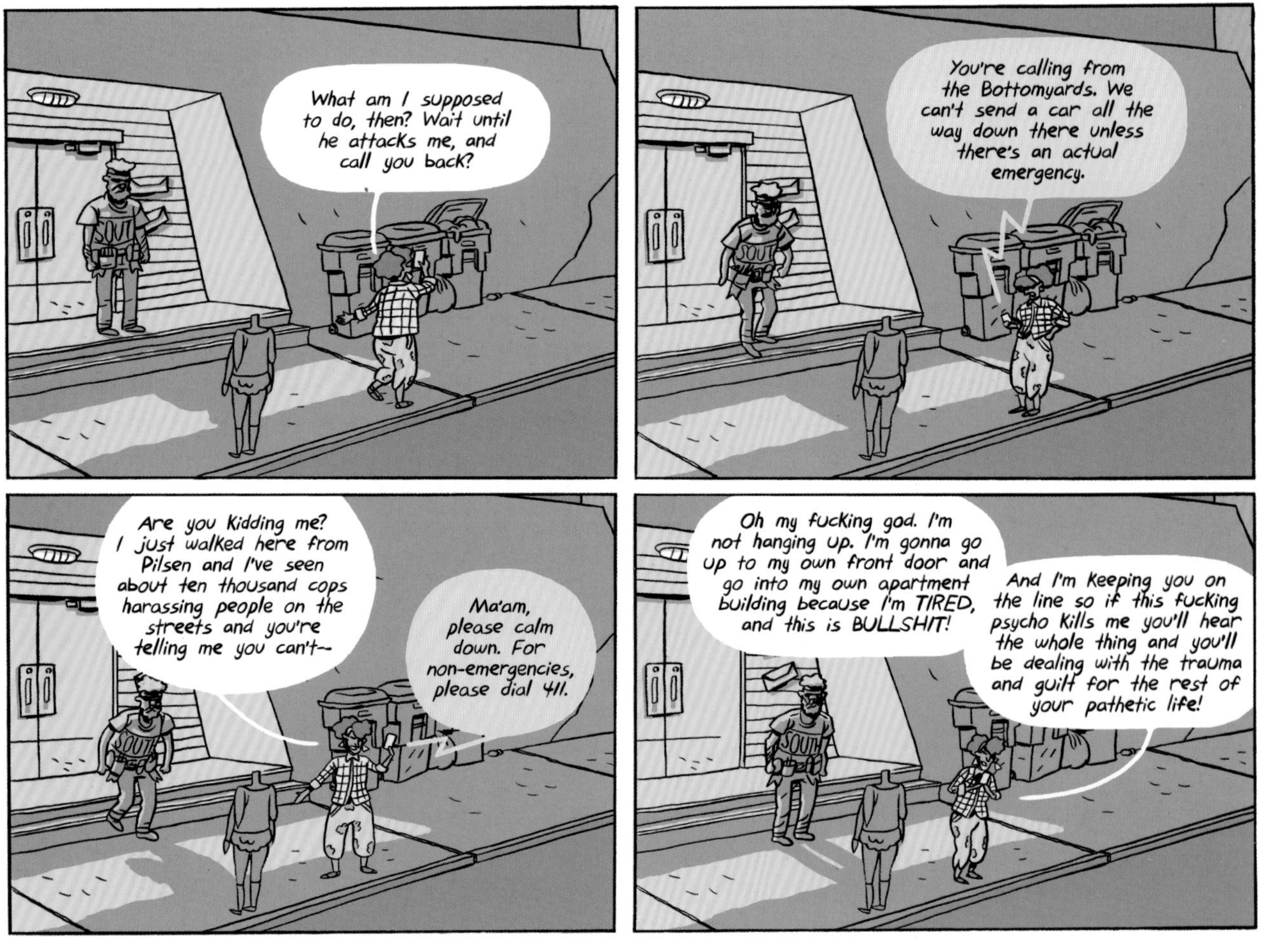

What am I supposed to do, then? Wait until he attacks me, and call you back?
You're calling from the Bottomyards. We can't send a car all the way down there unless there's an actual emergency.
SOUT
Are you kidding me? I just walked here from Pilsen and I've seen about ten thousand cops harassing people on the streets and you're telling me you can't--
Ma'am, please calm down. For non-emergencies, please dial 411.
Oh my fucking god. I'm not hanging up. I'm gonna go up to my own front door and go into my own apartment building because I'm TIRED, and this is BULLSHIT!
And I'm keeping you on the line so if this fucking psycho kills me you'll hear the whole thing and you'll be dealing with the trauma and guilt for the rest of your pathetic life!

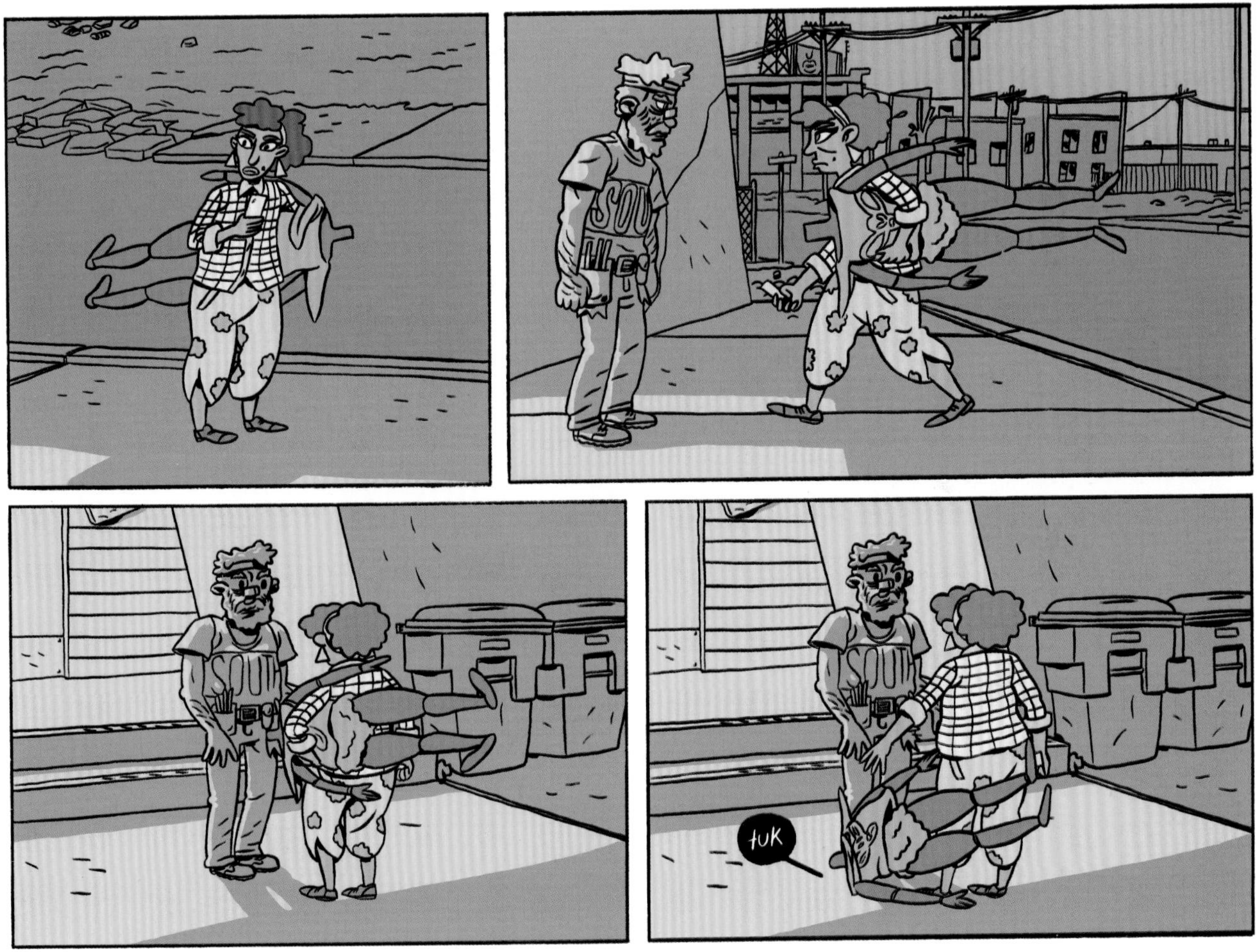
tuk

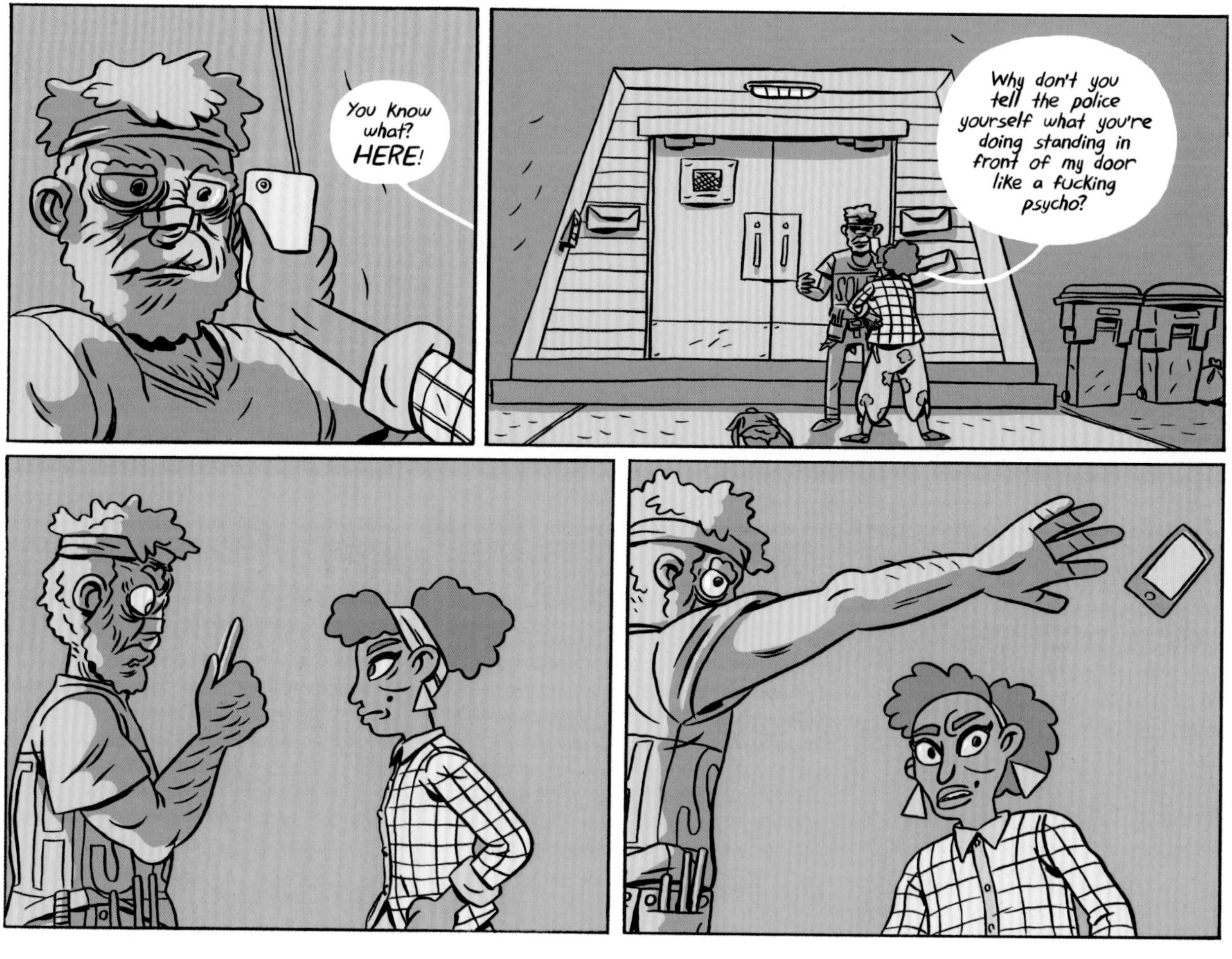
You know what? HERE!
Why don't you tell the police yourself what you're doing standing in front of my door like a fucking psycho?

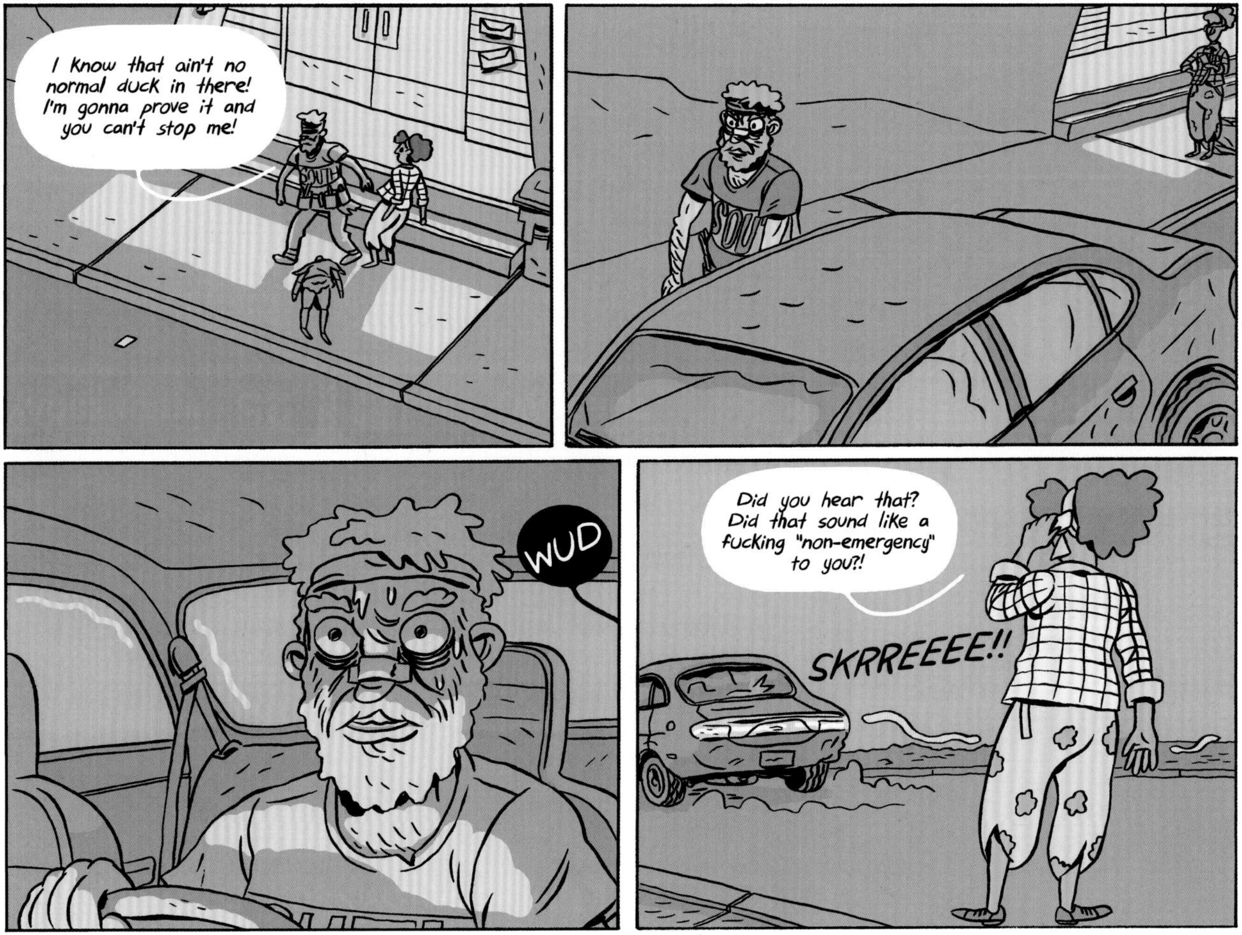

I know that ain't no normal duck in there! I'm gonna prove it and you can't stop me!
WUD
Did you hear that? Did that sound like a fucking "non-emergency" to you?!
SKRREEEE!!

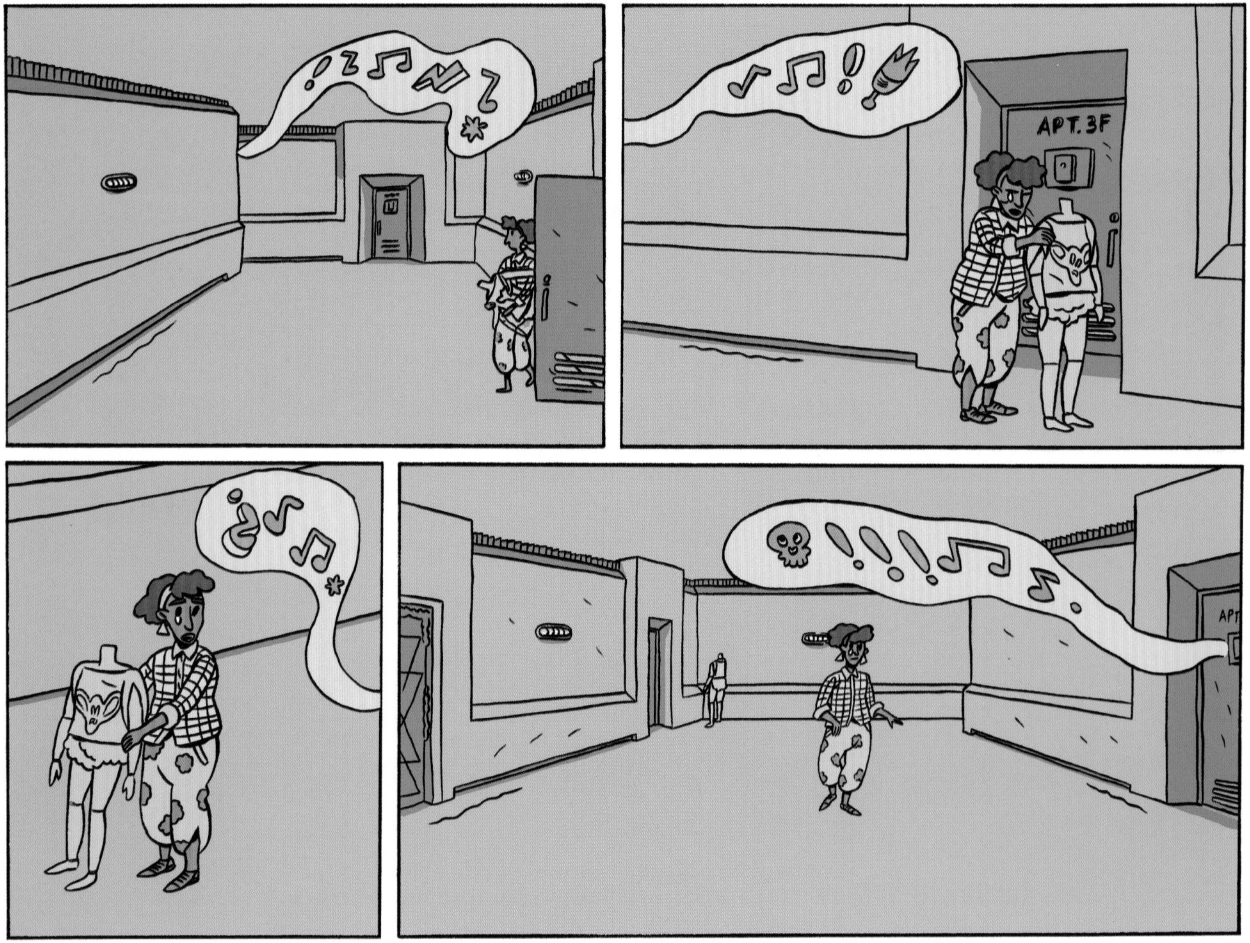
APT. 3F

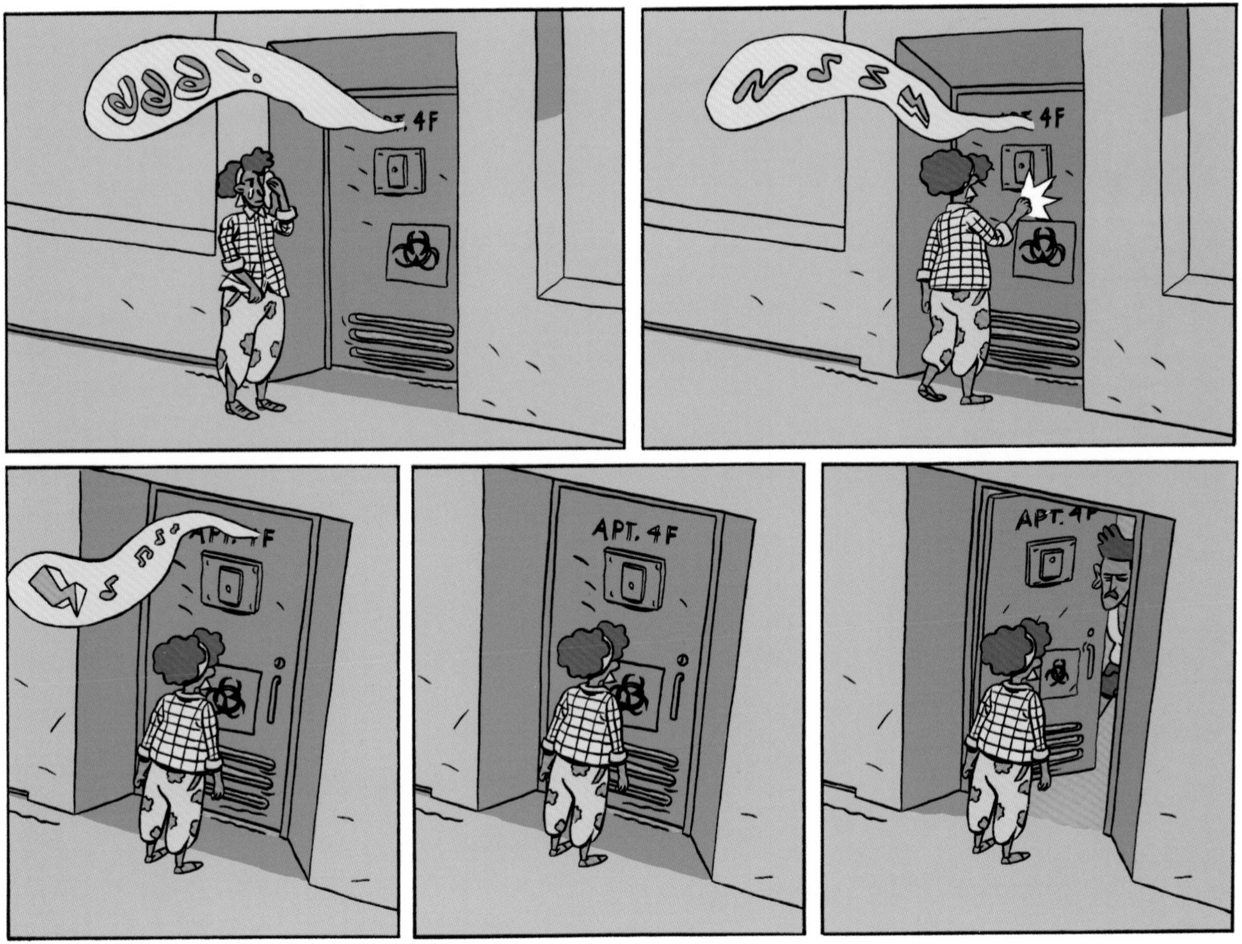
APT. 4F

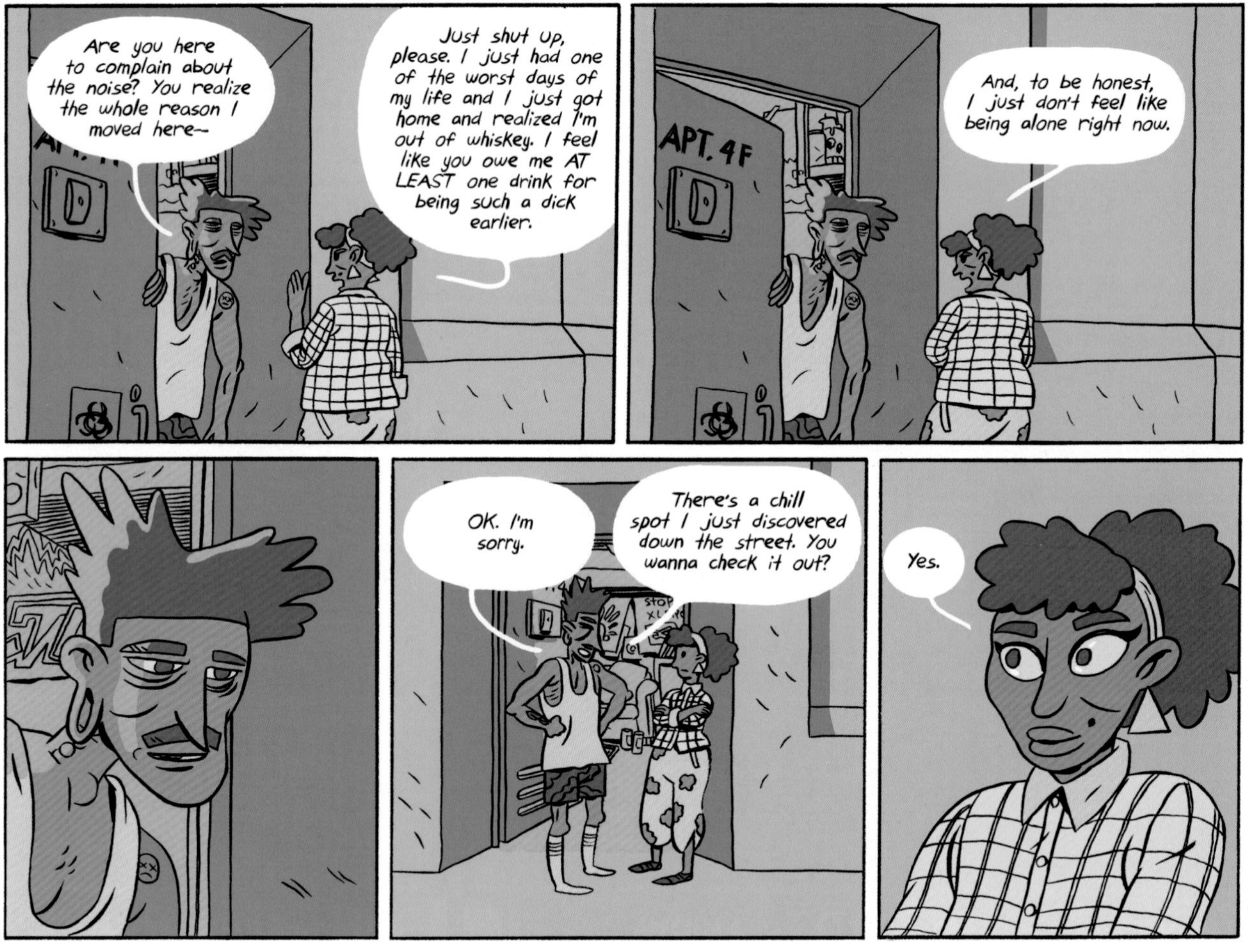
Are you here to complain about the noise? You realize the whole reason I moved here—
Just shut up, please. I just had one of the worst days of my life and I just got home and realized I'm out of whiskey. I feel like you owe me AT LEAST one drink for being such a dick earlier.
APT. 4F
And, to be honest, I just don't feel like being alone right now.
OK. I'm sorry.
There's a chill spot I just discovered down the street. You wanna check it out?
Yes.

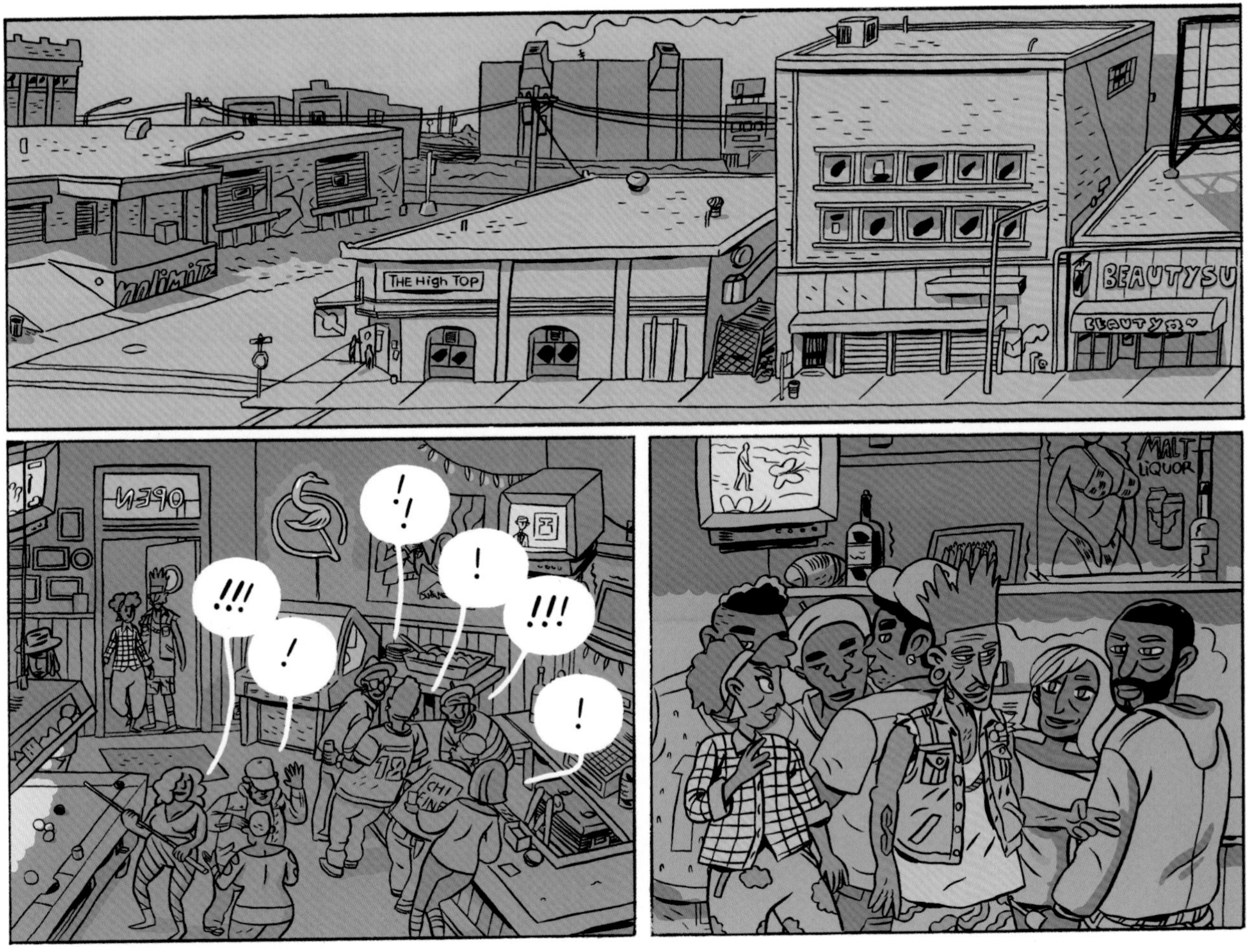
THE High TOP
BEAUTYSU
OPEN
!
!
!!!
!
!
!!!
!
MALT
LIQUOR

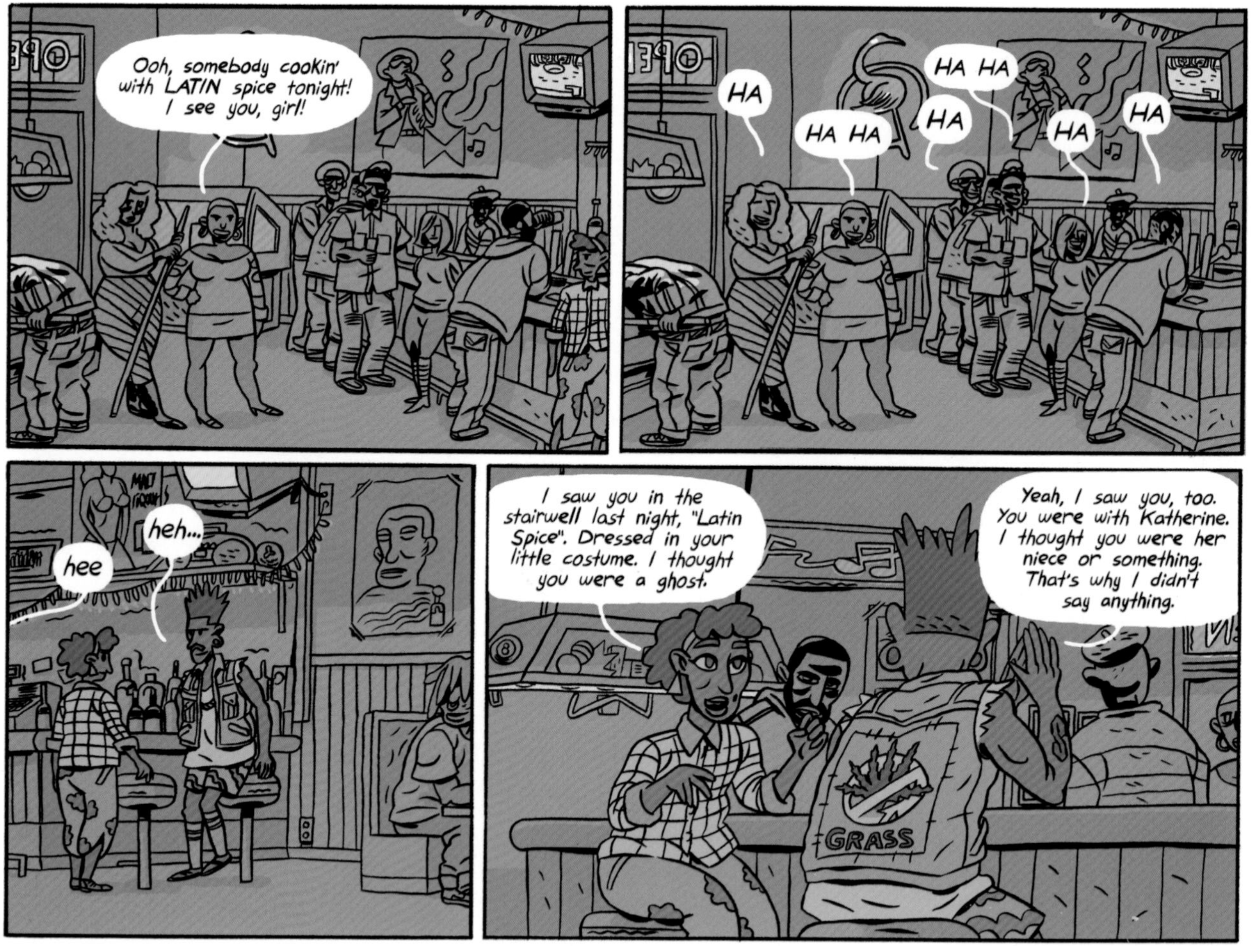
Ooh, somebody cookin' with LATIN spice tonight! I see you, girl!
HA
HA HA
HA HA
HA
HA
HA
hee
heh...
I saw you in the stairwell last night, "Latin Spice". Dressed in your little costume. I thought you were a ghost.
Yeah, I saw you, too. You were with Katherine. I thought you were her niece or something. That's why I didn't say anything.
GRASS

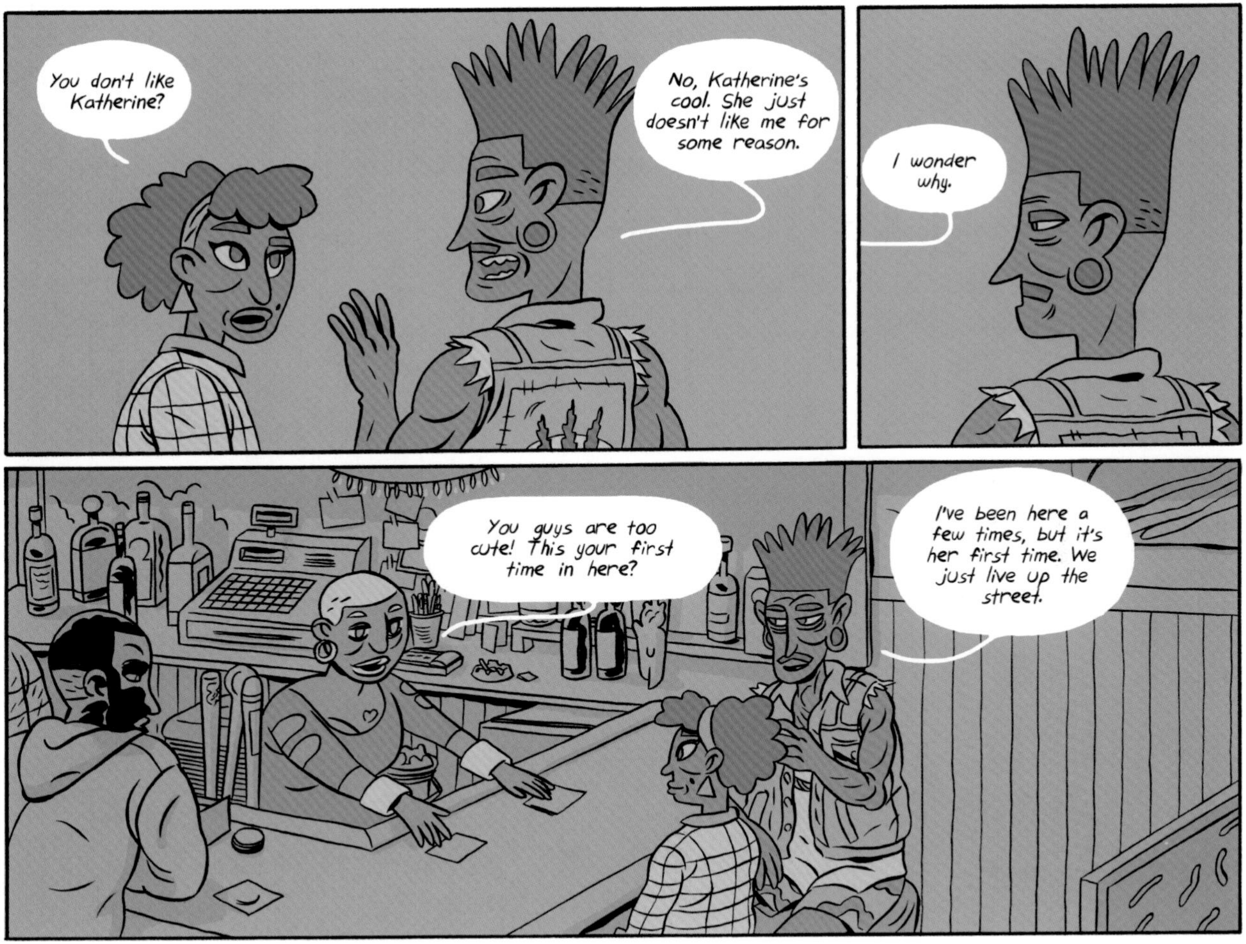
You don't like Katherine?
No, Katherine's cool. She just doesn't like me for some reason.
I wonder why.
You guys are too cute! This your first time in here?
I've been here a few times, but it's her first time. We just live up the street.

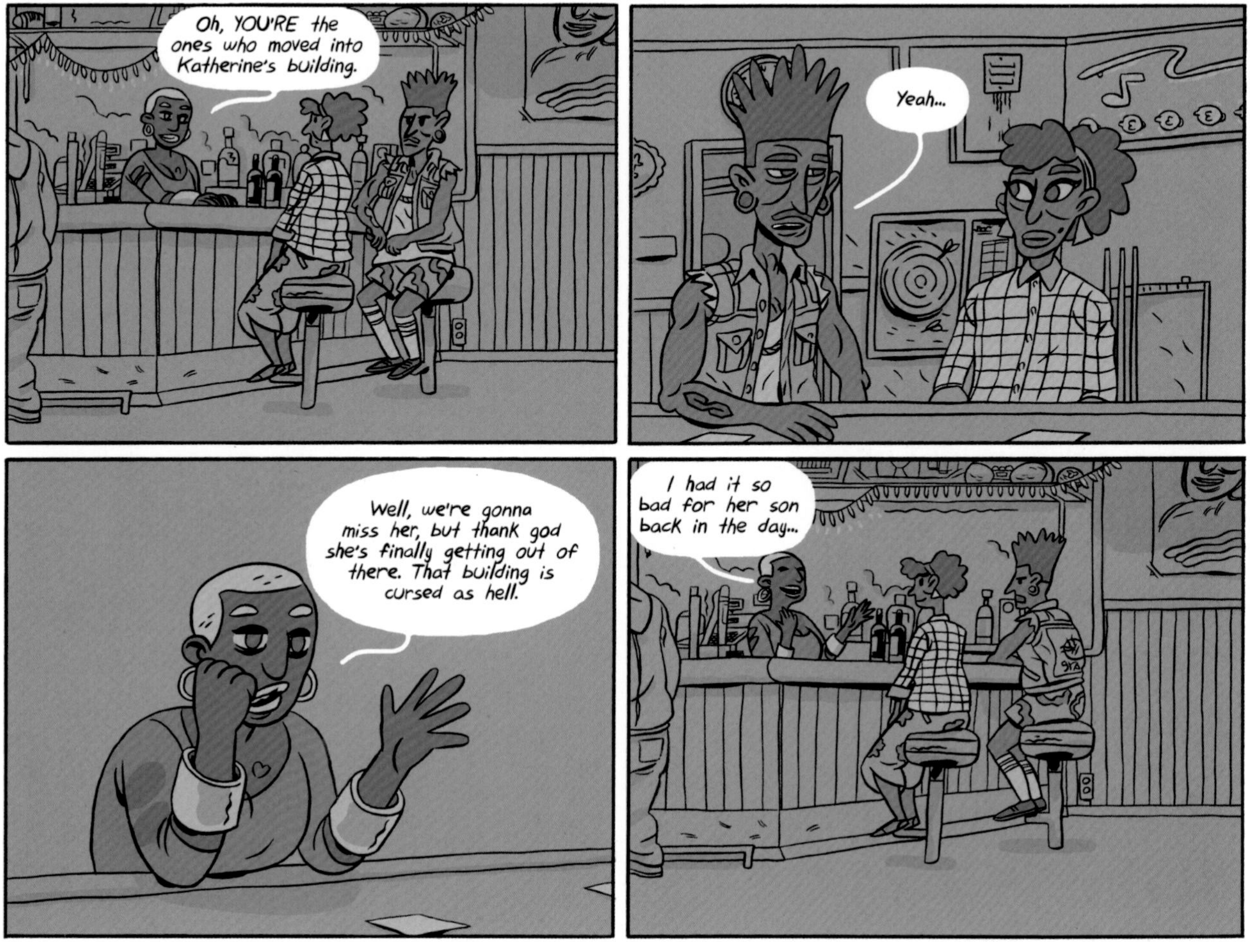
Oh, YOU'RE the ones who moved into Katherine's building.
Yeah...
Well, we're gonna miss her, but thank god she's finally getting out of there. That building is cursed as hell.
I had it so bad for her son back in the day...

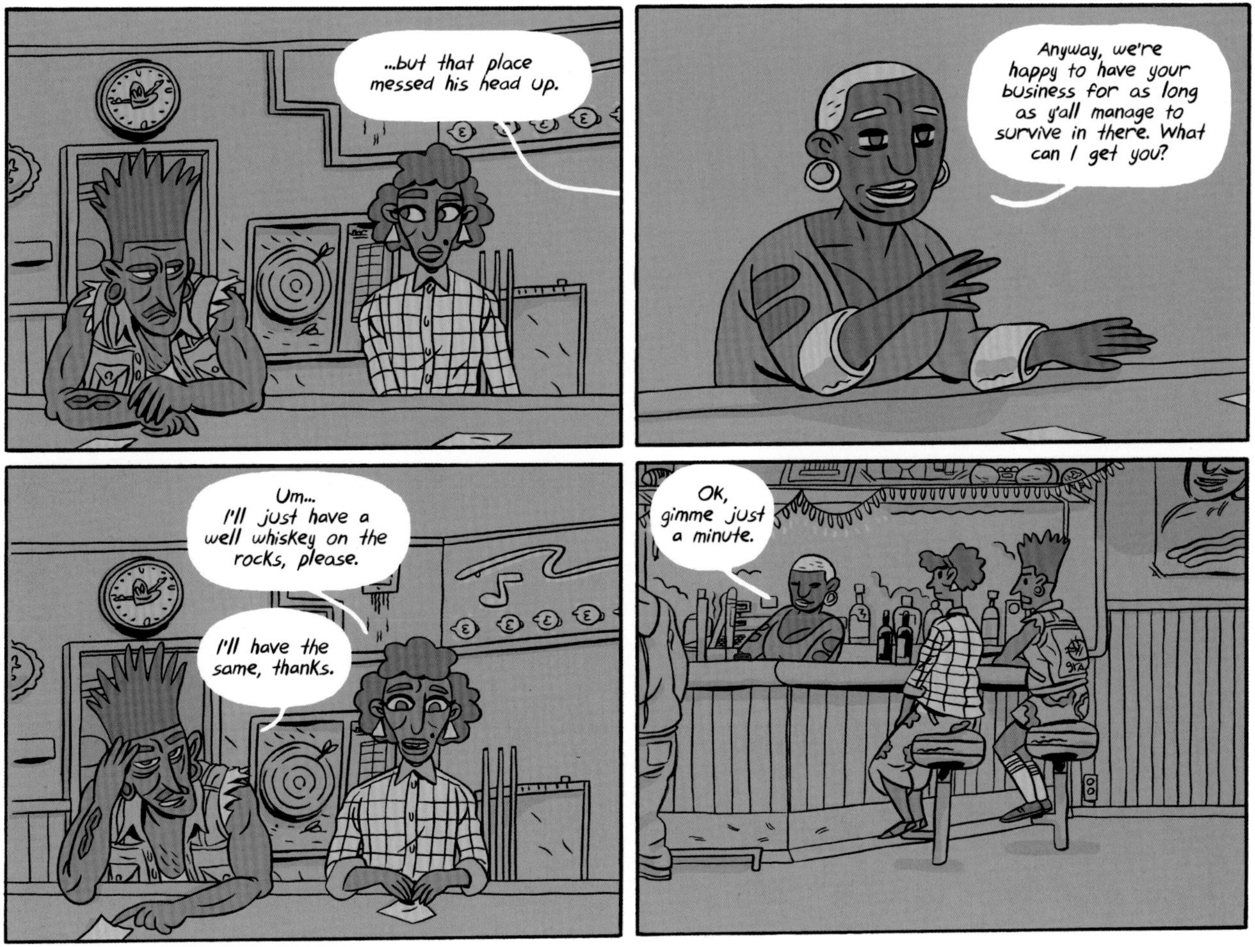
...but that place messed his head up.
Anyway, we're happy to have your business for as long as y'all manage to survive in there. What can I get you?
Um... I'll just have a well whiskey on the rocks, please.
I'll have the same, thanks.
OK, gimme just a minute.

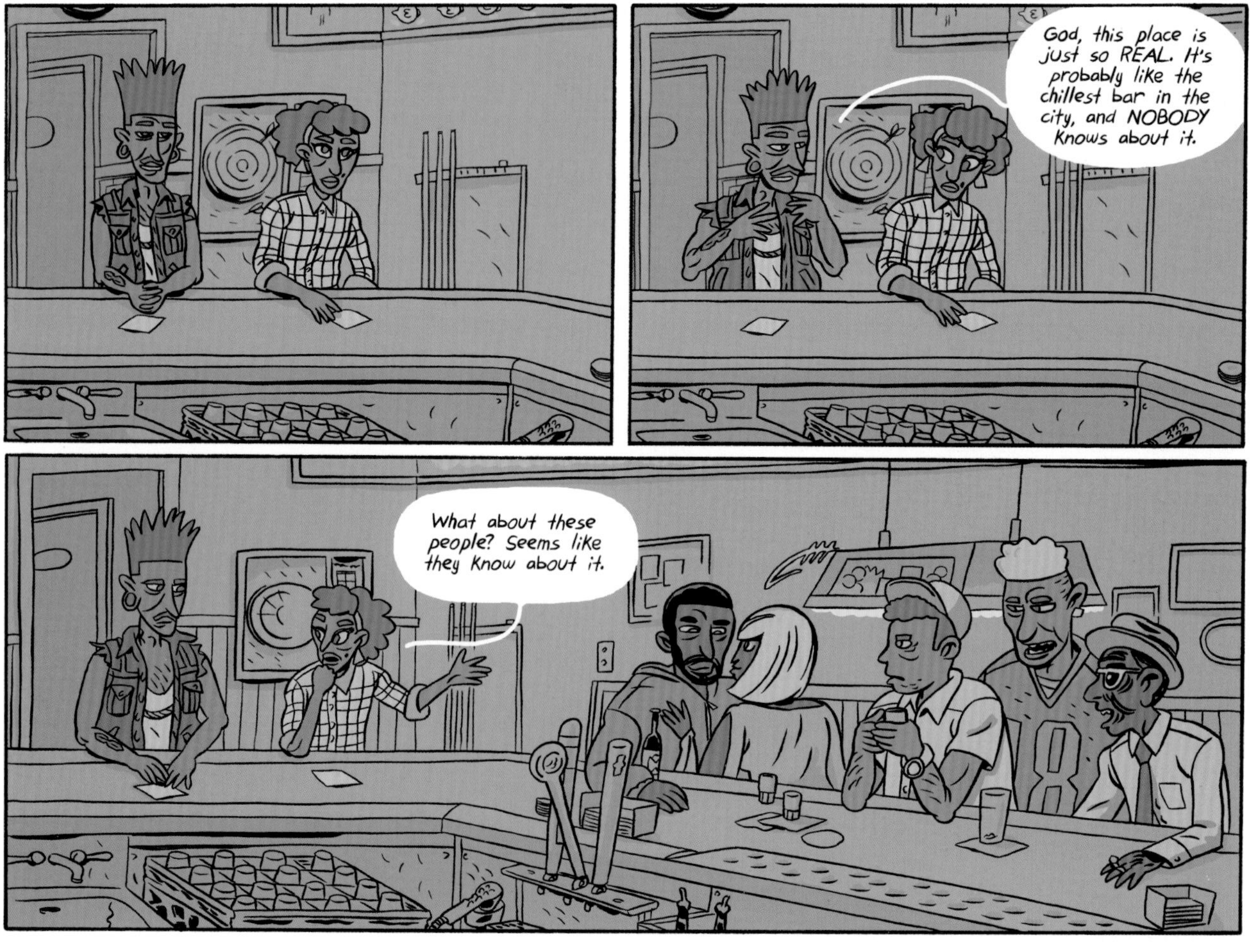
God, this place is just so REAL. It's probably like the chillest bar in the city, and NOBODY knows about it.
What about these people? Seems like they know about it.

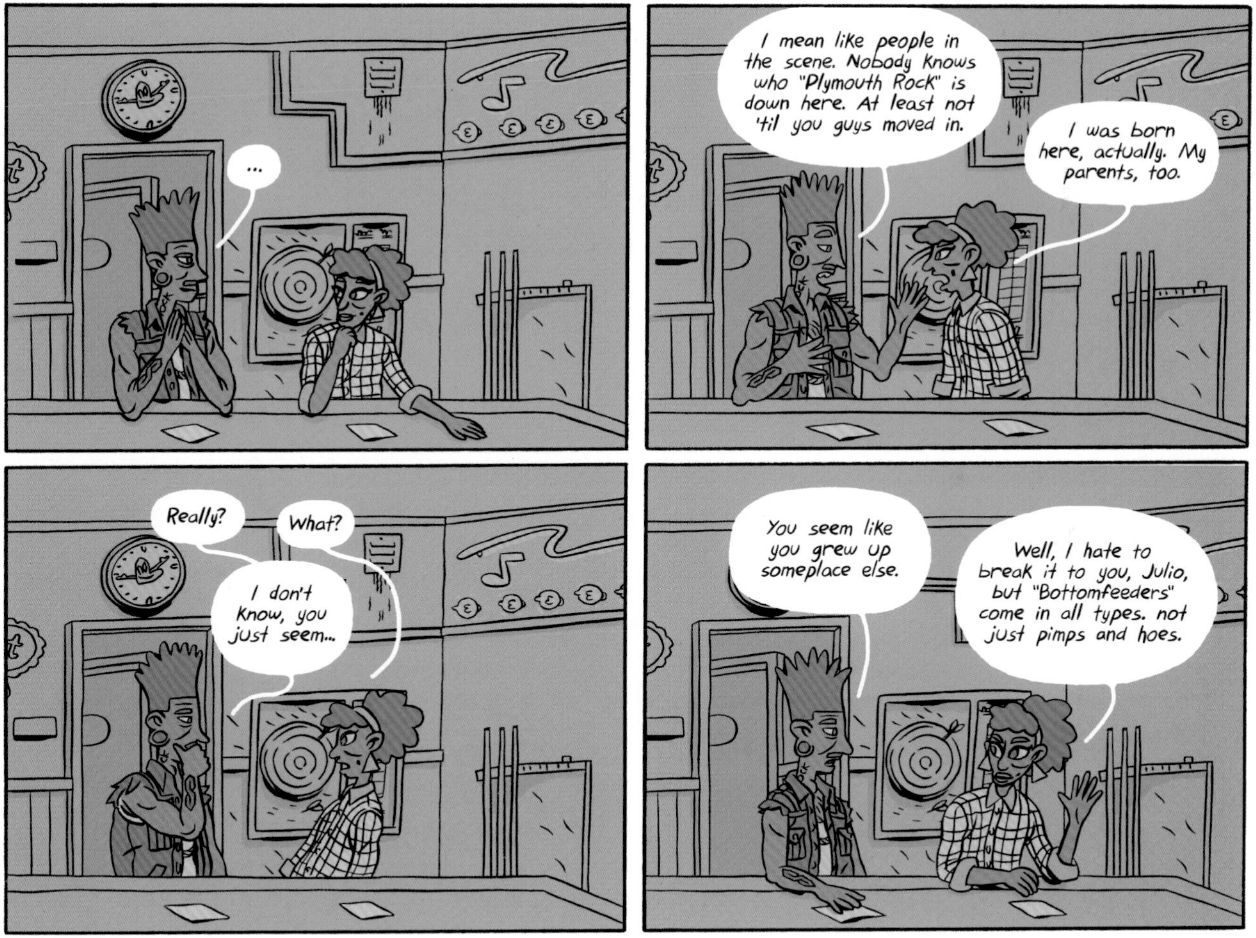
...
I mean like people in the scene. Nobody knows who "Plymouth Rock" is down here. At least not 'til you guys moved in.
I was born here, actually. My parents, too.
Really?
What?
I don't know, you just seem...
You seem like you grew up someplace else.
Well, I hate to break it to you, Julio, but "Bottomfeeders" come in all types. not just pimps and hoes.

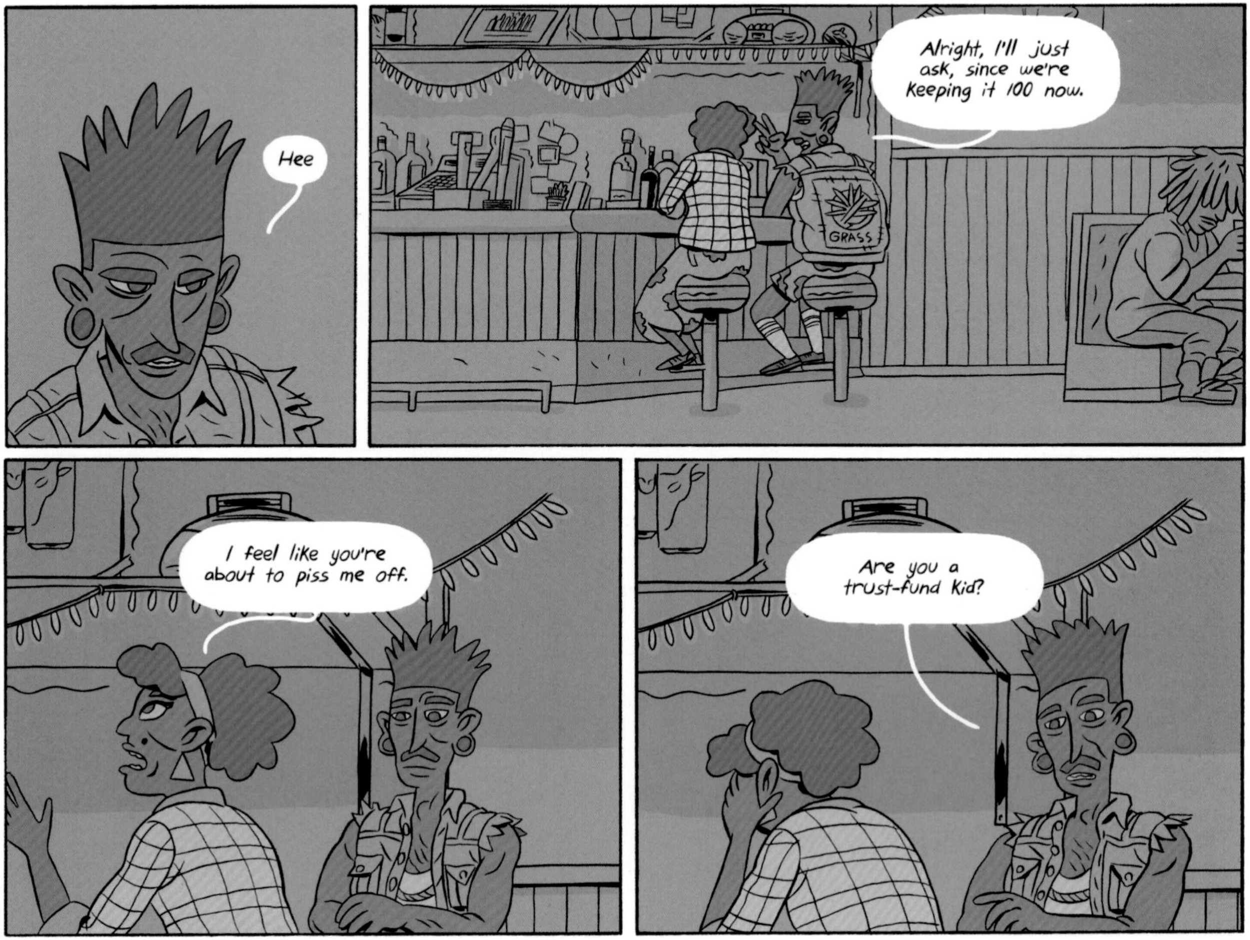
Hee
Alright, I'll just ask, since we're keeping it 100 now.
GRASS
I feel like you're about to piss me off.
Are you a trust-fund kid?

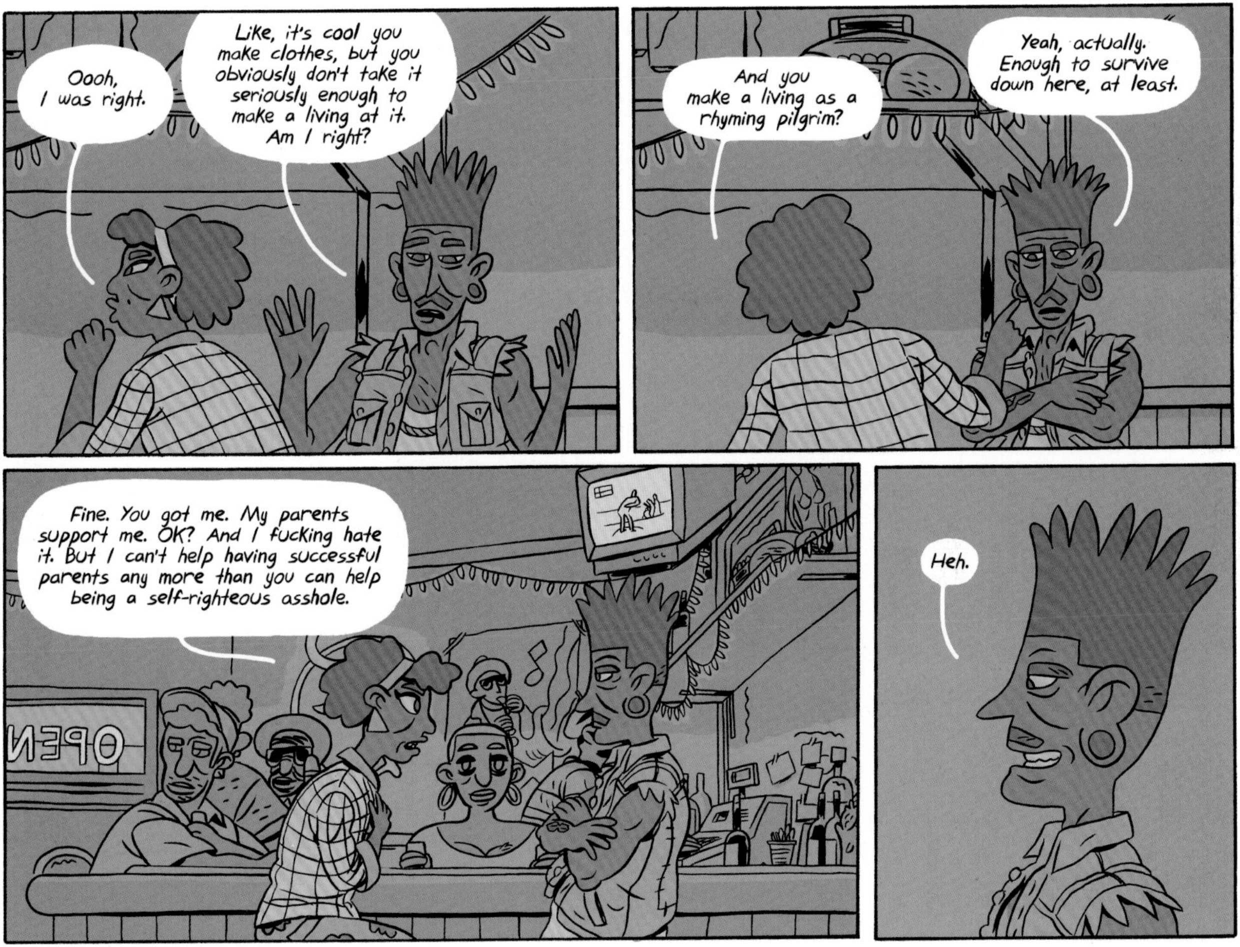
Oooh, I was right.
Like, it's cool you make clothes, but you obviously don't take it seriously enough to make a living at it. Am I right?
And you make a living as a rhyming pilgrim?
Yeah, actually. Enough to survive down here, at least.
Fine. You got me. My parents support me. OK? And I fucking hate it. But I can't help having successful parents any more than you can help being a self-righteous asshole.
OPEN
Heh.

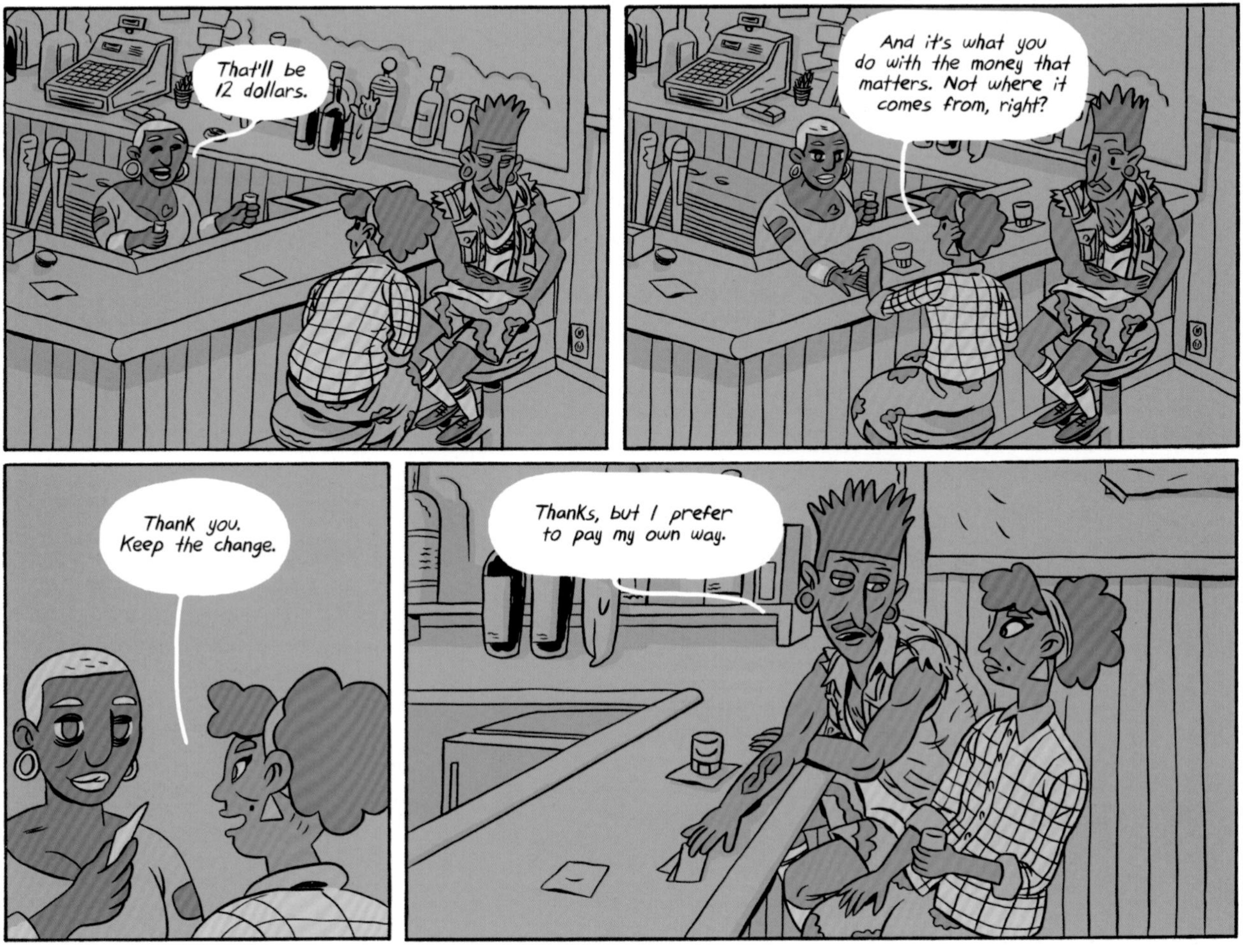
That'll be 12 dollars.
And it's what you do with the money that matters. Not where it comes from, right?
Thank you. Keep the change.
Thanks, but I prefer to pay my own way.

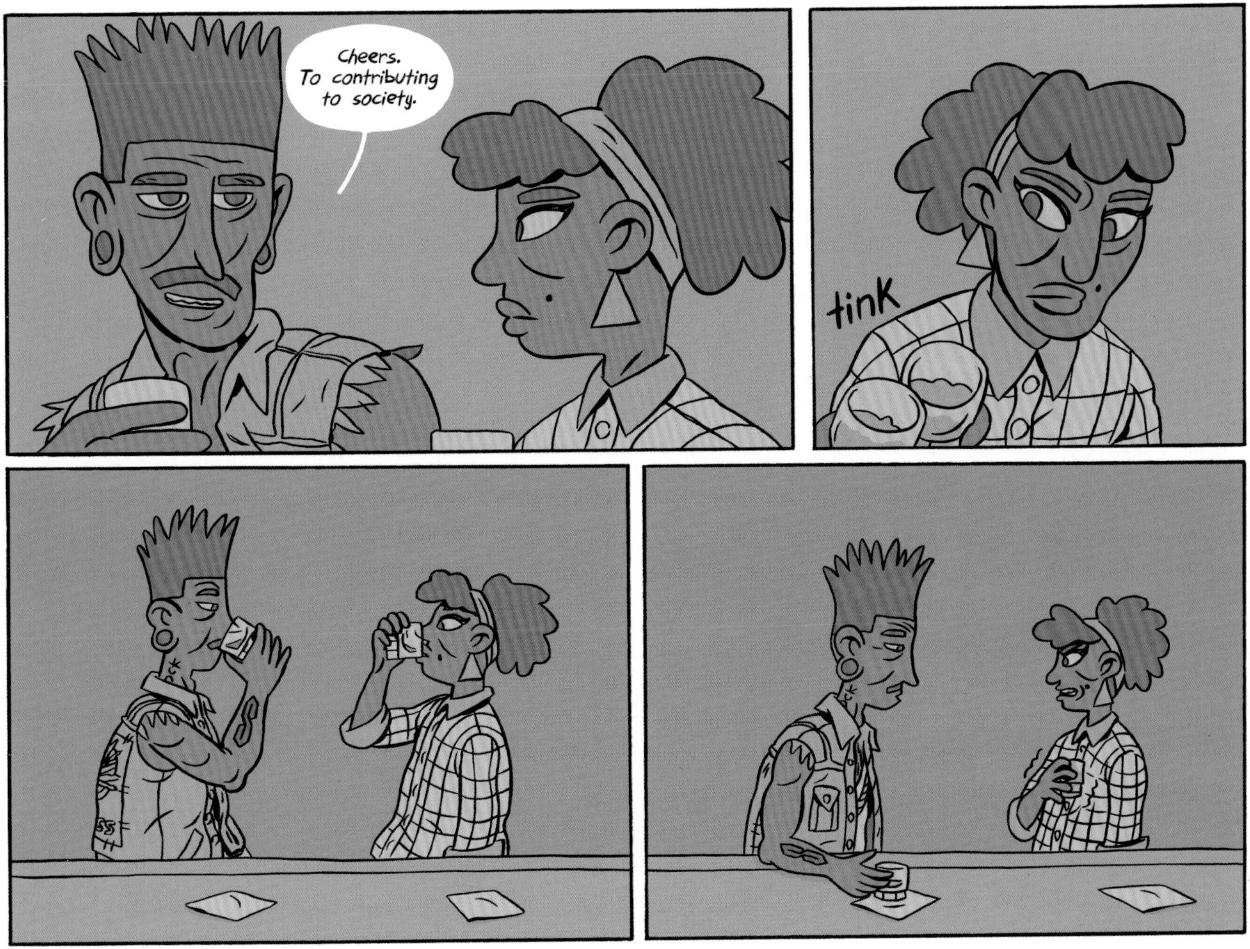
Cheers. To contributing to society.
tink

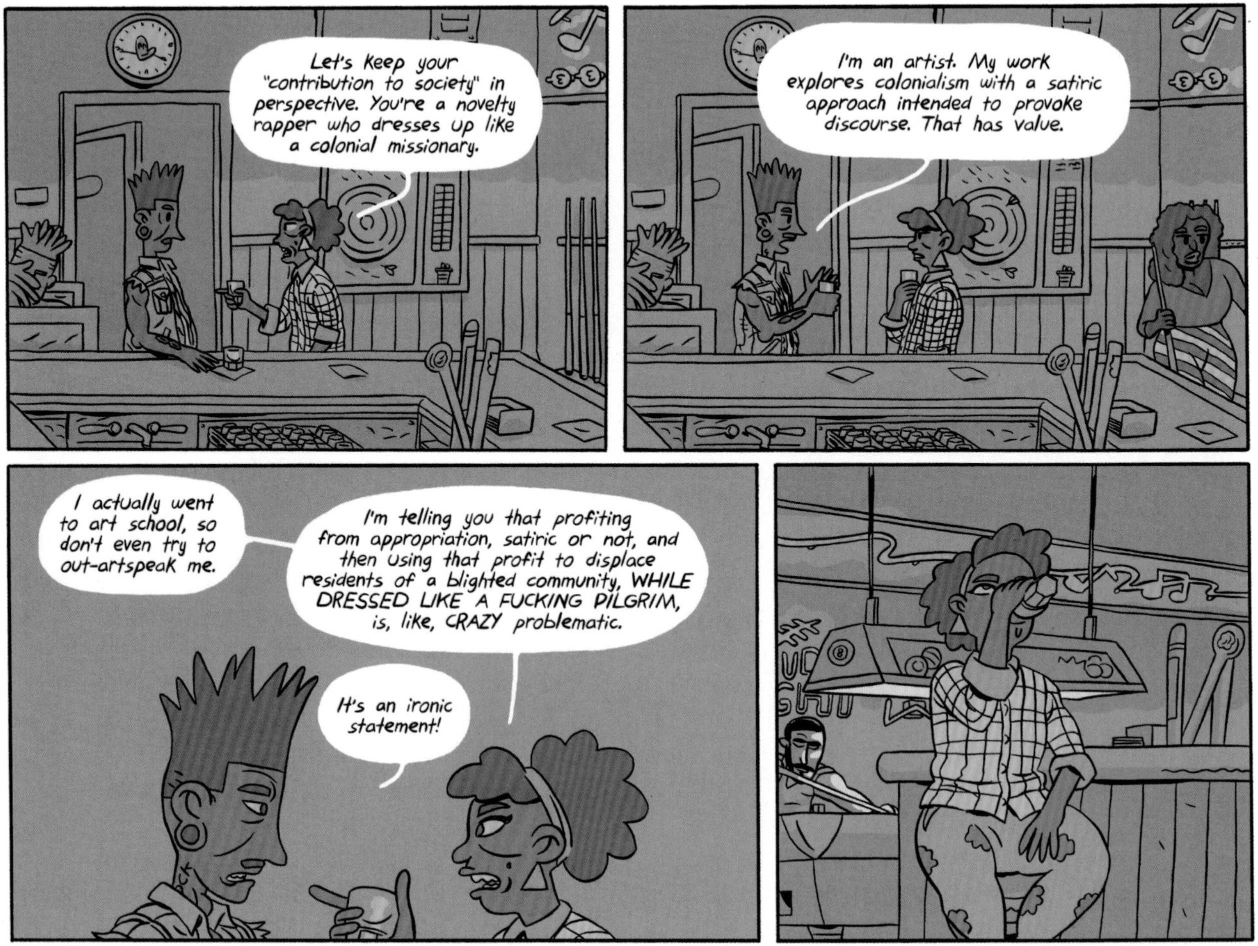
Let's keep your "contribution to society" in perspective. You're a novelty rapper who dresses up like a colonial missionary.
I'm an artist. My work explores colonialism with a satiric approach intended to provoke discourse. That has value.
I actually went to art school, so don't even try to out-artspeak me.
I'm telling you that profiting from appropriation, satiric or not, and then using that profit to displace residents of a blighted community, WHILE DRESSED LIKE A FUCKING PILGRIM, is, like, CRAZY problematic.
It's an ironic statement!

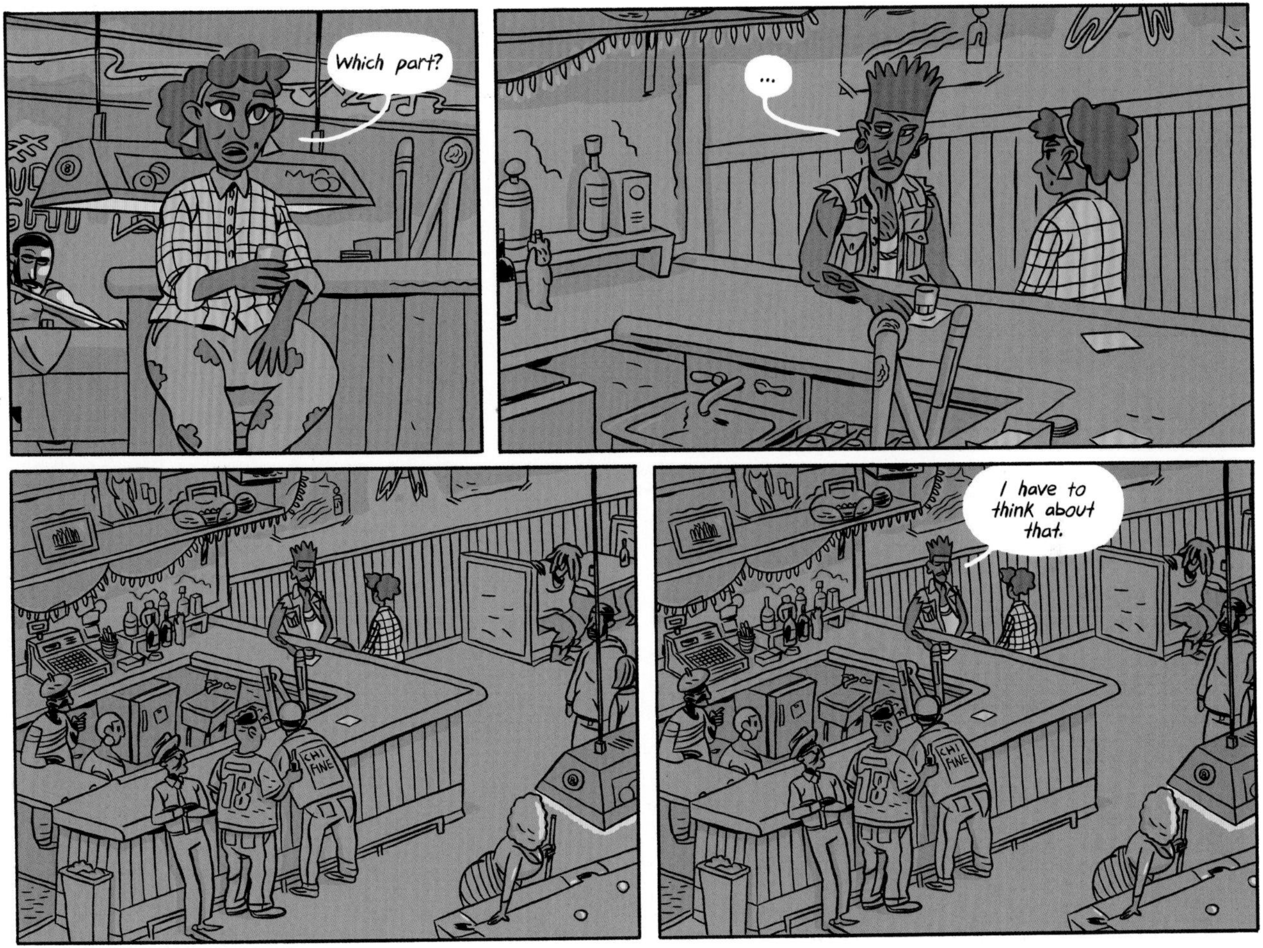
Which part?
...
I have to think about that.
CHI FINE
18

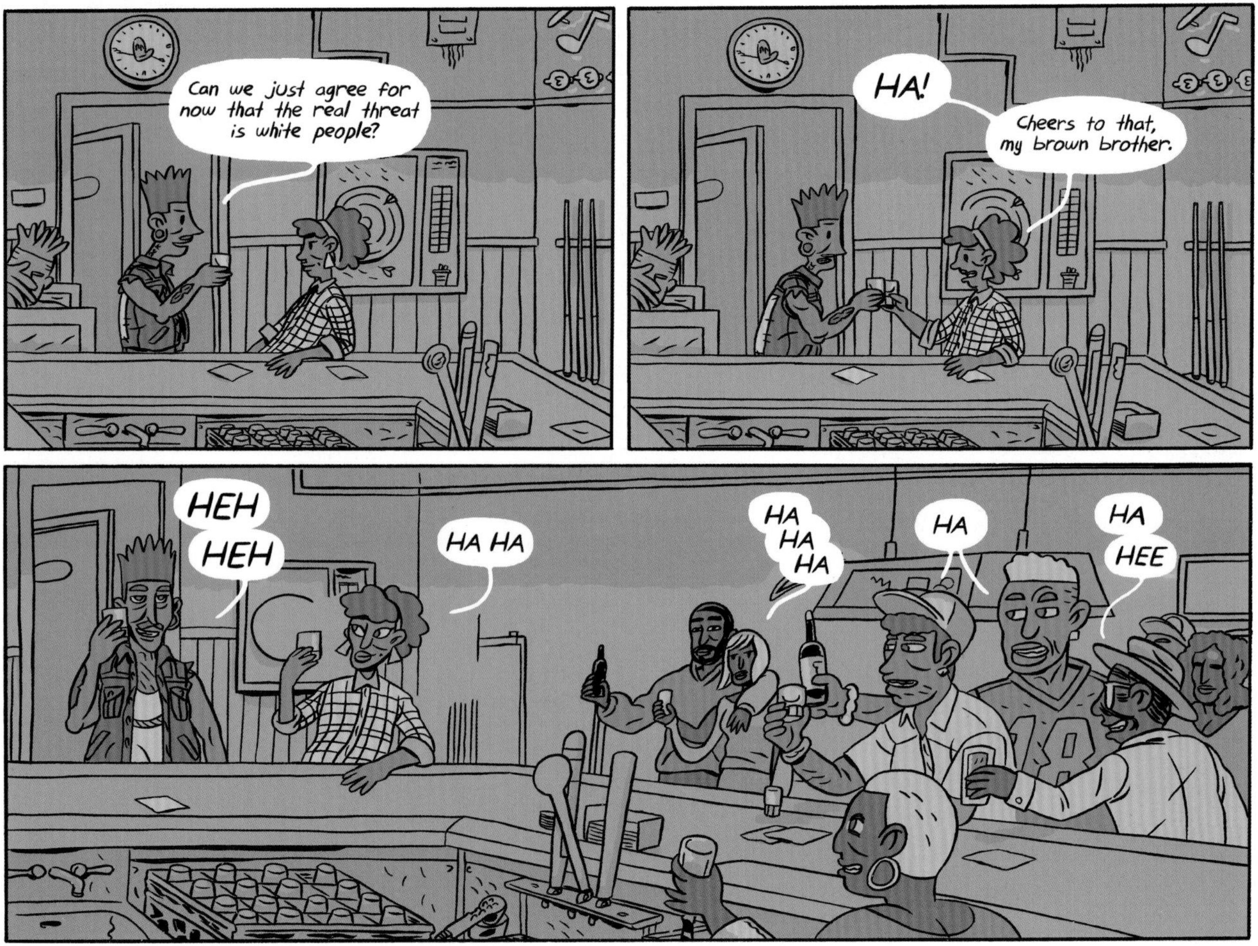
Can we just agree for now that the real threat is white people?
HA!
Cheers to that, my brown brother.
HEH
HEH
HA HA
HA
HA
HA
HA
HA
HEE

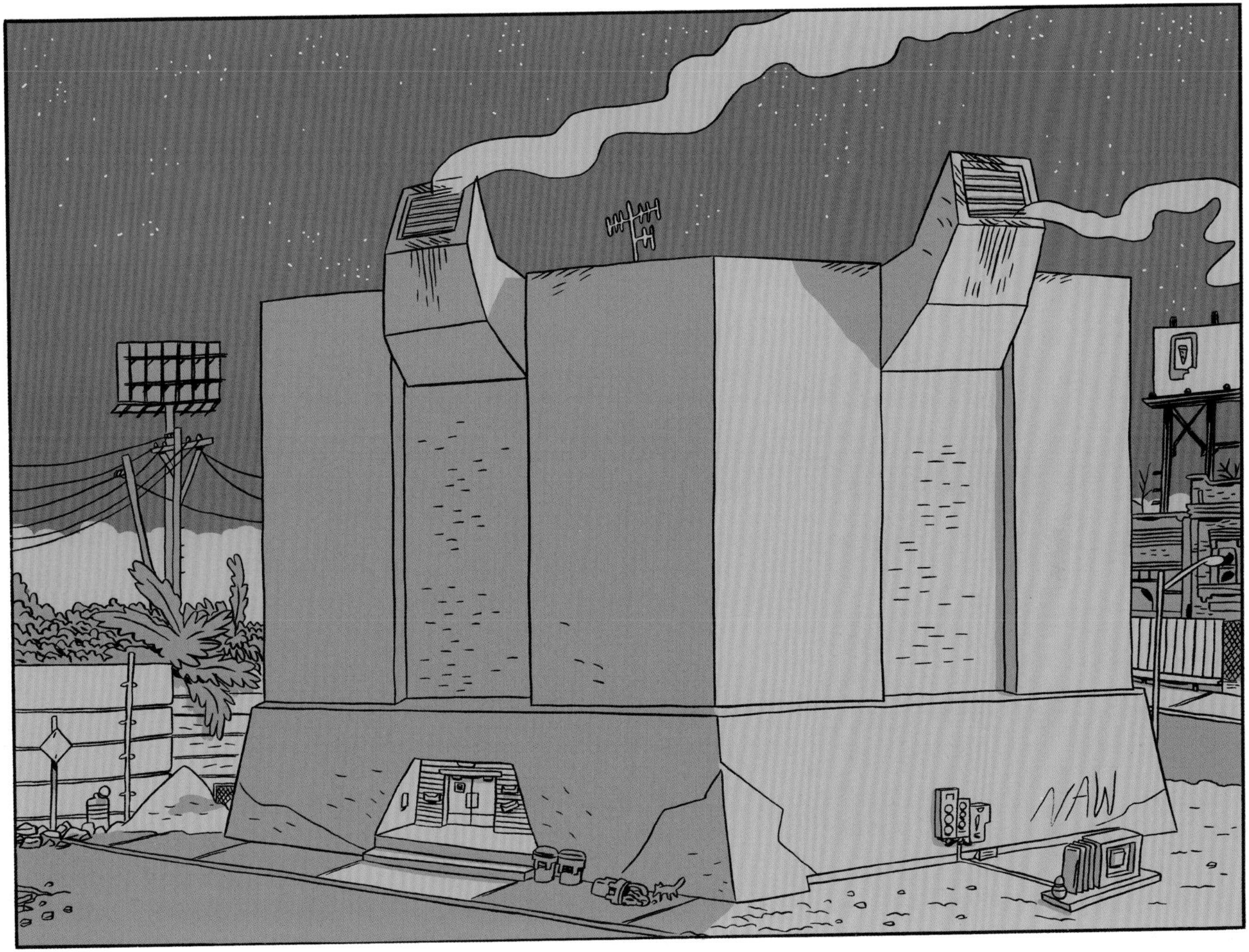
NAW

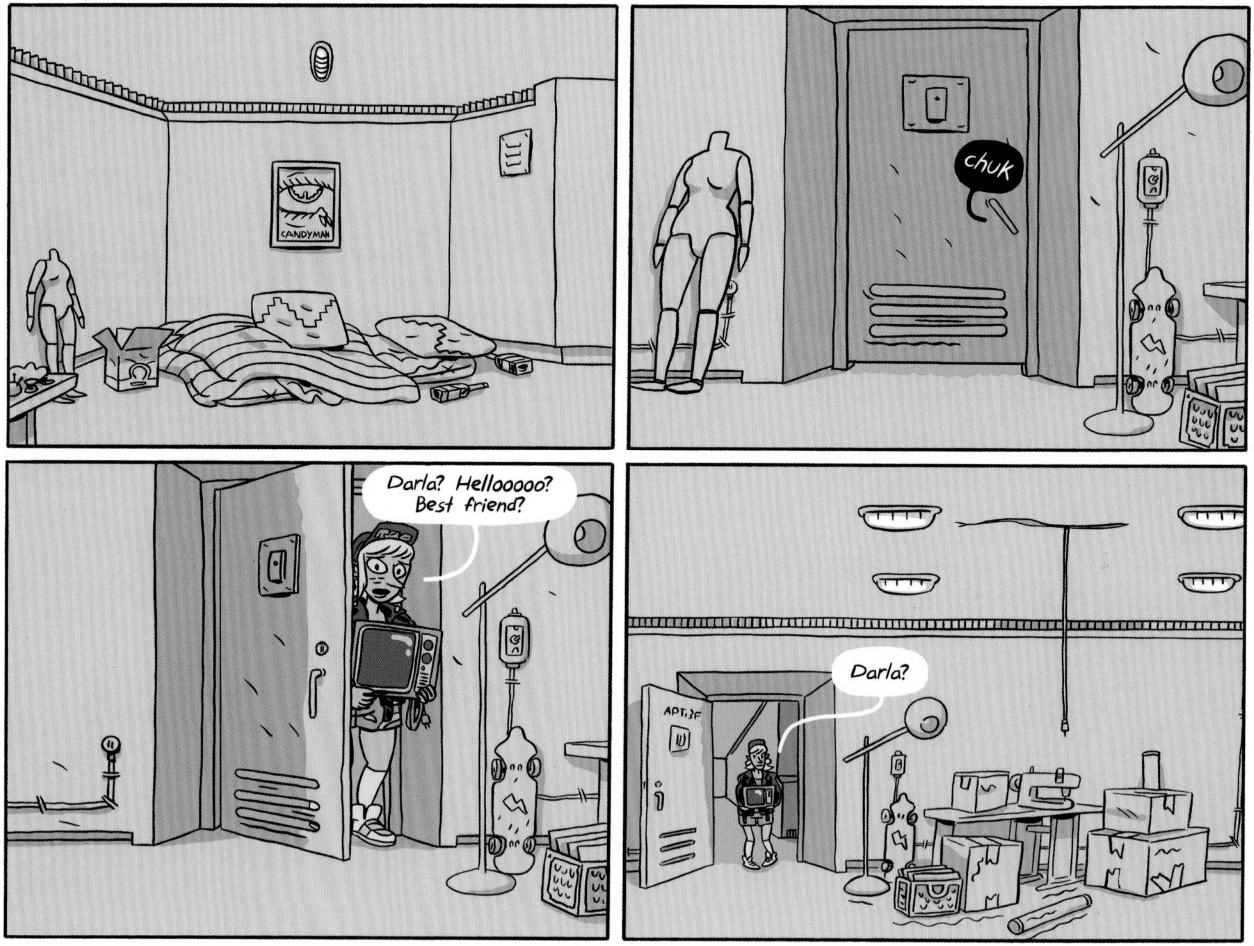
CANDYMAN
chuk
Darla? Hellooooo? Best friend?
APT. 3F
Darla?

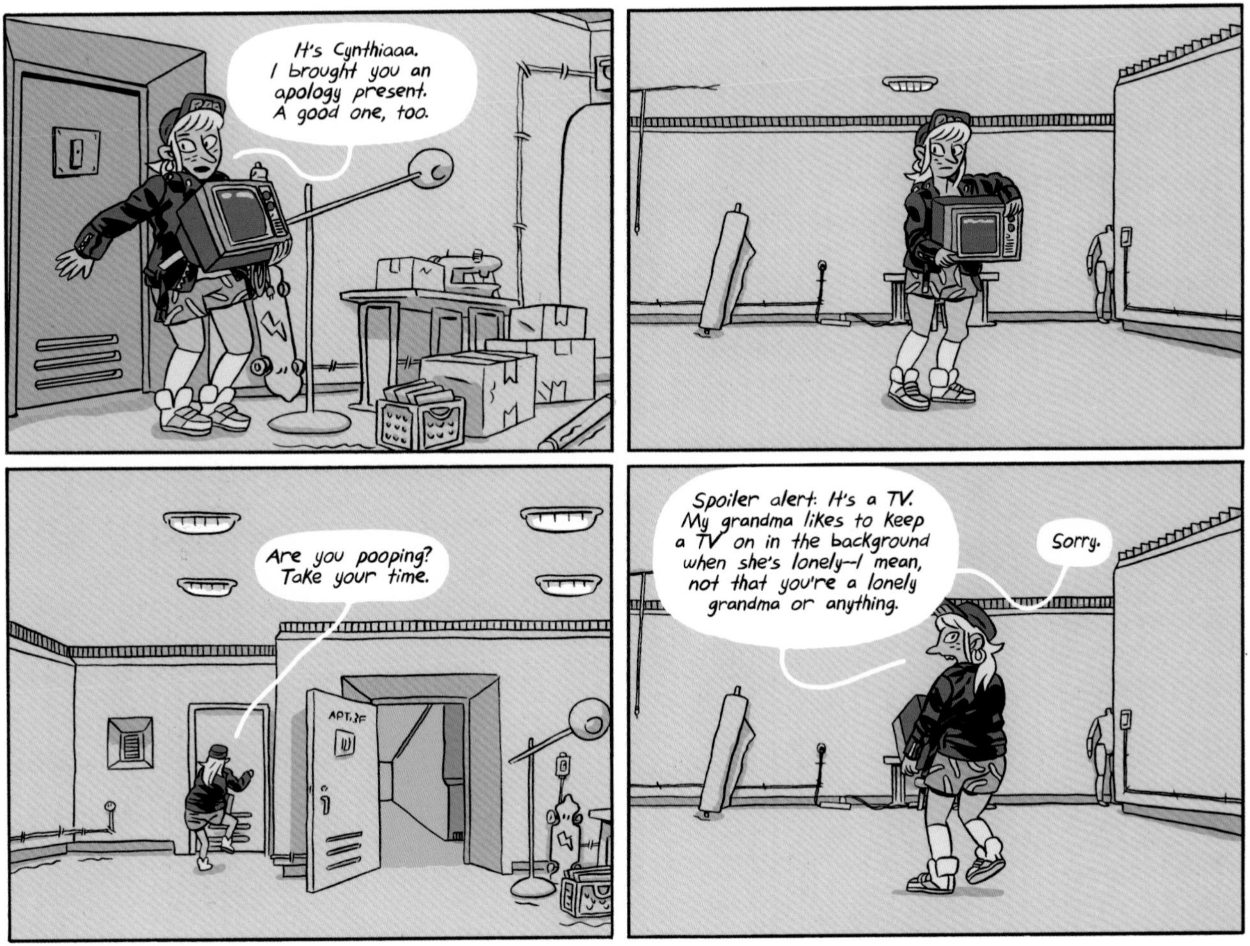
It's Cynthiaaa. I brought you an apology present. A good one, too.
APT. 3F
Are you pooping? Take your time.
Spoiler alert: It's a TV. My grandma likes to keep a TV on in the background when she's lonely--I mean, not that you're a lonely grandma or anything.
Sorry.

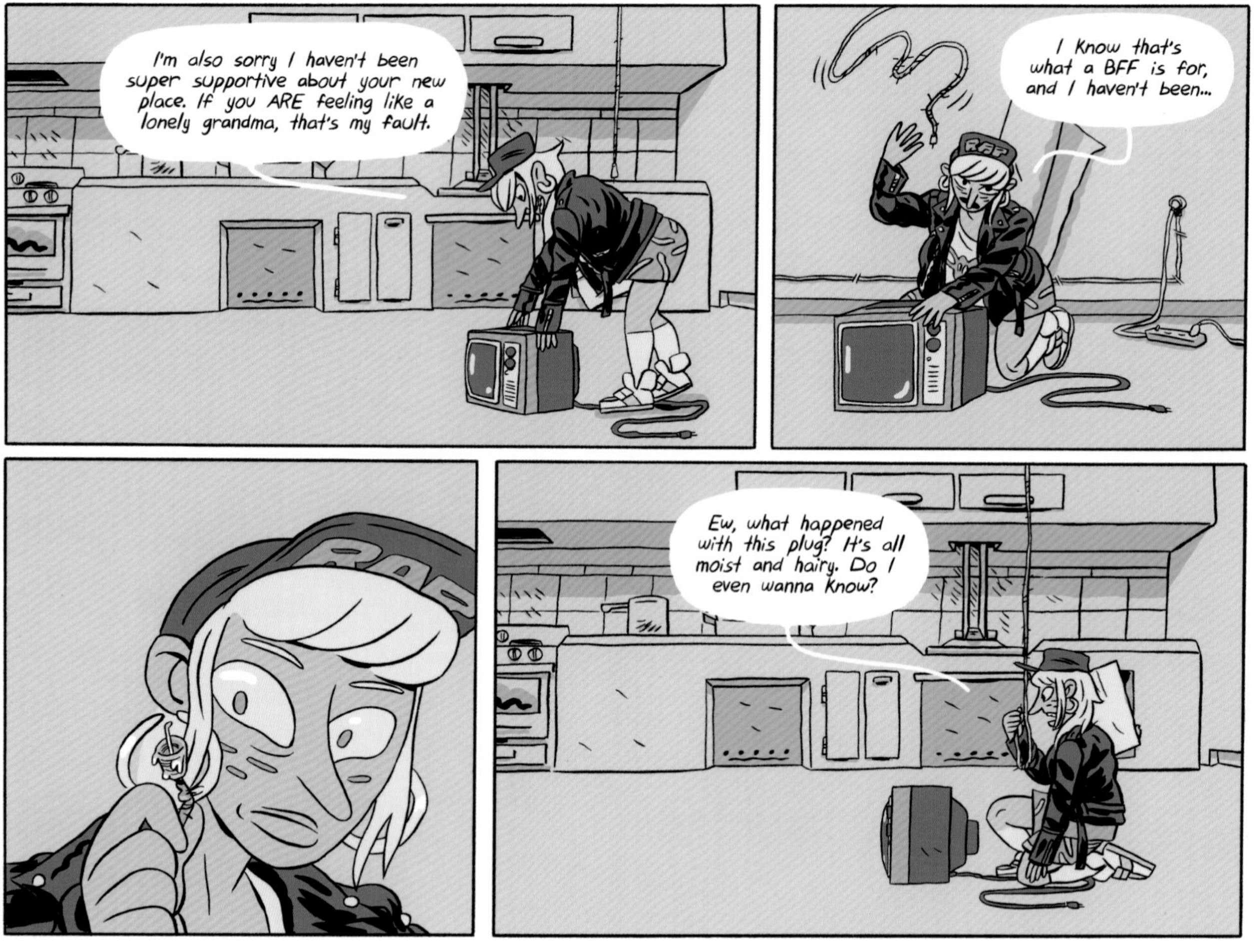
I'm also sorry I haven't been super supportive about your new place. If you ARE feeling like a lonely grandma, that's my fault.
I know that's what a BFF is for, and I haven't been...
Ew, what happened with this plug? It's all moist and hairy. Do I even wanna know?

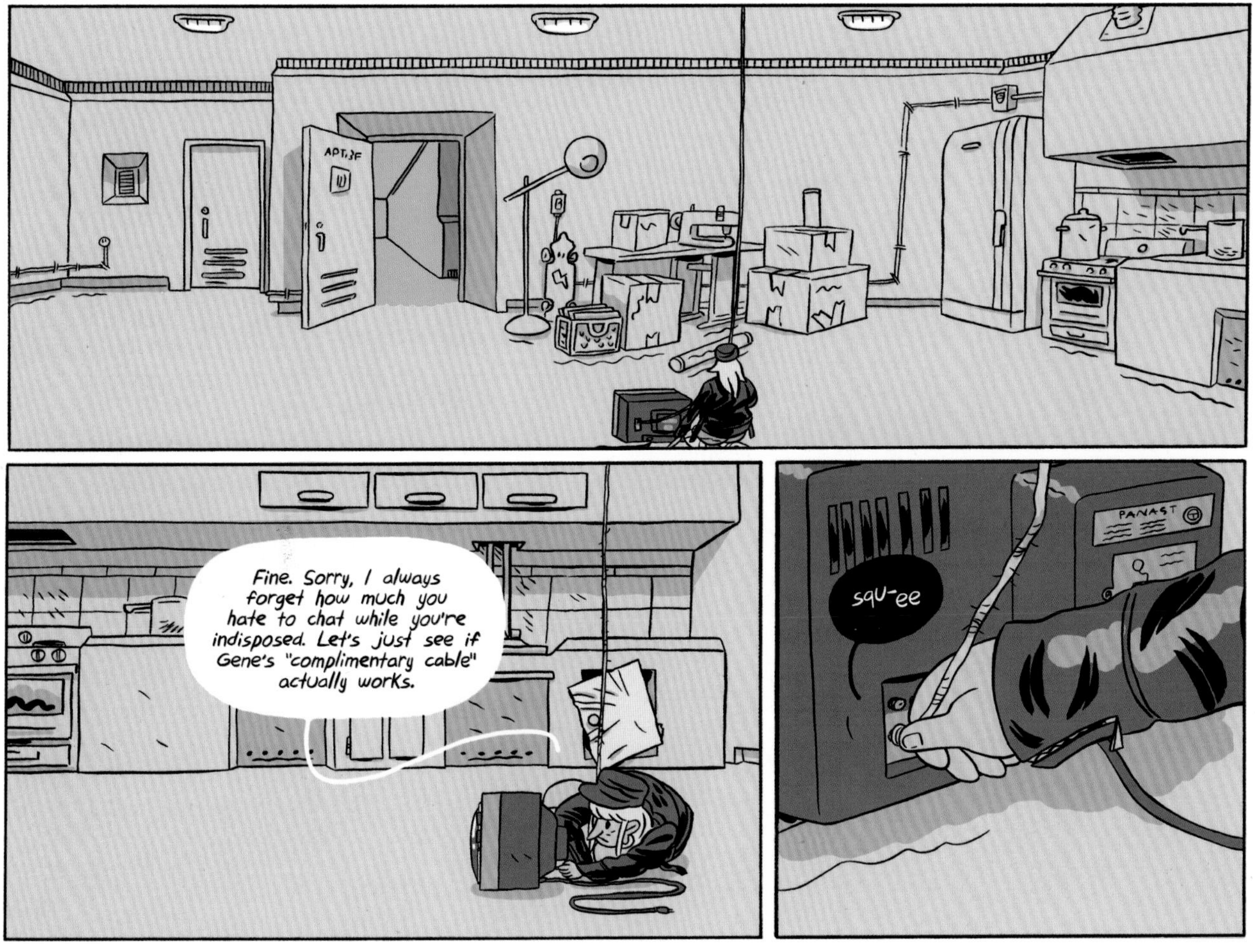
APT. 3F
Fine. Sorry, I always forget how much you hate to chat while you're indisposed. Let's just see if Gene's "complimentary cable" actually works.
squ-ee
PANAST

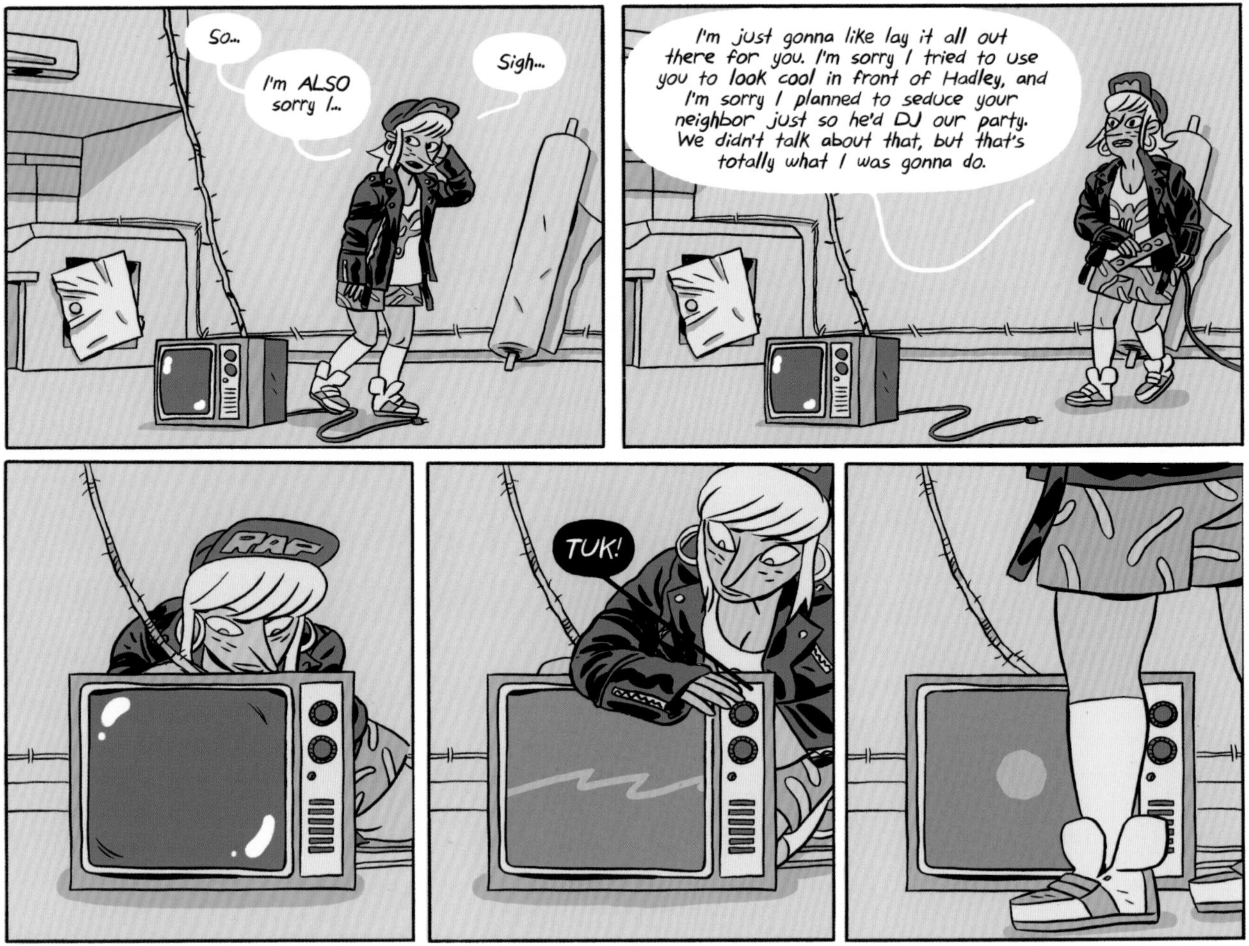
So...
I'm ALSO sorry I...
Sigh...
I'm just gonna like lay it all out there for you. I'm sorry I tried to use you to look cool in front of Hadley, and I'm sorry I planned to seduce your neighbor just so he'd DJ our party. We didn't talk about that, but that's totally what I was gonna do.
RAP
TUK!

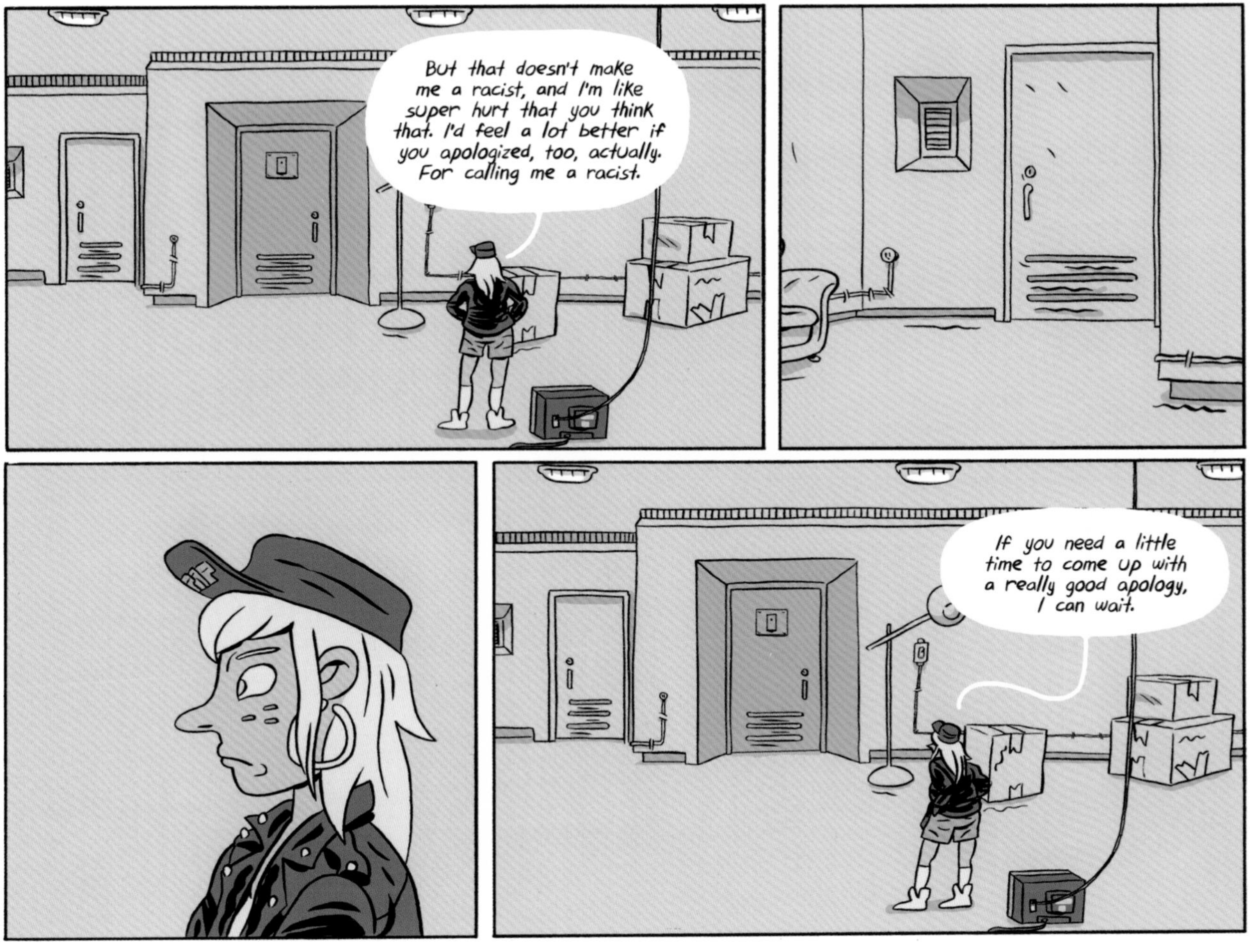
But that doesn't make me a racist, and I'm like super hurt that you think that. I'd feel a lot better if you apologized, too, actually. For calling me a racist.
If you need a little time to come up with a really good apology, I can wait.

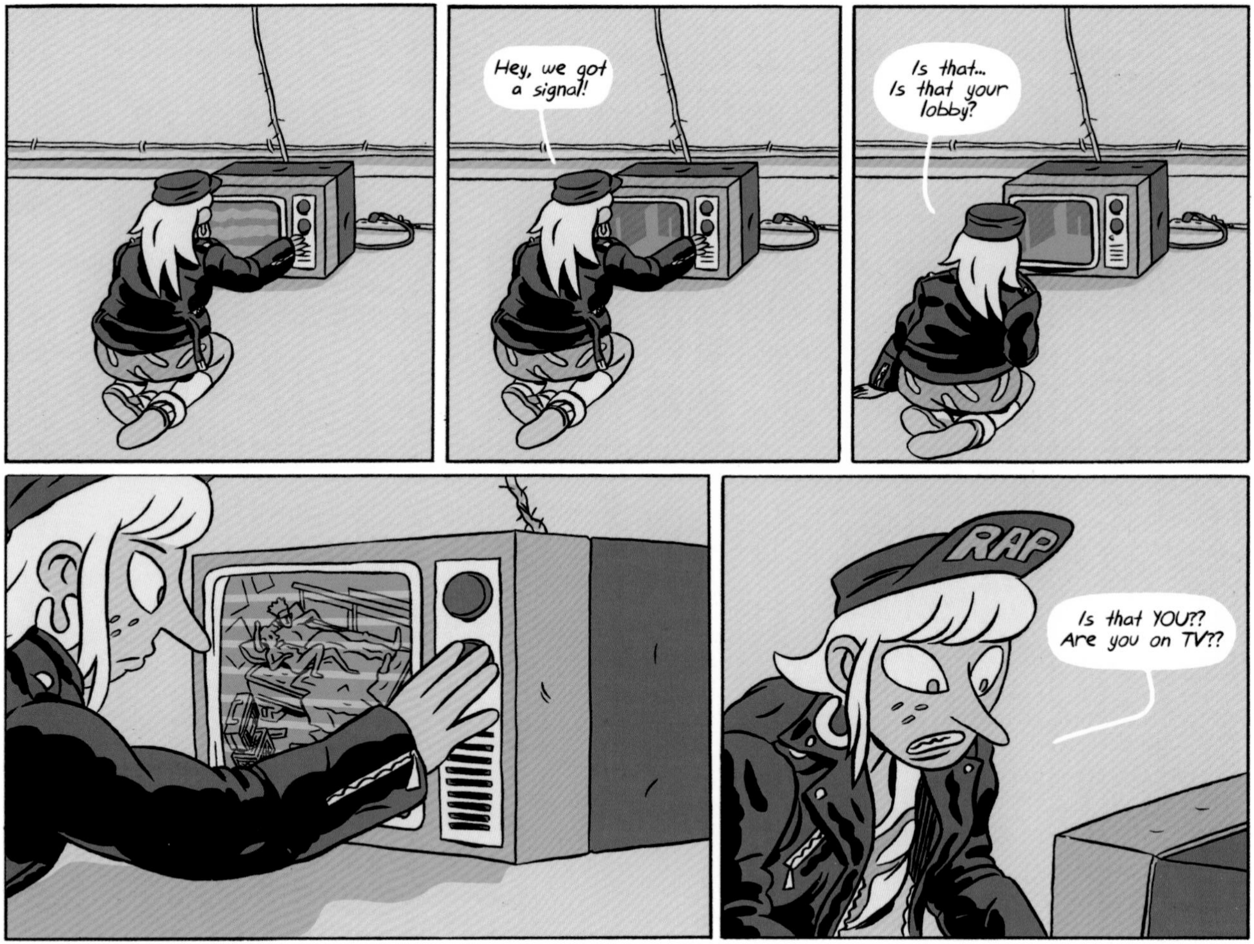
Hey, we got a signal!
Is that... Is that your lobby?
RAP
Is that YOU?? Are you on TV??

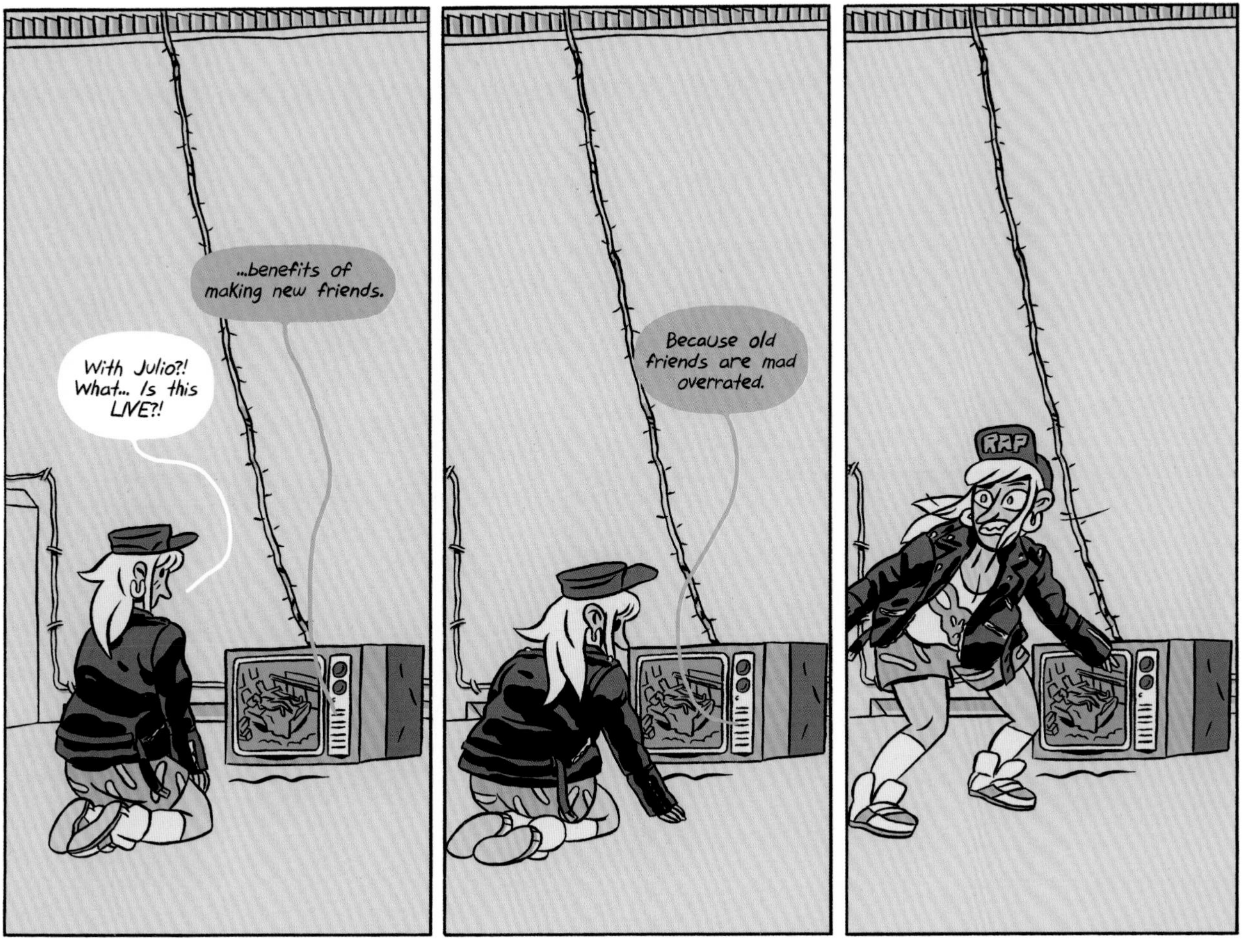
...benefits of making new friends.
With Julio?! What... Is this LIVE?!
Because old friends are mad overrated.
RAP

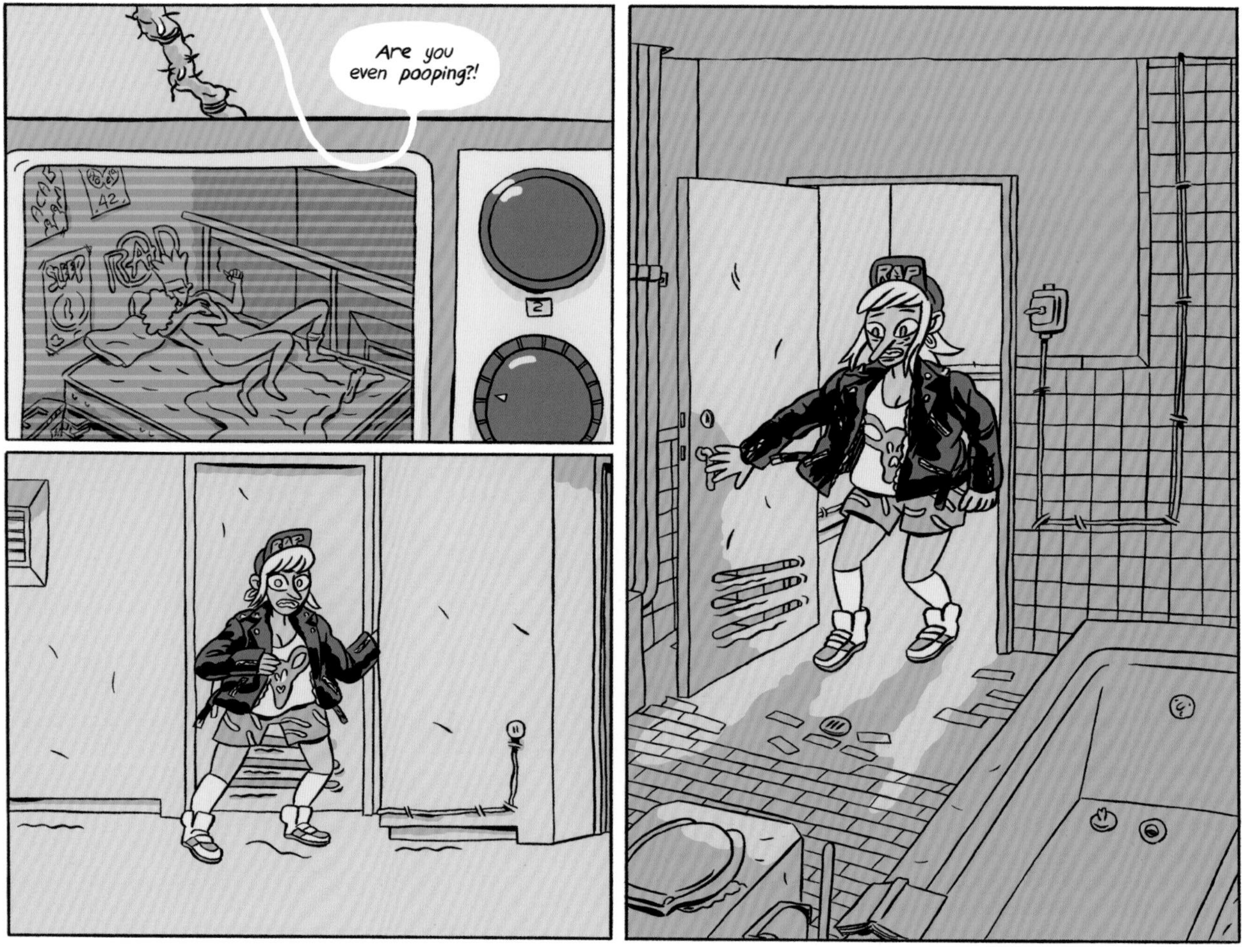
Are you even pooping?!

Alright, Latin Spice, I need coffee.

Oh, I have an automatic machine. There's already hot coffee in the kitchen.

Don't trip. I have a very special relationship with my French press.

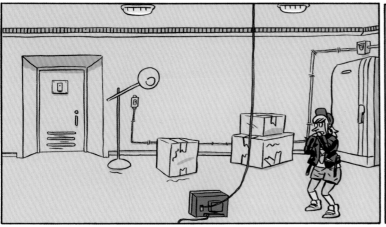

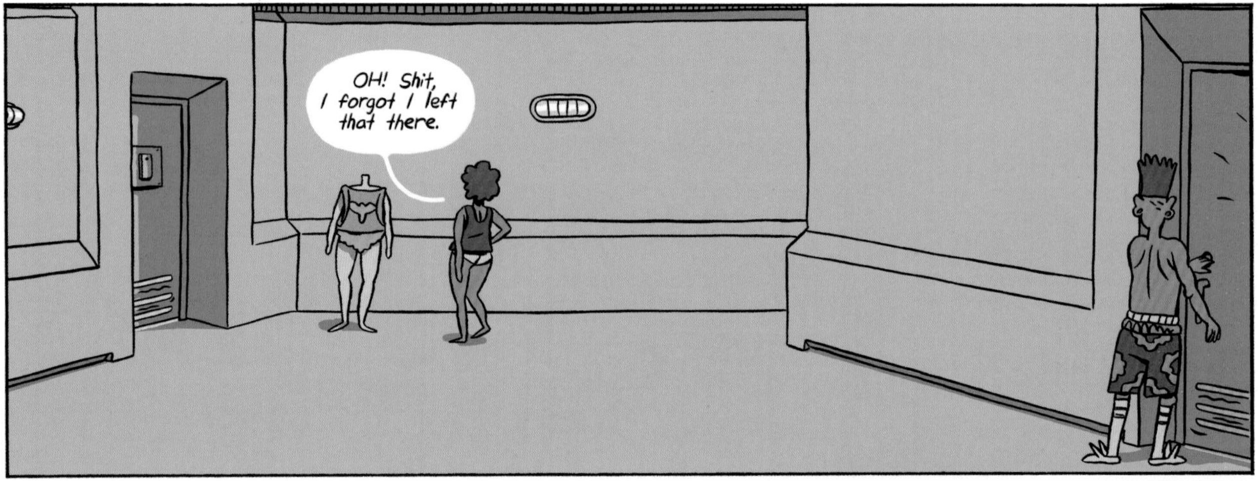
OH! Shit, I forgot I left that there.

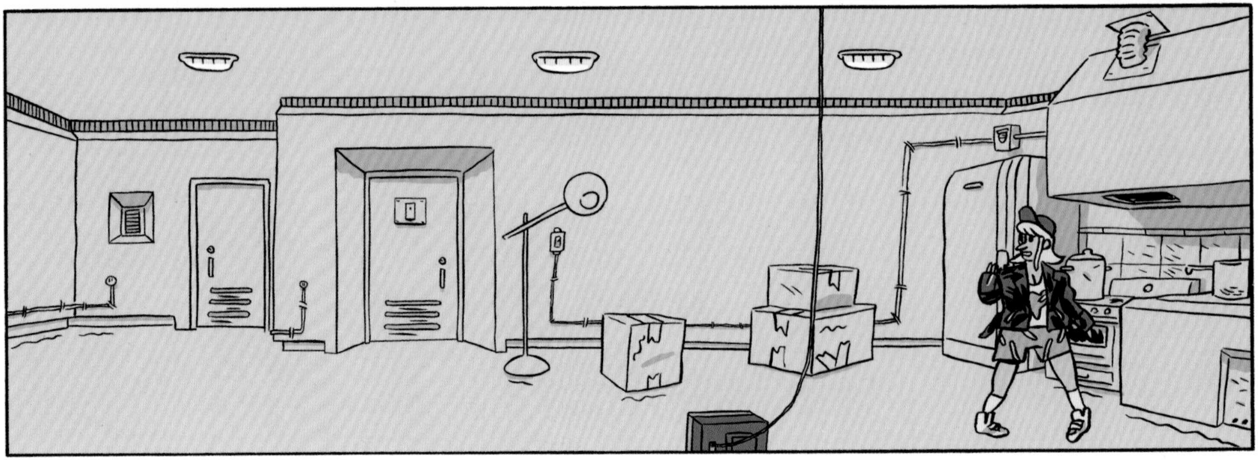

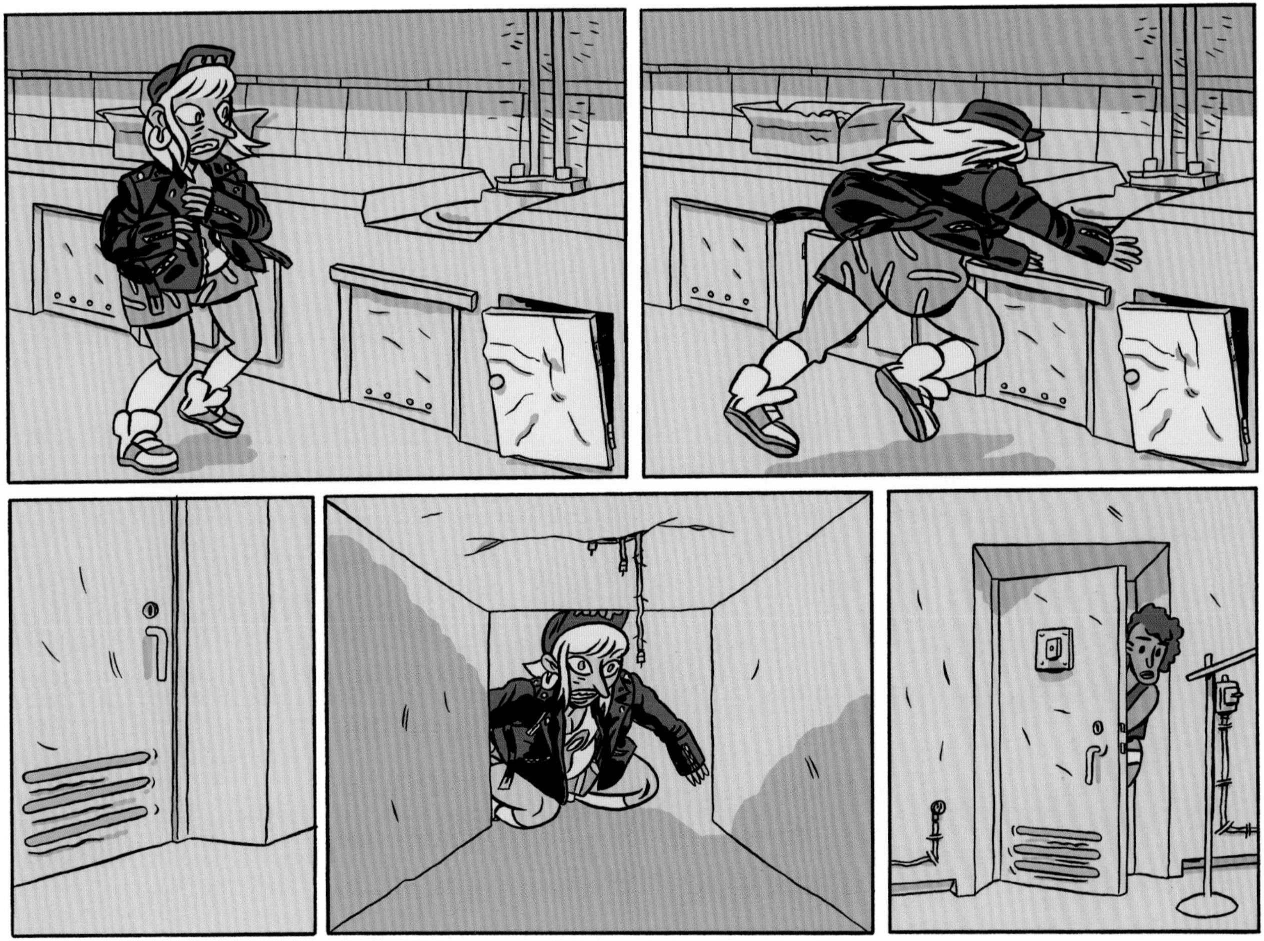

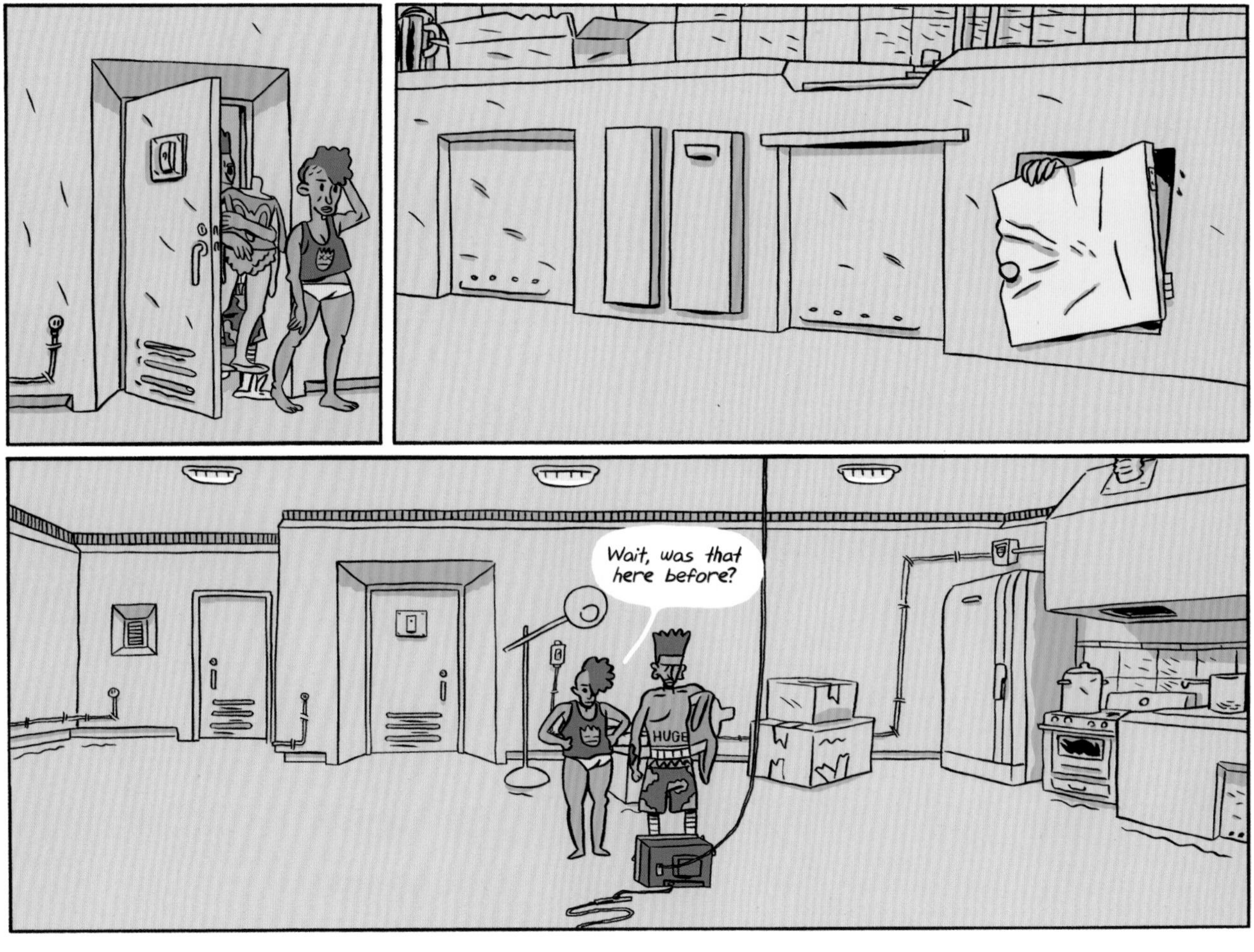
Wait, was that here before?
HUGE

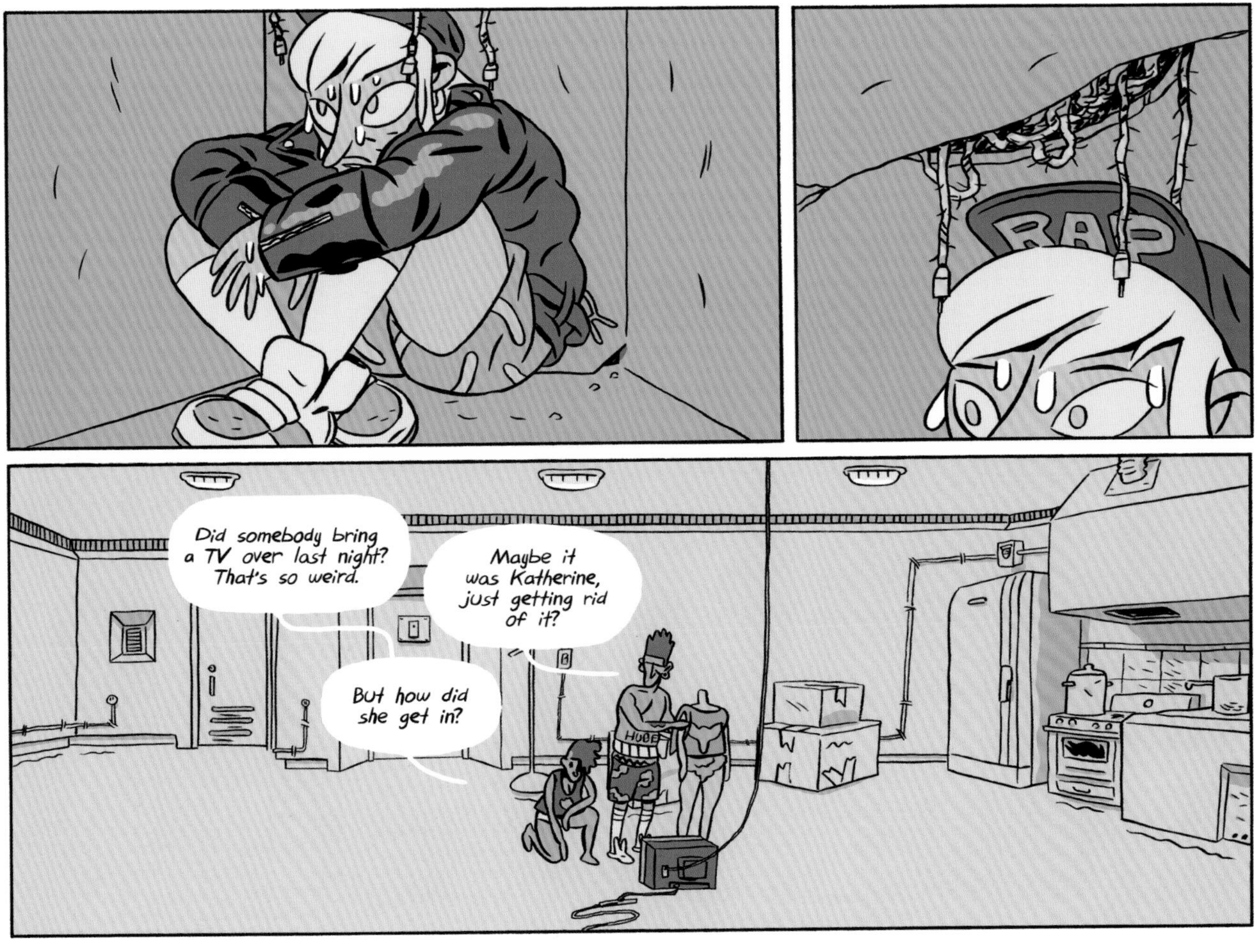
RAP
Did somebody bring a TV over last night? That's so weird.
Maybe it was Katherine, just getting rid of it?
But how did she get in?

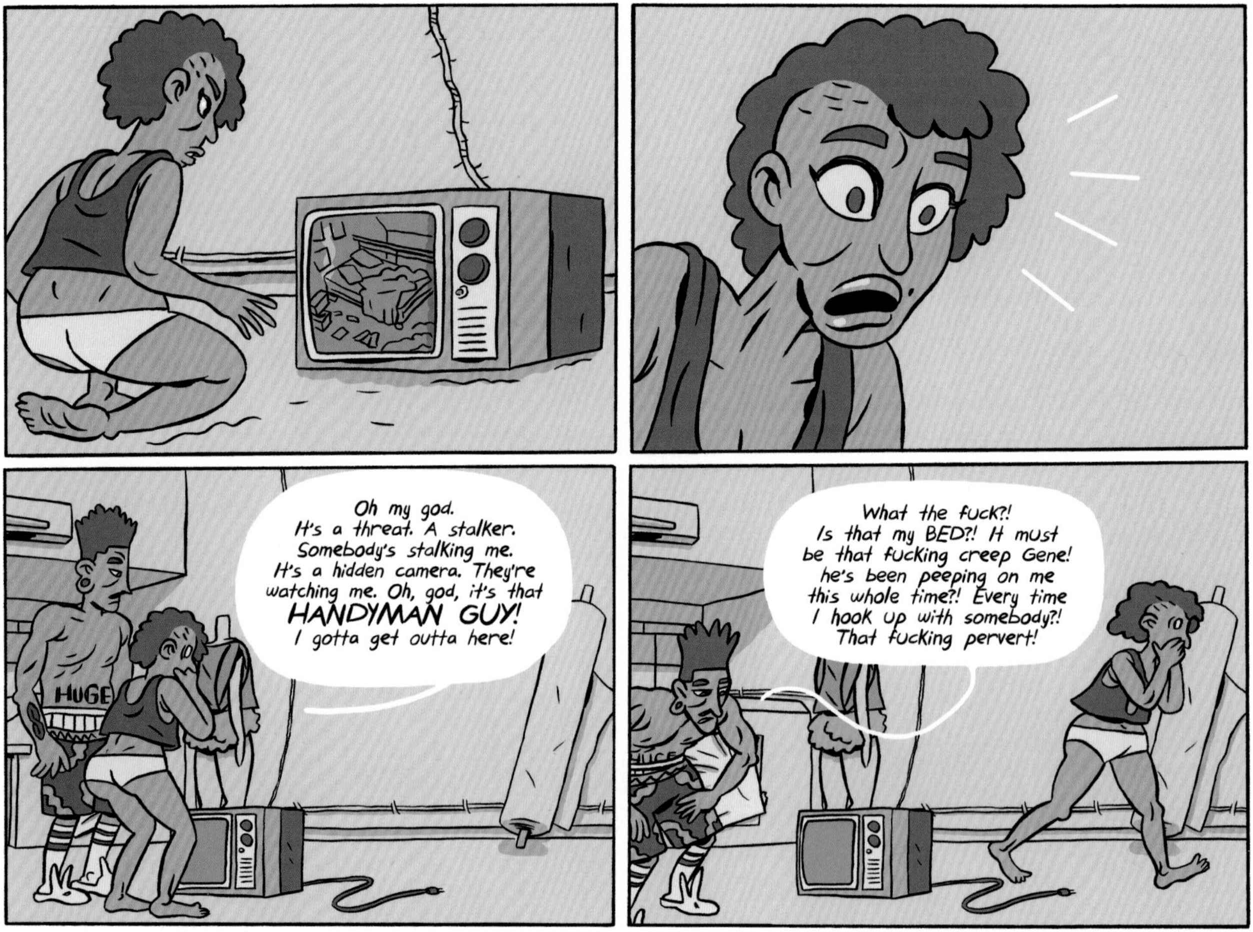
Oh my god. It's a threat. A stalker. Somebody's stalking me. It's a hidden camera. They're watching me. Oh, god, it's that HANDYMAN GUY! I gotta get outta here!
HUGE
What the fuck?! Is that my BED?! It must be that fucking creep Gene! he's been peeping on me this whole time?! Every time I hook up with somebody?! That fucking pervert!

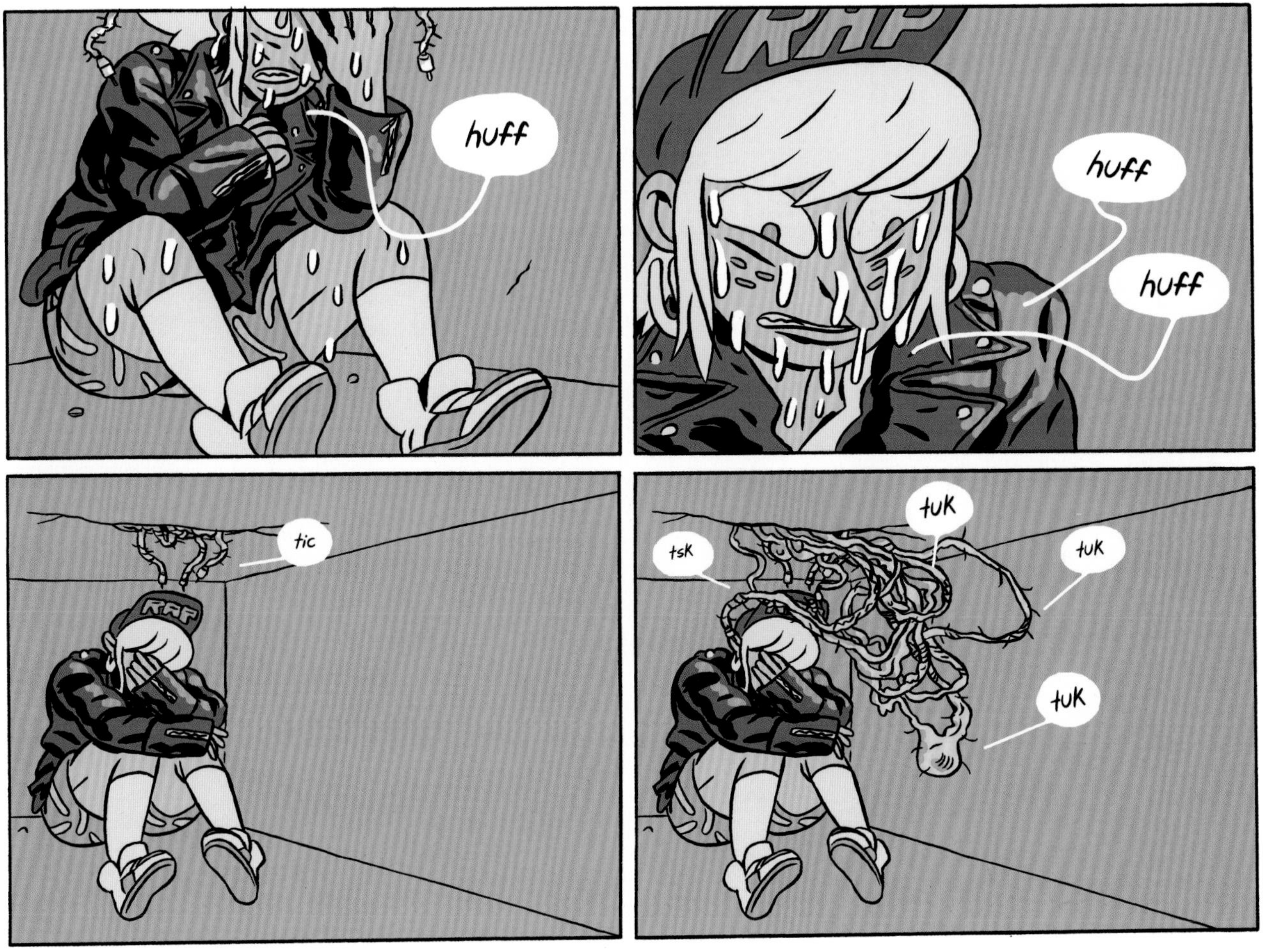
huff
huff
huff
tic
tsk
tuk
tuk
tuk

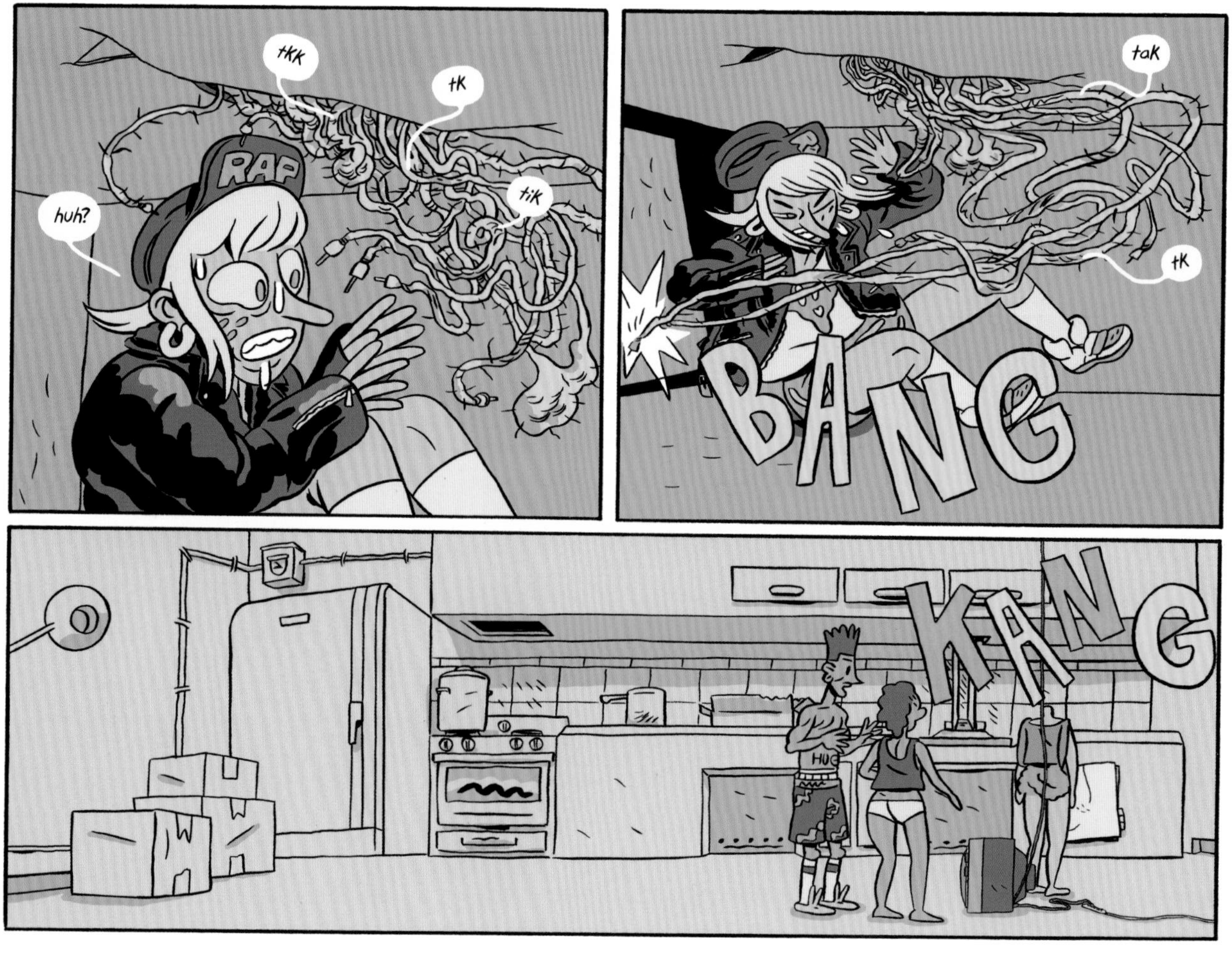
RAP
huh?
tkk
tk
tik
tak
tk
BANG
KANG
HUG

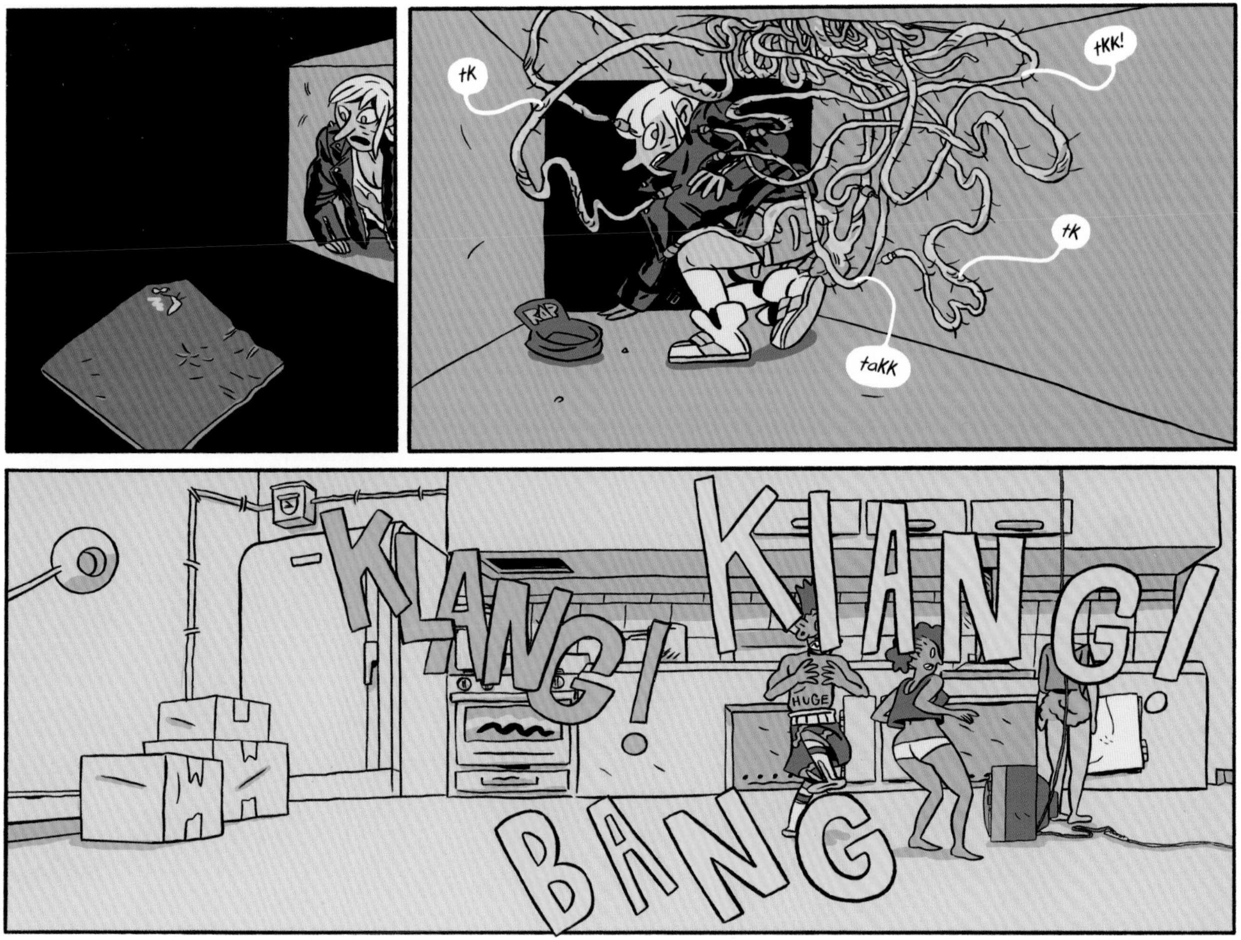
tk
tKK!
RAP
tk
taKK
KLANG!
KLANG!
HUGE
BANG

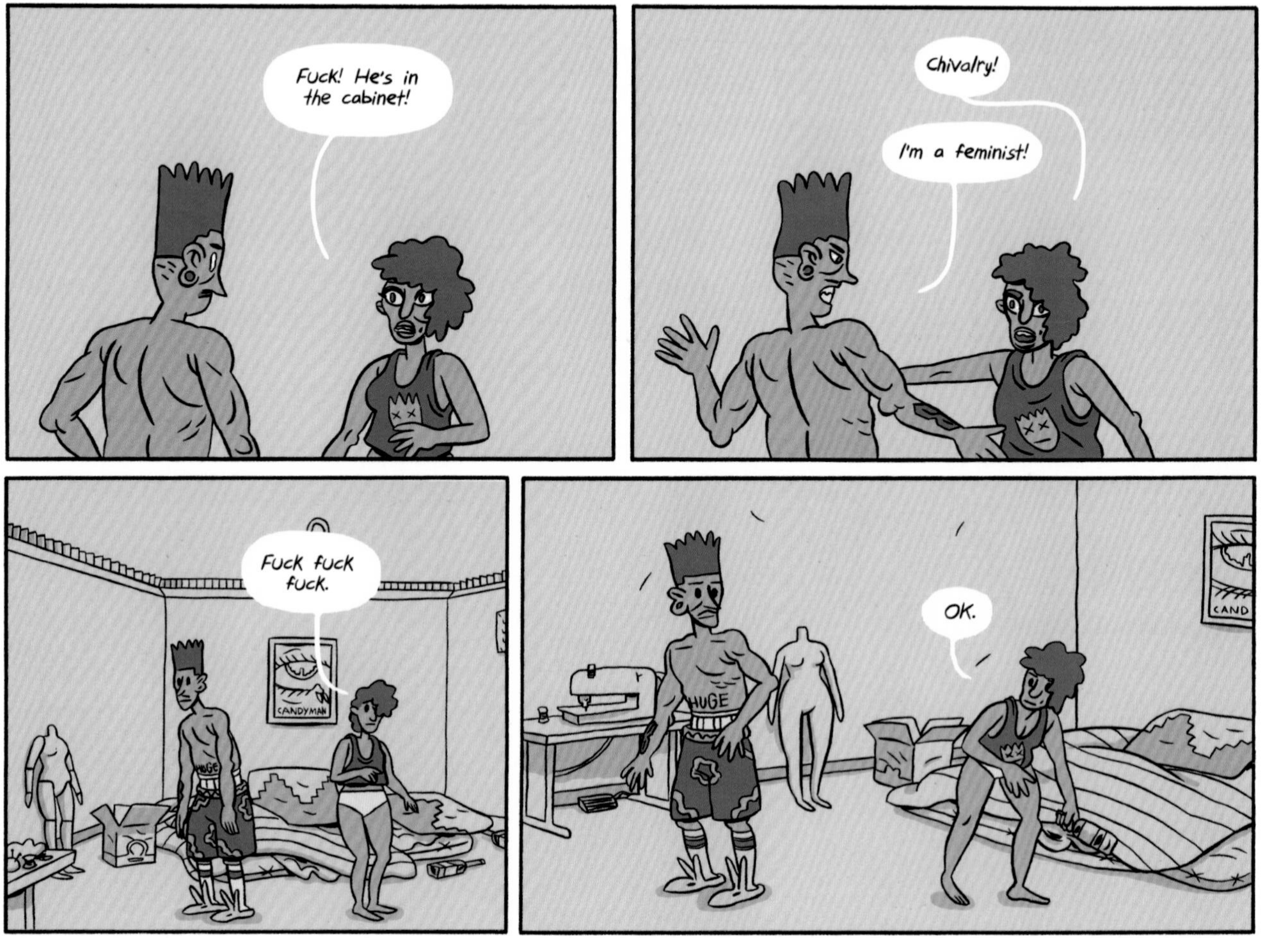
Fuck! He's in the cabinet!
Chivalry!
I'm a feminist!
Fuck fuck fuck.
CANDYMAN
HUGE
OK.
CAND

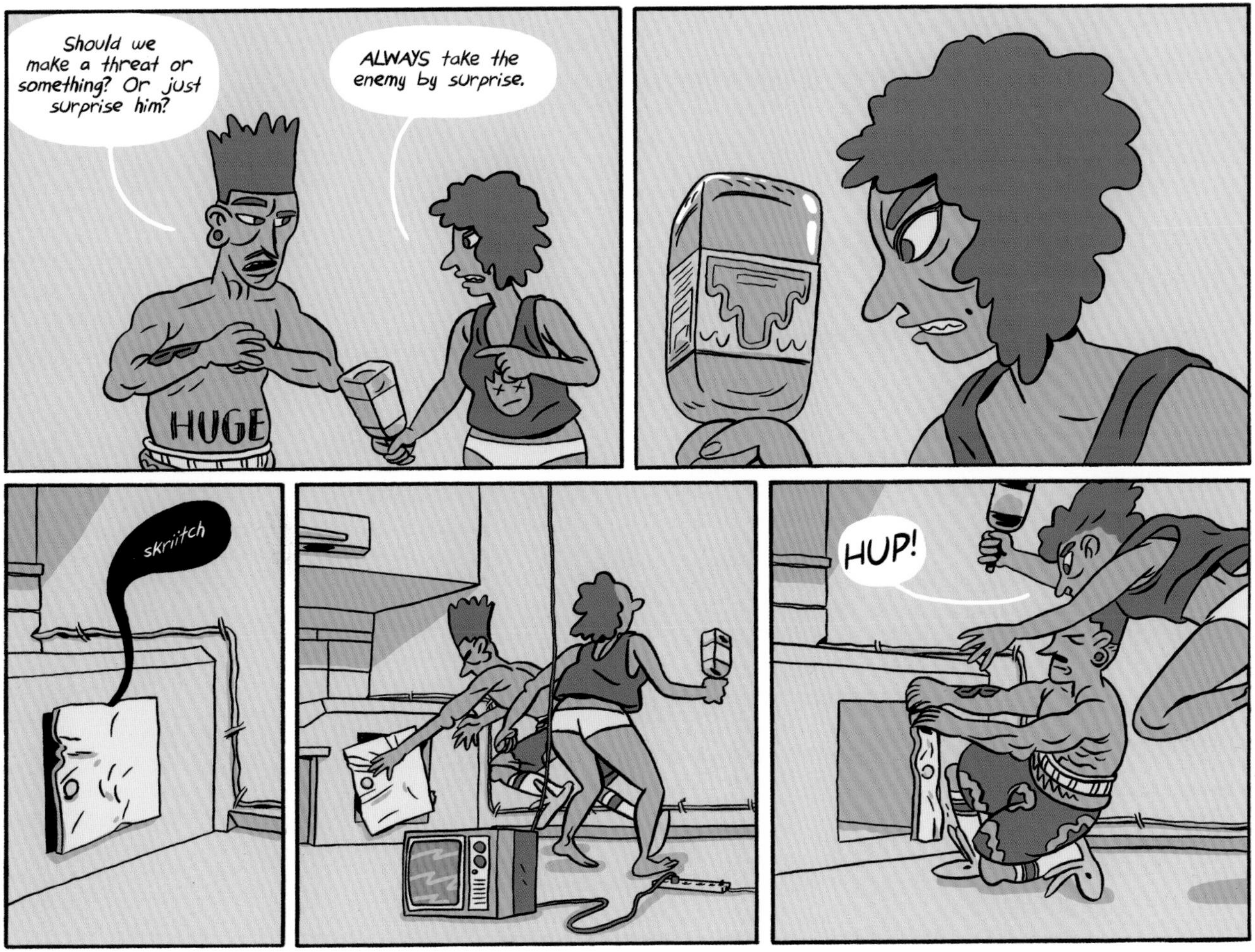
Should we make a threat or something? Or just surprise him?
ALWAYS take the enemy by surprise.
HUGE
skriitch
HUP!

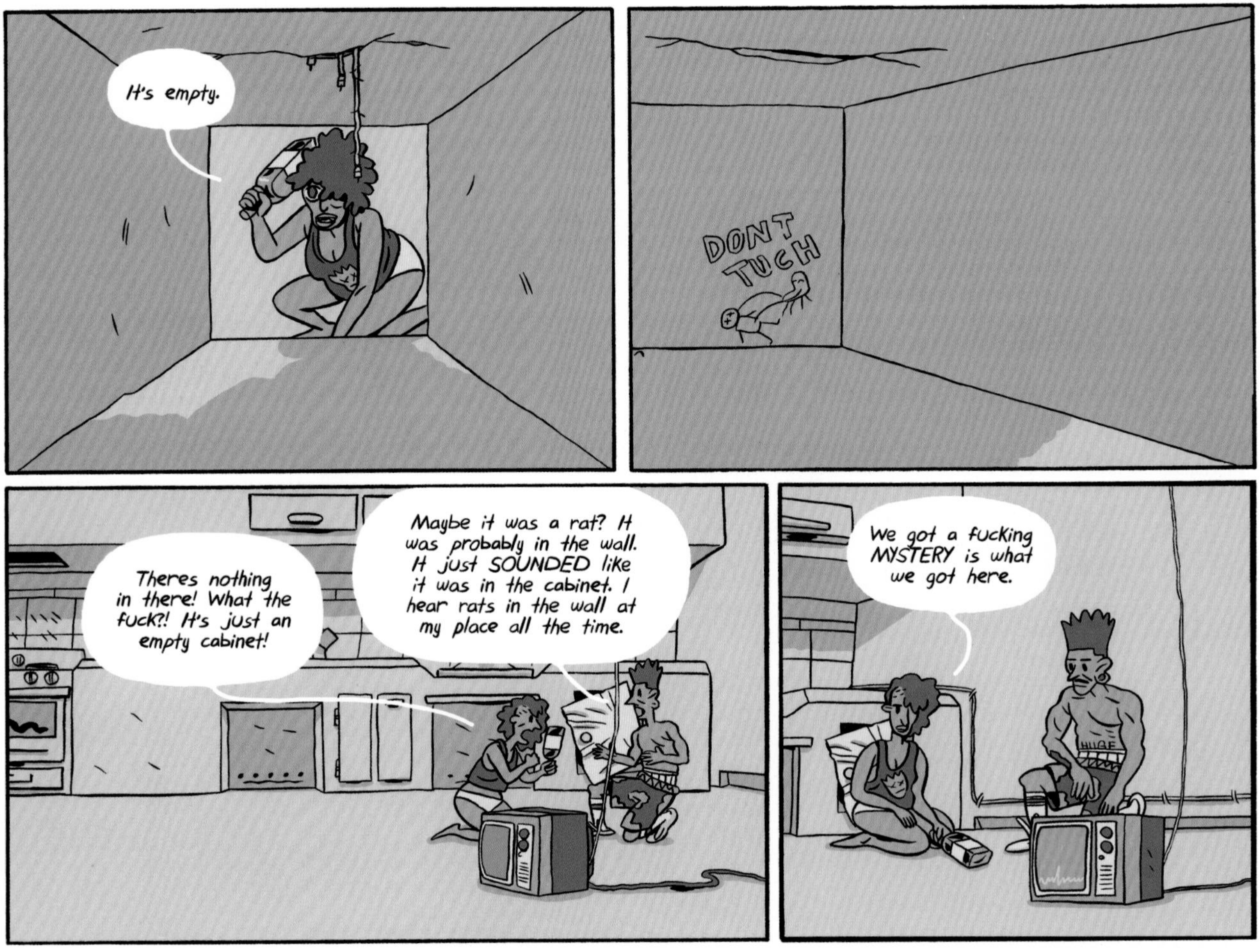
It's empty.
DONT TUCH
Theres nothing in there! What the fuck?! It's just an empty cabinet!
Maybe it was a rat? It was probably in the wall. It just SOUNDED like it was in the cabinet. I hear rats in the wall at my place all the time.
We got a fucking MYSTERY is what we got here.
HUGE

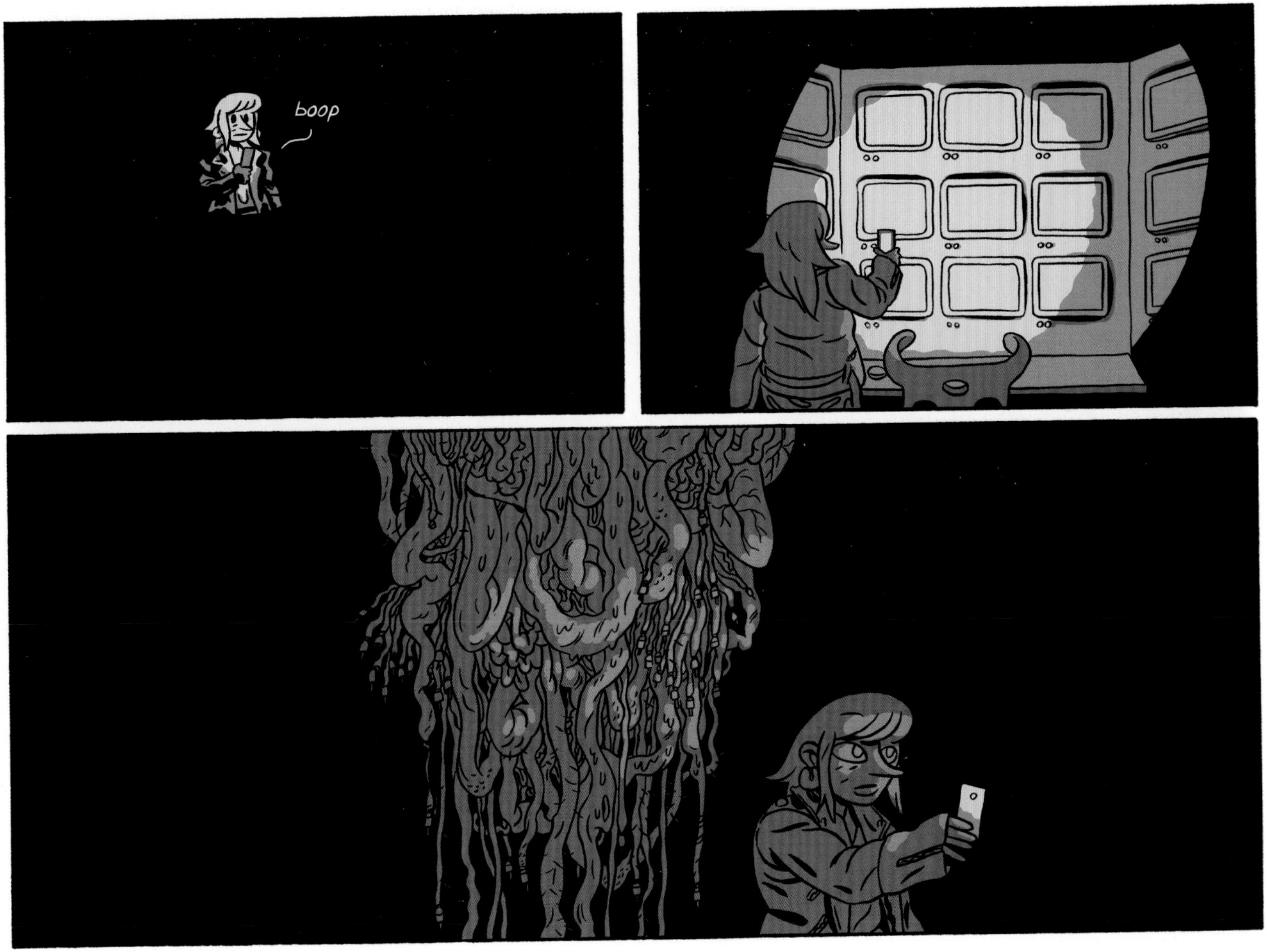
boop

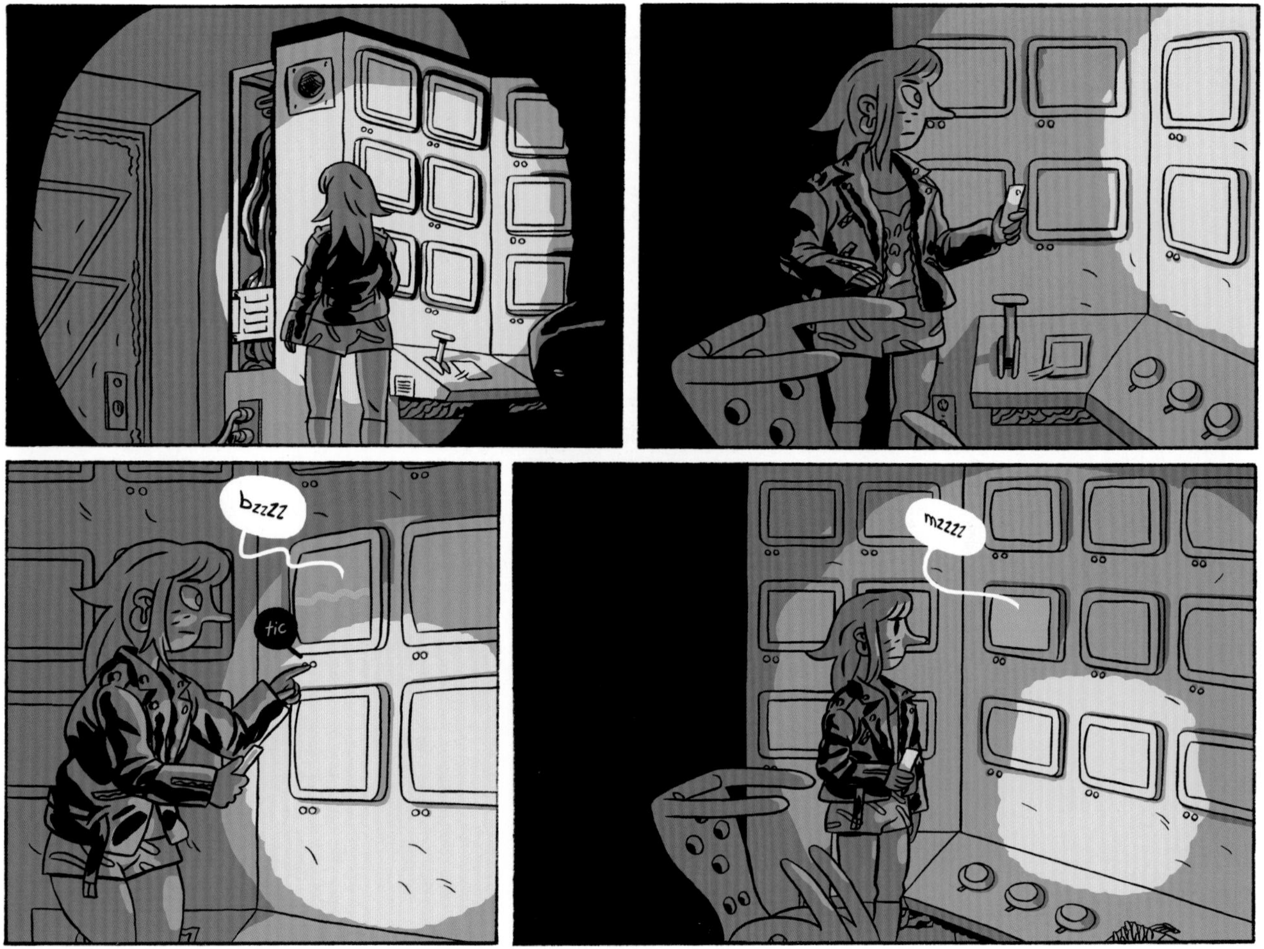
bzzzz
tic
mzzzz

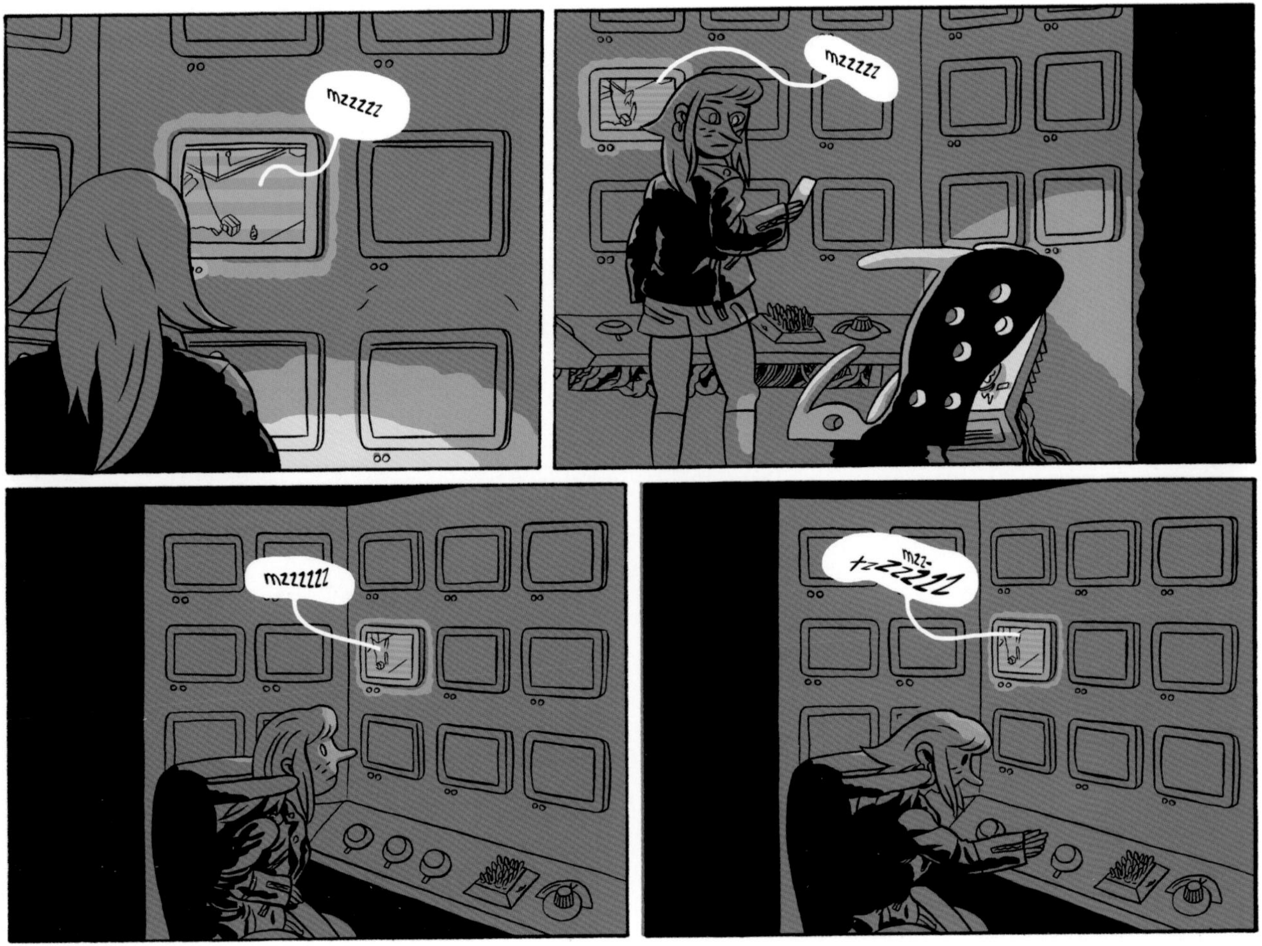
mzzzzz
mzzzzz
mzzzzzz
mzz-
tzzzzzzz

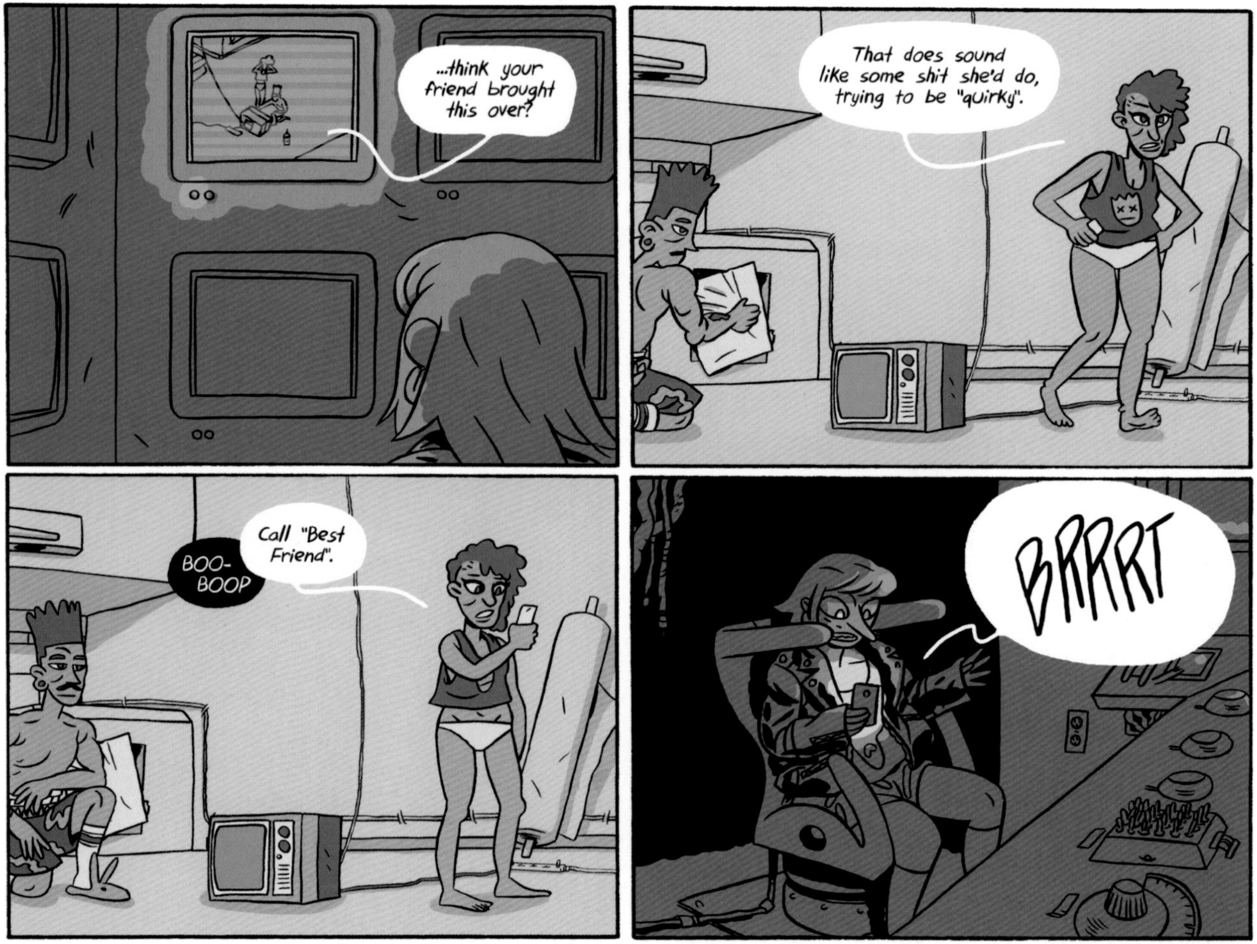

...think your friend brought this over?
That does sound like some shit she'd do, trying to be "quirky".
BOO-BOOP
Call "Best Friend".
BRRRT

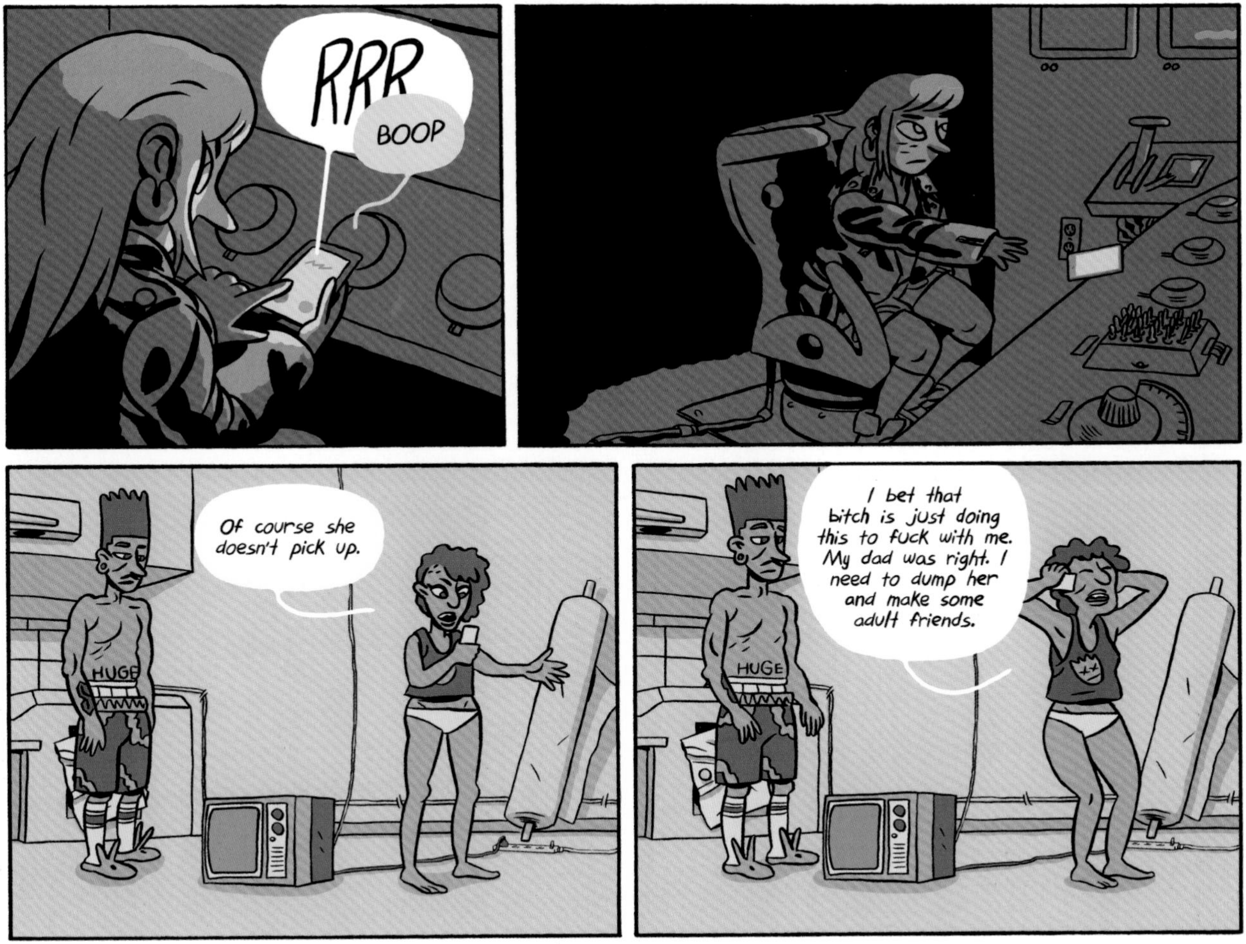
RRR
BOOP
Of course she doesn't pick up.
I bet that bitch is just doing this to fuck with me. My dad was right. I need to dump her and make some adult friends.
HUGE
HUGE

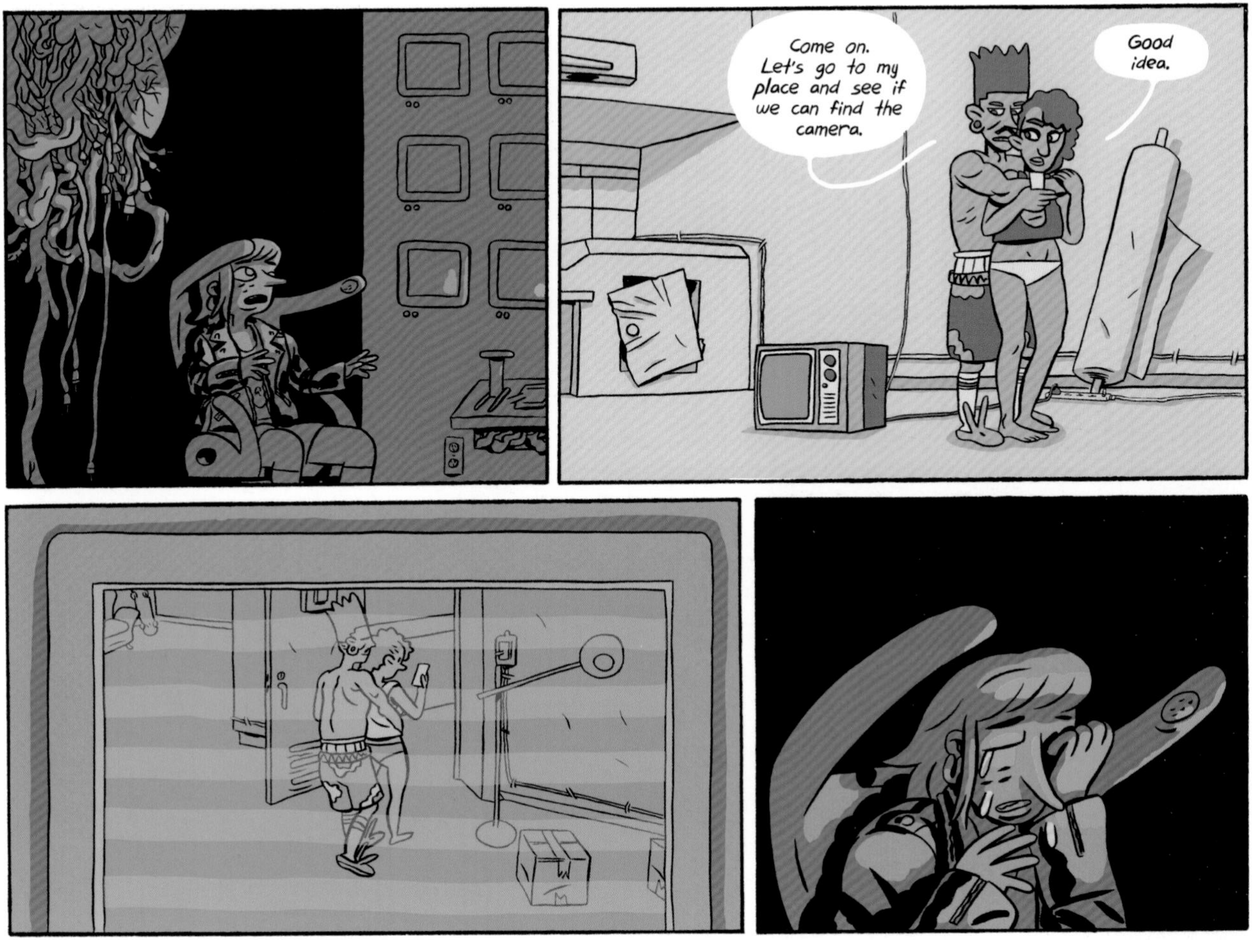
Come on. Let's go to my place and see if we can find the camera.
Good idea.

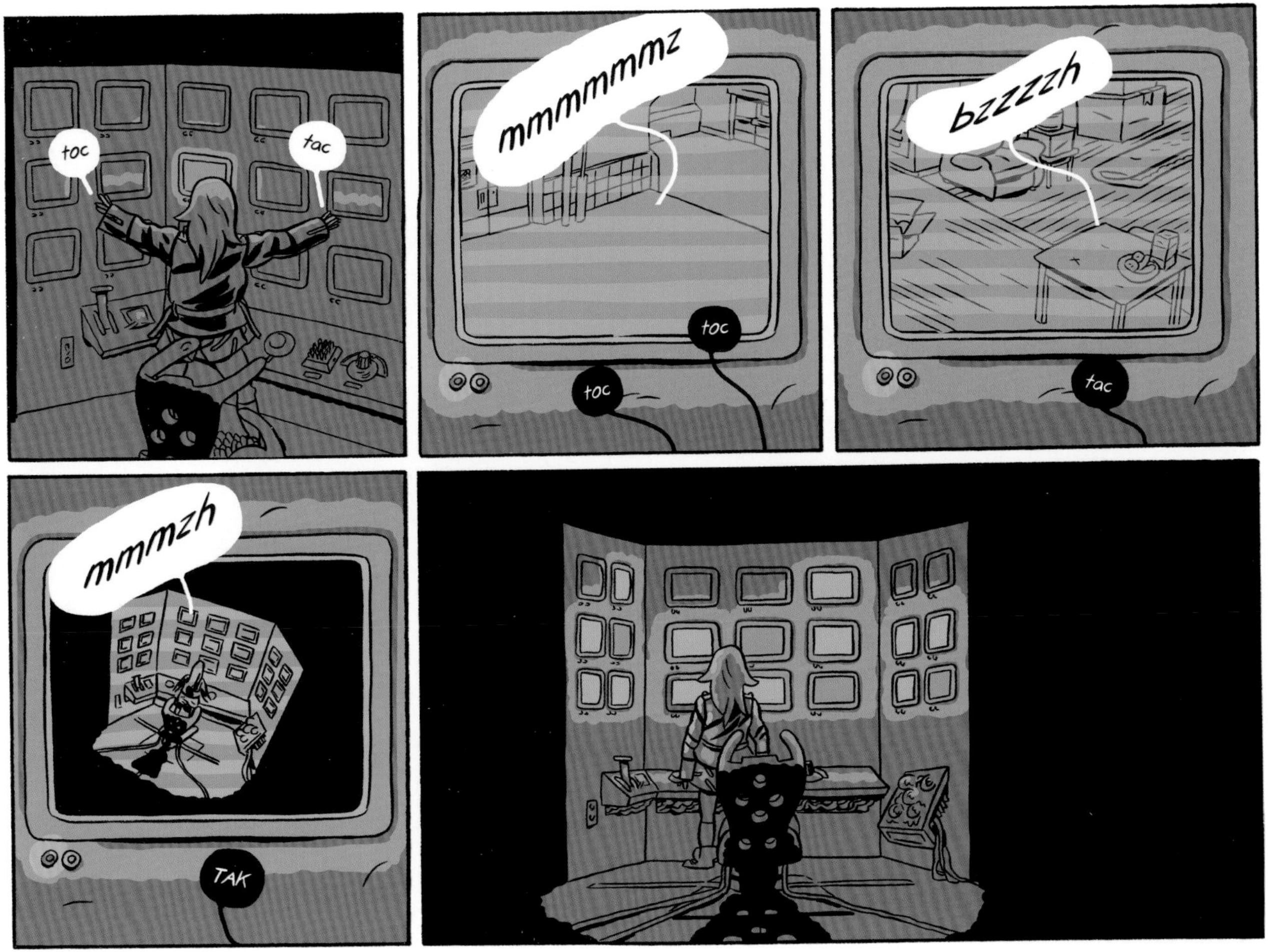
toc
tac
mmmmmmz
toc
toc
bzzzzh
tac
mmmzh
TAK

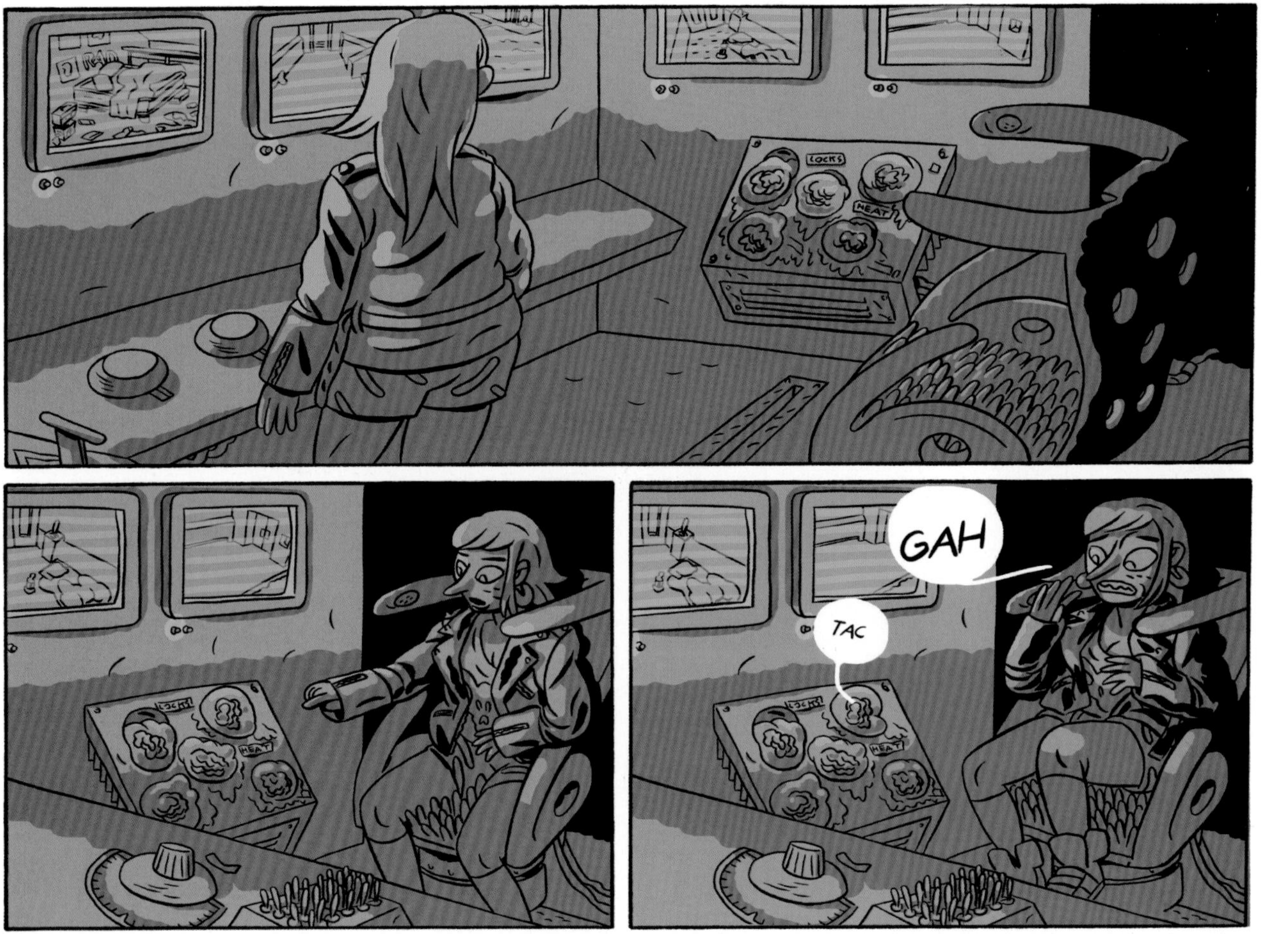
LOCKS
HEAT
LOCKS
HEAT
GAH
TAC
LOCKS
HEAT

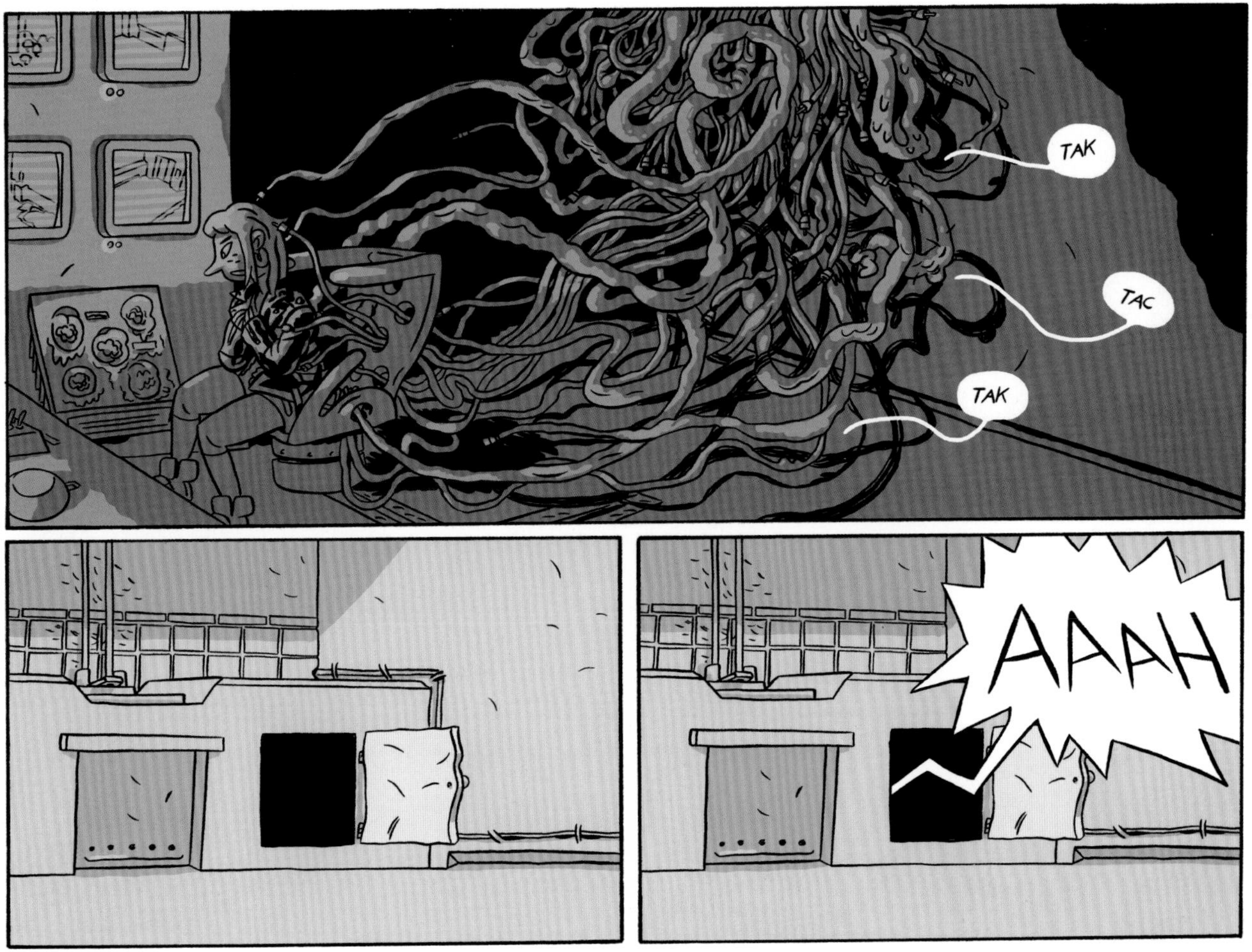
TAK
TAC
TAK
AAAH

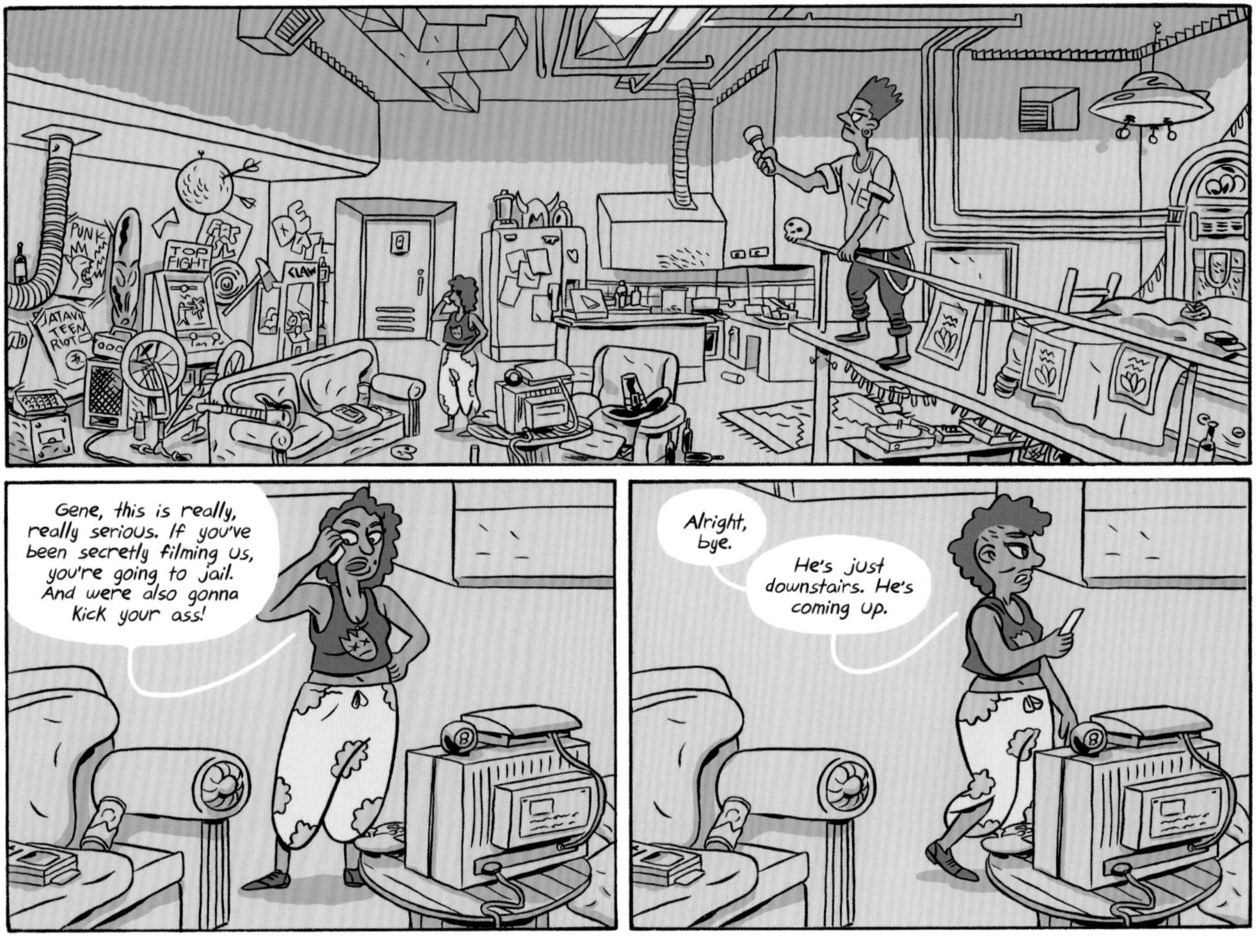
Gene, this is really, really serious. If you've been secretly filming us, you're going to jail. And were also gonna kick your ass!
Alright, bye.
He's just downstairs. He's coming up.

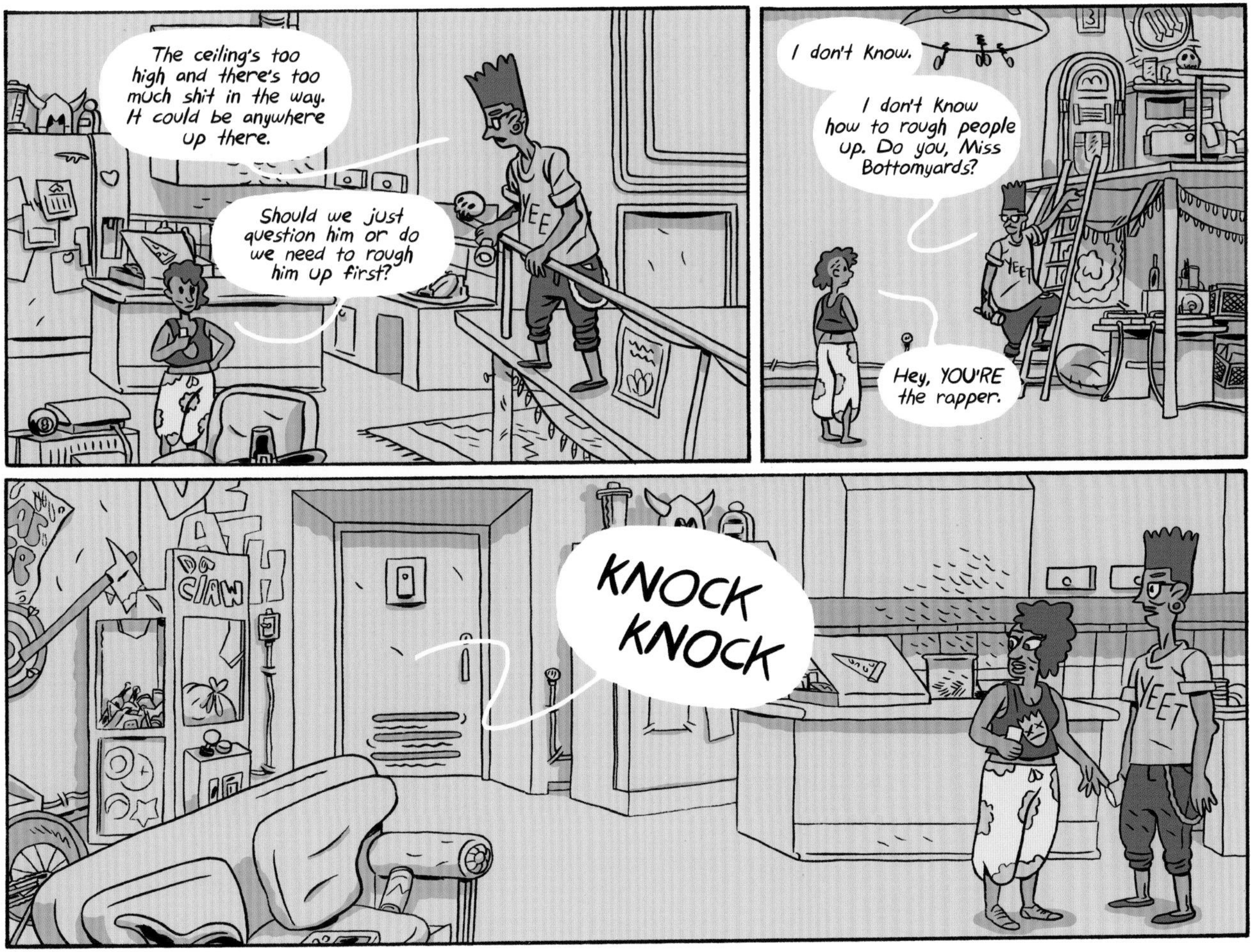
The ceiling's too high and there's too much shit in the way. It could be anywhere up there.
Should we just question him or do we need to rough him up first?
I don't know.
I don't know how to rough people up. Do you, Miss Bottomyards?
Hey, YOU'RE the rapper.
KNOCK KNOCK

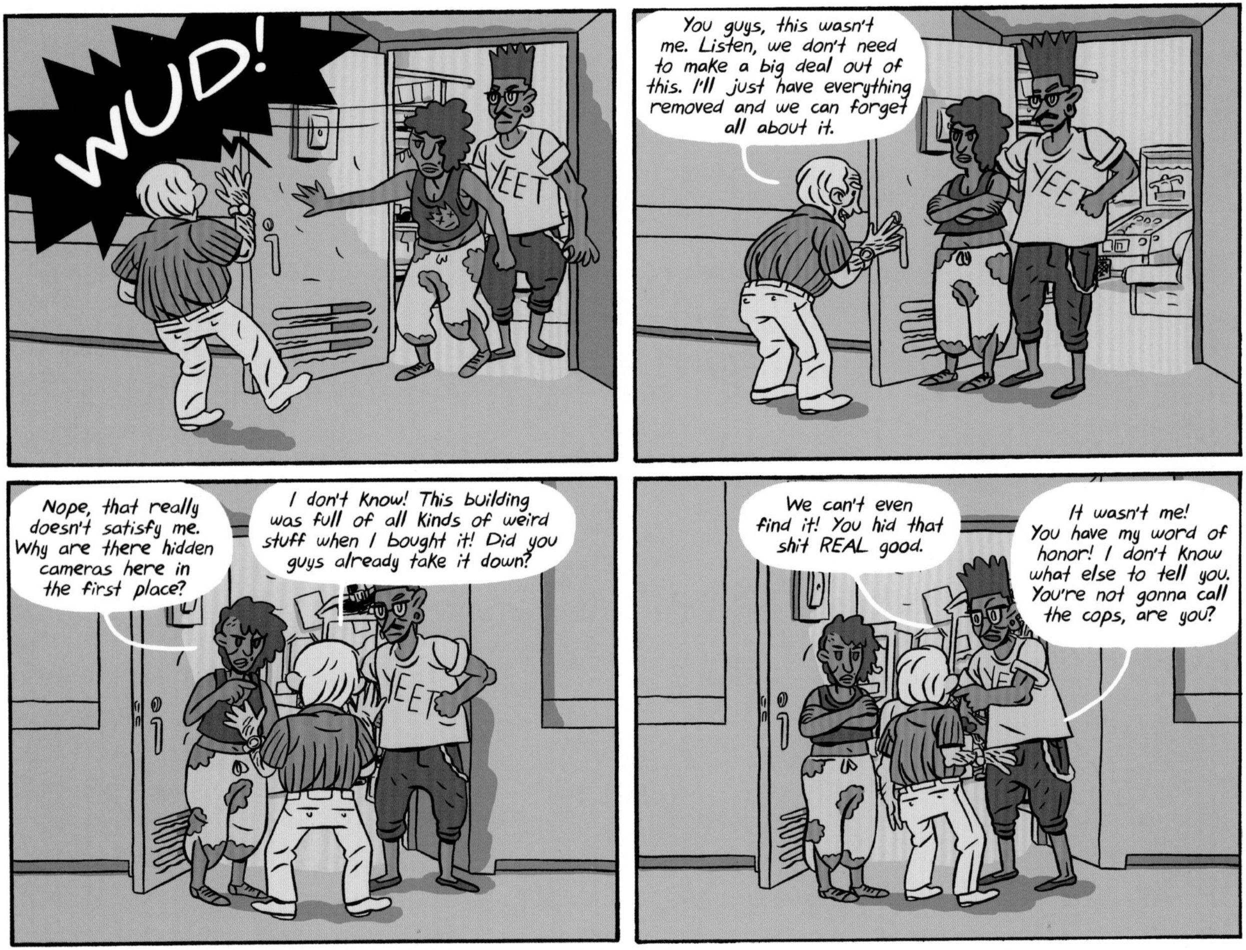
WUD!
You guys, this wasn't me. Listen, we don't need to make a big deal out of this. I'll just have everything removed and we can forget all about it.
YEET
Nope, that really doesn't satisfy me. Why are there hidden cameras here in the first place?
I don't know! This building was full of all kinds of weird stuff when I bought it! Did you guys already take it down?
We can't even find it! You hid that shit REAL good.
It wasn't me! You have my word of honor! I don't know what else to tell you. You're not gonna call the cops, are you?

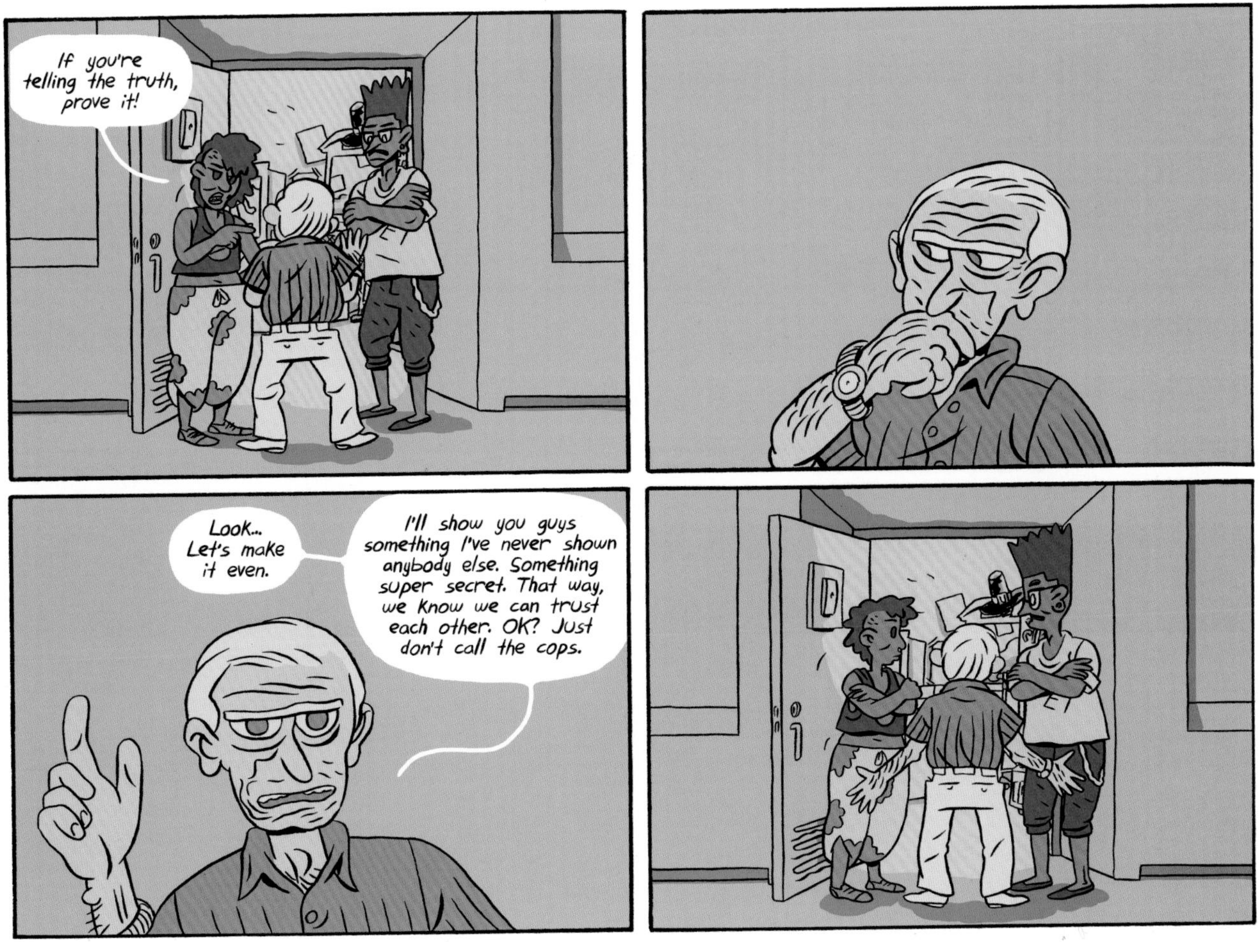
If you're telling the truth, prove it!
Look... Let's make it even.
I'll show you guys something I've never shown anybody else. Something super secret. That way, we know we can trust each other. OK? Just don't call the cops.

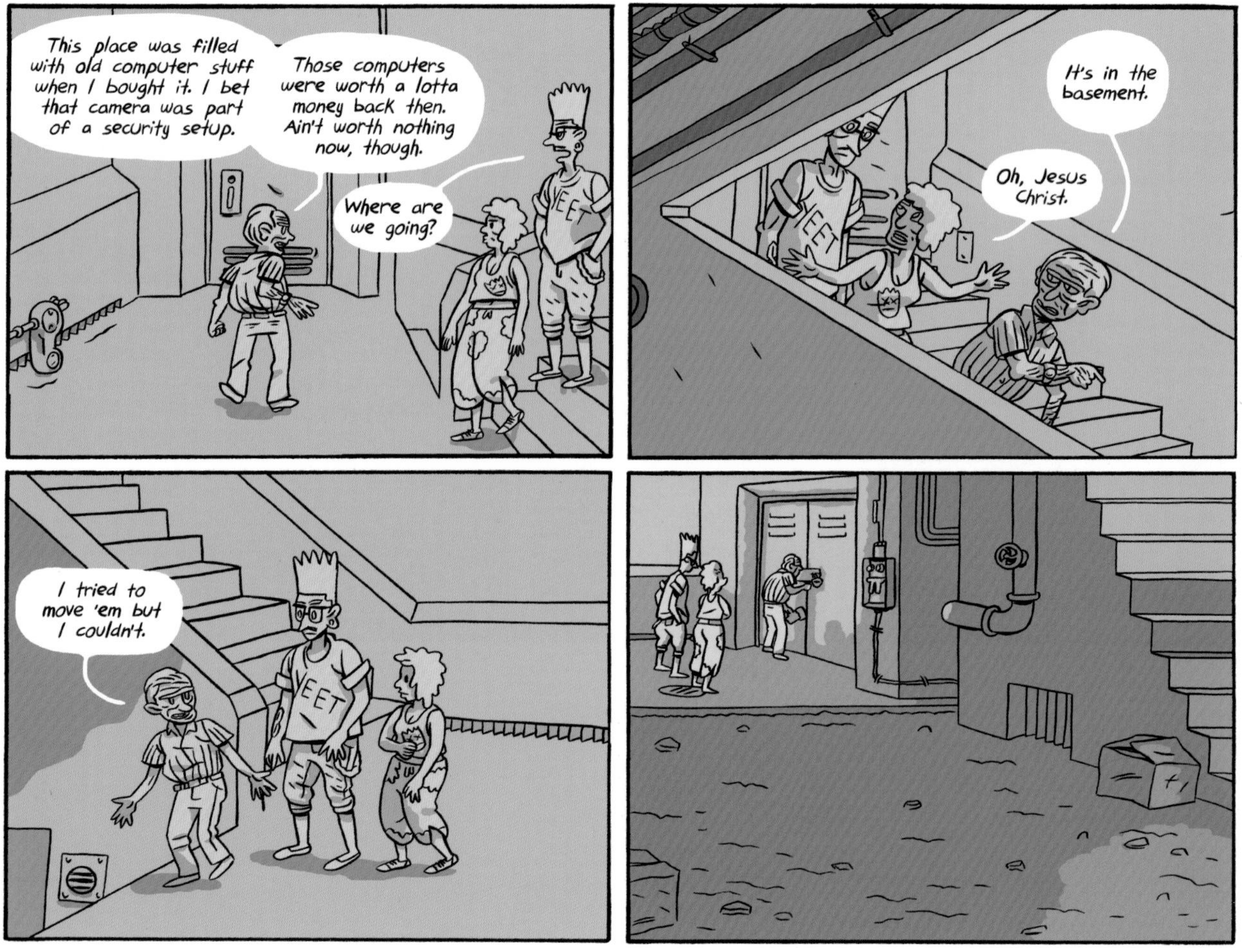
This place was filled with old computer stuff when I bought it. I bet that camera was part of a security setup.
Those computers were worth a lotta money back then. Ain't worth nothing now, though.
Where are we going?
YEET
It's in the basement.
Oh, Jesus Christ.
YEET
I tried to move 'em but I couldn't.
YEET

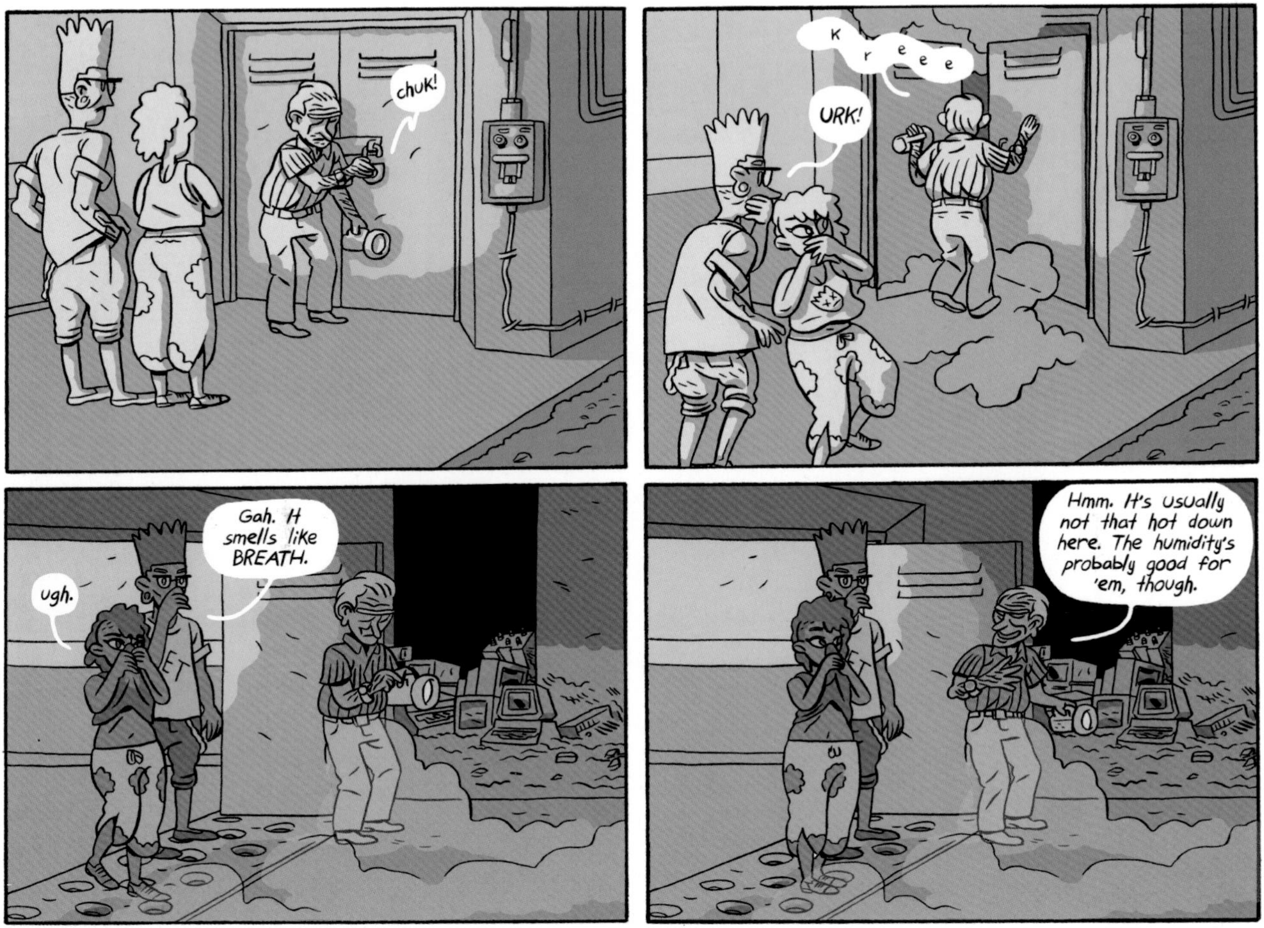
chuk!
Kreeee
URK!
ugh.
Gah. It smells like BREATH.
Hmm. It's usually not that hot down here. The humidity's probably good for 'em, though.

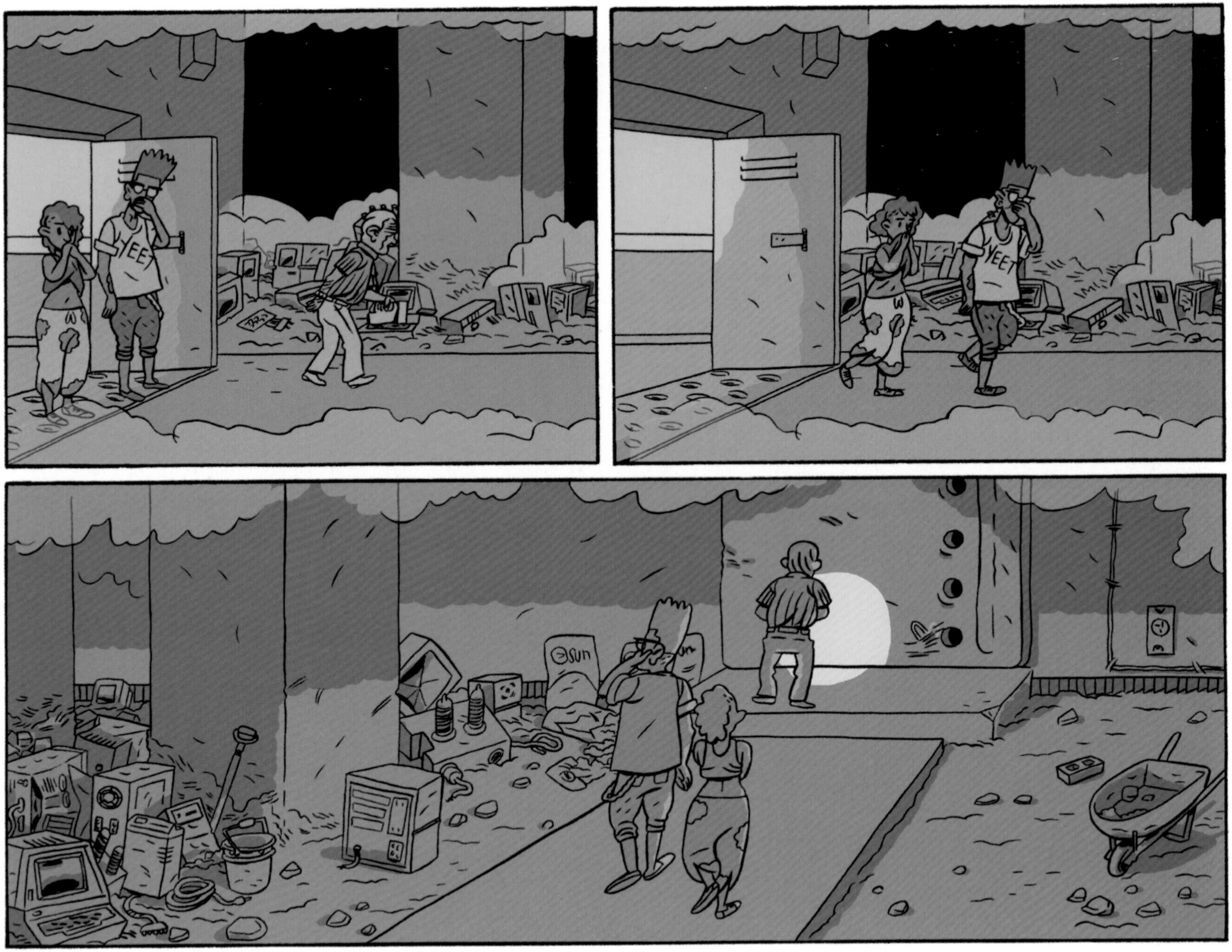
YEET
YEET
sun

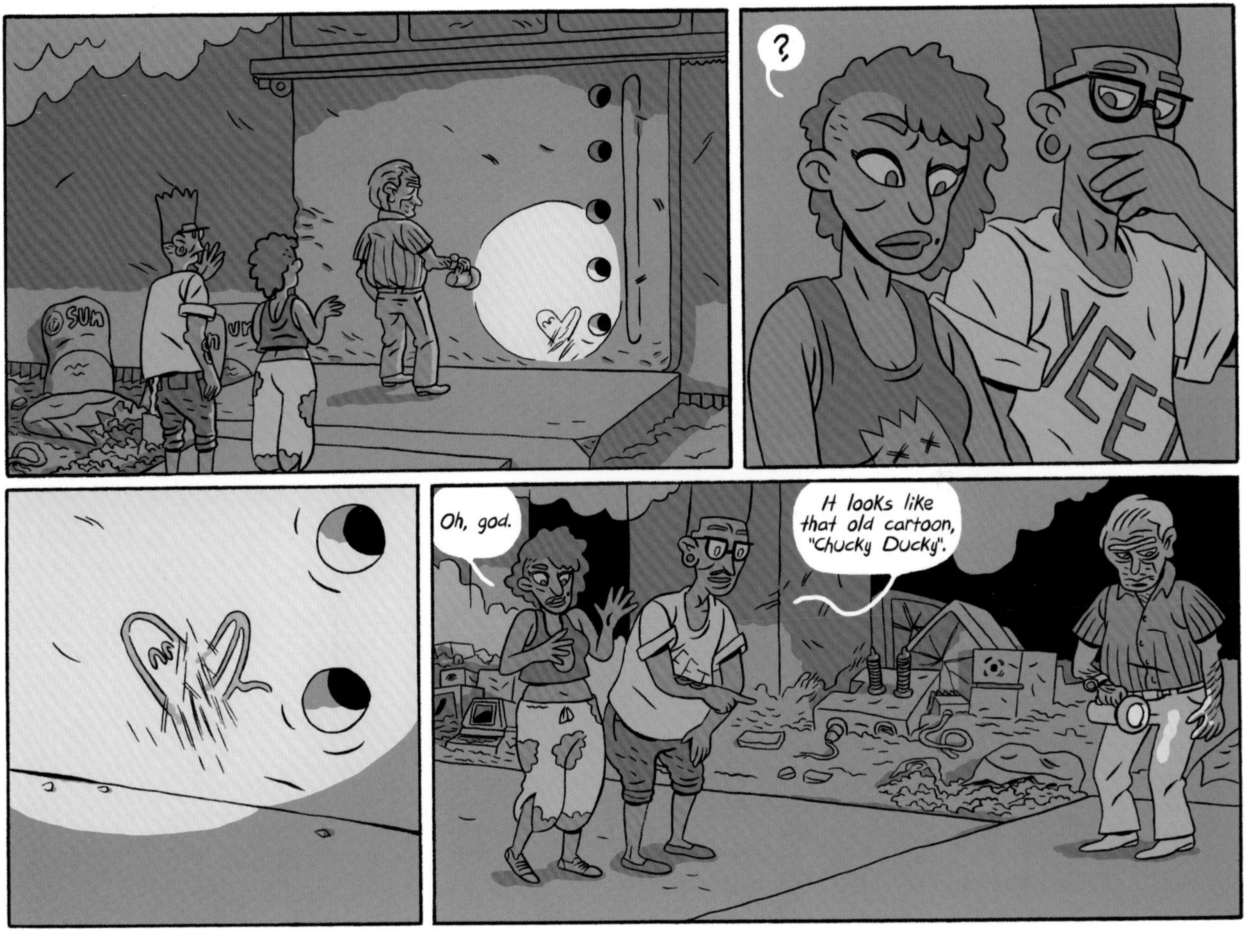
?
Oh, god.
It looks like that old cartoon, "Chucky Ducky".

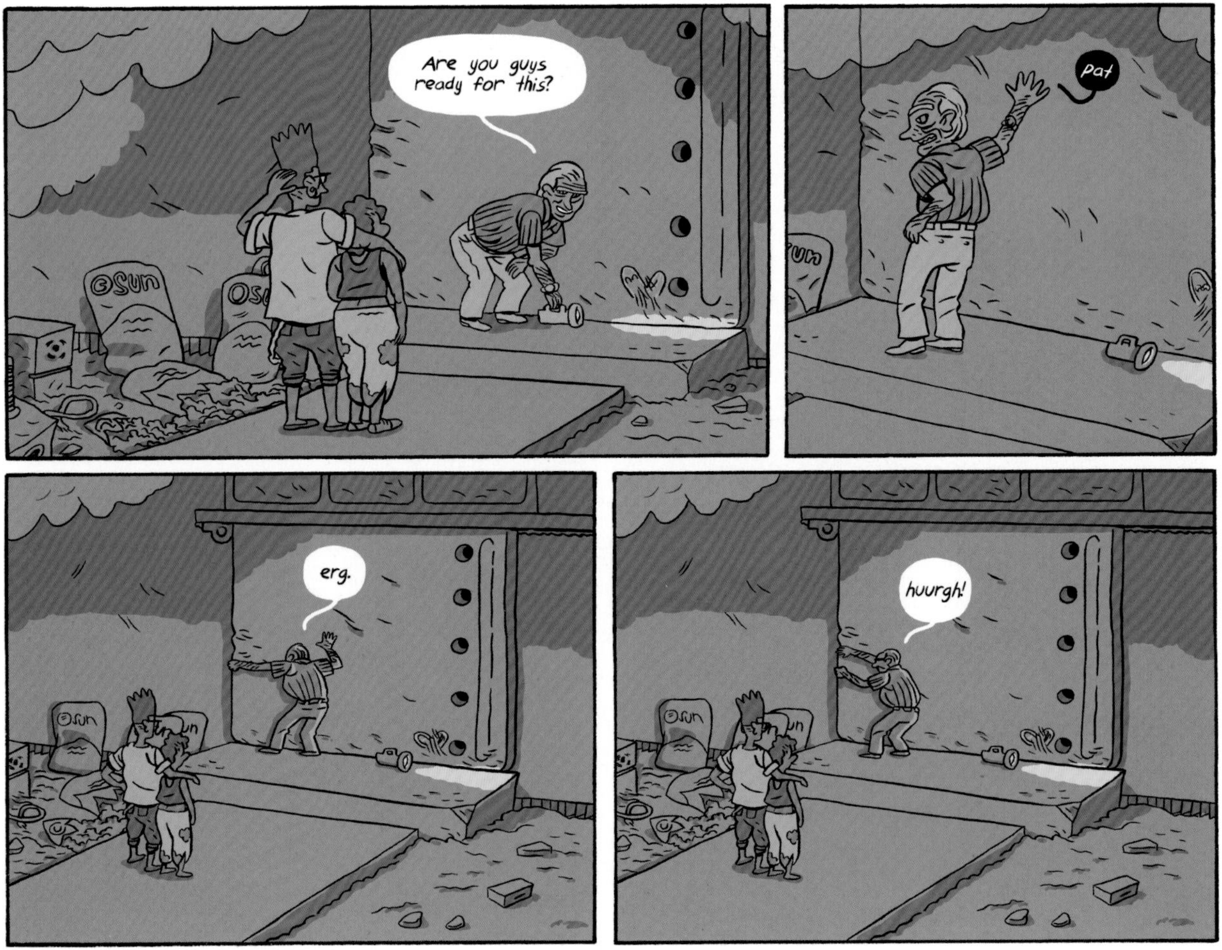
Are you guys ready for this?
pat
erg.
huurgh!

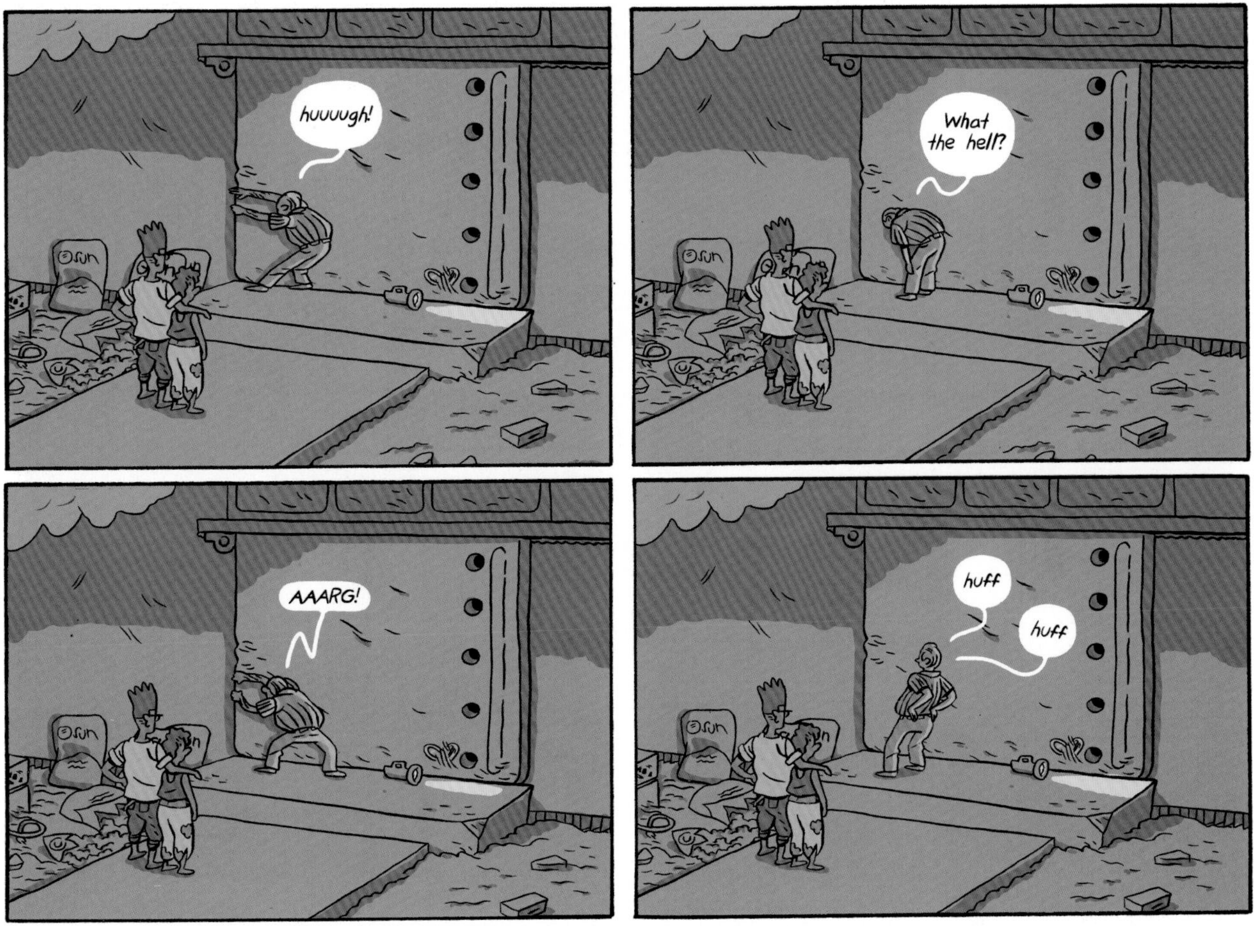
huuuugh!
What the hell?
AAARG!
huff
huff

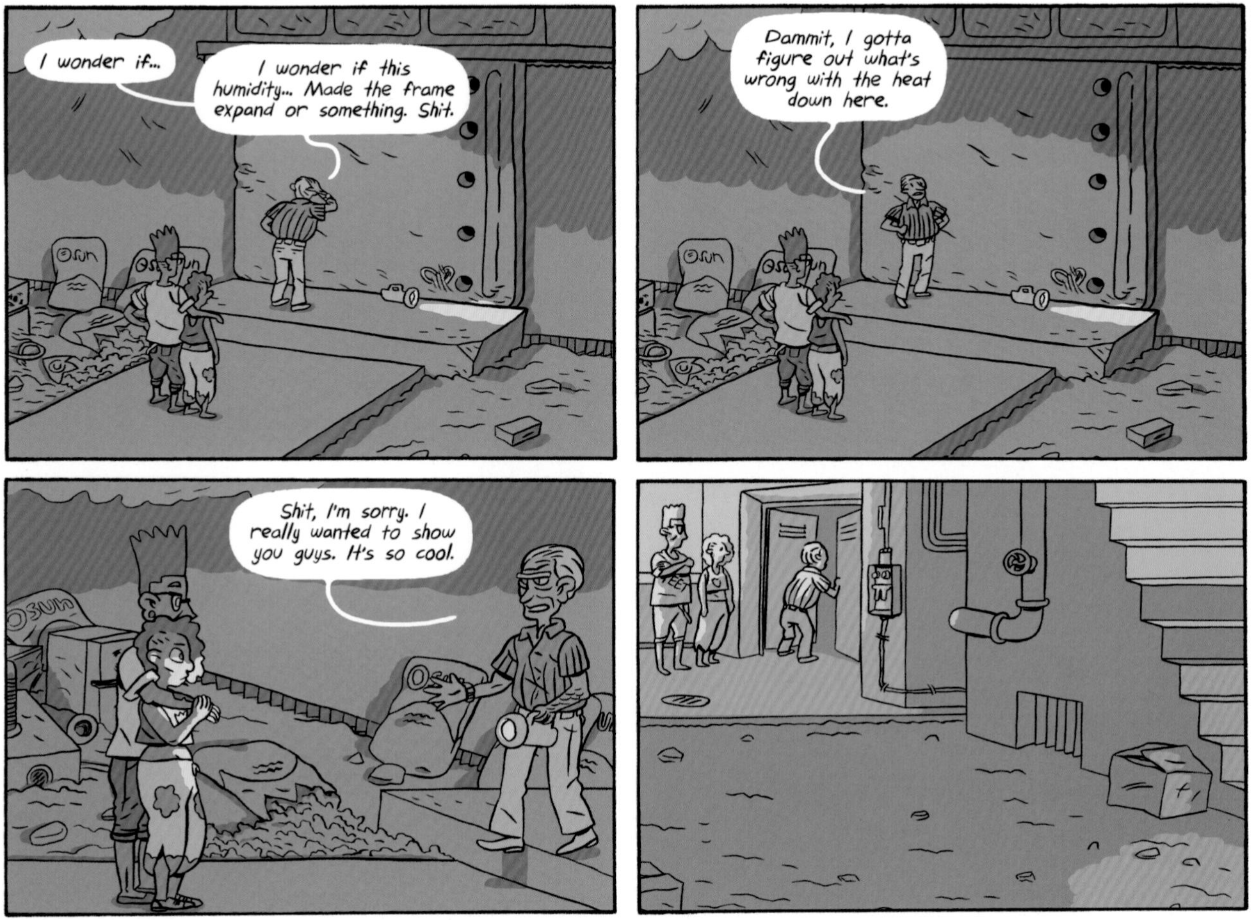
I wonder if...
I wonder if this humidity... Made the frame expand or something. Shit.
Dammit, I gotta figure out what's wrong with the heat down here.
Shit, I'm sorry. I really wanted to show you guys. It's so cool.

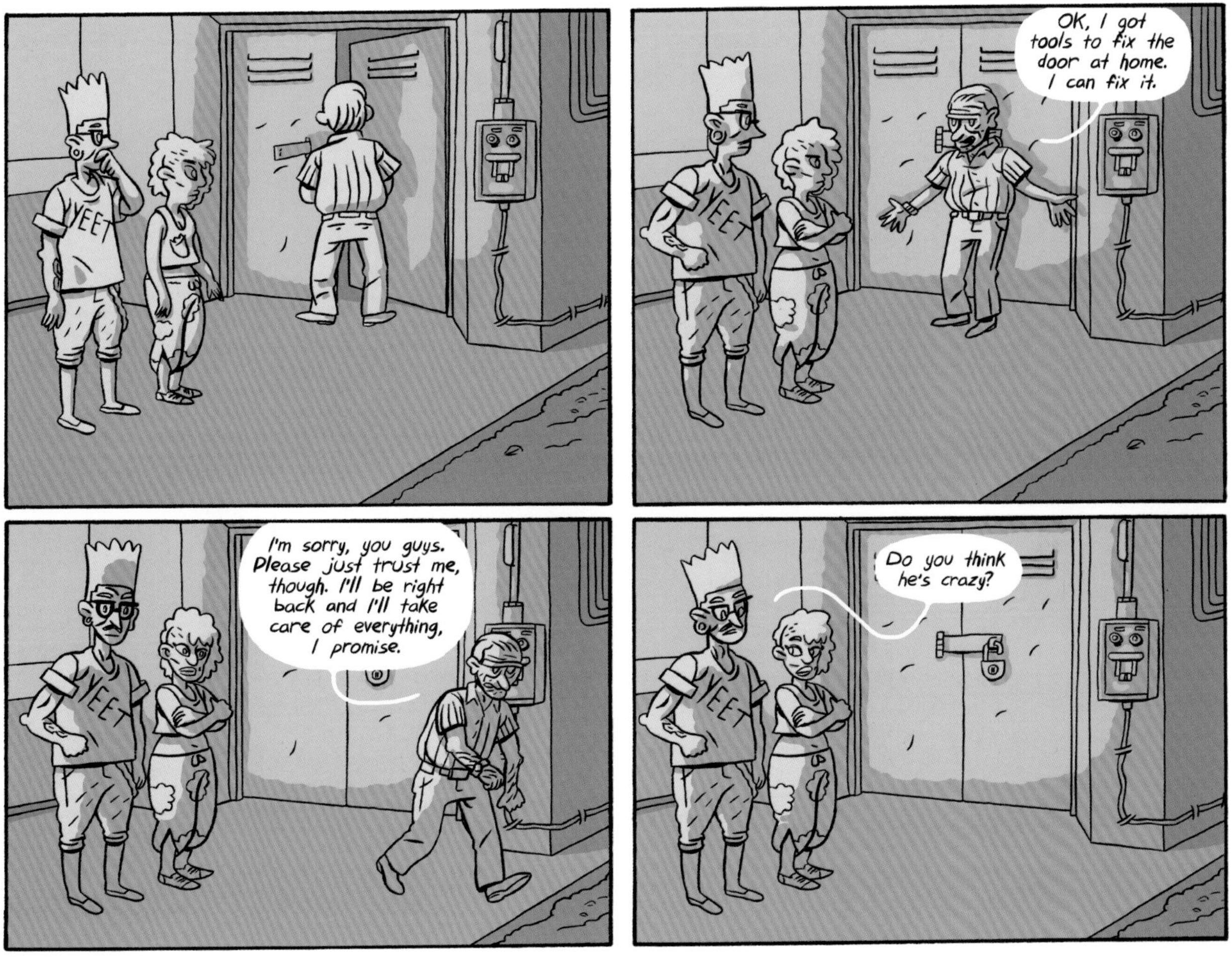
OK, I got tools to fix the door at home. I can fix it.
I'm sorry, you guys. Please just trust me, though. I'll be right back and I'll take care of everything, I promise.
Do you think he's crazy?
YEET

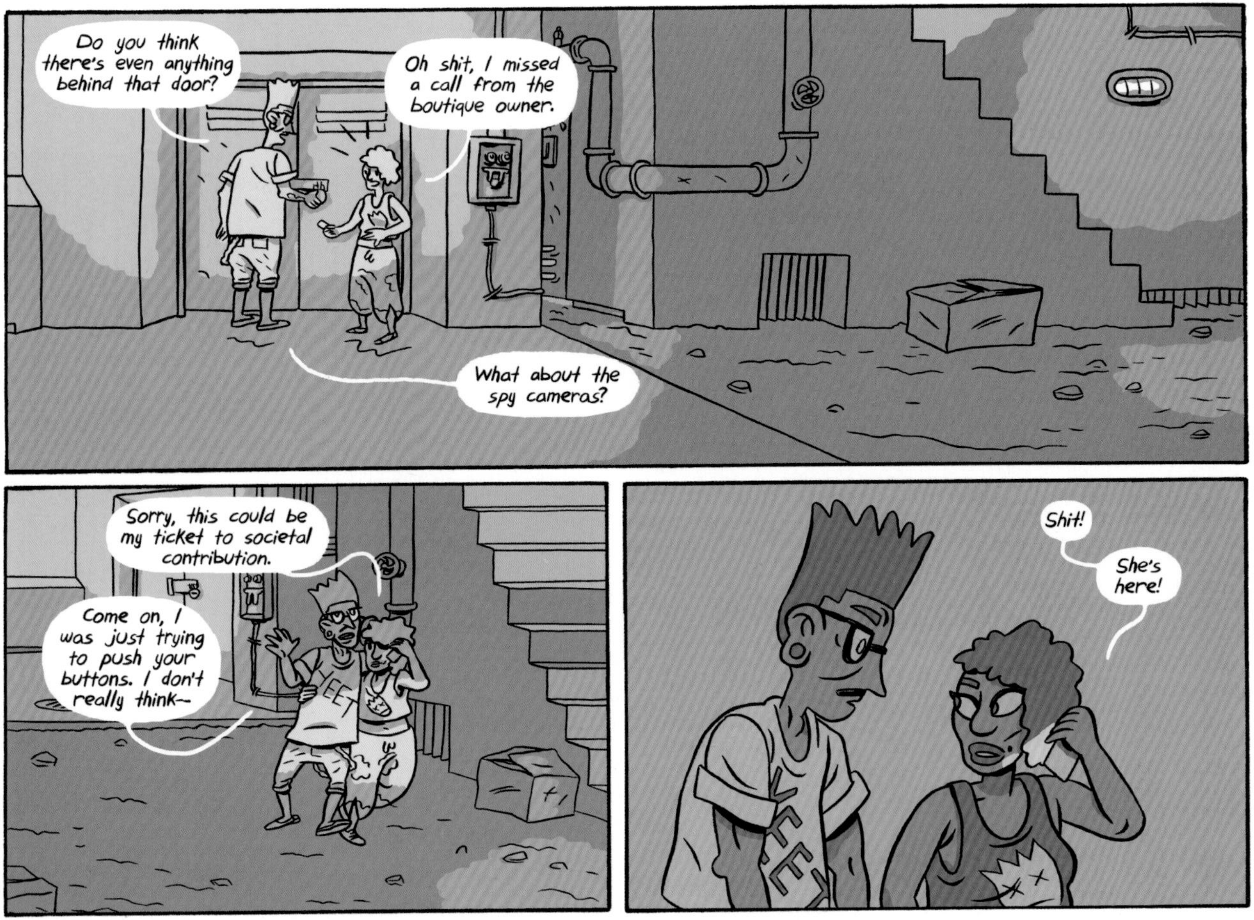
Do you think there's even anything behind that door?
Oh shit, I missed a call from the boutique owner.
What about the spy cameras?
Sorry, this could be my ticket to societal contribution.
Come on, I was just trying to push your buttons. I don't really think--
Shit!
She's here!

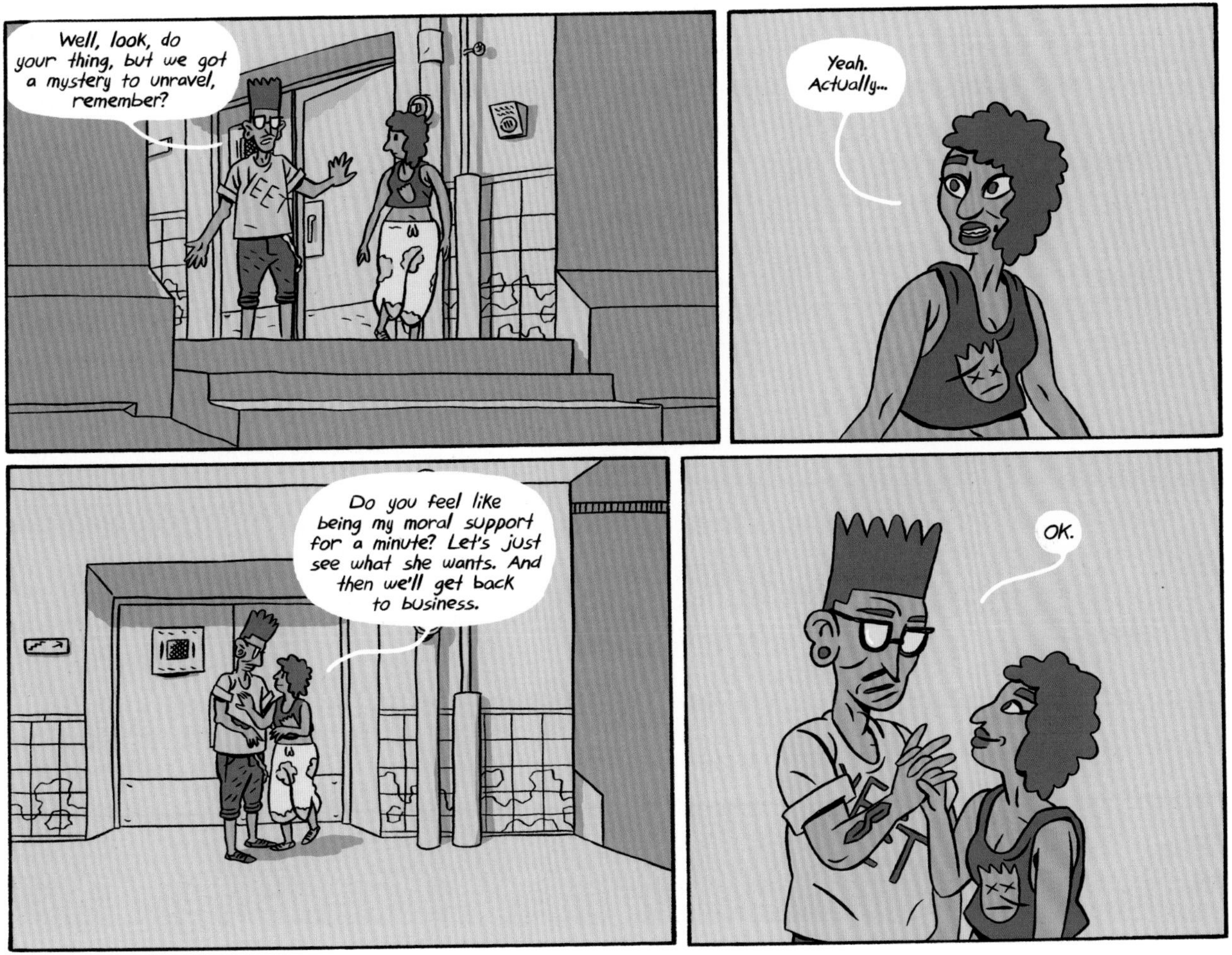
Well, look, do your thing, but we got a mystery to unravel, remember?
Yeah. Actually...
Do you feel like being my moral support for a minute? Let's just see what she wants. And then we'll get back to business.
OK.

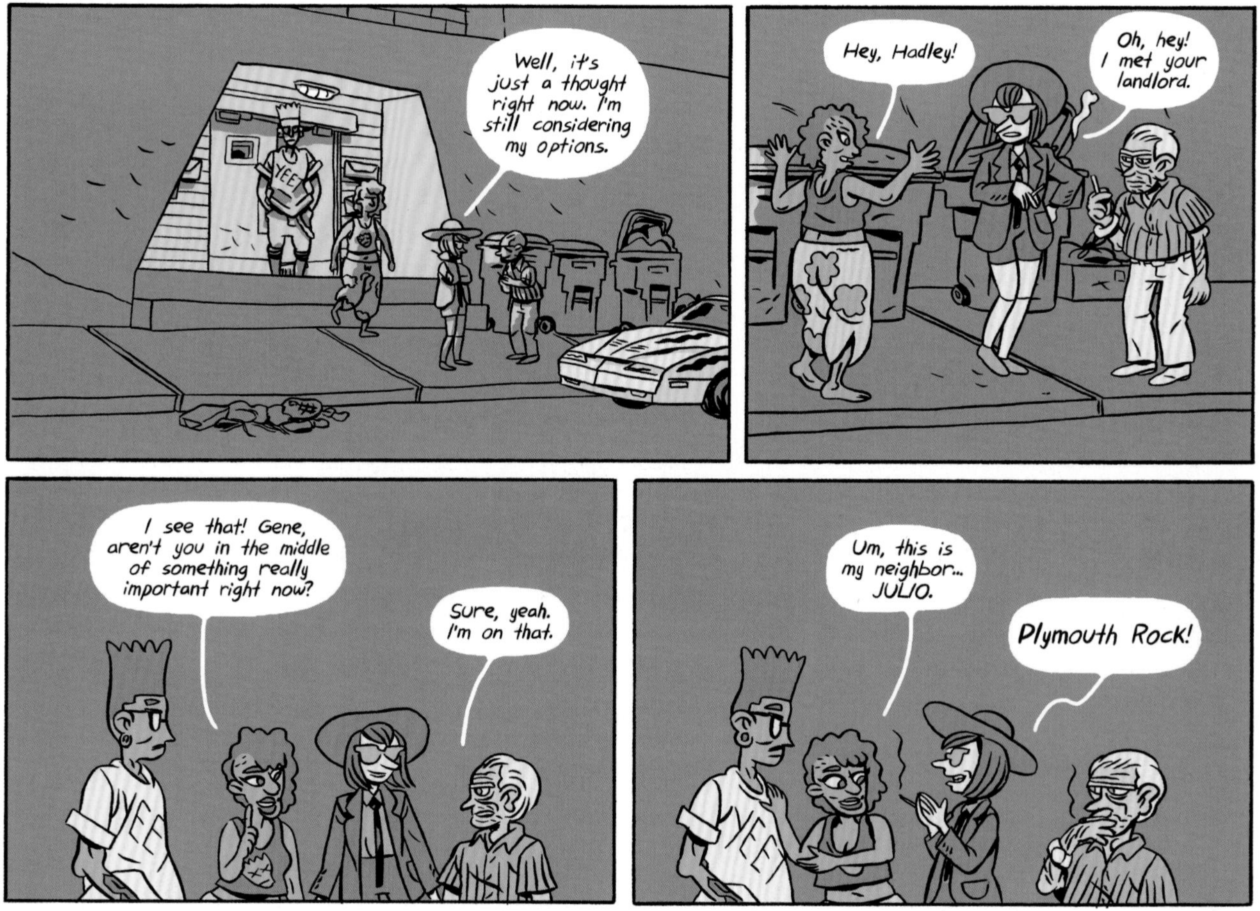
Well, it's just a thought right now. I'm still considering my options.
Hey, Hadley!
Oh, hey! I met your landlord.
I see that! Gene, aren't you in the middle of something really important right now?
Sure, yeah. I'm on that.
Um, this is my neighbor... JULIO.
Plymouth Rock!

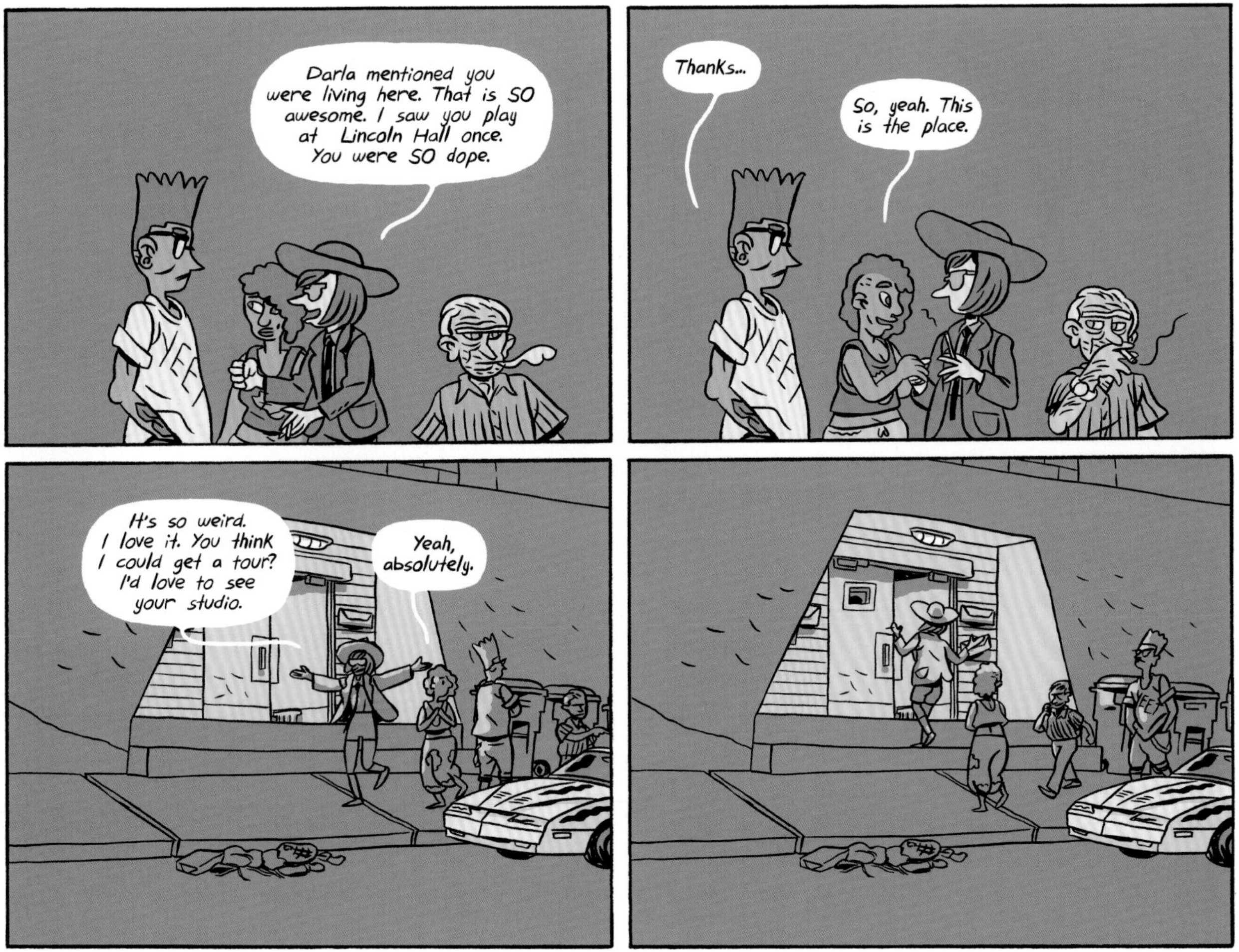
Darla mentioned you were living here. That is SO awesome. I saw you play at Lincoln Hall once. You were SO dope.
Thanks...
So, yeah. This is the place.
It's so weird. I love it. You think I could get a tour? I'd love to see your studio.
Yeah, absolutely.
YEE

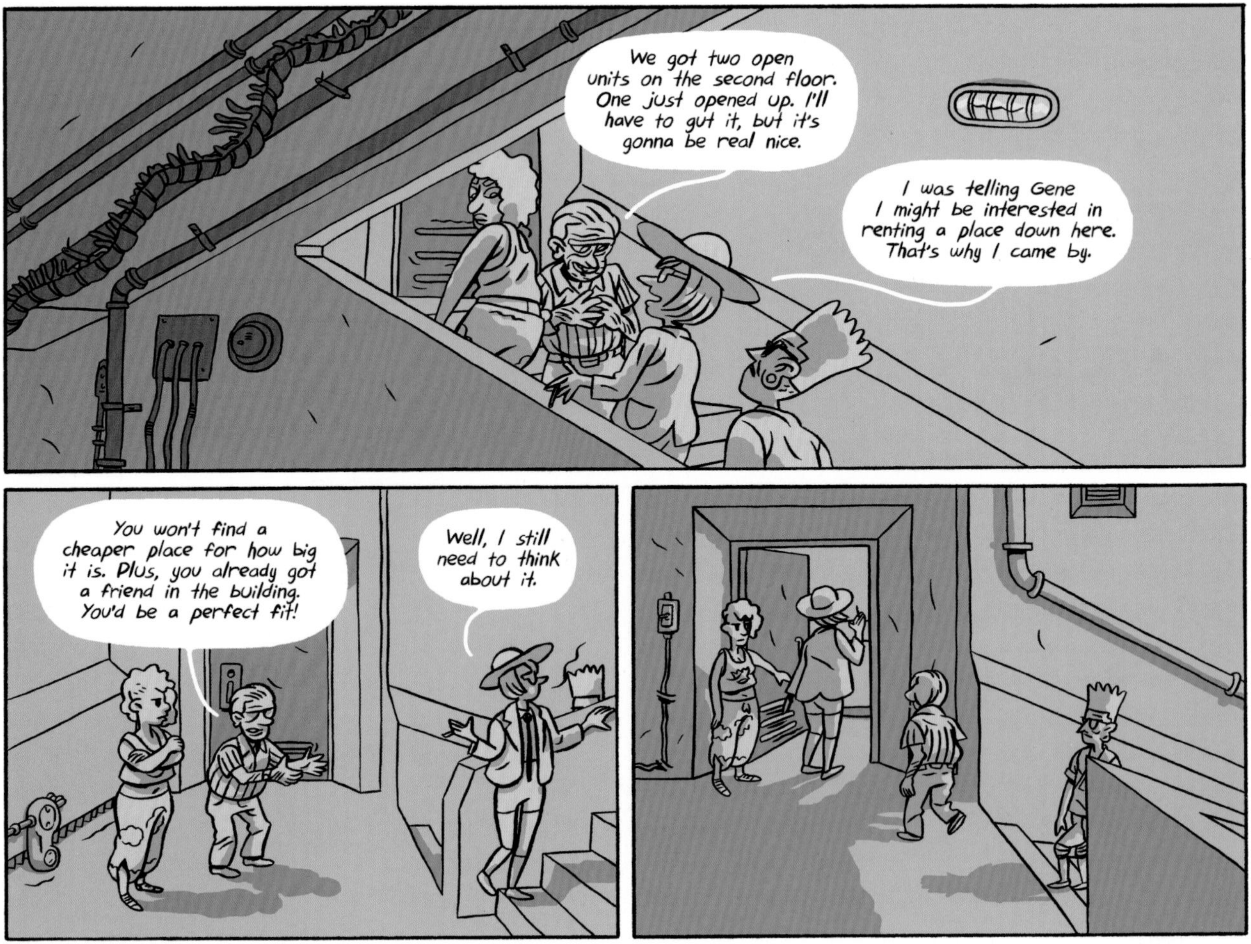
We got two open units on the second floor. One just opened up. I'll have to gut it, but it's gonna be real nice.
I was telling Gene I might be interested in renting a place down here. That's why I came by.
You won't find a cheaper place for how big it is. Plus, you already got a friend in the building. You'd be a perfect fit!
Well, I still need to think about it.

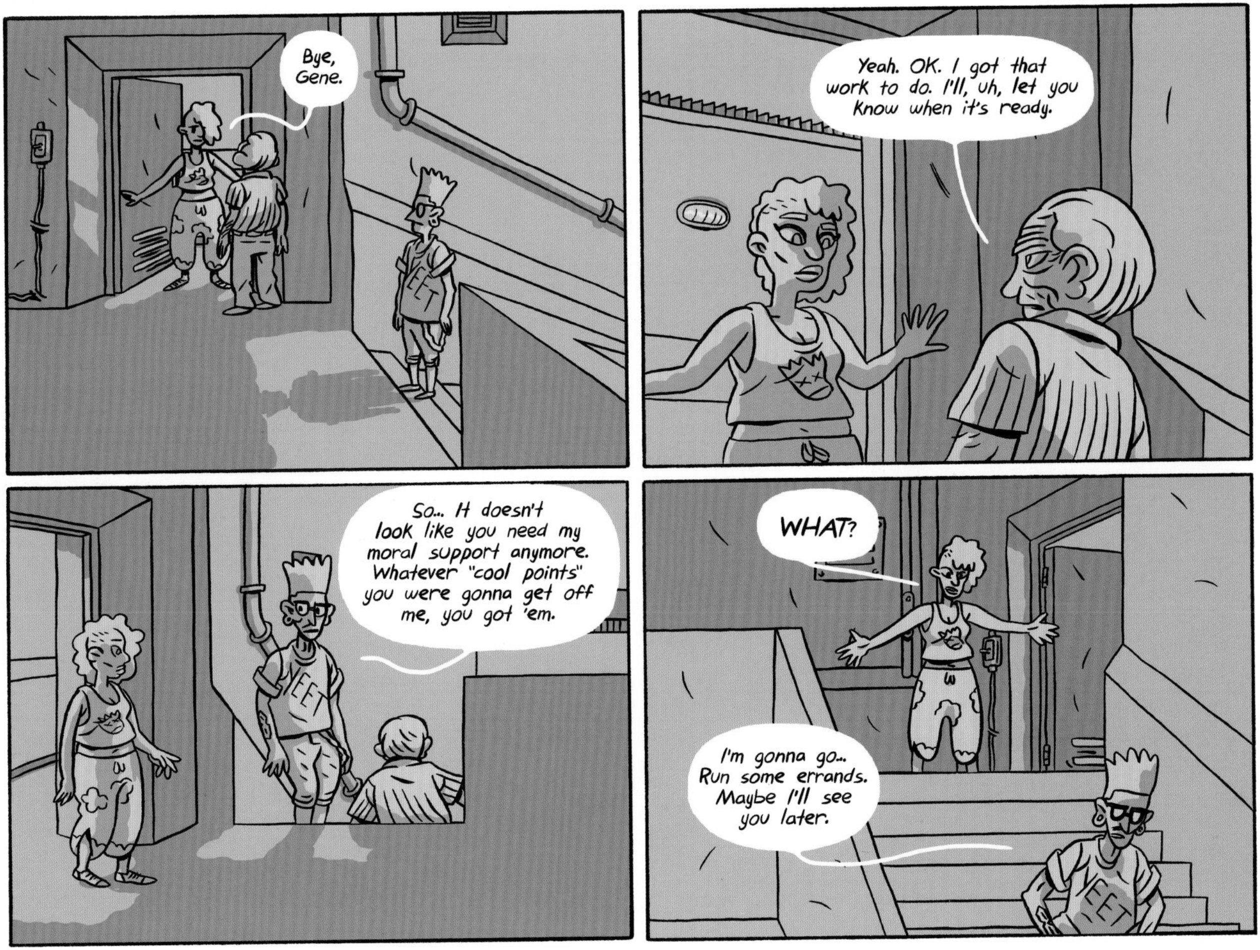
Bye, Gene.
Yeah. OK. I got that work to do. I'll, uh, let you know when it's ready.
So... It doesn't look like you need my moral support anymore. Whatever "cool points" you were gonna get off me, you got 'em.
WHAT?
I'm gonna go... Run some errands. Maybe I'll see you later.

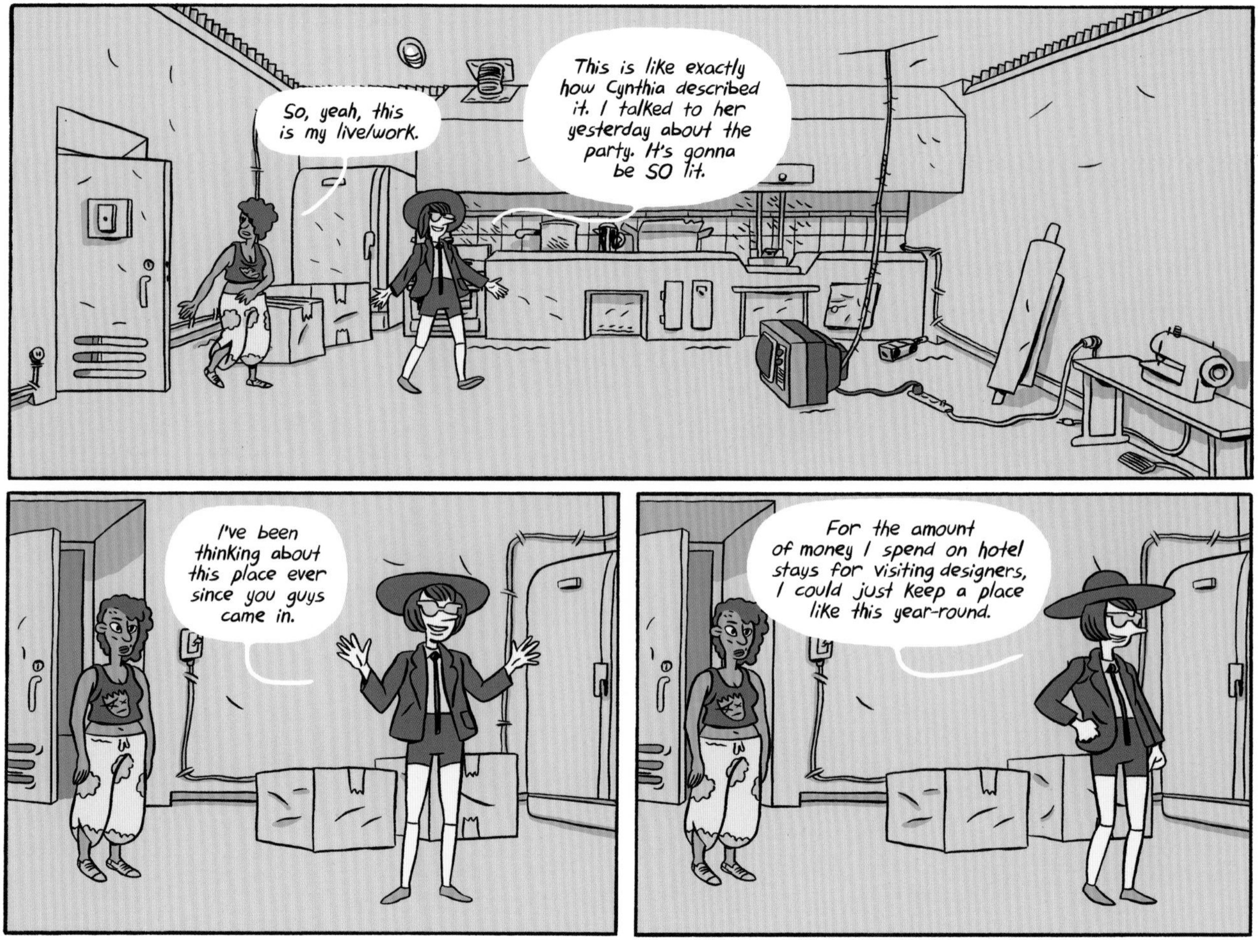
So, yeah, this is my live/work.
This is like exactly how Cynthia described it. I talked to her yesterday about the party. It's gonna be SO lit.
I've been thinking about this place ever since you guys came in.
For the amount of money I spend on hotel stays for visiting designers, I could just keep a place like this year-round.

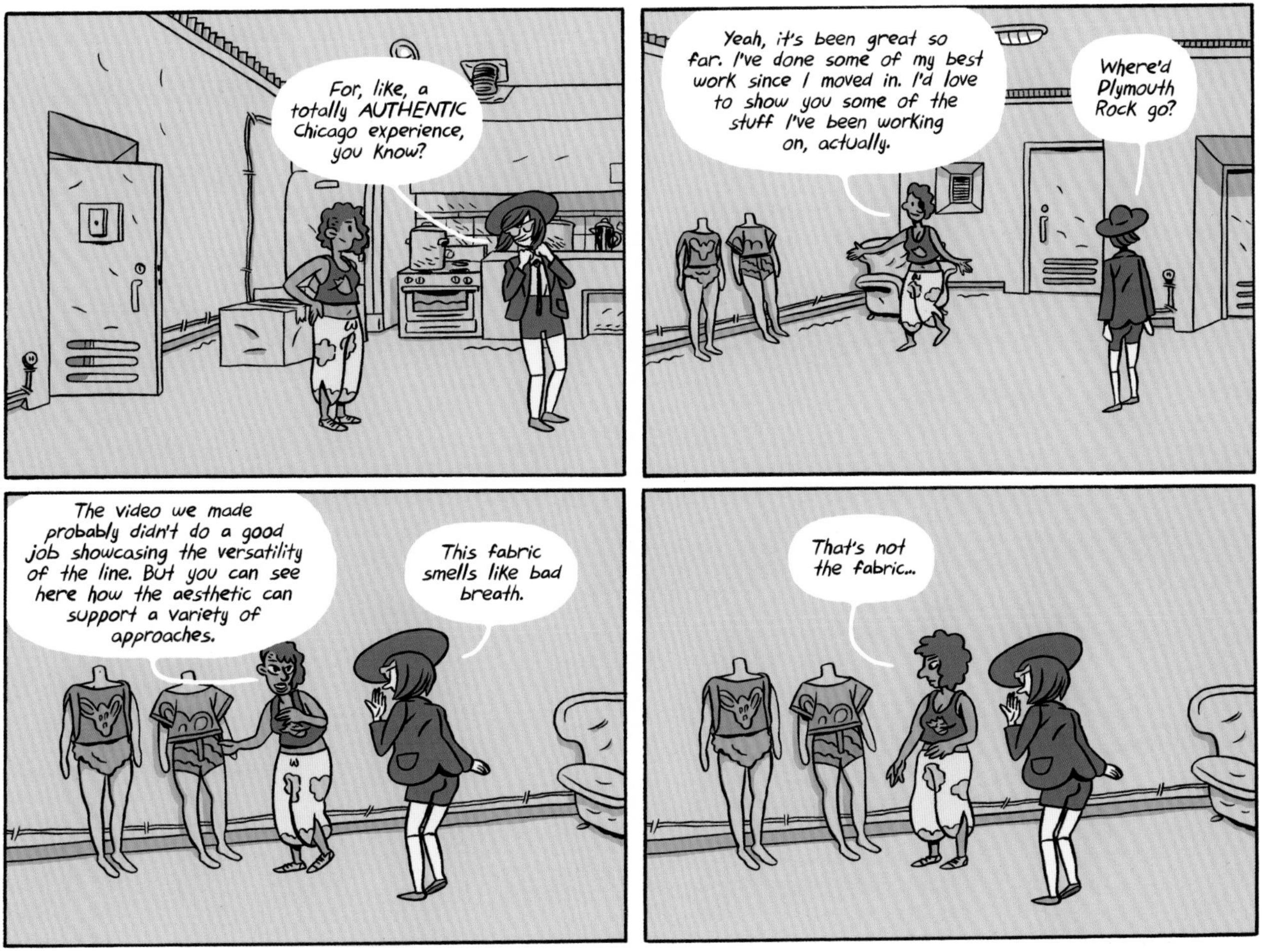
For, like, a totally AUTHENTIC Chicago experience, you know?
Yeah, it's been great so far. I've done some of my best work since I moved in. I'd love to show you some of the stuff I've been working on, actually.
Where'd Plymouth Rock go?
The video we made probably didn't do a good job showcasing the versatility of the line. But you can see here how the aesthetic can support a variety of approaches.
This fabric smells like bad breath.
That's not the fabric...

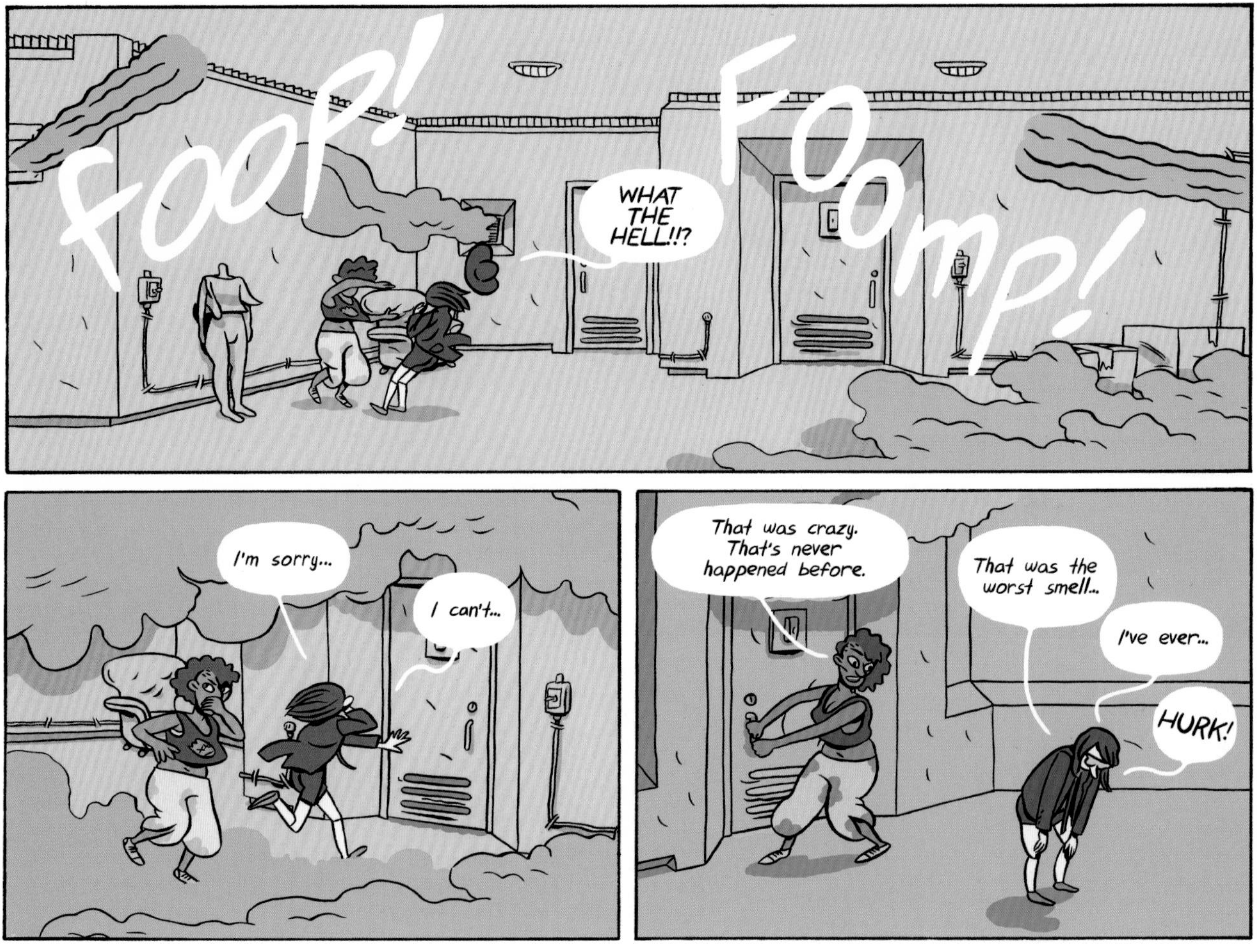
FOOP!
FOOMP!
WHAT THE HELL!!?
I'm sorry...
I can't...
That was crazy. That's never happened before.
That was the worst smell...
I've ever...
HURK!

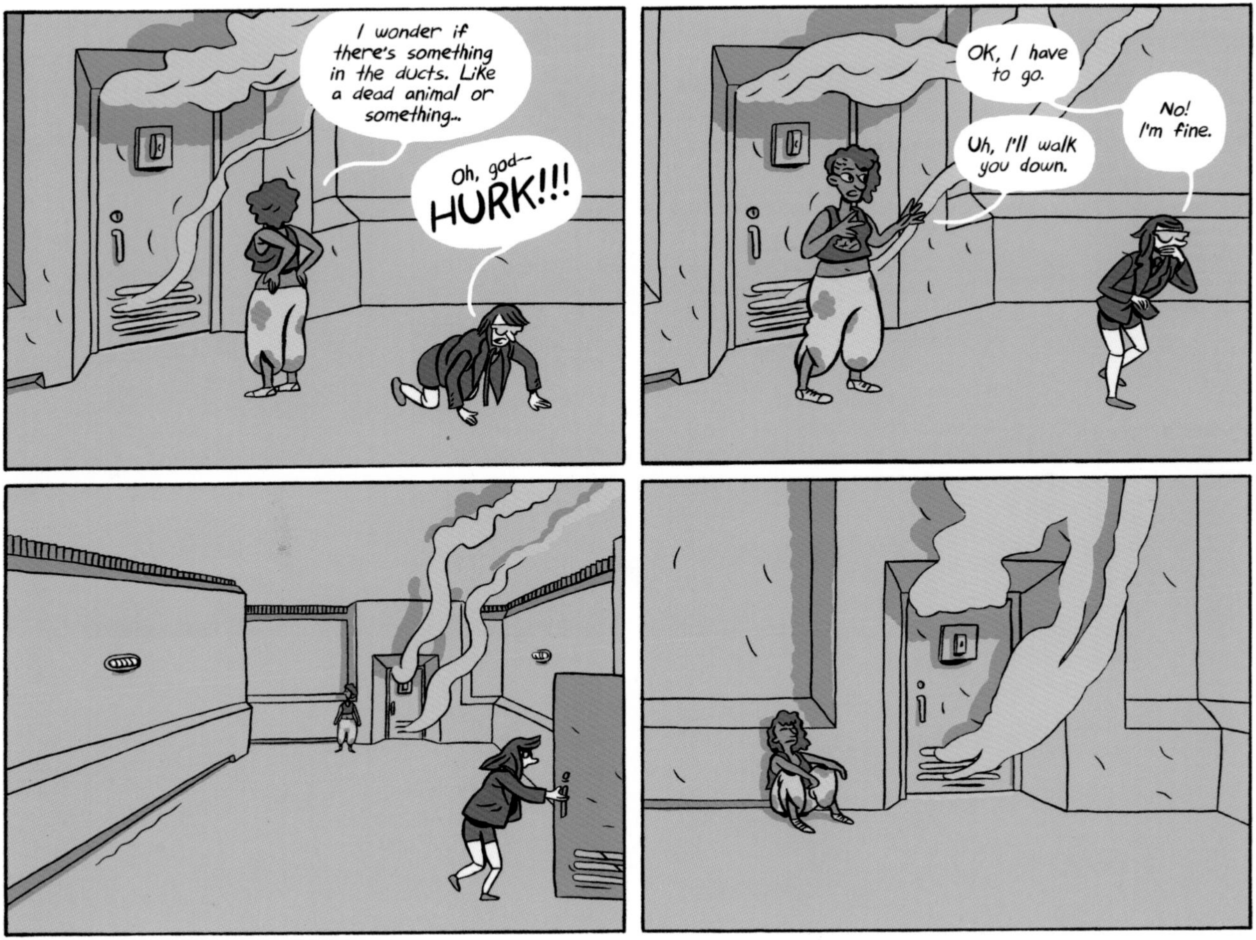
I wonder if there's something in the ducts. Like a dead animal or something...
Oh, god--
HURK!!!
OK, I have to go.
Uh, I'll walk you down.
No! I'm fine.

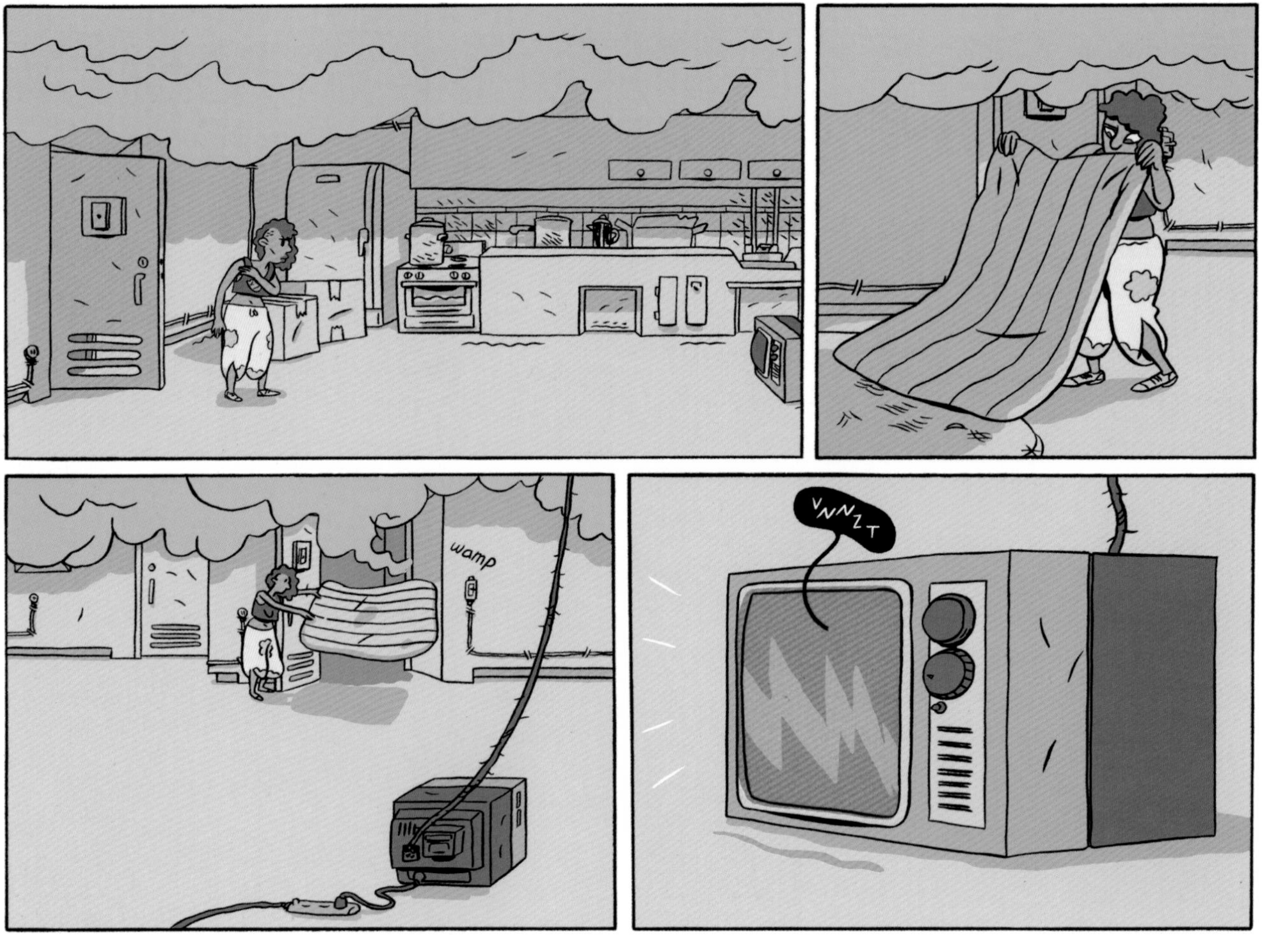
wamp
VNNZT

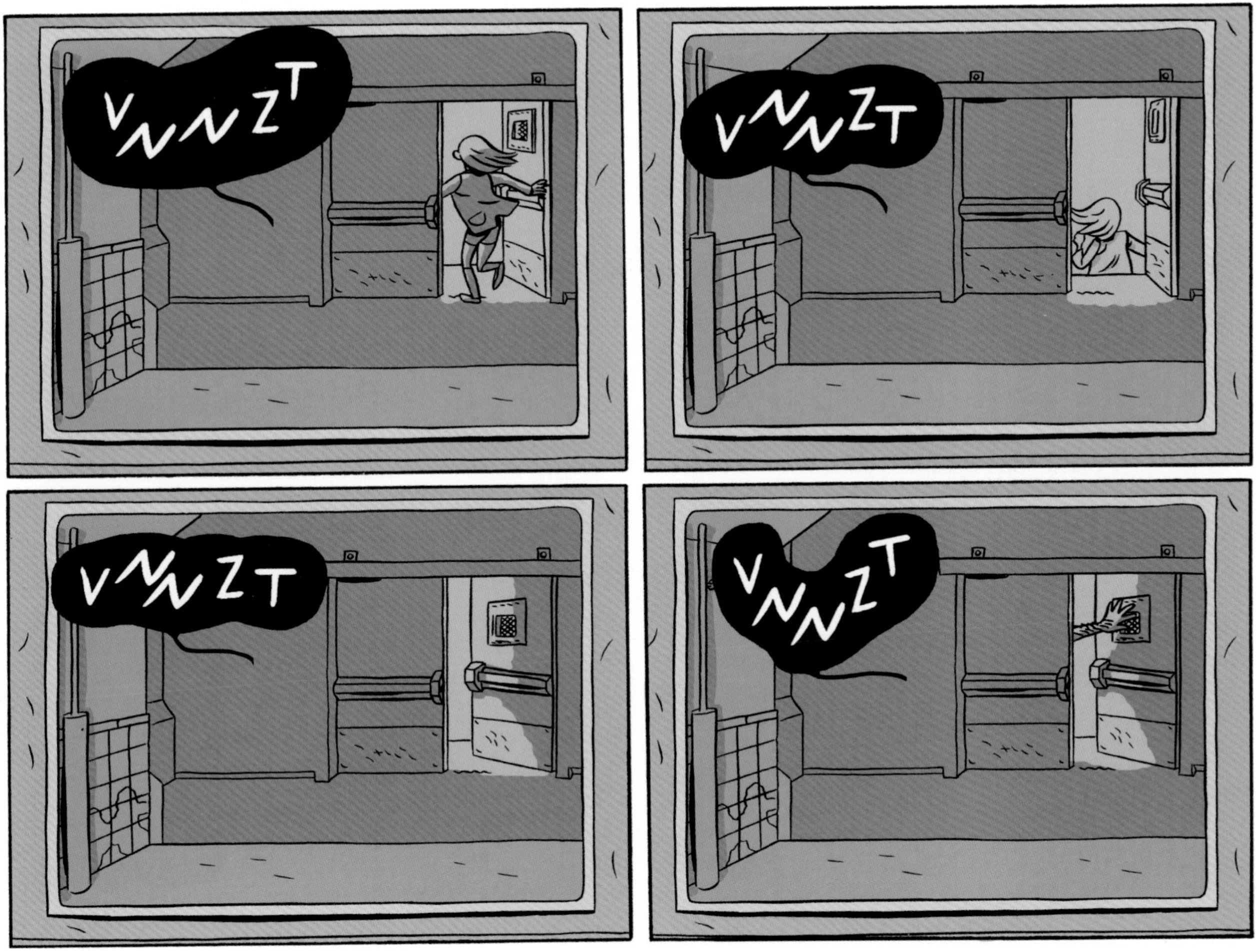
VNNZT
VNNZT
VNNZT
VNNZT

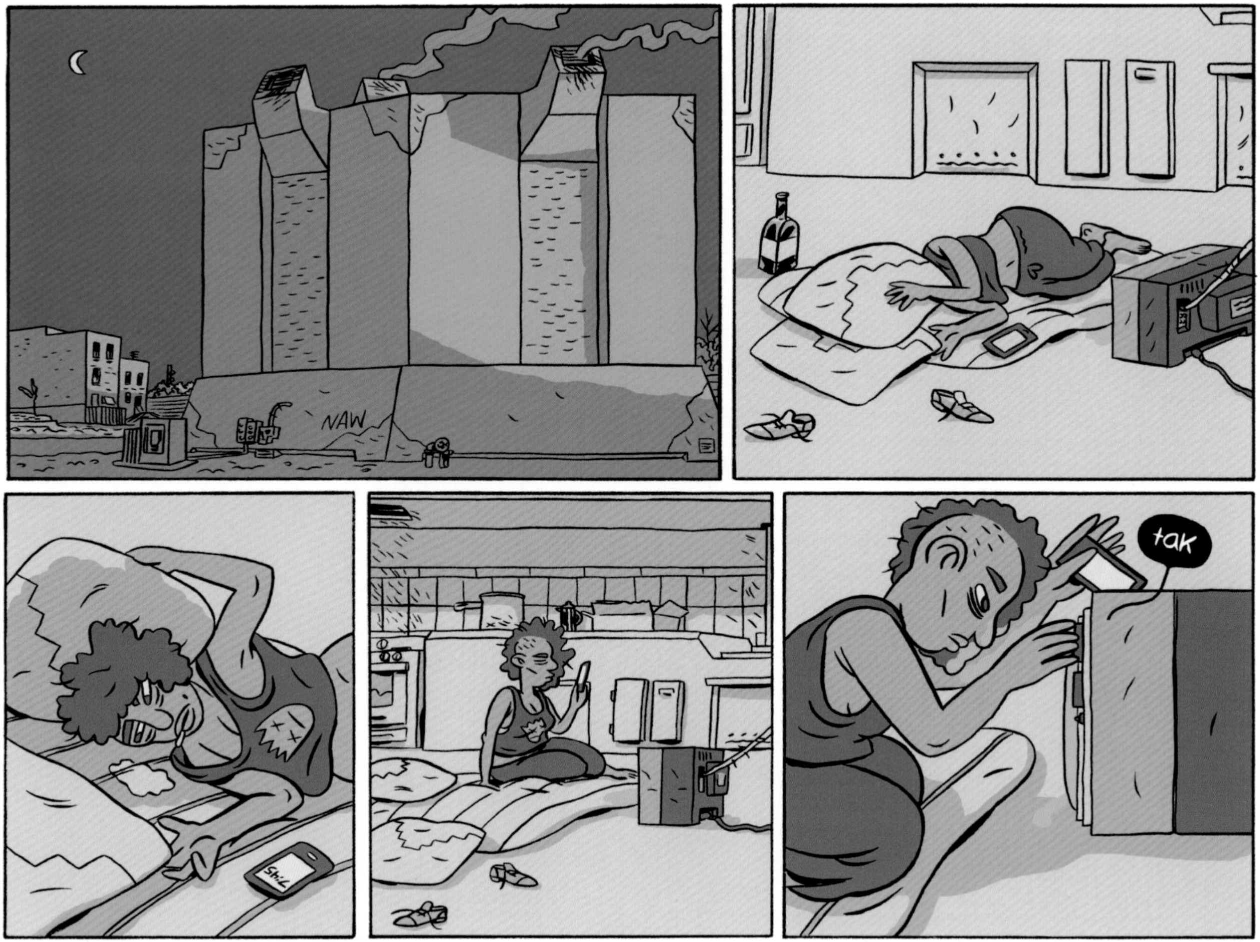
NAW
Shit
tak

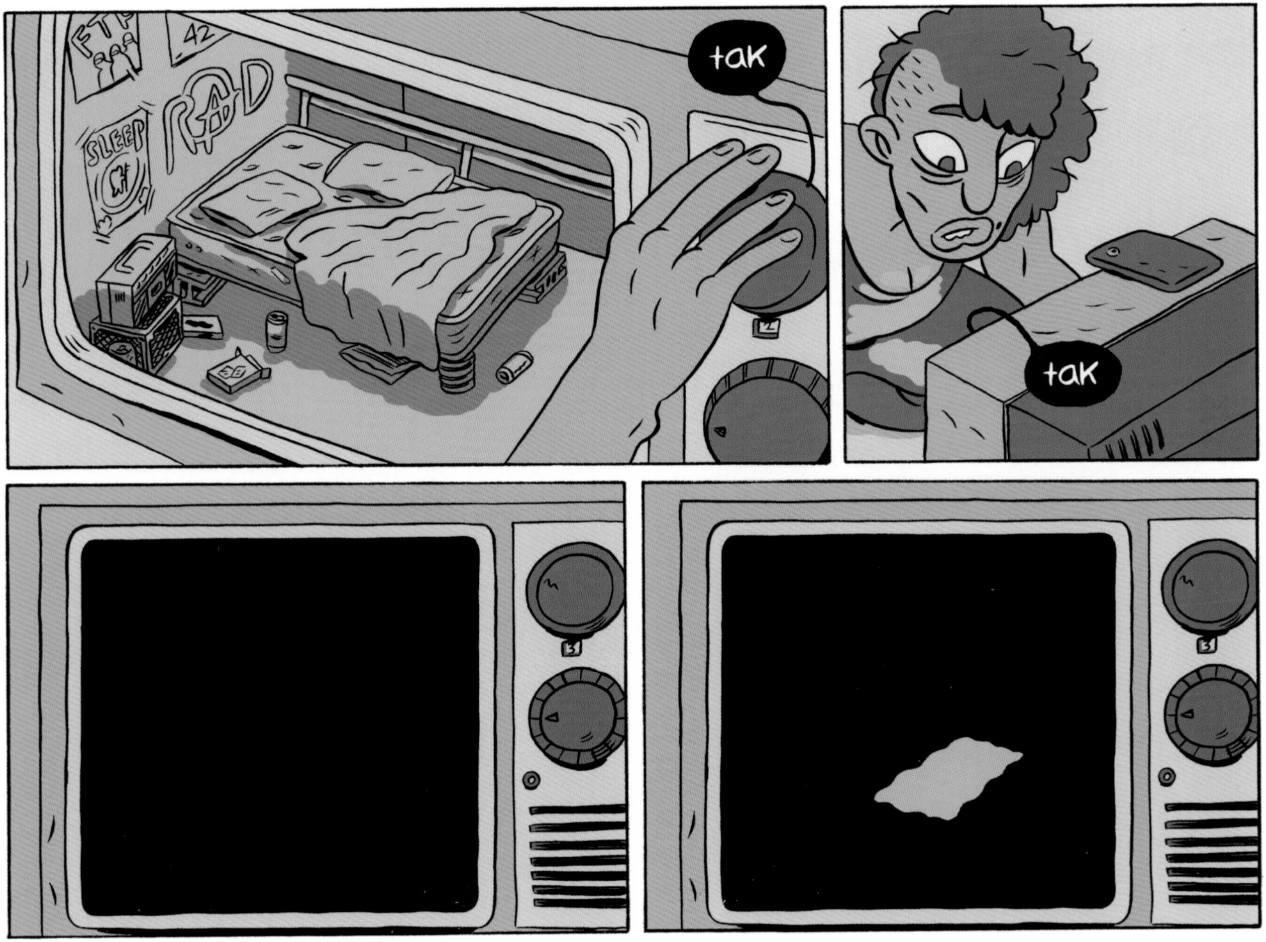
42
SLEEP
RAD
tak
tak

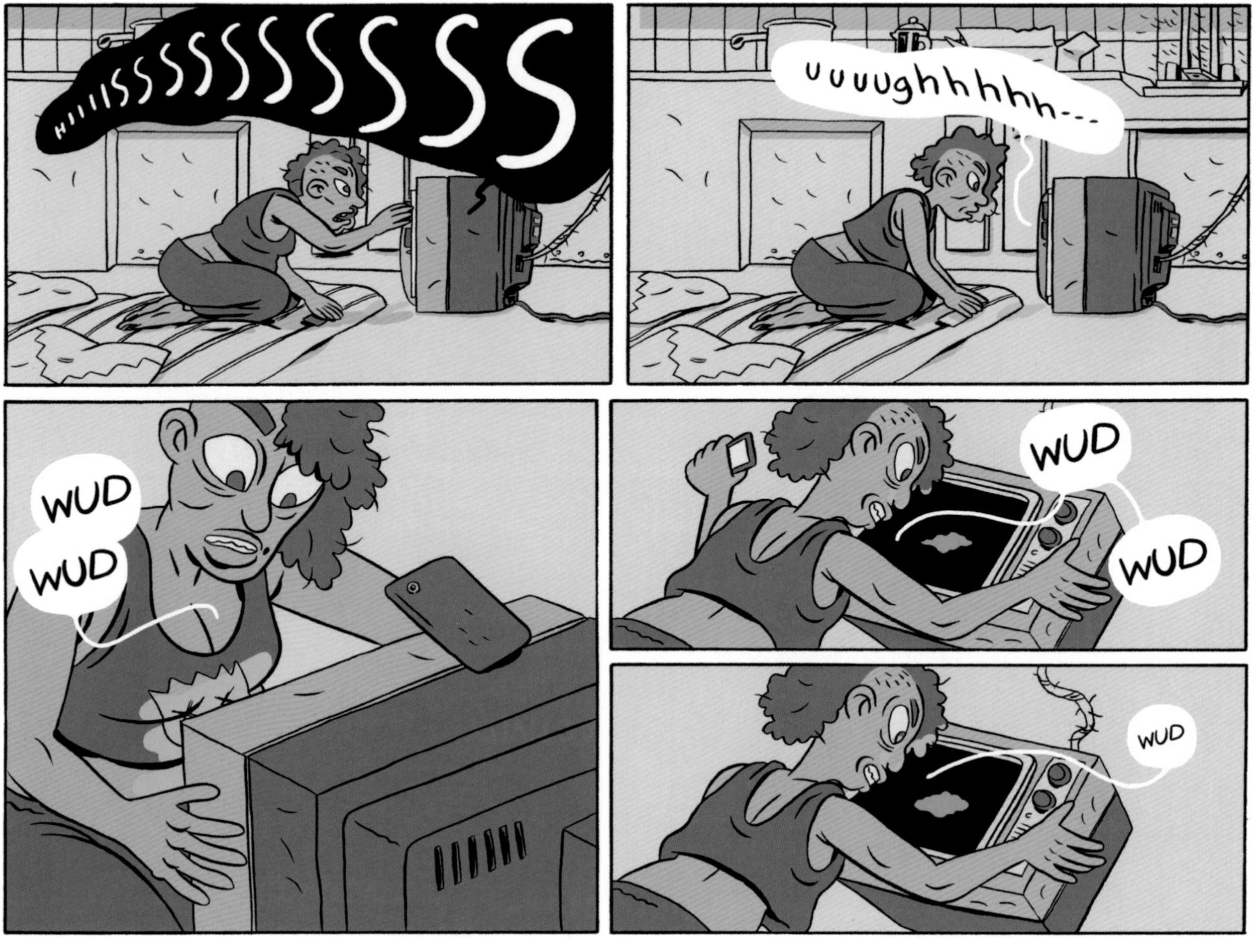
HIIIISSSSSSSSSSSS
uuuughhhhh---
WUD
WUD
WUD
WUD
WUD

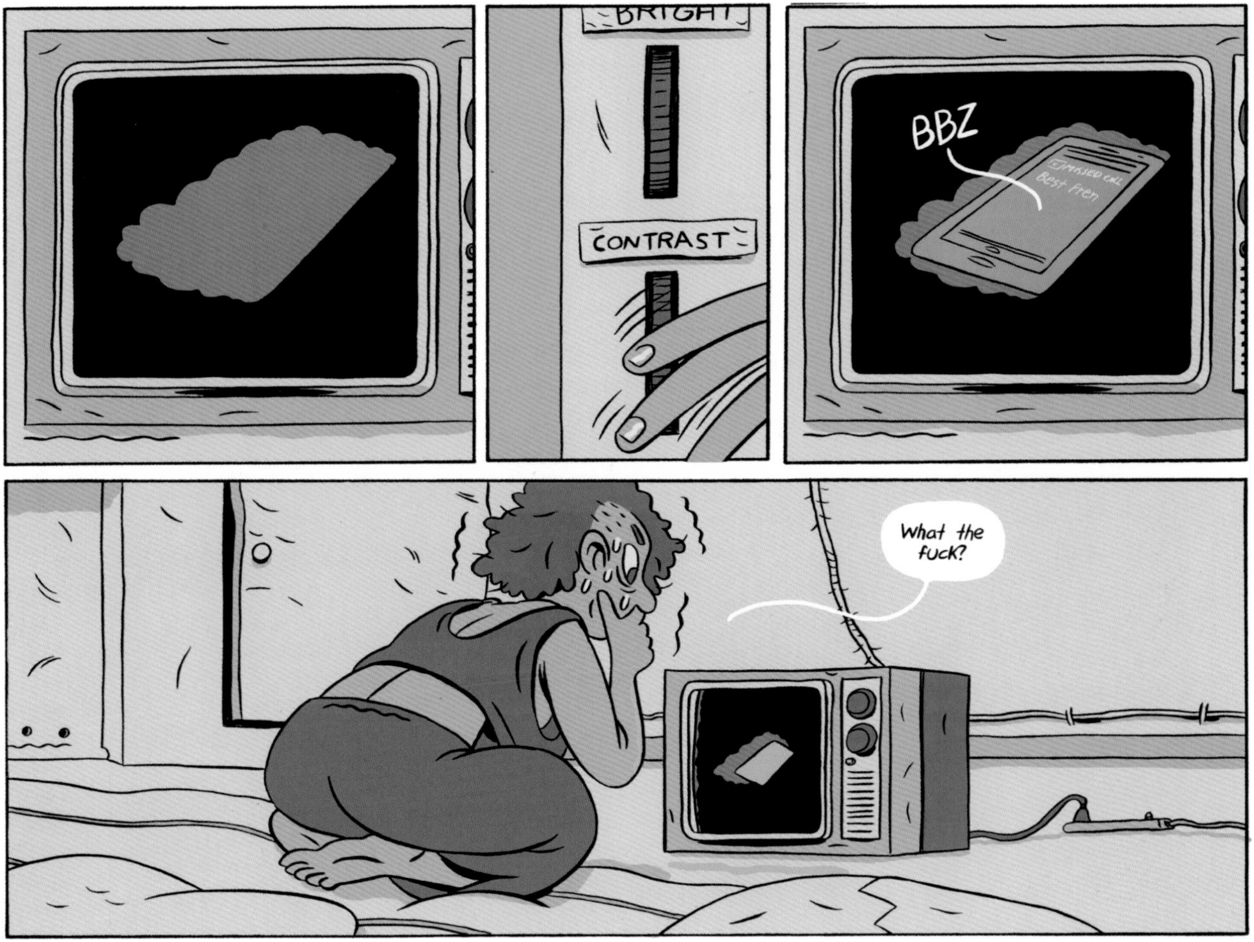
BRIGHT
CONTRAST
BBZ
MISSED CALL
Best fren
What the fuck?

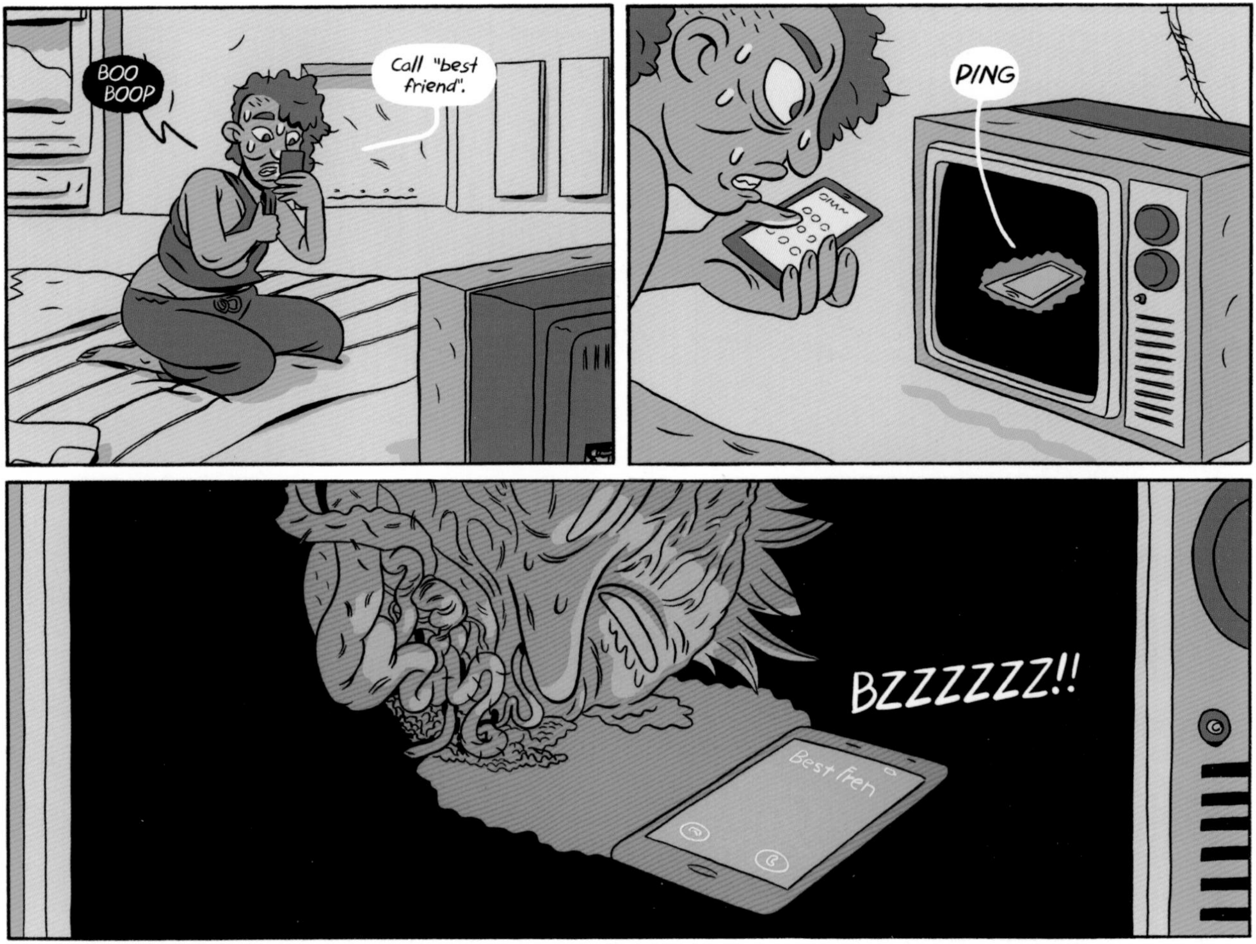
BOO BOOP
Call "best friend".
PING
BZZZZZZ!!
Best fren

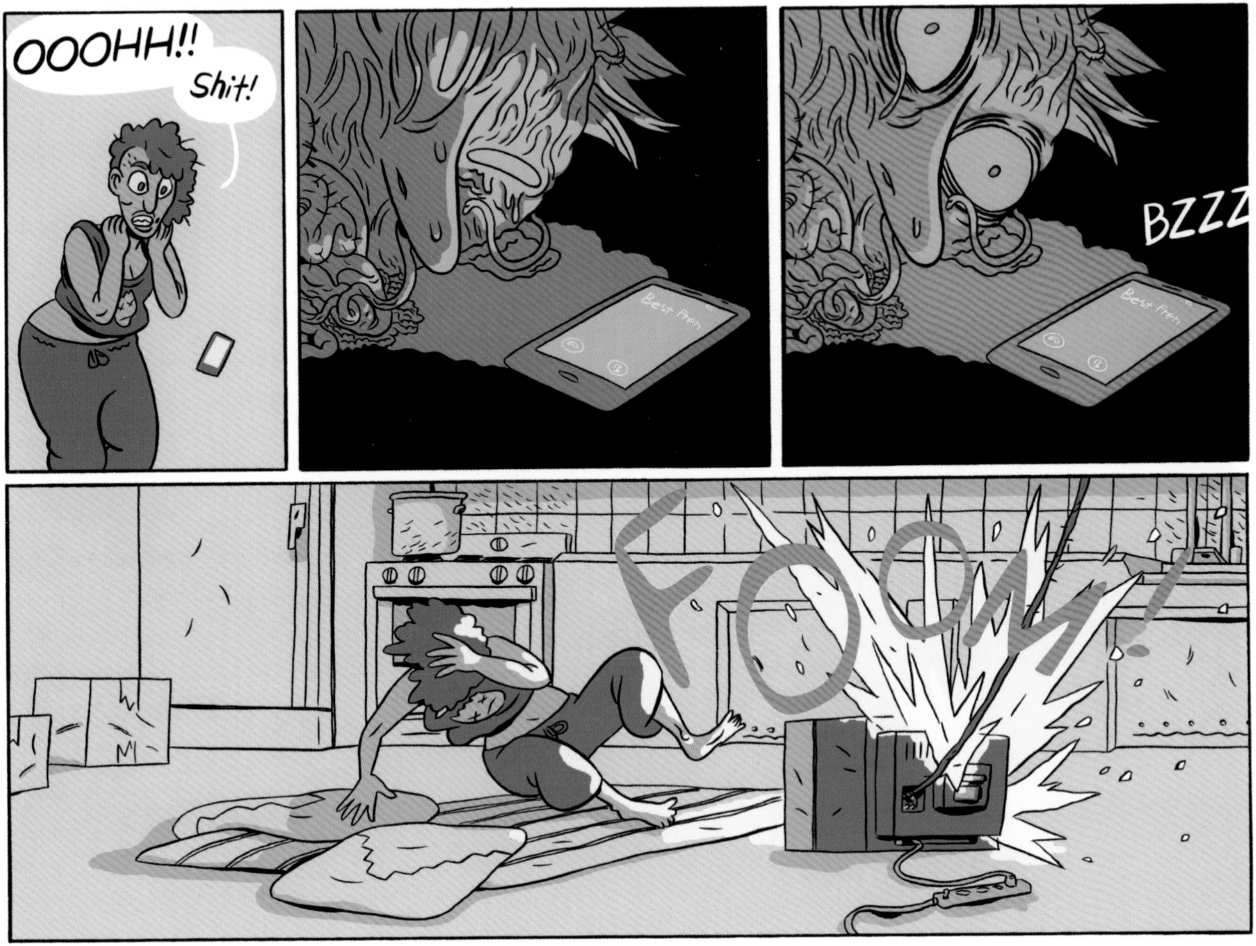
OOOHH!!
Shit!
Best Freh
Best Freh
BZZZ
FOOM!

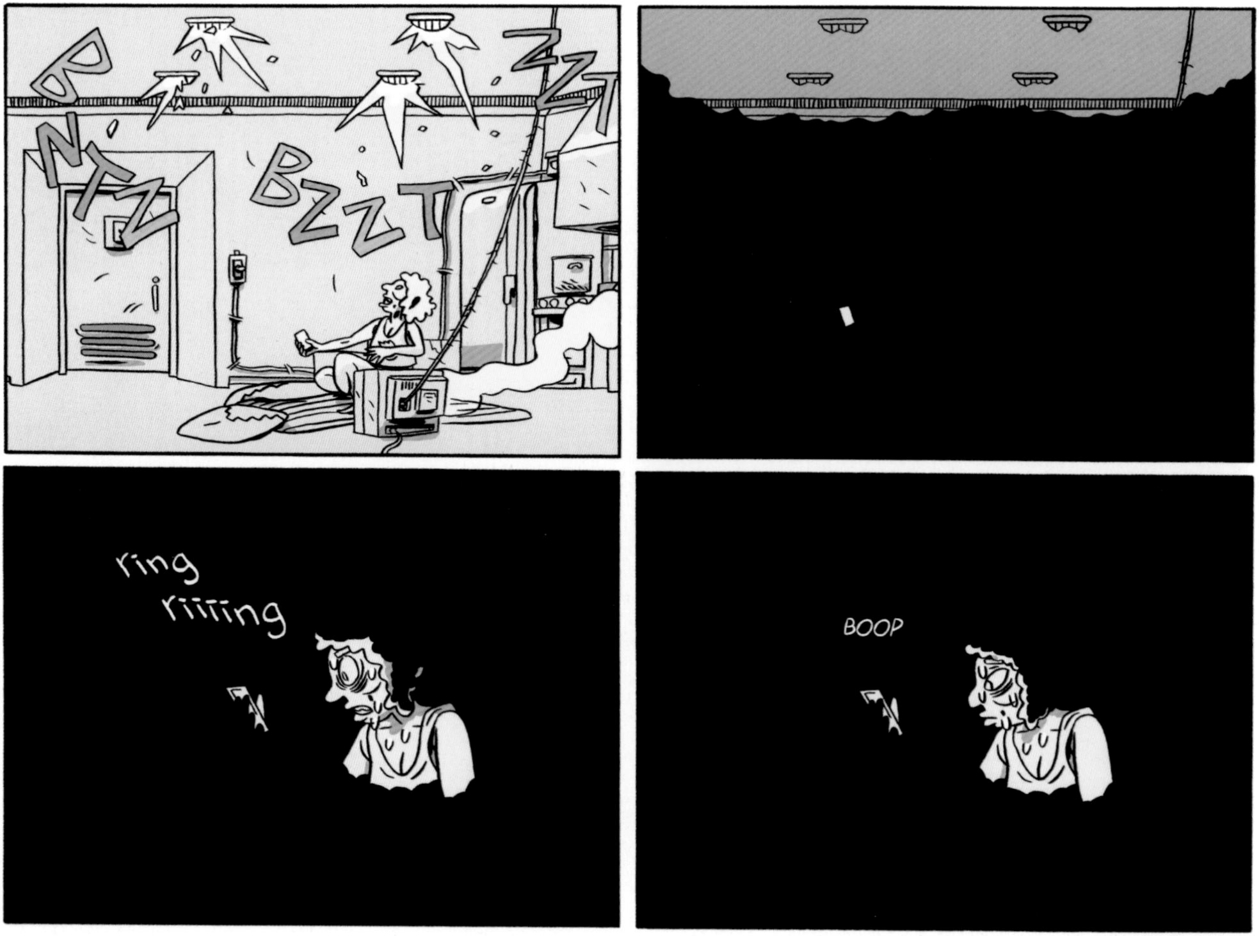
BNTZZ
BZZZT
ZZT
ring
riiiing
BOOP

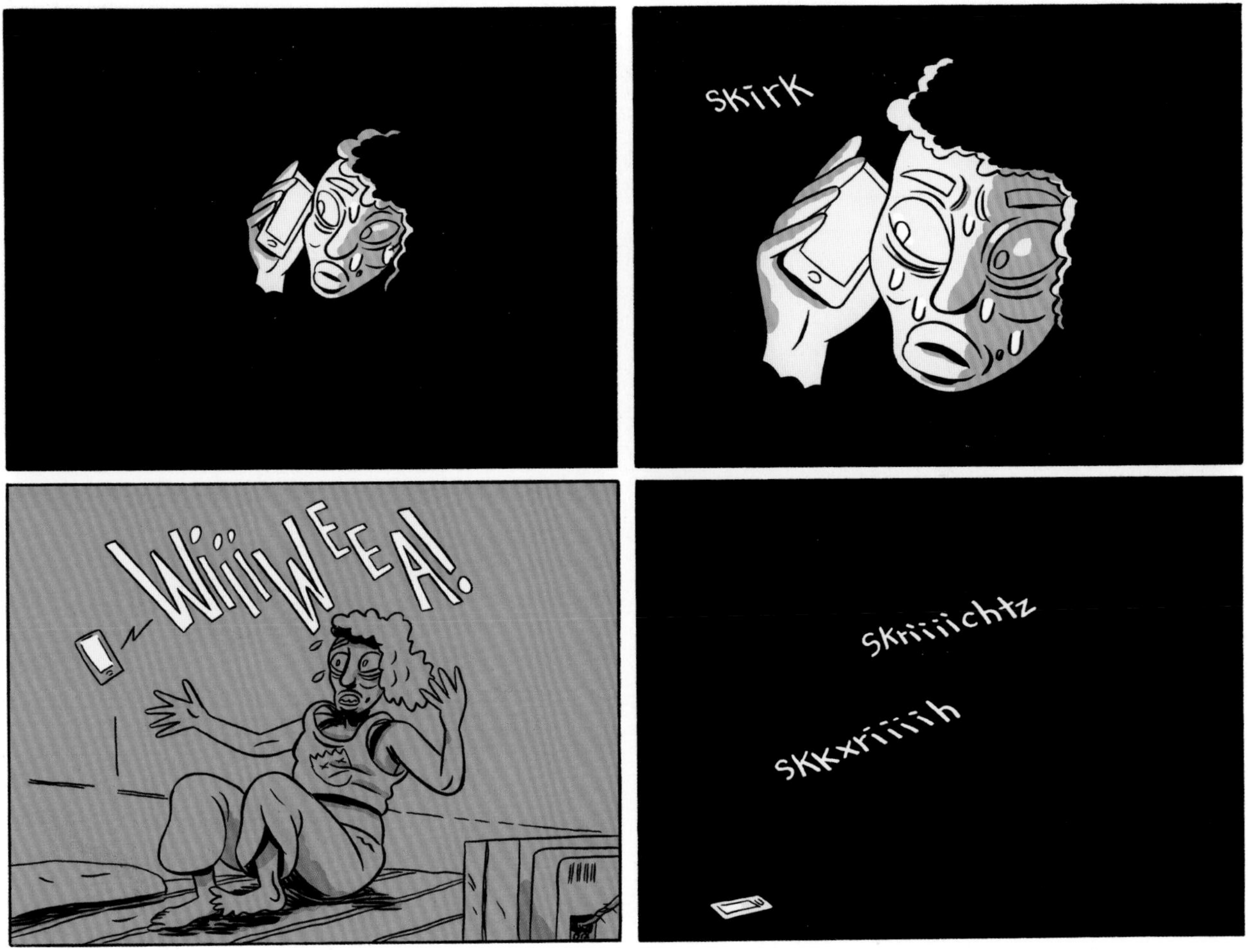
SKirK
WiiiWEEA!
Skriiiichtz
SKKxriiiiih

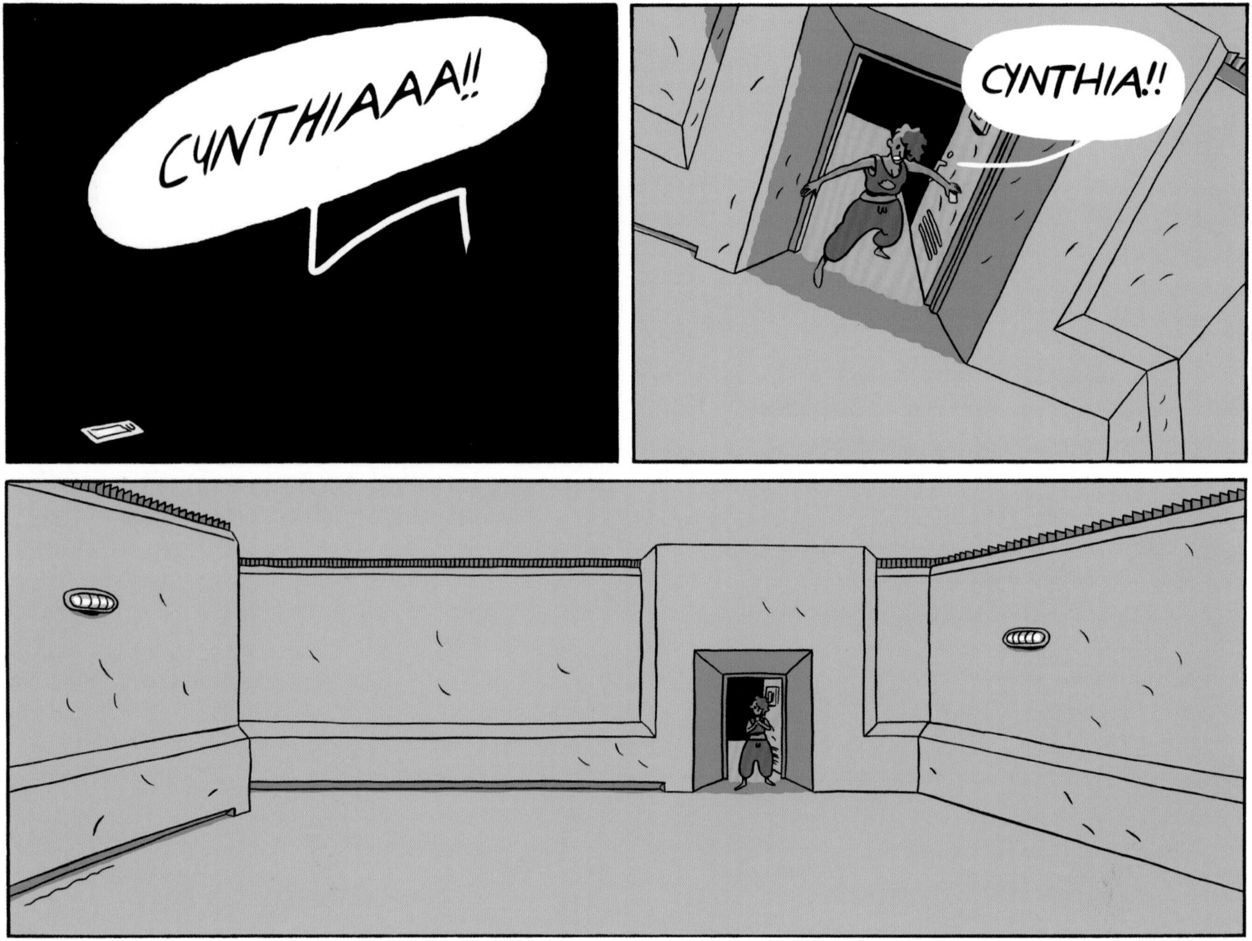
CYNTHIAAA!!
CYNTHIA!!

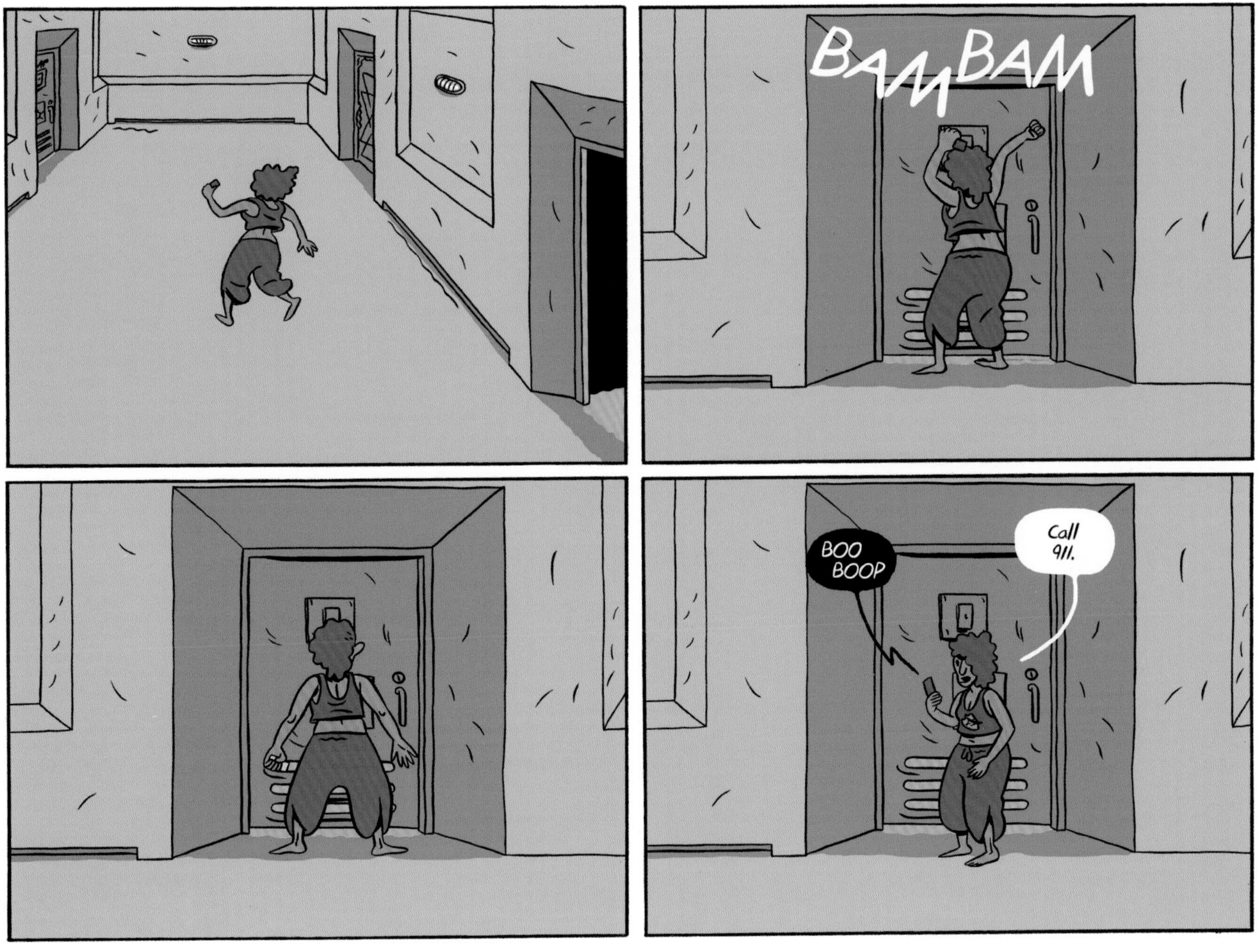
BAM BAM
BOO BOOP
Call 911.

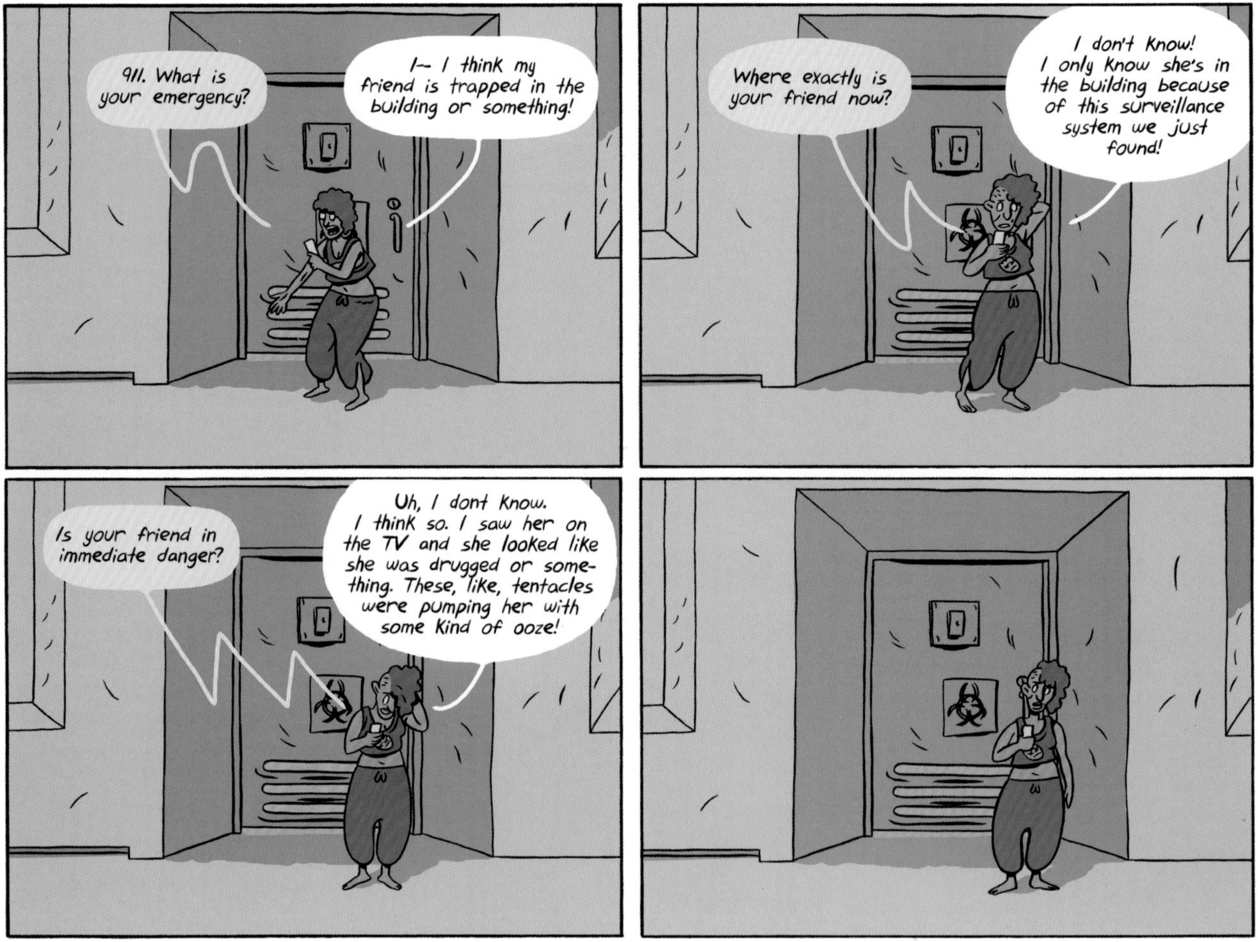

911. What is your emergency?
I– I think my friend is trapped in the building or something!
Where exactly is your friend now?
I don't know! I only know she's in the building because of this surveillance system we just found!
Is your friend in immediate danger?
Uh, I dont know. I think so. I saw her on the TV and she looked like she was drugged or some-thing. These, like, tentacles were pumping her with some kind of ooze!

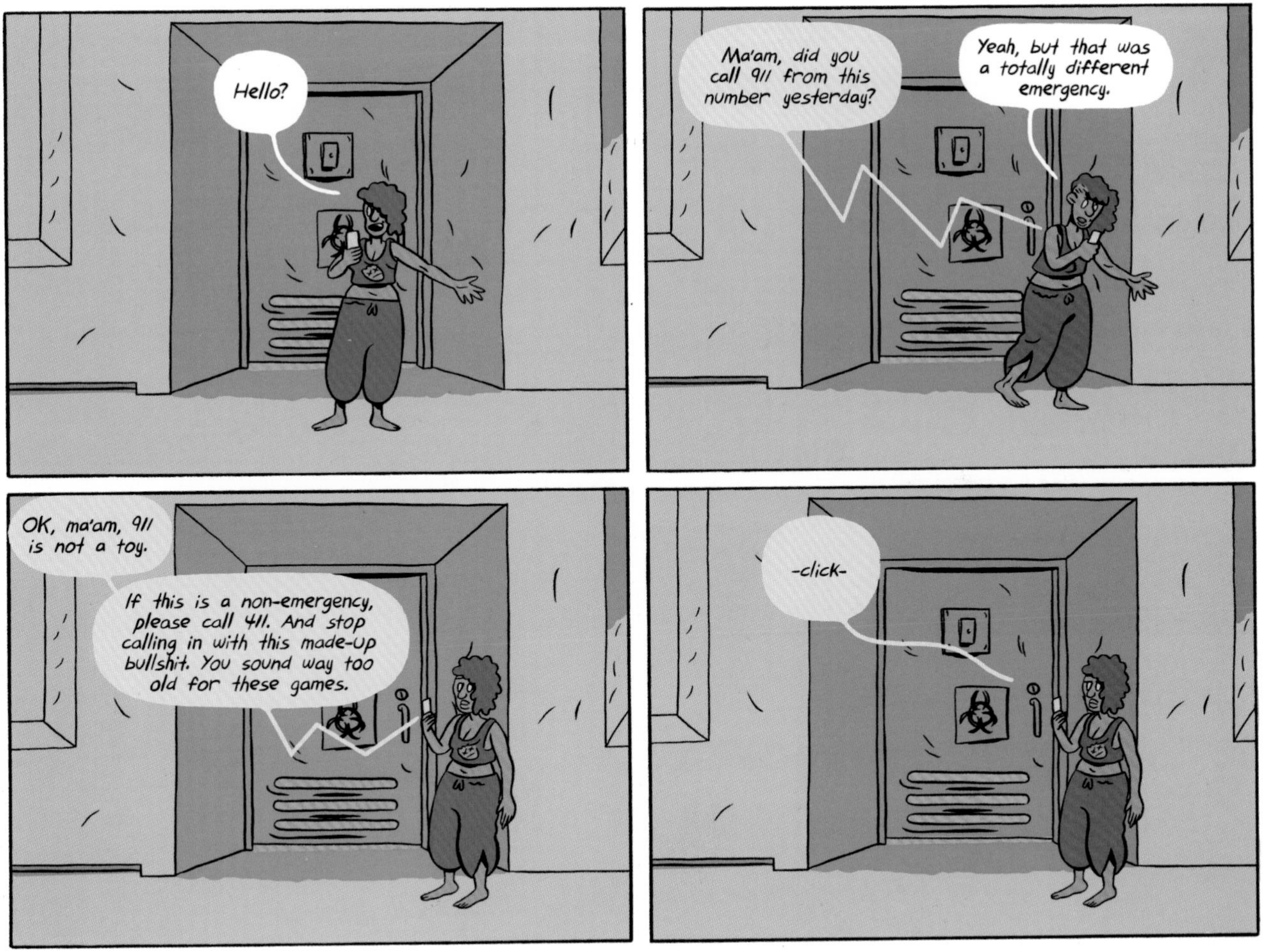
Hello?
Ma'am, did you call 911 from this number yesterday?
Yeah, but that was a totally different emergency.
OK, ma'am, 911 is not a toy.
If this is a non-emergency, please call 411. And stop calling in with this made-up bullshit. You sound way too old for these games.
-click-

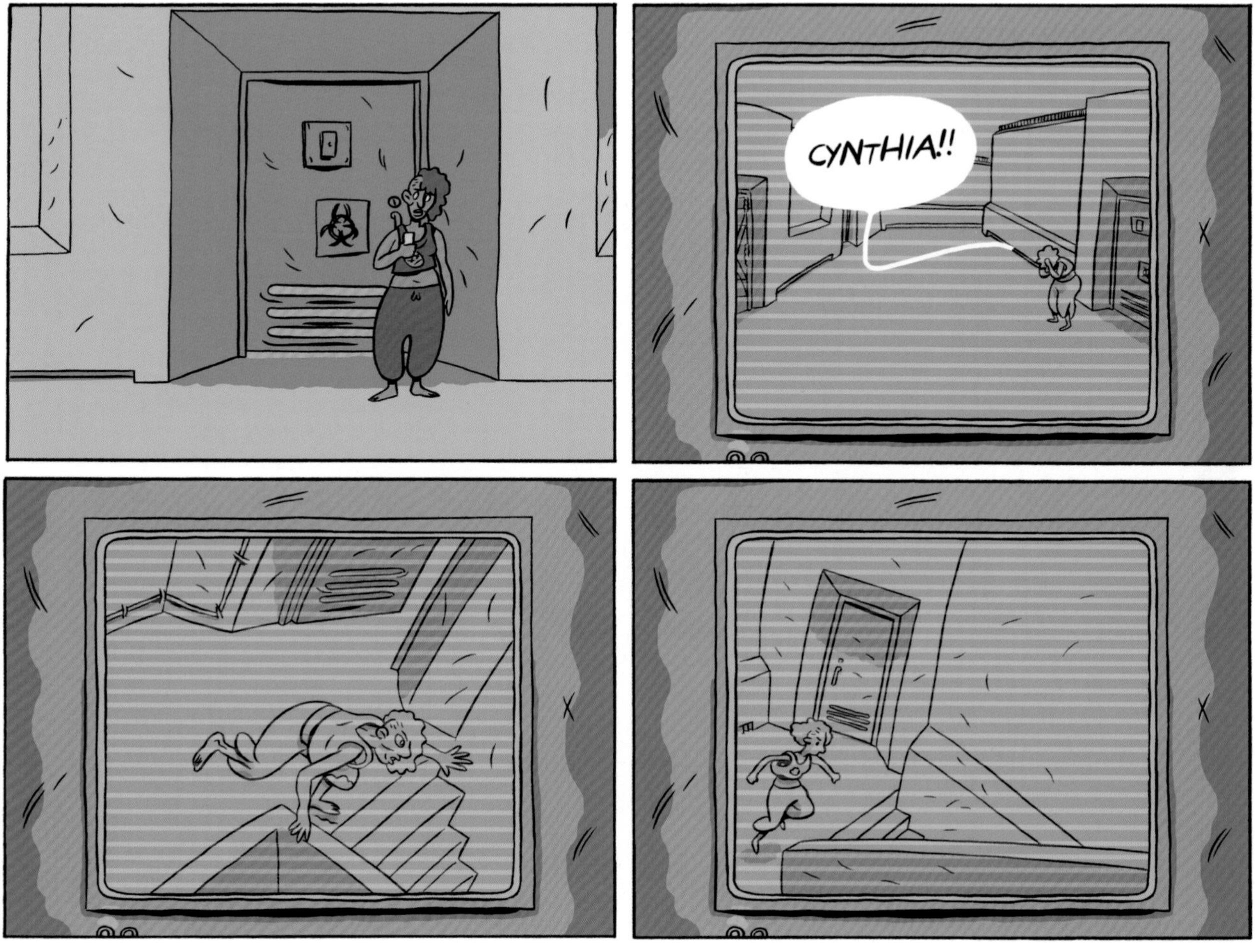
CYNTHIA!!

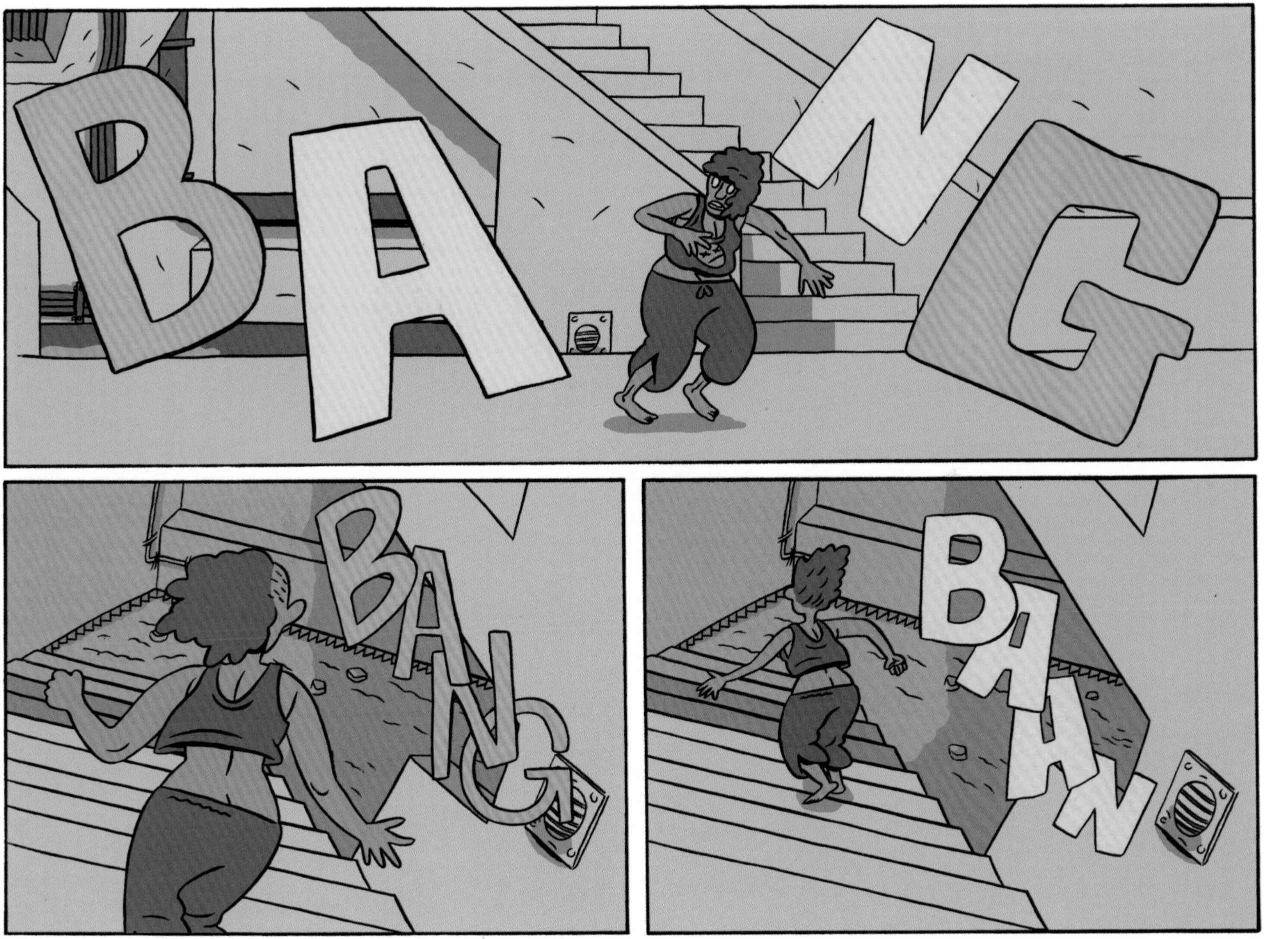
BANG
BANG
BANG

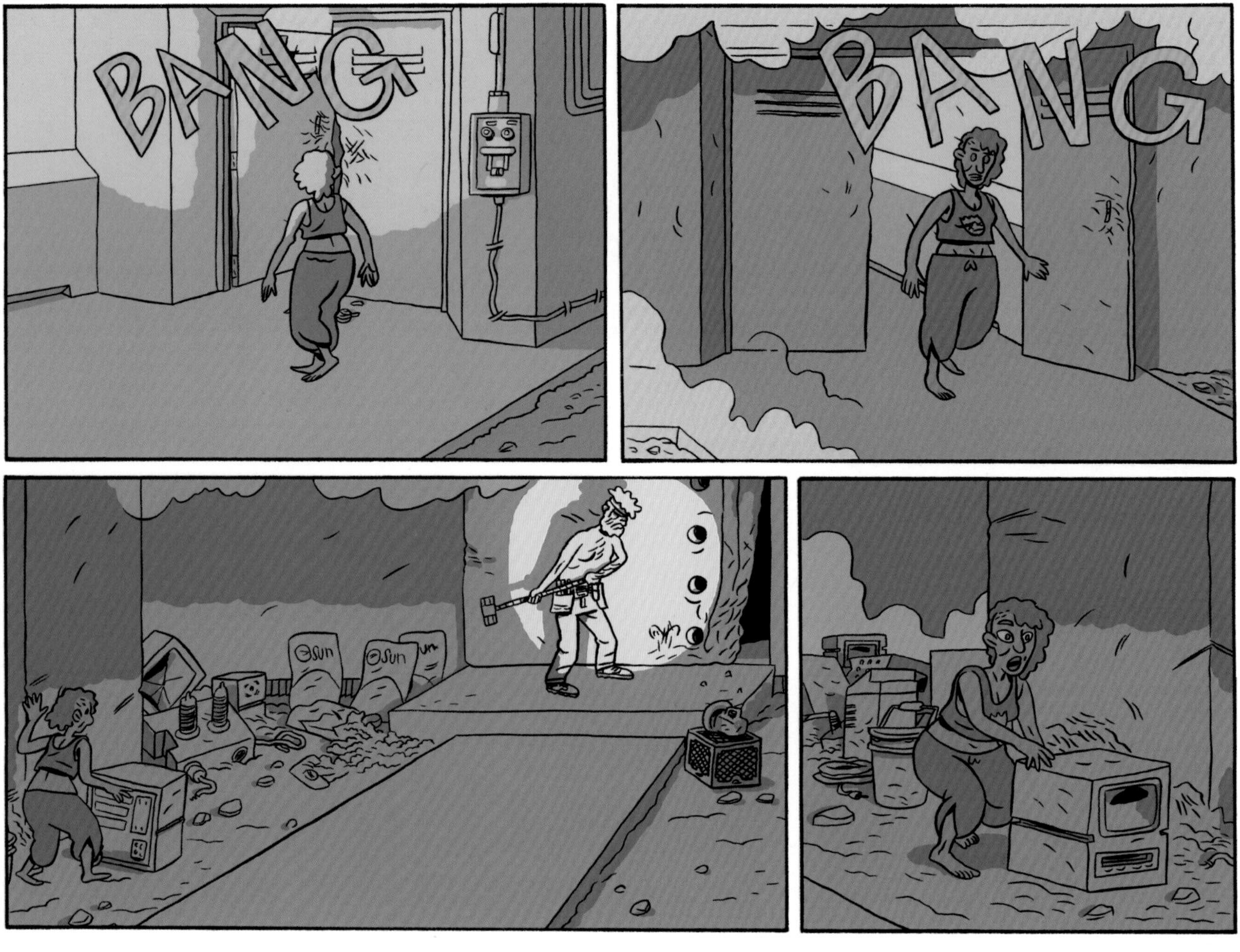
BANG
BANG

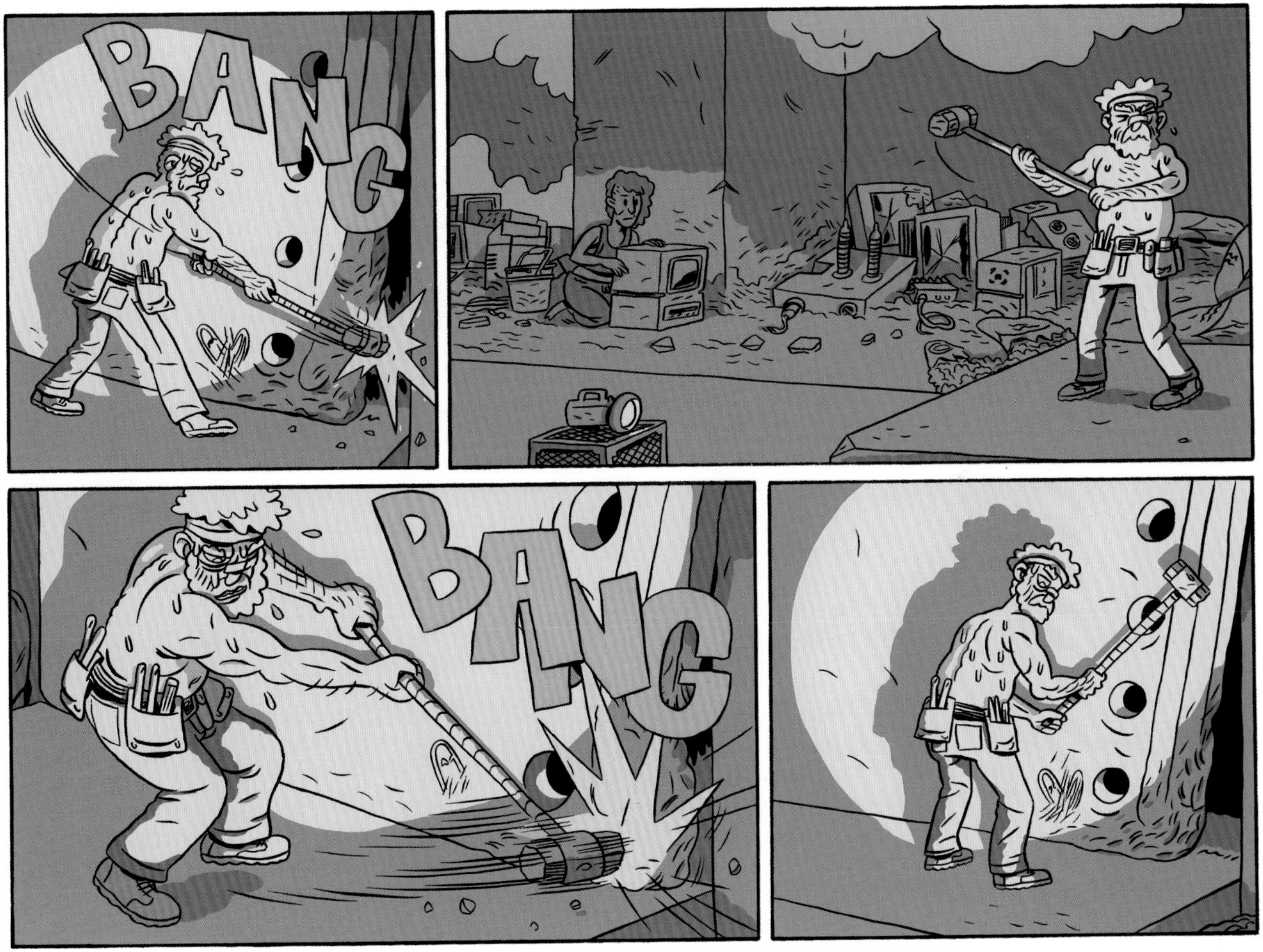
BANG
BANG

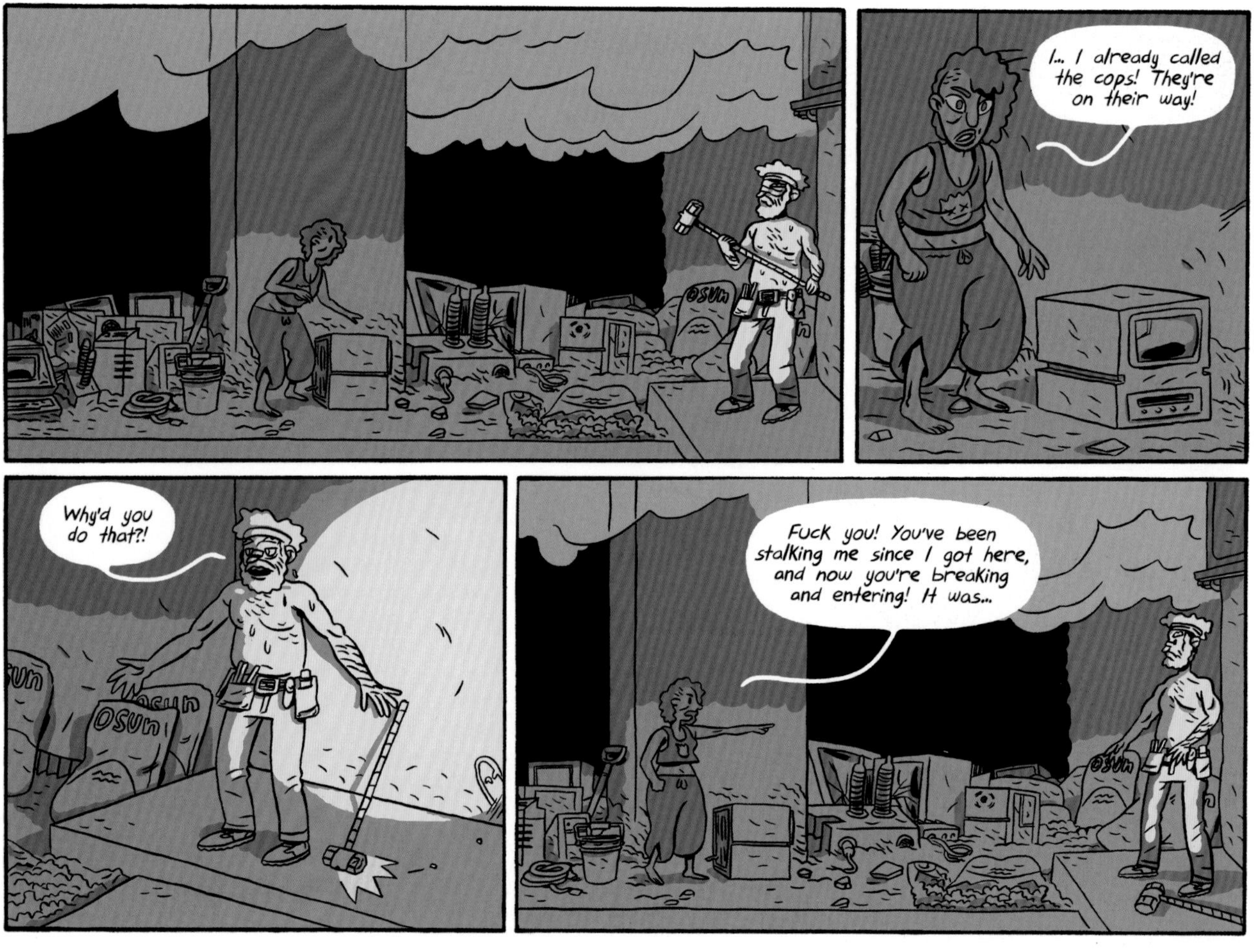
I... I already called the cops! They're on their way!
OSUn
Why'd you do that?!
Fuck you! You've been stalking me since I got here, and now you're breaking and entering! It was...

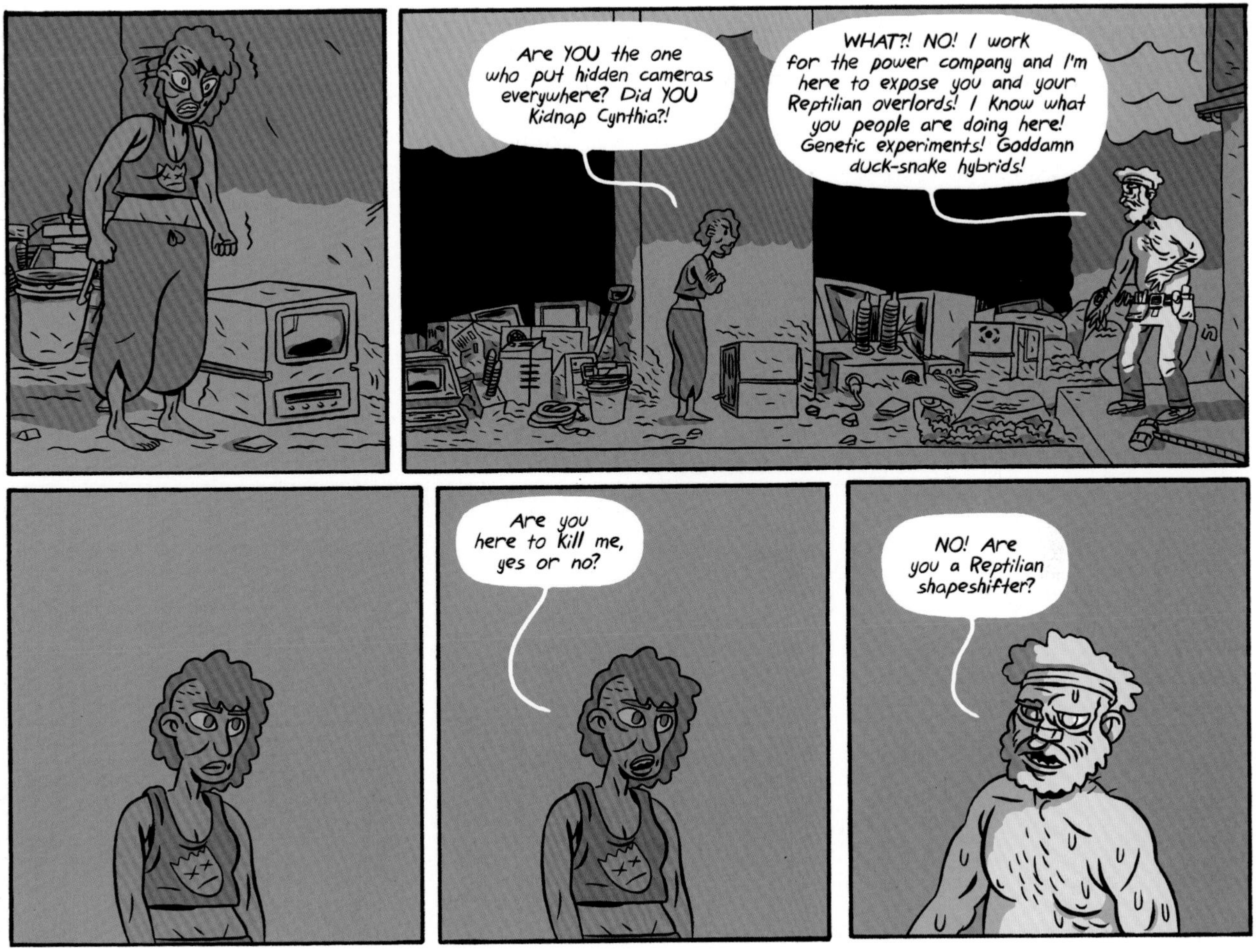
Are YOU the one who put hidden cameras everywhere? Did YOU Kidnap Cynthia?!
WHAT?! NO! I work for the power company and I'm here to expose you and your Reptilian overlords! I Know what you people are doing here! Genetic experiments! Goddamn duck-snake hybrids!
Are you here to Kill me, yes or no?
NO! Are you a Reptilian shapeshifter?

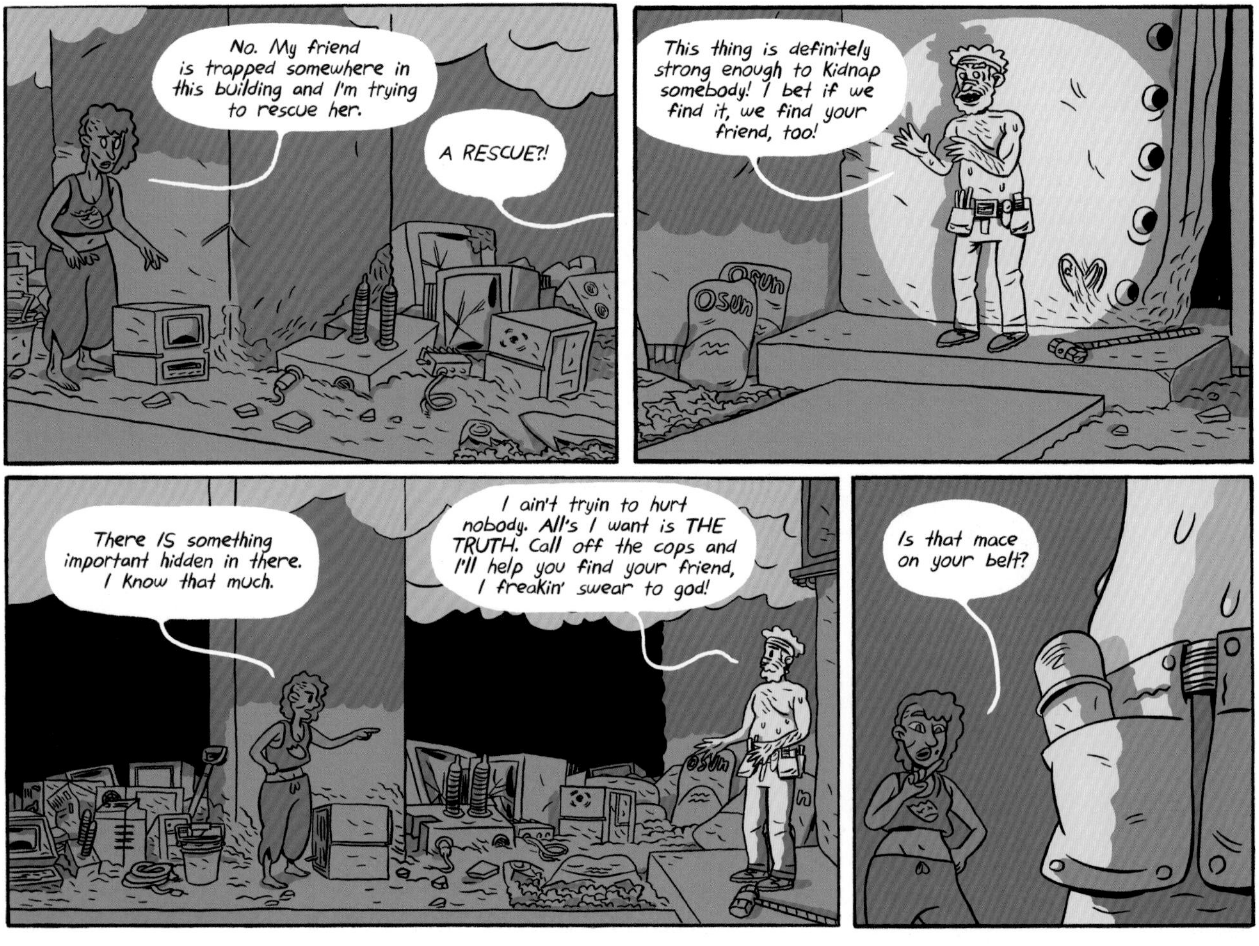
No. My friend is trapped somewhere in this building and I'm trying to rescue her.
A RESCUE?!
This thing is definitely strong enough to Kidnap somebody! I bet if we find it, we find your friend, too!
OSUN
OSUN
There IS something important hidden in there. I Know that much.
I ain't tryin to hurt nobody. All's I want is THE TRUTH. Call off the cops and I'll help you find your friend, I freakin' swear to god!
Is that mace on your belt?

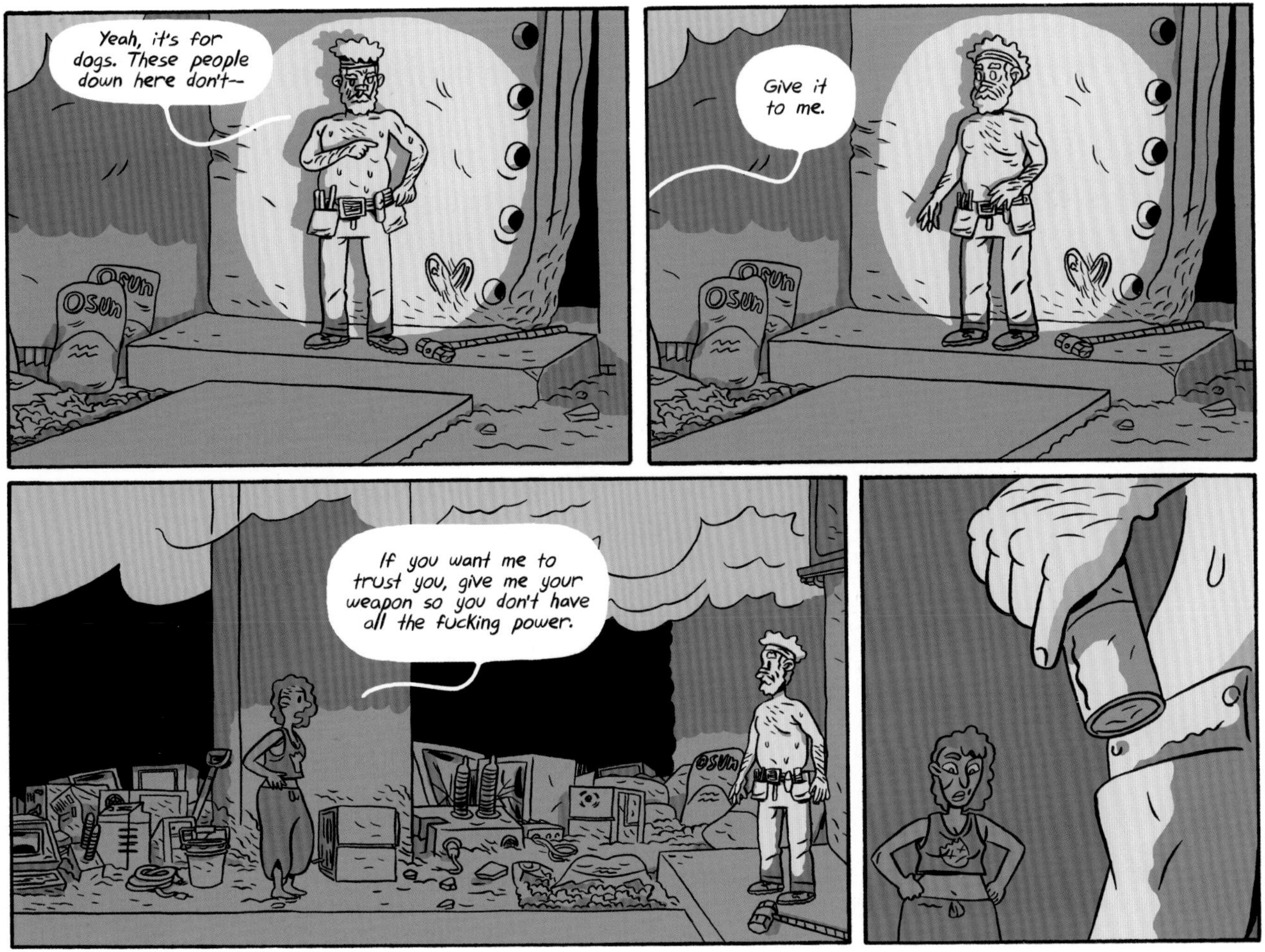

Yeah, it's for dogs. These people down here don't--
OSUN
OSUN
Give it to me.
OSUN
OSUN
If you want me to trust you, give me your weapon so you don't have all the fucking power.
OSUN

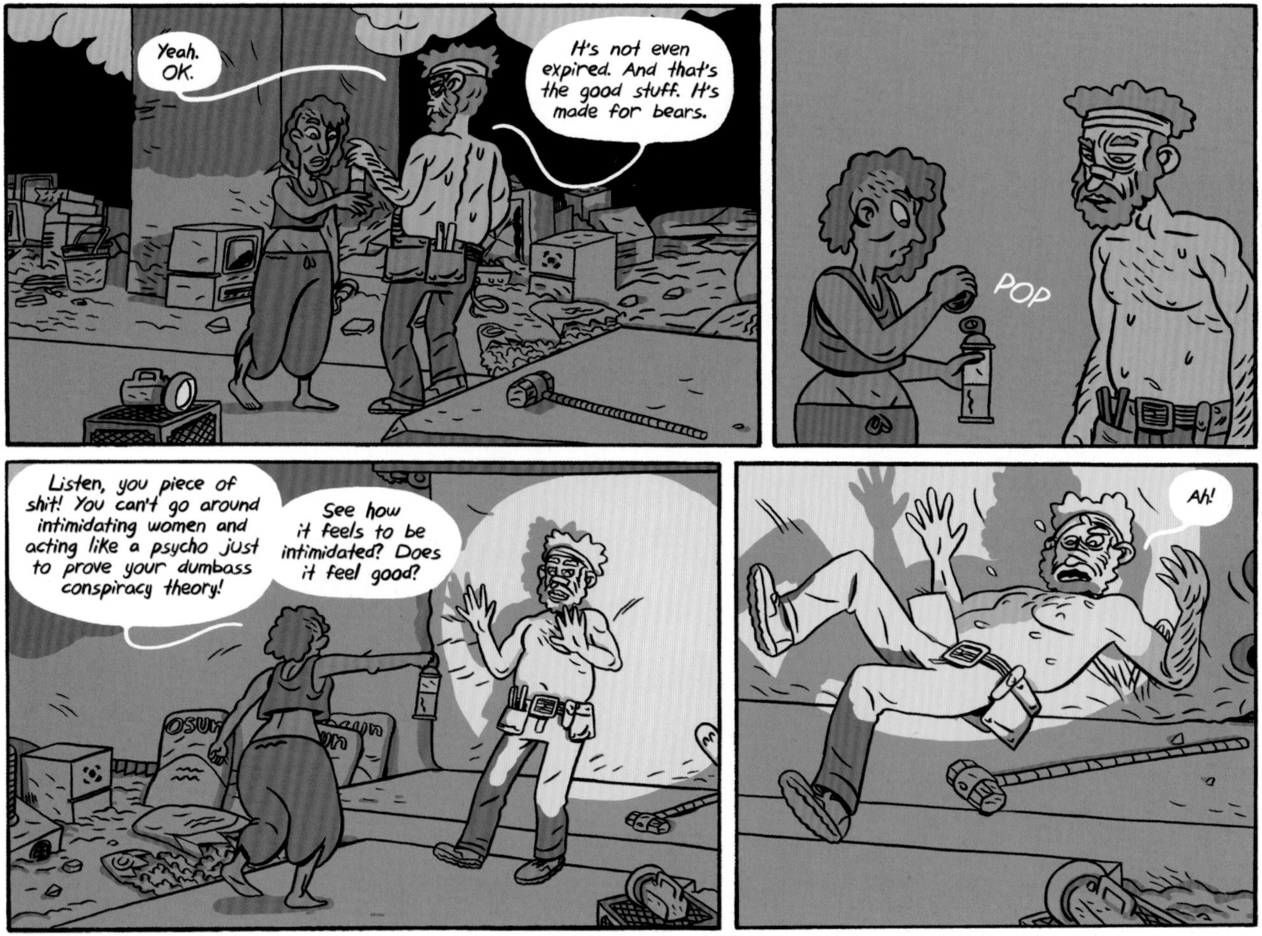
Yeah. OK.
It's not even expired. And that's the good stuff. It's made for bears.
POP
Listen, you piece of shit! You can't go around intimidating women and acting like a psycho just to prove your dumbass conspiracy theory!
See how it feels to be intimidated? Does it feel good?
Ah!

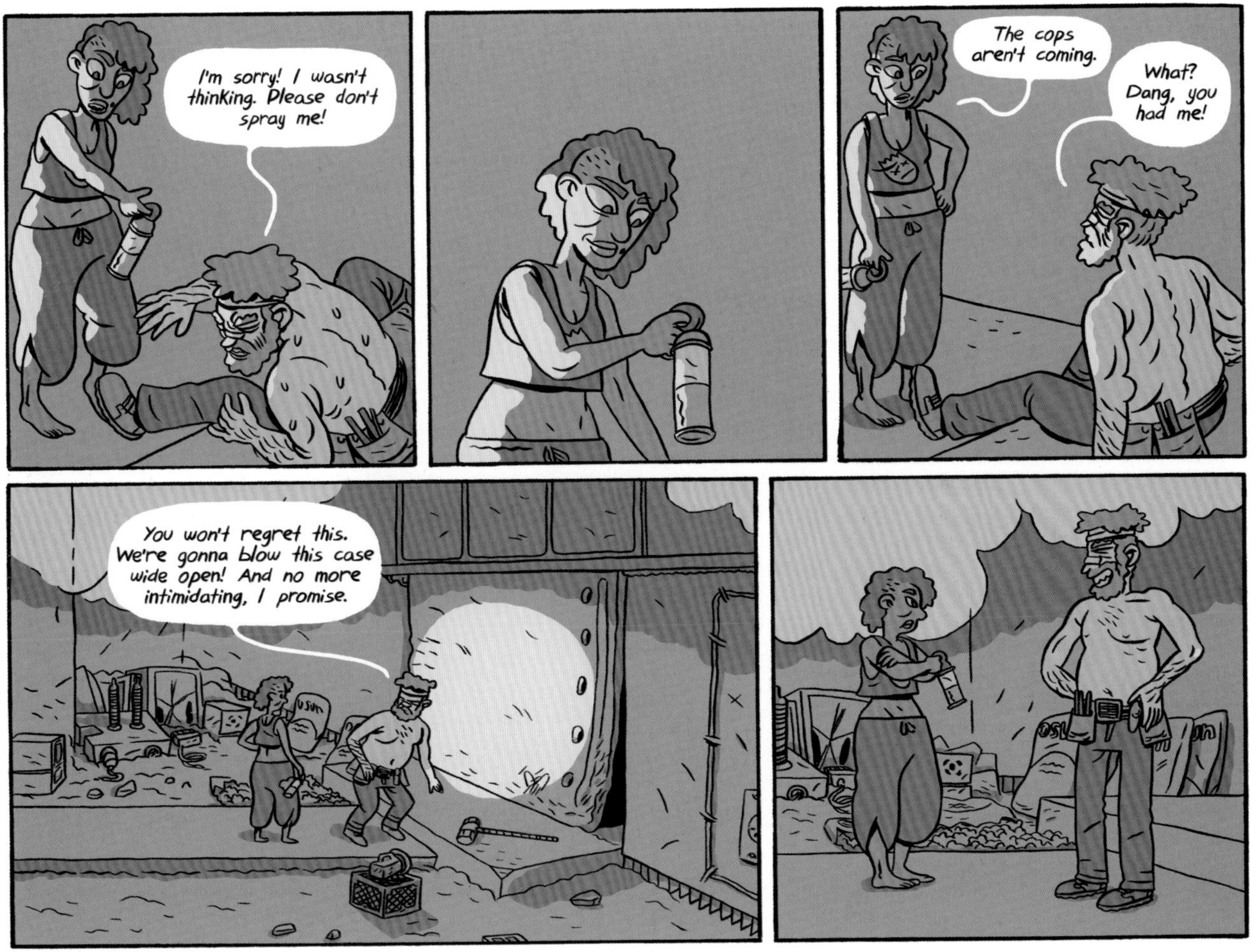
I'm sorry! I wasn't thinking. Please don't spray me!
The cops aren't coming.
What? Dang, you had me!
You won't regret this. We're gonna blow this case wide open! And no more intimidating, I promise.

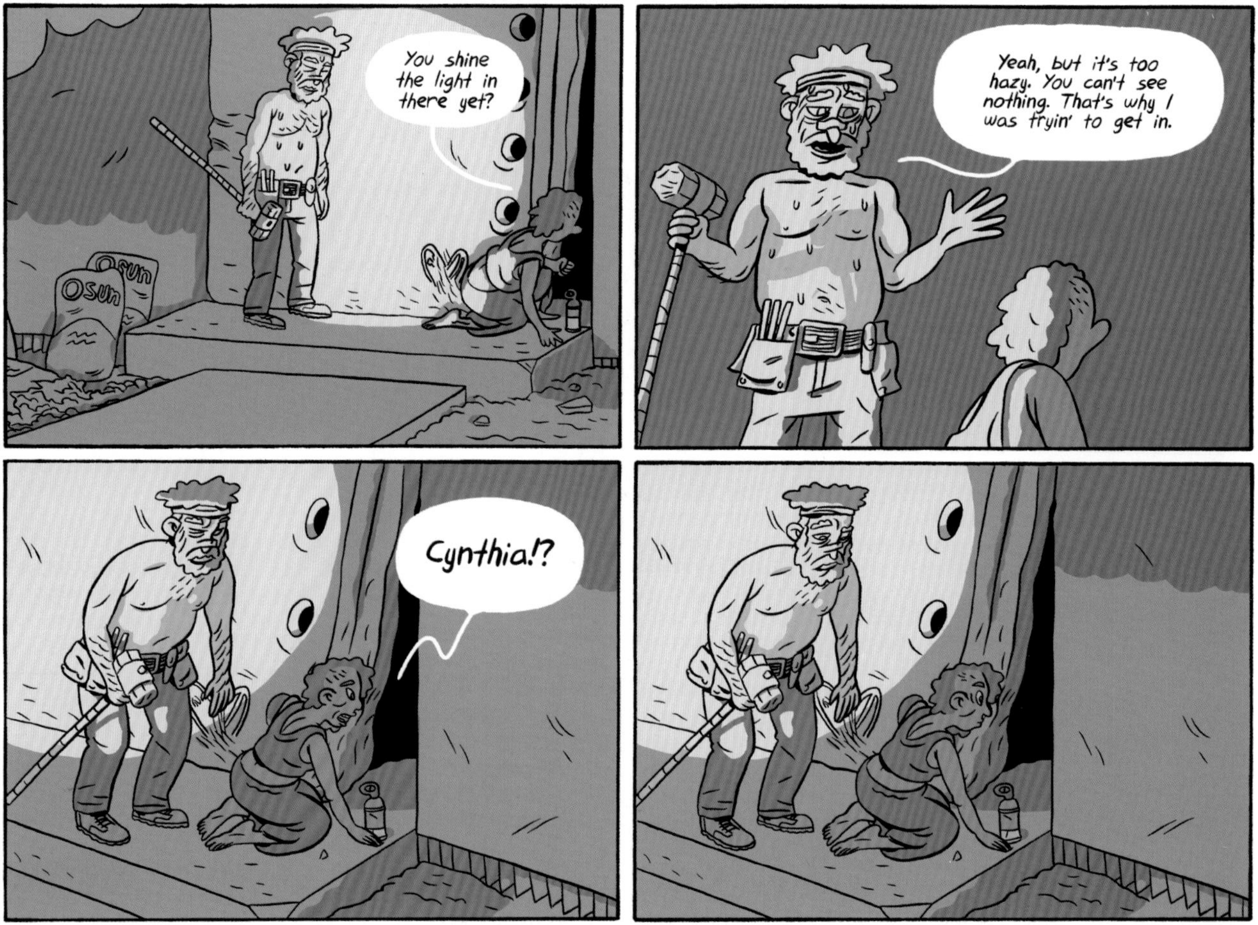

Osun
Osun
You shine the light in there yet?
Yeah, but it's too hazy. You can't see nothing. That's why I was tryin' to get in.
Cynthia!?

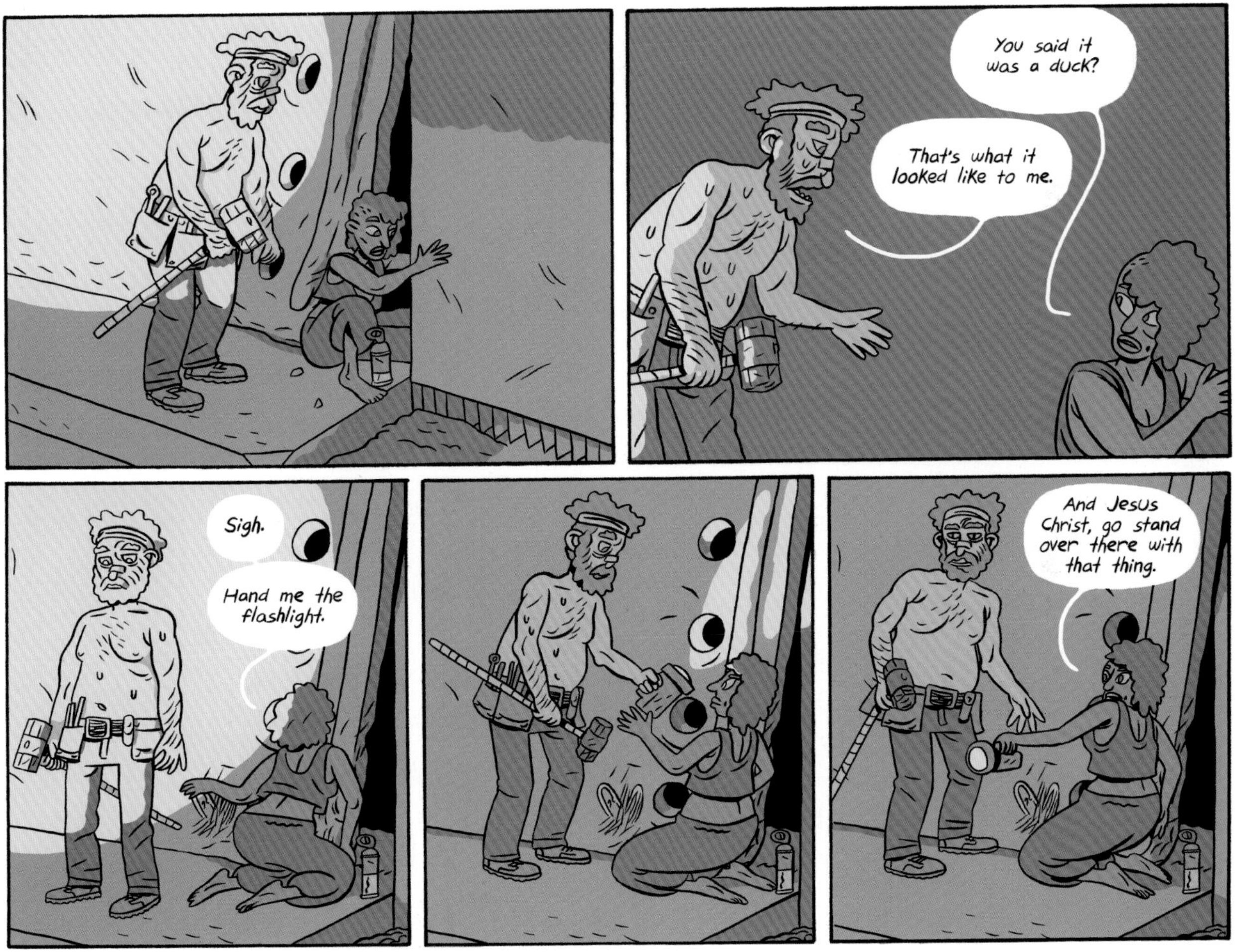
You said it was a duck?
That's what it looked like to me.
Sigh.
Hand me the flashlight.
And Jesus Christ, go stand over there with that thing.

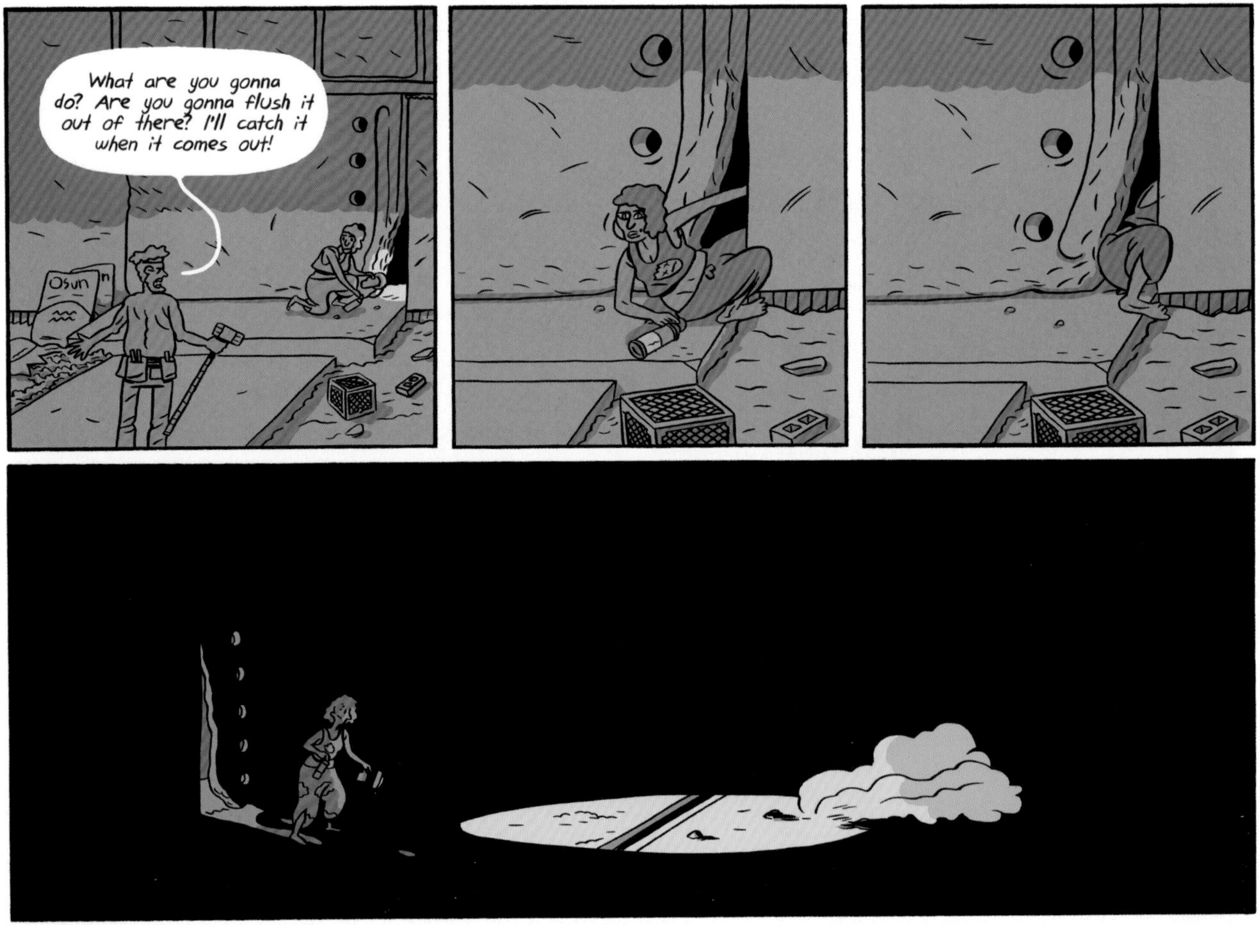
What are you gonna do? Are you gonna flush it out of there? I'll catch it when it comes out!
Osun

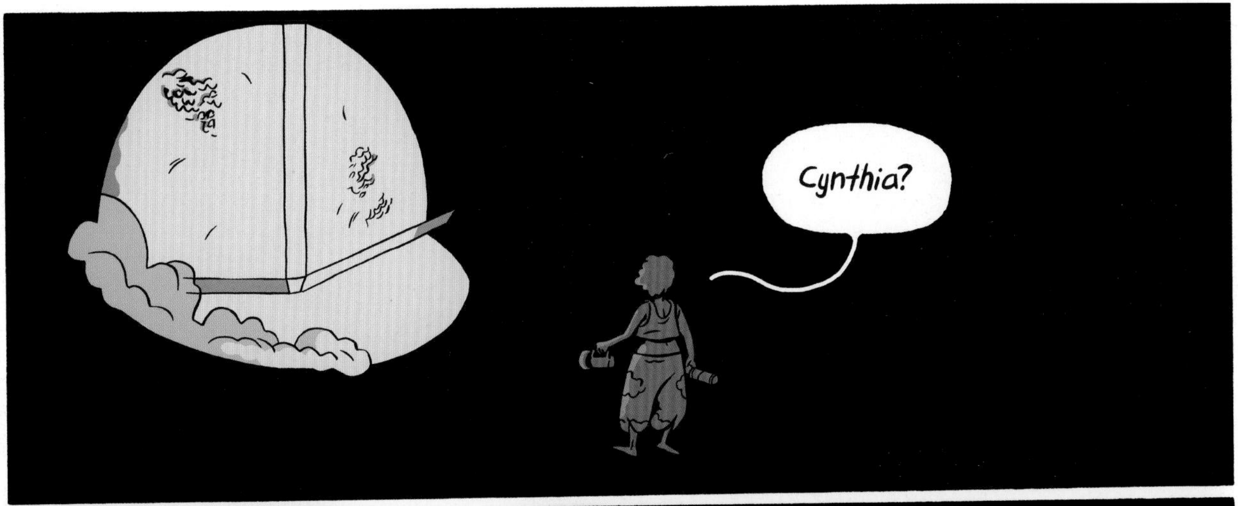
Cynthia?

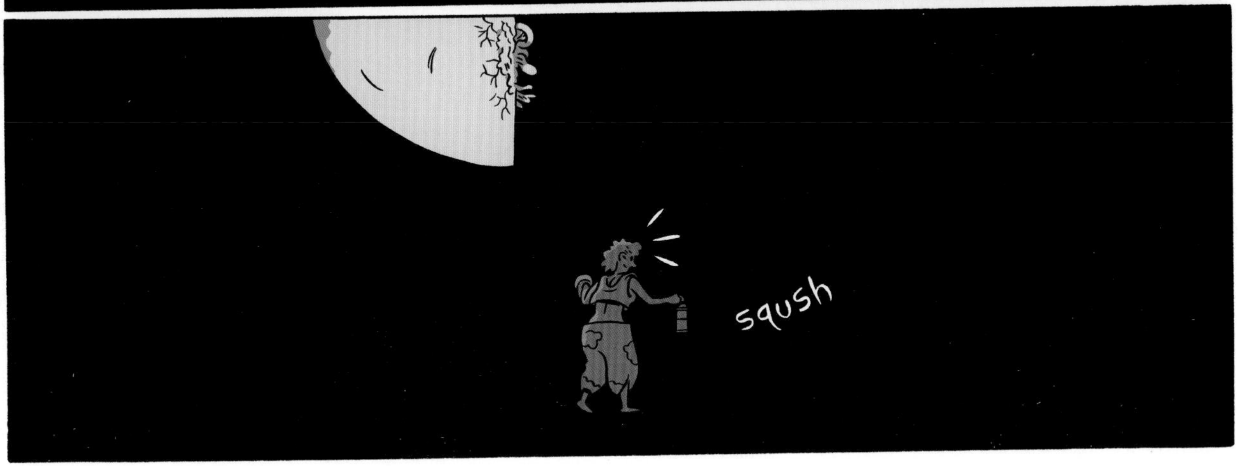
sqush

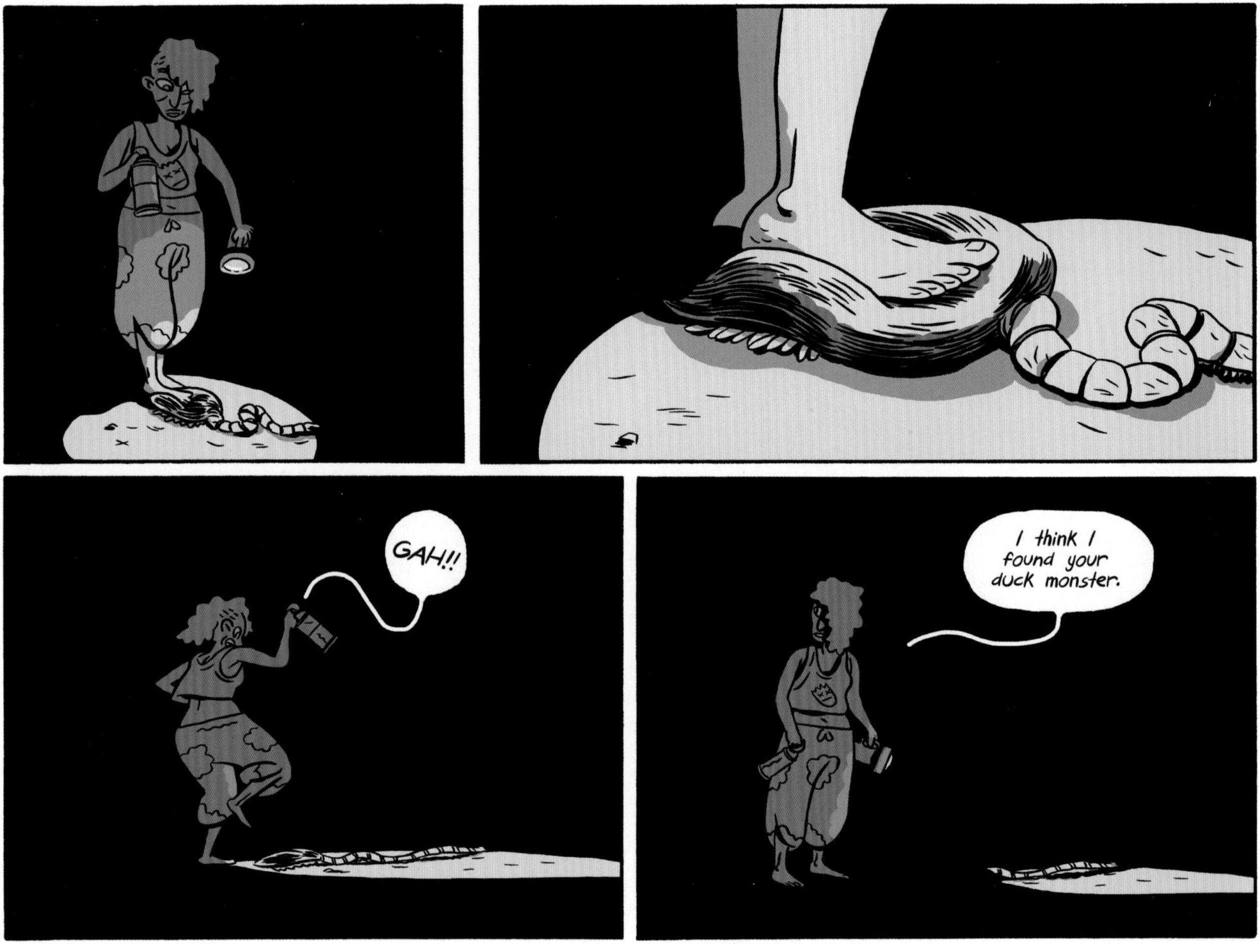
GAH!!
I think I found your duck monster.

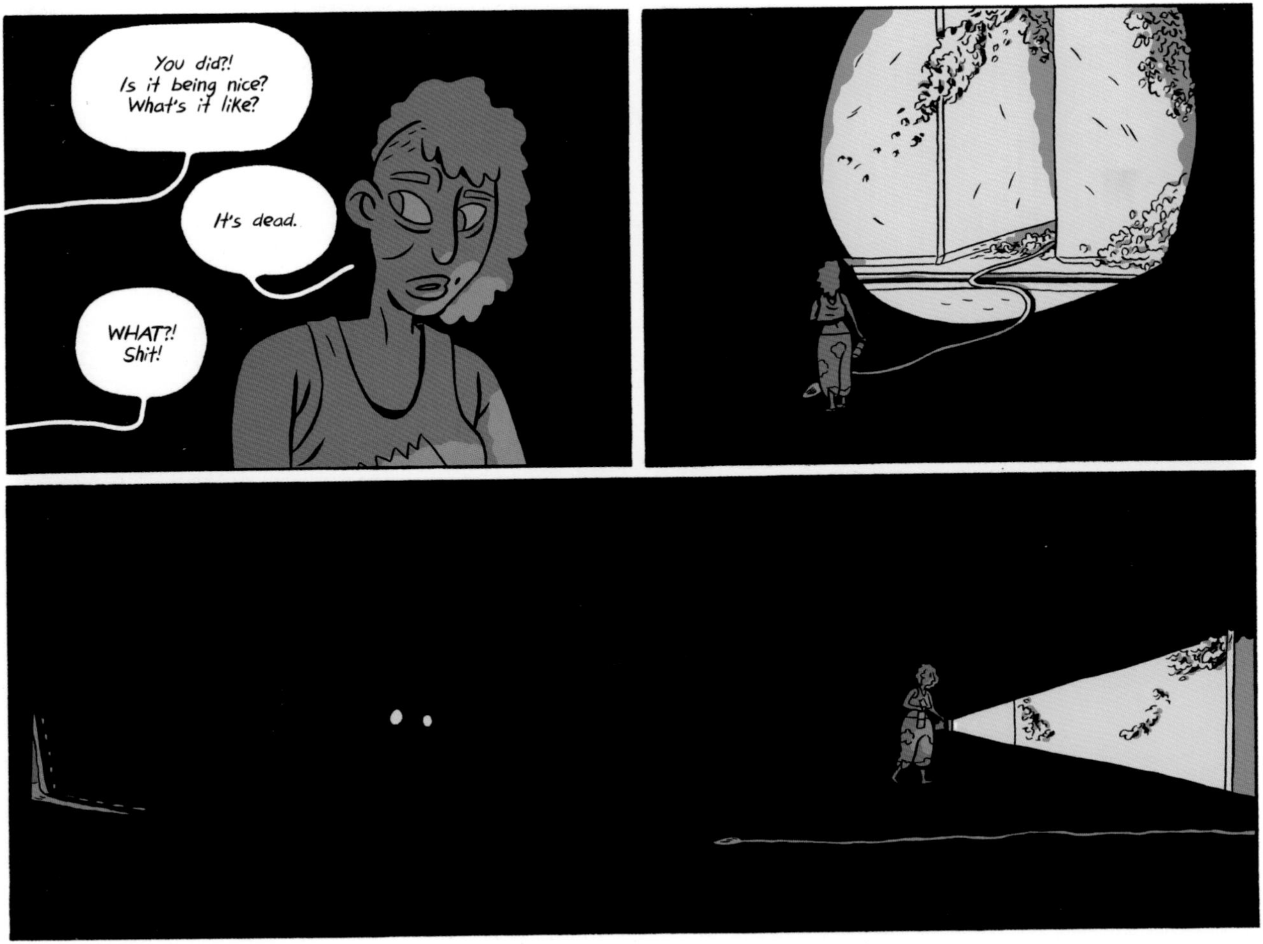
You did?!
Is it being nice?
What's it like?
It's dead.
WHAT?!
Shit!

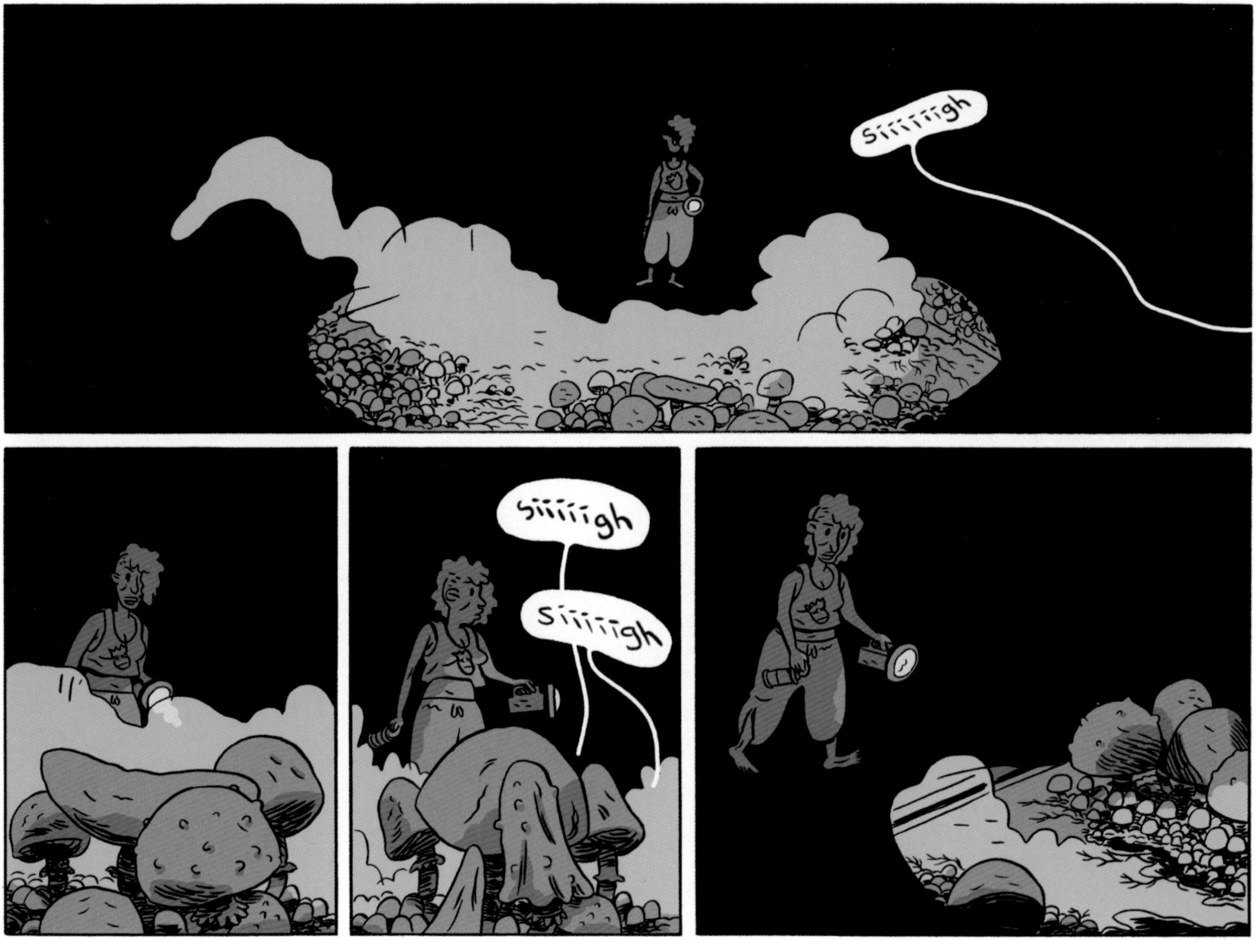
Siiiiiigh
Siiiiigh
Siiiiigh

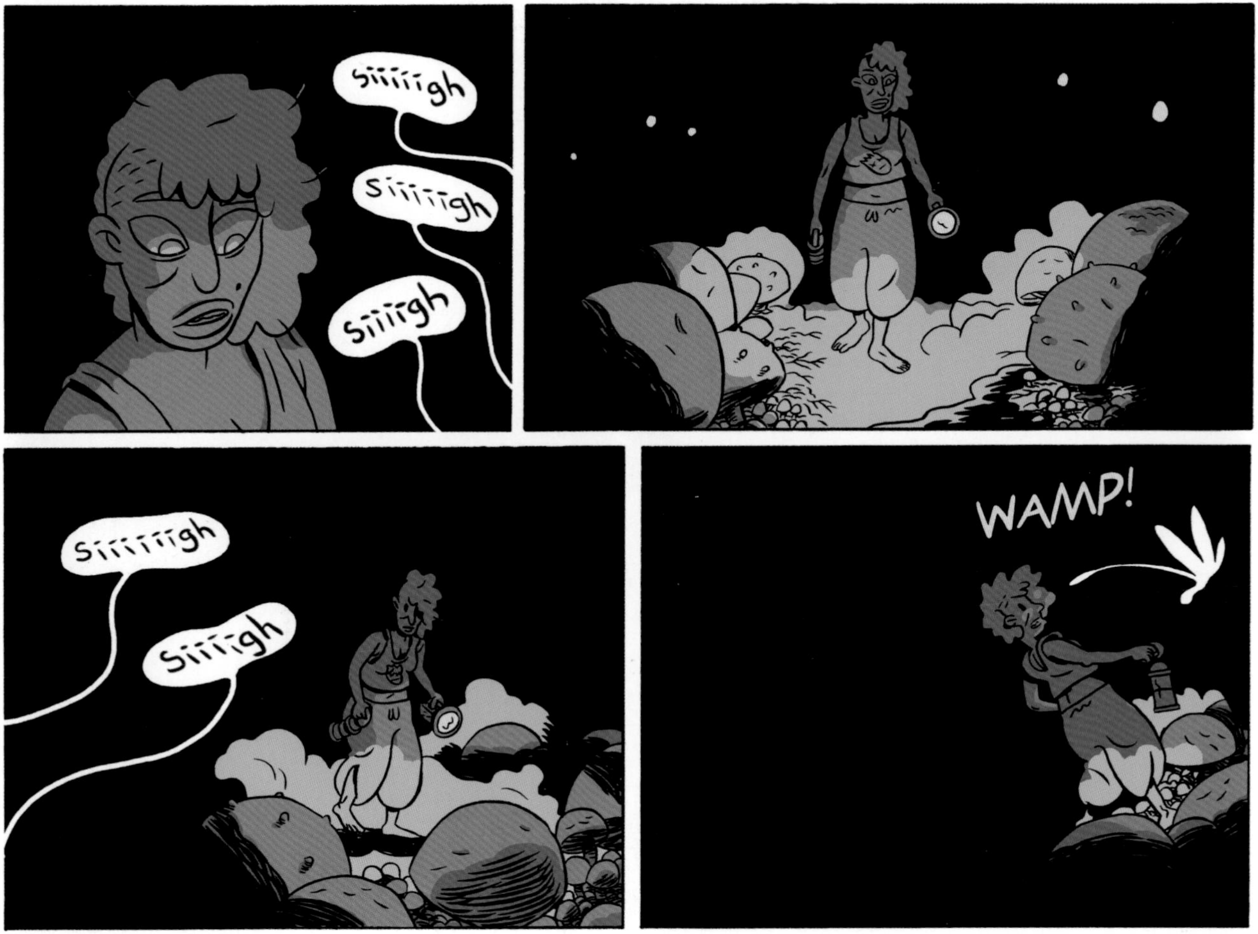
Siiiiigh
Siiiiigh
Siiiigh
Siiiiiigh
Siiiigh
WAMP!

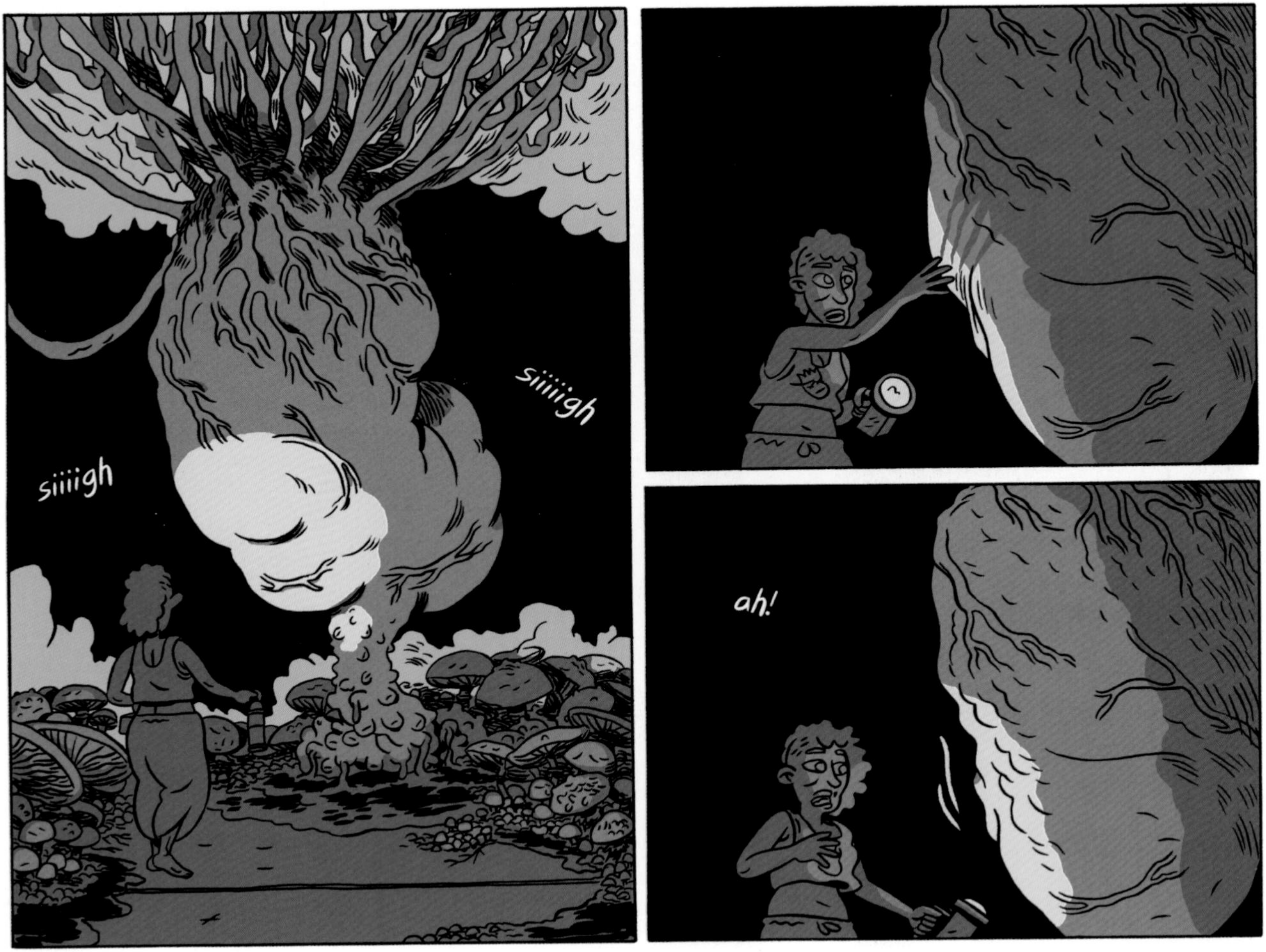
siiiigh
siiiiiigh
ah!

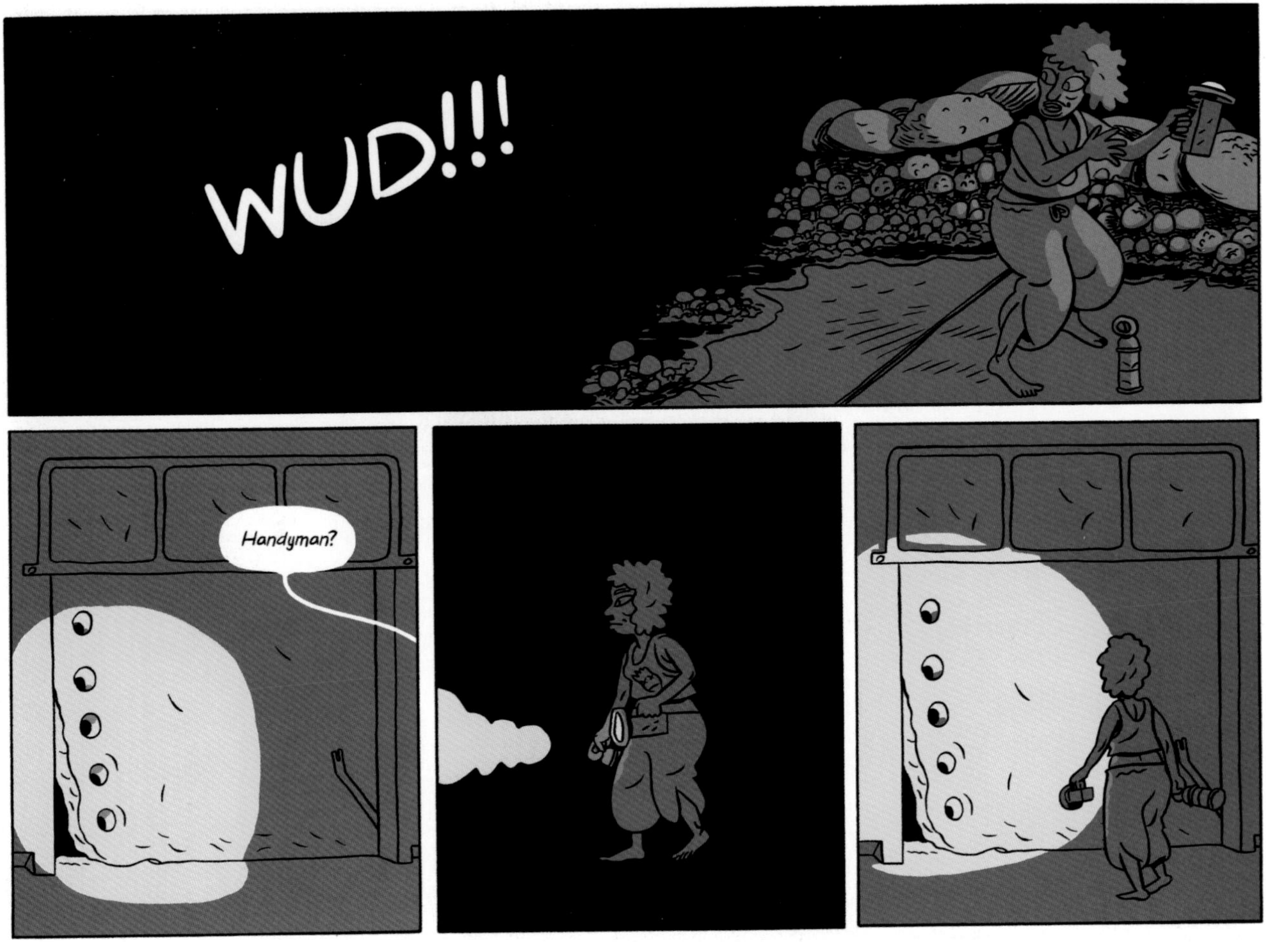
WUD!!!
Handyman?

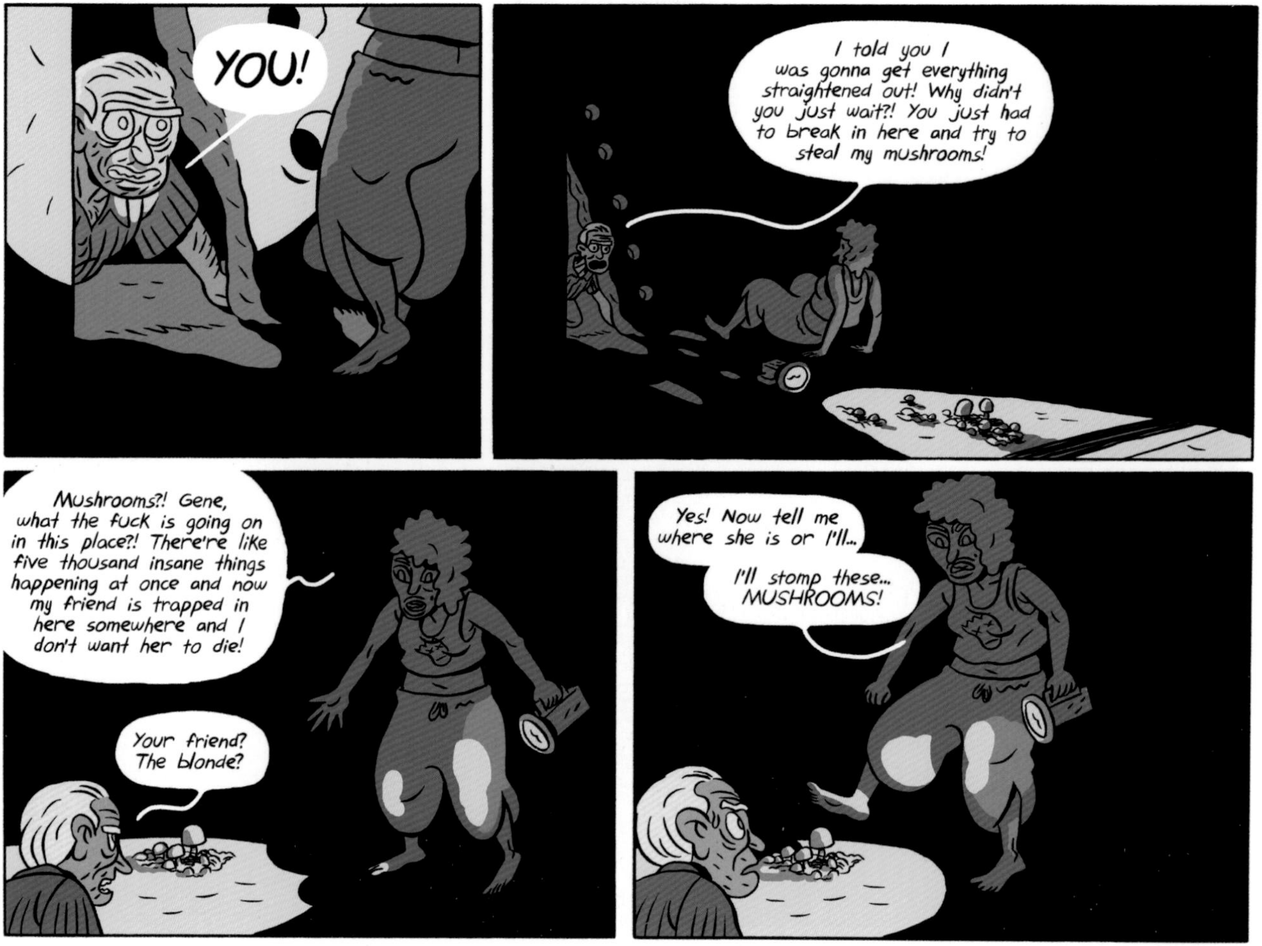
YOU!
I told you I was gonna get everything straightened out! Why didn't you just wait?! You just had to break in here and try to steal my mushrooms!
Mushrooms?! Gene, what the fuck is going on in this place?! There're like five thousand insane things happening at once and now my friend is trapped in here somewhere and I don't want her to die!
Your friend? The blonde?
Yes! Now tell me where she is or I'll...
I'll stomp these... MUSHROOMS!

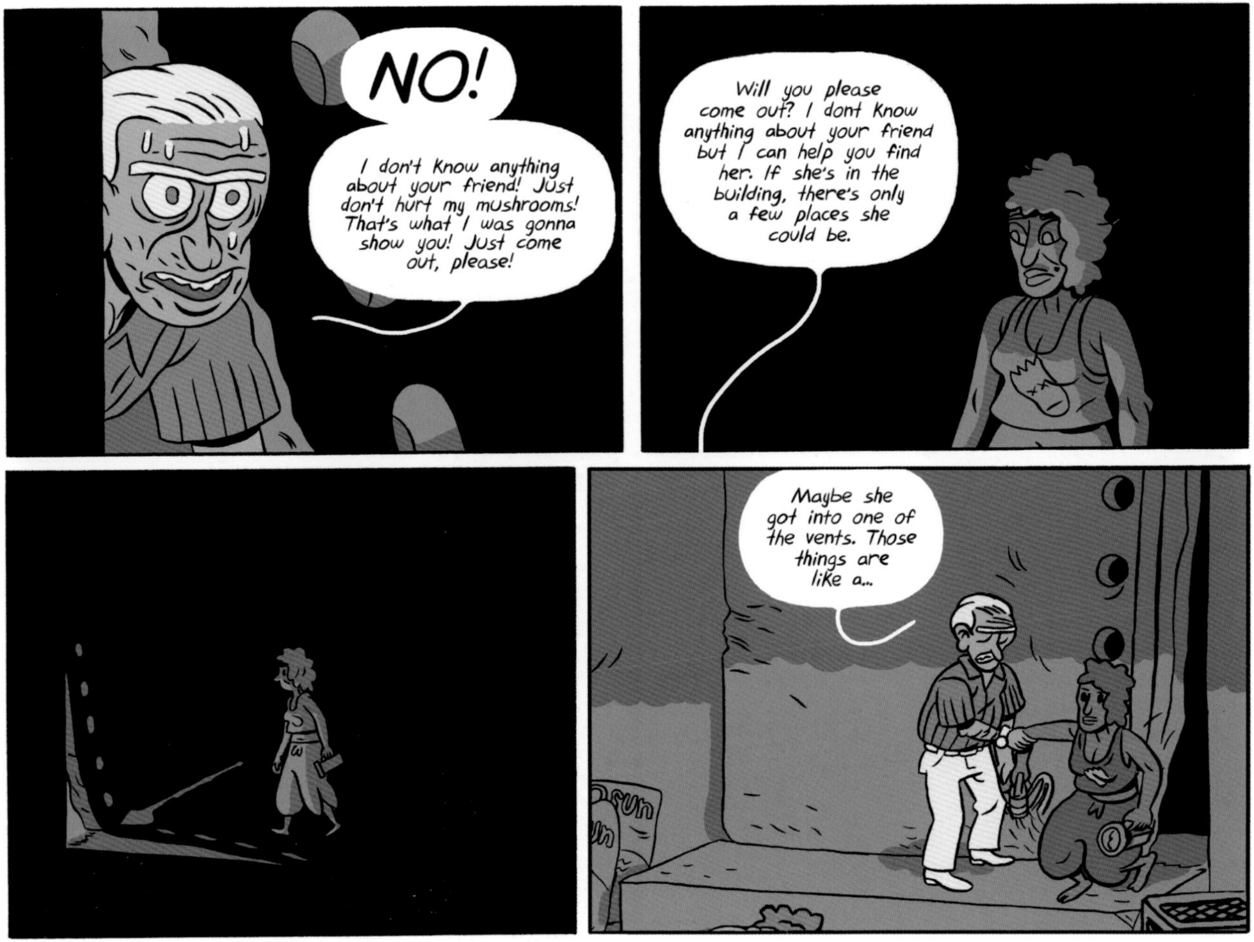
NO!
I don't know anything about your friend! Just don't hurt my mushrooms! That's what I was gonna show you! Just come out, please!
Will you please come out? I dont know anything about your friend but I can help you find her. If she's in the building, there's only a few places she could be.
Maybe she got into one of the vents. Those things are like a...

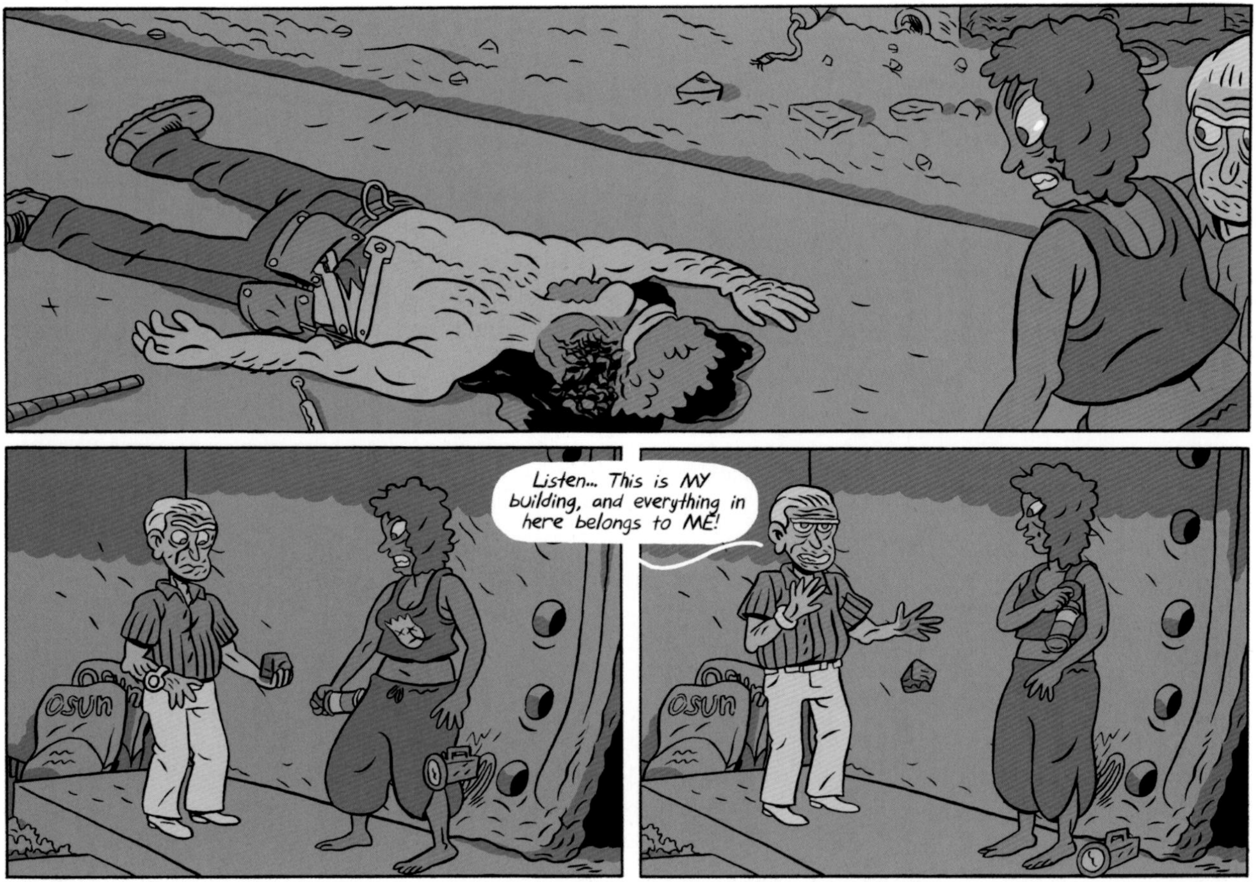
OSUN
Listen... This is MY building, and everything in here belongs to ME!
OSUN

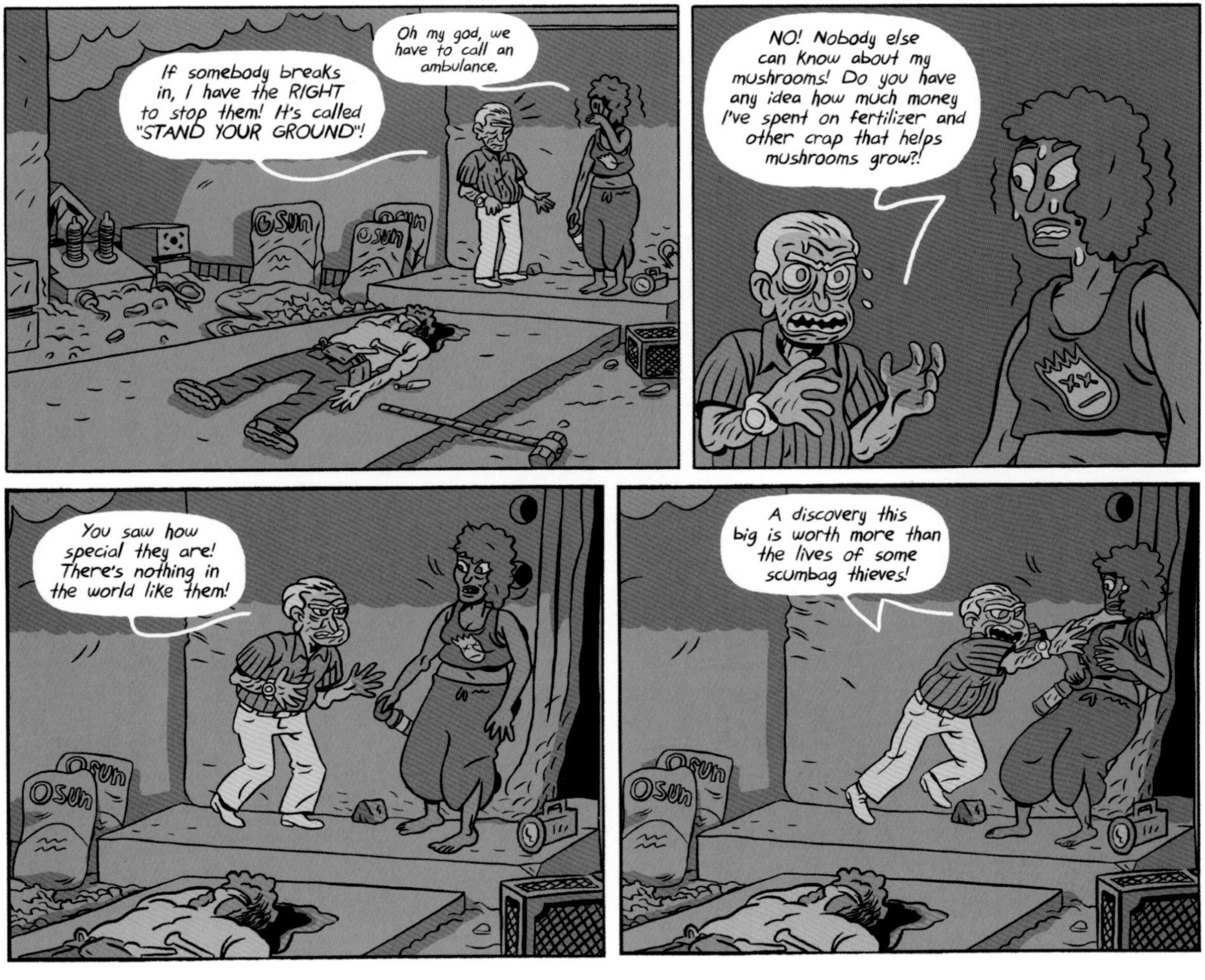
If somebody breaks in, I have the RIGHT to stop them! It's called "STAND YOUR GROUND"!
Oh my god, we have to call an ambulance.
OSUN
OSUN
OSUN
NO! Nobody else can know about my mushrooms! Do you have any idea how much money I've spent on fertilizer and other crap that helps mushrooms grow?!
You saw how special they are! There's nothing in the world like them!
OSUN
OSUN
A discovery this big is worth more than the lives of some scumbag thieves!
OSUN
OSUN

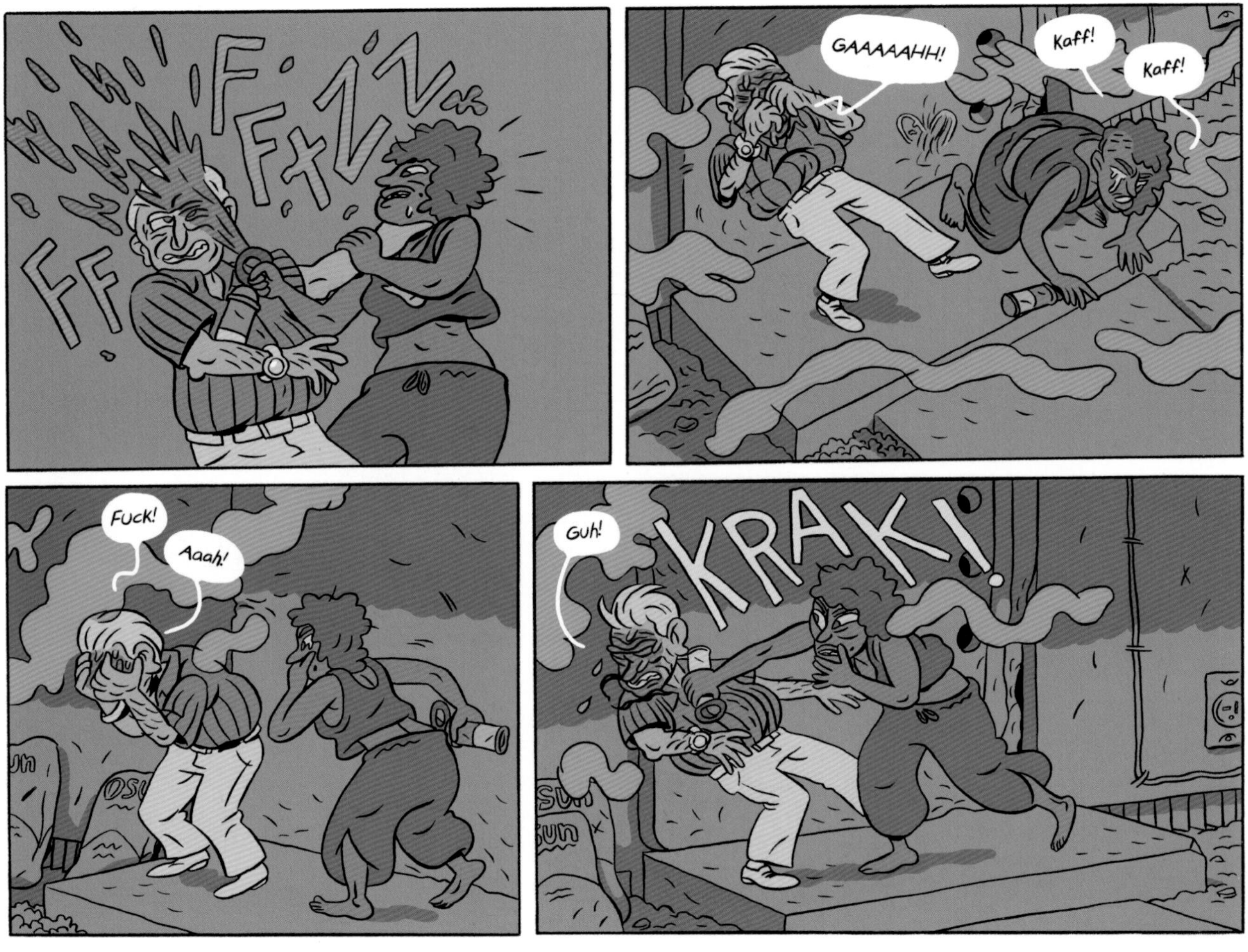
GAAAAAHH!
Kaff!
Kaff!
Fuck!
Aaah!
Guh!
KRAK!

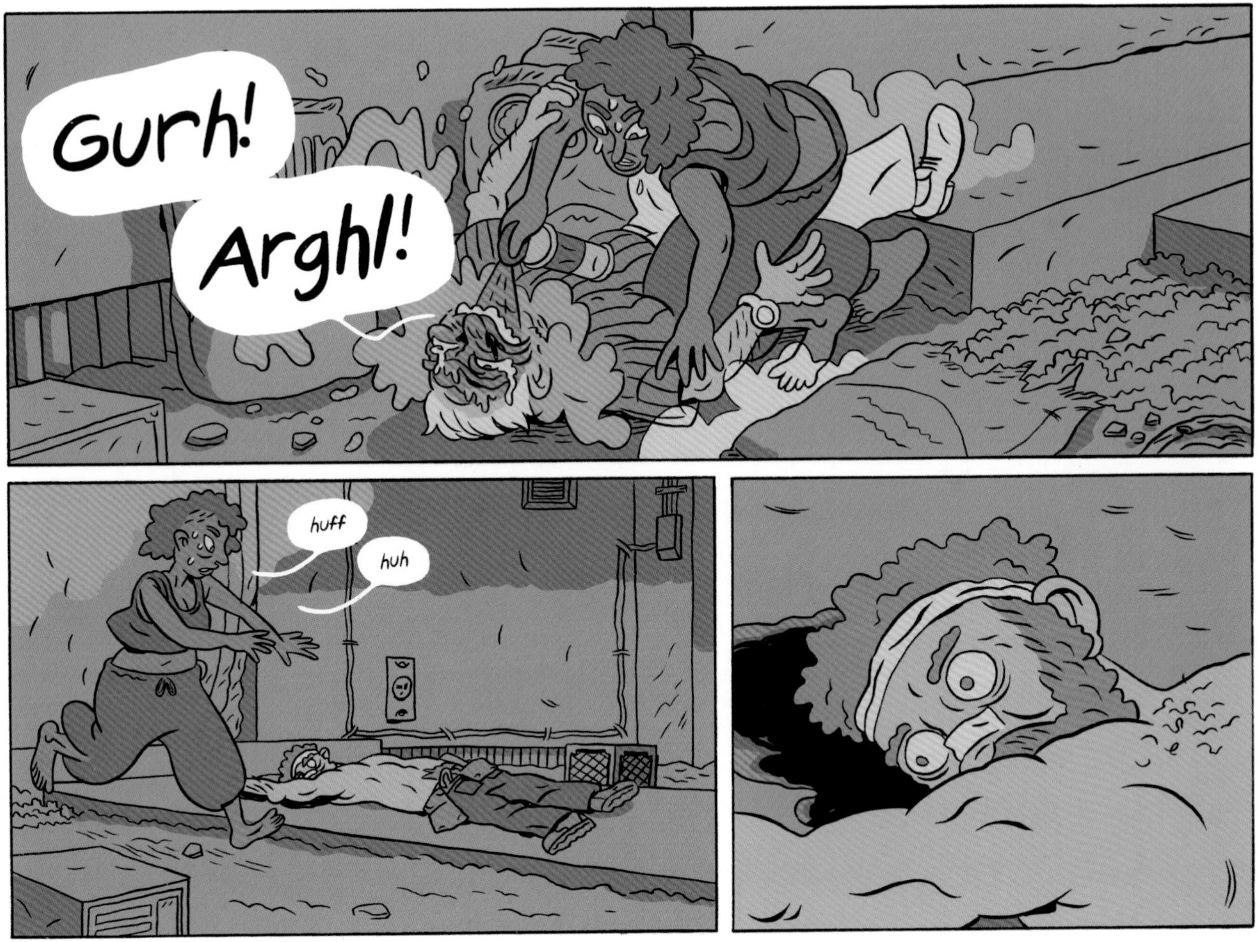
Gurh!
Arghl!
huff
huh

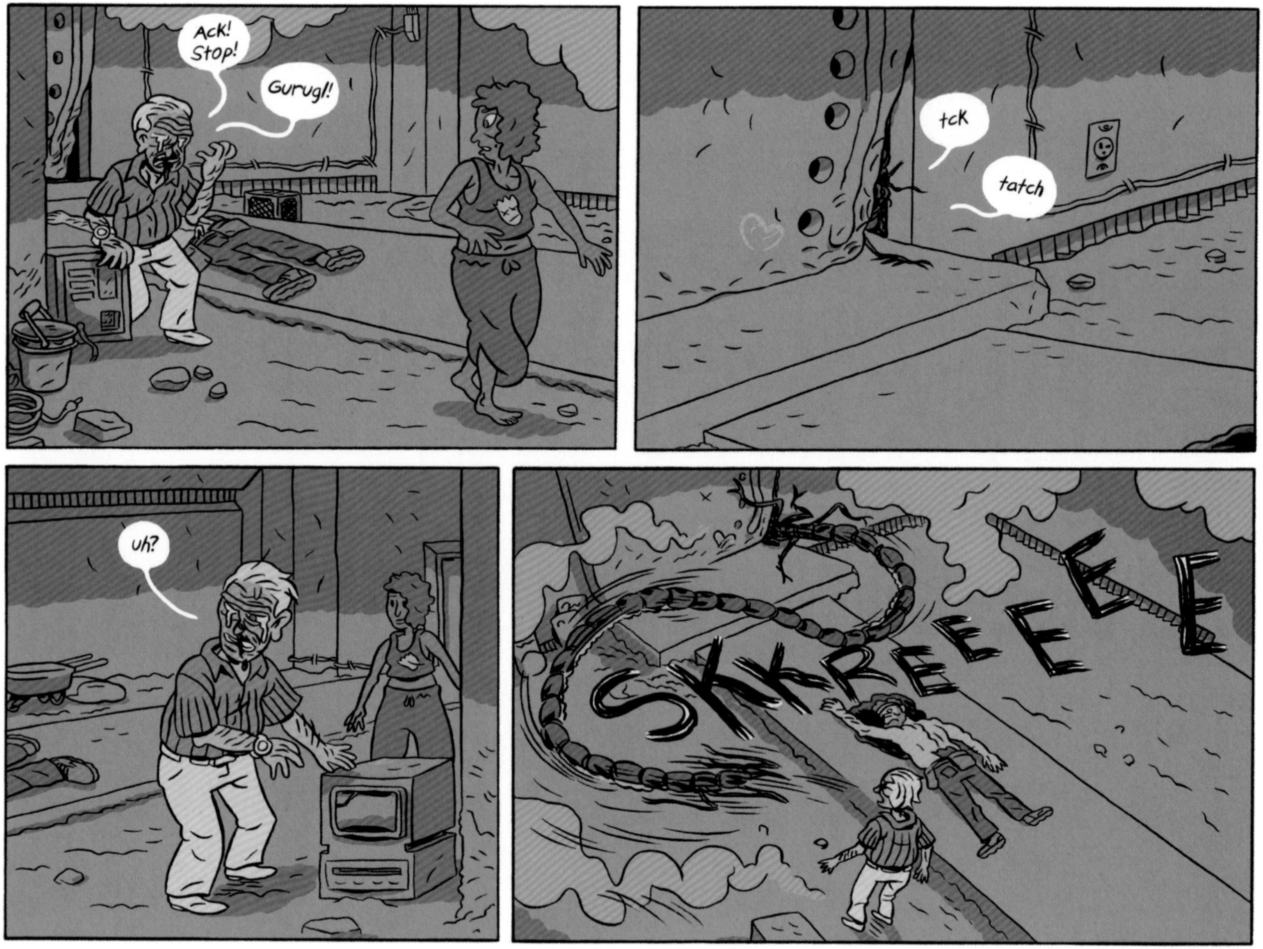
Ack! Stop!
Gurugl!
tck
tatch
uh?
SKKREEEEE

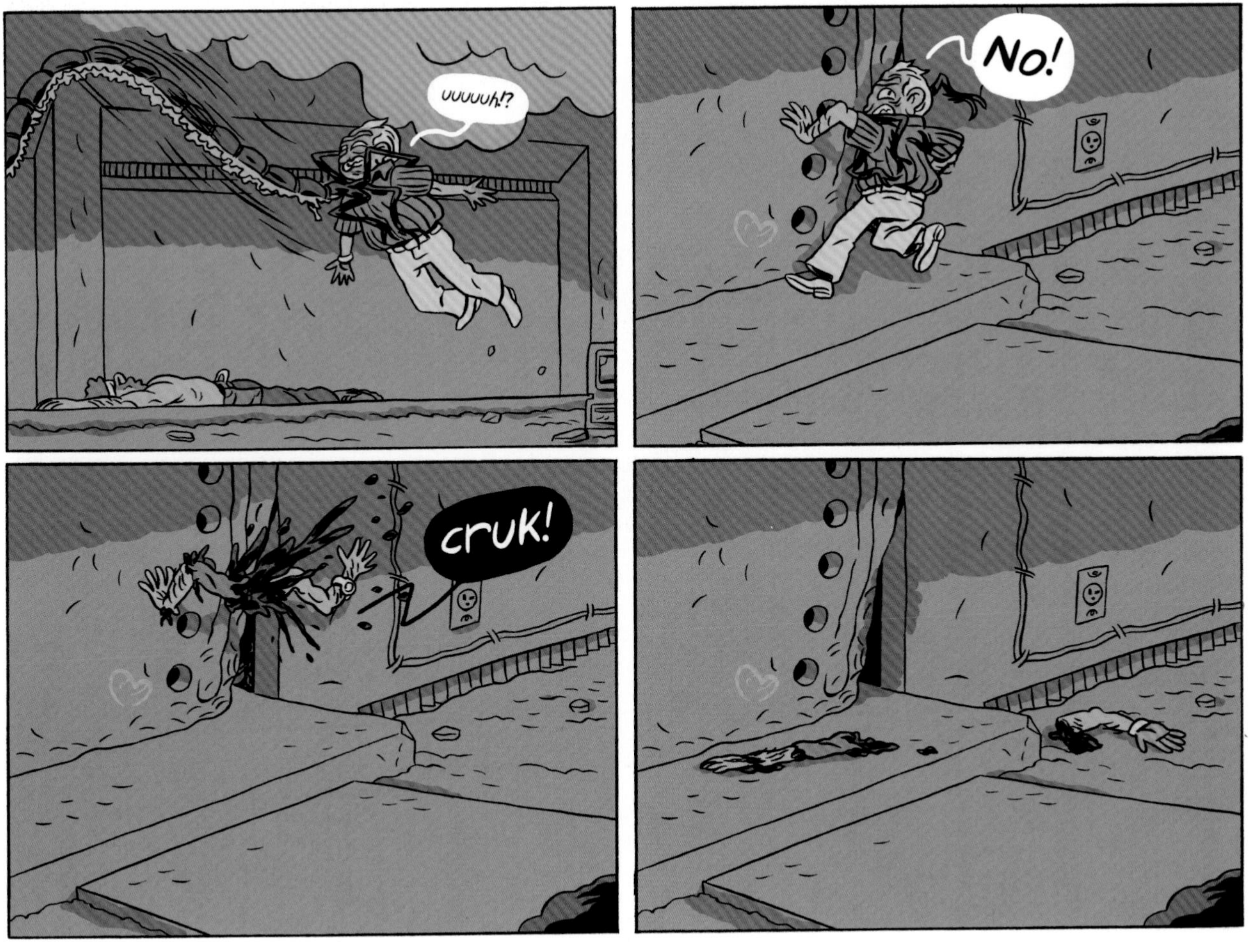
uuuuuh!?
No!
cruk!

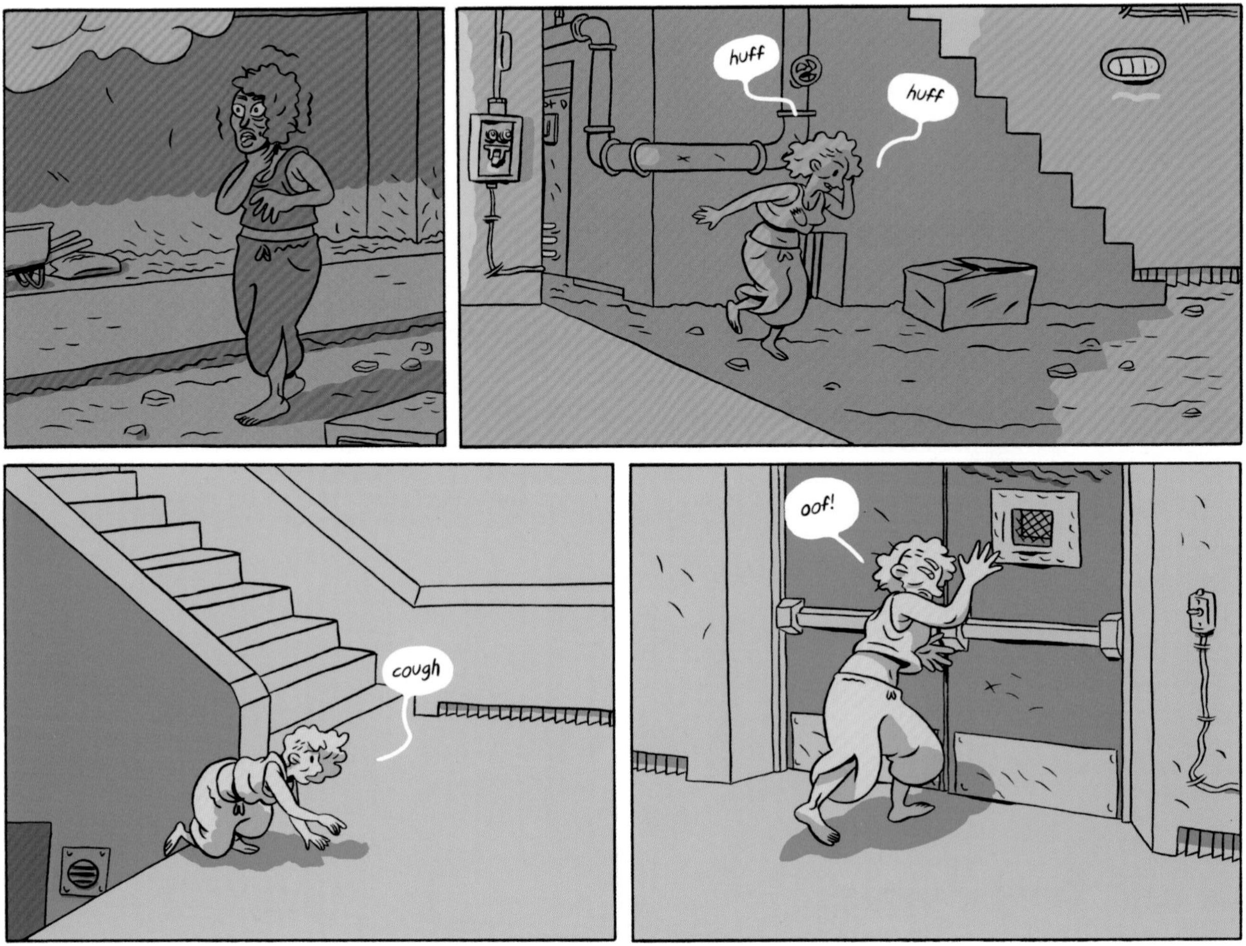
huff
huff
cough
oof!

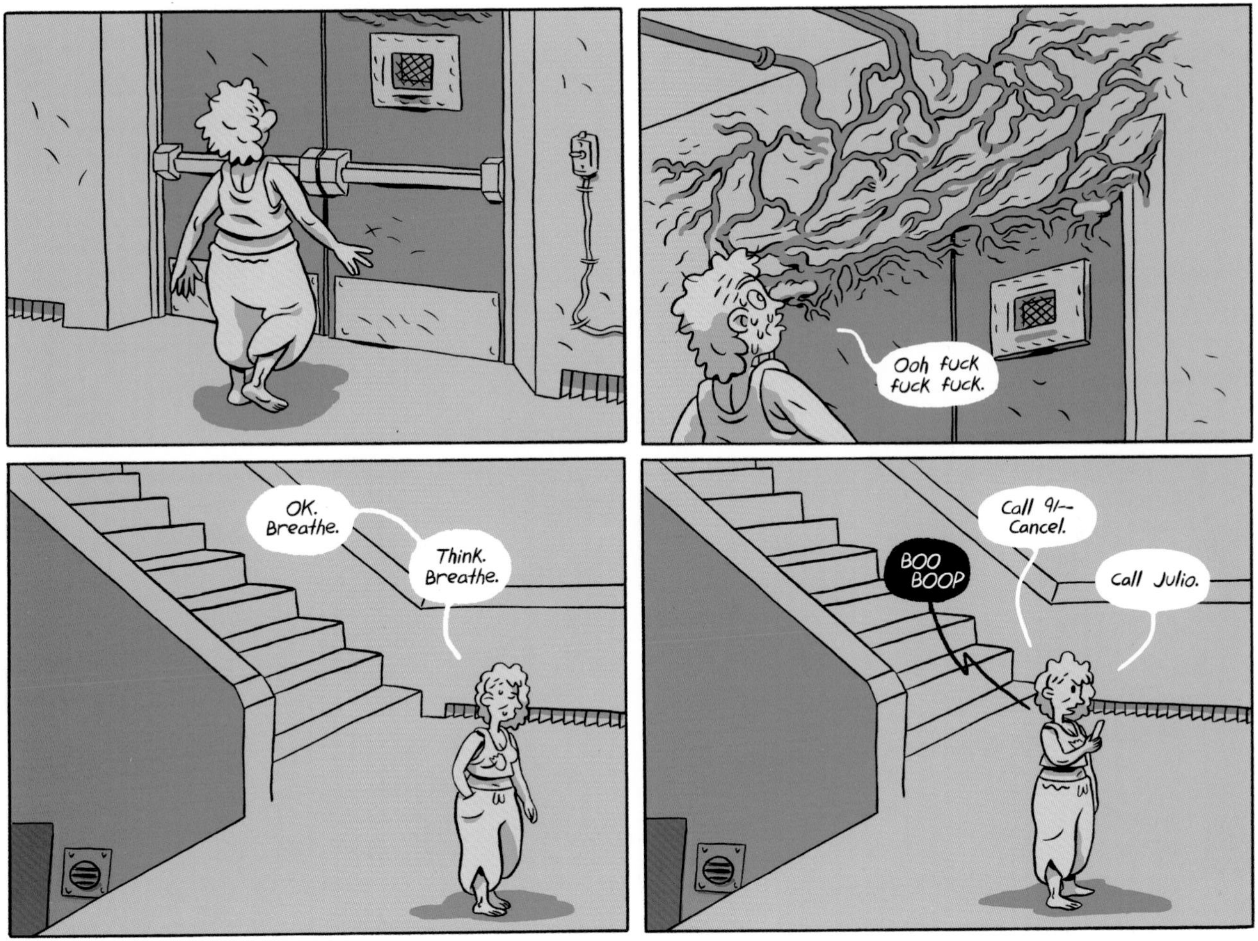

Ooh fuck fuck fuck.
OK. Breathe.
Think. Breathe.
Call 911--
Cancel.
BOO BOOP
Call Julio.

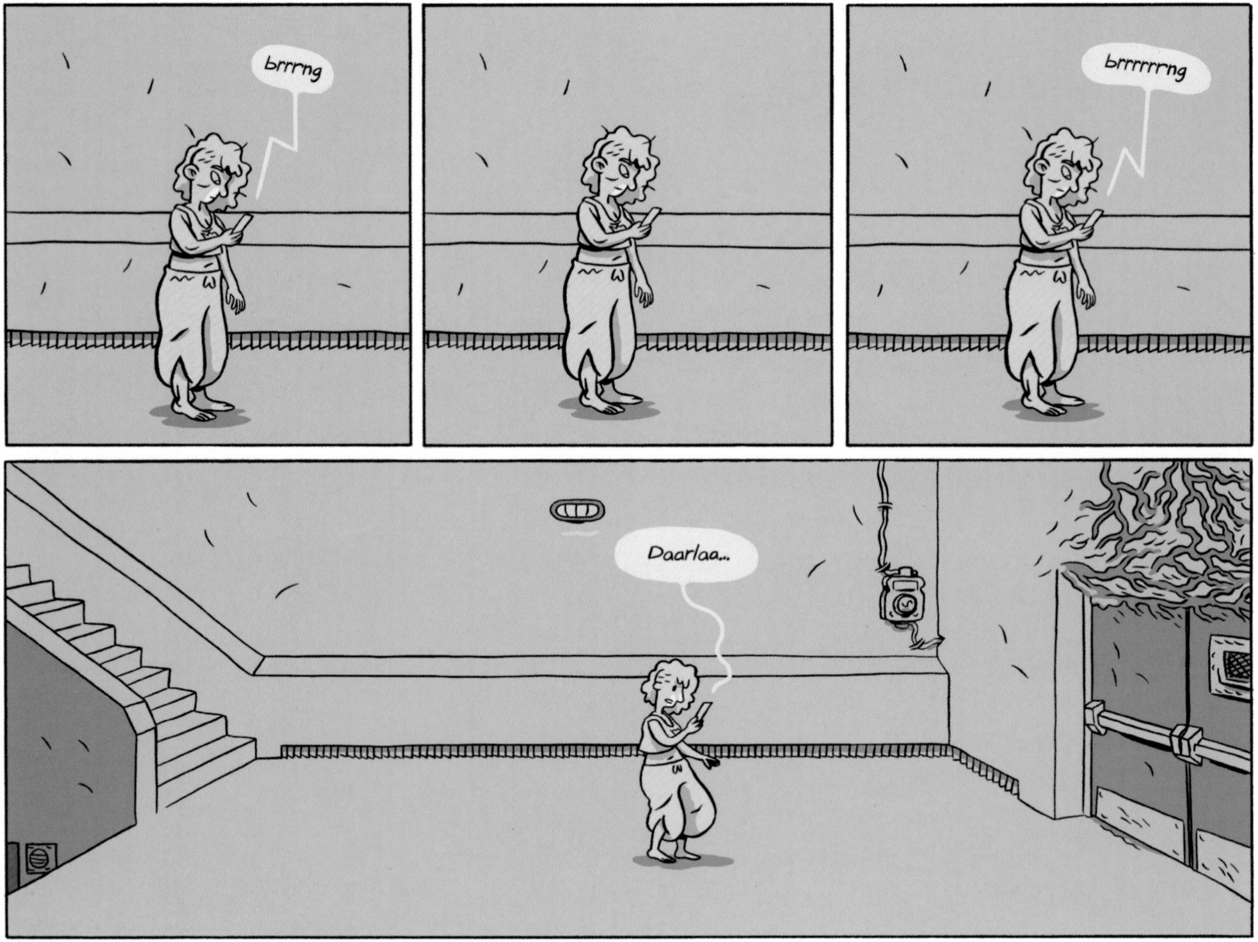
brrrng
brrrrrrng
Daarlaa...

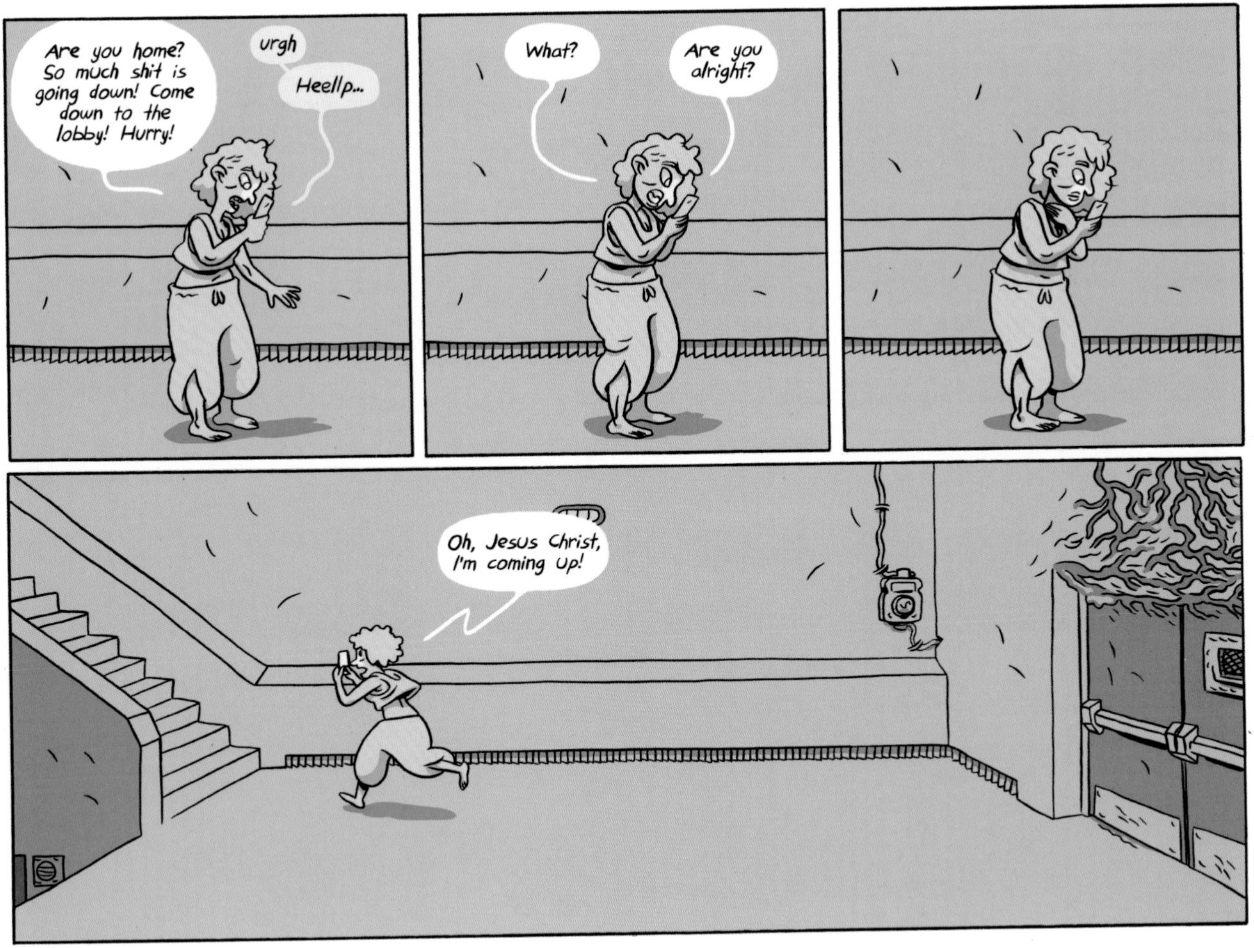
Are you home? So much shit is going down! Come down to the lobby! Hurry!
urgh
Heellp...
What?
Are you alright?
Oh, Jesus Christ, I'm coming up!

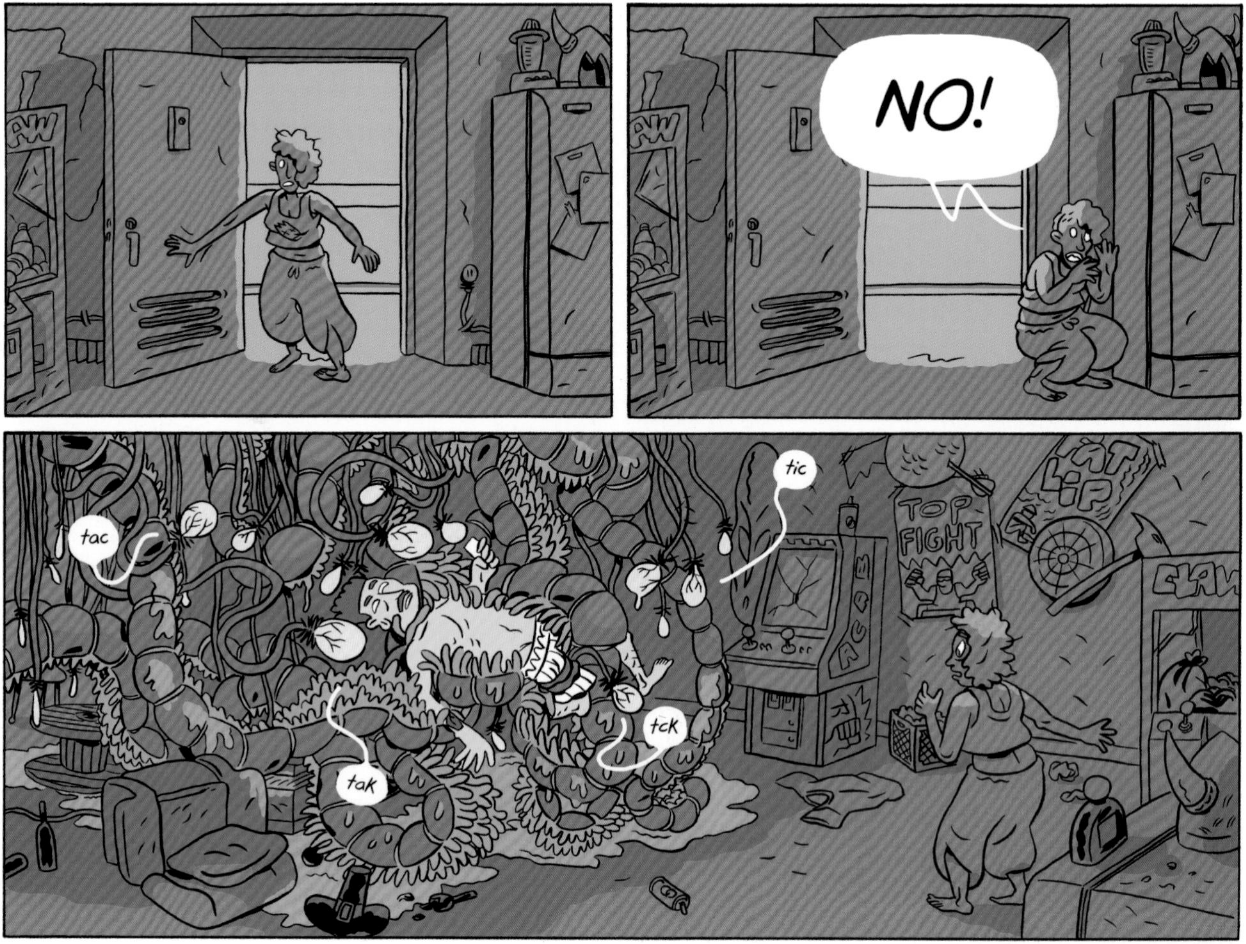
CLAW
NO!
tac
tic
tak
tck
TOP FIGHT
FAT LIP
CLAW

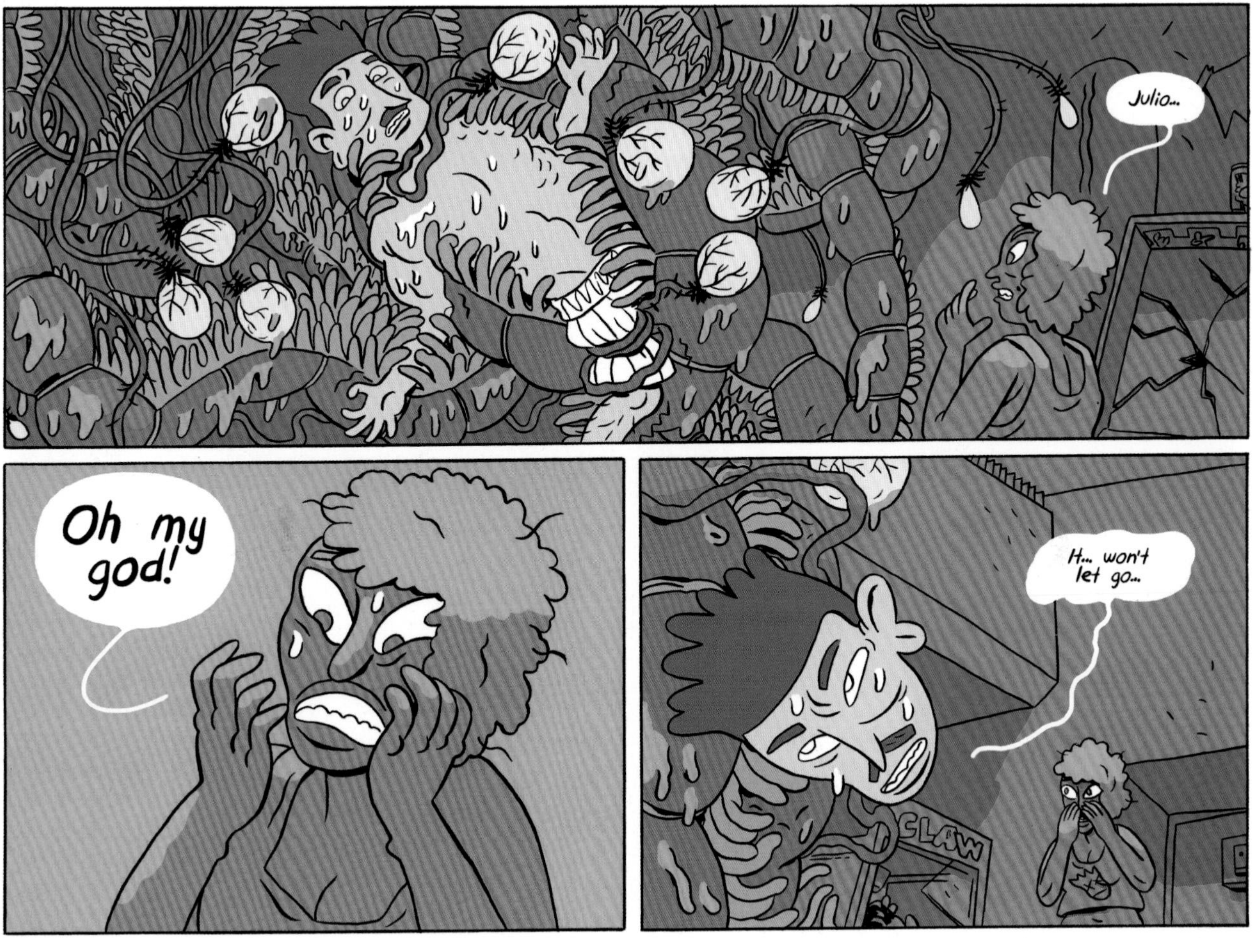
Julio...
Oh my god!
It... won't let go...
CLAW

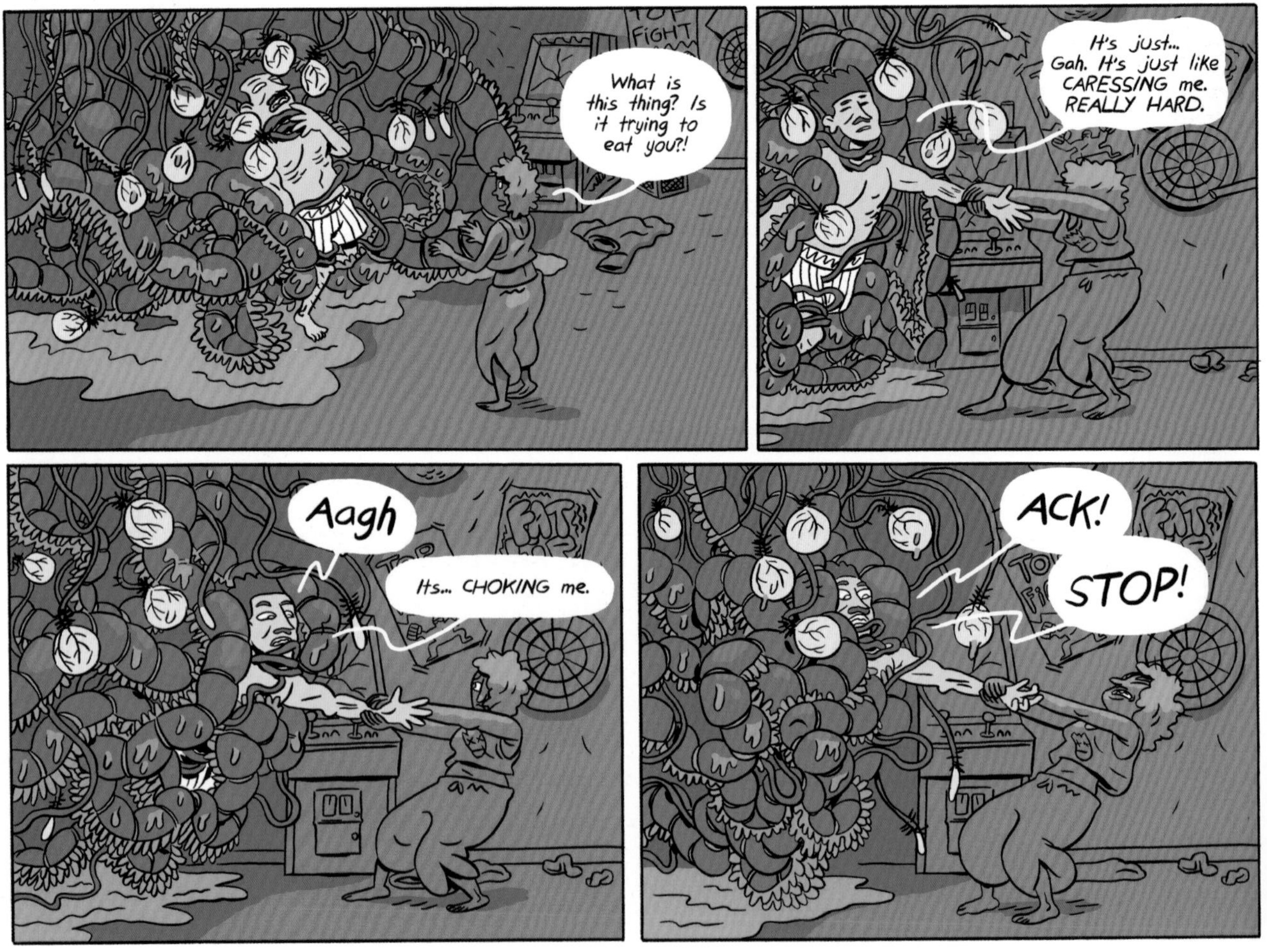
What is this thing? Is it trying to eat you?!
It's just... Gah. It's just like CARESSING me. REALLY HARD.
Aagh
Its... CHOKING me.
ACK!
STOP!

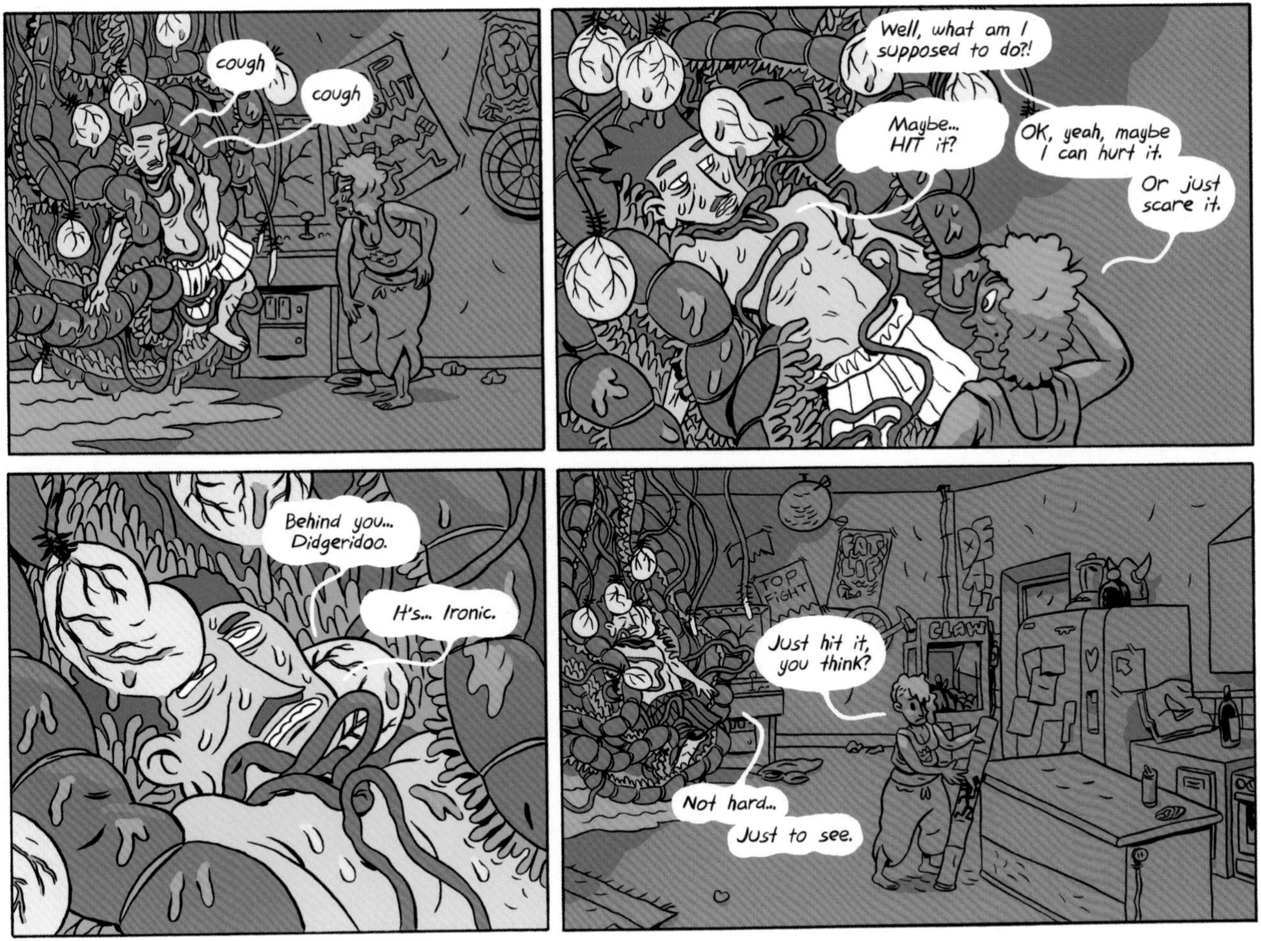

cough
cough
Well, what am I supposed to do?!
Maybe... HIT it?
OK, yeah, maybe I can hurt it.
Or just scare it.
Behind you... Didgeridoo.
It's... Ironic.
TOP FIGHT
CLAW
Just hit it, you think?
Not hard...
Just to see.

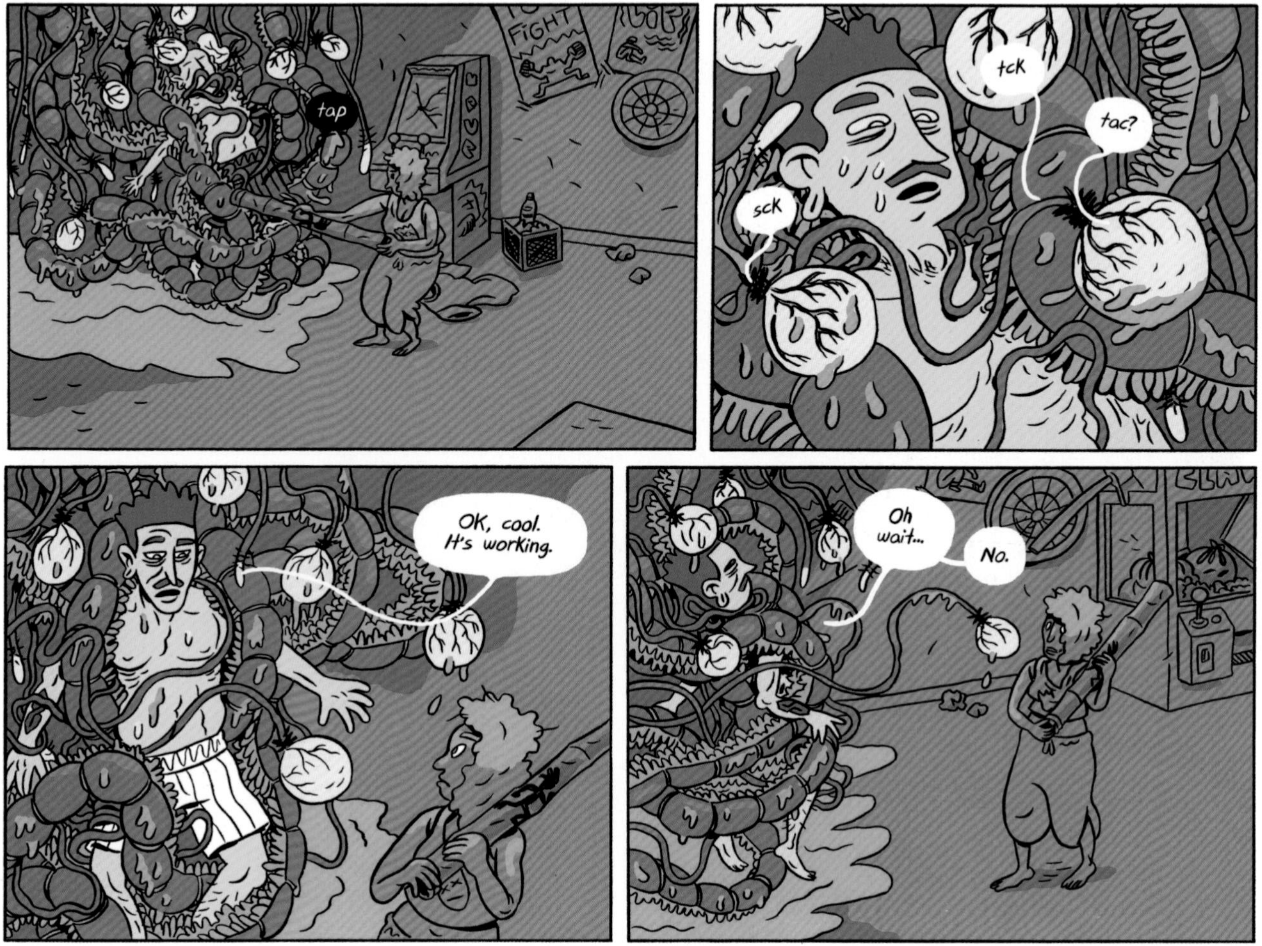
FIGHT
tap
tck
tac?
sck
OK, cool. It's working.
Oh wait...
No.

OW! um...
Fuck, OK. HIT IT AGAIN! HURRY!!
HURK!
WOK!
SKREEEEE
SKREEEEEE

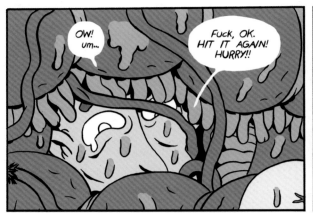

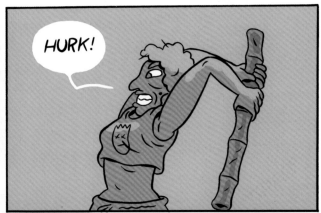

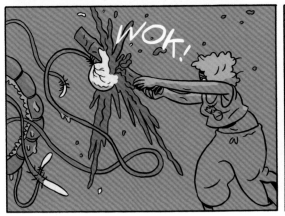

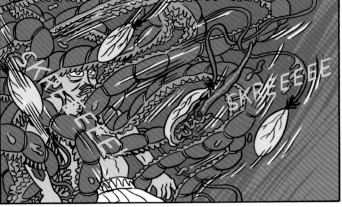

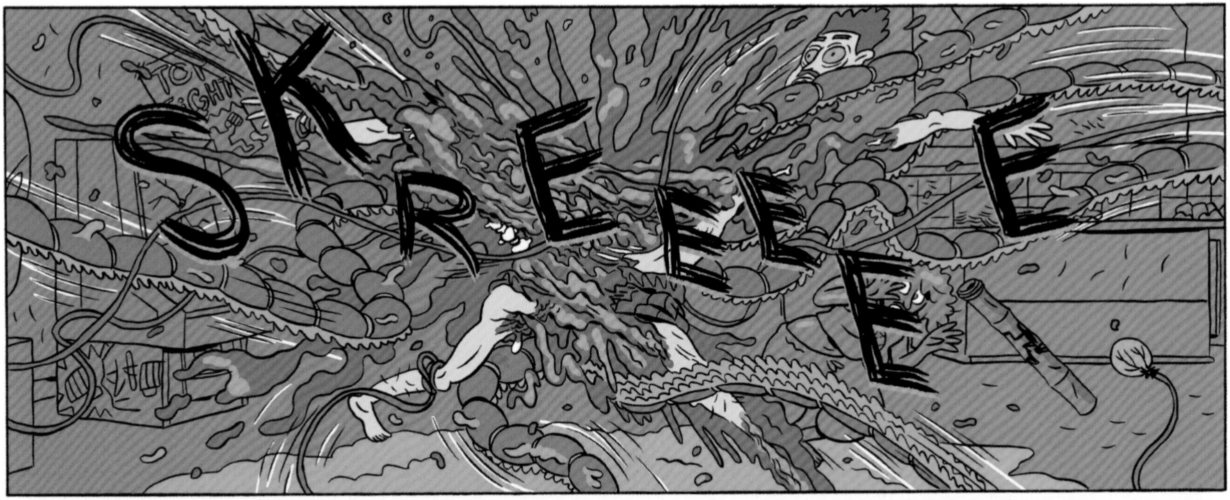
SKREEEEEE

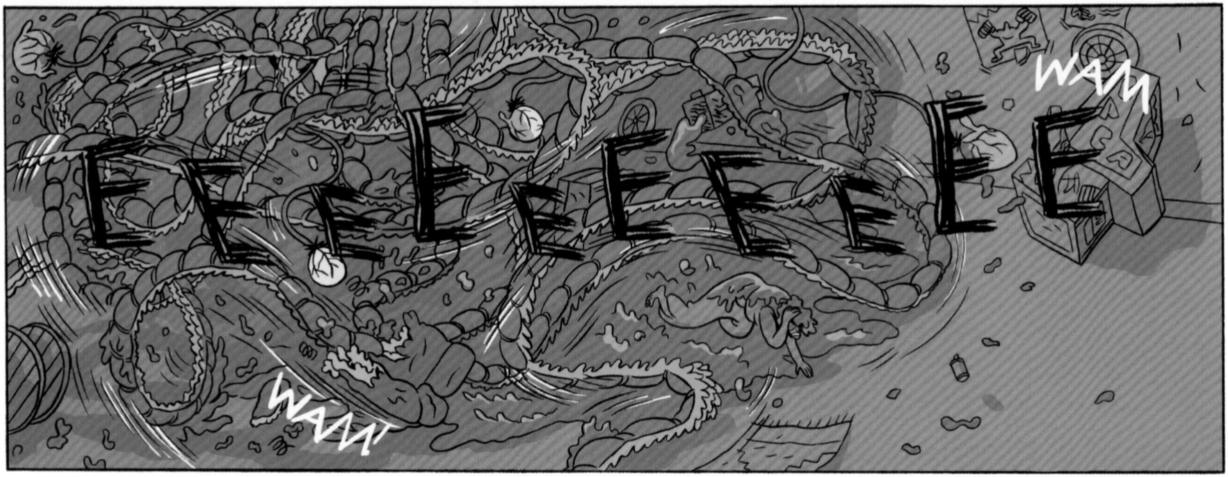
WAM
EEEEEEEEE
WAM

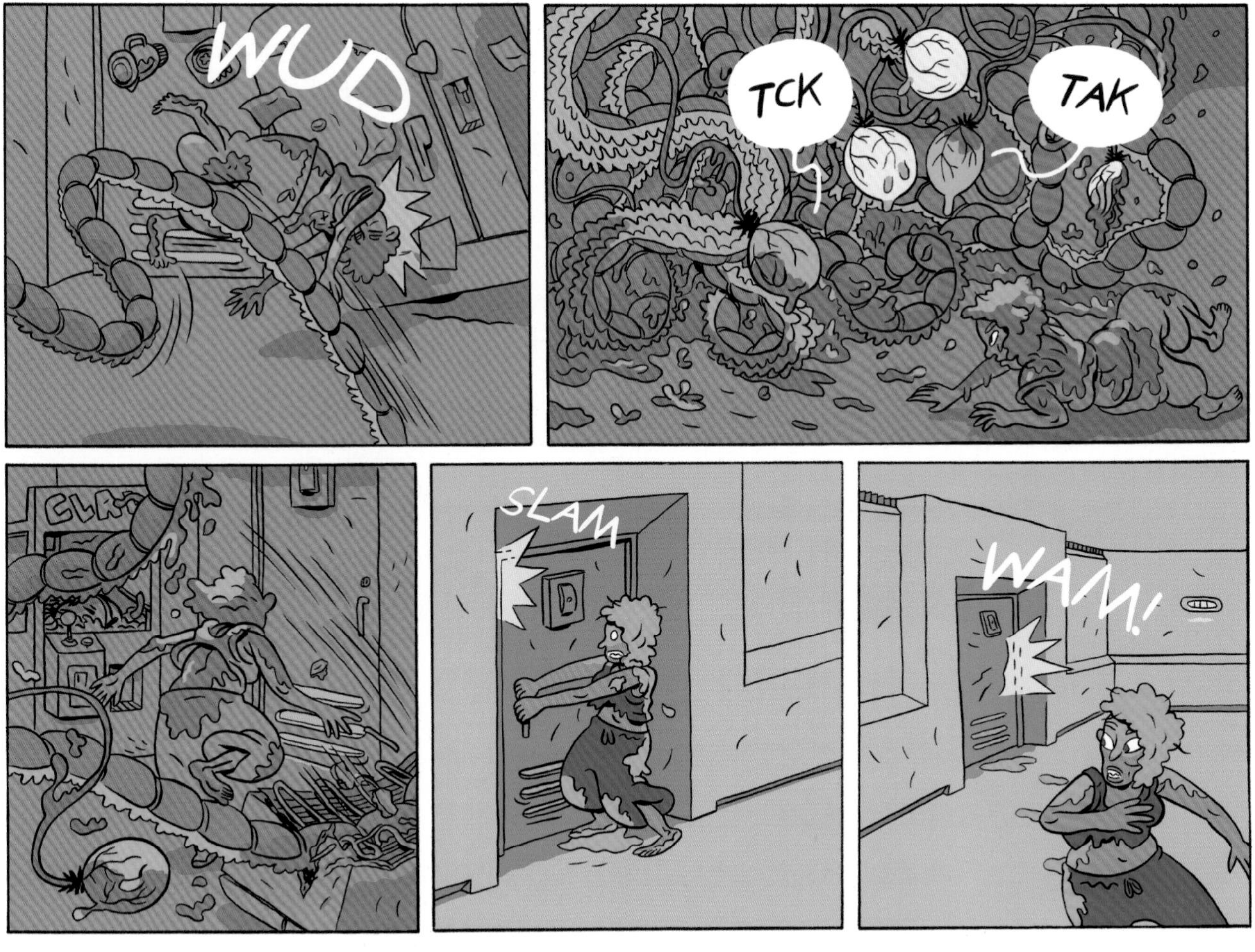
WUD
TCK
TAK
SLAM
WAM!

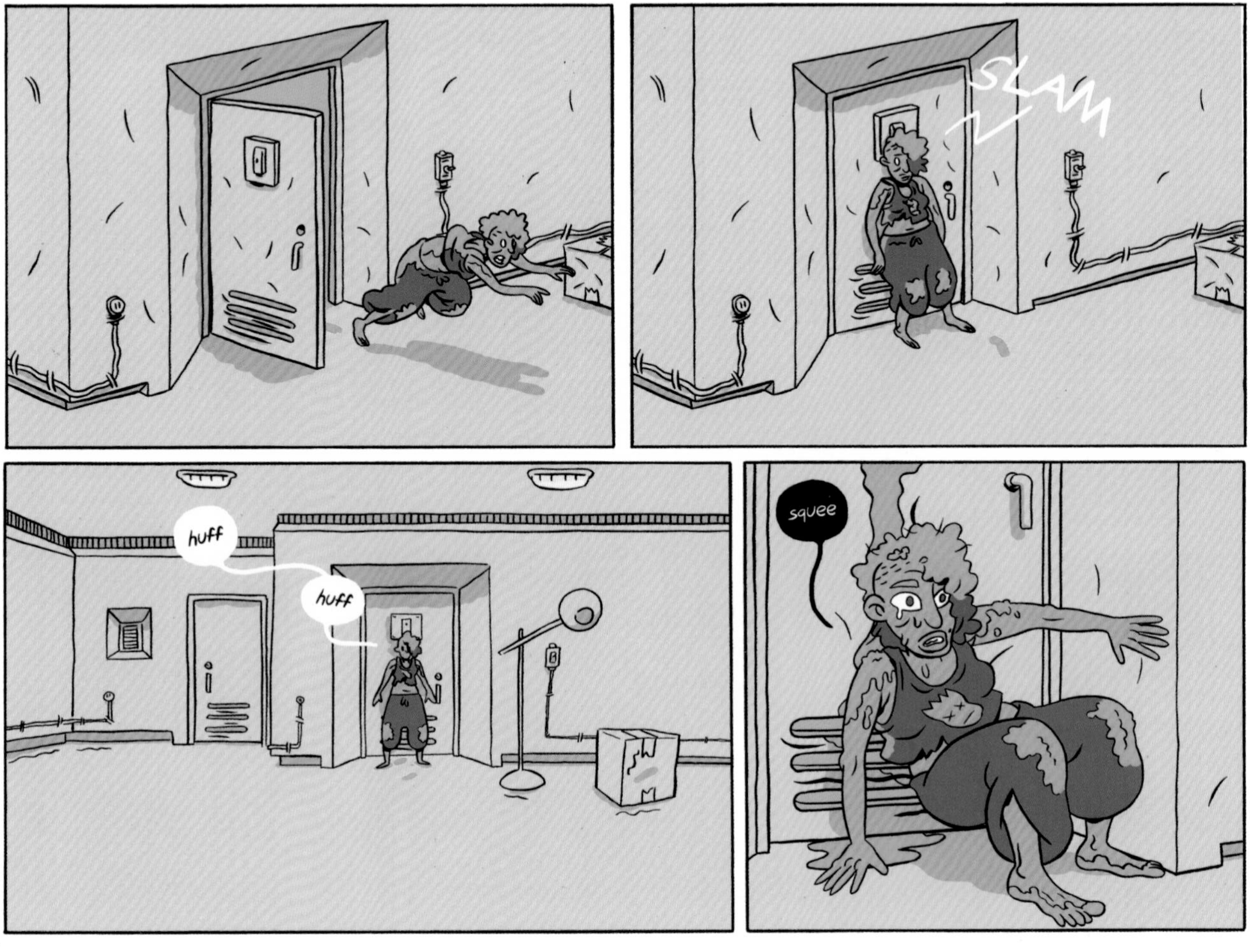
SLAM
huff
huff
squee

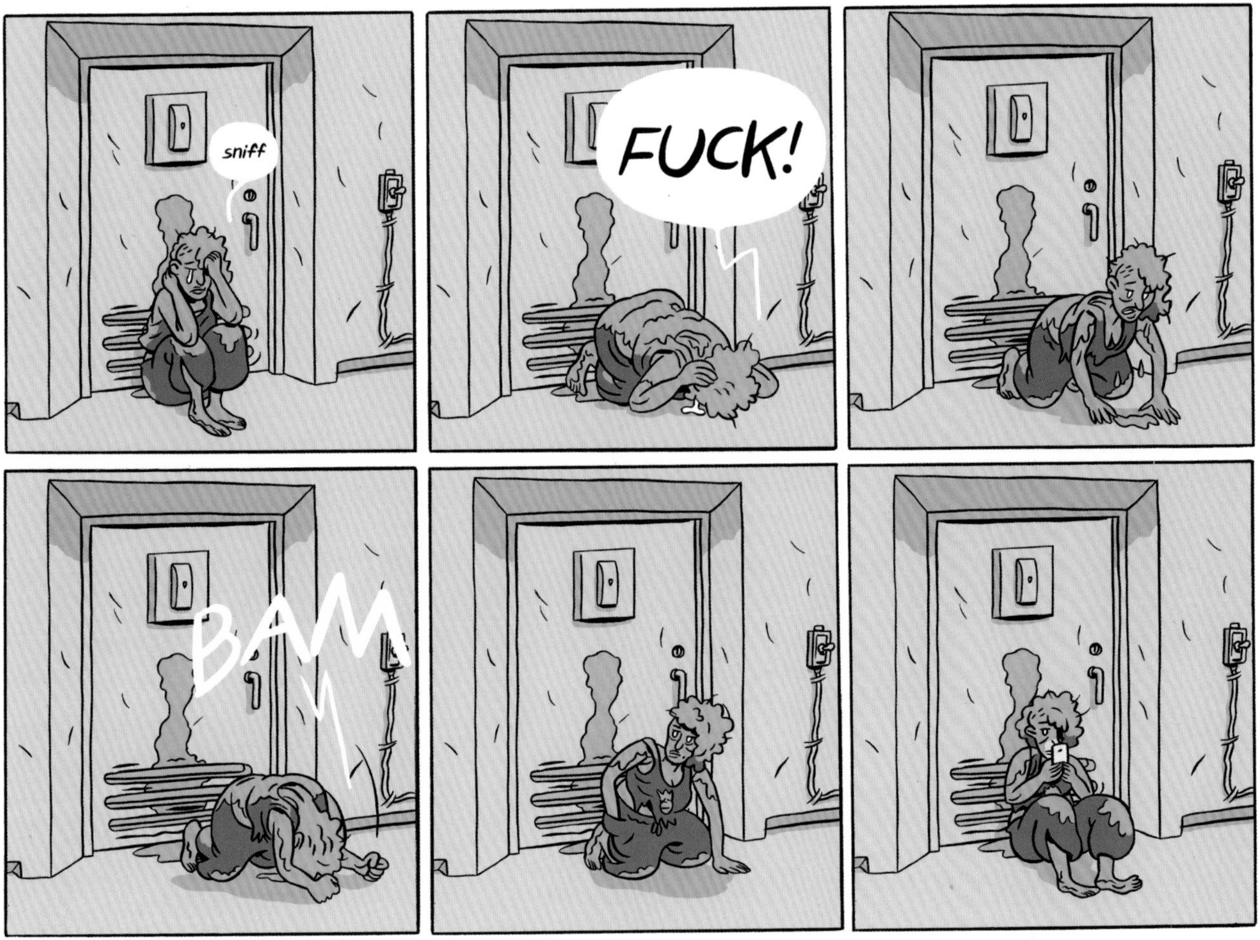
sniff
FUCK!
BAM

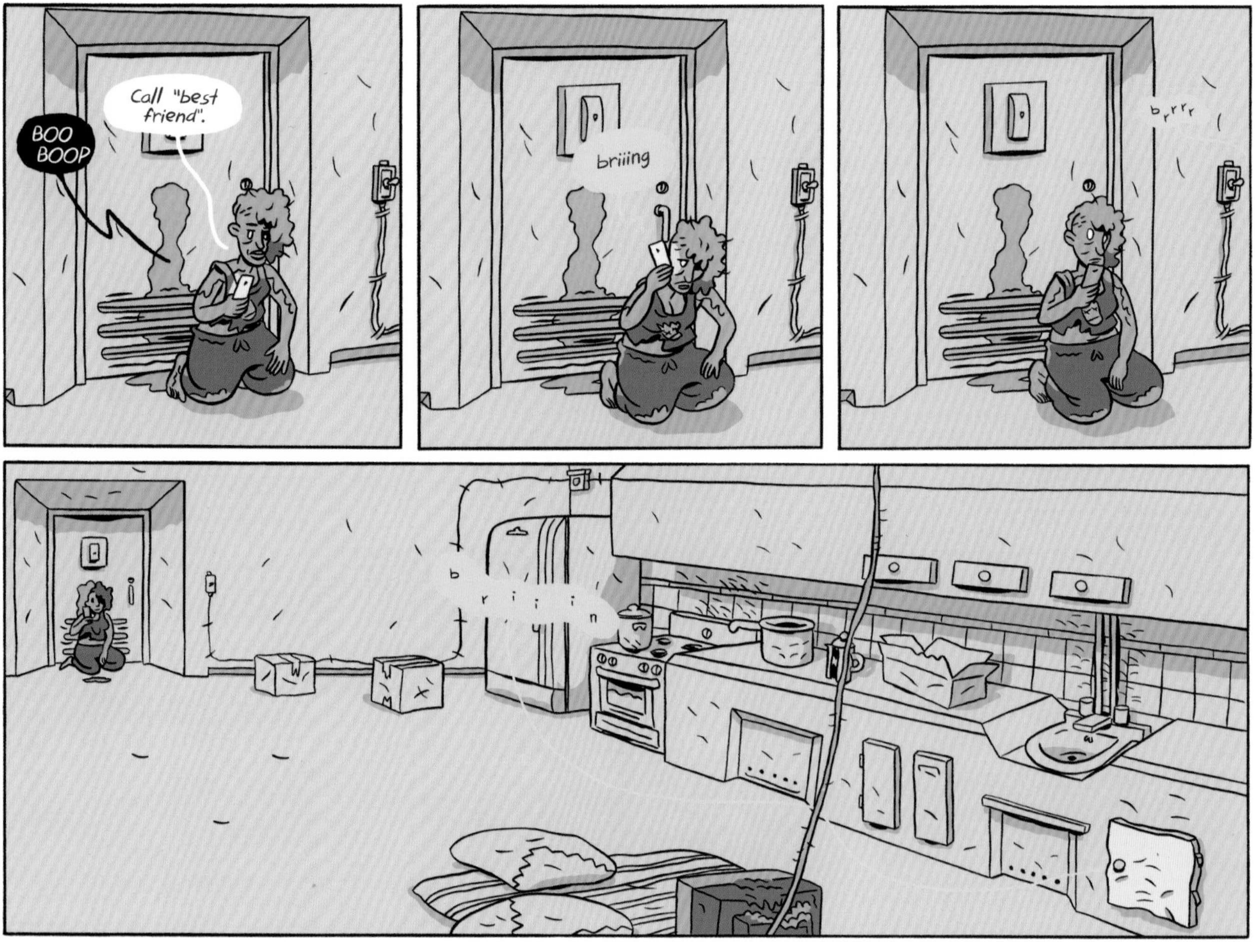
BOO BOOP
Call "best friend".
briiing
brrrr
briiin

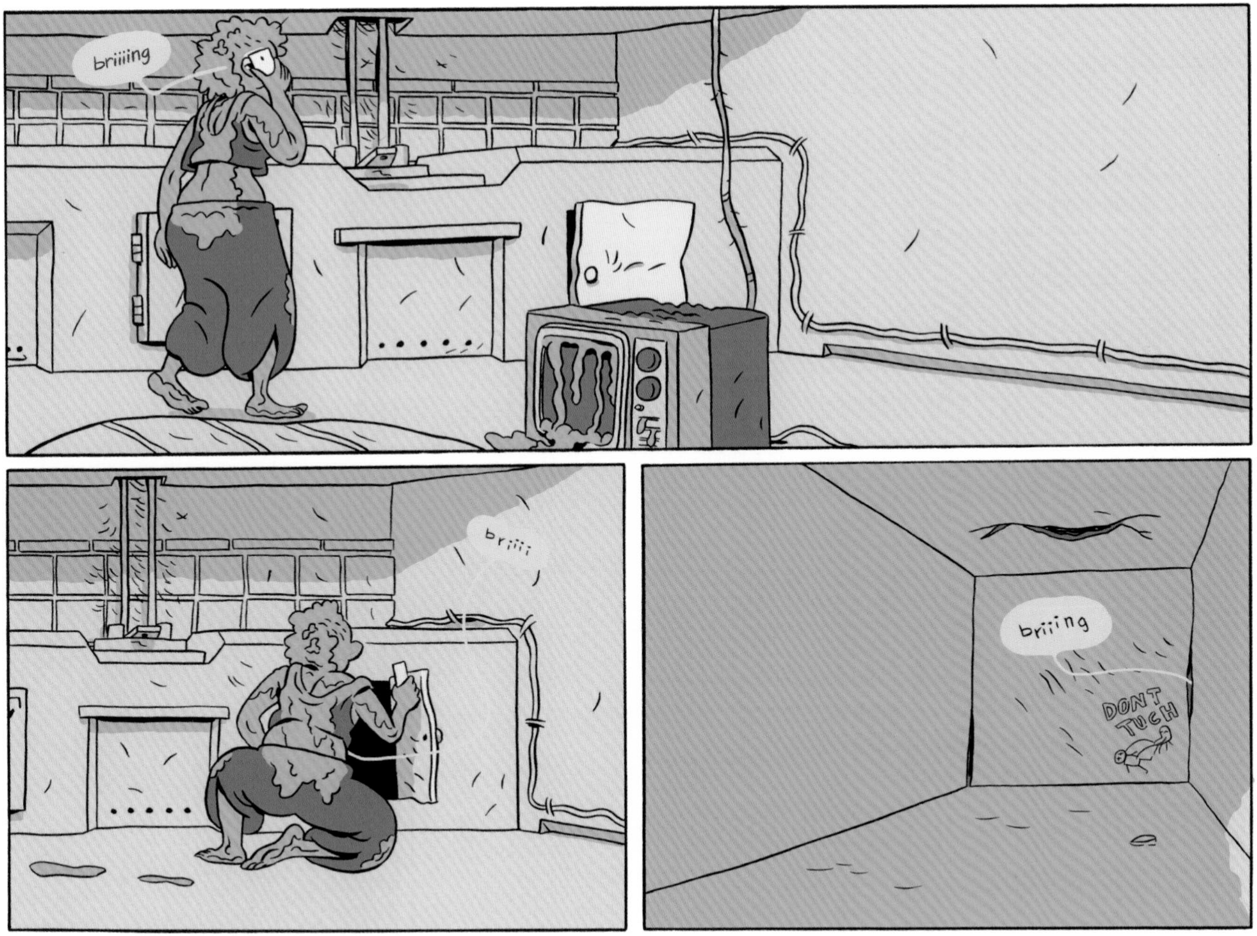
briiiing
briiii
briiing
DONT TUCH

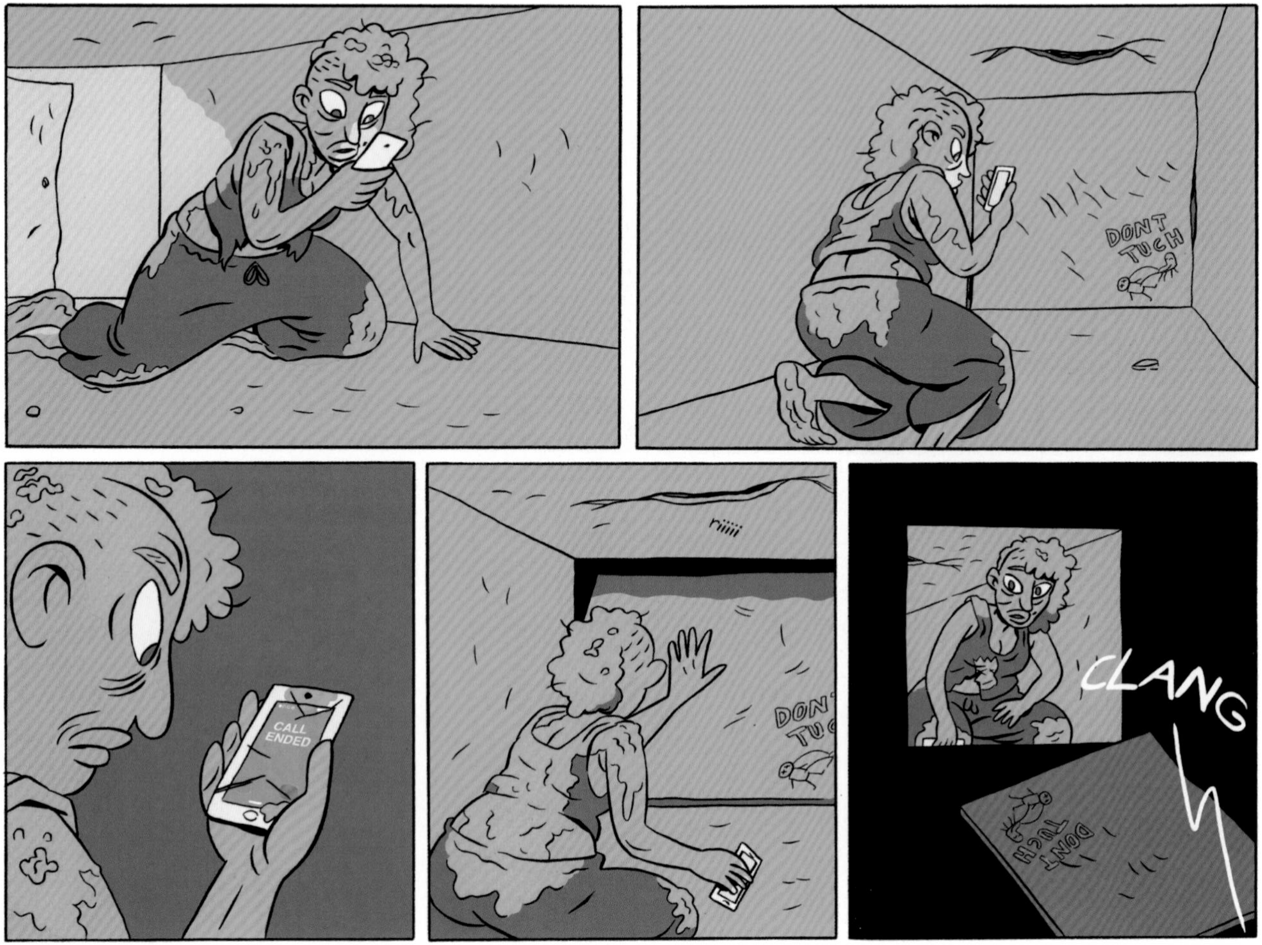
DONT TUCH
CALL ENDED
riiiii
CLANG
DONT TUCH

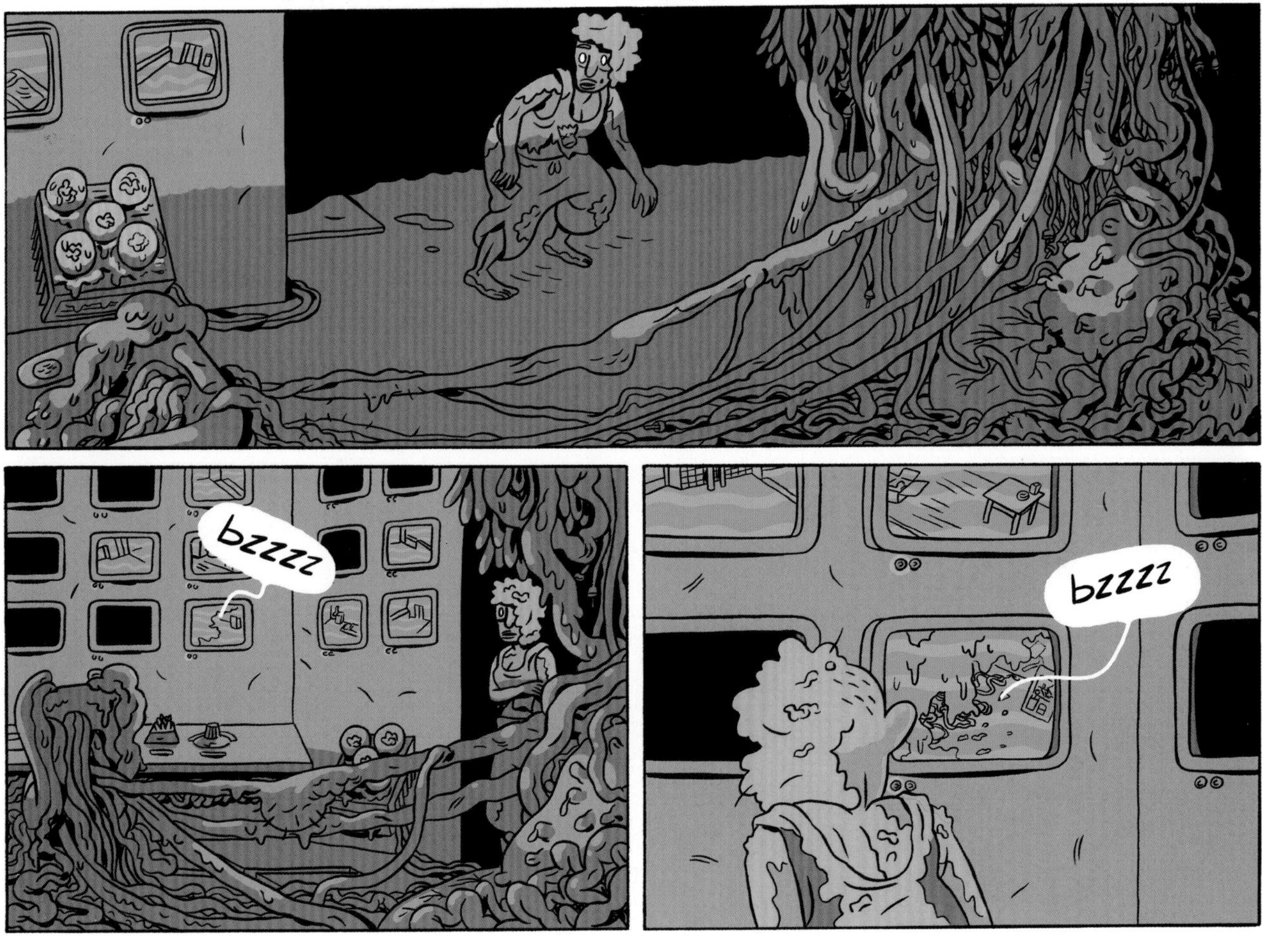
bzzzz
bzzzz

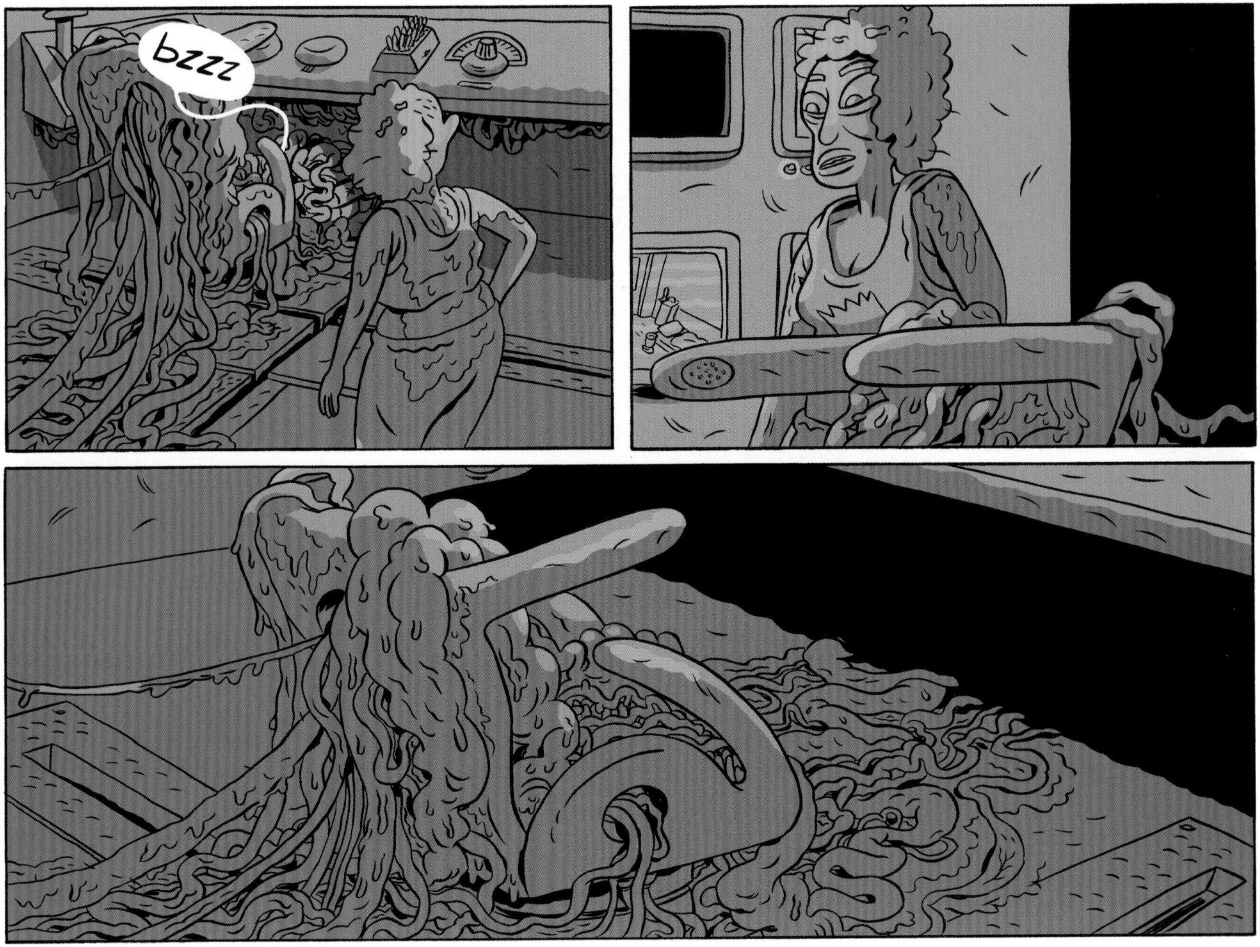
bzzz

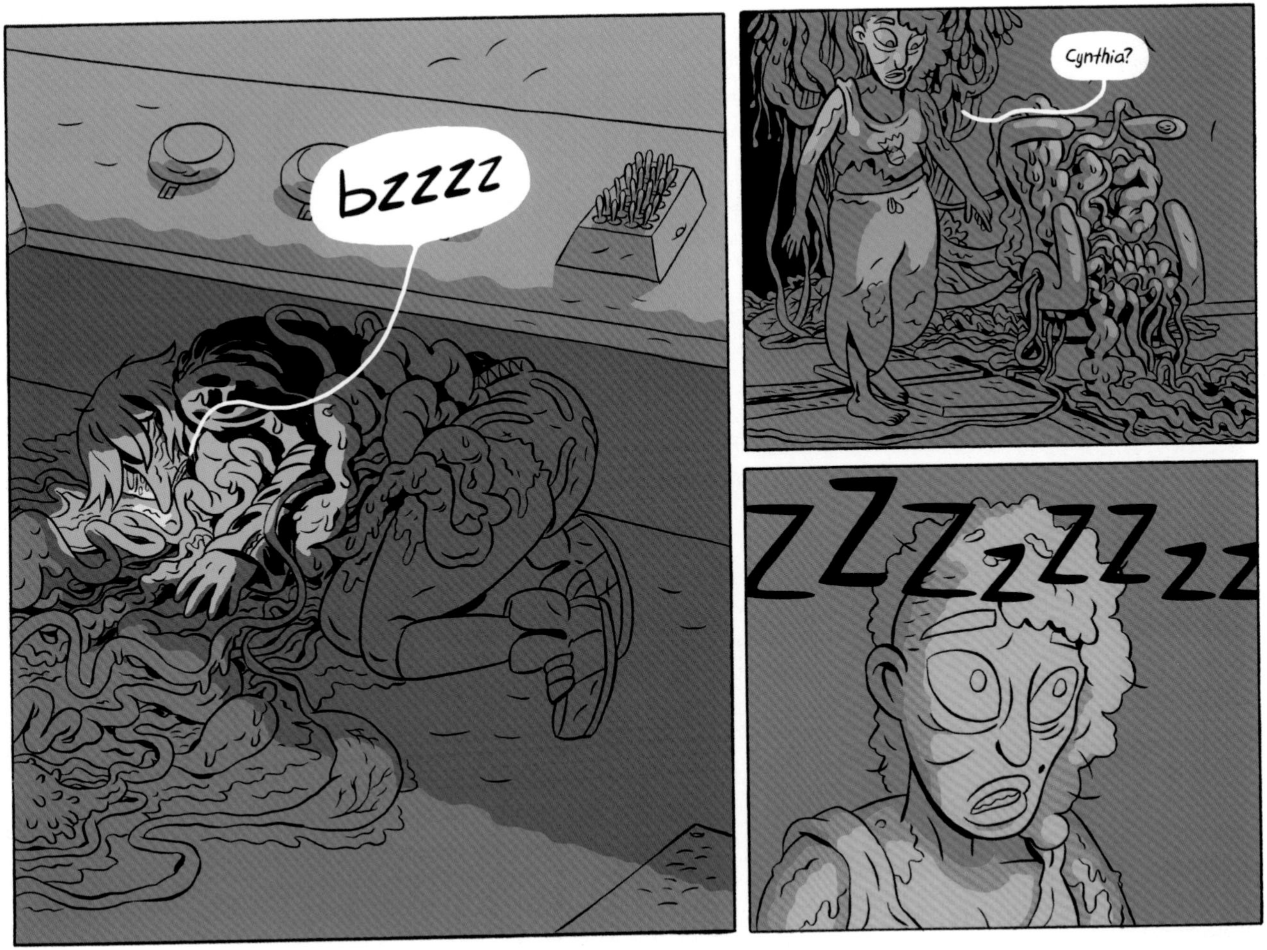
bzzzz
Cynthia?
ZZZzZZZzz

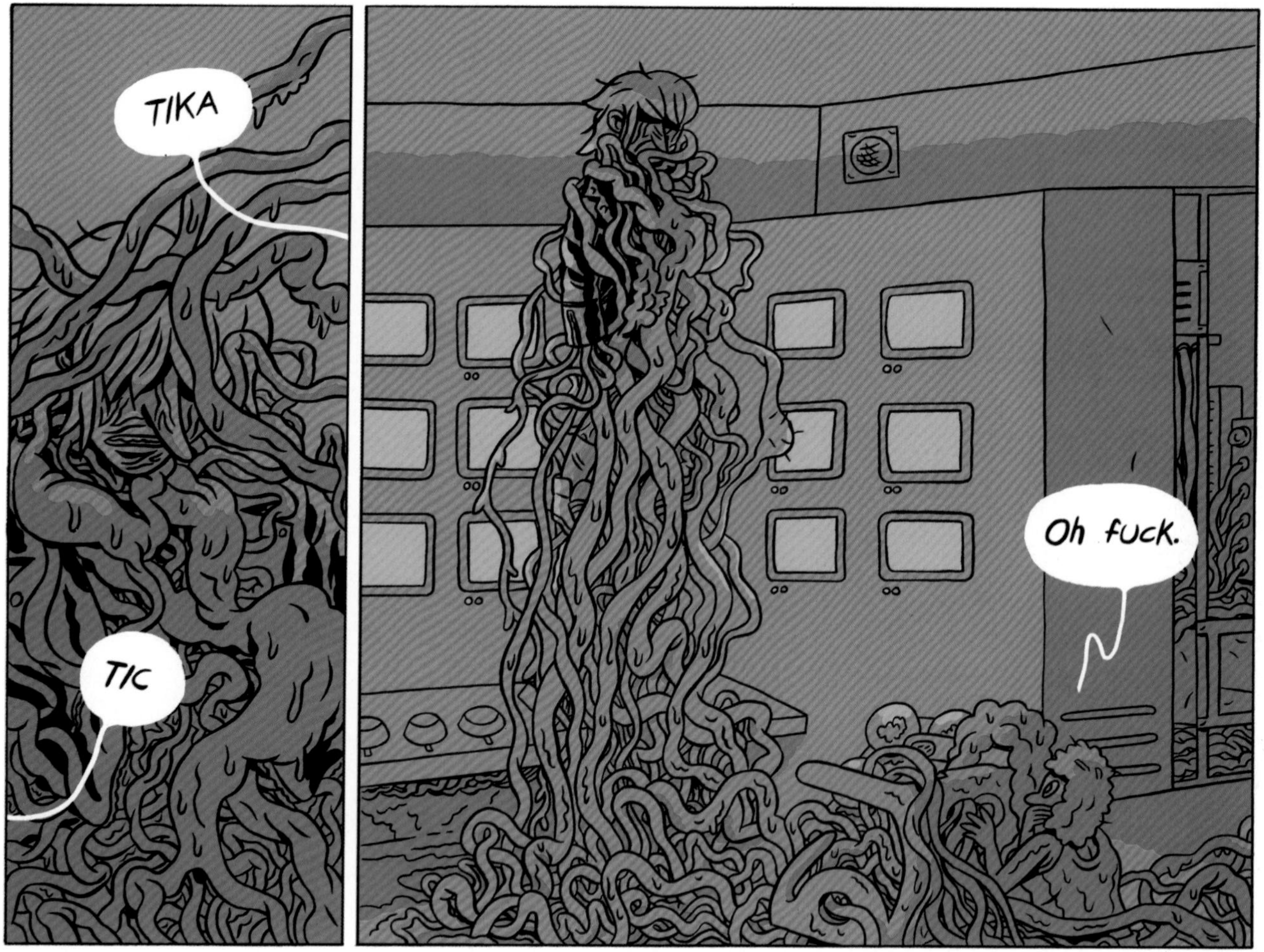
TIKA
TIC
Oh fuck.

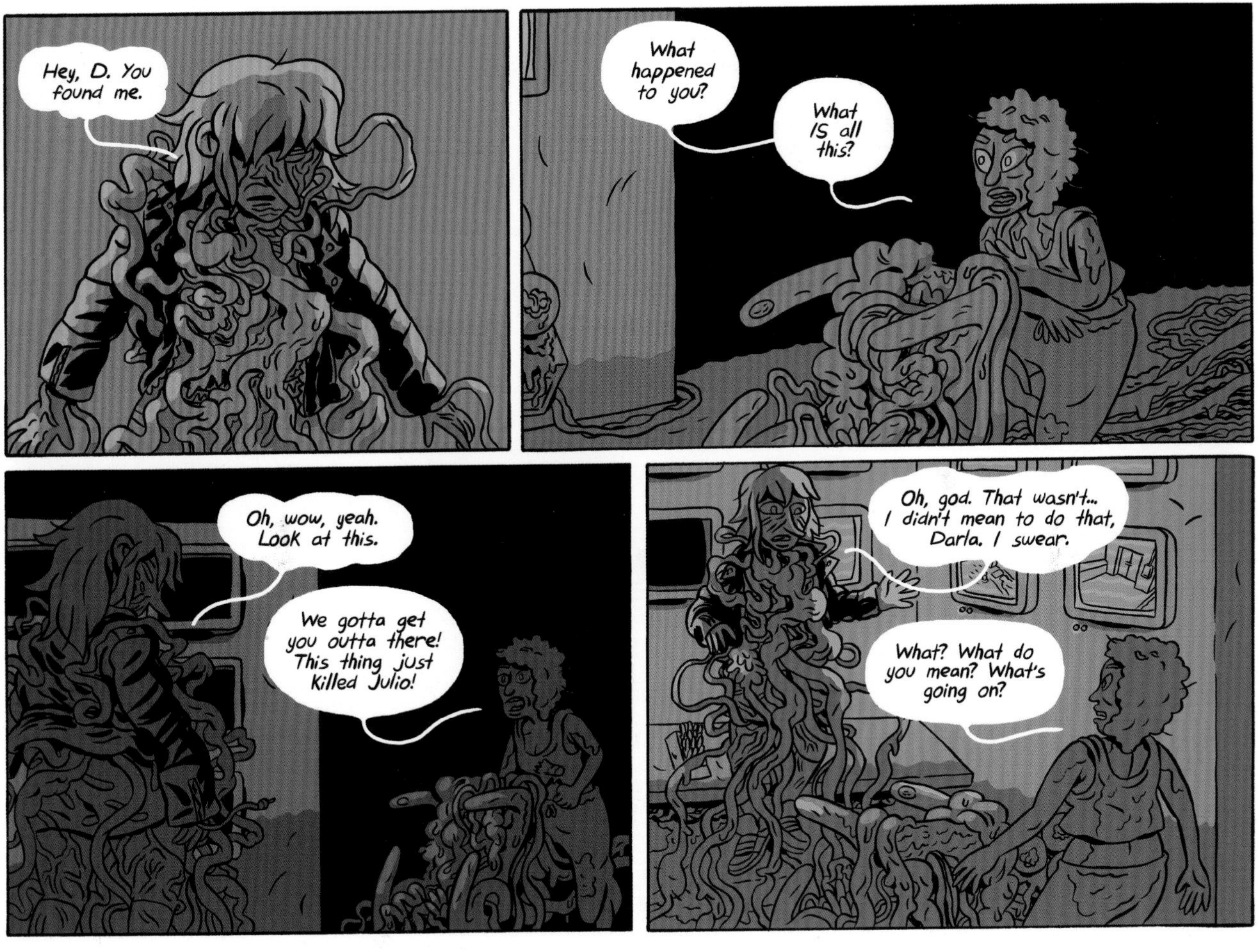
Hey, D. You found me.
What happened to you?
What IS all this?
Oh, wow, yeah. Look at this.
We gotta get you outta there! This thing just Killed Julio!
Oh, god. That wasn't... I didn't mean to do that, Darla. I swear.
What? What do you mean? What's going on?

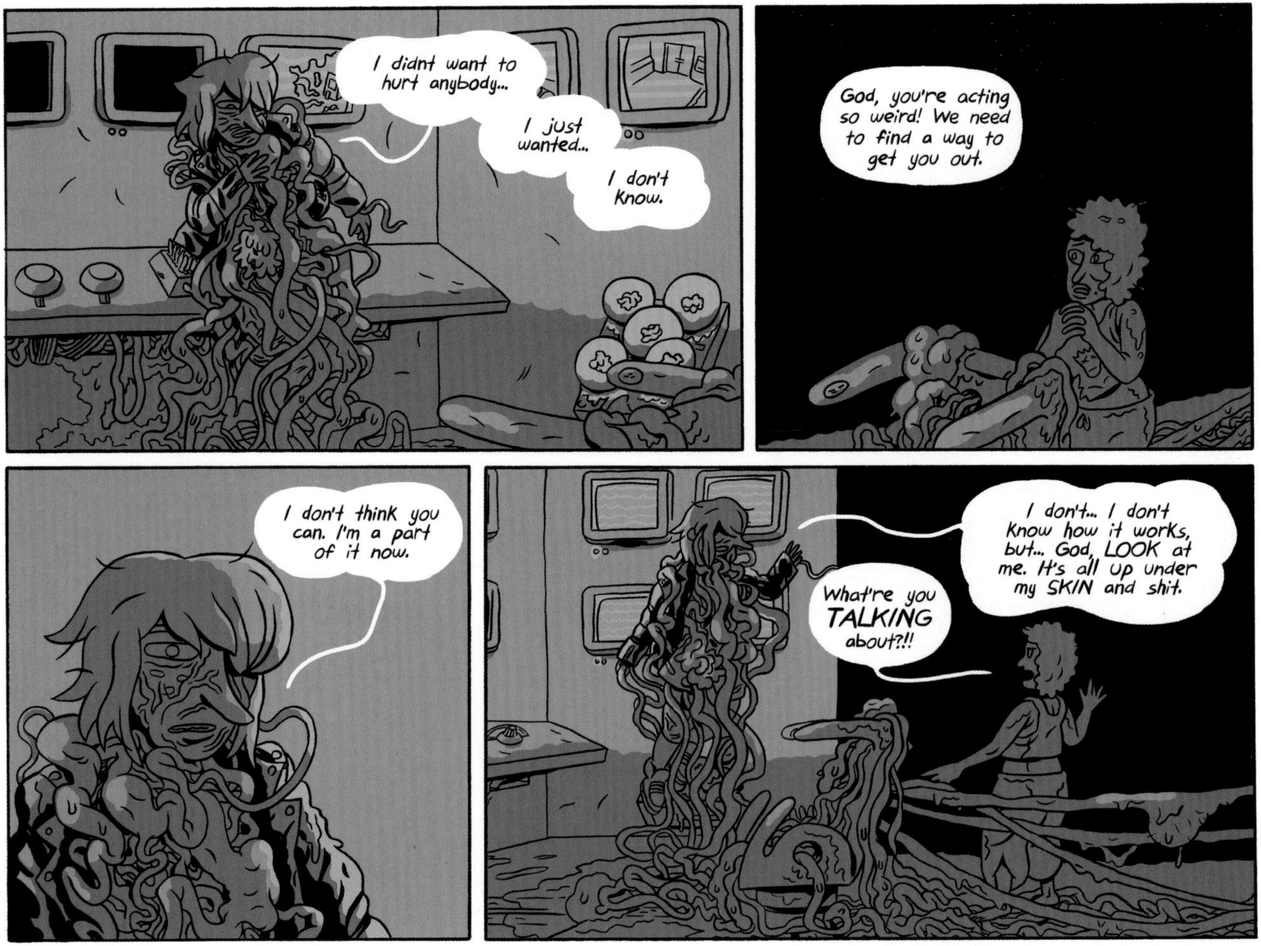
I didnt want to hurt anybody...
I just wanted...
I don't know.
God, you're acting so weird! We need to find a way to get you out.
I don't think you can. I'm a part of it now.
I don't... I don't know how it works, but... God, LOOK at me. It's all up under my SKIN and shit.
What're you TALKING about?!!

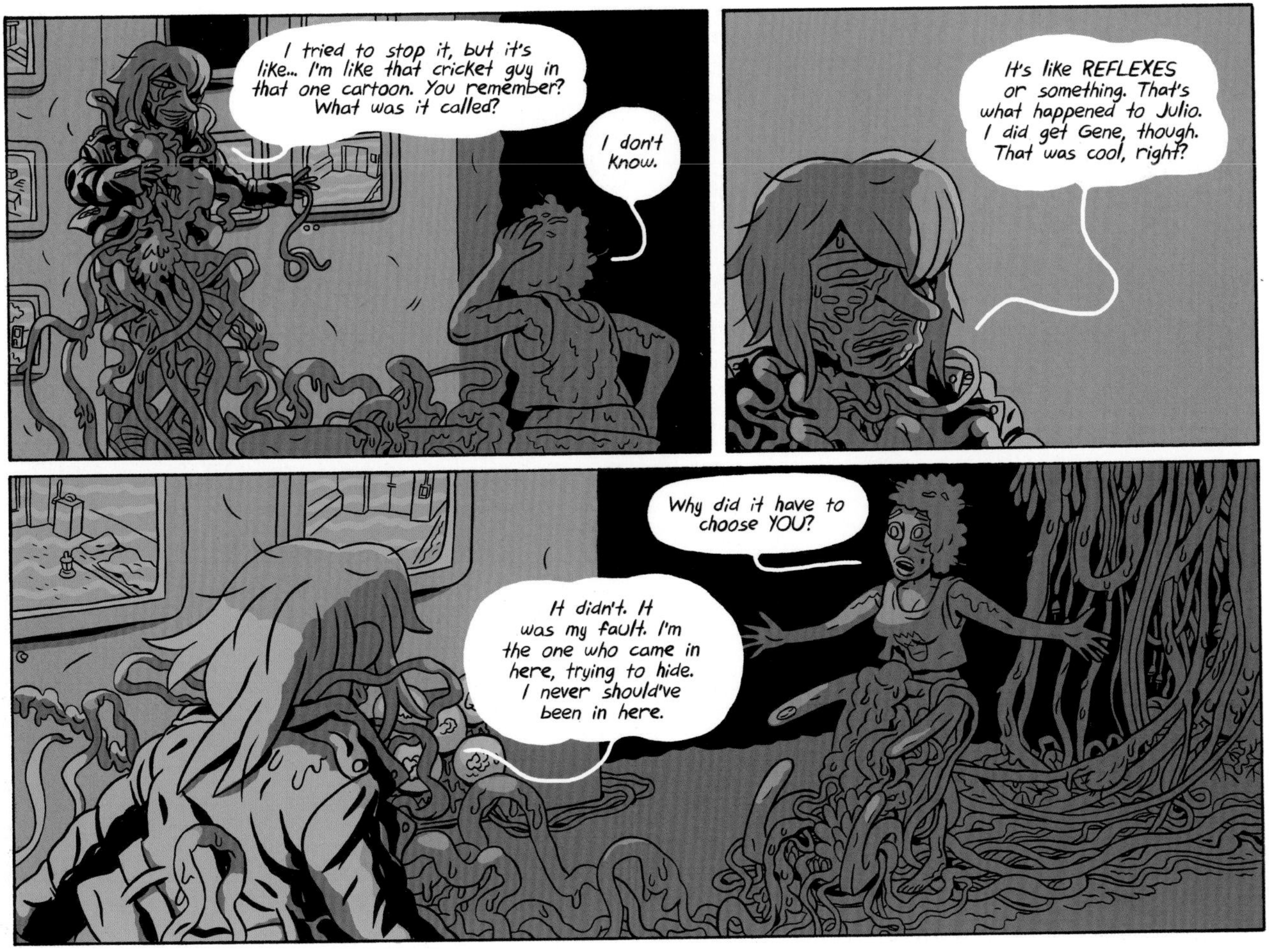
I tried to stop it, but it's like... I'm like that cricket guy in that one cartoon. You remember? What was it called?
I don't know.
It's like REFLEXES or something. That's what happened to Julio. I did get Gene, though. That was cool, right?
Why did it have to choose YOU?
It didn't. It was my fault. I'm the one who came in here, trying to hide. I never should've been in here.

Does it hurt?

No. It's uncomfortable, but like not in a bad way. I don't know what it's putting in me, but it makes it feel OK.

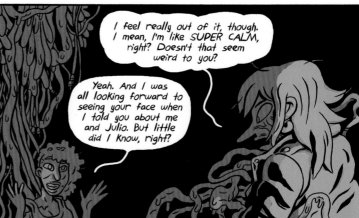

I feel really out of it, though. I mean, I'm like SUPER CALM, right? Doesn't that seem weird to you?

Yeah. And I was all looking forward to seeing your face when I told you about me and Julio. But little did I know, right?

Hahaha. I can't BELIEVE you hooked with him! He was such a dick to us!

Sniff.

Julio's OK once you get to know him...

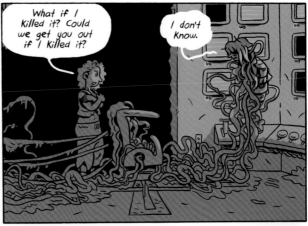

What if I killed it? Could we get you out if I killed it?

I don't know.

Well, I don't know what to do, Cynthia! 911 flagged my number, and I can't even leave the building to get help 'cause SOMEBODY sealed the stairwell with her wall tentacles!

Ugh, I'm sorry. I didn't mean to do that, either. I saw you running toward the door and I couldn't help it.

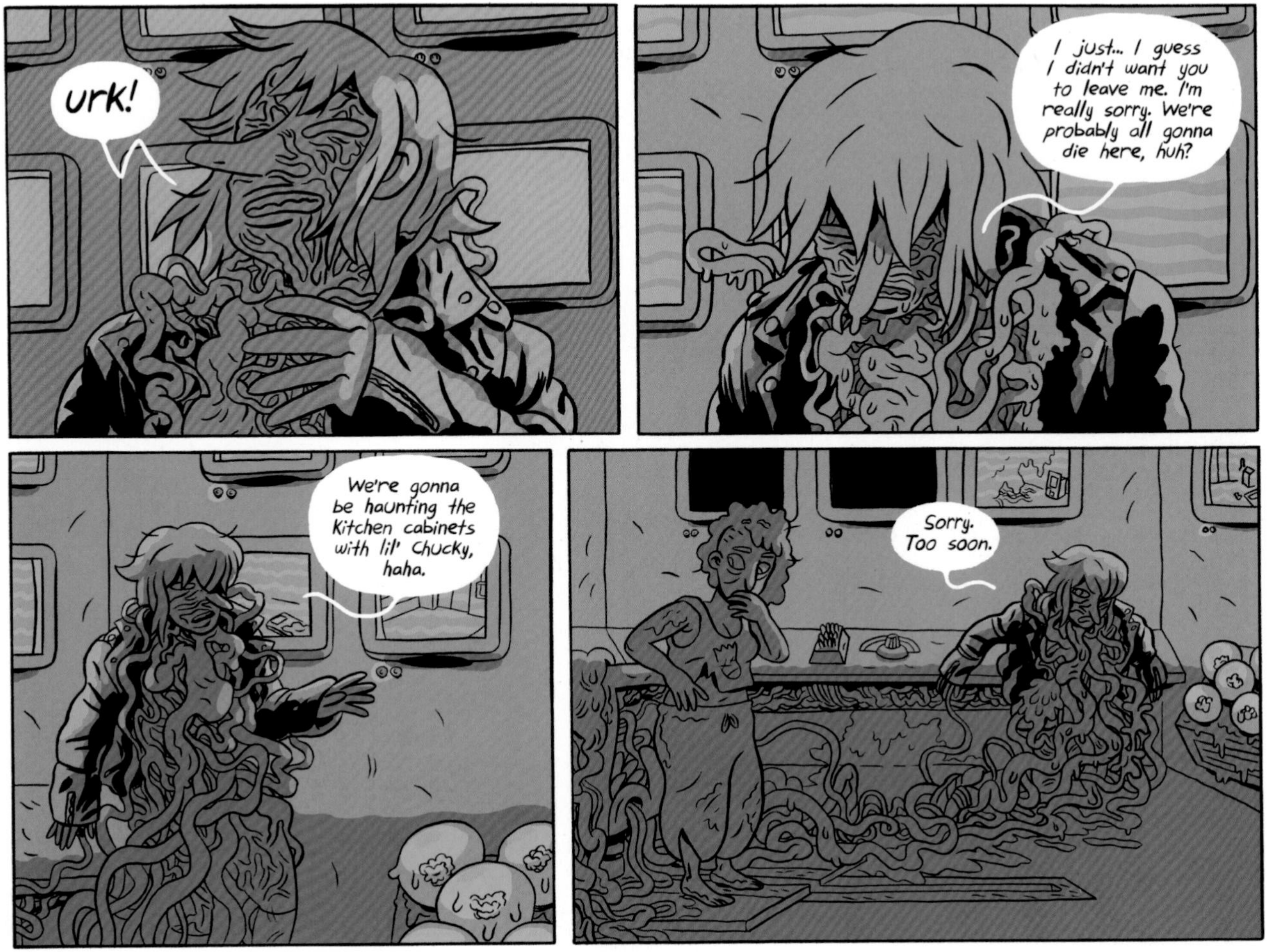
urk!
I just... I guess I didn't want you to leave me. I'm really sorry. We're probably all gonna die here, huh?
We're gonna be haunting the kitchen cabinets with lil' Chucky, haha.
Sorry. Too soon.

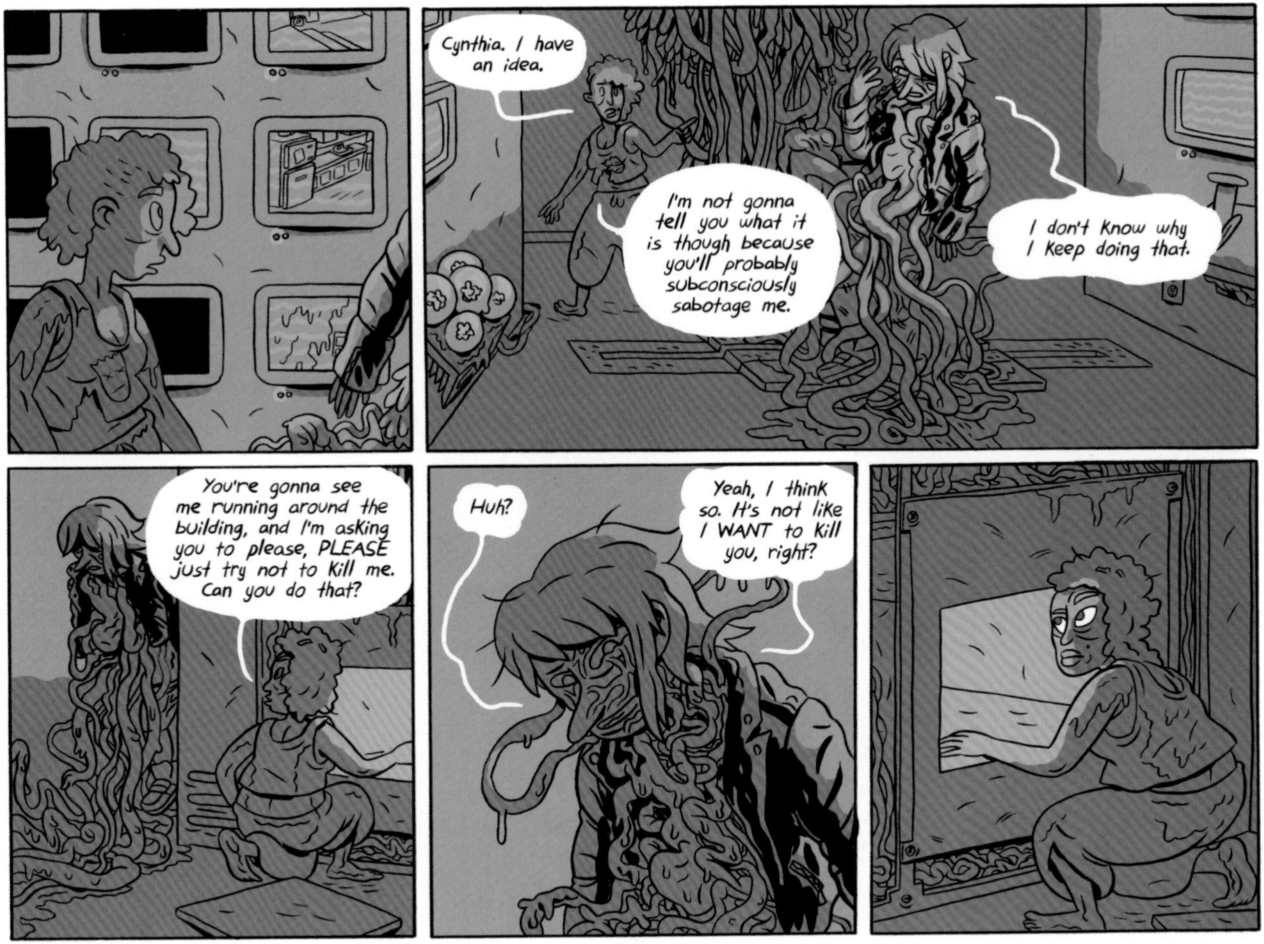
Cynthia. I have an idea.
I'm not gonna tell you what it is though because you'll probably subconsciously sabotage me.
I don't know why I keep doing that.
You're gonna see me running around the building, and I'm asking you to please, PLEASE just try not to kill me. Can you do that?
Huh?
Yeah, I think so. It's not like I WANT to kill you, right?

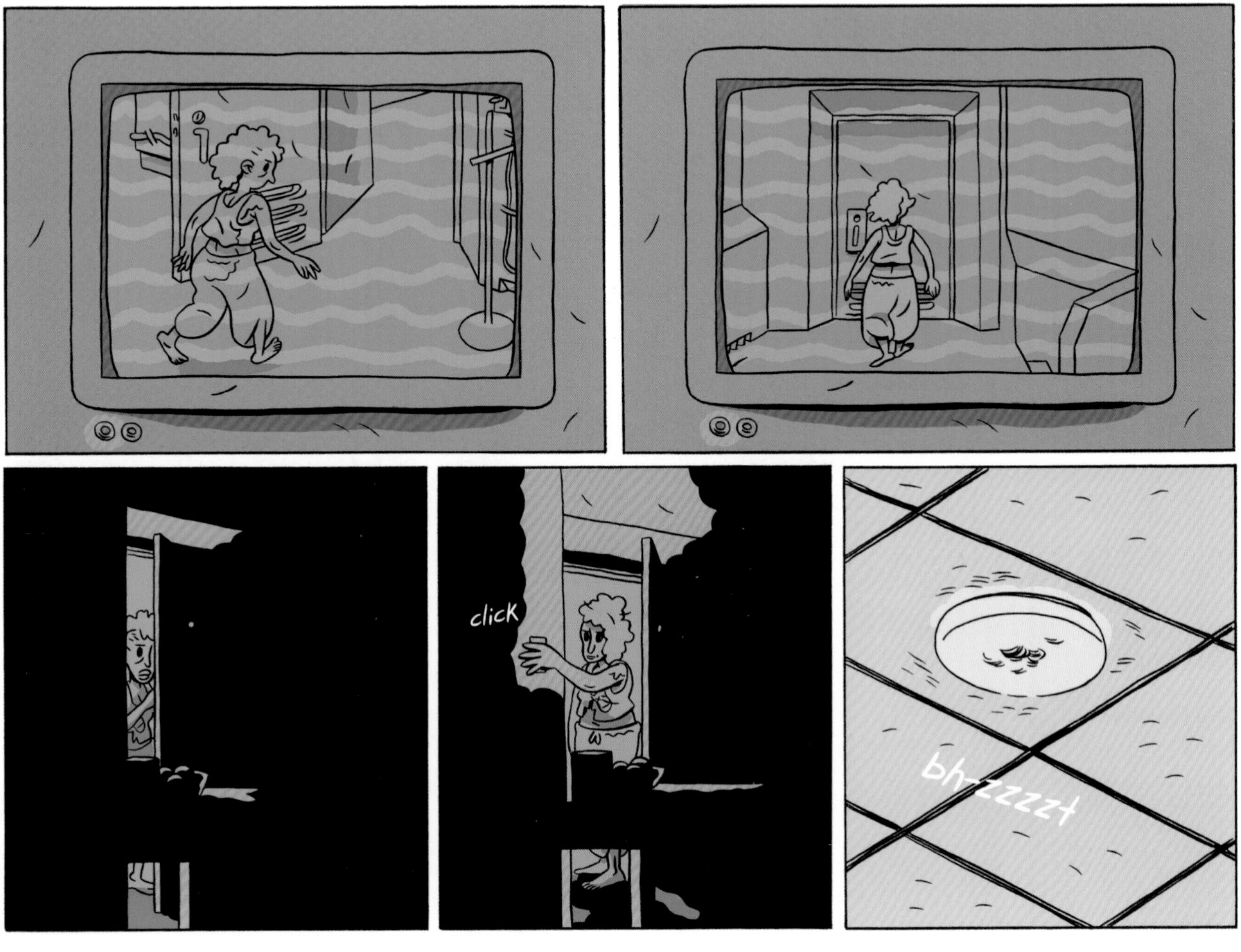
click
bh-zzzzzt

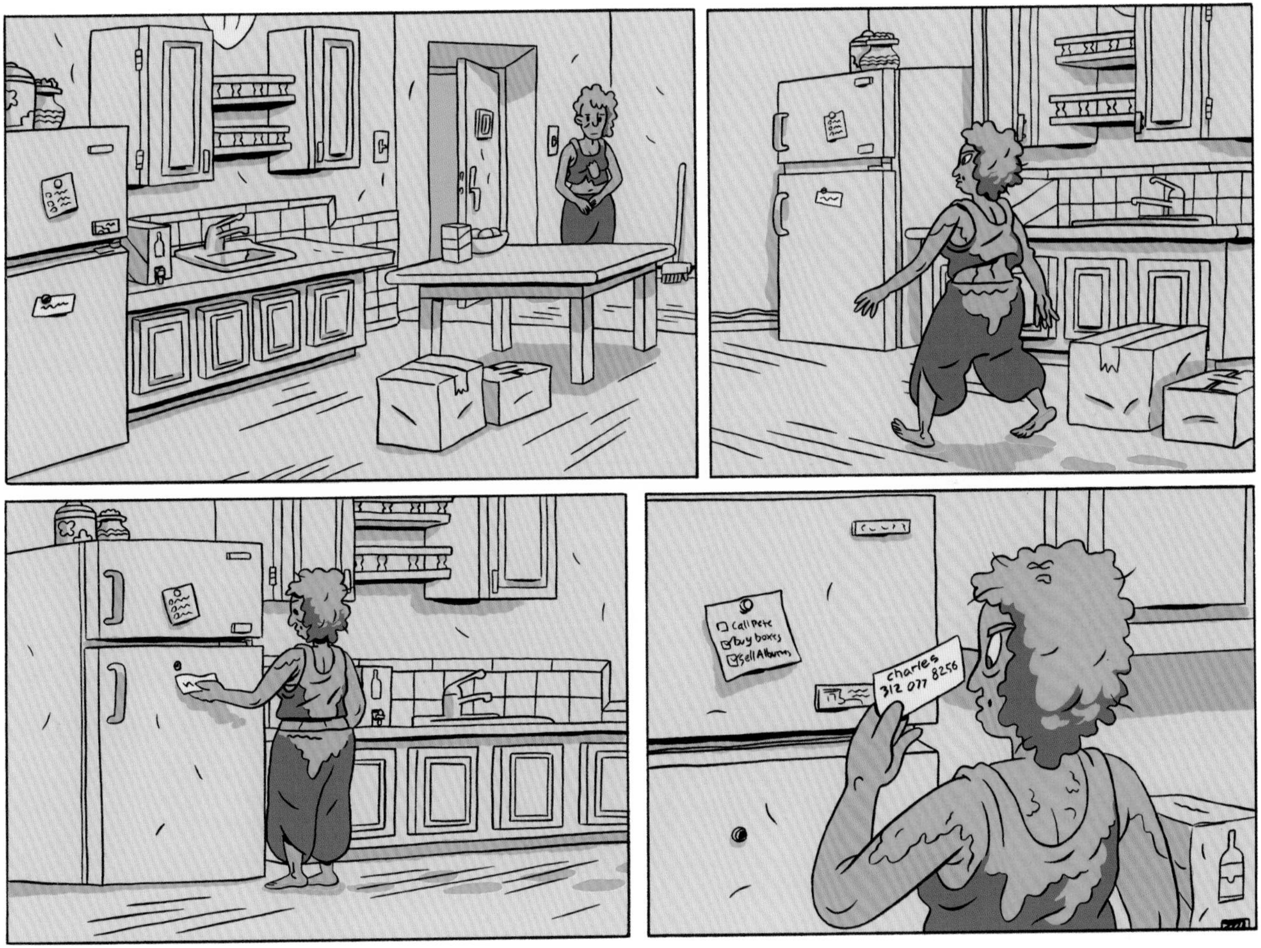
Call Pete
buy boxes
Sell Albums
charles
312 077 8256

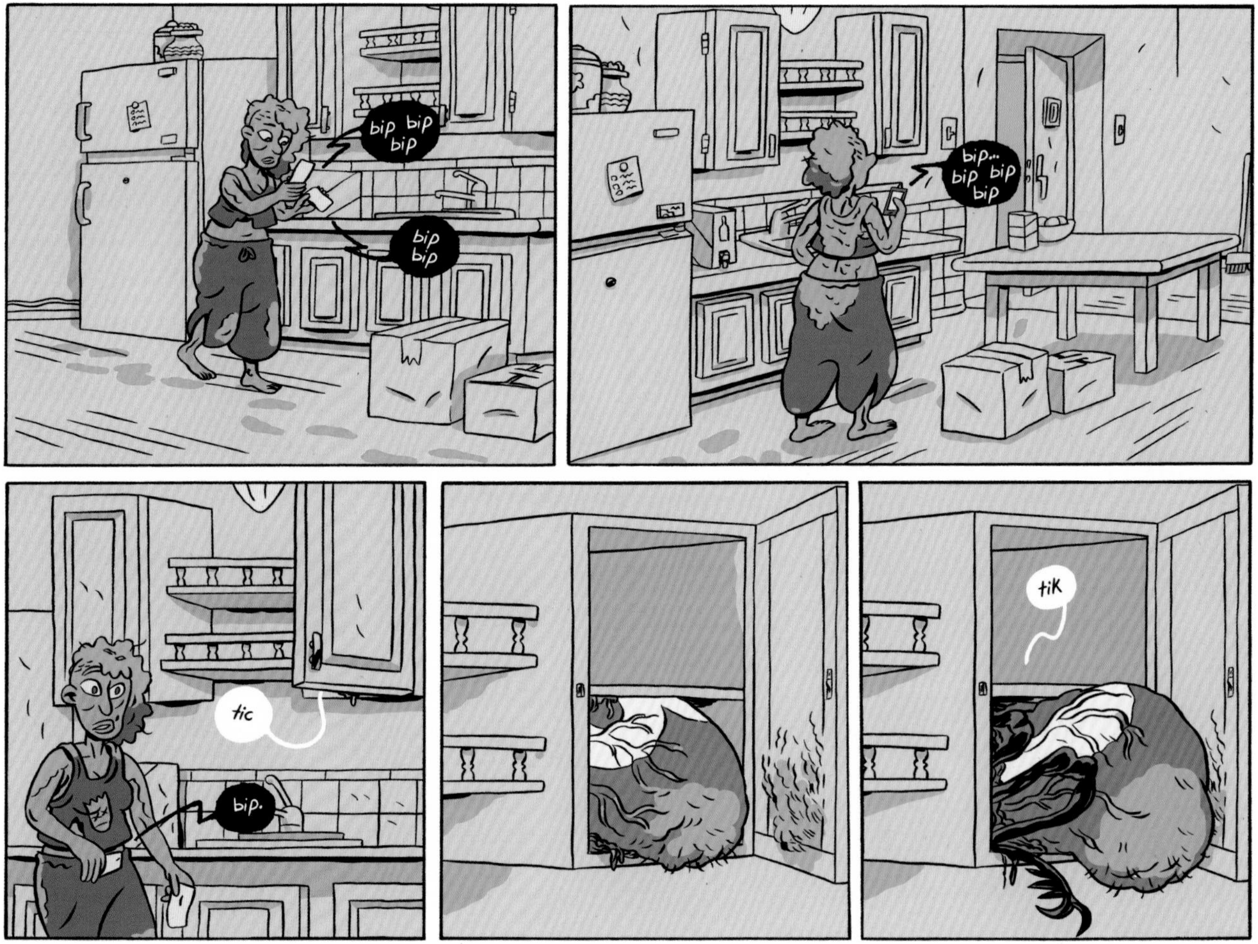
bip bip bip
bip bip
bip... bip bip bip
tic
bip.
tik

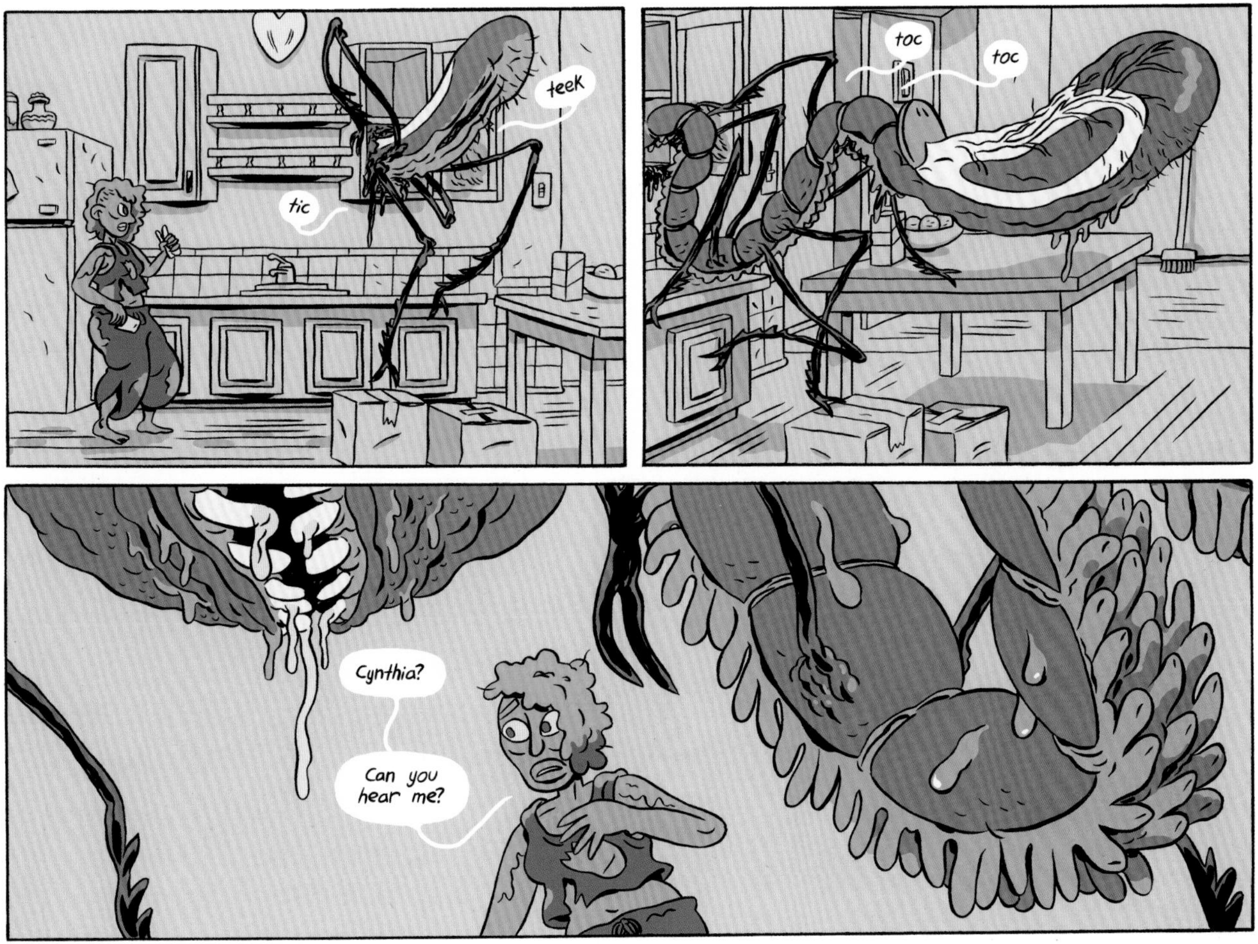
teek
tic
toc
toc
Cynthia?
Can you hear me?

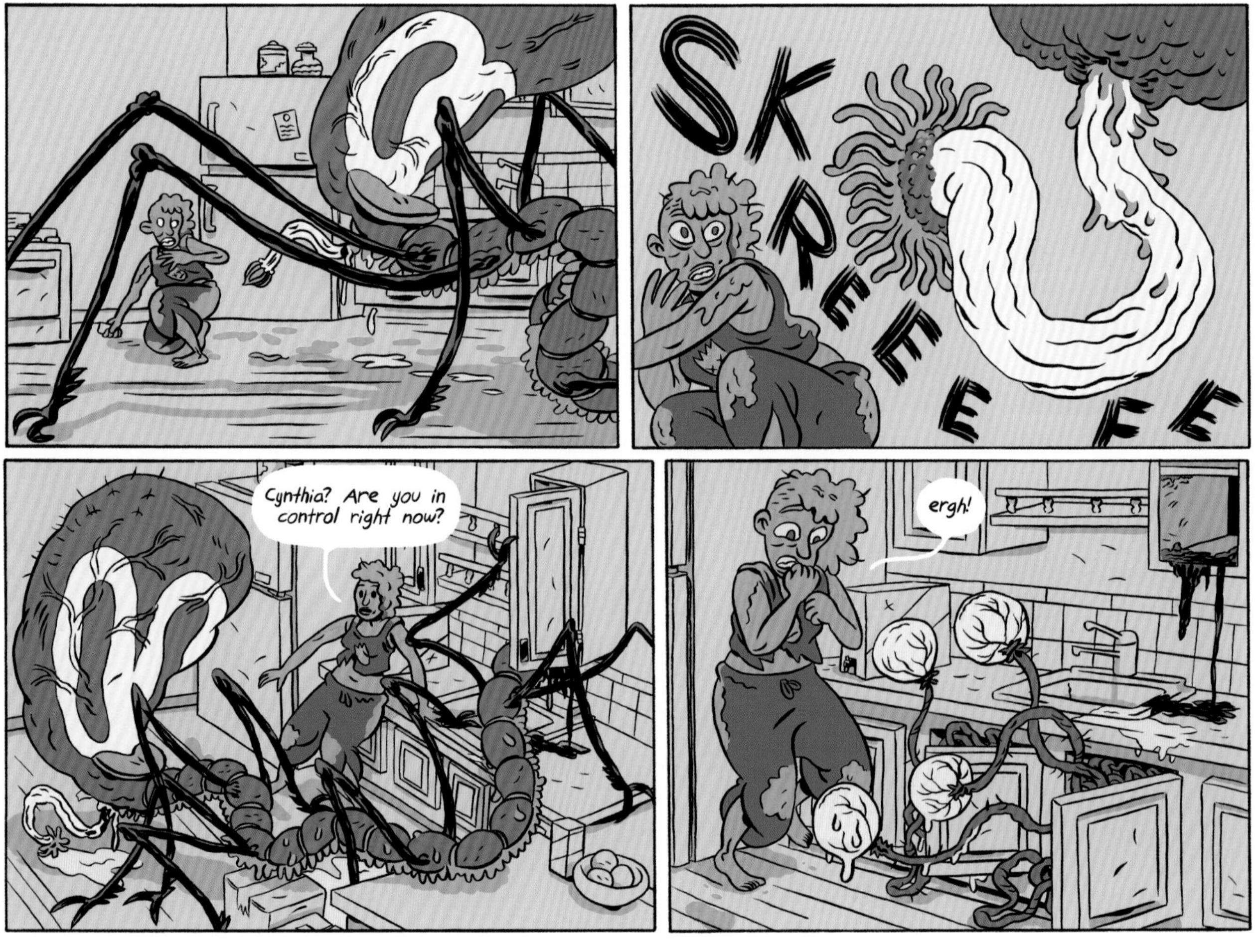
SKREEEEEEE
Cynthia? Are you in control right now?
ergh!

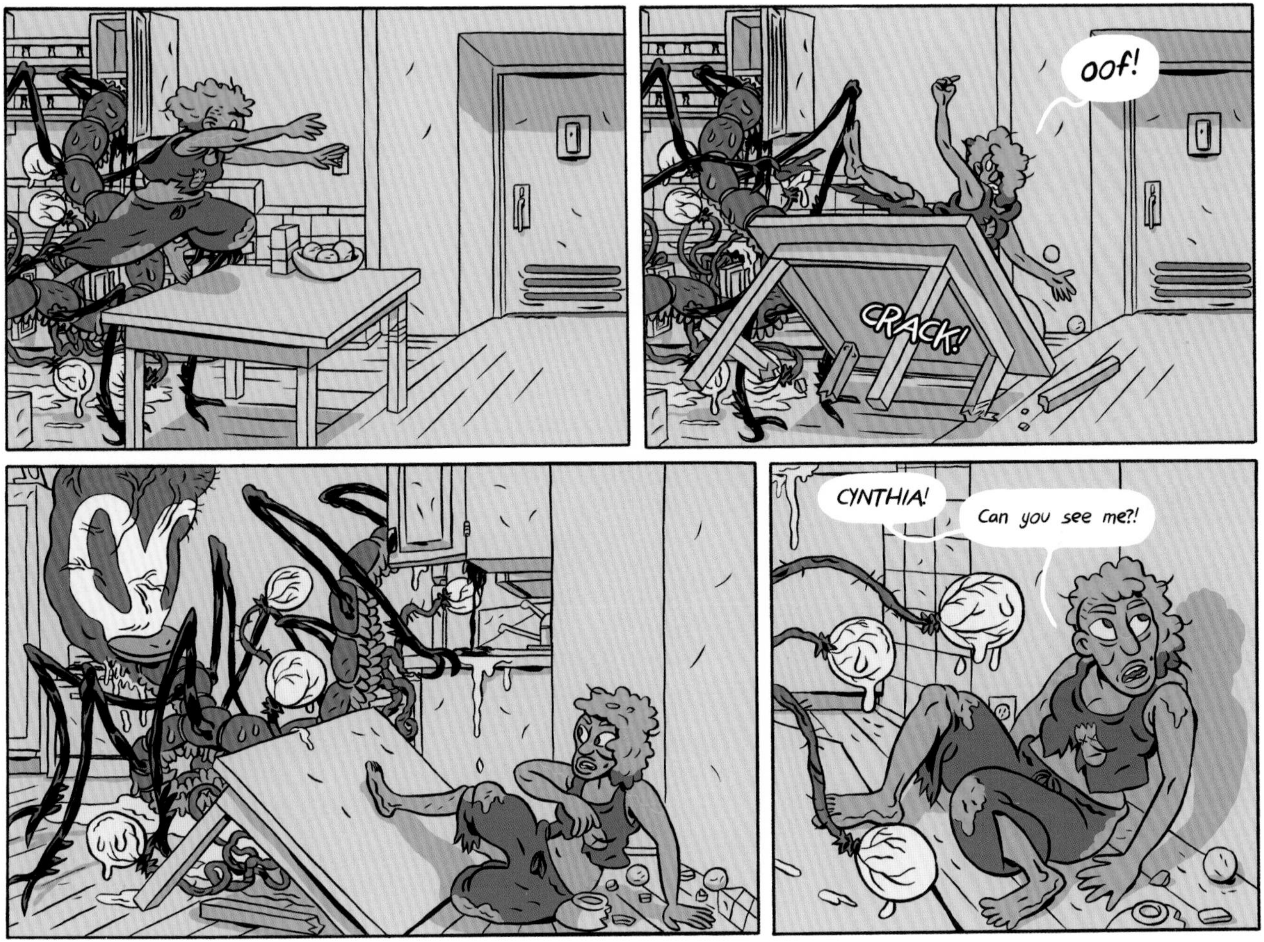
oof!
CRACK!
CYNTHIA!
Can you see me?!

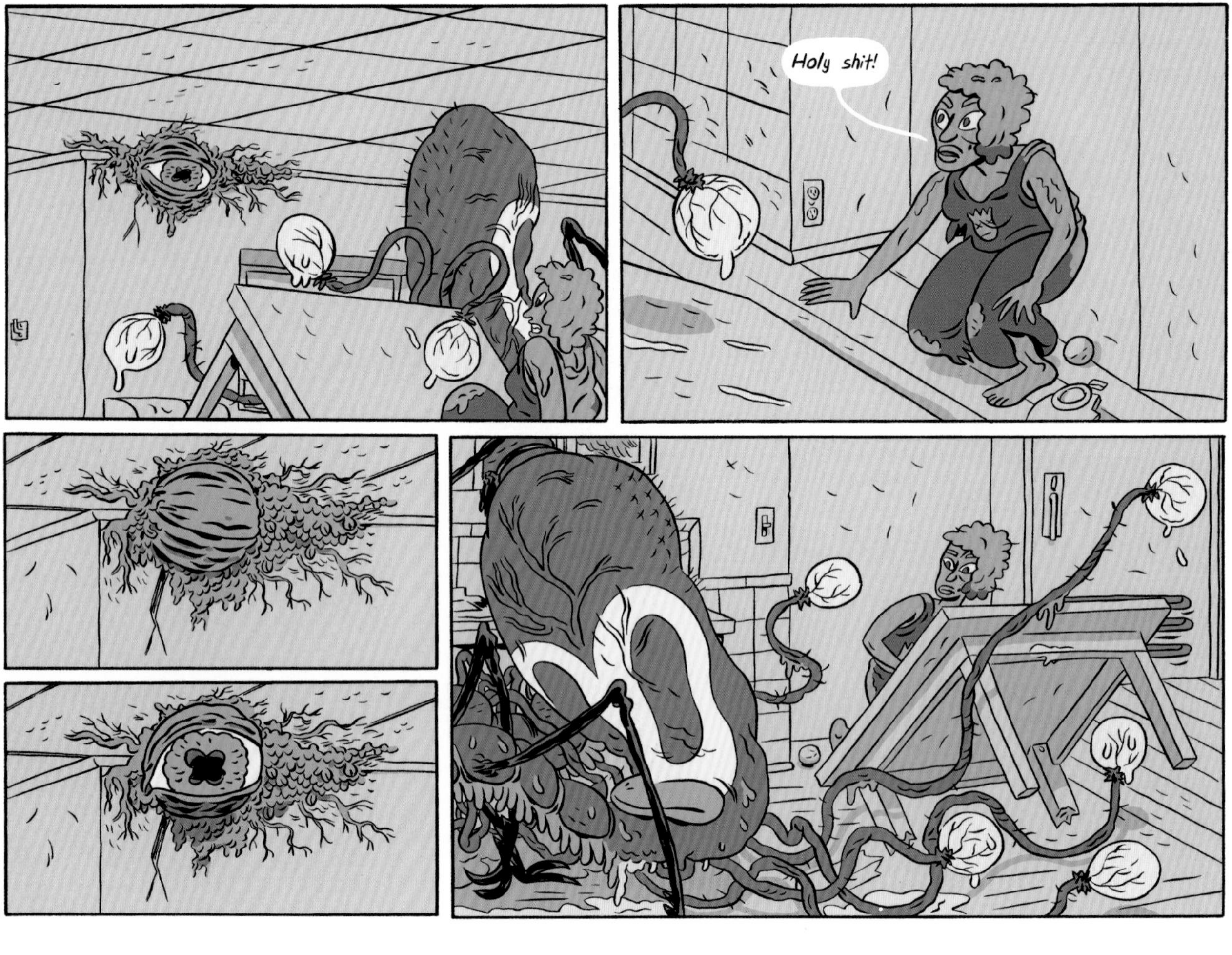
Holy shit!

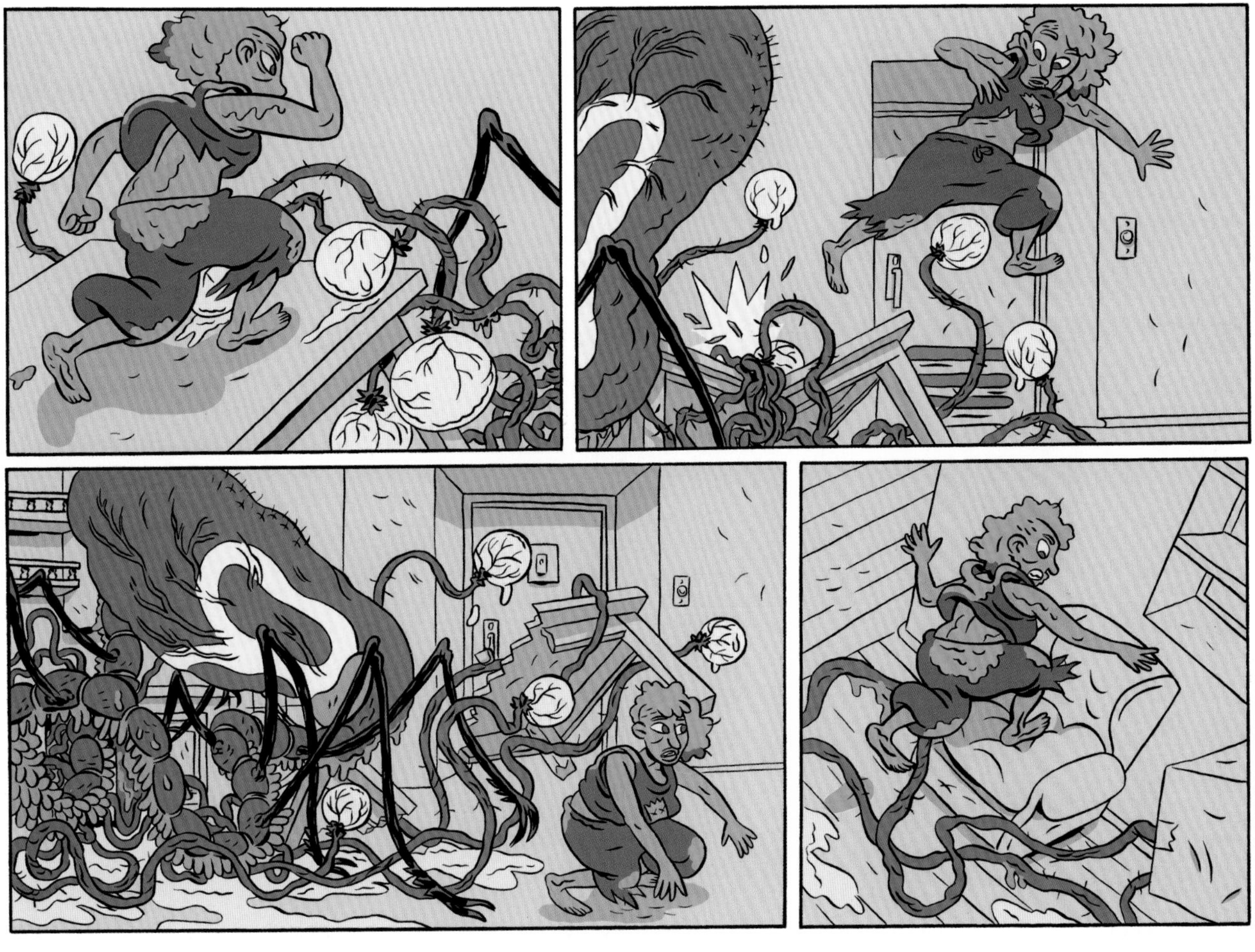

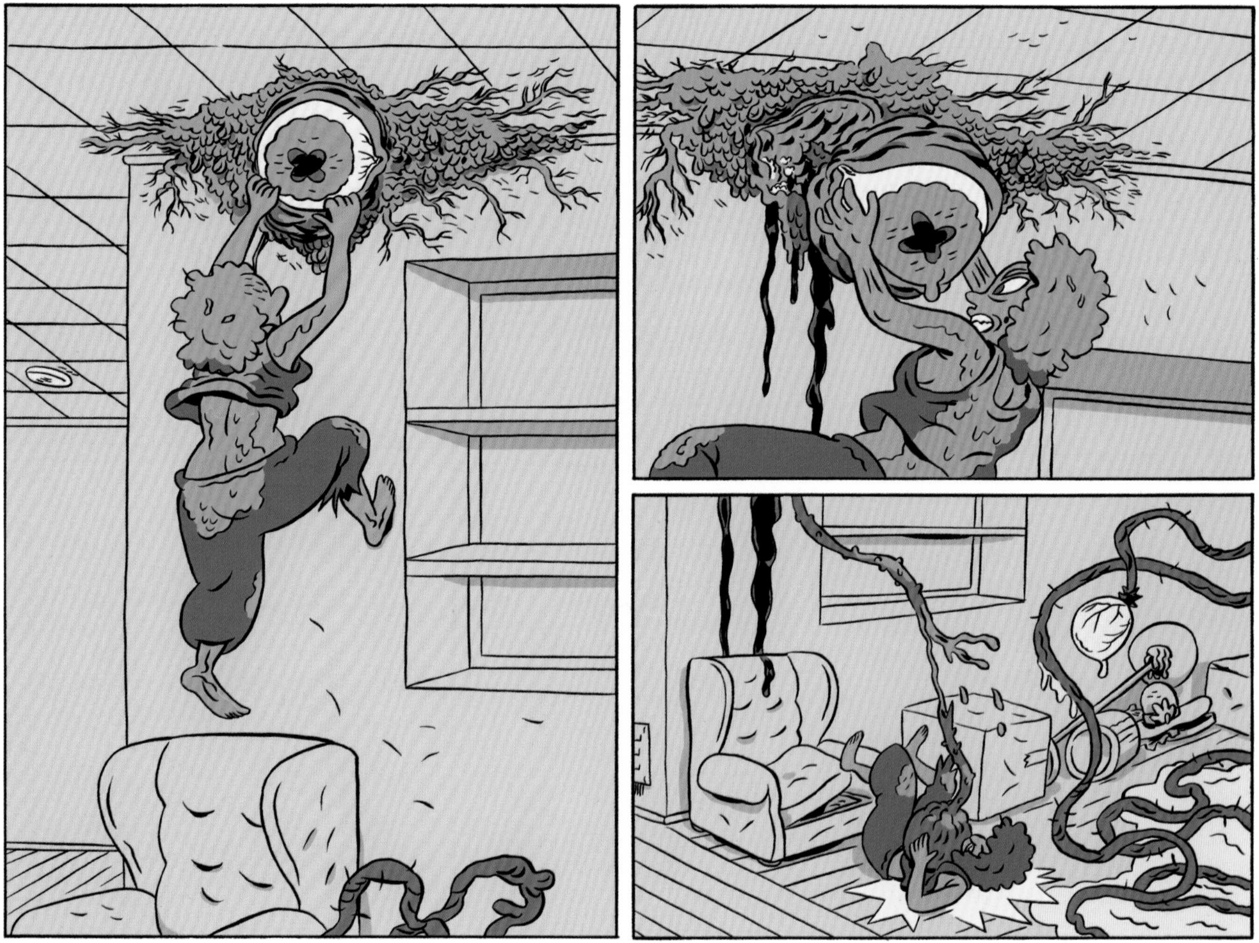

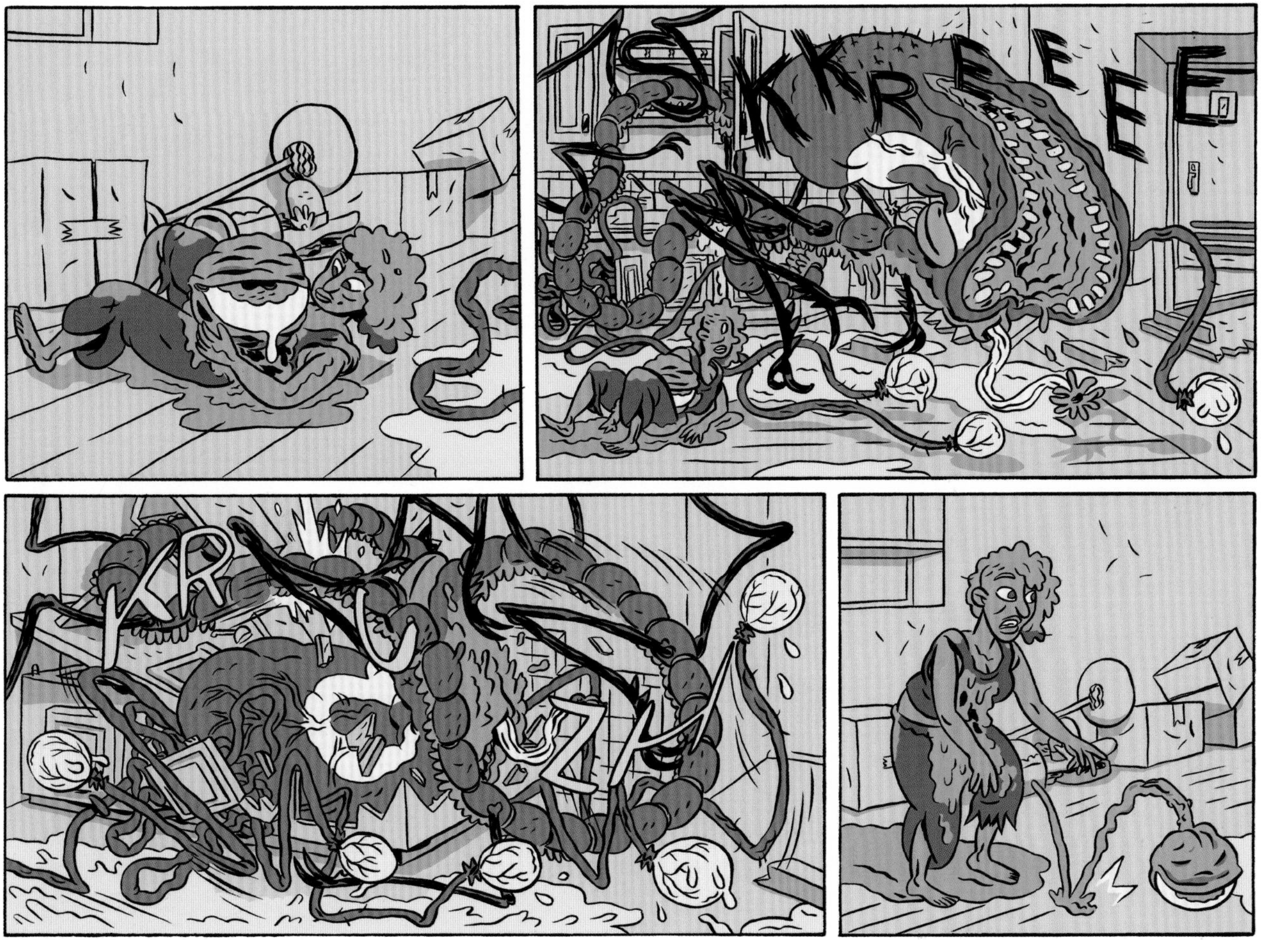
SKKREEEE
KRUZK

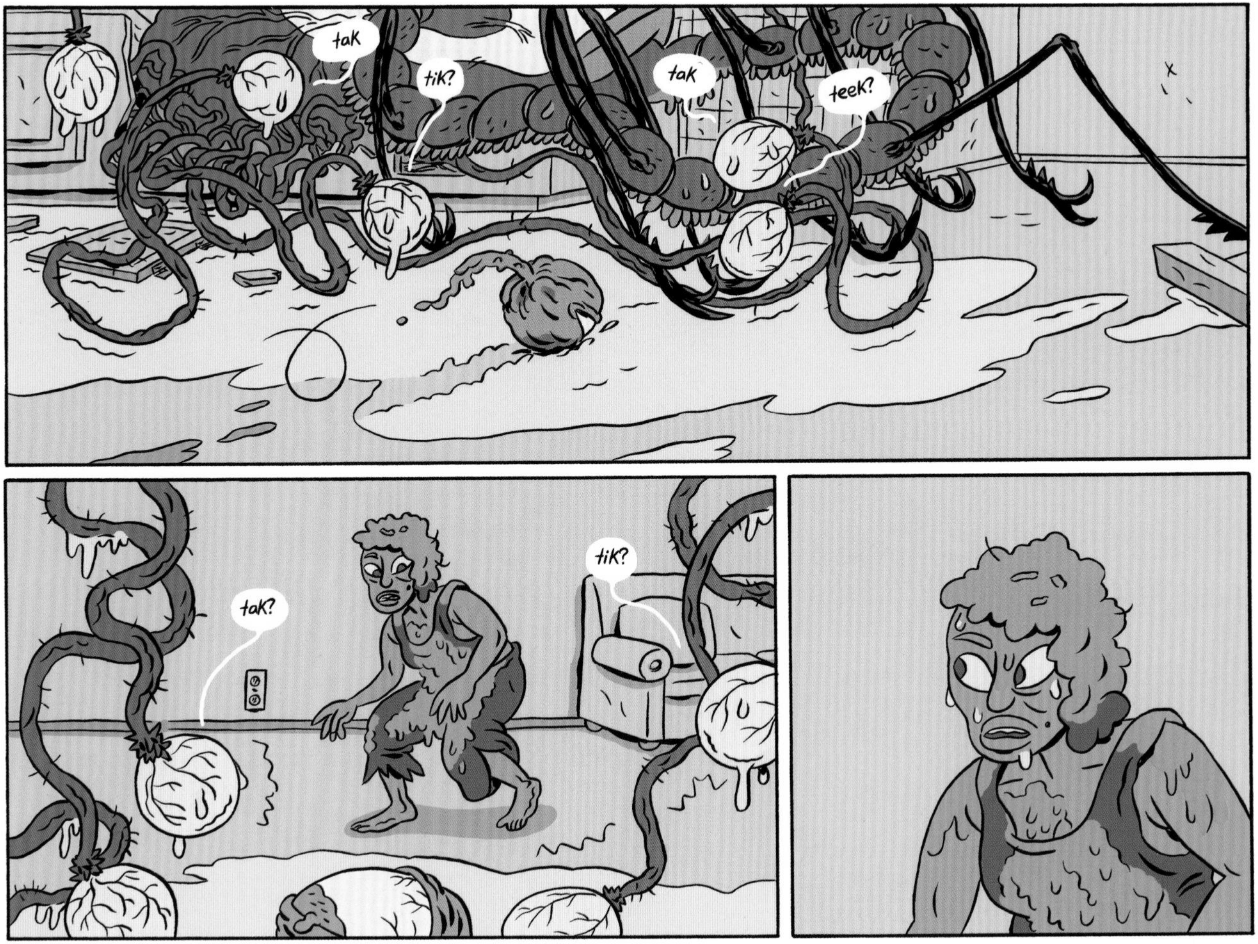
taK
tiK?
taK
teeK?
taK?
tiK?

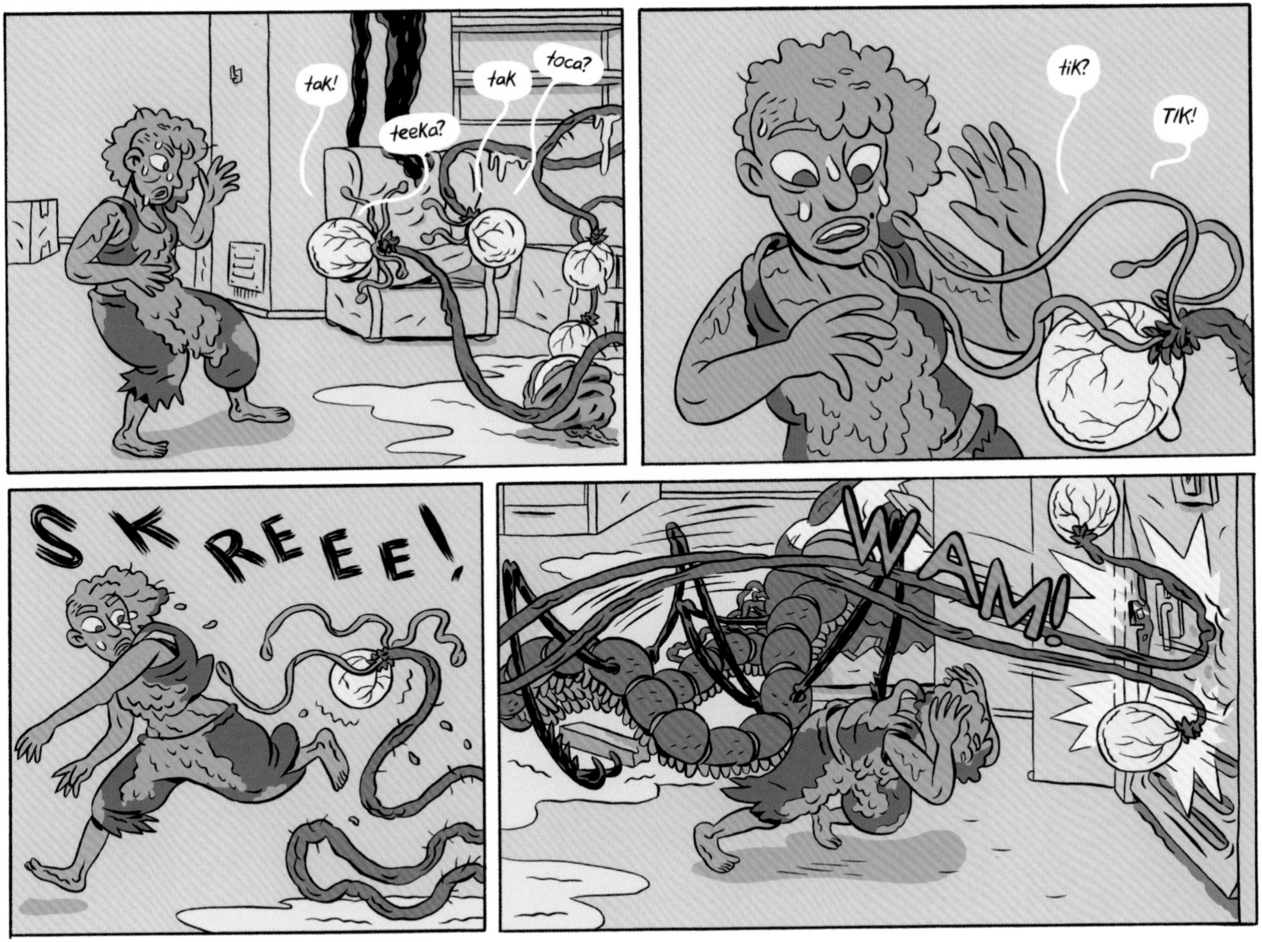
tak!
teeka?
tak
toca?
tik?
TIK!
SKREEE!
WAM!

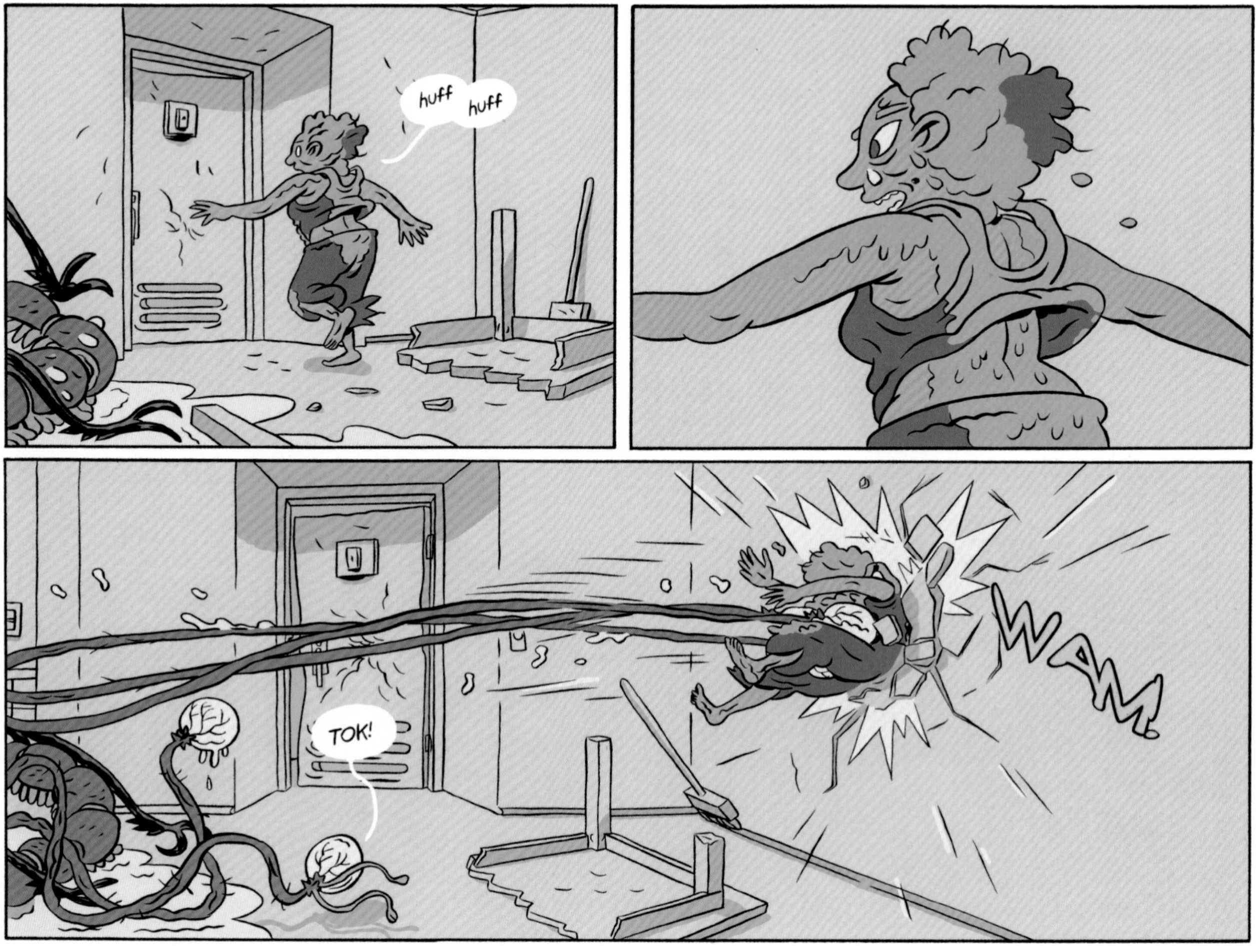
huff huff
TOK!
WAM!

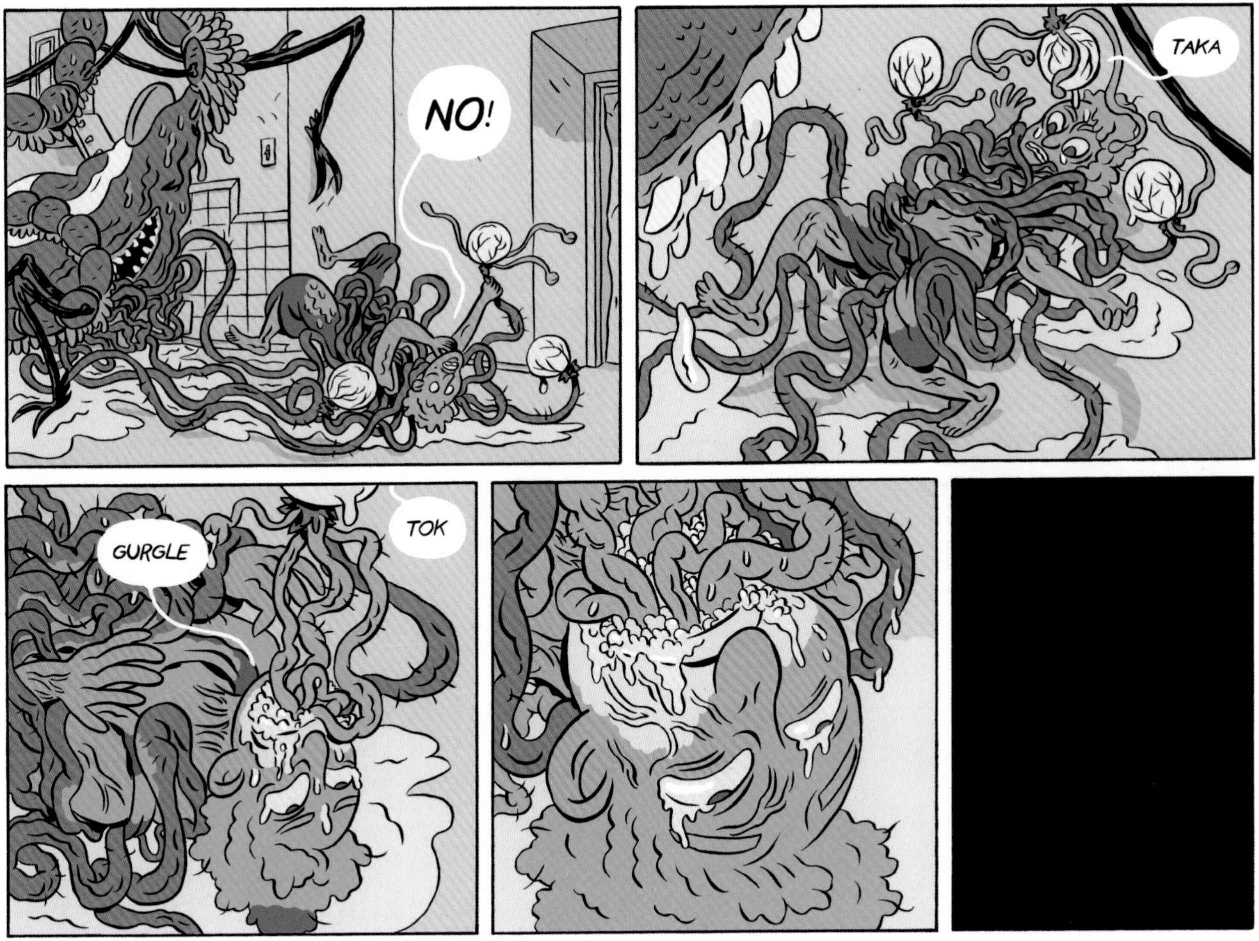
NO!
TAKA
GURGLE
TOK

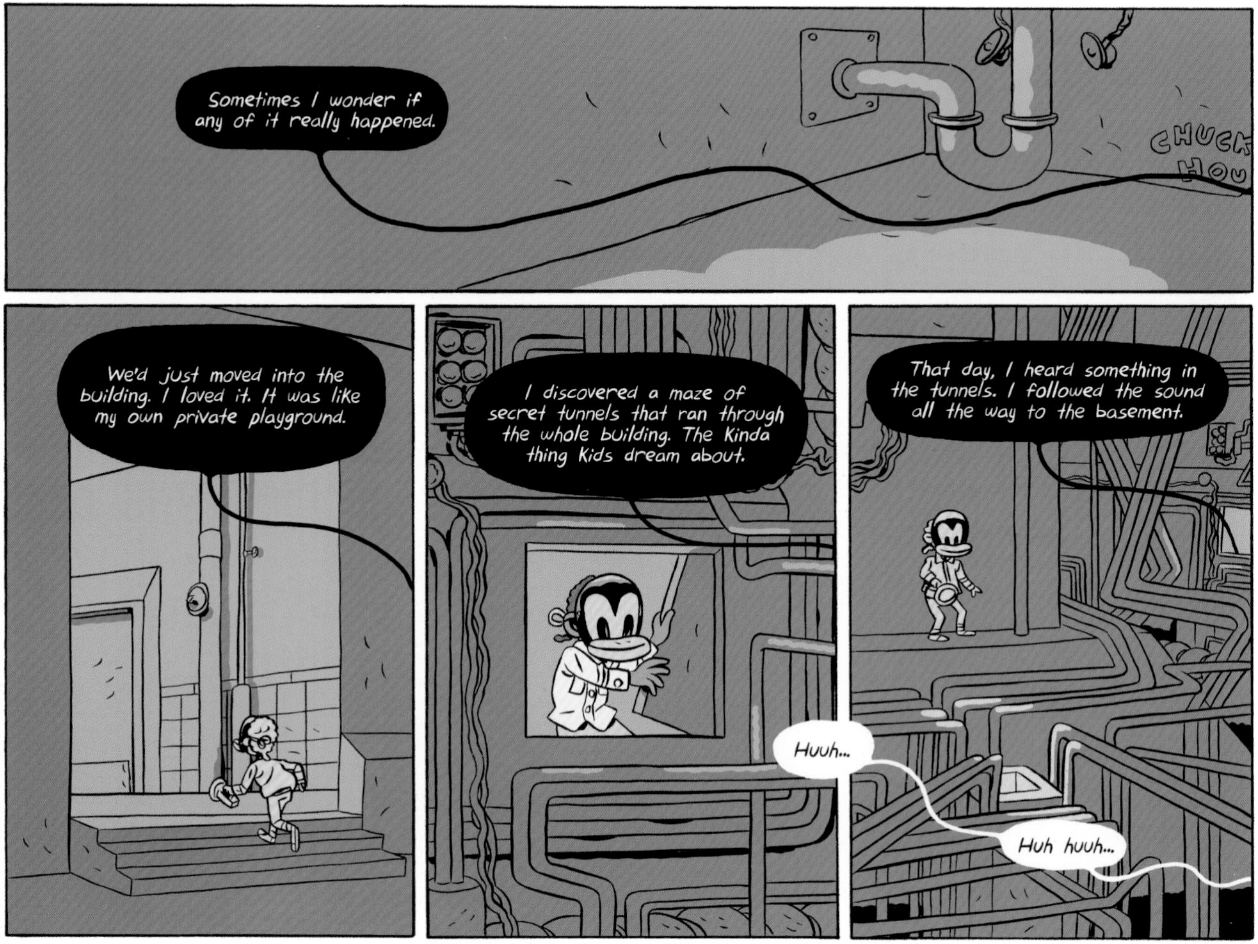
Sometimes I wonder if any of it really happened.
CHUCK HOU
We'd just moved into the building. I loved it. It was like my own private playground.
I discovered a maze of secret tunnels that ran through the whole building. The Kinda thing Kids dream about.
That day, I heard something in the tunnels. I followed the sound all the way to the basement.
Huuh...
Huh huuh...

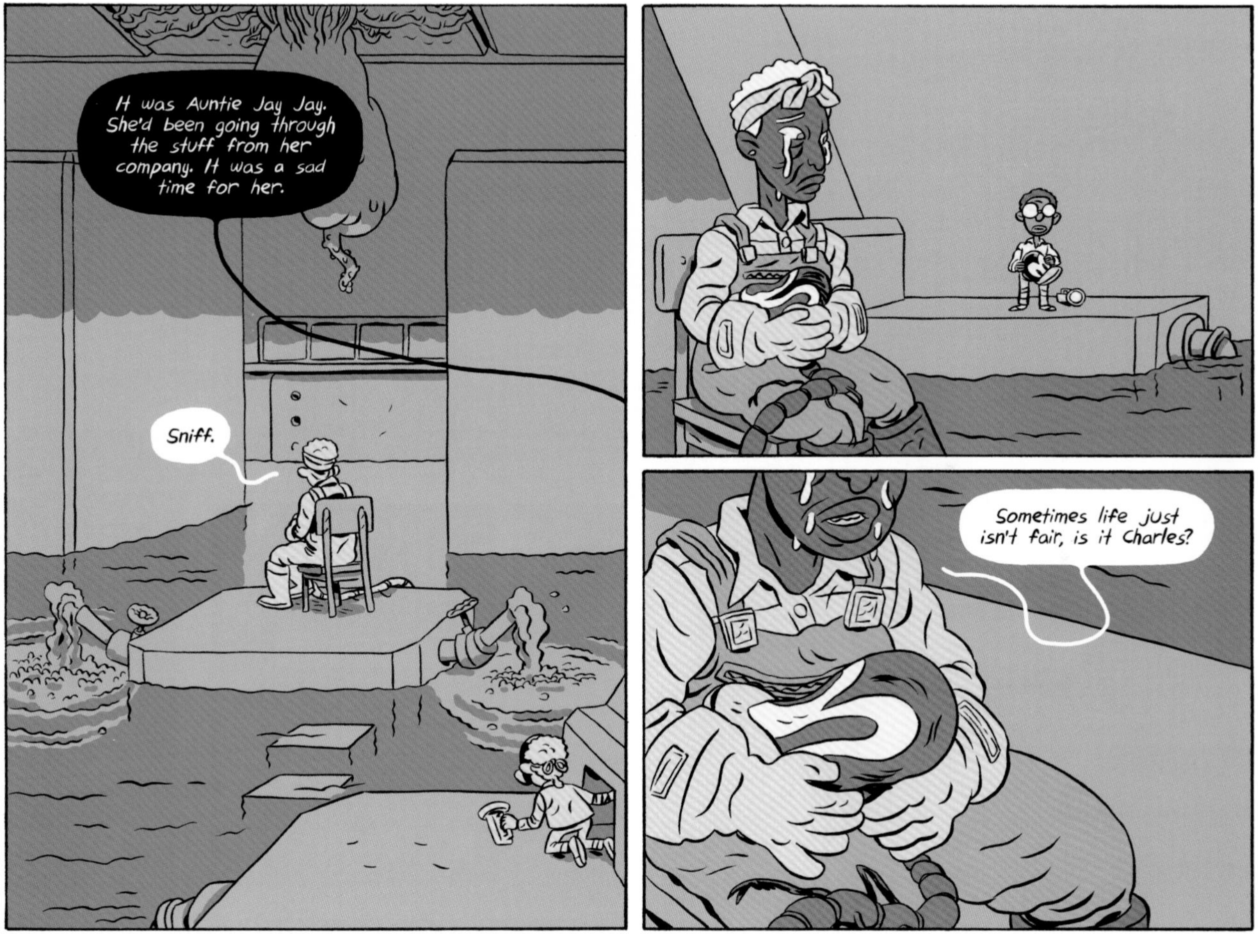
It was Auntie Jay Jay. She'd been going through the stuff from her company. It was a sad time for her.
Sniff.
Sometimes life just isn't fair, is it Charles?

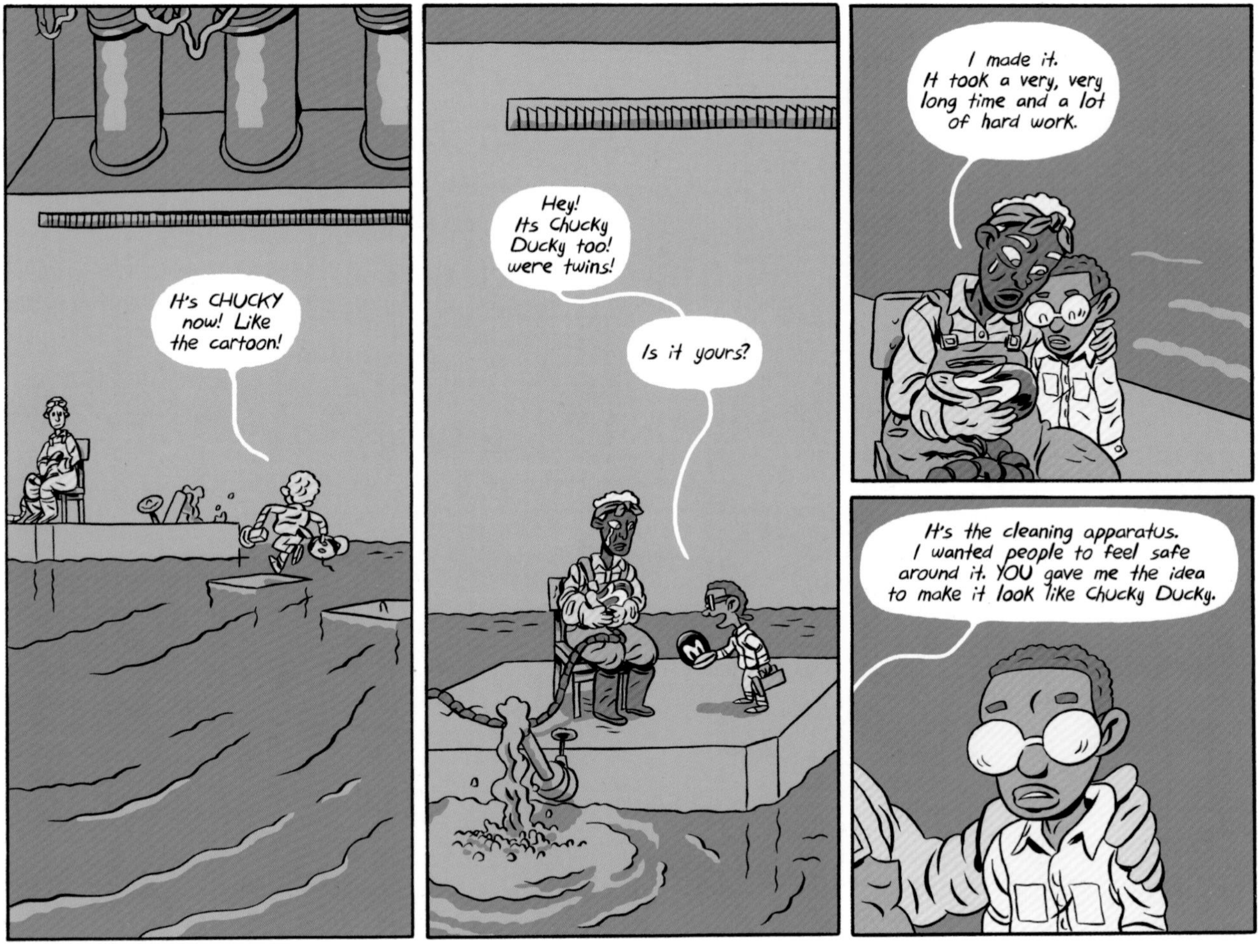

It's CHUCKY now! Like the cartoon!
Hey! Its Chucky Ducky too! were twins!
Is it yours?
I made it. It took a very, very long time and a lot of hard work.
It's the cleaning apparatus. I wanted people to feel safe around it. YOU gave me the idea to make it look like Chucky Ducky.

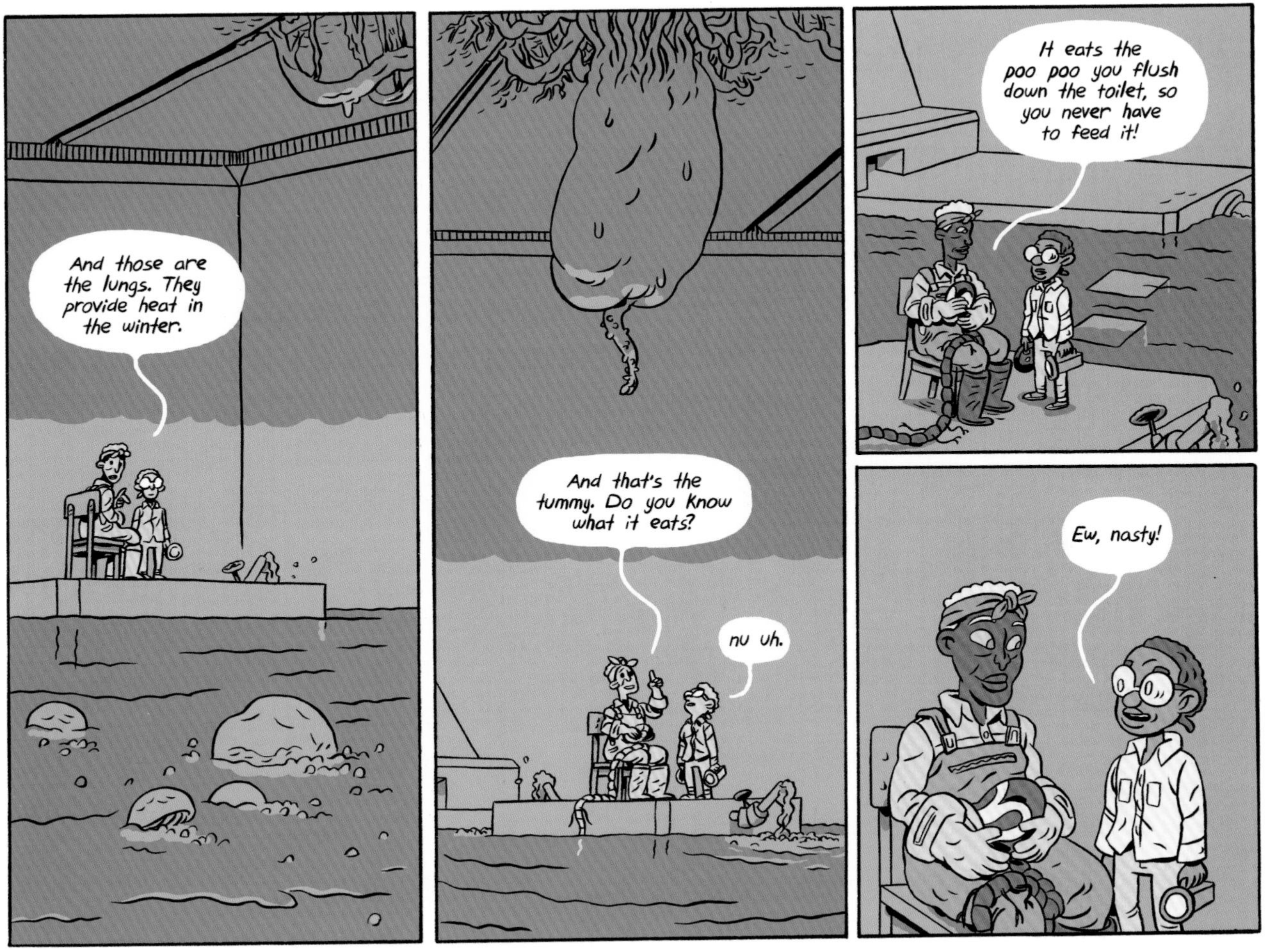
And those are the lungs. They provide heat in the winter.
And that's the tummy. Do you know what it eats?
nu uh.
It eats the poo poo you flush down the toilet, so you never have to feed it!
Ew, nasty!

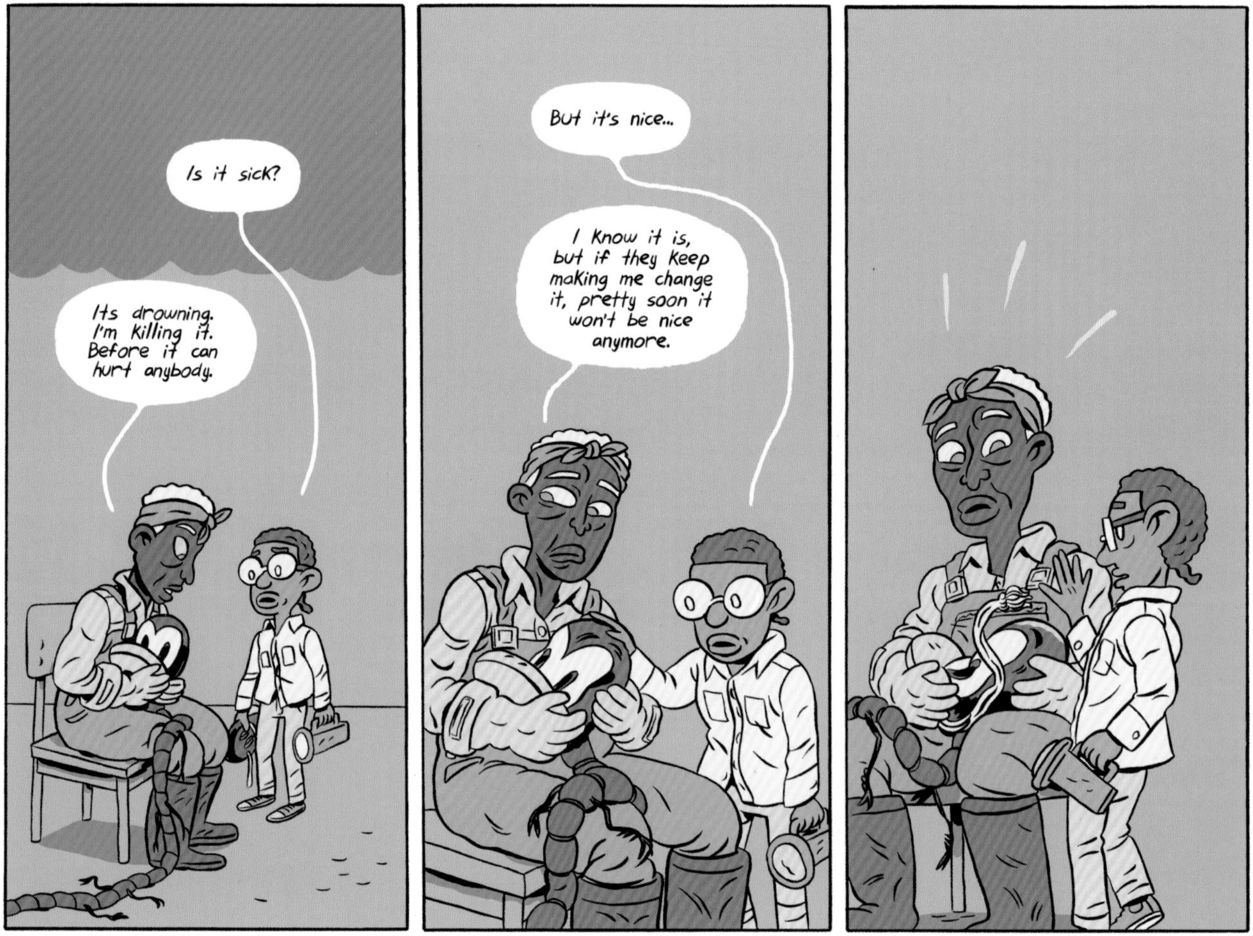
Is it sick?
Its drowning. I'm killing it. Before it can hurt anybody.
But it's nice...
I know it is, but if they keep making me change it, pretty soon it won't be nice anymore.

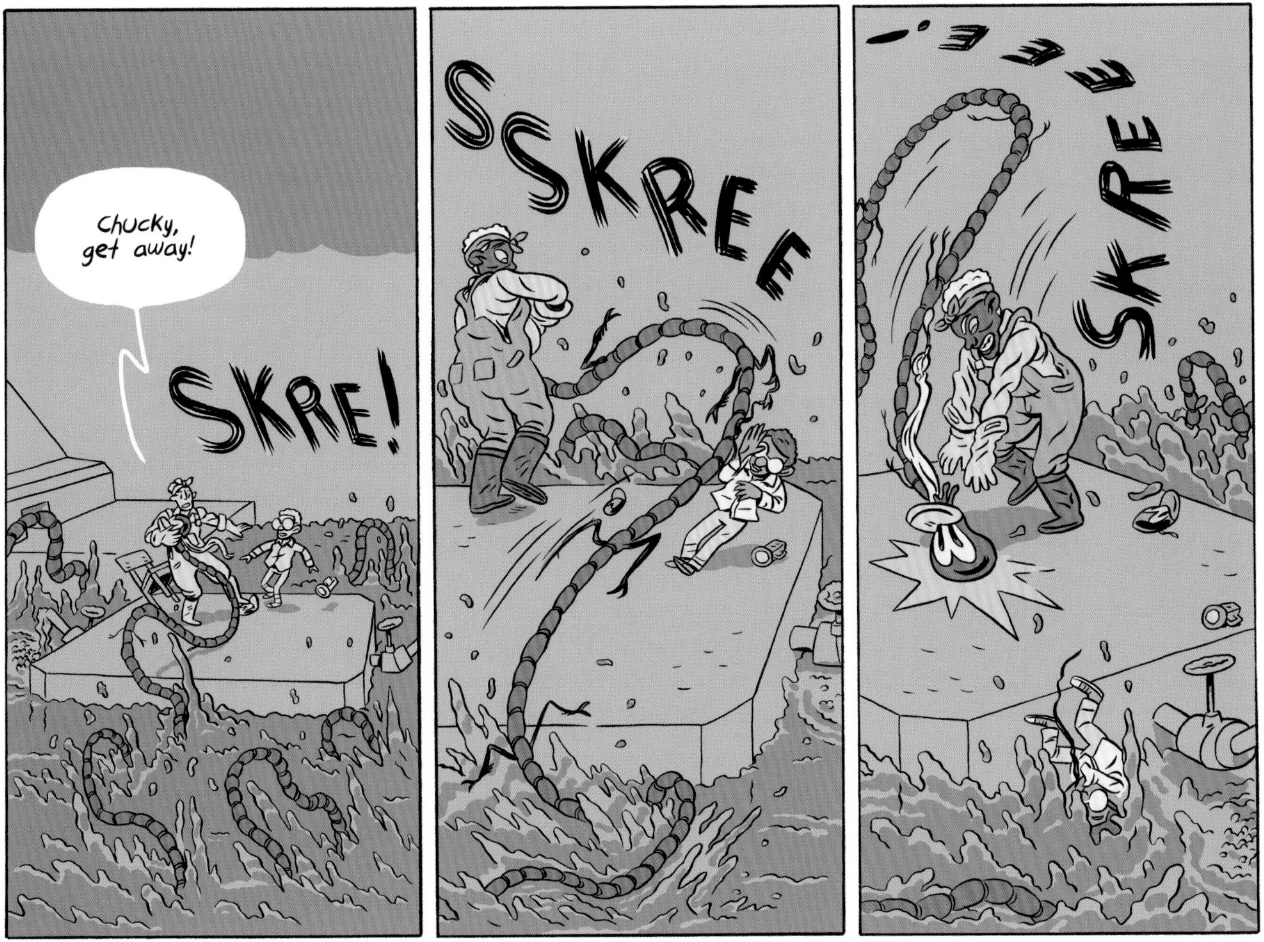

Chucky, get away!
SKRE!
SSKREE
SKREEEEE!

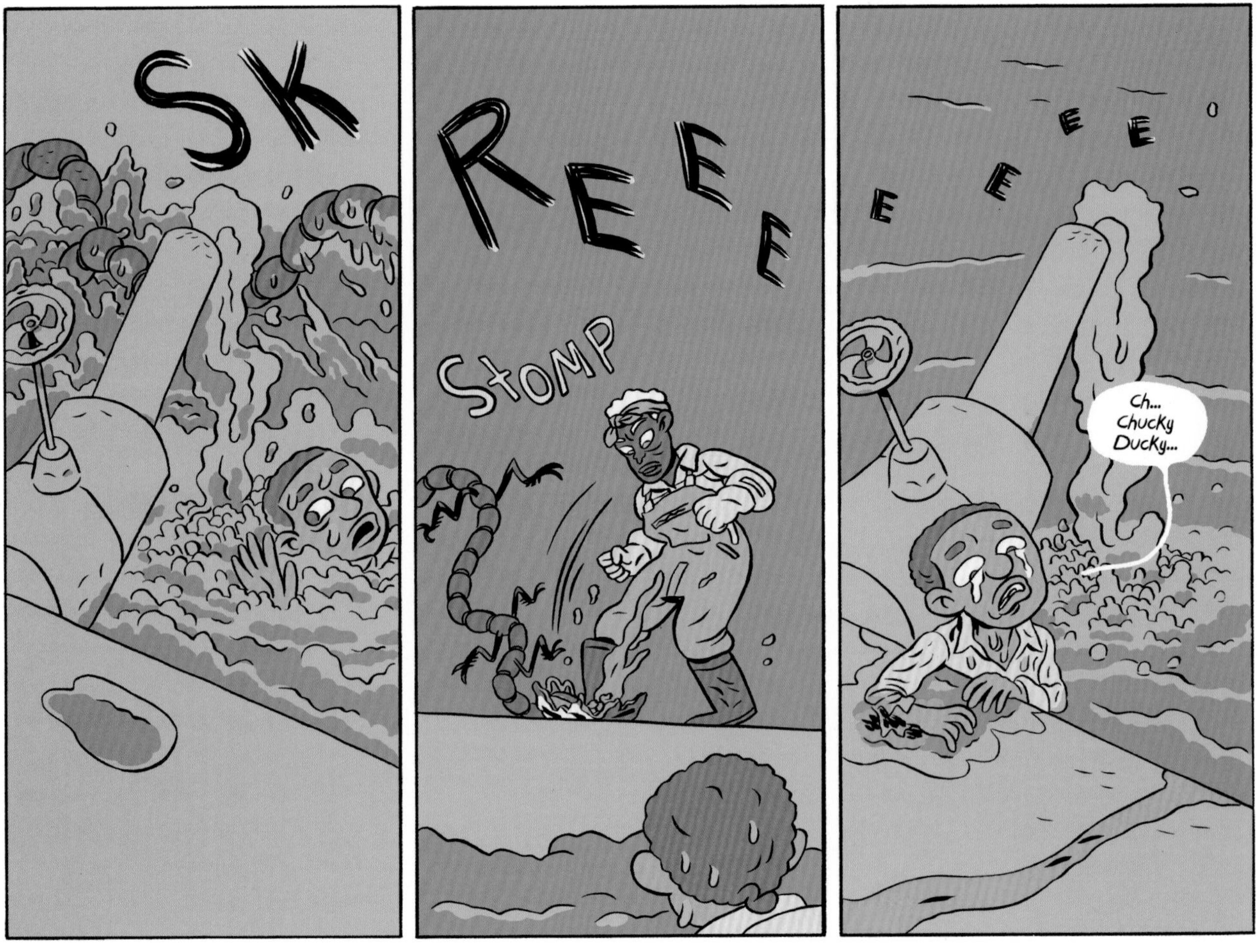
SK
REEE
EEEEE
STOMP
Ch... Chucky Ducky...

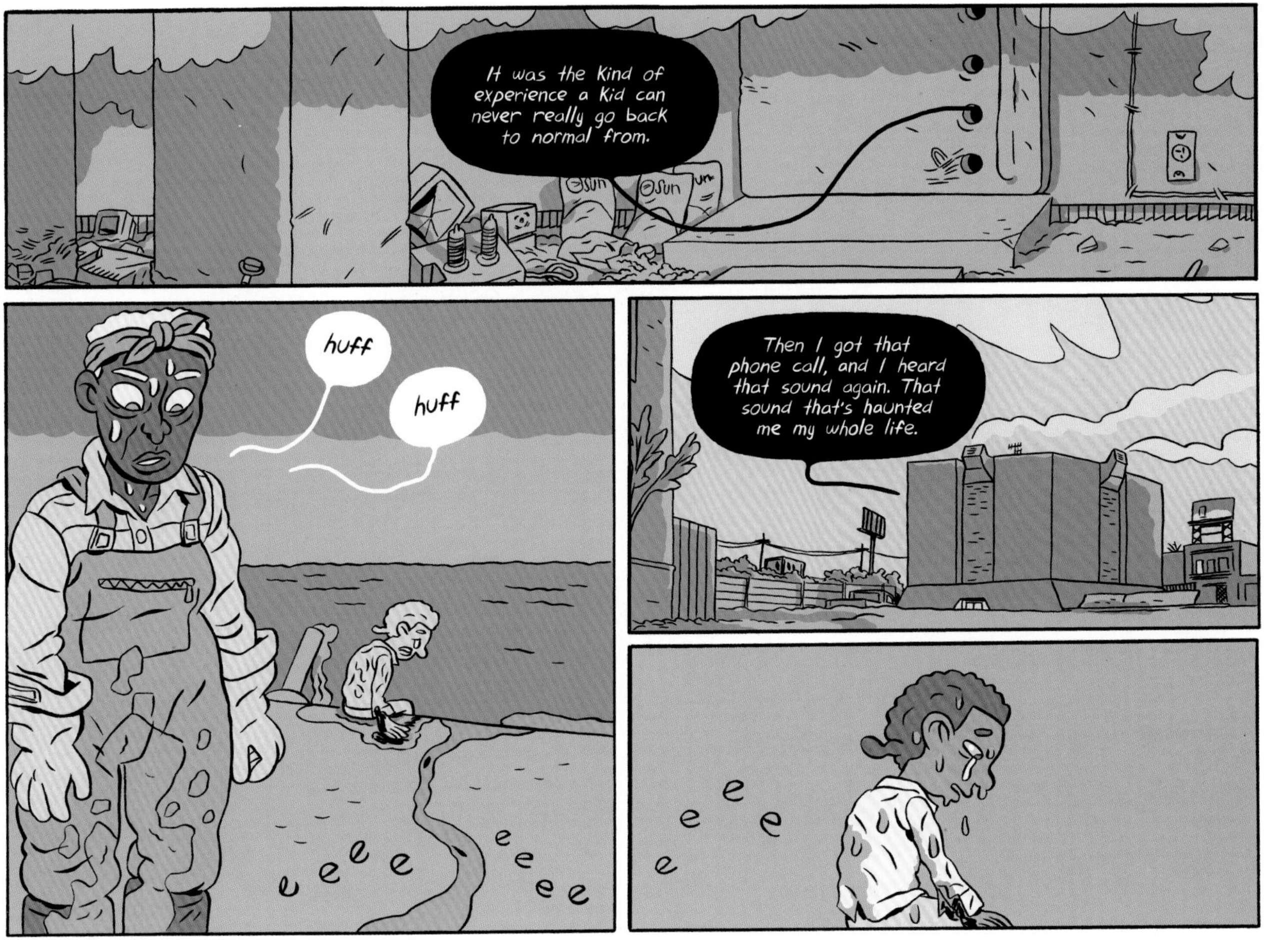
It was the kind of experience a kid can never really go back to normal from.
huff
huff
eeee
eeee
Then I got that phone call, and I heard that sound again. That sound that's haunted me my whole life.
eeee

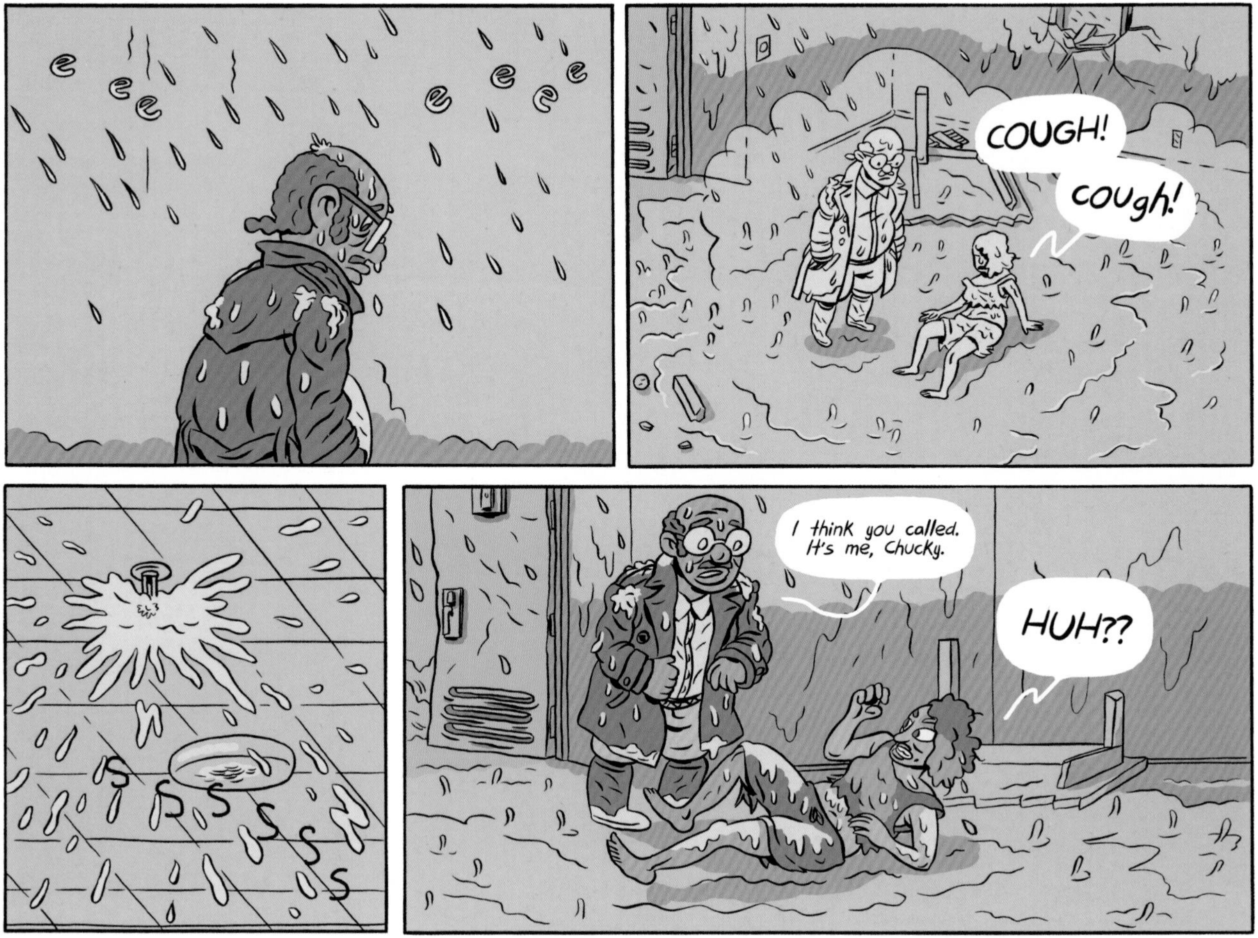
e ee e e e e e
COUGH!
cough!
SSSSSS
I think you called. It's me, Chucky.
HUH??

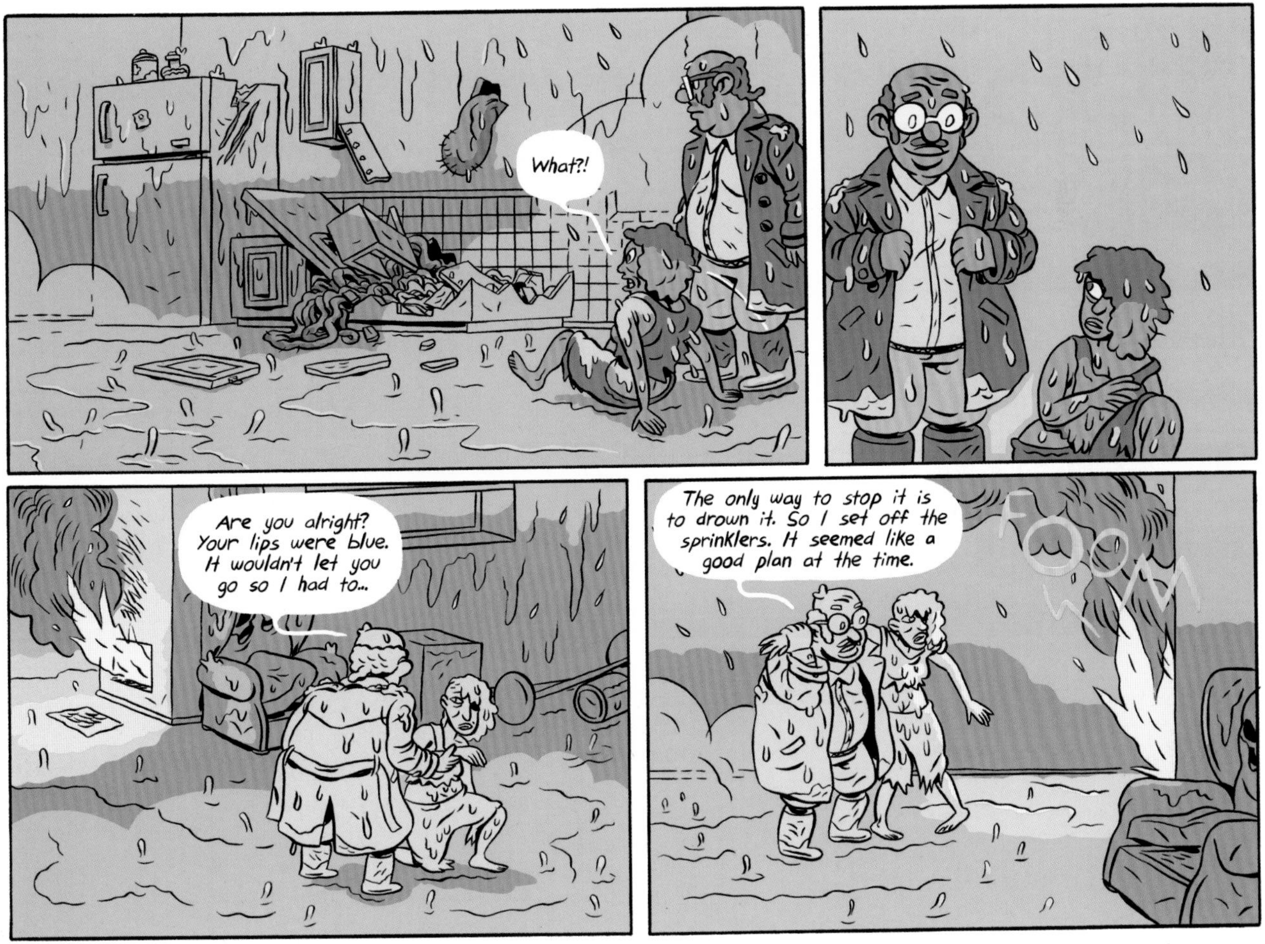
What?!
Are you alright? Your lips were blue. It wouldn't let you go so I had to...
The only way to stop it is to drown it. So I set off the sprinklers. It seemed like a good plan at the time.
FOOM

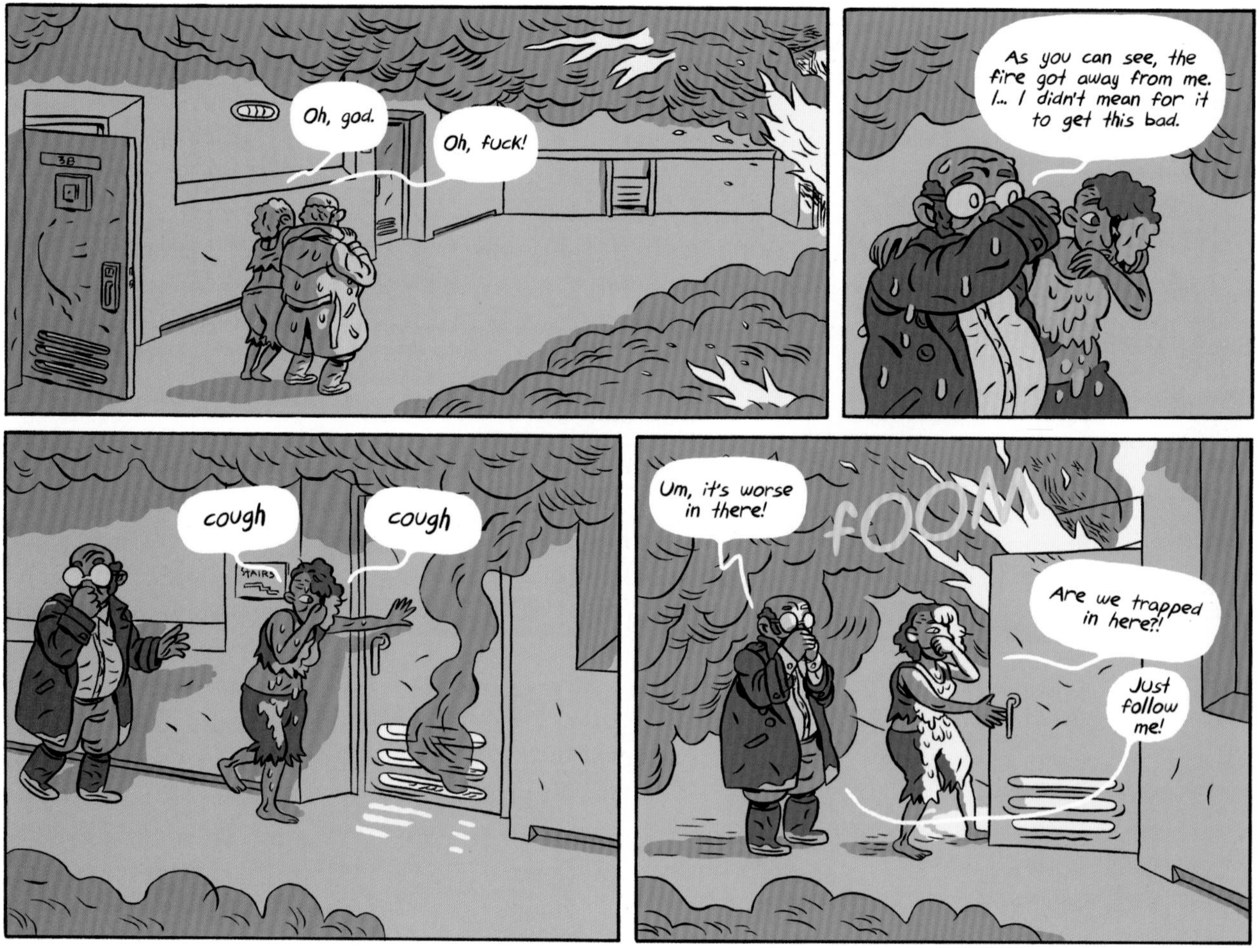
Oh, god.
Oh, fuck!
As you can see, the fire got away from me. I... I didn't mean for it to get this bad.
cough
cough
Um, it's worse in there!
FOOM
Are we trapped in here?!
Just follow me!

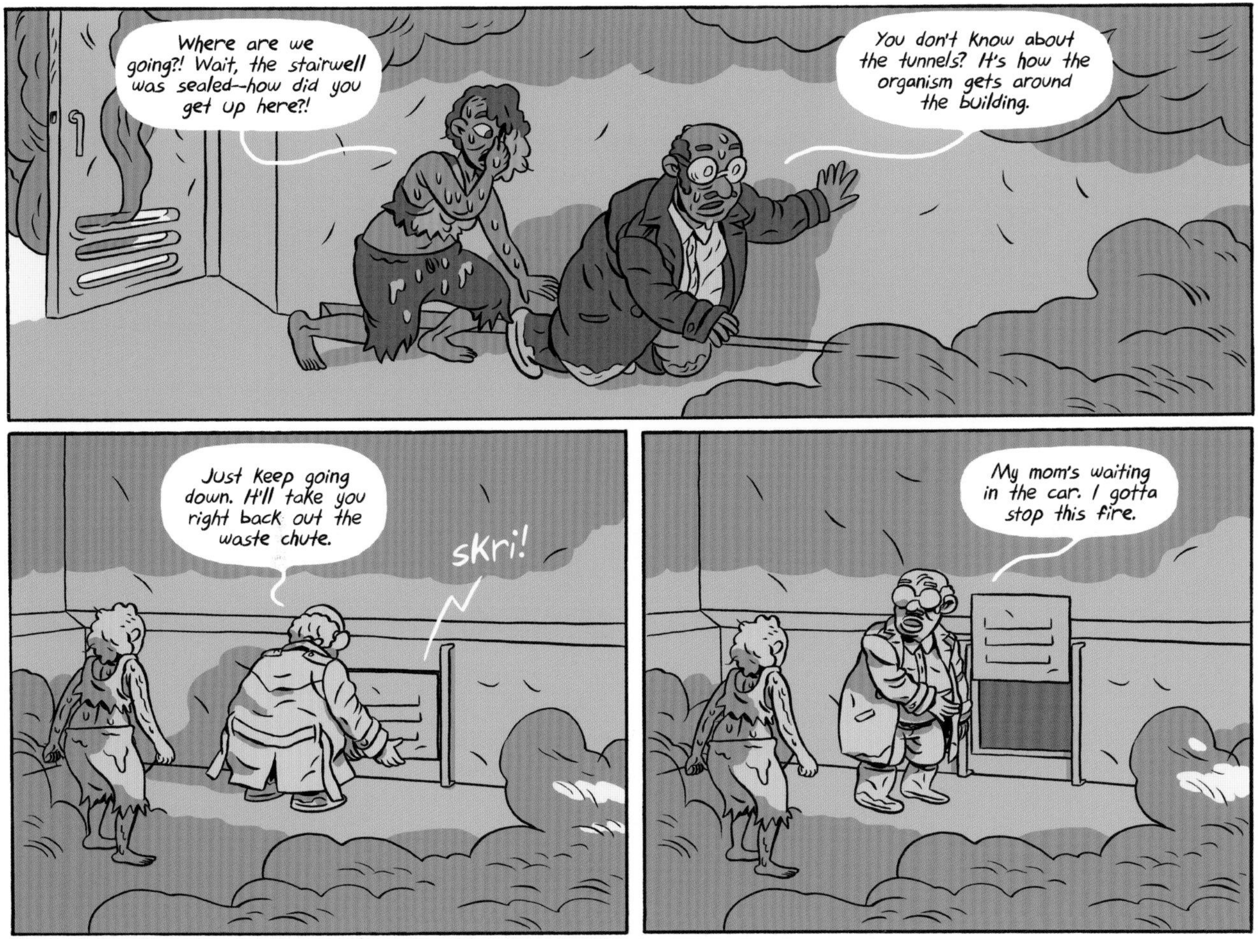
Where are we going?! Wait, the stairwell was sealed--how did you get up here?!
You don't know about the tunnels? It's how the organism gets around the building.
Just keep going down. It'll take you right back out the waste chute.
skri!
My mom's waiting in the car. I gotta stop this fire.

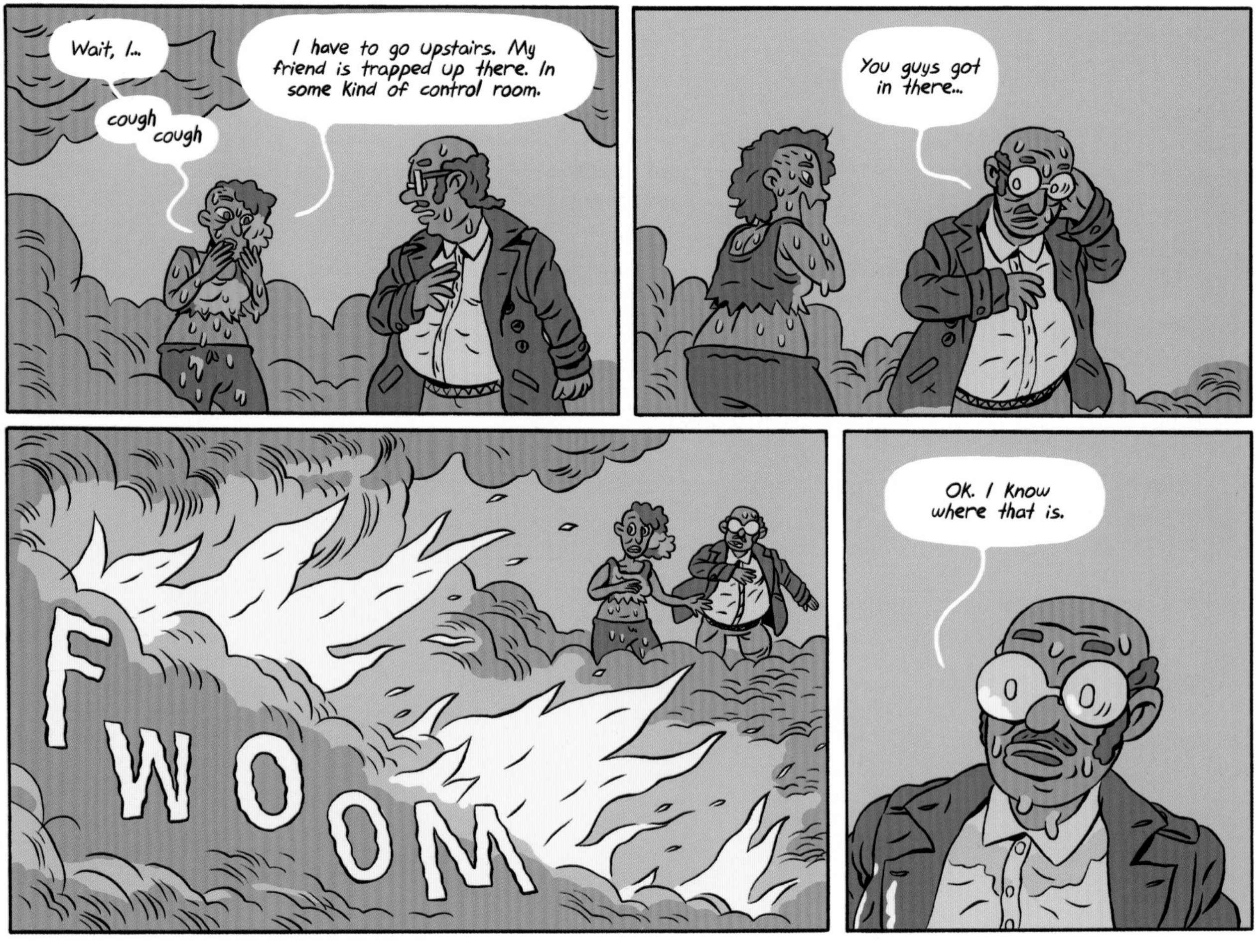
Wait, I...
cough cough
I have to go upstairs. My friend is trapped up there. In some kind of control room.
You guys got in there...
FWOOM
OK. I know where that is.

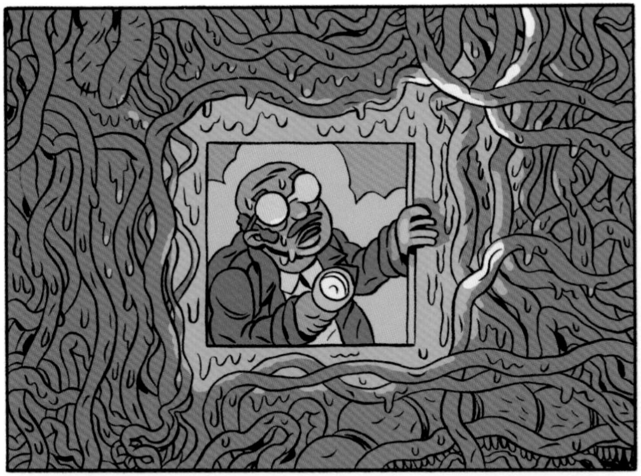
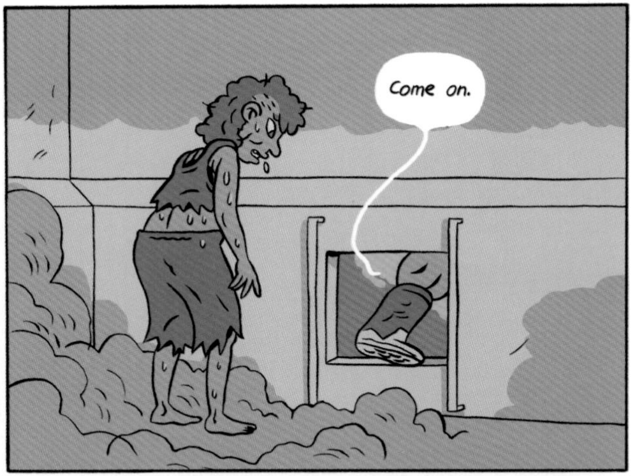
Come on.
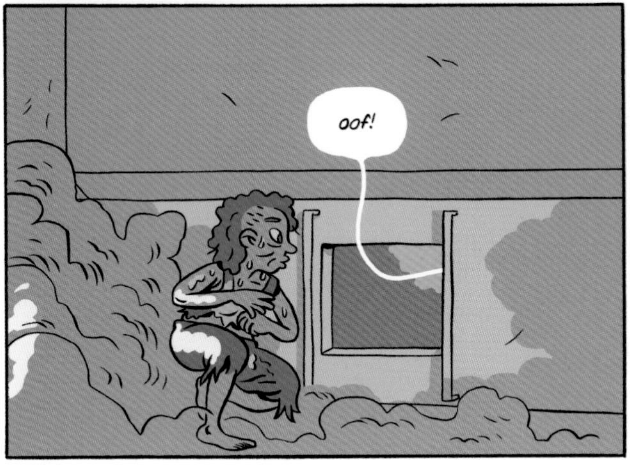
oof!
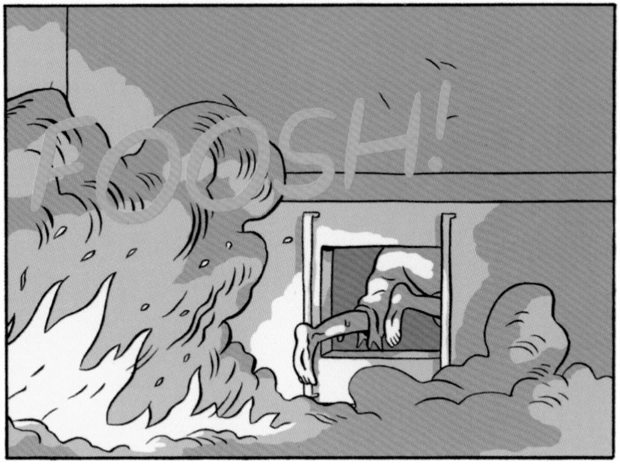
FOOSH!

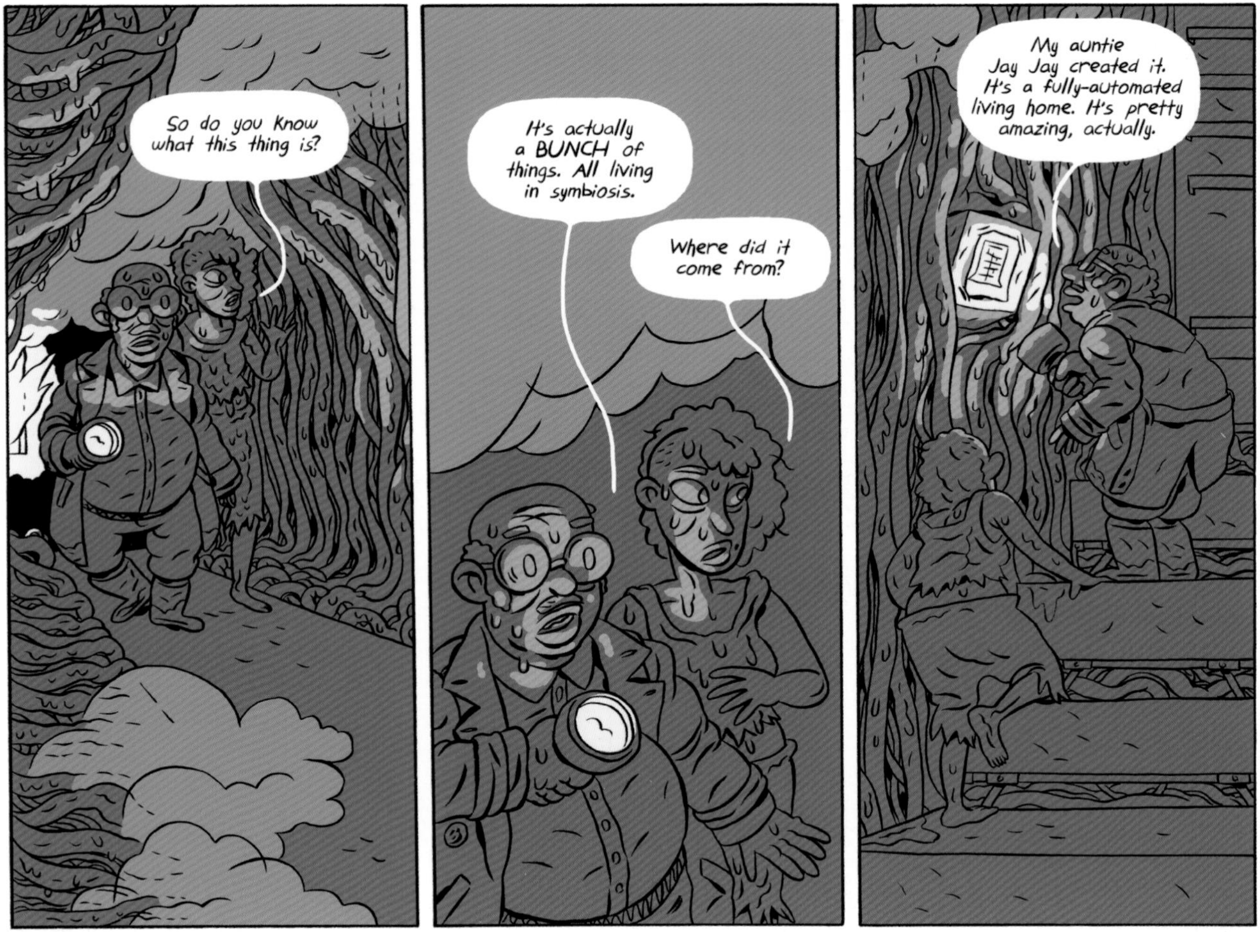
So do you know what this thing is?
It's actually a BUNCH of things. All living in symbiosis.
Where did it come from?
My auntie Jay Jay created it. It's a fully-automated living home. It's pretty amazing, actually.

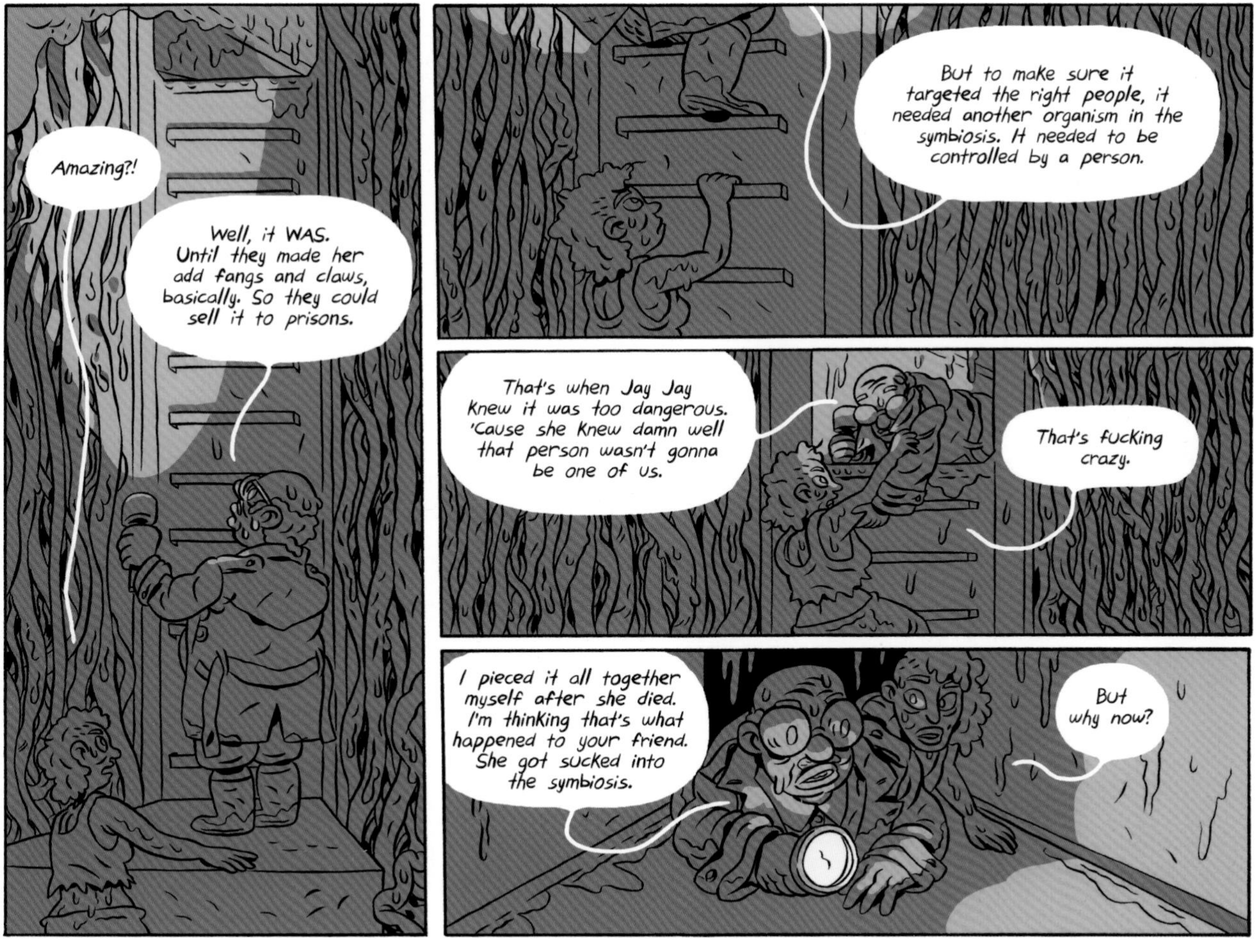
Amazing?!
Well, it WAS. Until they made her add fangs and claws, basically. So they could sell it to prisons.
But to make sure it targeted the right people, it needed another organism in the symbiosis. It needed to be controlled by a person.
That's when Jay Jay knew it was too dangerous. 'Cause she knew damn well that person wasn't gonna be one of us.
That's fucking crazy.
I pieced it all together myself after she died. I'm thinking that's what happened to your friend. She got sucked into the symbiosis.
But why now?

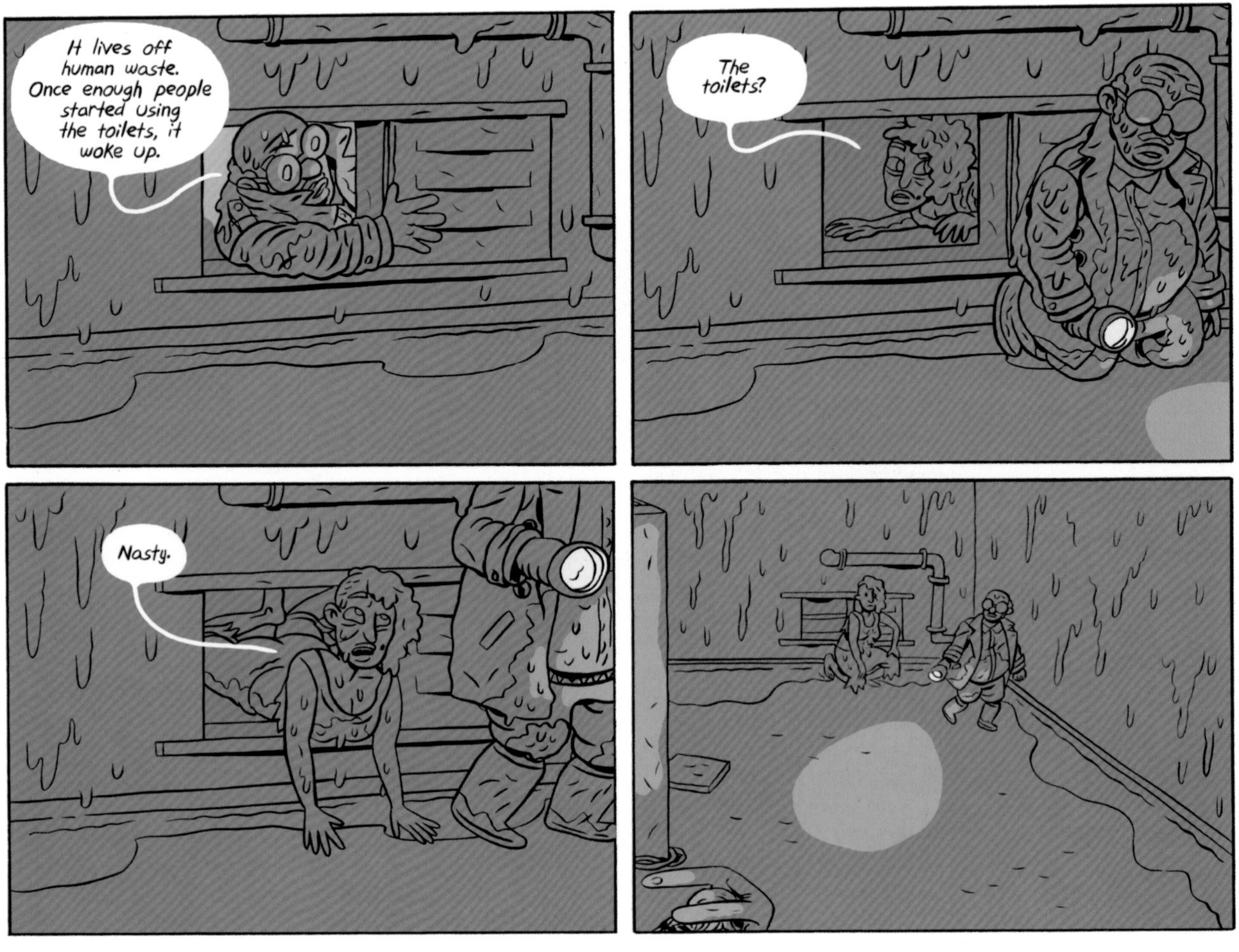
It lives off human waste. Once enough people started using the toilets, it woke up.
The toilets?
Nasty.

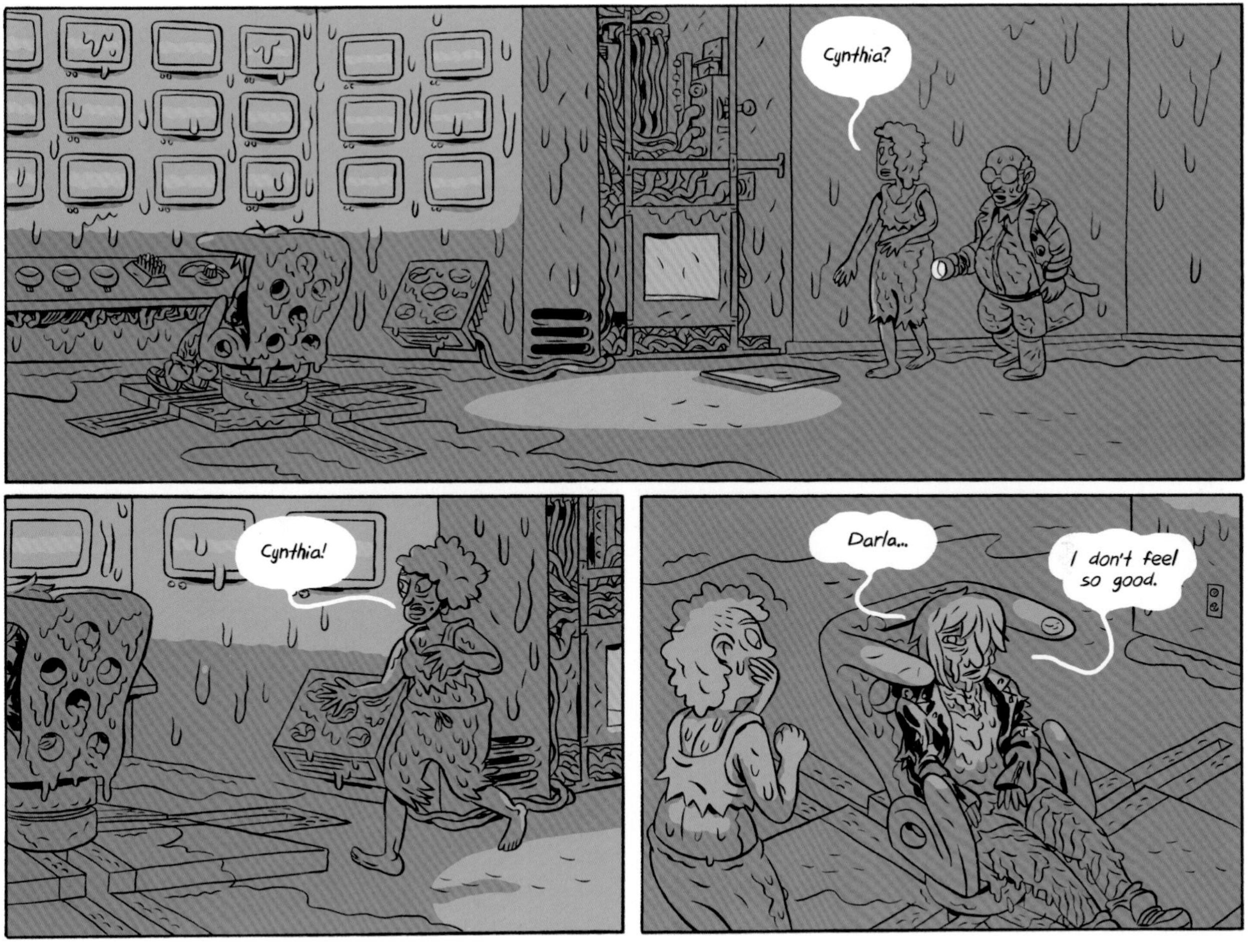
Cynthia?
Cynthia!
Darla...
I don't feel so good.

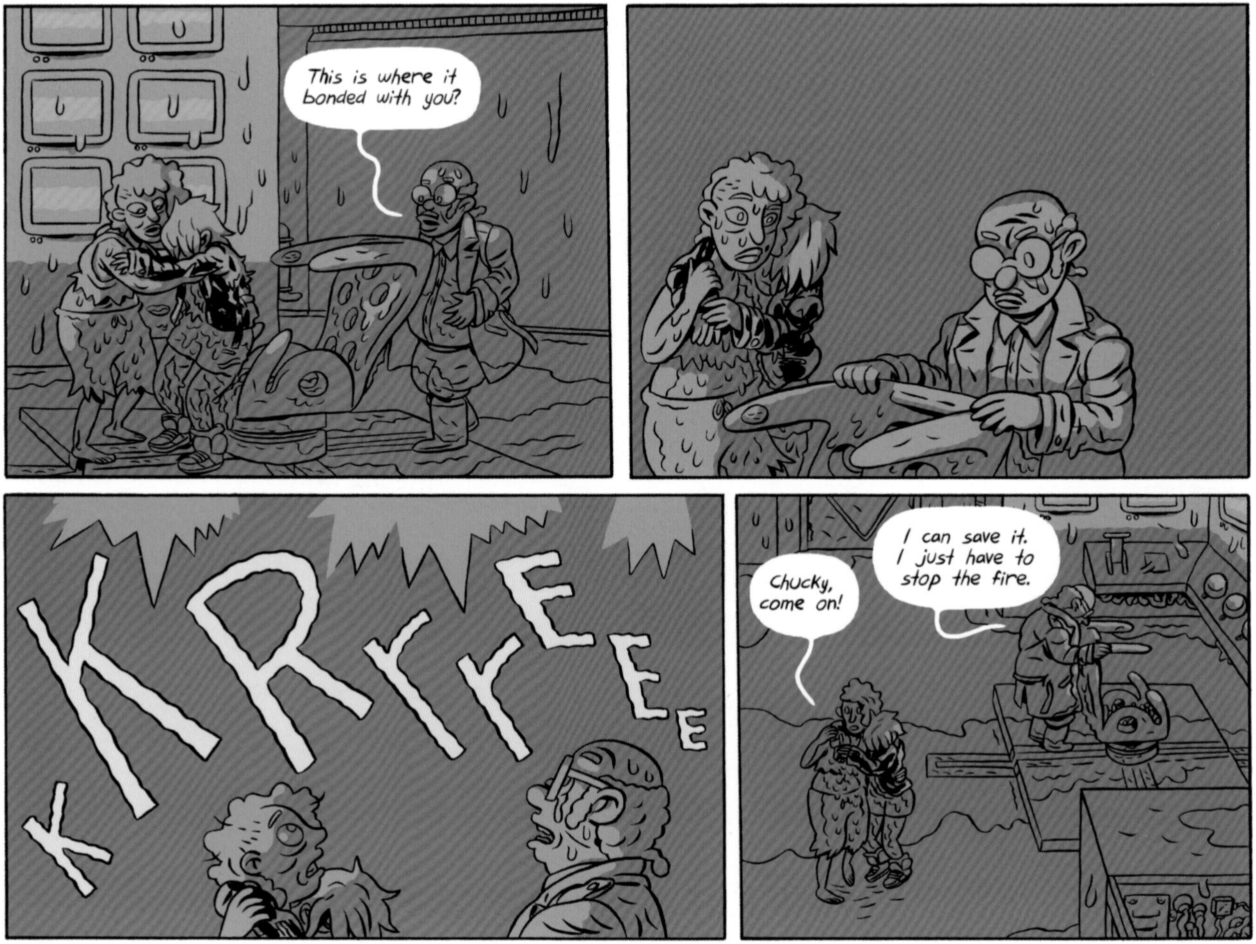
This is where it bonded with you?
KRrrEEEe
Chucky, come on!
I can save it. I just have to stop the fire.

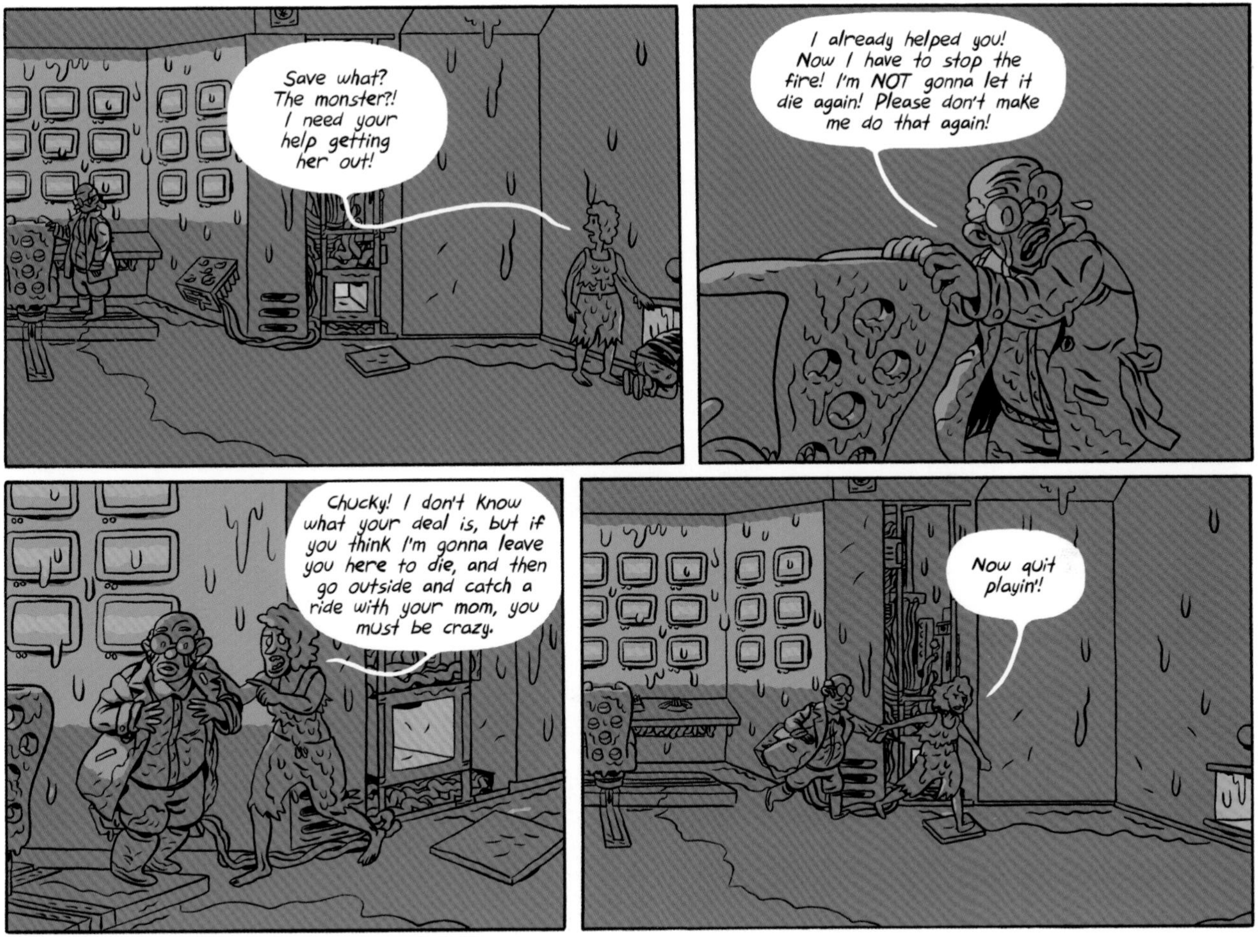
Save what? The monster?! I need your help getting her out!
I already helped you! Now I have to stop the fire! I'm NOT gonna let it die again! Please don't make me do that again!
Chucky! I don't know what your deal is, but if you think I'm gonna leave you here to die, and then go outside and catch a ride with your mom, you must be crazy.
Now quit playin'!

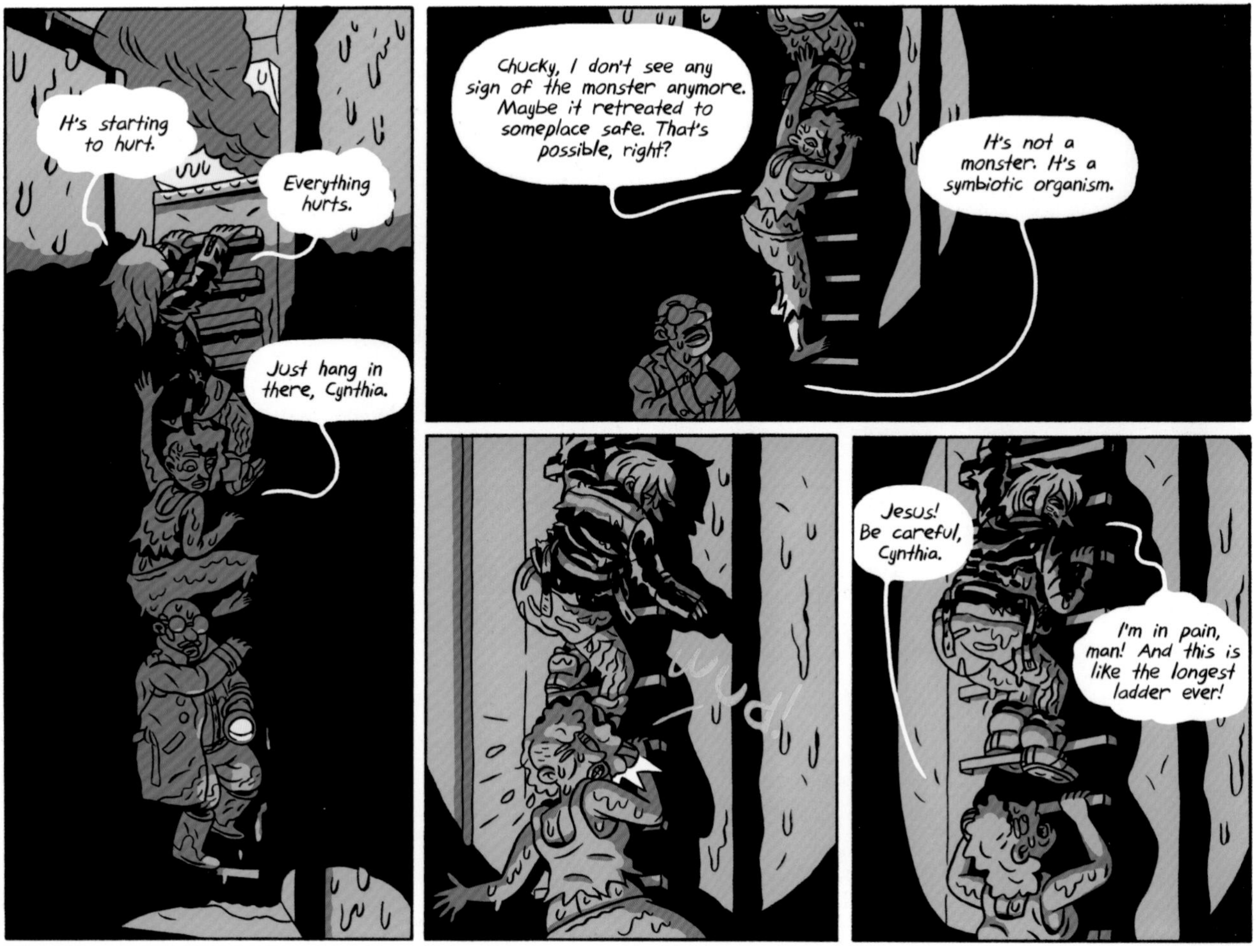

It's starting to hurt.
Everything hurts.
Just hang in there, Cynthia.
Chucky, I don't see any sign of the monster anymore. Maybe it retreated to someplace safe. That's possible, right?
It's not a monster. It's a symbiotic organism.
Jesus! Be careful, Cynthia.
I'm in pain, man! And this is like the longest ladder ever!

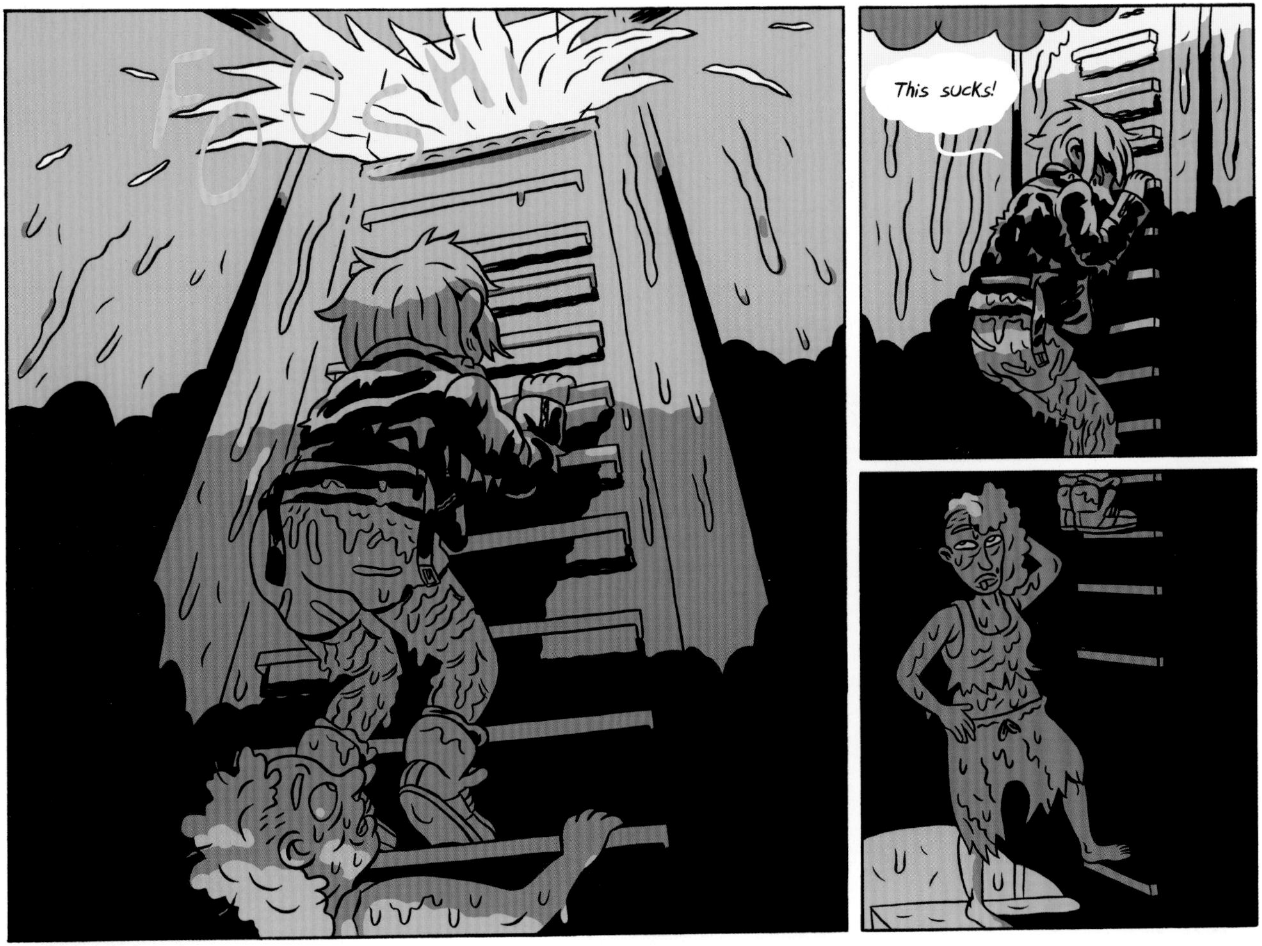
FOOSH!
This sucks!

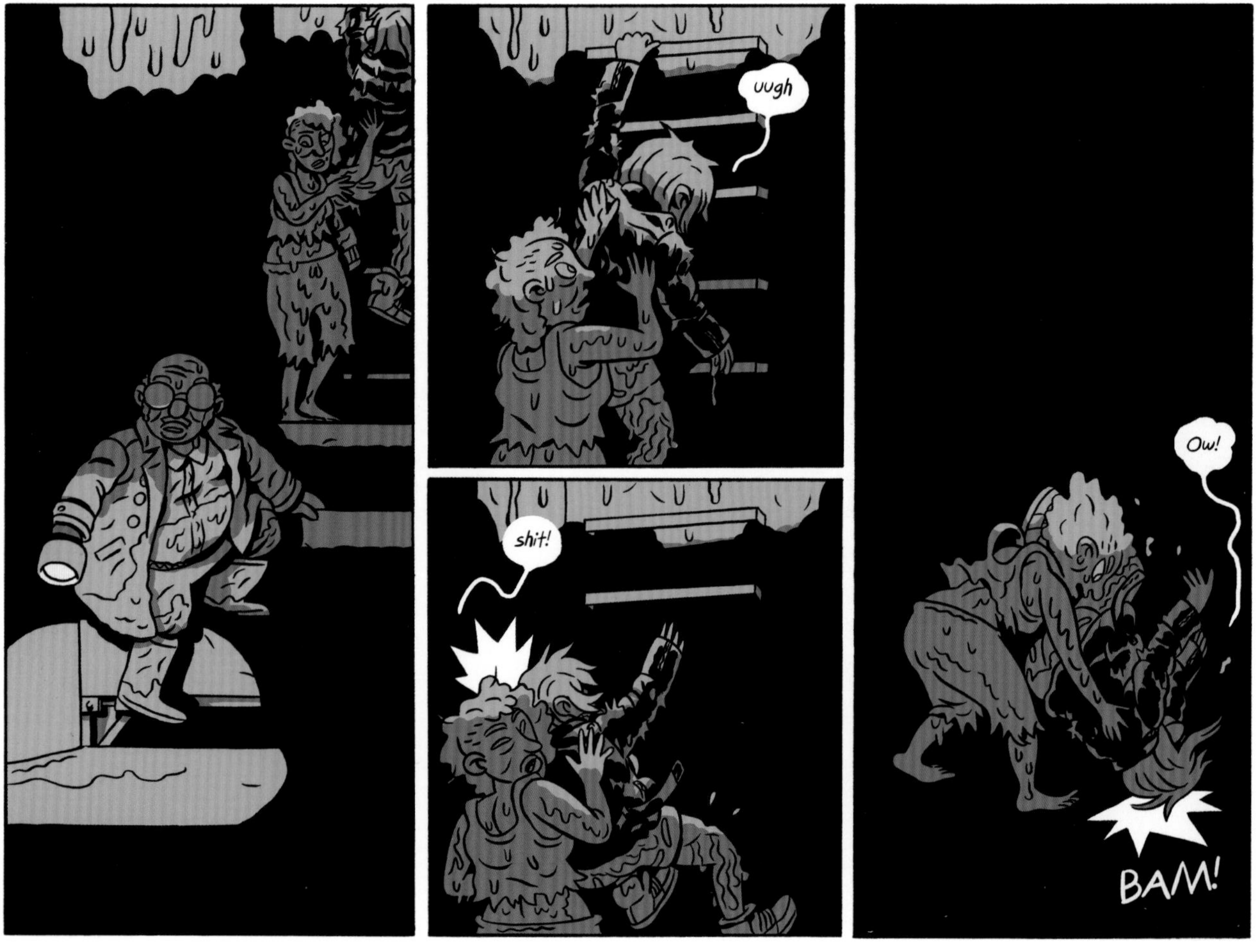
uugh
shit!
Ow!
BAM!

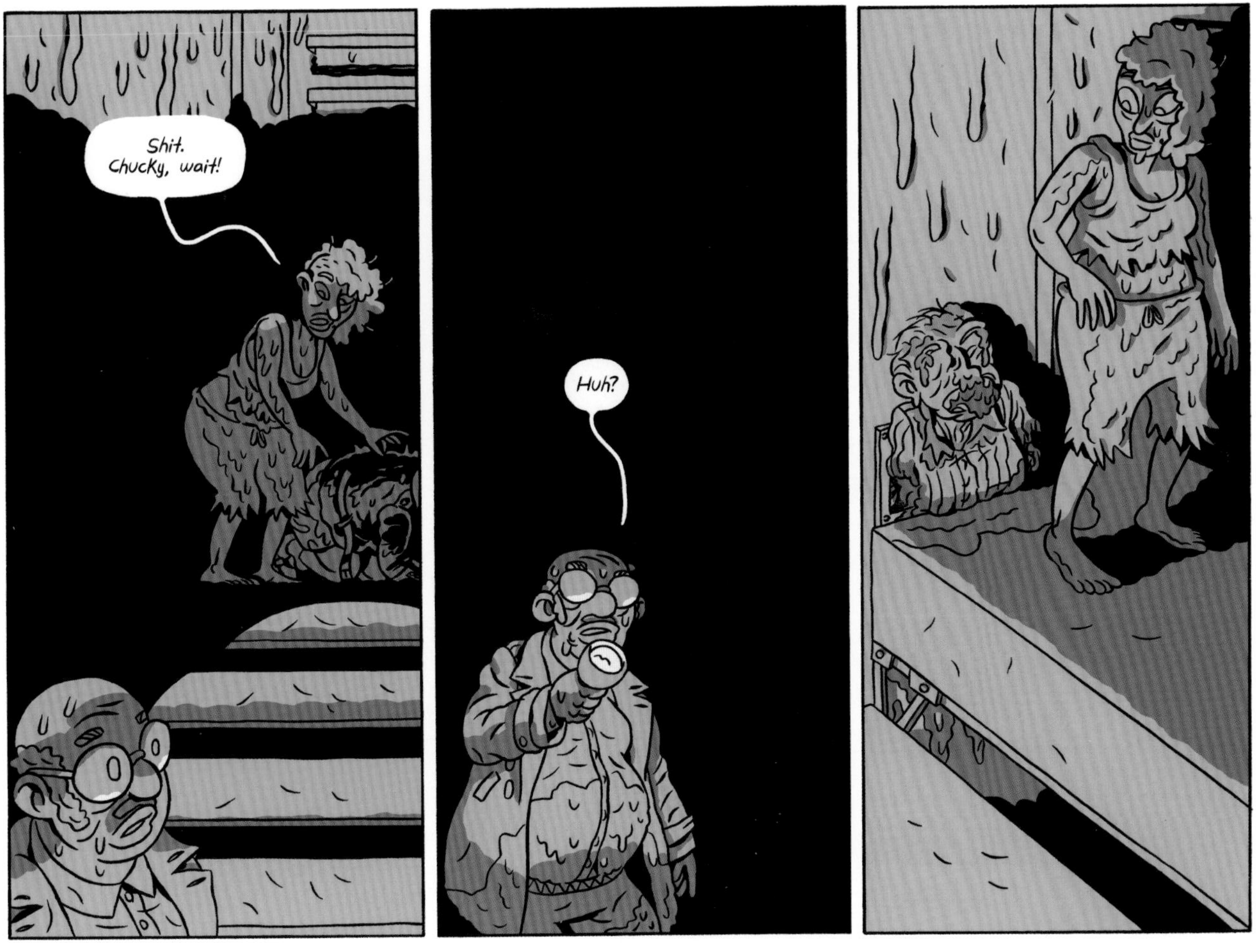
Shit.
Chucky, wait!
Huh?

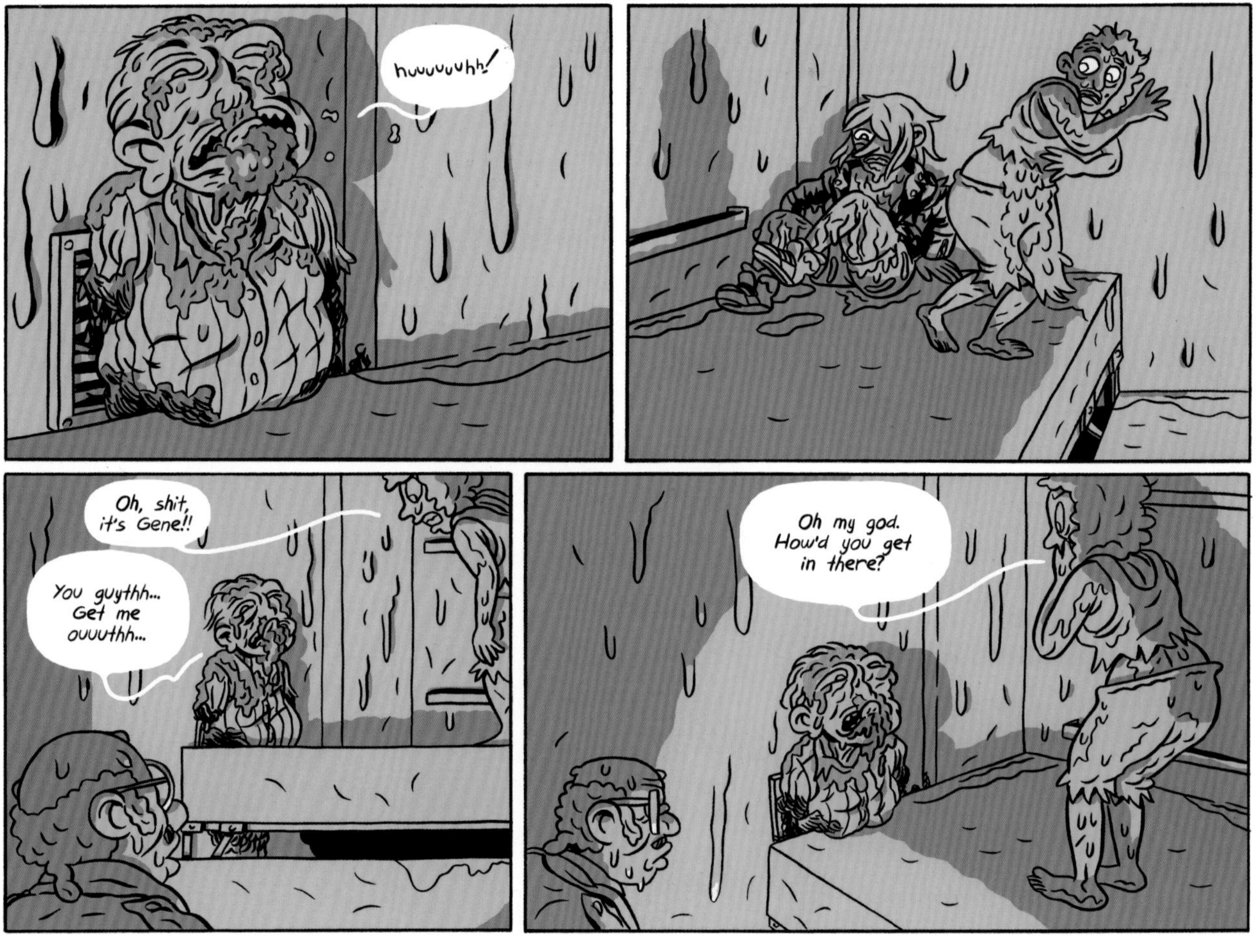
huuuuuuhh!
Oh, shit, it's Gene!!
You guythh... Get me ouuuthh...
Oh my god. How'd you get in there?

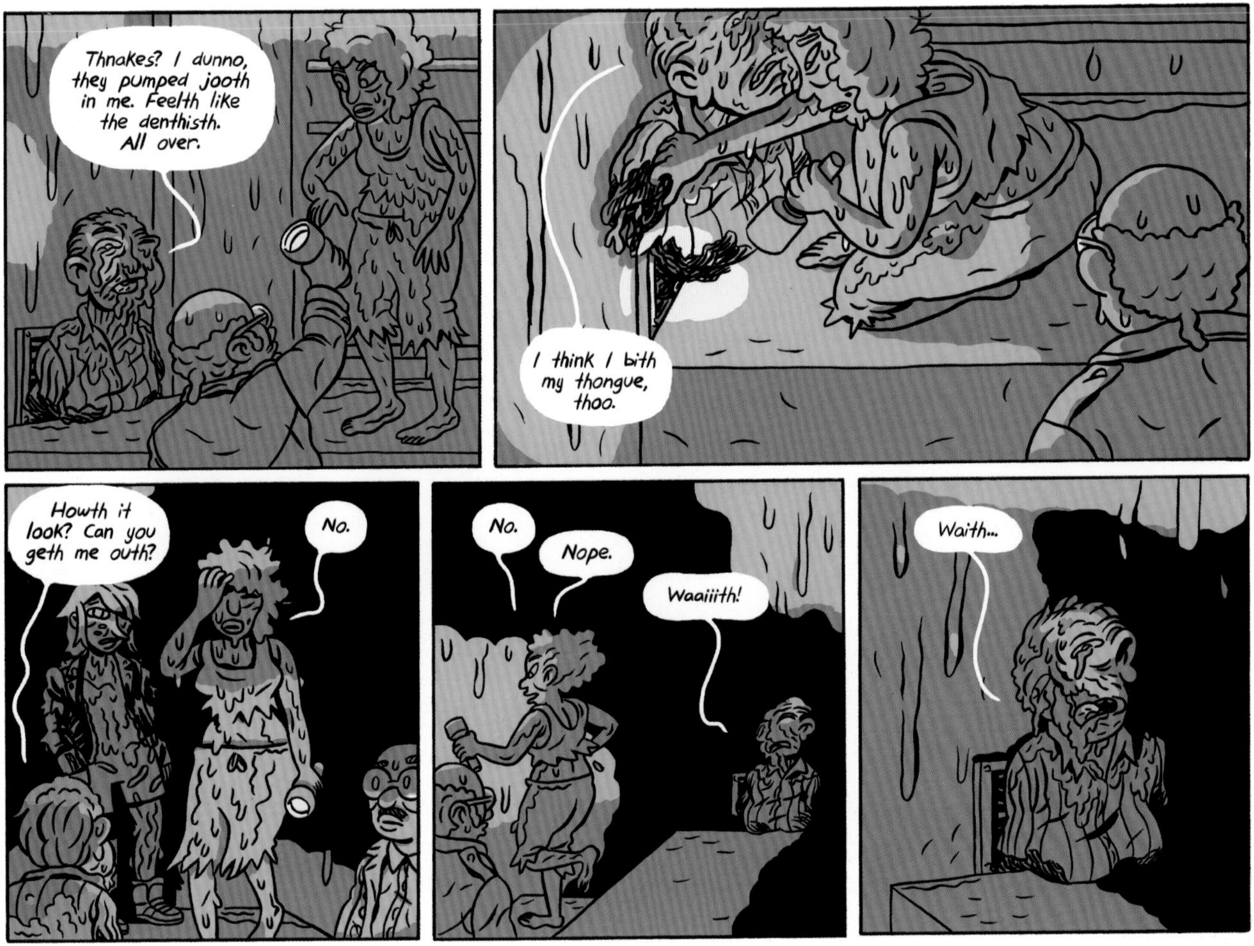
Thnakes? I dunno, they pumped jooth in me. Feelth like the denthisth. All over.
I think I bith my thongue, thoo.
Howth it look? Can you geth me outh?
No.
No.
Nope.
Waaiiith!
Waith...

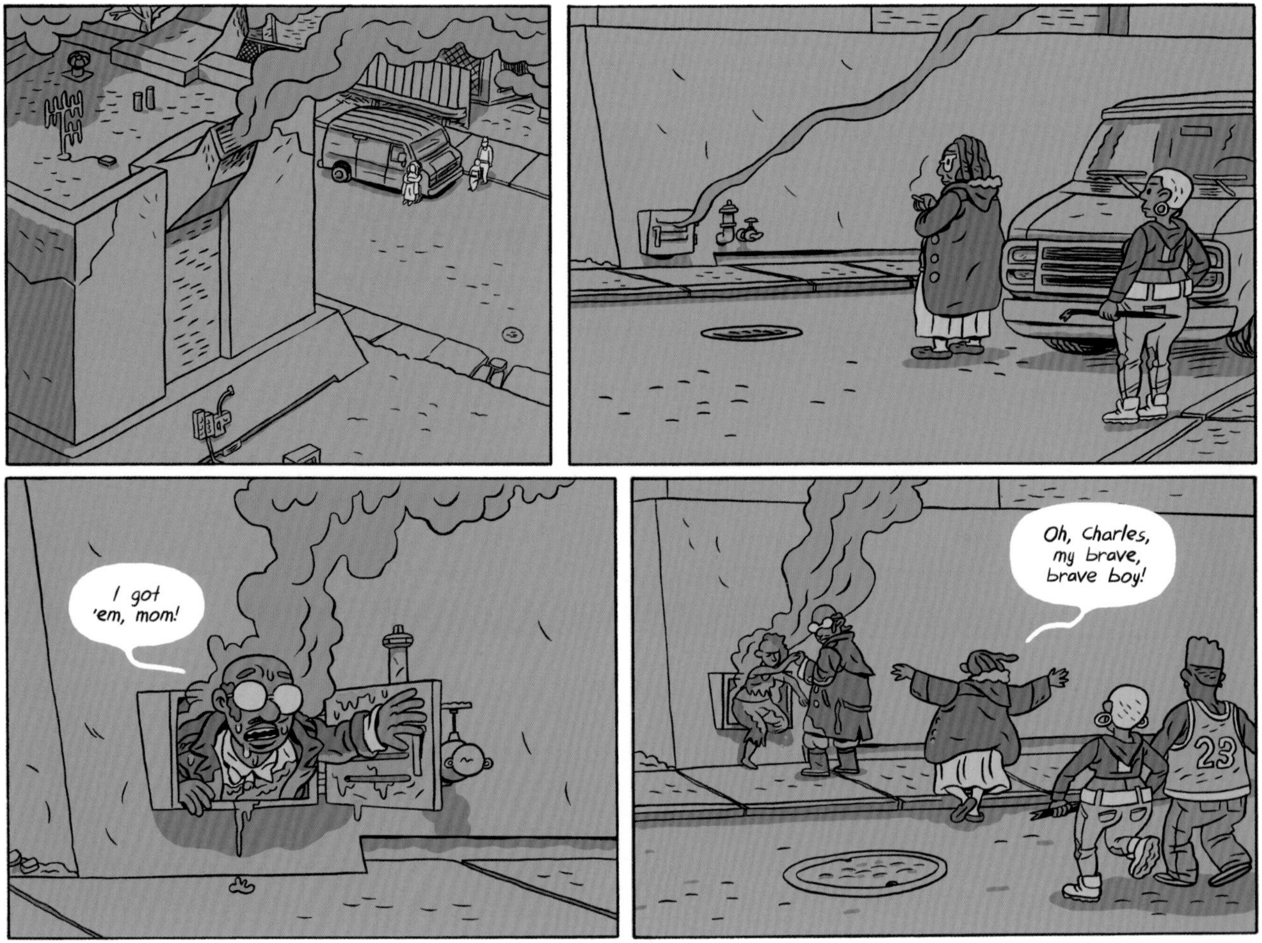
I got 'em, mom!
Oh, Charles, my brave, brave boy!

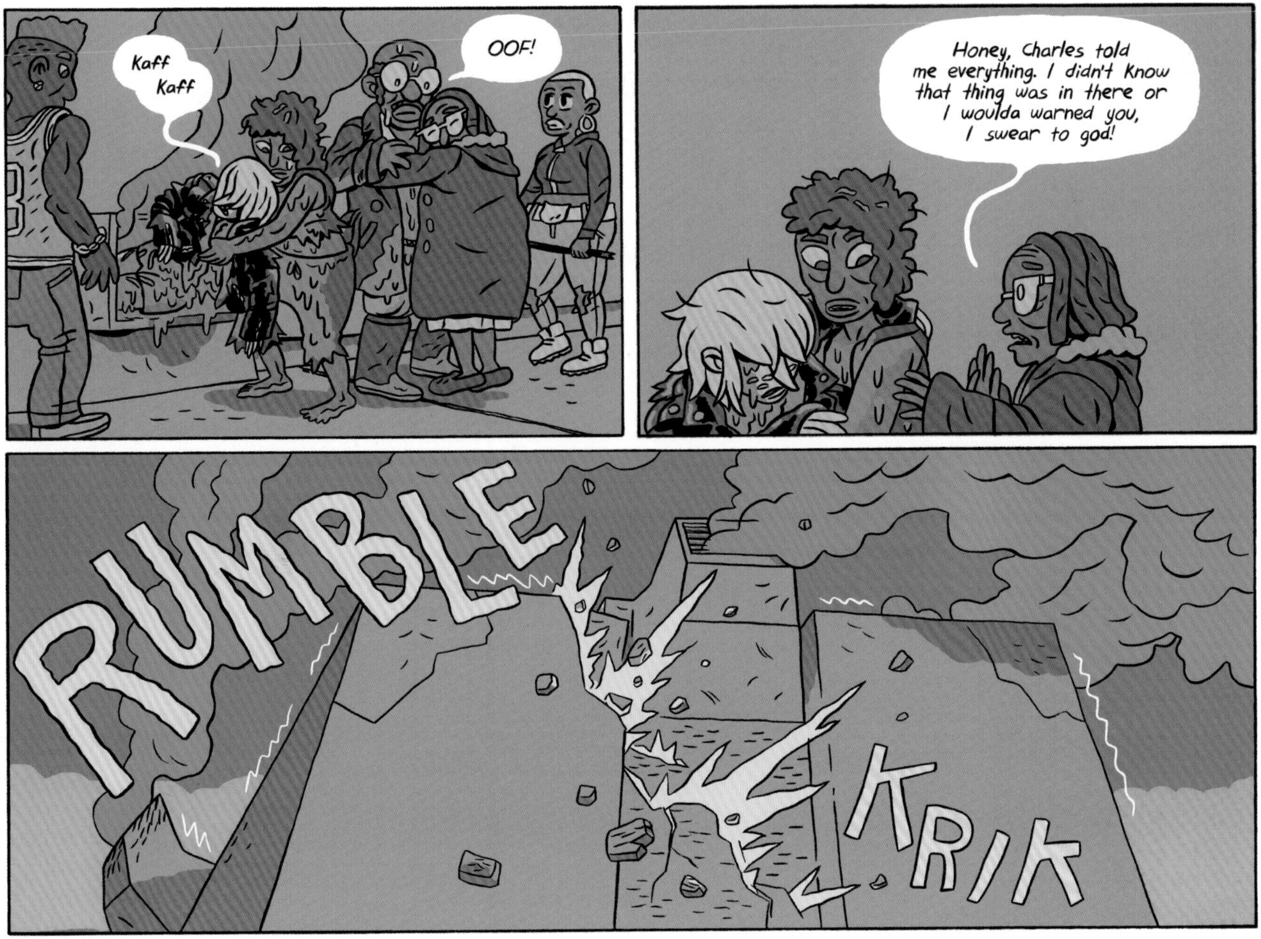
Kaff
Kaff
OOF!
Honey, Charles told me everything. I didn't know that thing was in there or I woulda warned you, I swear to god!
RUMBLE
KRIK

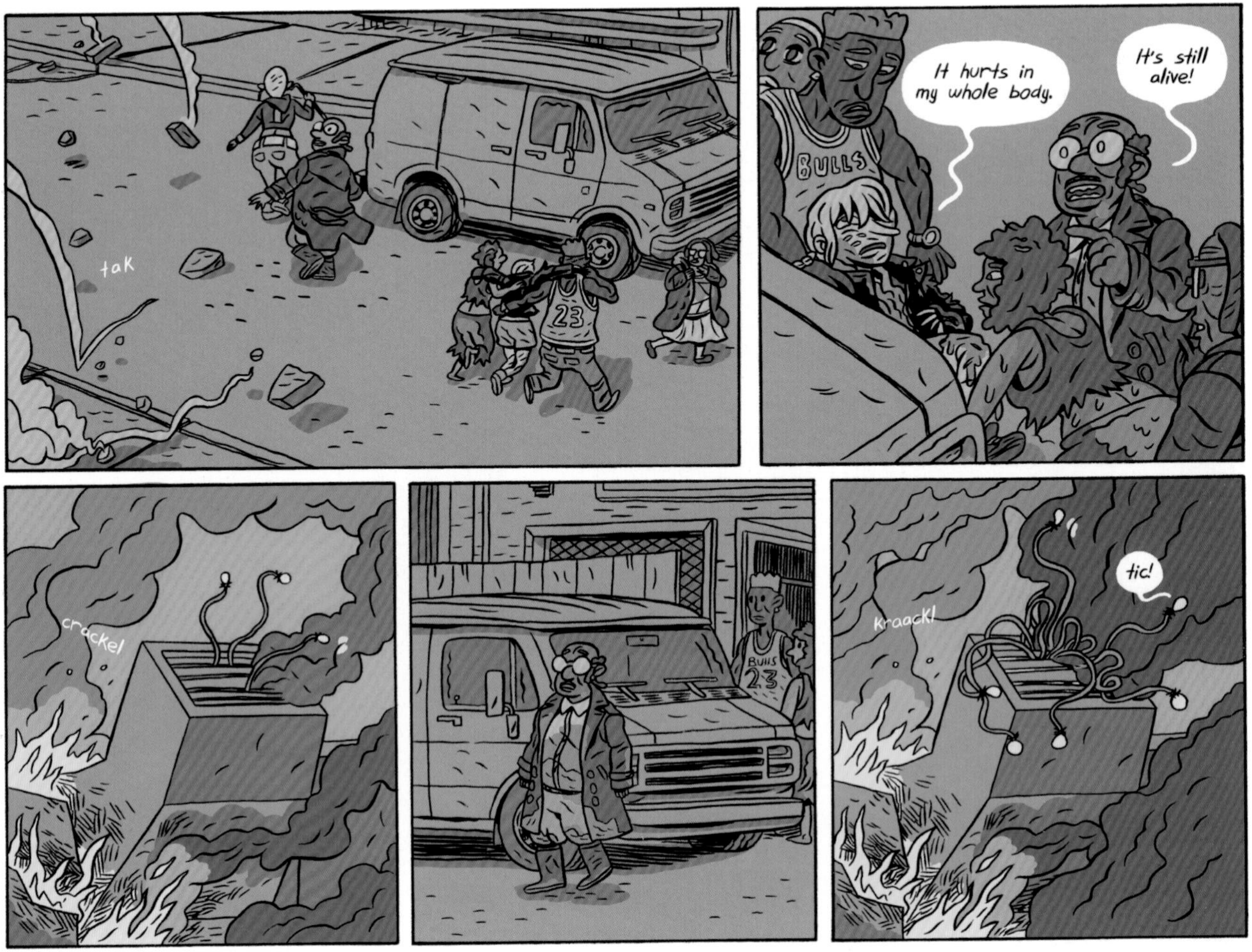
tak
23
BULLS
It hurts in my whole body.
It's still alive!
crackel
BULLS 23
kraack!
tic!

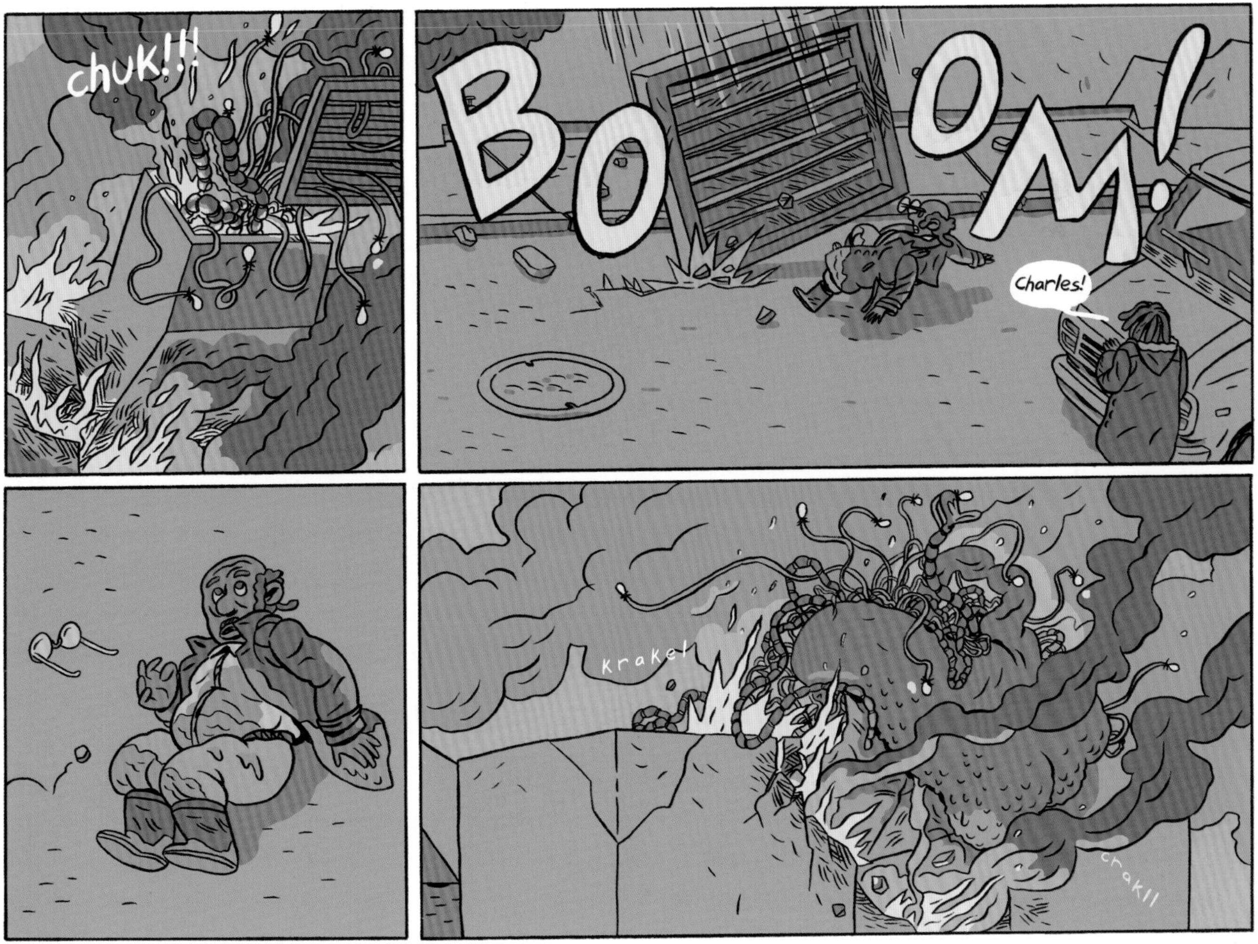
CHUK!!!
BOOM!
Charles!
krakel
crakll

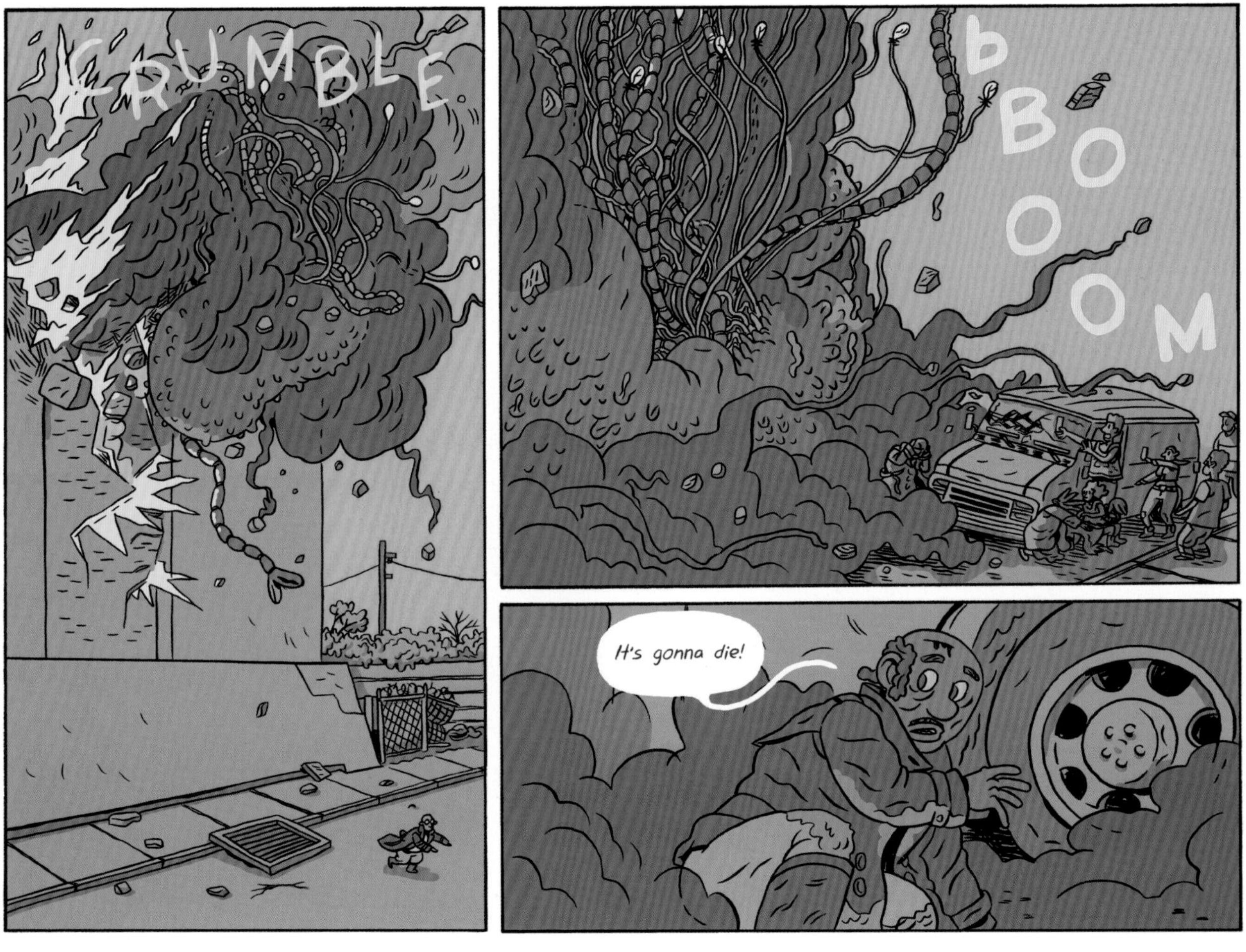
CRUMBLE
BBOOOM
It's gonna die!

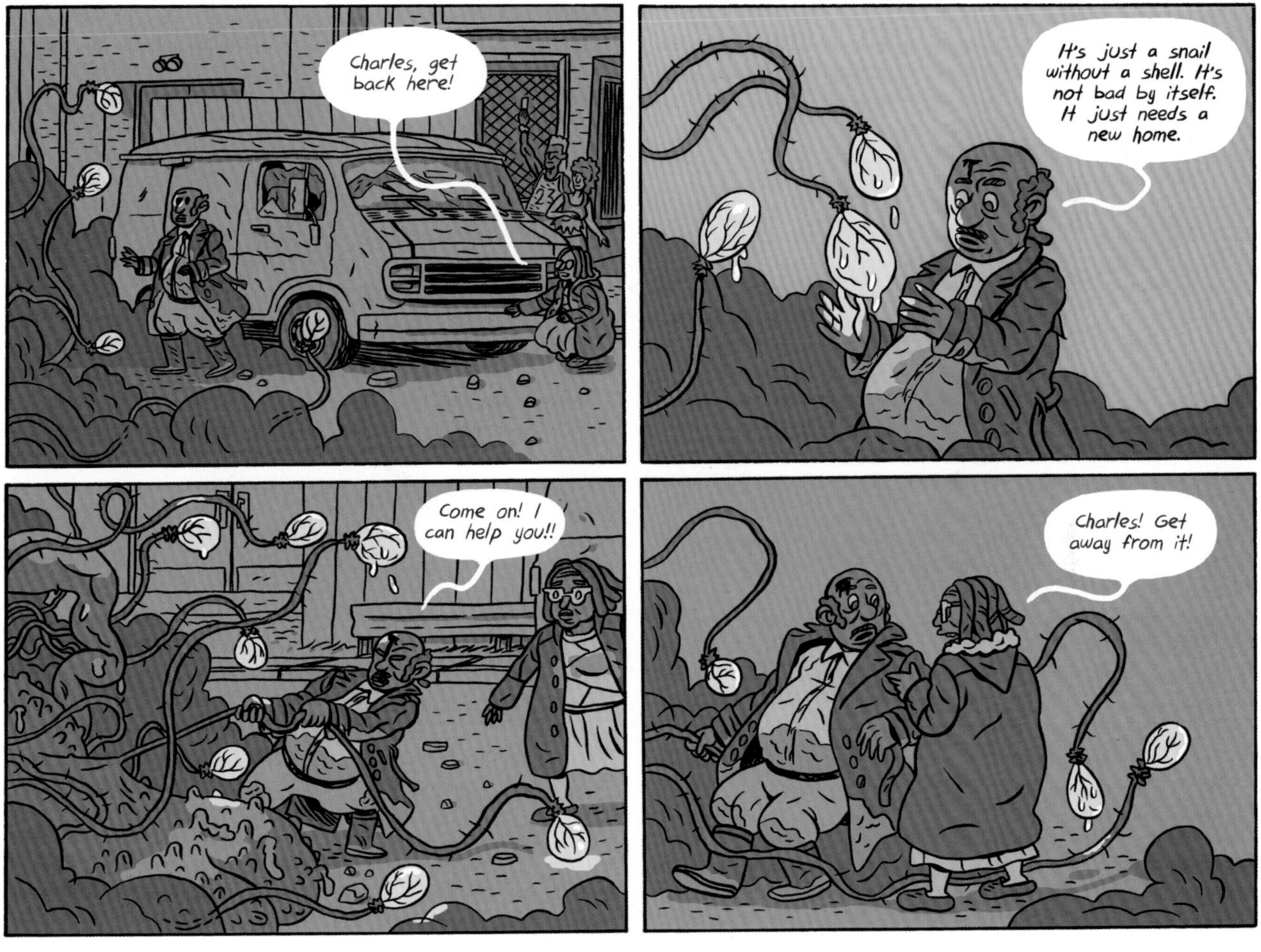
Charles, get back here!
It's just a snail without a shell. It's not bad by itself. It just needs a new home.
Come on! I can help you!!
Charles! Get away from it!

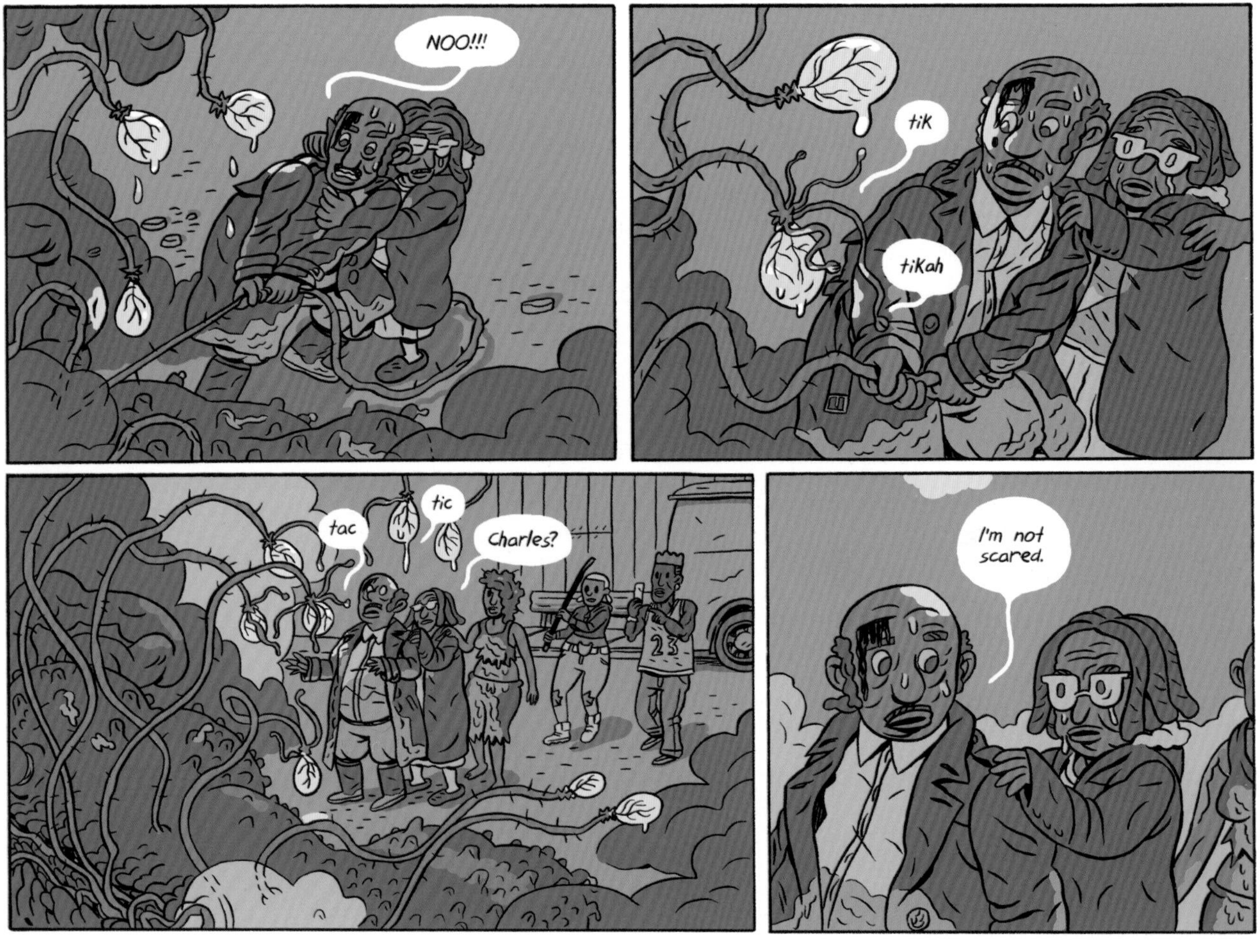
NOO!!!
tik
tiKah
tac
tic
Charles?
I'm not scared.

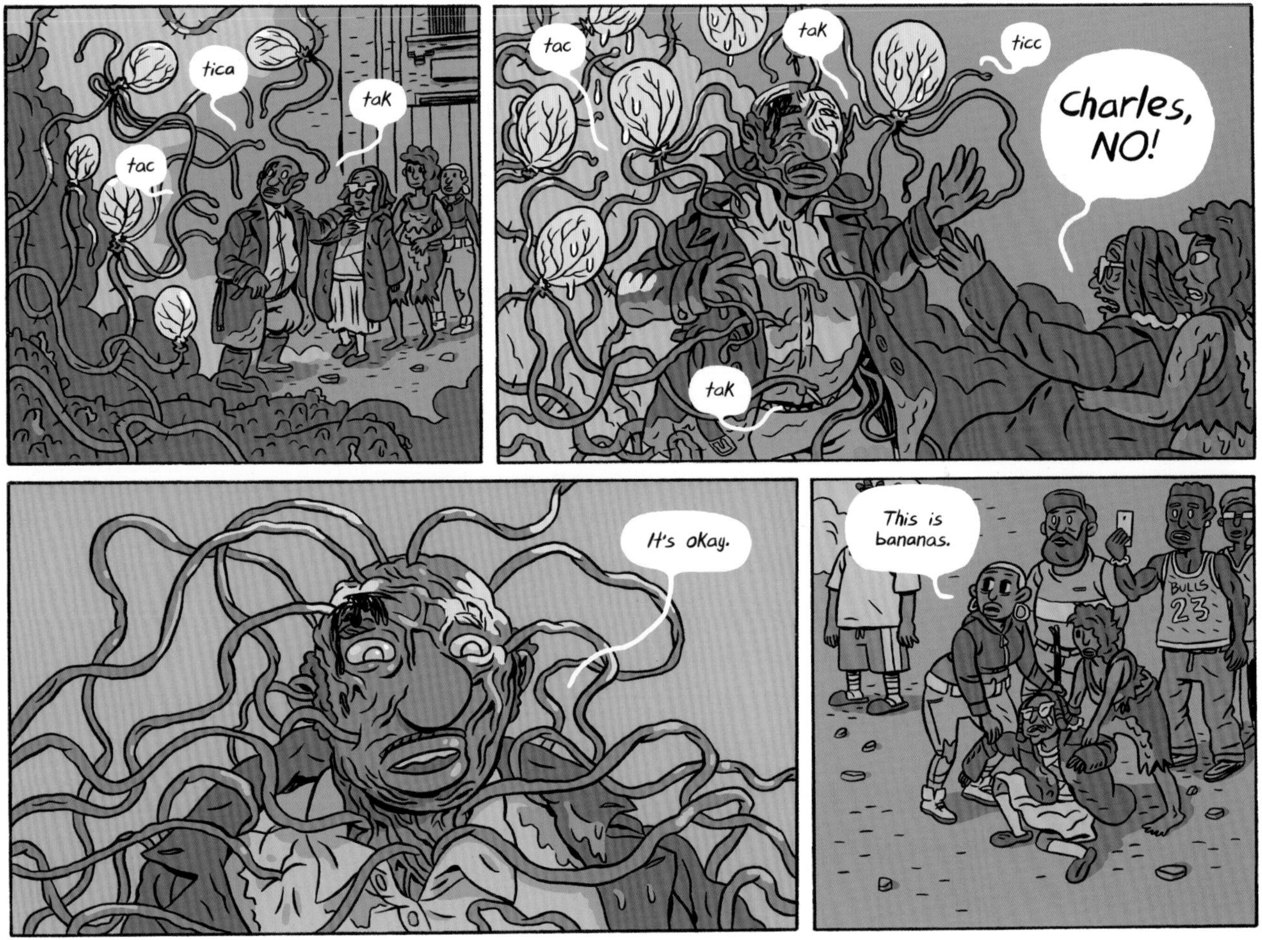
tica
tak
tac
tac
tak
ticc
Charles, NO!
tak
It's okay.
This is bananas.

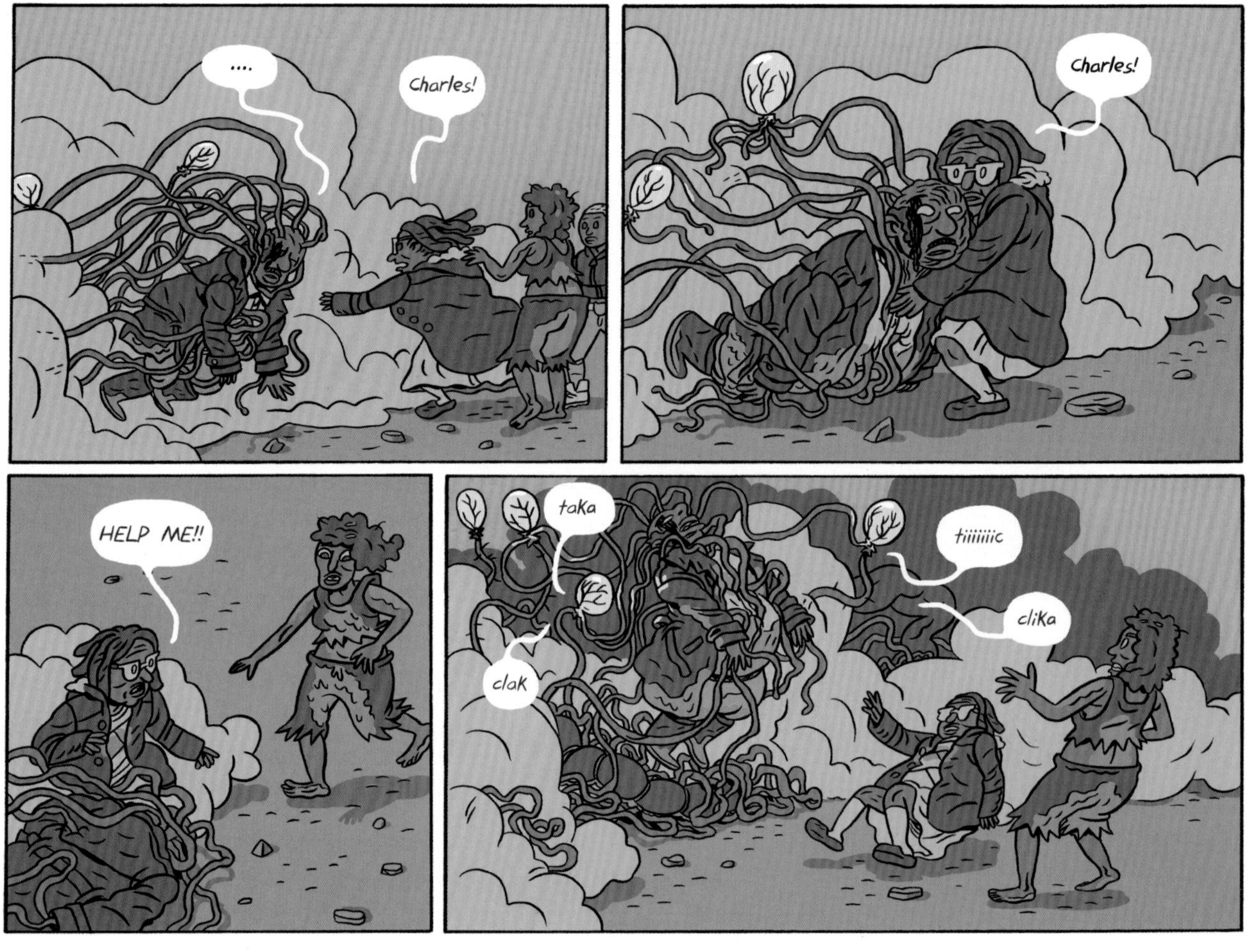
....
Charles!
Charles!
HELP ME!!
taka
clak
tiiiiiiic
clika

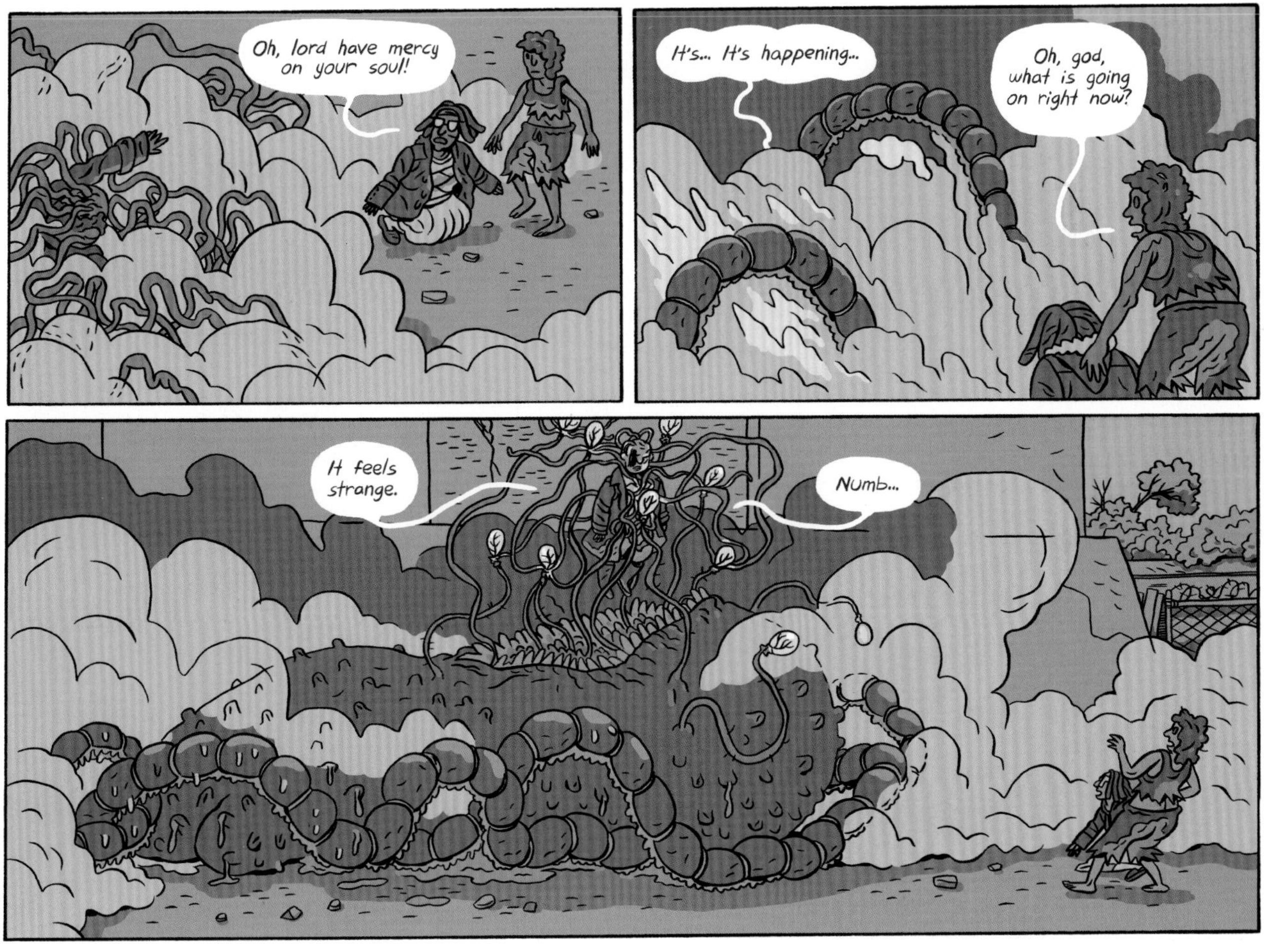
Oh, lord have mercy on your soul!
It's... It's happening...
Oh, god, what is going on right now?
It feels strange.
Numb...

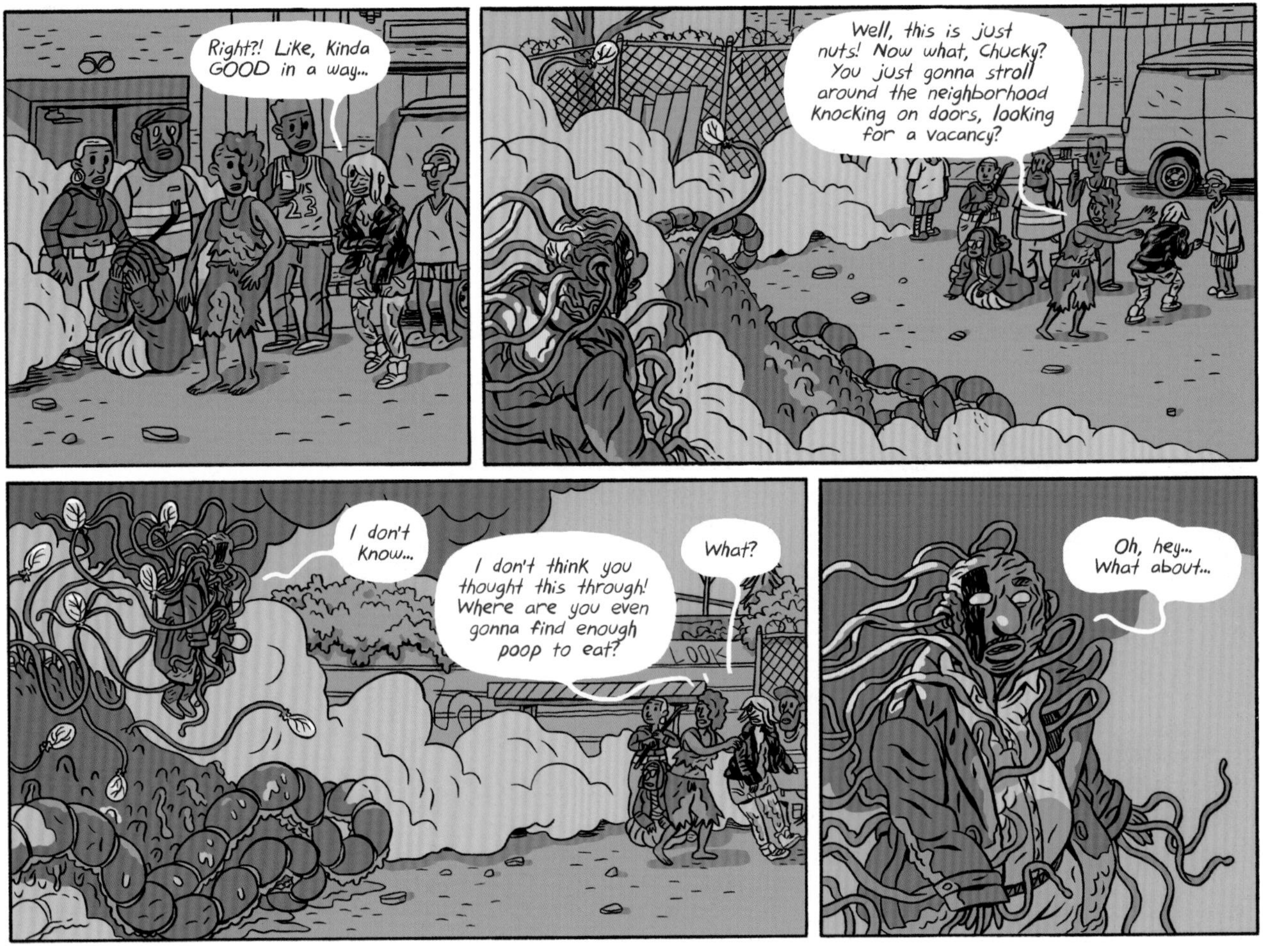
Right?! Like, kinda GOOD in a way...
Well, this is just nuts! Now what, Chucky? You just gonna stroll around the neighborhood knocking on doors, looking for a vacancy?
I don't know...
I don't think you thought this through! Where are you even gonna find enough poop to eat?
What?
LOOK
Oh, hey... What about...

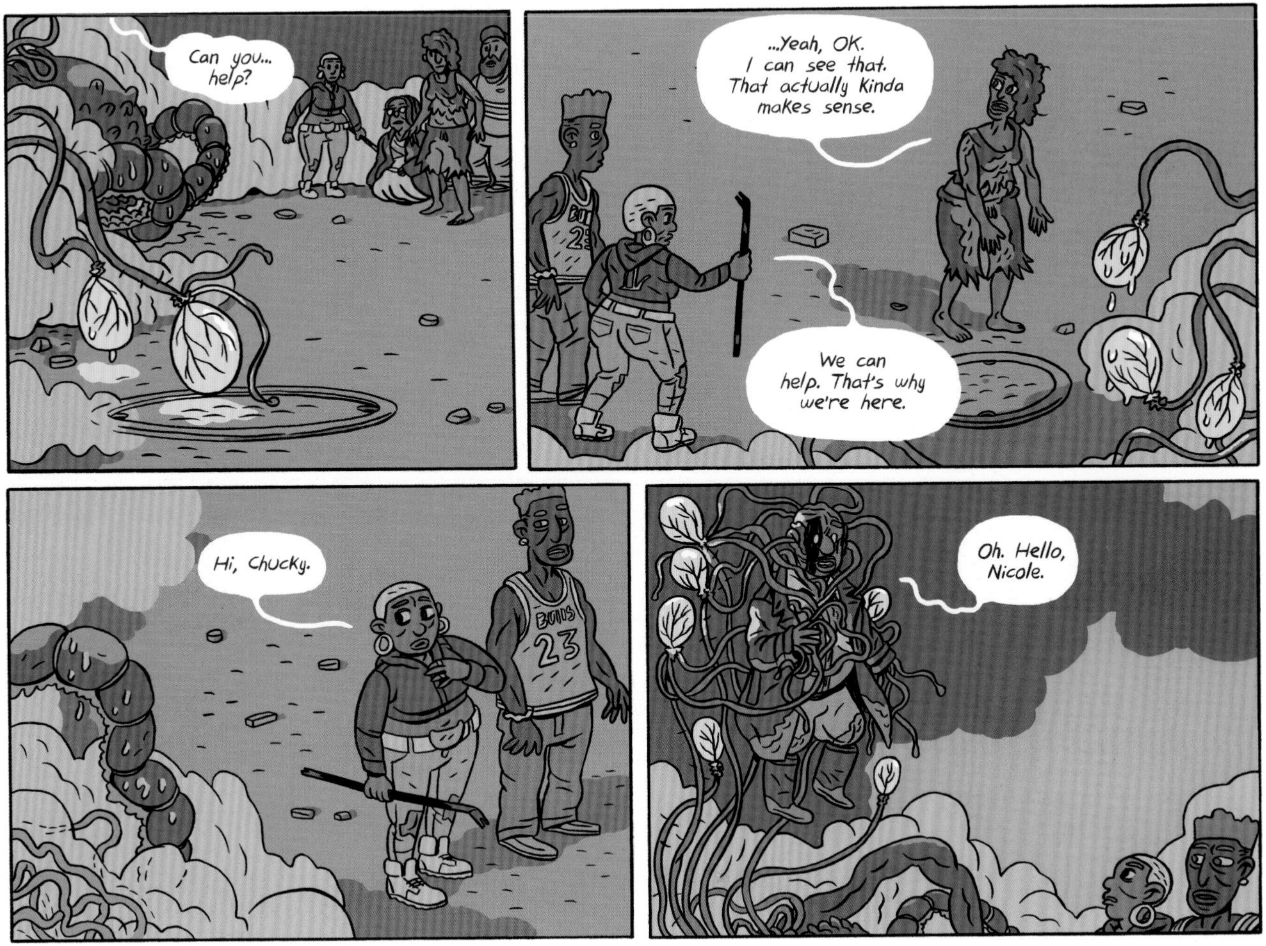
Can you... help?
...Yeah, OK. I can see that. That actually kinda makes sense.
We can help. That's why we're here.
Hi, Chucky.
Oh. Hello, Nicole.

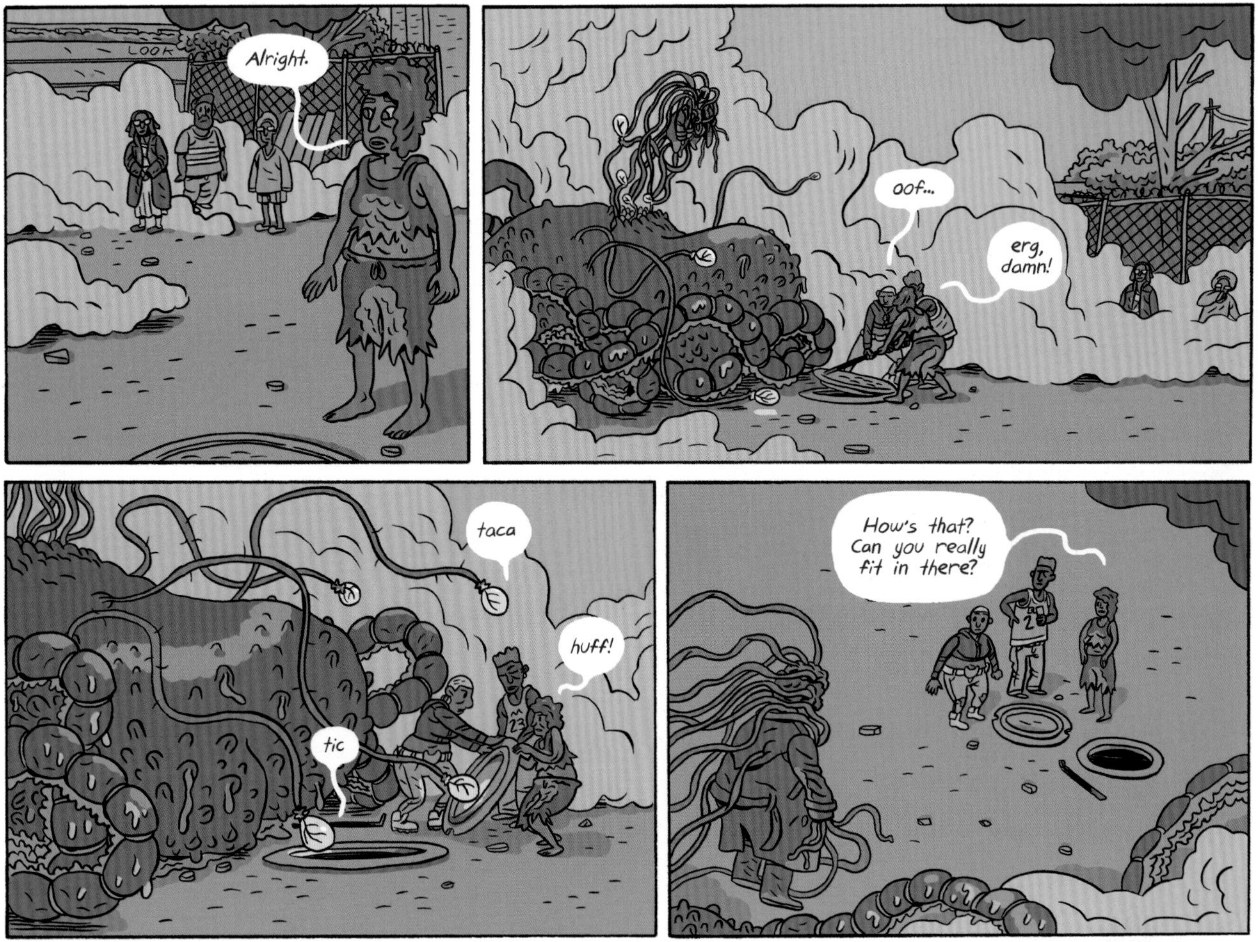
LOOK
Alright.
oof...
erg, damn!
taca
huff!
tic
How's that? Can you really fit in there?

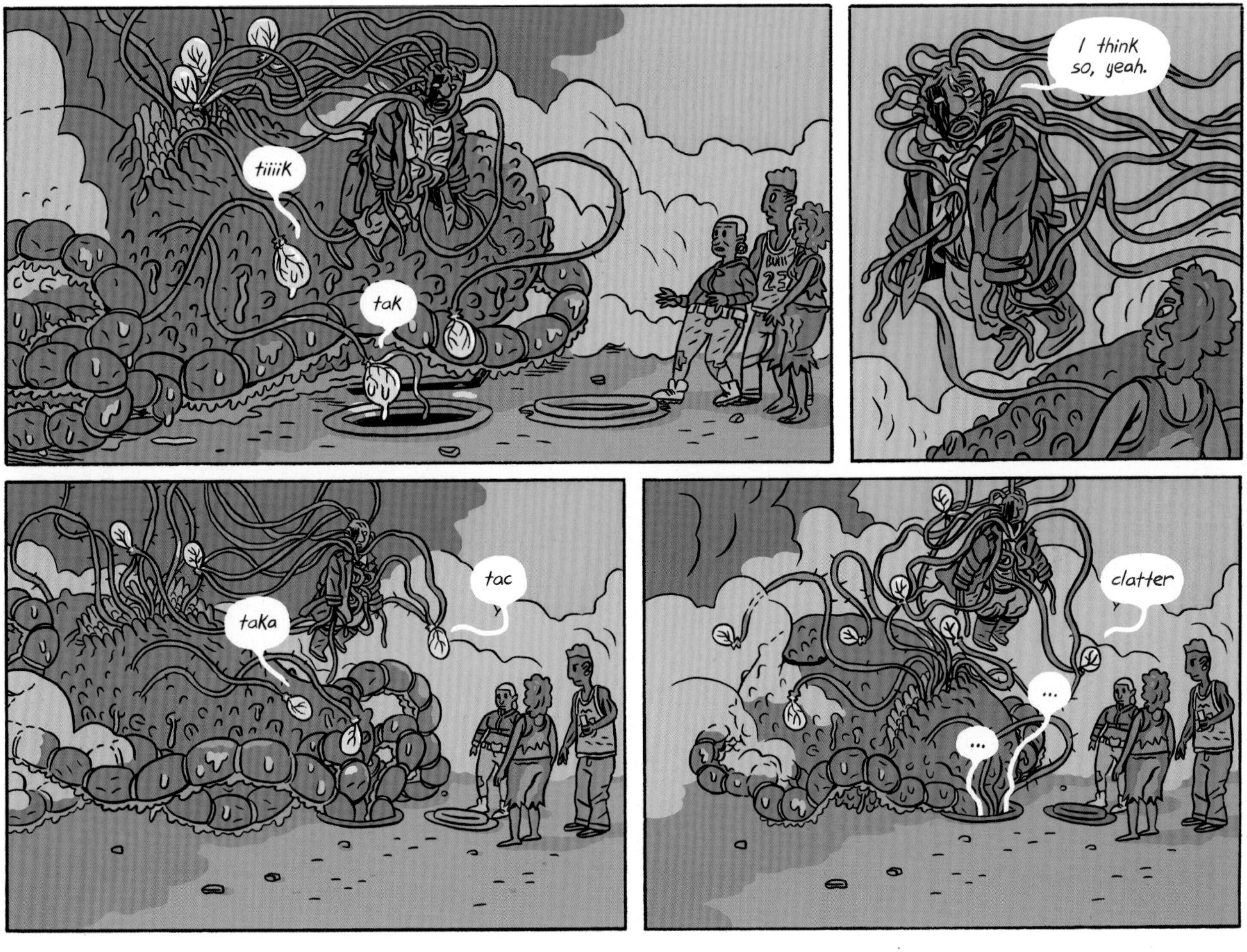
tiiiiK
tak
I think so, yeah.
taka
tac
clatter
...
...

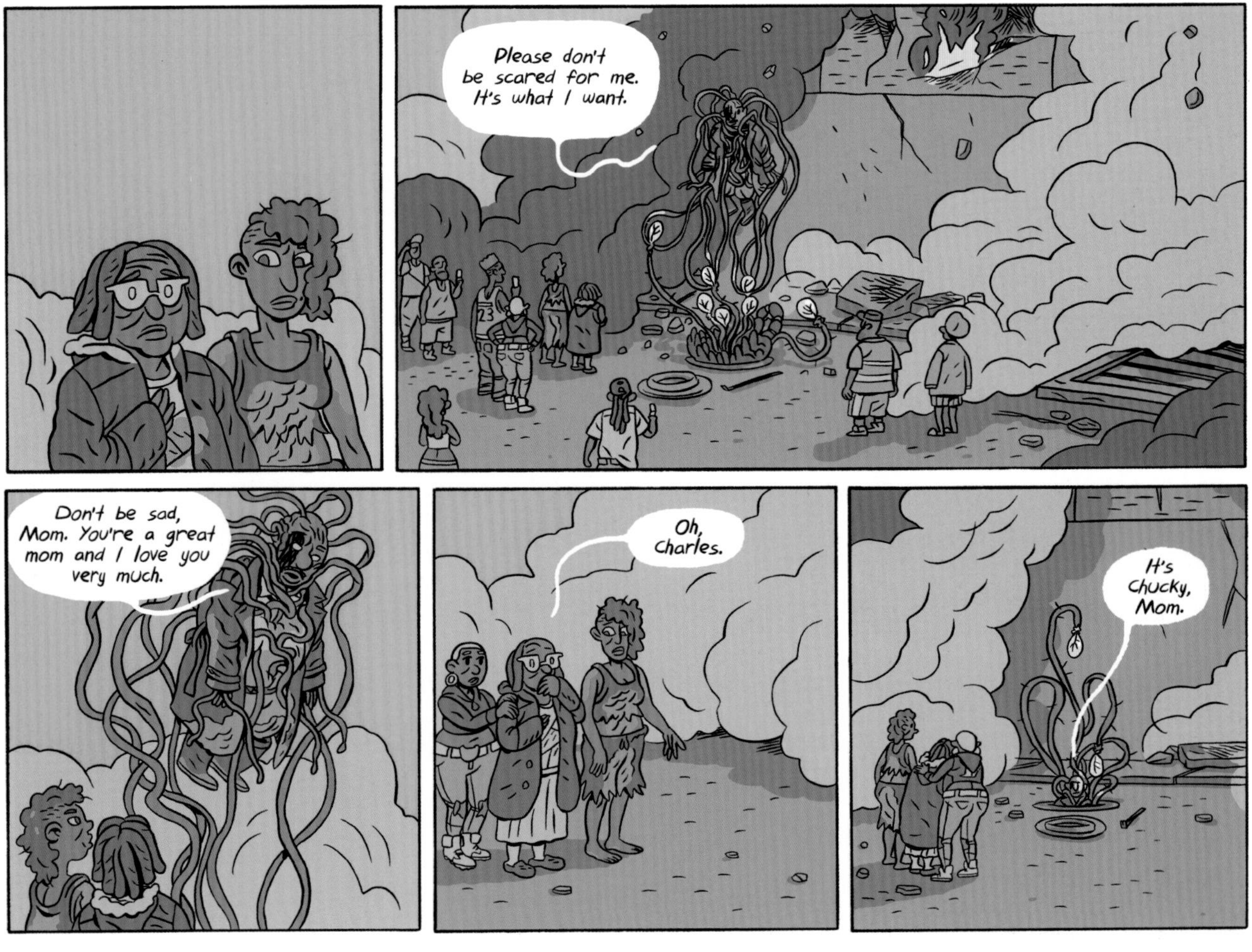
Please don't be scared for me. It's what I want.
Don't be sad, Mom. You're a great mom and I love you very much.
Oh, Charles.
It's Chucky, Mom.

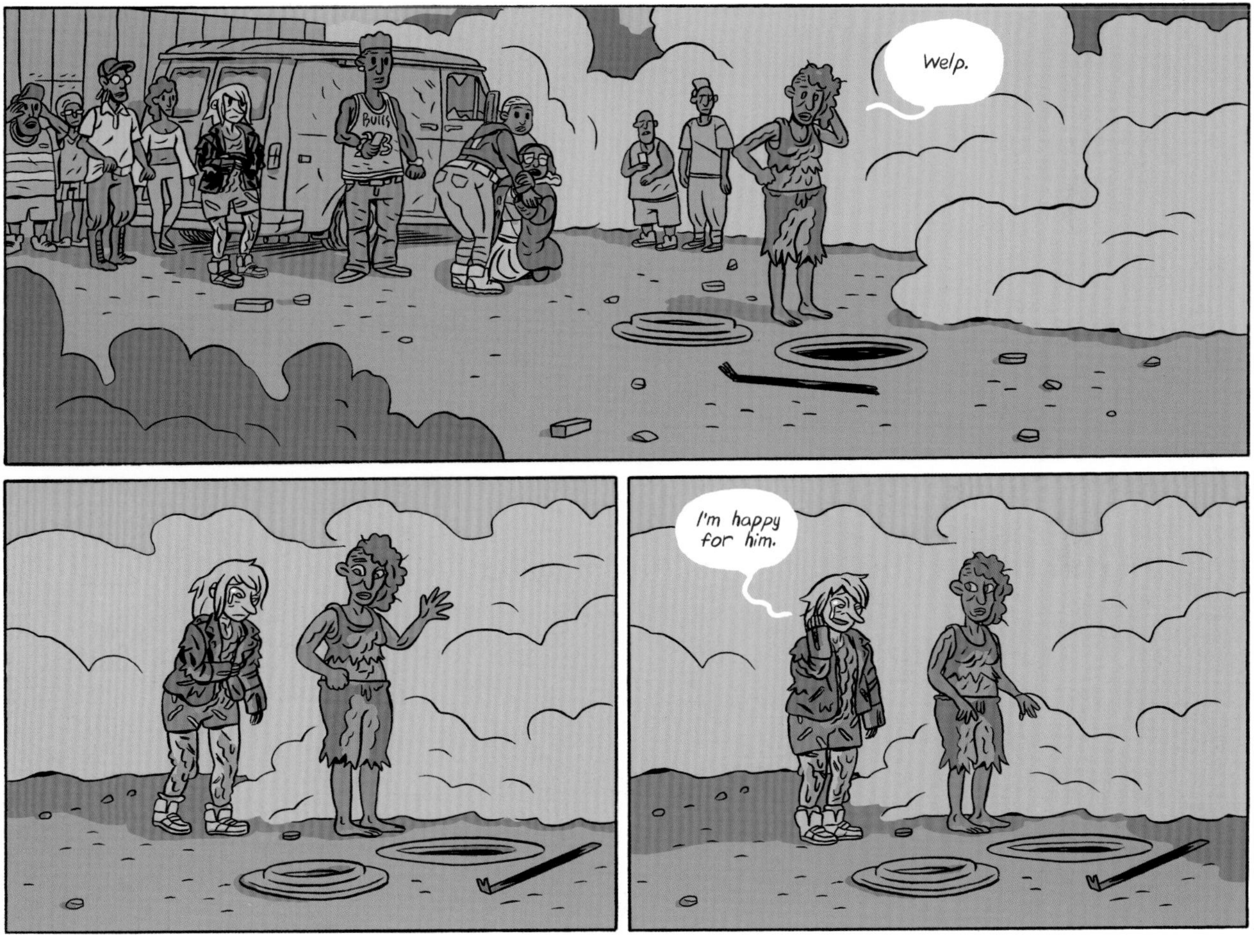
Welp.
I'm happy for him.

SCREEH!
MONSTER in my CLOSET
MONSTER IN MY CLOSET
We're back with an update to a bizarre story that's made headlines around the world.
Cynthia Morgan, an innocent young woman raised in a nice, wealthy suburb, was nearly KILLED last week when a violent mutant animal ATTACKED her in her own squalid BOTTOMYARDS apartment.
We go now to Pat Potash with the latest...
heh!
Wait, YOUR apartment?

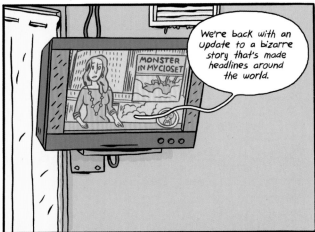

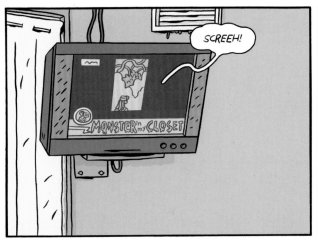

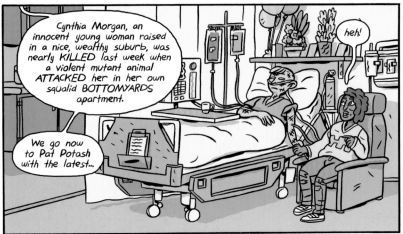

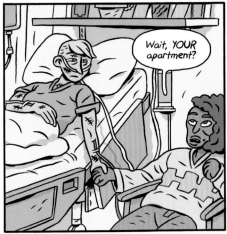

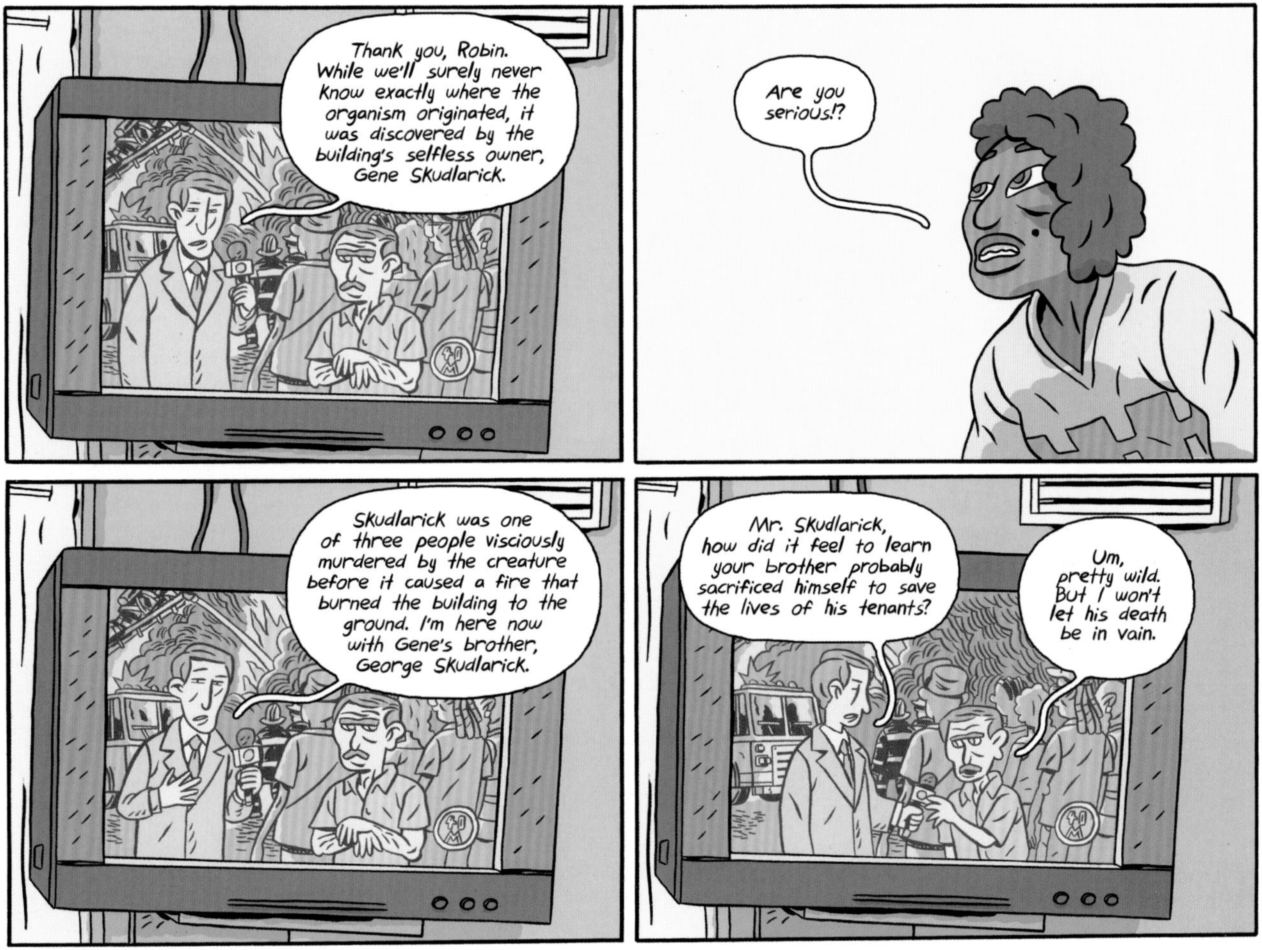
Thank you, Robin. While we'll surely never know exactly where the organism originated, it was discovered by the building's selfless owner, Gene Skudlarick.
Are you serious!?
Skudlarick was one of three people visciously murdered by the creature before it caused a fire that burned the building to the ground. I'm here now with Gene's brother, George Skudlarick.
Mr. Skudlarick, how did it feel to learn your brother probably sacrificed himself to save the lives of his tenants?
Um, pretty wild. But I won't let his death be in vain.

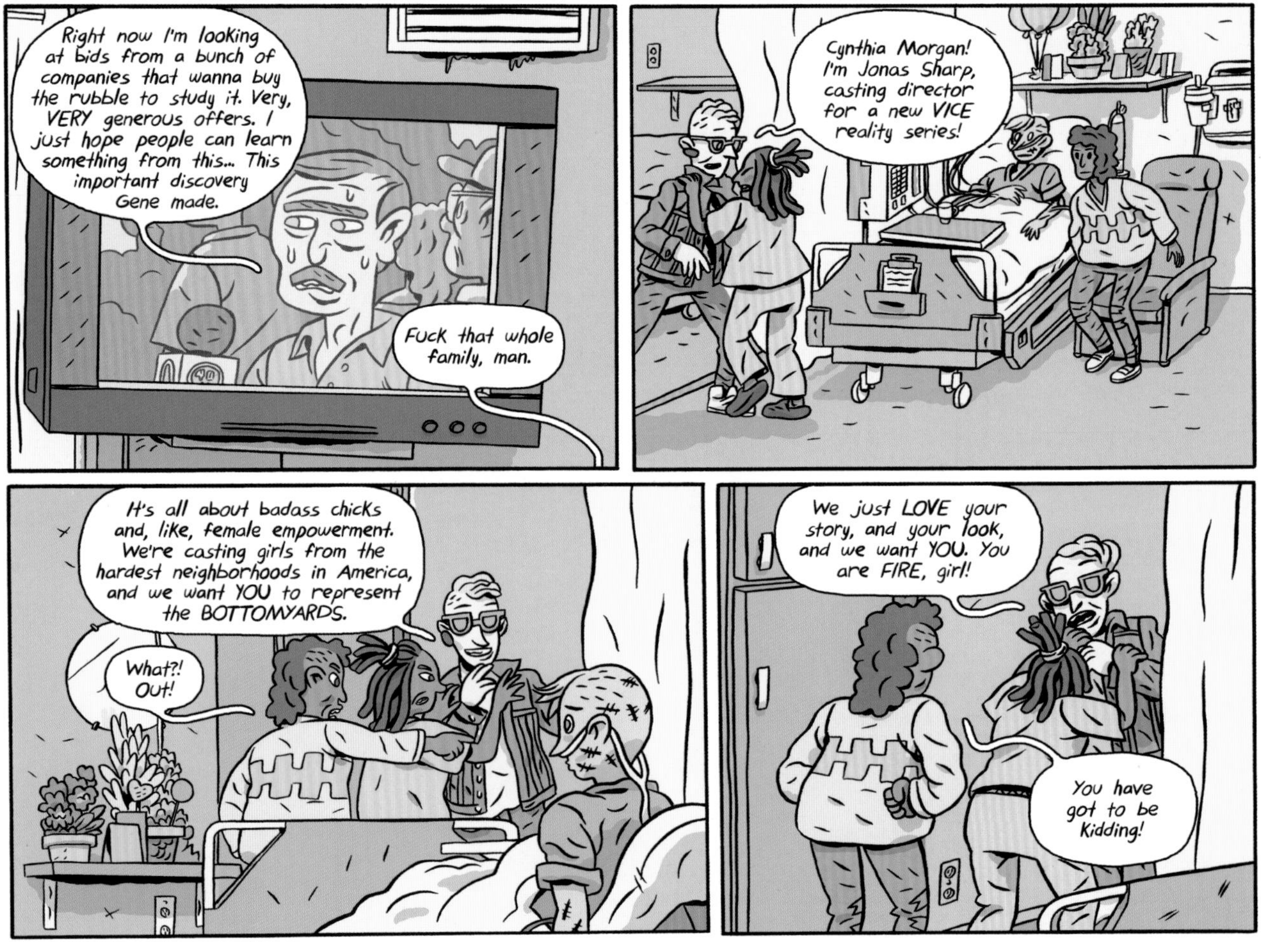
Right now I'm looking at bids from a bunch of companies that wanna buy the rubble to study it. Very, VERY generous offers. I just hope people can learn something from this... This important discovery Gene made.
Fuck that whole family, man.
Cynthia Morgan! I'm Jonas Sharp, casting director for a new VICE reality series!
It's all about badass chicks and, like, female empowerment. We're casting girls from the hardest neighborhoods in America, and we want YOU to represent the BOTTOMYARDS.
What?! Out!
We just LOVE your story, and your look, and we want YOU. You are FIRE, girl!
You have got to be Kidding!

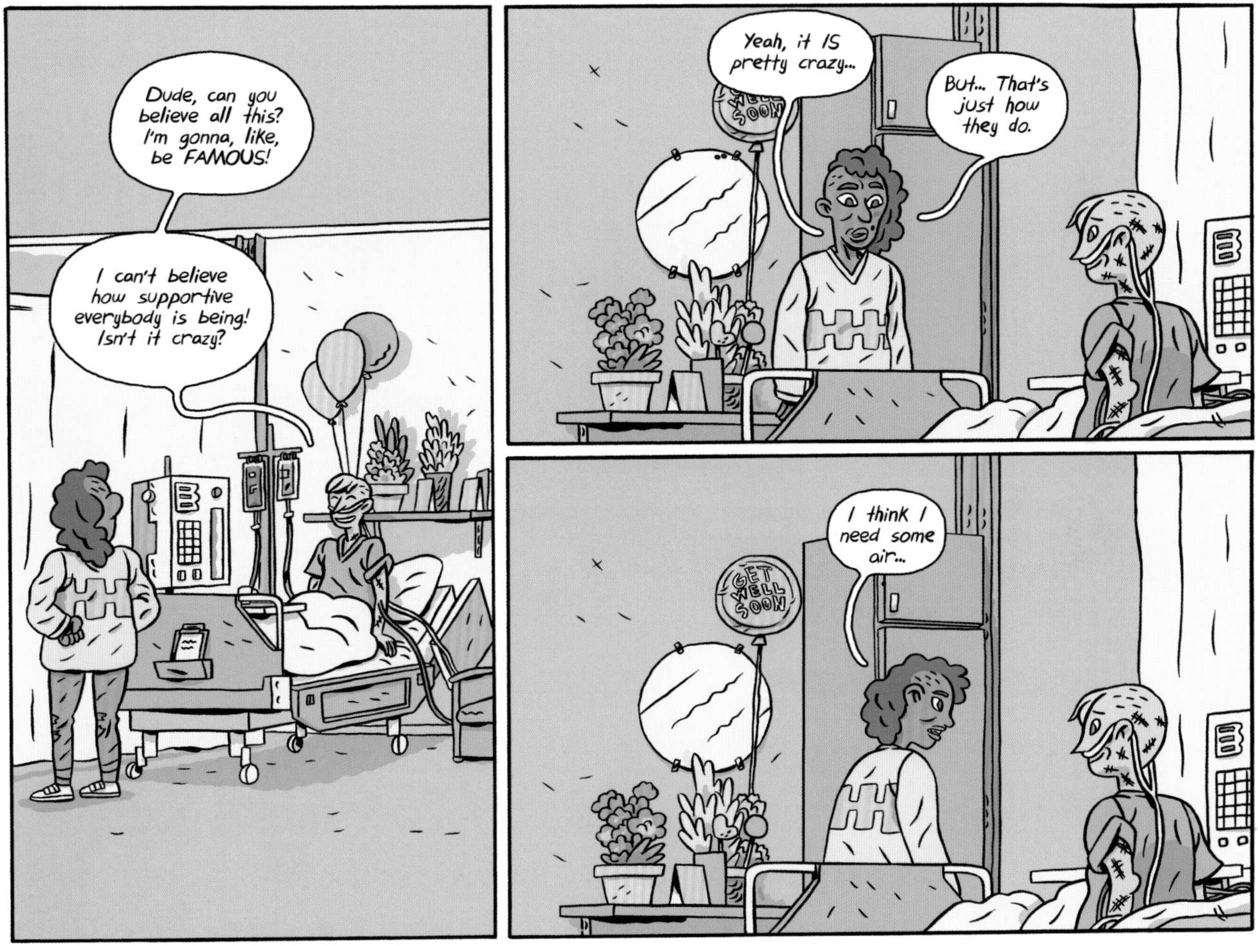
Dude, can you believe all this? I'm gonna, like, be FAMOUS!
I can't believe how supportive everybody is being! Isn't it crazy?
Yeah, it IS pretty crazy...
But... That's just how they do.
I think I need some air...
GET WELL SOON

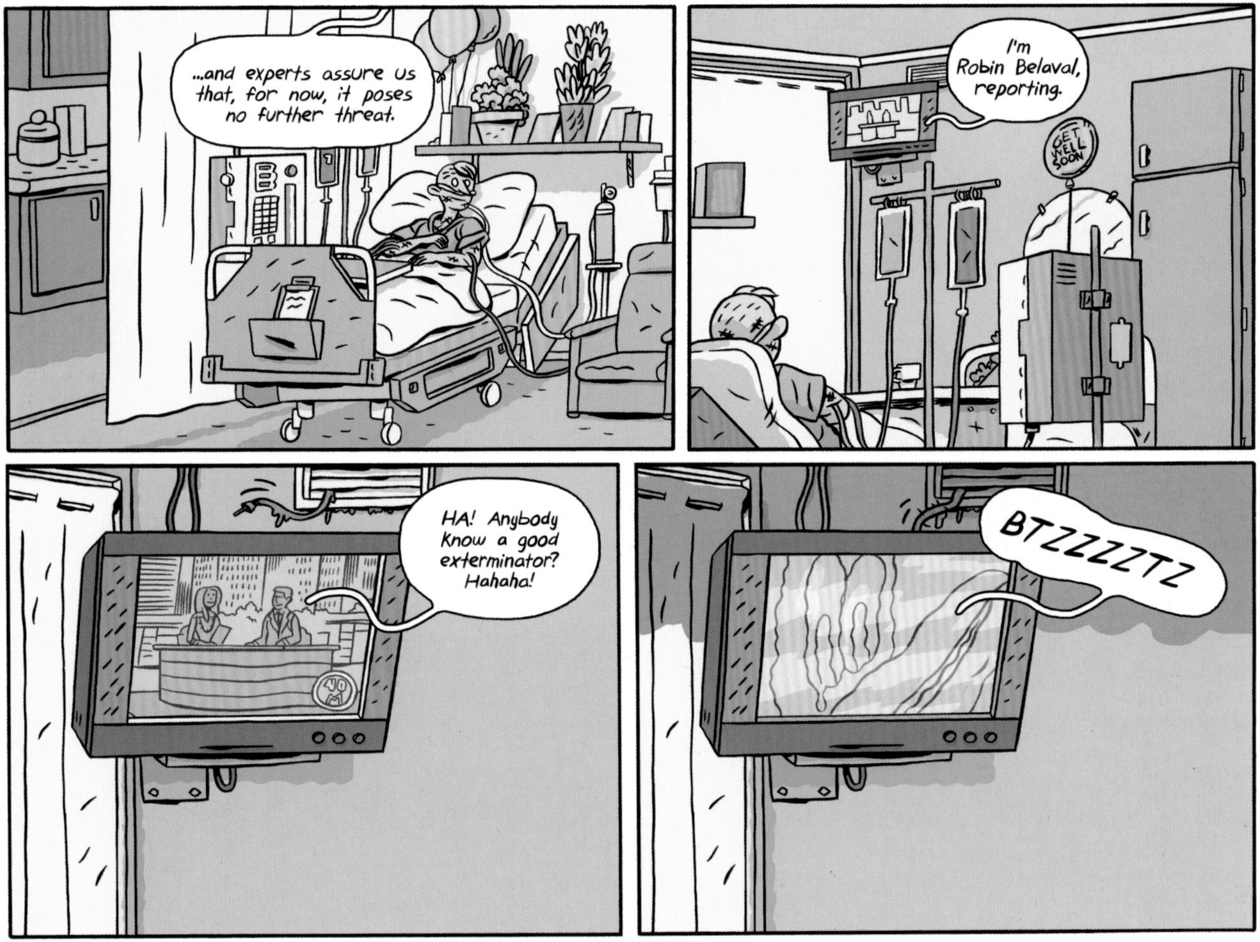
...and experts assure us that, for now, it poses no further threat.
I'm Robin Belaval, reporting.
GET WELL SOON
HA! Anybody know a good exterminator? Hahaha!
BTZZZZZTZ

MMMM
BTZZ
Uh oh.

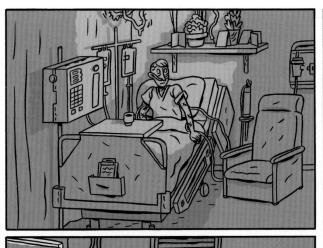

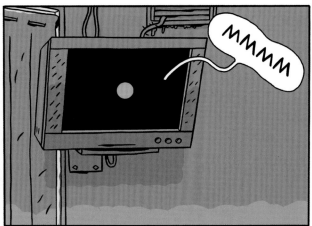

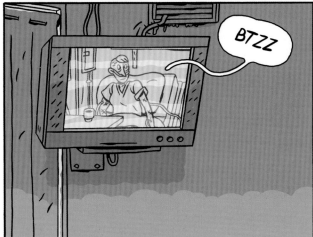

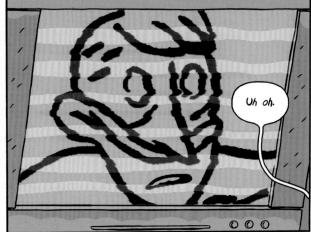

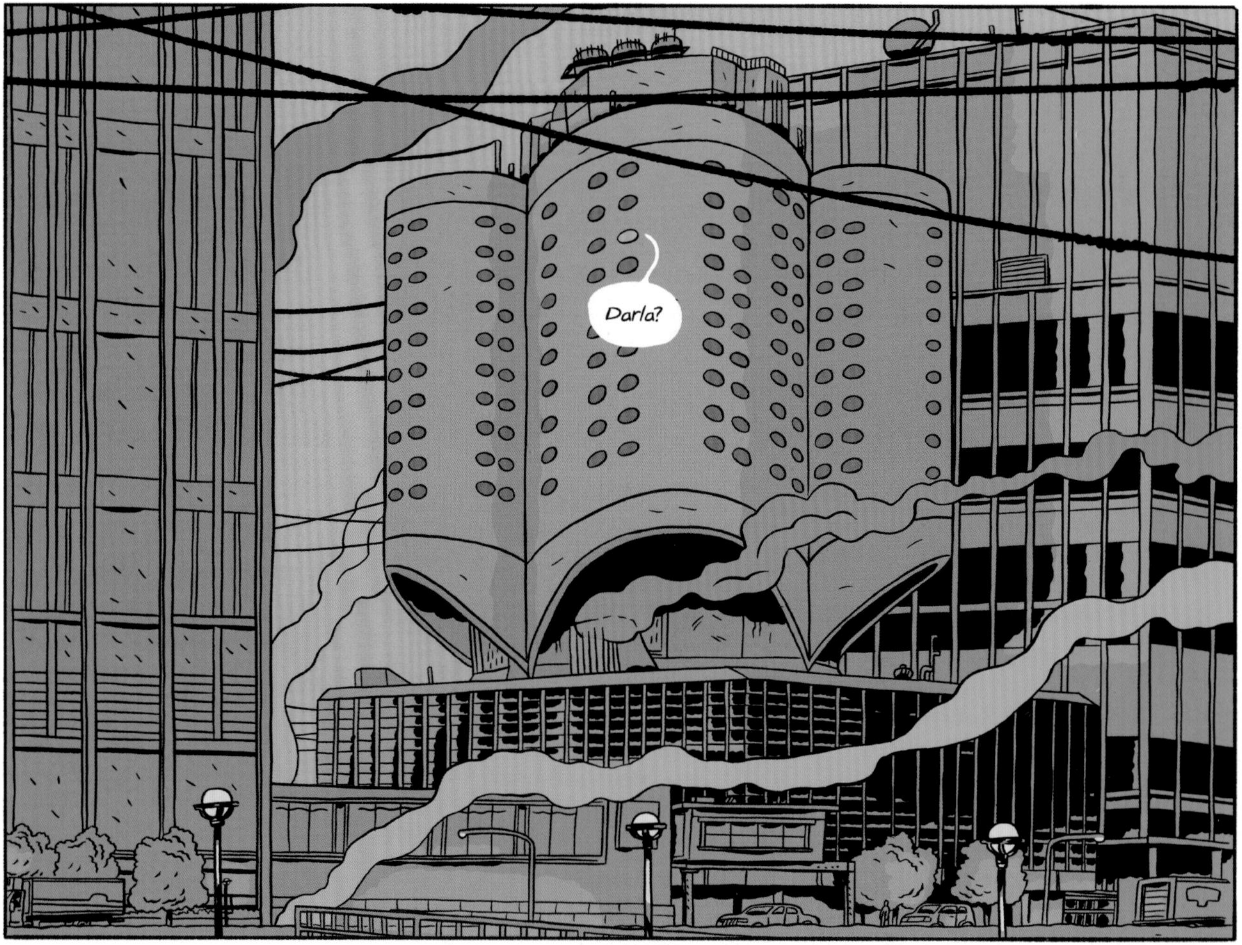
Darla?

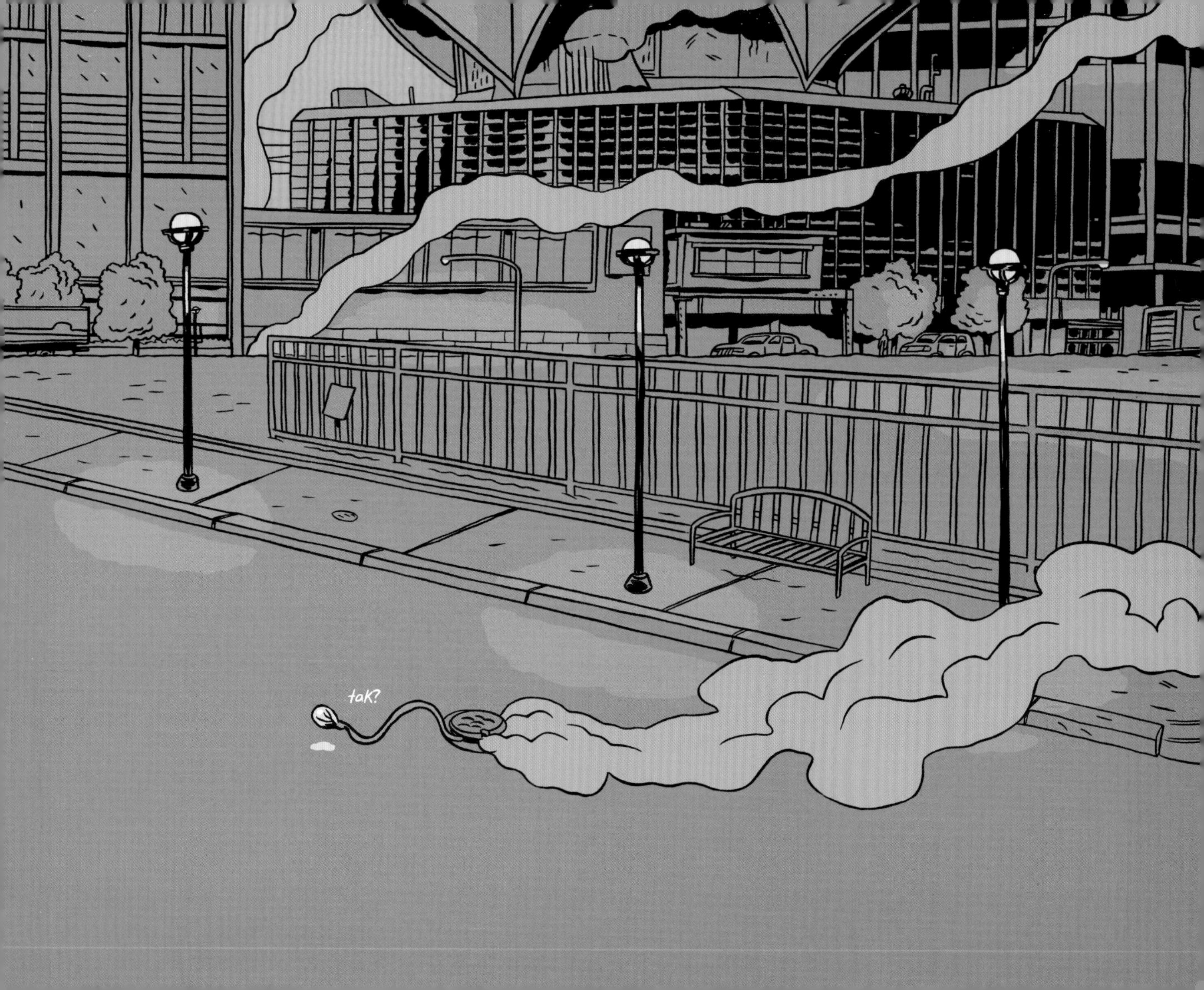
taK?

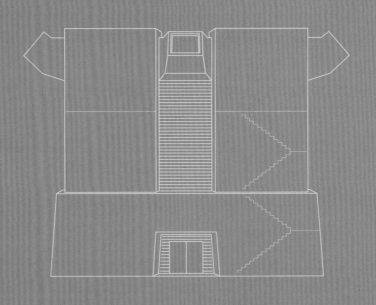

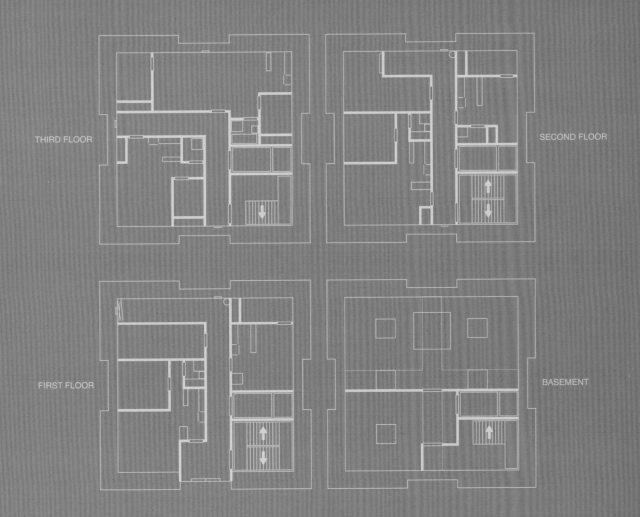

THIRD FLOOR

SECOND FLOOR

FIRST FLOOR

BASEMENT

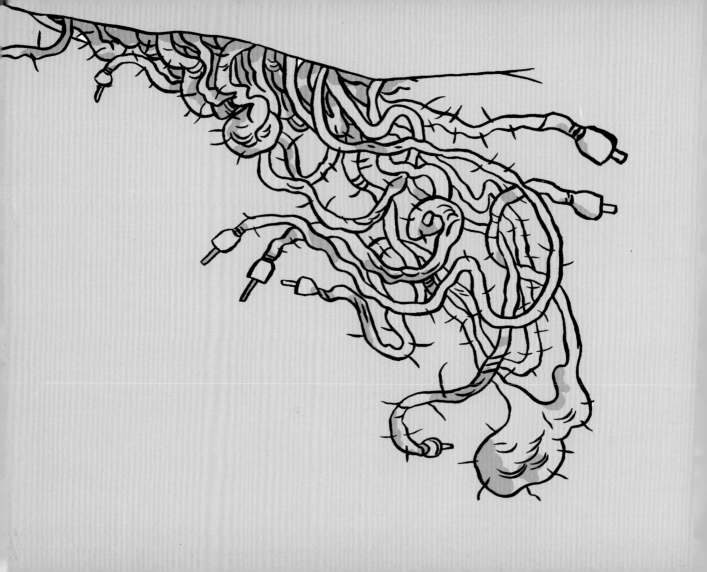